NICOLA

A Place in the Sun

HarperCollins*Publishers*

HarperCollins*Publishers*
77–85 Fulham Palace Road,
Hammersmith, London W6 8JB

This paperback edition 1993
1 3 5 7 9 8 6 4 2

Previously published in paperback by Grafton 1988
Reprinted three times

First published in Great Britain by
Grafton Books 1987

ISBN 0 586 06876 7

Set in Times

Printed in England by Clays Ltd, St Ives plc

To my dear friend Anne Parratt
and her family of Melbourne, Australia
who throughout the writing of the Askham Chronicles
have sustained me with their encouragement
and support, this final volume
is lovingly dedicated.

Family Tree of the Earls of Askham

From (vol. 1) *Never Such Innocence* (ends 1915) to the beginning of (vol. 4) *A Place in the Sun (*

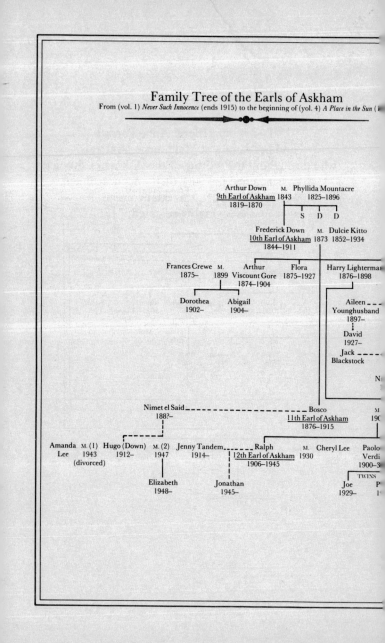

Arthur Down
9th Earl of Askham 1843
1819–1870

M. Phyllida Mountacre
1825–1896

S   D   D

Frederick Down
10th Earl of Askham 1873
1844–1911

M. Dulcie Kitto
1852–1934

Frances Crewe   M.   Arthur   Flora   Harry Lighterman
1875–   1899   Viscount Gore   1875–1927   1876–1898
Arthur 1874–1904

Dorothea   Abigail
1902–   1904–

Aileen ___
Younghusband
1897–

David
1927–

Jack ___
Blackstock

N

Nimet el Said _____ Bosco   M
188?–   11th Earl of Askham   190
1876–1915

Amanda   M.(1)   Hugo (Down)   M.(2)   Jenny Tandem _____ Ralph   M.   Cheryl Lee   Paolo
Lee   1943   1912–   1947   1914–   12th Earl of Askham   1930   Verdi
(divorced)   1906–1945   1900–3

TWINS

Elizabeth   Jonathan   Joe   P
1948–   1945–   1929–   1

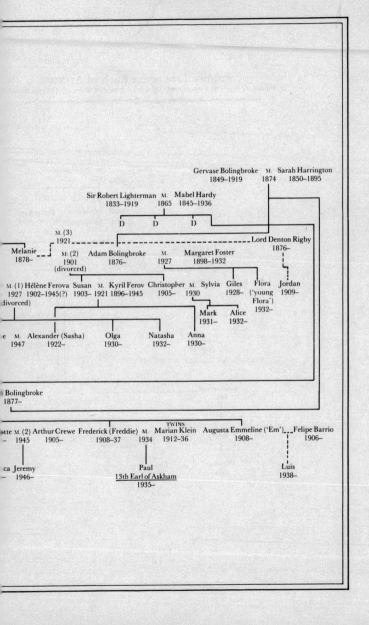

Gervase Bolingbroke M. Sarah Harrington
1849–1919   1874   1850–1895

Sir Robert Lighterman M. Mabel Hardy
1833–1919   1865   1845–1936

D   D   D

M. (3)
1921 --- Lord Denton Rigby
Melanie   1876–
1878– ---
                M: (2) Adam Bolingbroke   M.   Margaret Foster
                1901   1876–   1927 1898–1932
                (divorced)

M. (1) Hélène Ferova Susan M. Kyril Ferov Christopher M. Sylvia Giles Flora Jordan
1927 1902–1945(?) 1903–1921 1896–1945 1905–   1930   1928– ('young 1909–
divorced)   Flora')
                                            Mark   Alice   1932–
                                            1931–   1932–

e M. Alexander (Sasha)   Olga   Natasha   Anna
1947   1922–   1930–   1932–   1930–

Bolingbroke
1877–

tte M. (2) Arthur Crewe Frederick (Freddie) M. TWINS Augusta Emmeline ('Em'), _ Felipe Barrio
–   1945   1905–   1908–37   1934 Marian Klein 1908–   1906–
                                                1912–36

ca Jeremy   Paul   Luis
–   1946–   13th Earl of Askham   1938–
                              1935–

Contents

PART 1

The Visit

January 1949–October l951

CHAPTER 1

Anna Ferov was eighteen when she returned to visit her mother's family at Askham Hall, having lived most of her life abroad. The last time she was there was as a girl of three and now she was a young woman: tall, lissom, aristocratic, handsome rather than beautiful – with a touch of evil. After all, she was the daughter of Kyril Ferov and, if the sins of the fathers are not rightly visited upon their children, may not some taint of inheritance touch them?

Born in 1930, after her father was released from a Siberian labour camp, Anna was eight years younger than her brother, Sasha, who had brought her down to the Hall to meet the family. There was certainly nervousness on both sides about the visit as her grandfather, Adam Bolingbroke, aunts, uncles and cousins gathered to receive her. They were anxious to see how this young woman, isolated from them by the war, had turned out and she, for her part, was concerned to make an impression. The Askhams as a clan were so daunting, so legendary, so many stories about them had been told by her grandmother, Lady Melanie, that even someone with the self-confidence of young Anna could be forgiven for momentarily faltering.

But first impressions on both sides were good. One could almost have detected an audible sigh of relief as Anna survived the scrutiny of the family to pass with distinction. She was one of them.

After the greetings, the awkward tea in the lounge, the breaking of ice, her two cousins, Olga and Natasha, took

Anna upstairs to show her her room, give her a chance to freshen up after her journey.

Anna liked her room. It was at the back of the Hall, overlooking the lake and, arms akimbo, she stood in front of the window, her head slightly to one side.

'I remember being here when I was a little girl. I think it was for old Lady Askham's funeral. I remember . . .'

'You couldn't possibly remember that!' Olga, who was exactly the same age as Anna, came and stood beside her. 'We were too small. It must have been when cousin Freddie died.'

'Mummy never came back to England for that funeral,' Anna said in that firm, positive tone of voice that also seemed to distinguish her from her youthful relations. She shook her head, tossing back her long hair with its reddish tint. It was a curious, rather beautiful colour which, together with her green eyes and high Slav cheekbones, made her a creature of fascination. She had a pale translucent skin and a wide, sensuous mouth which, if the rest of her had not been so interesting, could have been quite ugly. As it was, it added to her un-English appearance; a sure sign that half of her was Russian. Anna sat on the side of the bed laying a long hand by her side and studying the ring on her finger. One could tell she was foreign because, although she was not engaged, she wore a ring on that finger in the manner of some continental girls – a large topaz set in fine filigree, a ring that a much older woman might have worn.

Anna did, in fact, look much older than eighteen and the two cousins stared at her in awe.

She stared back at Olga and Natasha who looked at her shyly, self-consciously. Why did some people, they seemed to be asking, develop so quickly – others stay behind?

'We know that our mother *killed* someone,' Natasha

14

ventured at last and then stifled the remark by girlishly clutching her mouth and starting to giggle. For it seemed such a terribly rash, brave thing to say; but Anna nodded as though she could give them years in feminine wisdom. Being Anna she was, of course, unshockable.

'That was a long time ago. You must remember that since then your mother was a heroine in the war.'

'No one knows where she is now,' Olga said sadly. 'We think she's dead.'

Anna was not to be outdone. 'My father also disappeared, and we think he's dead too. That happened to many, many people in the war, you know, thousands and thousands, millions perhaps. Even in Venice we saw the pictures of Belsen and Auschwitz. Your mother was in Auschwitz?'

As a tear trickled from the corner of Natasha's eye, Anna swiftly rose and went over to her.

'We were all very much affected by the war,' she said, putting an arm round her. 'But it's over now.'

Natasha felt so grateful to Anna for that warm, comforting arm . . . She knew she loved her. It was the spell that Anna wove.

Gazing round the oval table in the family dining-room late that evening Rachel Askham was glad that this room, at least, had survived the refurbishment of Ralph's wife, Cheryl. She had sent everything of value in the Hall to the sale-rooms, stripped the walls of ancient plasterwork and employed a fashionable designer of the thirties to refurnish and redecorate in a style that was already dated. The dining-room had remained unscathed because Ralph had put his foot down just in time and the centrepiece of the room remained: a solid walnut table from the time of Queen Anne, its cabriole legs adorned with intricate

15

acanthus and shield carvings rising from clawed feet firmly clasping round, wooden balls.

The design of the dining-chairs on which they sat was baroque, upholstered with raw silk, the top rails and splay backs intricately worked with an inlaid seashell motif attributed to William Kent.

The walls were hung with red silk and those family portraits which Cheryl had consigned, thankfully, to the attic and not the sale-room. Many of them had been, or were, in the process of being lovingly restored on the orders of Jenny, who knew how important family ties were to her husband's family.

Rachel could see that Bobby, too, was very taken by his niece, had been seated next to her and had grown quite animated as the dinner progressed, with Jenny rather flustered and nervous at one end of the oval table and Hugo, assured and reassuring, at the other. Jenny had never presided over such a family gathering since she'd been married to Hugo because of the deep division that had occurred in the family when they nearly went to court over the fate of the Hall. This reunion was also an attempt to heal a deep wound.

Anna wove a definite spell over everyone, her aunt thought, watching her charm at work on Bobby. Everyone seemed to hang on Anna's words in a way that was odd for someone of her age. Despite her youth she looked about twenty-three and there was nothing demure in the striking dinner dress she wore of kingfisher blue silk, moulded to her figure, the material ruched at the hip, and a rather bold V neckline. The other girls of Anna's age, her cousins, wore pretty party frocks that were much younger, more suitable, gathered at the waist and with high or rounded necks, in pretty pastel colours.

Olga, Natasha and their cousin Angelica Verdi looked

what they were: pretty teenage girls. Anna looked a woman.

Rachel thought that maybe this sophistication was due to the fact that Anna had had an unusual upbringing, living mostly alone with her mother Susan; a father who came and went, often for long periods, thus imbuing the family atmosphere not only with a hint of mystery but with considerable uncertainty.

Finally he had disappeared for good. No one had heard of him since 1942, except for a possible sighting in Berlin in 1945 which could not now be checked up on as the person who had seen him was dead.

Susan had taken Anna to Venice; and what sort of life was that for a girl in wartime, cut off from family, surrounded by people who might well have regarded her as alien? Anna reminded Rachel of others she had known who had had strange childhoods, some of them in her own family. She looked at her three grandchildren, Joe, Pascal and Angelica, sitting opposite Anna and as transfixed by her as anyone else. Had they not grown up fatherless and in the shadow of the war, fearful that their own mother might not return from it?

With her long memory, Rachel could recall the small child who had come over, in the days when Kyril and Susan were still together, for the funeral of Dulcie, Lady Askham, in the winter of 1934. Anna was just three and there was no hint in that far-off day of the tantalizing woman she would turn into. If Anna were like this now one could not help wondering what she would be like in a few years' time.

Her daughter Em, sitting next to her, followed Rachel's gaze.

'Surely you're not hooked by Anna, too?' she whispered.

'She *is* rather intriguing,' Rachel smiled, 'but I was

17

looking at Joe and Pascal and thinking how dissimilar they'd grown. They used to be quite alike.'

'But they were never identical twins.'

'No, but they looked more alike than they do now. Pascal is somewhat beefier. He's very taken by Anna.'

'Everyone is taken by Anna.' Em gazed at her relations who sat round the table: her sister Charlotte and her husband Arthur; Anna's grandfather Adam Bolingbroke, her Uncle Bobby and his wife Aileen, rather prim and severe-looking in an evening dress of grey grosgrain; Hugo, the host and present incumbent of the Hall, Em's last surviving brother, and his wife Jenny who wore the harrassed look she always did when entertaining, as though she missed the hordes of servants both in dining-room and kitchen who went with the Hall in pre-war days, thus making the task of the hostess relatively simple. There was Sasha, Anna's brother, a good-looking young man with reddish brown curly hair who had the attraction, but not quite the same mysterious quality, that so intrigued everyone about his sister, and there was Princess Irina, their Russian grandmother.

There was Sasha's young wife Stefanie, who was, in many ways, the most classically beautiful woman present, though some would have given this accolade to Charlotte and some to her daughter Angelica. Still others, perhaps, to Natasha. Not yet twenty-one, Stefanie was already a mother and that act of motherhood seemed to have enhanced her girlhood beauty, brought it to maturity. And, maybe, the air of sadness she habitually wore enhanced it more. Stefanie, melancholic by nature, guilt-ridden, seldom smiled and her peerless kind of beauty made her air of tragedy so much harder to understand except for those who knew, as the family did, about her mother who had vanished in the war.

Now Hugo was standing up and making a speech,

difficult for him because he was a taciturn young man, of the family yet also not of it, someone whom only the happiness of marriage had made secure. Lifting his glass he said:

'I'd like to propose a toast. But, first of all, I'd like to say how pleased Jenny and I are to have you all here – the family in the family's house. I want you to feel that, wherever you live, you all share in this house and that Anna is particularly welcome here and must think of it as much a home as Venice.' As everyone murmured appreciatively Hugo lowered his head and then raised it again, eyes on Bobby. 'I'd especially like to thank Bobby for being here, and Aileen, of course. I want them to know how very welcome they are – as you all are, and to tell you all that Jenny and I want you to come more often. My toast is, then, to the Family.'

Everyone stood up, raised their glasses and drank to the family and as they sat down Sasha remained on his feet, his hand out for silence.

'I'd like to thank Hugo for his generous speech, particularly on behalf of Anna who has been made so welcome by you all. As you know the Ferovs are very late additions to the Askham family but now, having well and truly married into it, we feel that we belong. The strength of the family is that it has flung its tentacles so far. I'd particularly like to remember tonight those who are not here: Ralph and Freddie, my cousins, Stefanie's mother, Hélène, our grandfather Alexei, and my father Kyril whose fate we have never discovered. I would also like to remember my mother and grandmother in Venice and to say how much we miss them.' Sasha paused for a moment as if wondering if he had forgotten anyone, then he took his glass in his hand and raised it in front of him.

'To absent friends and the beloved dead.'

19

'Absent friends and the beloved dead,' everyone murmured.

Rachel felt the tears spring to her eyes and there was such a lump in her throat that she could hardly swallow her wine. When they sat down again and everyone began talking, rather self-consciously, Joe murmured: 'Are you all right, Gran?'

'Perfectly all right, dear.' Rachel's eyes were still bright. 'Unfortunately, or coincidentally, I don't know, the words Sasha used just now were the very same words that your great-grandmama used the Christmas before she died, "absent friends and the beloved dead". Suddenly I seemed to see her sitting here in this room and those days came so vividly back to me.'

Just then everyone stood up to go into the drawing-room for coffee and Joe took her arm and surreptitiously kissed her cheek.

Joe was a favourite of Rachel's. He was a slight, softly spoken boy with striking Renaissance looks: hooded eyes, high cheekbones and pale, bloodless lips. Like Charlotte's two other children by Paolo Verdi he had thick black hair, a lock of which always fell over his forehead. Joe was an intense young man, close to Rachel because he followed the profession of journalism and had worked on a provincial newspaper instead of going to university like his brother, Pascal. Em had recently taken him on the family paper, *The Sentinel,* because it was a possibility that, one day, Joe might succeed her.

The family drawing-room on the first floor above the dining-room had also been partly restored and refurnished, though not with the priceless antiques that graced the dining-room.

The room had been repainted, but all the intricate original plaster work on the ceiling – the octagons, quatrefoils, lozenges, rosettes, coronals of leaves and flower sprays – that had been removed on Cheryl's orders could never be replaced. It now looked like a rather ordinary, large but comfortable lounge furnished with deep sofas and easy chairs with loose covers. It was a functional, family room. The carpet could be rolled back for dancing, which was not, as in the old days, in the huge ballroom which could accommodate five hundred people and a string orchestra. Only ghosts lived there now.

Although Rachel had been born in 1877 and the year now was 1949 – some would think a lifetime away from those far-off days when Queen Victoria had yet another twenty-four years to reign – making her seventy-two, no one ever though of her as an old lady. She was tall and upright and her looks, though faded, were recognizable from the years of her youth – fair hair, pale skin, very blue eyes. There was now more white in her hair which she wore in a style that hardly ever changed: softly waved in front and pinned in a large bun at the nape of her neck. There was an aura of pre-Raphaelite painting about Rachel yet it was deceptive.

In many ways she was a formidable woman, having endured much suffering – the loss of a husband and two sons in the wars that had occupied the twentieth century – and overcome it. She still drove a car, gardened vigorously and went for long walks with her dogs at least once a day in all weathers. She was formidable yet she was loved, particuarly by her surviving children and grand-children. Those who knew her well appreciated her most, but those who didn't found her a little daunting. She was, indeed, the matriarch of the family.

Anna decided she didn't like her. She felt Rachel's piercing appraisal had been critical, whereas Anna was used to flattery and, as she followed the throng from the dining-room to the drawing-room, she kept well away from her great-aunt. Joe's gaze, however, lingered once he had settled Rachel in a chair by the fire and he watched Anna as she drifted across the room with the two Lighter-man sisters. Jenny had stayed behind to organize coffee, and Hugo and Sasha had gone up to the billiards-room to see if it was warm enough to play. The Hall was huge and the heating bill so expensive that parts of it remained unheated.

'Are *you* taken by Anna?' Rachel eyed her grandson curiously.

'She's unusual,' Joe nodded gravely. 'Intriguing, yes. But like? I'm not so sure.'

He looked at his grandmother and smiled. In many ways Joe was another mystery, a boy she'd helped raise when his mother was away in the war; yet could she with truth say she knew him? His twin Pascal was warm and outward-looking, extrovert and impulsive; but Joe was cautious, controlled, even a little evasive. It was difficult to know quite what Joe was thinking, a trait he'd shown even as a small child. Did he like Anna? Or was he critical of her? Hard to tell.

'There's something about Anna that reminds me of . . .' Rachel paused as if wondering whether to go on.

'Of, mother?' Em stood on one side of her, smoking a cigarette.

'I was going to say Cheryl, but . . .'

'She's not a *bit* like Cheryl,' Em said in her robust fashion.

'Not to look at, but . . .' Rachel paused again.

'I thought everyone *detested* Uncle Ralph's wife,' Joe expostulated. 'That's not a very nice thing to say.'

'No one detested her at all at first,' Em said quickly. 'She was very popular. I think that's what Gran means.' Em frowned at her mother and saw, with relief, Stefanie strolling towards them with Charlotte.

'Where's your grandmother?' Rachel said, greeting her.

22

'She's gone to powder her nose, Aunt Rachel.' Stefanie flopped down beside Em while Charlotte went to the fire to light a spill for her cigarette. Charlotte wore a close-fitting evening dress and Rachel thought her figure hadn't changed since the thirties. Although she was over forty she could be a mannequin even now, only, of course, she never would because she was so busy being a hostess for Arthur. Also, unlike the thirties, she no longer needed the money as Arthur was a wealthy man with many directorships in the City.

Charlotte did look beautiful, though somehow wistful, Rachel thought, with a tinge of sadness in her face, as though she missed the war years . . . or was it because of what had happened in the war years? Excitement, adventure . . . and passion. Did Charlotte miss passion in her happy, uneventful marriage?

'The men are all going to play billiards.' Charlotte removed her cigarette from her mouth. 'I thought that kind of thing went out with the war.'

'What kind of thing?' Joe perched on the floor by his mother, his arms round his knees.

'Men leaving the women. I wondered for a moment earlier on if they were all going to stay behind tonight and drink port!'

'Jenny certainly wouldn't allow *that*!' Rachel said firmly. 'She doesn't believe in it.'

It was not surprising. Hugo's wife Jenny, a country girl, hadn't been brought up to it. Before the war when all the Askhams did all the right things, like dressing for dinner and leaving the men to their port, Jenny had been growing up on a farm in Cumberland. First she had been Ralph's girlfriend and then Hugo married her after his death. She was the mother of Ralph's son, Jonathan, born in 1945 and asleep upstairs.

The arrival of Princess Irina Ferov, flanked by her

granddaughters, was a welcome diversion. After her strolled Sasha and Hugo, and one of the hired helpers for the evening wheeled in a trolley with coffee. Before the war this would have been brought in by the butler, trailed by footmen and maids, not a homely old body in a flower-patterned overall. Hugo was the first owner of the Hall not to have a butler, and much else had gone too.

Once the village of Askham had provided most of the staff the Hall needed but now, although many of the people who lived there had once been in the service of the Askhams, their children no longer were.

As soon as Anna saw her grandmother she came over to be with her while Joe held out a chair to the Russian Princess to sit in. Irina gratefully sank into it, rubbing her hands.

'Isn't it cold?' she said, her accent still very pronounced. 'Do you think we'll have snow? Isn't my granddaughter enchanting?' She gazed at Anna and clasped her hand. 'Do you know, I haven't seen my baby since before the war? Since Susan quarrelled with Bobby . . .'

'That's all made up now, Babushka,' Anna said.

'*Everyone* quarrels with Bobby,' Irina grunted, 'except me, of course. *I* never quarrel with Bobby!' Irina, who depended on Bobby, gave a sly, rather mischievous smile.

Princess Irina, widow of Prince Alexei of the noble house of Ferov, was some four years older than Rachel but the two women had never been close. There was no animosity. They were simply not each other's type and no one knowing them would expect them to have anything in common. The Princess lived for pleasure, luxury and fun and had had all in full measure at some time in her life. She had also known poverty, anxiety and grief as well as exile from her native home. She had lost a son and a daughter as well as her husband in the Second World War and other relatives and friends in the First.

24

Yet her ebullience enabled her to rise to each new challenge, and now, in her mid seventies, she felt she had found her particular place in the sun. Surely, nothing could dislodge her from it now?

Didn't they all, after all, deserve a place in the sun for all they had endured? Few members of the family in this room had escaped deprivation and suffering as a result of the war. But Irina didn't want to think of the war, but of a time much further away. In a nostalgic mood, warmed by wine and a plentiful supply of brandy, Irina reminded Rachel of her visit to Russia in 1921.

'Anna would not be here now were it not for your visit, would she, Rachel?'

'Indeed she would not,' Rachel said, smiling, 'and hardly anyone in this room would be here, except Bobby, had Bosco and I not met in Egypt in 1898. Such is the way of life, isn't it, Irina?'

'You're right,' Irina nodded, a hand touching Rachel's arm. 'But she has something, my granddaughter, has she not? Something special?'

'She's a lot like Kyril,' Irina sighed – sadness followed happiness so quickly.

Rachel agreed. 'More like Kyril than Sasha is.'

'Oh, Sasha has *nothing* of Kyril in him at all! Sasha takes after my side of the family. But Kyril was clever and so is Anna. Anna will go far.' As Irina sighed again Rachel noticed she had referred to Kyril in the past, as if he were indeed dead. 'I love all my grandchildren equally, of course,' Irina said quickly. 'One is *so* thankful to have relations, to have survived at all after all that has happened. To think that we are all sitting here together, in comfort with our loved ones, whereas . . .' Irina once more sighed lugubriously.

Rachel knew what was going to happen. Any moment now and the Princess would dissolve into tears; memories

25

of the past would come tumbling out, all this nostalgia was too much for her Slav soul. Regularly Irina, by recollection and reminiscence, was able to drum up enough misery to half drown herself.

Despite her years of misfortune Irina remained an attractive, well-preserved woman, who looked younger than she was. Rachel remembered the Princess's hair being as many colours as Joseph's coat over the years. She had seen it auburn, black, briefly grey when the Princess was feeling depressed; but now it was a kind of mauve colour which went well with her magenta lips and violet cheeks, the dark eyes, thickly edged with kohl, almost as bright and piercing as they had been in the thirties.

In these latter years the Princess had reluctantly discarded the court dress, which she had first worn at the celebration of 300 years of the Romanov dynasty and was for just such special occasions, for a lace affair that came from the wardrobe of her former friend and patroness, Dulcie Askham. Dulcie's dress had much in common with the clothes worn by Queen Mary. Even now they were considered unfashionable for dowagers but, somehow, they suited Irina's slightly plump but statuesque figure, the pronounced corseted bosom not unlike that of the old Queen.

By now the commotion in Irina's part of the room had drawn the attention of everyone else. The girls stopped their chattering and Bobby and Adam looked up. Anna attempted to comfort her while Stafanie put an arm round her shoulder. Charlotte looked at her mother and raised her eyes to the ceiling. It was all so familiar on any family occasion when Irina had had a little, perhaps, too much to drink. Almost predictable.

'There, there,' Anna said. 'There is no need to cry, Babushka,' and she murmured a few words of the Russian she had learned from her father before he left them for good.

Irina's attention-grabbing techniques were familiar to Bobby and they irritated him. Hélène had been his first wife; Stefanie, Natasha and Olga were his daughters. Whether he liked it or not – and he didn't – Irina was part of his family, part of his life. Ever since the end of the war he had let her live at his country home on the banks of the Thames, Robertswood, which had been used from 1940 to 1945 as a convalescent home for officers. It was thanks to her, too, to her taste and good judgement, her capacity for hard work when the occasion arose, that it was being restored to its pre-war glory as one of the finest country homes in England.

Still, Irina was an irritant. He stood looking down at her broodingly.

'What is it this time, Irina?'

'So unsympathetic,' Irina said petulantly, screwing her handkerchief into her eyes.

'Not at all,' Bobby replied.

'Babushka is thinking about the past,' Stefanie explained to her father. 'It always has this effect on her.' Stefanie's memory went back years, to life with her grandmother in pre-war Paris.

'Don't think about the past then, Irina,' Bobby said tetchily, as though such things could be put easily out of one's mind. 'Why don't you put on the gramophone or play cards?' He looked around for Hugo. 'The young ones can dance. There are plenty of them about. Where's Hugo, where's Pascal, where's Sasha? I want to speak to Sasha, anyway.'

Bobby hated gloom and introspection. His briskness, though deeply resented by Irina, made her dry her eyes and as she stuffed the handkerchief up the sleeve of her Queen Mary dress everyone suddenly got very busy.

27

Sasha and Hugo appeared, Pascal and Arthur were sent for and Natasha, who loved dancing, started to roll back the carpet. As the music started on the wind-up gramophone Charlotte began to tap a foot.

'Come and dance,' Hugo said, placing an arm round her waist.

'What about Anna?' Charlotte asked, gliding with him on to the hastily improvised dance floor.

'What about her?'

'Shouldn't she have the first waltz?'

'I think Pascal will claim that privilege. He's susceptible.'

'He's susceptible to everyone, that's the problem.' Charlotte sighed and gazed at the other twin still chatting with his grandmother. 'I wish Joe were, too.'

'Joe will be waiting for someone special,' Hugo's arm tightened round her waist. 'He's the type.'

It was true that a minute or two later Pascal, lured by the sound of the music, appeared and immediately reached out to lead Anna on to the floor. She proved as adept at the quickstep as at charming her relations, and Sasha was about to join them with Stefanie when Bobby took his arm and whispered something to him. Sasha looked puzzled, talked rapidly to Stefanie and then the pair of them left the room with Bobby.

'I wonder what that was about?' Arthur enquired of Rachel as he gallantly led her on to the small square of carpetless floor.

'One of Bobby's mysteries,' Rachel replied, trying to get into step. 'I'm too old for this sort of thing, you know.'

'That's nonsense,' Arthur said. 'Charlotte said you were fined for speeding the other day.'

'Nearly,' Rachel laughed guiltily. 'It was such a nice policeman though, and he let me off. Gave me a caution though . . .' Rachel looked slyly at Arthur, who pressed his cheek against hers. He did love her.

Bobby led Sasha and Stefanie to a small study on the ground floor, a functional, ill-furnished room which had been many things since Dulcie's day, when it had been a parlour. During the war it was the school office and graffiti still remained on the walls, drawn by idle East End evacuees waiting for the morning's reprimand from Cheryl.

'What a horrible place,' Bobby said, shivering. 'Really, this house has completely gone to pot. I thought Hugo was going to make something of it.'

Bobby leaned down and turned up the gas fire which was needed to complement the erratic central heating. Sasha and Stefanie stood watching him, aware of his irritation that he had lost the chance to turn the family home into a luxurious hotel, and the reasons for it, perhaps justified. Bobby was a successful entrepreneur and had the gift of Croesus with everything he touched. He had made several fortunes over the years and still got richer by the minute while his investments grew and multiplied, some silently, some noisily, on the Stock Exchange and commodity markets of the world.

It was not difficult to imagine now that Bobby may have been right, and the family wrong, to oppose his acquisition of the large house that had once needed so many servants to run it. The building as such extended over many centuries, but was finally enlarged in the eighteenth by the spendthrift fifth Earl, both as an exercise in self aggrandisement and to house his many children. But now, except for a few rooms, Askham Hall was sparse; it was chilly, the central heating antiquated, and people tended to huddle round fires as they were in the drawing-room upstairs. Jenny and Hugo were spartan, outdoor types who seemed not to notice the cold; but Bobby froze when he was there and even Rachel, who prided herself on her fortitude, was glad to return to the comfort of Darley Manor, the home she still shared with Adam ten miles away. It was here that she brought up her orphaned grandson Paul, and where she had helped to rear her niece and nephew Flora and Giles after their mother's death.

Bobby went on grumbling and muttering, rubbing his hands together and blowing on them rather dramatically, while Sasha drew chairs up to the fire, made sure that the curtains were tightly drawn to keep out the draught and the door closed. Still it was cold. Then he put off the main light so that the glow from the solitary table lamp made the room seem softer and more comfortable, giving the illusion of added warmth. Sasha, as usual, tried to make life easier while Stefanie huddled in her chair, every bit as cold and disgruntled as her father.

When they were together it was easy to see that they were related. Bobby, dark haired, blue eyed, had been a beautiful child, the son of Melanie and Harry Lighterman who had been killed at Omdurman. Melanie had been a celebrated beauty and Harry a good-looking man, moustached, Victorian, saturnine, a well-trained member of a famous regiment, the 17/21 Lancers, who had also taken part in the Charge of the Light Brigade. Yet Harry had never seemed destined for heroism, but maybe the satisfying and predictable career of an army officer or, eventually, the running of his father's successful business which had proved the basis of Bobby's subsequent fortune.

But Harry had been cut off in his prime and his widow had married not once but twice more, never satisfied, never really happy. Thus Bobby, though wealthy and greatly loved by his grandparents who had brought him up, could be said to have had a deprived childhood, though in a different way from his daughters. Bobby had too much and they too little.

'Better?' Sasha said, smiling at Stefanie, when he had done his best to insulate the room.

'Not much,' Stefanie rubbed her arms. 'I can't stay here for more than a night. The bedroom is as cold as this.'

'I'll warm you,' Sasha said tenderly, but it appeared to be of small comfort to her. As Bobby lit a fresh cigar she asked, 'What did you want us for, Father?'

'I wanted to talk to you about the future,' Bobby said.

'Our future?' Stefanie looked surprised.

'Yours and Sasha's.' Bobby blew out his match and settled back in his chair. 'Let's forget about all this,' he airily waved his hand as if to dismiss the shabby room and its contents. 'It was never my wish to fall out with the rest of the family by trying to take the Hall from them. Of course, they are only my family in a broad sense; you two are my intimate family and it is you and my grandson I am thinking of.' Bobby turned his gaze on Sasha.

'Now I know, Sasha, that you are not a poor man. Your mother settled a handsome endowment on you and your grandmother, my mother, has not been ungenerous. You have never been extravagant and yet you must feel a little insecure now that you have a family.'

'I have been looking for work, Uncle,' Sasha said defensively.

'I know, my boy, I know.' Bobby held up a hand. 'Something compatible with your interests – machines or aircraft. Why not? I'm not accusing you of being idle for one minute. I know that since you came back from abroad you've been looking around, which is why I want to snap you up before you find something. I've talked to you before about joining the business, Sasha. That was when I still had hopes that it would interest David, my natural

31

heir. But David . . .' Bobby sighed and shrugged his shoulders, a man suddenly overwhelmed by a deep sadness. 'No hope there, I'm afraid. I'd like *you* to come in with me with the idea that eventually you will succeed me, Sasha, as the head of the Lighterman empire.'

Sasha, sitting next to Stefanie, leaned forward, a note of apprehension in his voice.

'I have no experience of business, Uncle. I don't even know if it's what I want.'

'You can find out,' Bobby said. 'There no compulsion. Frankly, I think it will suit you to the ground. Your war record . . .'

'I can't see what Sasha's war record has to do with this,' Stefanie said, sitting up and lighting a cigarette, snapping her purse firmly shut afterwards. 'Personally, I don't think he should be involved . . .'

'But why not?'

'Because,' Stefanie paused to stare at her father, 'I think the less he has to do with you the better. You already interfere too much in our lives. Why you should try to make up now for all the neglect of me and my sisters, I don't know; but I'm not having you seducing my husband in an effort to do it. The whole idea is quite monstrous.' Stefanie brandished the cigarette in her hand like a weapon. 'You're trying to control us, that's what it is, getting at me through him. Well, frankly, Father, I don't want it. I'm sure Sasha doesn't want it and if he says he does he's a hypocrite. Do you think we even *like* you? The answer is No: never have and never will – you can stay on your own, Lord Lighterman.' Stefanie paused and looked at her husband.

'Come on, Sasha.'

'I can't,' Sasha said, looking at the ground, utterly wretched.

'What do you mean, you *can't*?'

'I can't leave Uncle like this. Whether I work for him

or not isn't the point. You've been so rude that I think you should apologize.'

'Apologize!'

'Yes, apologize. This weekend was an attempt to welcome Anna, to let bygones be bygones. I know your father made a great effort coming down here at all. The Hall meant a lot to him; it was the family home – his family's home, just as much as it was Hugo's. He may have made it into a hotel but it would still have been a beautiful home.'

'Like a country home,' Bobby said, pleased and gratified by Sasha's stand. 'Restored with all the finest furniture.'

'Now it's like a huge cold barn,' Sasha said. 'I don't think Hugo's ancestors would have approved. I think he took on too much, much as I like him. I see Uncle's point of view, Stefanie. *Please,* now that your father is trying to be generous, can't you just be nice to him?'

'Too late,' Stefanie said, gathering her things up from her chair. 'Much too late.'

It was well after midnight when Anna kicked off her shoes and lay on her bed, still wearing the evening gown she'd bought in Paris on her way over to England. She still felt excited and pleased with herself, aware of her effect on her relations, the power that she had just acquired over them as well as over her family and friends in Venice.

Anna had been aware of this power quite early in her life. People had always paid her compliments, hung on her words, sought her opinions, even the nuns in the convent where she'd been educated. Reverend Mother used frequently to send for Anna just for a chat, as though rubbing shoulders, as Anna did, with the great and noble would somehow rub off on her, too.

Anna had been a grave girl and she was now a grave

young woman. No one would call her fun; but her power was to mesmerise and fascinate, to bewitch.

Here at Askham, seat of her mother's maternal family, Anna felt at home: rich, powerful. It was a home that one day she would like to own, this or one like it; to be the chatelaine, restore the Hall to its former splendour and people it with servants, furnish it with antiques. She could see herself poised on the balustrade just above the hall, ready to descend, while, gathered below, were a throng of eager admirers waiting to acclaim her. It was a fantasy, but much of Anna's life was a fantasy: a longing for the unreality of the dream.

She had wanted to come to England; she was excited to be here. Despite the apparent glamour of a life in a Venetian palazzo, the excitement of sophisticated cosmopolitan friends, Anna Ferov at eighteen was a bored, rather discontented young woman. She was bored with the blatancy of the marriage stakes; the automatic supposition that all a young woman wished to do was marry; she was bored with the ceaseless lunches, dinners and parties, the furtive afternoon drinking sessions that went on in the homes of young women like herself when their parents were away. Instead of opening new vistas, life seemed to be closing in on her, cutting off escape routes, shutting doors, until her mother, sensing her daughter's discontent, had suggested a visit to the family, not seen since well before the War.

Susan, her mother had married Kyril Ferov in Russia in 1921 and had lived a life of stylish elegance, even luxury, which owed nothing to her alliance to an impoverished Russian émigré family who had settled in Paris. Susan was a clever woman, and her daughter took after her. Susan knew the value of family and connections, the importance of money and possessions. She was not the sort of person to say that happiness came from the heart.

Susan Ferov had made much of her own life from unhappy beginnings and she was ambitious for her children. But Sasha was not the sort of man who would push his way ahead, shoulder people aside as she would, or Anna, or her brother Bobby, who had done so for so many years with such conspicuous success. Though Sasha had had a distinguished and arduous time in the War he was one of nature's gentlemen: polite, considerate, courteous. He had married Stefanie to give a name and identity to her unborn child by another man. Stefanie had accepted this courtesy as a right, even though she didn't love him.

Anna didn't like Stefanie very much. She hated people who were permanently discontented and did nothing about it. Anna didn't like to mope around, but to be ever up and doing things. She was not a reader and she was not a thinker. She was not yet a schemer; but that would come.

Satisfied with her day, with the visit so far, she quickly took off the rest of her things, carefully hung the dress on a hanger, cleansed and creamed her face, got into bed and was soon asleep – assured of sweet dreams.

CHAPTER 2

Stefanie's quarrel with her father cast a blight over the family party for the rest of that weekend in the winter of 1949. Bobby left the following morning without taking his leave of Jenny who, ever conscious of her family responsibilities, at first thought it was something to do with the old row over the Hall with Hugo. Bobby would never have thought of the inconvenience he was putting people to, the misinterpretation of his motives. He was angry with his daughter and, through her, his son-in-law, who found himself torn both ways, seeing both points of view.

Bobby had been a bad father to his daughters, who had suffered considerably because of his selfishness. When he divorced their mother he had wanted to put them out of his mind as well. In the hardness of his heart he had banished them all to France without even giving them sufficient to live on: the girls, he had claimed, were heiresses, would come into money on their maturity, and in the meantime he gave them the most miserable of stipends on which to live in case the Ferov family, whom he hated, used it all.

It was an awful way to grow up and it was understandable that Stefanie should feel hatred for her father. But Sasha felt he had to look to the future, too: they both had and, as Bobby had said, he was not a rich man and Stefanie's bounty, too, was dependent on Bobby's goodwill. Her inheritance could be revoked by him at any stage he wished and he had already threatened to do it once before when Stefanie was involved with a man of whom he disapproved.

The day after the row was a Sunday and some of the family were preparing to leave anyway. Anna, used to luxury and a much warmer climate, found the Hall, despite its ancient grandeur, its appeal to her sensibilities, too chilly for her. She willingly agreed to travel back to London with the Crewes rather than face the displeasure of her uncle and the consequent bad atmosphere at Robertswood where she had been due to go on to with Princess Irina.

Anna travelled up in Arthur's large Bentley, sitting at the back between her cousins Joe and Angelica. Charlotte rode beside Arthur in the front. Pascal had his own car and had gone straight back to Durham where he was studying engineering. Pascal was the very first member of the Askham family not to have gone to Oxford or Cambridge but to have preferred a provincial university. He was one of the new breed of youngster produced by the war and the post-war climate.

All the Verdi children were Italianate in appearance – dark haired, olive skinned, black eyed – after their racing-driver father Paolo, who had been killed when his baby daughter was only nine months old. Angelica had thus grown up without a father's love and care, as her mother had, as Bobby had. It seemed a tradition in the modern annals of the Askham family – since 1900 – that too many of its youngsters were reared by one parent. Paul Askham, the young Earl, was growing up without either parent alive. Yet a large, close family such as this one was able to enfold its less fortunate members in a wide umbrella of love and care, as Rachel had raised Paul and helped Adam with the motherless Giles and Flora. However, as the Verdi children grew up they seemed to show those symptoms of insecurity brought about by a fatherless upbringing, and a sense of the danger their mother had been in during the war.

37

Except for her colouring, Angelica was a replica of her mother in her youth – tall, slim and with a mass of black hair whereas Charlotte's was a deep chestnut. Angelica, like Charlotte, had style and, left on her own, she would have developed this; but her mother had managed to suppress it in order to try and keep her daughter young. Thus, whereas Anna looked like a mature woman at eighteen, Angelica looked like a typical teenager; she wore classical jumpers, well-cut skirts and tailored dresses bought mostly for her by her mother at Harrods or Harvey Nichols. Compared to Anna, Angelica had felt very gauche indeed and did so now, sitting beside her in the car as they travelled up to London. Anna had her long legs crossed and she smoked a tipped cigarette. She wore a fur coat that an older, richer woman might envy and a small beaver hat with a jaunty feather. She wore lipstick and mascara, and rouge on her pale cheeks. Charlotte thought she overdid it and felt critical but Angelica, who hadn't seen her cousin since they were both small, was mesmerised, every bit as much as the Lighterman girls. Together they had whispered about her whenever they got the chance, almost tongue-tied in her presence.

Charlotte was worried about Stefanie, whom she regarded as a daughter, having been the last one of the family to see her mother alive. Together they had been in Auschwitz, but Hélène had to stay behind when Charlotte was moved on and that was the last anyone heard about her.

Charlotte knew that Stefanie was disturbed and wilful and Bobby was cussed, imperious and narrow-minded. It didn't make for a good combination in father and daughter.

Arthur glanced at Charlotte and put a hand over hers, momentarily taking his eyes from the road.

'Don't brood on it,' he said.

38

'I can't help it. It was such a horrible way to end the weekend. Awful, especially, in front of Anna.'

'Oh, I don't mind,' Anna said, puffing smoke towards the narrow opening in the window. 'Don't think of me. We have family brawls of our own, I assure you.'

'Really?' Angelica looked interested. Could this imperious being actually stoop to a *row*? 'I can't imagine either you or your grandmother . . .'

'You should hear us when we're all at it. One time Mother went off after the most frightful scene and stayed in a hotel on the Grand Canal, catching the first train out in the morning. Mother never thought of *me*.'

'All families have their rows,' Charlotte agreed. 'But this is a little more serious than that. It concerns Sasha, but Stefanie is so unforgiving. He doesn't know what to do. I feel more sorry for him than anyone else.' She half turned so that she could see Anna and smiled.

'All this must be so much Greek to you, but a lot of it goes back to the war when Sasha became very dear to us. He was so brave and, of course, I was very close to Stefanie's mother, whom I loved. She helped save Sasha too . . .'

'I know that,' Anna said in her low voice with a hint of an accent. Growing up to speak Russian, French and Italian, as well as her native English, it could perhaps be forgiven her. It certainly added to her fascination. 'I know all about Hélène in the War, and you too, Charlotte. We are very proud of you.' Her tone sounded patronizing.

'There's no need for that!' Charlotte was aware that she was blushing, amazed at the ability of so young a girl to bring this about. She couldn't remember blushing since she was Anna's age. When Anna paid a compliment one felt not only grateful but actually flattered. It was quite ridiculous the power she had established over the family in such a short time. Maybe it was because they hadn't

39

seen her for so many years . . . Charlotte turned her head away and stared at the road.

There was something about Anna that made her uncomfortable, even though she was old enough to be her mother.

The Crewes lived in some splendour in one of those large old houses whose gardens backed on to Holland Park. Arthur, who had spent most of the war on the Burma Railway, having been captured at the fall of Singapore, had recovered remarkably quickly afterwards. This was largely thanks to his marriage to Charlotte, whom he had loved for many years, even before the war began.

It had been difficult for Charlotte to settle down to civilian life and peacetime, but Arthur was the ideal person to be married to because he was a gentle and considerate man, very much in love.

Arthur, a younger son of the Earl of Crewe and Carstairs, was distantly related to the Askham family. He was one of those fortunate people whose experiences in the war had left them relatively unmarked. He didn't suffer from any traumas or nightmares afterwards, or any sense of guilt about the number of fellows who had perished on the railway while he had lived.

After marriage to Charlotte, Arthur had gone into the City, taking up a number of directorships he had been offered, thanks partly to family contacts and partly to men he had served with in the RAF. He had become an insurance broker, a member of Lloyd's, and he was able to keep Charlotte in the style of an earl's daughter, though Charlotte had never craved luxury and her life as a mannequin in the thirties followed by her wartime experiences had made her ready for anything.

At the turn of the year of 1949 people hoped for less gloom than in 1948, which had been one of foreboding

40

with a Communist coup in Czechoslovakia, widespread shortages in England, including newsprint and cigarettes, which were sometimes only obtainable under the counter. There had been a dock strike and a steep rise in the cost of living. Labour was struggling to keep its promise of a brave new world, but its welfare plans were being eroded and there was still widespread rationing. The Communist coup in Czechoslovakia had made Churchill speak in ominous tones of the menace of a third world war.

Somehow, as always, the upper classes remained relatively unscathed. They were touched, of course, by general shortages, rationing and so on. But the rise in the cost of living, which particularly affected the middle classes and those on fixed incomes, presented little problem to households such as the Crewes. Trade, commerce of all kinds, was a great healer between nations and the city was rapidly recovering from the effects of the War despite the trauma of a Labour Government. After all, investment and the making of money was the best way to prosperity and Arthur Crewe, having effectively shut out his past, was there among the top.

Until the arrival of Anna Ferov the Crewe household could have been considered a reasonably happy and contented one. Afterwards all this changed, but it is impossible to say whether the blame could be laid directly at Anna's door or whether it would have happened anyway. Charlotte's three children had had a restless, disturbed childhood, much as the family had tried to help them. There was a mother living and working in France, boarding-school in England, a toing and froing that the War interrupted, only to result in the complete disappearance of their mother.

After the marriage in 1945 the twins and Angelica, who had known Arthur most of their lives, accepted him as a father – Angelica even called him 'father'. He was especially tender with her but, by the time their mother married Arthur, the boys were seventeen and they called him by his Christian name.

Joe and Angelica still lived at home and so, of course, did Jeremy, the youngest member of the family, Charlotte and Arthur's son born in 1946. There was a small but adequate staff – a cook, a maid who lived in plus a daily gardener and a daily woman. Arthur had a chauffeur, an ex-RAF batman, who drove him daily to and from the City.

It was thus a compact, well-organized household capably presided over by Charlotte, who became a simple housewife and mother after a life of activity and excitement.

She never thought very much about it, the daily routine, but when she did she compared it quite favourably to her lifestyle before, except that she knew something was missing that she would never replace. In many ways she didn't want to, but sometimes she did if she dared let herself think about it: excitement, danger, even the threat of death.

But Charlotte's life wasn't purely domestic. She was on the committees of many organizations to do with refugees and others displaced by the War. She took an active part in Arthur's political life – he was nursing a northern constituency and she travelled about a lot with him.

Anna had been with them a few weeks when, one morning, Charlotte put down the phone after talking to her mother. Charlotte swallowed a cup of coffee as she consulted some notes for a speech she had to make that afternoon, on behalf of Arthur, to a Conservative women's group, when Angelica put a head round the door.

'Can I have a word, Mummy?'

'I'm terribly busy, darling, won't tonight do?'

'I'd rather it were now.'

'Of course,' Charlotte put away her notes, surreptitiously glancing at her watch. She had made it a rule, and she tried to keep to it, that the children and Arthur came first, everything else second.

She smiled at Angelica and then noticed she still had on her dressing-gown.

'Aren't you well, darling?'

'Quite well, Mummy,' Angelica yawned. 'Late night.'

'So I heard,' Charlotte frowned. 'I don't think Anna is a very good influence on you.'

'Oh, Mummy! Don't be so prejudiced. Didn't *you* have a few late nights when you were young?'

'I suppose so,' Charlotte continued to look worried. 'Things were different in those days, though. Somehow one didn't worry so much about the young. At least, I don't think they did.'

'Anna's leaving, anyway,' Angelica said.

'Oh, is she?' Charlotte tried to keep the relief out of her voice. 'Is she going to tell me?'

'Of course she is,' Angelica sank on to the sofa. 'She's going to take a flat.'

'Isn't she going back to Venice?'

'Not yet. She loves London.'

'So I noticed.' Charlotte thought she had time for just one more cup of coffee and poured some from the pot.

'You don't like Anna much, do you, Mummy?'

'I hardly ever see Anna, to tell you the truth,' Charlotte said. 'She doesn't seem to get up until about noon and is never here in the evenings.'

'Neither are you. That's just an excuse, though. I can tell there is something about her you don't like.'

'Not exactly dislike,' Charlotte said carefully. 'Perhaps I don't really understand her. She's like her mother, you know. Susan was only a few years older than we were and

43

yet we always thought she was enormously remote and sophisticated. Then when she went and got married – eloped if you please!' Charlotte laughed at the memory. 'Oh yes, darling, mother and daughter are very alike. Of course I don't dislike Anna but I do find her,' Charlotte searched for the most tactful word, 'unrestful.'

Angelica, head on chest, appeared lost in thought. Then she raised her head.

'Would you mind if I shared a flat with her? It would be such fun!'

'But Angelica . . .' Charlotte wanted desperately to say the right thing. 'You have a . . . perfectly good home here.'

'But it's not the same, is it?'

'All the freedom you want.'

'Yes, but can't you understand?'

'I can understand, but you're only eighteen.'

'Other people go away to university at that age. Can't I make you understand, Mummy?'

'I can understand, but not with Anna,' Charlotte said suddenly. 'On that I have quite made up my mind.'

'Why not?'

'I don't have to give you my reasons. I'm your mother.'

'You do, you do.' Angelica jumped up and stamped her foot on the floor. 'You do. You treat me like a baby, and you *do*! If you don't let me go I shall run away and you won't know where I am.'

The family were used to violent eruptions from Angelica – she was a creature of moods, highs and lows, infinitely volatile. It was as though her hold on life were finely balanced – she could go this way or that. Often Angelica reminded Charlotte of a time bomb and for this she blamed herself. Angelica's childhood had been far from secure, she was away from her mother for long periods. Then, when a girl most needs her mother, the early years of adolescence, she had disappeared during the war, no one knew whether she were alive or dead. When she did return, Angelica deliberately adopted a casualness, a flippancy that had never quite left her.

'Anna is no good at all for Angelica. I should never have invited her,' Charlotte said to Arthur in bed that night. He had travelled down from the constituency he was nursing and she'd met him at the station. He'd had a business dinner to which she was invited and now, at last, they were alone. Most of their serious talks had to be conducted like this – in the dead of night or the early hours.

'Charlotte,' Arthur murmured from the depths of a terrible weariness he invariably felt at the end of his frenetic day. 'You can't blame Anna for *everything*. You and your mother seem to have a thing about her.'

'But she was supposed to be coming to England for a few weeks. She's been here nearly four months. What kind of "visit" is that?'

'Well then, if she wants to go now, let her.'

'But why with my daughter! Of course the problem is that she hasn't got enough money. Susan has kept her on a tight rein. I can see why; she is very extravagant. What do you think the effect of her example on Angelica will be?'

'Terrible,' Arthur was nearly asleep. 'But you'll have to let her go. No mother should hang on to her children for ever.'

Soon Arthur was snoring gently; but Charlotte couldn't sleep. Anna wasn't in and Angelica, excluded also from Anna's exciting night life, was sulking in her room.

Charlotte knew that Anna would use the malleable Angelica for her own ends. It was then that Charlotte found herself forced to confront the real reason for her dislike of this cousin from abroad – it wasn't because of

Susan, but Kyril. She was Kyril's daughter and, in many ways, this seemed to Charlotte like the mark of Cain. Too much was suspected about Kyril to make one feel wholly comfortable with his progeny. Unfair this might be, but it was a fact. Sasha had proved himself loyal, sensitive, sincere, a darling beloved by all the family. But Anna? Charlotte felt a little prickle of fear that the security and happiness she'd had since the war were about to disappear; that danger was returning to her life, yet again.

Anna had a habit of getting her own way. She did it quite insidiously so that hardly anyone ever knew it had happened. She would sow the seeds and other people would do the work. When it came down to it no one could really point the finger at Anna. If there were witnesses, they would say the same thing about her behaviour as a child or small girl: others always got the blame.

Despite their sympathy, the family thought that, on the whole, Charlotte made an awful fuss when she opposed Angelica and Anna sharing a flat together. Em was all for independence and she approved of it. She had no hang-ups about Anna at all – no share in Charlotte's misgivings. She even found a flat for the girls, round the corner from her own in Redcliffe Gardens not far from Earls Court Station, and not too far from Charlotte, if it came to that.

It was futile for Charlotte to point out that she didn't like Anna's lifestyle, because everyone called her old-fashioned.

Rachel sympathized, but she could remember Charlotte at the same age as Anna and Angelica and, if anything, Charlotte had been a little worse. In fact, in many ways Rachel had given Charlotte more freedom than Angelica was allowed by her mother.

In the summer Anna went abroad again to meet her mother in Paris and travel with her to Venice. While she

46

was away Charlotte had the flat redecorated at her own expense and refurnished to her own taste. As it was a rented, furnished flat, she was throwing an awful lot of money away and people said she was interfering. It was like doing up the baby's nursery all over again, the baby she was reluctant to let grow up.

In the summer, too, the Crewe family always did those jolly holiday things that families liked to do: they spent a lot of time in the country at their own house or those of various friends; monied, titled people like themselves. They went up to Scotland for the glorious twelfth and shot grouse and fished in the Tweed from the family seat of the Kittos.

They liked to travel about as a family with a family identity. Even Pascal, who liked his freedom, felt he had to be with them and Joe was the only one who was allowed to escape because he had a job.

Joe spent a lot of that summer in London because he was working on a local paper in Kent and it was easy for him to come home at nights. He was a solitary person and liked having the place to himself.

Thus Joe was alone in the house when a cable came from Anna announcing her imminent arrival at Victoria Station and asking someone to meet her.

'Typical,' Joe thought, but he dutifully went and stood on the platform as the boat train came puffing in and, eventually, Anna descended, immediately to be surrounded by porters with a mountain of baggage, like a visiting celebrity. When she saw him, Anna threw her arms out and gave him a theatrical embrace.

'Joe! How sweet of you to come!'

'Not at all,' Joe felt himself blushing.

'Where are the others?'

'In Scotland. I only got your telegram by chance.'

Anna clicked her fingers. 'I should have remembered

47

they'd be in Scotland. Mummy wanted me to stay on but I couldn't wait to get back.' Anna began directing the porters to precede her. Joe was aware that she did indeed look lovely and smelt fragrant. He discovered he was extremely nervous in her presence.

'Have you a car?' Anna enquired.

'Taxi,' Joe replied. 'I don't drive a car.'

'Still, it *is* sweet of you to come, anyway.'

By the time Anna and all her baggage were safely stowed away, Joe felt exhausted. Anna counted her pieces of luggage several times and undertipped the porters, sending them away disgruntled. Eventually Joe climbed into the seat beside her and mopped his brow.

'Hot,' he said.

'It *is*,' Anna agreed, 'but you should be in Venice. At least it doesn't stink in London.'

As Joe leaned forward and gave the address of the Earls Court flat Anna said suddenly:

'Have you a key?'

'Key?'

'To the flat,' Anna said. 'I left it with Angelica. Your mother said she wanted to redecorate. Her interference was the price we had to pay to win Angelica's freedom.'

'I don't think Mother meant it that way,' Joe blushed again.

'Oh, I'm sure she didn't.' Anna put a surprisingly cool hand over his. 'What a *beastly* thing for me to say. But it means we can't get into the flat, can we?'

'Why not?'

'No key.'

'You'll have to stay at our place,' Joe said. 'There's plenty of room.'

Joe never thought of himself as in danger from his cousin.

* * *

Joe Verdi at twenty was a tall, rather introspective young man with the classical Verdi good looks. Pascal and Joe were very unalike, Pascal being devoted to all forms of physical exercise and crazy about cars. Joe was cerebral, an aesthete. His Aunt Em considered his judgement so good, so balanced that he had already written leaders for her paper. She would gladly have given Joe a job, but he was only a few years in the journalistic profession and the family didn't want to be accused of nepotism. However, both Rachel and Em, the journalists in the family, thought highly of his ability and were proud of him. He was certainly seen as a future editor of *The Sentinel*.

Joe felt himself quite out of the class of his cousin Anna. Her flamboyance distressed him. He liked people who were self-effacing. He was not especially good, or comfortable, in the presence of women but Anna was family and, as family, had to be met, accommodated. It was not only good manners. It was expected.

He probably imagined, nevertheless, that he could leave his cousin in her room and forget about her.

But as soon as Anna had freshened herself up from the journey she descended to the kitchen, where Joe was thinking about getting something to eat. Anna sat on the kitchen table and swung her long brown legs.

'You're very domesticated, aren't you? Anything to drink around here?'

'Of course,' Joe said politely. 'What would you like?'

'Gin and T please,' Anna said. 'Then why don't we go out and eat?'

'Good idea,' Joe said, thinking it would be less awkward in company.

But Anna was good company. She talked about Venice and the family and made him laugh. They went to a nearby restaurant in Holland Park that had recently opened. Anna said she'd go anywhere as long as it wasn't

Italian, and this was one of those hybrid restaurants that were springing up after the war. There were not many of them because there was still rationing, but some people were venturing out, possibly in anticipation of a boom when derationing finally came.

'Where's your mother now?' Joe asked, when they were half-way through the meal.

'She's gone to New York. She's going to open one of her shops there. She calls them gallerias,' Anna pronounced it *ga-le-ria* with a strong emphasis on each syllable, 'but I call them shops. Don't you?'

'I suppose so,' Joe said, smiling. 'Rather swanky shops.'

'Mother is frightfully good on furniture. Grandma says she's a connoisseur, in the world class.'

'That's good,' Joe said. He was a little bit afraid of Aunt Susan, too.

They got home quite early and Anna went to bed, saying she was tired but, later that night, as Joe sat at his desk writing up some notes from the day's reporting jobs, he heard a footfall behind him and felt a hand on his neck. He turned with an exclamation but Anna, smiling, held up a finger to her lips and whispered: 'Shhhhh . . .'

'There's no one here to hear,' Joe said irritably. 'You startled me.'

'Sorry. I couldn't sleep. I saw your light. Do you always stay up so late?'

'Usually,' Joe said. 'I can concentrate when it's quiet and dark.'

Anna let go of his shoulders and flopped on his bed, exposing her bare legs, the hem of a lacy nightie. Anna seemed thoroughly at home and Joe eyed her nervously, not knowing whether to go on with what he was doing or stop. Finally he said: 'Don't think me terribly rude but do you mind? This has got to make the afternoon edition of my paper tomorrow.'

'Don't you ever relax?' Anna said. 'Or don't you like girls?' Joe stared at the legs, aware of the colour suffusing his cheeks, unable to stop it. 'Or didn't you think my approach would be quite so blatant?' Anna went on relentlessly. 'Are you a virgin, Joe?'

Joe got up and began to pace up and down in front of her, glad of the sudden breeze from the open window on his face.

'I didn't realize this evening would be like this, Anna. Maybe I should go to a hotel?'

'Oh, *Joe*.' Anna sat up and swung her legs over the side of the bed so that she sat with both feet on the floor. 'I'm just joking, kidding, you know. You are a bit of a fall guy. So nice, so polite. I bet you don't have any fun at all, do you?'

'I would never have dreamt of inviting you here if . . . After all, you're a *cousin*.' Joe sounded affronted.

'I see you can't take a joke.' Anna stood up and gazed at him, arms akimbo. 'I think you must be a pansy.' Then she turned and walked through the open door, back to her room.

After she'd gone Joe threw a shoe at the door, and when he sat down at his desk again he was trembling.

Anna never really minded offending people very much. The whole episode with Joe, though unexpected, amused her and she slept very well after it, as she always did. When she came down to breakfast he had gone and the daily woman was pottering about, all the other staff being on holiday.

Mrs Brown asked how long Miss Ferov would be staying and Miss Ferov replied that she didn't know. It would depend. She hadn't really intended to seduce Joe and the bit of fun the night before had gone sour and seemed rather unkind by morning. She didn't imagine that he was a pansy for a moment, but he clearly was not attracted by her, and it saved one's pride to be offensive. She thought she'd had rather too much to drink at dinner.

'Well, Mr Joe's gone and you'll have the house to yourself,' Mrs Brown said. 'Stay as long as you like, Miss,' and she went up to do the bedrooms.

But it was hot in London and most of Anna's friends were away. She rather regretted returning so early when most people were still on holiday. Her mother had given her a lift as far as Paris in her car but Paris was empty too, and Anna, always restless, felt England was the place to be.

But was it? She lit a cigarette and stared at her coffee-cup.

Perhaps England in the countryside. Yes, that was it. She got up to telephone her Russian grandmother and discovered that a lot of family were expected for the weekend.

Suddenly alive again, Anna called out to Mrs Brown that her plans had changed and she would, after all, be leaving again that day.

Bobby liked to think of himself as a family man and, though there were some who found this concept amusing, nevertheless it was true. He was the father of four children and the pivot of a rather large, diffuse family. While Paul was in his minority many regarded him as its head. Bobby was also a man of extreme wealth, the owner of two large houses stuffed with treasures that, if sold even on the depressed post-war market, would increase his fortune by half as much again.

His grandfather, Sir Robert Lighterman, had laid the foundation of Bobby's fortune from humble beginnings as a grocer's boy. He had left to his grandson a huge mansion in Manchester Square in London, which Bobby had recently given to the nation.

The Lighterman Collection had been opened by Royalty and thus set the seal on Bobby's prestige and munificence.

Yet Bobby was a lonely man. Not many people liked him. His second wife, Aileen, avoided his company whenever she could, occupying herself with charitable causes. His only son David, of whom Bobby had had such hopes, had rejected his parents, their lifestyle and fortune and gone to America where he was trying to build a reputation as a jazz musician. Of his three daughters, rather like the daughters of King Lear, only one really loved Bobby, Natasha, the youngest, though only one really hated him – Stefanie, the eldest.

Stefanie Ferov was a complex young woman whose life had been dominated by grief, by restlessness, by fear. Insecurity was perhaps the paramount reason for all this because she had been older than the others when they were all expelled from her father's home.

For over a year, however, Stefanie had been married to her cousin Sasha, who was not the father of her son Nicky, but who had adopted him. He regarded Nicky as his own child and he loved him.

But Stefanie's problems continued even after a marriage that should have made her happy and restored to her the sense of security which she had lost. Sasha was a loving and indulgent husband, a capable man, even a strong one. He had some income of his own and Bobby had given them a house for their wedding present and, for tax reasons, had made over Robertswood to them as their country home.

But of course the dominant presence was still his. He continued to regard it as his home, whatever the deeds said, and he came and went as he pleased. He had a comfortable suite on the first floor and an excellent housekeeper in the form of his ex-mother-in-law, Princess Irina. Irina, thankful for a permanent roof over her head, had done her best to help restore it since the war. She had grown up in gracious houses and palaces in Russia and her taste was unerring. She, too, had a large suite on the first floor, at the opposite end of the wide-fronted house from Bobby's.

When they were there Stefanie and Sasha had rooms on the second floor which also contained some guest rooms. The large attic, which had formerly housed the servants, was no longer used for this purpose. The house was looked after mainly by cleaning women from the nearby town, and the small resident staff lived in two cottages in the grounds, and renovated stables some distance from the house. There was a butler, three maids, a cook, a handyman and four gardeners, though only one of them was resident.

In the days of Sir Robert the house had as many servants as Askham Hall, but two wars had changed this state of affairs. People no longer wanted to go into domestic service, attitudes had changed. Bobby was considered lucky to have so many resident staff, but he could pay good wages and local residents were eager to work for him because of the unusually high rates he was able to pay. Thus a small army of overall-clad ladies descended on the house every morning and left it at about four o'clock, rather like workers clocking in and out from a factory. A stream would emerge from the gate, and wait in the lane outside for the local bus and over the years there were few changes, because working in the house was so popular.

Summer was undoubtedly the time of year when the countryside around the house was seen at its best, the verdant greenery of the valley through which the broad

Thames flowed down, through London, to the estuary. The house had been built by Sir Robert in the 1870's, a huge, turreted redbrick mansion with four gables and a great mock-gothic portico. Many had named it a folly, but from the river it looked imposing and anyone who could afford to live there was envied.

There were many such houses up and down the country – Askham Hall was one – which had also been turned into other use during the war and many of them had never become homes again.

Bobby loved to get his family together. He felt he could relax at Robertswood and be himself: that charming, if erroneous, vision he had of the idea that he was a typical English country gentleman.

For this weekend in August he had invited just his immediate family, because the main purpose of the party – and Bobby always had a purpose for everything – was to persuade Sasha, still wobbling on the brink, to join him in running the Lighterman empire.

There had been many discussions since Bobby had first issued the invitation several months before. He had not been deterred by Stefanie's reaction, as the last thing he ever expected from her was co-operation. To him Stefanie was a rather disagreeable nuisance. He had long ago stopped trying to woo her affection.

Stefanie was his daughter and he had a duty to her, he accepted that, rather late in the day; but he didn't have to like her. But he did like his nephew and son-in-law, Sasha. He was very fond of him indeed. He hadn't liked Sasha very much as a boy, before the war, but he had grown to admire him and, as far as he was capable of affection, even to love him.

Aileen wasn't at the house party that August weekend after Anna returned from Venice. She had made an excuse to go and visit her father in Scotland. Olga was

55

there, with a friend from Cambridge called Max who was studying physics, and Sasha had invited a comrade from the War, a fellow gunner called Royce Buxton. Sasha was expansive and hospitable and never forgot old friends.

Natasha had been staying with her grandmother for several weeks already, on holiday from school. Anna travelled down with Bobby, who collected her from the Crewe home in Holland Park.

Bobby liked his niece. She was the sort of smart woman he took to, and a great and welcome surprise when she had first appeared on the scene the previous January. Until he and Susan had fallen out he had always got on with her, and he still admired her, even though they had very little to do with each other. What had happened had happened a long time ago and, if the immediate cause of the quarrel was forgotten, Susan and Bobby had drifted apart. Susan with her family near her seldom came to London. She felt she no longer had a home in England.

But Anna was good company. She and Bobby chatted all the way down, sitting comfortably in the back seat of the car chauffeured by the excellent Reeve, who had been with Bobby since the twenties. Reeve and Bobby were almost exactly the same age and Reeve valeted for him too and generally mothered him because Aileen was so often away.

'I thought you'd just come for a visit,' Bobby told her, chuckling, exhaling smoke from his cigar through the open window of the car into the English countryside. 'It looks to me as though you've come to stay.'

'Mother said the same thing,' Anna smiled and touched his arm. 'She sent you her best by the way, and Granny,' Anna leaned over and her lips brushed his cheek, 'she sent you a kiss.'

Bobby always felt vaguely uncomfortable when his

mother was mentioned. He was not a man much troubled by conscience, but he was dogged by a sense of guilt about his mother. She had not been to England since before the War and he had only once been to Venice. But Bobby and Melanie were fond of each other and they corresponded. He sent her gifts. Bobby always thought that if you gave people things it made up for the lack of more personal forms of contact.

Still, it was good of his mother to remember at least to send him a kiss. He squeezed Anna's arm.

'It's good to see you, dear. You're like a fresh breeze bringing a new mood, new ideas. I'm glad you didn't just come for a short visit but may spend some time here. I hear you've taken a flat?'

'Charlotte's not too pleased, I'm afraid. Angelica's sharing it with me.'

'Charlotte has become very set in her ways since the war,' Bobby said testily. 'She makes a baby of Angelica. Compared with the experiences my daughters have had Angelica has been over-protected.' Bobby looked searchingly at Anna. 'But what will you do in your flat?'

'What do you mean, what will I "do", Uncle Bobby?' Anna appeared startled.

'I mean have you got a lot of friends in London?'

'I expect I'll look for a job,' Anna crossed her legs and Bobby was reminded how shapely they were. He shook his head.

'Jobs, that's all girls can think about these days. With the better-off classes there is no need. Yet my daughters have the same idea. It was having a "job" that was the undoing of Stefanie. She met that frightful man and we all know what happened there.' Bobby pursed his mouth glumly.

'But you don't disapprove of women working, do you, Uncle Bobby?'

57

'I do in a way,' Bobby admitted. 'It began after the First War, you know. I was nineteen when the war ended and everyone wanted to work. It was quite unnecessary. But people also wanted to enjoy themselves then and now they're not so keen on that. The twenties were very gay and I wouldn't say the immediate post-war years this time have been. Work, work, work. It's so gloomy and, for women, so unecessary.' He put an avuncular hand on her knee. 'There is no need for you to work at all. Have all the fun you can and look around for a nice husband.'

'You wouldn't, say, employ *me*, Uncle Bobby, would you?' Anna said slyly, noticing how delicate and well kept his hand was. There was something slightly precious about her uncle, a smallish man, neat and well preserved but powerful. There was, perhaps, something rather Napoleonic about Bobby.

'*Employ* you? Can you type?'

'Not in that way, but as you want to employ Sasha; as an executive.'

'But you've no experience!' Bobby expostulated.

'Neither has he.'

'He was in the Air Force, he's a man . . .' Bobby paused, sensing he may have offended this rather exacting young woman. 'Besides, he's a lot older than you. Please, my dear Anna, get rid of all these notions and concentrate on being a woman.'

They got to Robertswood at about six in the evening of Friday and found the rest of the company already assembled. Max and Royce were introduced to the new arrivals and Anna was shown to her room next to her grandmother's suite on the first floor. Irina was overjoyed at having most of her grandchildren together under one roof and, despite Bobby's tacit disapproval, the meal that evening was a Russian one and Irina kept on lapsing into the language into which she had been born. Indeed, a majority of the people round the table spoke it. Irina had little lapses of memory due to emotion, to be so over-joyed, but no one minded very much. Wine flowed freely and inhibitions were released. Stefanie even managed a smile for her father, to be quite pleasant, and Bobby took it as a good sign for the discussions he intended to have that weekend.

After dinner, as usual, there was coffee in the drawing-room and Sasha and Royce went off to play billiards.

Anna thought Royce looked rather interesting and watched with some regret as Sasha led him out of the room. Men, meeting them and thinking about them, occupied quite a good deal of Anna's time.

Uncle Bobby had urged Anna to concentrate on being a woman and, in one aspect, she was very keen to do this. In Italian society the sexual mores were still hypocritical and stifling. It was most unusual to go out alone with a man; indeed it wasn't possible. Young people went around in groups and even parties were likely to be overseen by parents.

Anna's knowledge of sex was limited to a few furtive gropings and she was ashamed of her inexperience. She knew it was contrary to the impression she made on people and in a way she played on it; she used it to entice men.

But Anna had had no intention of trying to seduce her cousin Joe Verdi earlier in the week and had spent a lot of time wondering why she behaved as she did. She was slightly ashamed of herself and, had he been around, would have apologized. She had even toyed with the idea of sending him a letter. But how did you apologize to someone for calling them a pansy? She felt uncomfortable to even think of what she'd said. It was a horrible thing to do.

Anna supposed the point was that she saw in Pascal and Joe the opposite poles of sexuality: Joe was withdrawn and Pascal was a flirt, like her. She suspected that had she lounged on Pascal's bed he would pretty soon have been beside her, and in a way she was trying to test Joe. But why? It was not nice and it certainly was not ladylike. Her mother would be horrified. It was unforgivable.

Someone like Royce Buxton, however, who was quite old and looked as though he had lived, might be the step to advancement in a girl's sexual career that she was looking for. However, she didn't see him again that night and went rather forlornly and chastely to bed in the next room to her grandmother.

She was just about to put out the light when there was a timid knock on the door. She sat up, wondering if that sexual message had managed to transmit itself across the dining-room.

'Come in,' she called, slightly breathless, but a white, plump, rather gnarled old hand came round the door, followed by a bright birdlike nose and a pair of twinkling eyes.

'Babushka,' Anna said, sinking back on her pillows.

'Who did you think it was, my *dotchinka*?' Irina said mischievously, advancing into the room with the dainty steps she had learned in the court of the last Tsar. One hand now clasped her quilted dressing gown around her and in the other there was a glass of milk which she held out to Anna.

'Oh Babushka!' Anna laughingly reached for it. 'How sweet of you. You shouldn't have done this.'

Irina's eyes sparkled with pleasure and, giving her the glass, she drew up a chair and sat down by the side of the bed.

'You've no idea the pleasure it gives me to have you all

here. My four granddaughters, my grandson . . .' Irina's voice trailed off. She had other grandchildren, too, from her children Evgenia and Dima, who still lived in France and whom she saw infrequently. One branch of the Ferov family had split itself off from the other. The war had done that to a lot of families. She put out a hand and gently touched Anna's hair, murmuring to herself.

'So grown up,' she said. 'So grown up. I remember when you were born.' Irina cupped her hands together and smiled while Anna started to sip her milk. 'Such a tiny baby; such a sweet one.' She continued to stroke her head and Anna bent it towards her like a cat, to please her grandmother.

Anna felt Irina was the one person she most truly loved in the world. She had seen so little of her and consequently the memories she had were pleasant ones. Irina was so warm and generous, a Slav. Red Russian blood throbbed in her veins. She had suffered and the suffering showed; but she'd survived. She'd courted the imperious Askhams, the menacing Nazis and the patronizing Bobby in order to stay alive: and she had. She was a survivor, a winner, someone who always landed on her two feet. Remembering, even from this point of time, how her grandmother had lived in Paris, Anna thought it was amazing how well she looked even though she was rather wrinkled and slightly stooped . . . not quite the *grande dame* of her former years.

'You're like my Kyril,' Irina crooned, hands running again through Anna's hair. 'Much more like him than Sasha. My Kyril, I wonder what became of him?'

Anna clutched Irina's hand as both their eyes filled with tears.

'What did become of Father, Babushka? Won't we ever know?'

Irina shook her head. 'In my heart I feel he is alive.

61

Like Hélène. I think she is alive, too.' She brushed the tears from her eyes. 'My poor Alexei I *know* is dead because I saw his poor body, shot through the head.' Irina put a trembling hand to her forehead. 'A clean, neat hole, like the work of a surgeon . . .'

'Hush, Babushka, hush. Don't distress yourself.'

But Irina was loosed once again on a flood tide of nostalia and reminiscence. Whenever she saw her family there was an almost irresistible urge to have a good cry . . . to wander down memory lane with them, weeping. It was quite an understandable, indeed perhaps necessary, outlet for a woman who was in her seventy-seventh year; who had seen two major wars which had altered the face of the world, and the destruction of most of the major monarchies reigning over it when she was a girl, including her own precious Tsar, Nicholas II.

While Anna listened to her grandmother she thought about her father, whom she hadn't seen since she was six. It had never been explained to her why her parents drifted apart because at the beginning it had seemed such a romantic story – a meeting in Russia when Susan was only eighteen, an elopement, a honeymoon cut short by the direct orders of Stalin. Uncle Bobby had come over to find his sister and he was even then a powerful man, dealing directly with the new Soviet government, the infant Bolshevik state, to supply it with much-needed vehicles and machinery.

When, many years later, her father was released, again it seemed to the lookers-on that the romance had started up again. There followed a few years of harmony during which Anna had been born.

Anna could still very vividly recall her father: not very tall but powerfully built with the reddish hair that she had inherited. His personality was powerful too, magnetic, and it seemed, as the years passed, to grow in her imagination so that it became almost God-like.

Everyone knew that a father was important for a growing girl and Anna had been deprived of hers too soon. Her grandfather, poor, feckless Prince Alexei, with his dreams and delusions of grandeur, was no substitute for that powerful, enigmatic figure.

Anna clutched her grandmother because she was a much stronger bond with her father than her mother, who no longer loved him. Irina had borne him and loved him as only a mother can love.

And, through her, Anna loved her father, and knew she always would.

Royce Buxton was about Sasha's age and, like Sasha, he had stayed on for a time in the RAF. He was an Australian without ties and he now worked for an engineering company as a salesman. Royce was a little out of his depth with Sasha's family, his uncle a lord. He was a simple, tennis-loving extrovert who seldom turned down a weekend invitation to try and ease his loneliness, his lack of ties when he wasn't working.

Anna rather took to the stocky, virile-looking Royce who had thick ginger hair, a pinkish complexion, very blue eyes and a walrus moustache. She went to considerable trouble to make him feel at home in her uncle's huge house.

They were both down early for breakfast and she offered to show him the house and took him in hand for the rest of the day, charming him out of his mind. Royce was most impressed, and not a little overawed, by the attention he was receiving from this rather sumptuous-looking woman with the red hair and fascinating eyes. He thought she must be about twenty-two or -three and he was flattered that she obviously liked him. Hands off

Sasha's sister, though, he knew that. Besides, he was a commercial salesman with little prospect of promotion, and she was the daughter of a prince and princess and the niece of a lord.

Later that afternoon Stefanie and Natasha sat in deck-chairs near the tennis court while Anna and Royce partnered Olga and Max at a vigorous game. Fourteen-month-old Nicky sat in his play-pen, staring ecstatically at a ball his grandfather had brought down for him. In small things Bobby was surprisingly considerate – or was it that he was his first grandchild, and one's grandchildren were so much more interesting than one's children because one could indulge them without having the responsibility? Nicky was an attractive, dark-haired child and Bobby flattered himself that his grandson resembled him when young. It was largely because of Nicky that Bobby had made up with Stefanie after the row at the party to welcome Anna – because of Nicky and the fact that he wanted Sasha in the business. Who could be better than Sasha, ready equipped with an heir to follow him?

No one had ever told Bobby that Nicky wasn't Sasha's son. The curious thing was that Bobby hadn't guessed; like many self-centred people, he was relatively uncurious about others. Sasha and Stefanie were married and, as far as he was concerned, Nicky was theirs. It never occurred to him to think of the man he had never met, Jack Blackstock, Stefanie's former lover and the father of her child.

But Stefanie knew whose son he was and, from the moment he was born, she had disliked him. Sometimes she could hardly bear to look at him so much did he, to her way of thinking, resemble Jack. Consequently she had never shown a mother's love for her baby and it had been left to Sasha to make up for her.

But, on that beautiful August day in the summer of

1949, it was hard to feel out of tune with the world, even when Bobby had taken Sasha away from them, saying that he wanted to walk by the river.

'I notice he didn't ask me,' Stefanie said, watching them walk away.

'Nor me,' Natasha smiled at her sister. 'But we didn't want to go, did we?'

'Not really.' Stefanie snuggled back in her chair, eyes closed to the hot sun. 'I bet I know what it's about.' She opened her eyes. 'Father will never give in about Sasha working for him. He's been so nice to me since the row, but he will never give in – and Sasha will work for him and it will be a disaster.'

'Why?'

'I know it will. What Sasha would like is some small business of his own, making cars or planes. He doesn't want to be the managing director of an empire!'

'They why doesn't he do what he wants to do?'

'It's difficult to know how to start. He hasn't enough capital and Father would never give it to him or lend it to him. Sasha's only hope is to do what he wants within the Lighterman empire . . .'

'That seems a good idea.'

'Do you ever think of Mother?' Stefanie asked abruptly.

'Sometimes.'

'I think of her all the time.'

'I know. You shouldn't. She's dead.'

'Babushka thinks she's alive.'

'*And* Uncle Kyril. I think they're both dead and so does everyone else.'

'I'm haunted by the fact that Mama . . .'

'I know,' Natasha reached for her hand. 'But try not to be. Accept what has happened and try to make it up with Father instead.'

'I wish *he* were the one who had died,' Stefanie said savagely. 'I wish . . .' But she leaned her head back, closing her eyes, and never said what it was she wished.

Natasha sighed. She did care, but she was a realist. She was also a conciliator, a peacemaker. She was a sunny, uncomplicated girl whose soft and appealing ways made her loved by all the family. She had been the one least affected by the experiences of the past; she missed her mother less than her sisters and she was the first to forgive her father. Yet she craved more affection from Bobby than he seemed able to give; he regarded Natasha with more detachment than the other two. It was Stefanie, because of her hostility, whom he most wanted to please.

Stefanie seemed to be dozing and Natasha started to watch the players on the court. She had noticed that Royce was taken with her cousin. Royce reminded her a bit of Jack Blackstock, Stefanie's boyfriend over whom there had been such a family row. He didn't resemble him in looks, but in manner. He was rather common, a bit too loud, not a gentleman. Natasha, however, although she was only seventeen, suspected that Anna wanted something from him that had nothing to do with any of these things. She was aware, too, of a sexual attraction about Royce and when, after the game, she saw Anna and Royce go off through the woods by the side of the house she wondered if they had gone to kiss.

That night after dinner Bobby announced that, after all, Sasha was going to come into the business with him. It had been agreed that afternoon, by the river. Stefanie had been informed and was happy about it. He had paused to look at Stefanie who had shown a kind of acquiescence that surprised most people.

Altogether it was a happy family party, happier than most people had expected, or could remember. After

66

dinner there was dancing in the ballroom to the new radiogram that Bobby had imported from America. Royce and Anna danced closely and Natasha decided that her surmise about them had been correct. She danced with her father, but he kept on looking at Sasha and Stefanie, a complacent smile on his face.

'I don't know how you did it,' Natasha said, following his gaze.

'Did what?' Bobby was so happy with the outcome of his conversation with Sasha and, later, Stefanie, that he looked at her benignly. 'Did what, my dear?'

'Persuaded Stefanie . . .'

'Oh, that was easy,' Bobby smiled. 'I promised her that if Sasha joined the company there would be lots of chances to visit Russia – I've kept up all my old contacts, you know. The mention of Russia had more effect on Stefanie than any offer of riches I could have made.' Briefly Bobby's eyes clouded, but quickly cleared again. 'For some reason your poor sister is still deluded enough to think your mother is alive and that, if she goes to Russia, she will find her.'

CHAPTER 3

'I can't help thinking you used my name,' Charlotte said.
'I knew Igor Stanislavsky in Paris before the War.'

'I had to use your name to get the interview, Mummy.
Why should he have seen me otherwise with so many
applicants for so few jobs?'

'Sneaky, I think,' Charlotte gazed fixedly at Anna.

'Nothing to do with me, Charlotte,' Anna said. 'I assure
you . . .'

'Most things seem to be these days.' Charlotte was
conscious of a constriction in her throat. 'Angelica seems
unable to take any decisions by herself . . .'

'Not true, Mummy!' Angelica said hotly. 'Just
because . . .'

'You make a frightful fuss about everything, Charlotte,'
Anna said mildly, screwing a cigarette into her holder and
crossing her legs. 'The war has happened, you know,
since you were a girl. My mother remembers, too, how
worried Aunt Rachel was when you wanted to go on the
stage.'

'True, but I never wanted to leave home. I never even
suggested it.'

'Things were very different then, you've got to admit
that.'

Things were very different, it was true. Charlotte
started to pour the tea the maid had just brought in,
following the unannounced arrival of her daughter and
cousin. Life seemed so full of surprises these days – most
of them unwelcome.

Arthur had been returned as Conservative Member for

the north country constituency at the election in February 1950 when Labour's majority was reduced from 136 to 7. This meant that Arthur had to spend a lot of time both in the House, in case there was a vote, and in the north nursing his own small majority in a middle-class area disillusioned by five years of a Labour Government.

Charlotte felt, nevertheless, that her own busy life had a futility to it but she knew that the reason was because, like the country and the rest of Europe, she hadn't properly recovered from the War. Arthur had settled down but she hadn't.

She turned to look at Angelica, head bowed, stroking the cat that had sauntered into the room. Her daughter's sleek, dark head still reminded her so much of Paolo, dead nearly twenty years. Angelica had only been nine months old when Paolo had been killed at the opening race in Monza in 1931. Charlotte had done her best, but she had had a living to earn. The children had eventually all been sent to school in England and, inevitably, saw very little of their busy, successful mother. Then in the war she had vanished altogether. The boys appeared to understand and were proud of her; but Angelica couldn't forgive her for volunteering for such a dangerous mission and mother and daughter, never very close, had grown further apart.

Anna and Angelica finished fussing over the cat, a Siamese that Arthur had given Angelica for a birthday.

'Don't you want to take Chow with you?' Charlotte passed her daughter's cup and then offered Anna a piece of cake. Anna shook her head.

'Mummy, it's not fair if we're out all day.'

'Anna isn't out all day.'

'Anna *is* out all day, Charlotte,' Anna said firmly.

'Having a good time,' Angelica laughed, perhaps a little enviously.

'Doing *what*, exactly?' Charlotte sat down and crossed her ankles neatly beneath her. Whatever time of day one saw Charlotte she was always perfectly dressed and groomed, favouring twin-sets and tweed skirts for home in the winter and casual Horrocks's frocks in the summer. Charlotte was never ever seen, except perhaps in intimate moments by her husband, without make-up or looking anything but her best. Sometimes it could be irritating.

'There's a lot to do in London, Charlotte,' Anna said. 'I couldn't really tell you what I do, but I do a lot.'

'Don't you get bored,' Charlotte asked, 'doing nothing?' She bit her lip. It was so difficult to say the right thing when Anna was around.

'Well, do *you* get bored doing nothing?' Anna raised her head, her eyes bright. Charlotte felt a flush steal over her cheeks which she hoped wasn't noticeable.

'I have a lot to do, Anna, especially since Arthur was elected. I try and go up to Yorkshire with him at least every other weekend and we have lots of entertaining to do, both for business and Parliament.'

'Yes, but it's not *work*, is it, Charlotte? And I think that's what you're accusing me of. The implication is I'm lazy. Yet you do all you can to prevent Angelica doing what *she* wants to do. I find you very contrary. She is nearly twenty. We're both quite big girls, you know.'

'Please don't be sarcastic, Anna. I know that. It's just that I have experience of life. Modelling is very demanding and tiring. Maybe because I did it myself I wanted Angelica to do something else. I think I'd even have preferred her to have gone on the stage. The fact is that she didn't consult me, and I find that hurtful. As for your life, of course it's your own to do as you wish . . .'

There was the sound of a taxi in the drive and Charlotte paused to look out of the window.

'Joe! Oh, it's Joe. Joe . . .'

Charlotte ran to the door and the two girls looked at each other. Anna stuck her thumb in the air.

'Round one to us. Round two to Joe, I think, for coming just in time. Where's he been?'

'America.' Angelica also jumped up and followed her mother into the hall, from which came glad cries of welcome while Anna sat sipping her tea and listening.

She knew she wasn't popular in the Crewe household, but not altogether why. She was one of those people who found it very difficult to evaluate hostility on the part of others or the reasons for it. She attributed it to some kind of jealousy, even on the part of her family. She rose to her feet just as Joe came into the room in front of his mother and sister. She put her cup and saucer on the tray and held out her hand, smiling.

'Welcome home, Joe.'

'Thank you,' Joe shook her hand politely but he turned away immediately, looking embarrassed. Anna hadn't seen him since the summer even though she shared a flat with his sister. Time had passed very quickly. Time doing nothing, as Charlotte would be the first to say. But Anna found that life passed in this way was pleasant. She'd spent Christmas in Paris and New Year in Rome. Most of January she was skiing with Italian friends in the Dolomites. Now it was spring again in England, over a year since she'd first arrived just for a visit.

As Charlotte fussed with the tea things, Joe produced presents from his bag which he gave to his mother and sister.

'Nothing for you, I'm afraid,' he said.

'I wouldn't have expected it.' Anna smiled at him again. 'You must come and see us in our flat. It's very cosy.'

'I'd like that,' Joe said, sitting down next to his mother. But he didn't sound enthusiastic.

71

As Charlotte met his eyes she was surprised to see mirrored there a mixture of anger and despair. She looked from Joe to Anna but neither gave anything away. She knew, though, that Joe had been hurt in some way and a current of anger ran through her against the only person who could be the cause: Anna.

Joseph Stalin at seventy seemed to Bobby to be not very different from the man he had last seen over twenty years before when, on a visit to Russia, he had negotiated the release of Kyril Ferov from his labour camp. Stalin was perhaps a little more thick-set, more lined than in those impossibly far-off days; but he had the same assurance and steadfast gaze that had so impressed Bobby. Since then he had become, of course, a world leader – the architect of Russia's victory in the war. To many he was also the greatest threat to peace.

Bobby and the Marshal had sat, with Sasha as inter-preter between them, in a pleasant room in the Kremlin for over an hour discussing events that had happened since their last meeting.

Finally Stalin said: 'It is you, Lord Lighterman, who first showed faith in the Soviet government as early as 1921. You have been a very good friend to us.'

Even during the purges in the thirties, Bobby thought, when men he had done business with, entertained and been entertained by, simply disappeared and were never seen and heard of again, he had maintained his friendship with Russia. Russia had been very grim in those days and, indeed, in some ways it was again. There had been optimism and a vigour about the twenties which was absent now after the terrible destruction and loss of life during the war when the Germans had reached the outskirts of Moscow, and the streets of Leningrad had been full of corpses.

'You have been consistent in your enthusiasm for the Soviet government,' Stalin continued, 'when others have failed us or betrayed us.'

Was this a reference to his friends who had disappeared in the purges, Bobby wondered? But he went on smiling and, as he did, tea in the samovar was brought in and little Russian cakes and delicacies. Stalin then turned his attention to Sasha, who had managed to merge himself in the background despite giving a very fluent and accurate two-way translation of the conversation.

'And you, young man,' Stalin's eyes glinted with approval. 'Ferov is your name, you say?'

'Prince Ferov and his family left Russia during the Revolution,' Bobby said, as Sasha automatically translated for him. 'But many of its members stayed loyal. His father, Kyril, for example, may well have served the Soviet Union in some exemplary fashion. He was last seen in Berlin with the Russian rank of colonel, but has disappeared.'

'Oh!' Stalin's eyes crinkled and he nodded. 'I will look into this.'

Sasha leaned forward.

'I would like to have news of my father if possible, Marshal. I have not seen him since the war. No one knows what happened to him. If . . .'

'I will look into it,' Stalin nodded again and half closed his eyes as if trying to recapture some distant memory.

'My daughter Stefanie is here with us,' Bobby said, acting on a prearranged plan. 'She is married to Sasha, whose dearest wish it is to take his wife to the Caucasian home of the Ferovs near Batum. Would this be possible, my dear Marshal . . . as a *very* great favour?'

Stalin half closed his eyes again in the characteristic mannerism that Bobby decided was meant to be unnerving, as though one's fate were in the balance.

'There will be nothing left of the family home in Batum,' Stalin replied, '*as* the family home, you understand. If it still exists it will be in use for the good of the people.' Stalin looked at his secretary sitting beside him, who was taking notes, and nodded. 'We will look into it . . . and if it is possible, Lord Lighterman, and I cannot promise it, it will be in return for favours from you . . . armaments, particularly, to guard our country against the west.'

'There is no need for you to fear attack from the west.' Bobby began to feel he was getting into very deep and murky waters, which reminded him slightly of the armaments crisis in the thirties concerning sales to the Nazis. 'The west is licking its wounds, too. Even in England we still have shortages, strict rationing and yet, unlike the Continent and yourselves, we were never invaded . . .'

'We suffered terribly,' Stalin said grimly. 'We need guns, Lord Lighterman, arms for defensive purposes.'

'I will have to see what I can do,' Bobby said. 'Certainly everything else, Marshall, if I cannot provide you with arms . . . tractors, machine tools, and so on. We are thinking of manufacturing cars again . . .' Bobby's lips were feeling dry.

'Guns, Lord Lighterman,' Stalin said softly and made a sign to signify that the interview was at an end.

The journey across Russia by train had taken almost as long as it had in those chaotic years after the Revolution when nothing ran on time and people, with their pathetic possessions in bundles, waited for days on stations for transport that never came. Trains in those days were fuelled by wood, so that every few miles they stopped in a forest clearing while more was cut to enable them to run along another few miles of track.

Yet since that time, thirty years before, Russia,

although still a backward country, was emerging as one of the great nations of the world, a rival to America for domination. The Russians' natural suspicion of foreigners and outsiders was enhanced by its experiences in the war when, virtually alone, it repulsed the mighty German army and turned the tide.

Yet the port and city of Batum, lying almost in sub-tropical conditions near the Turkish border, had changed only very little since 1921 when the Revolution was only four years old and had scarcely reached the southern parts of the country. There was still the thrust and bustle of a busy sea port, with liners calling from all parts of the world; still the gaily painted feluccas bobbing in and out among the oil tankers, the fishing smacks and the boats that plied along the coast of the Black Sea from Yalta in the Crimea to Trebizond on the Turkish coast.

But, unlike those far-off days of the brief courtship of his mother and father who had arrived in Batum on a small cruise boat from Yalta, Sasha and Stefanie were met at the station by a party functionary, there directly by command of Stalin. They were escorted to an old, large and pre-war limousine which was driven at great speed through the narrow winding streets of the old town, scattering pedestrians, donkeys, bicycles and assorted carts and vehicles in a way that would have been frowned upon in the days of the Tsar.

Batum had scarcely been touched by the war and recovered very quickly from it afterwards. Its polyglot population had, over the centuries, seen many oppressors come and go and, in that vast ocean of time, the advent of Hitler and jackboots was but a drop.

In the days when the Emperor of All the Russias, the Little Father, the last Tsar, Nicholas II, held sway, the Ferovs, hereditary princes whose dynasty parallelled that of the Romanovs, had had vast country estates, besides palaces in Moscow and Petrograd. The Moscow palace had rapidly been commandeered by participants in the 1917 Revolution, as Prince Alexei Ferov and his family fled to Paris.

But like many great Russian families, the Ferovs had their supporters of Lenin and these had stayed behind, most of them to disappear in the purges of the twenties and thirties. The last to go had been Kyril – where, or how, none of his family knew.

The Ferov estate in the shadow of the great Caucasian Mountain range was a two-storey house of comfortable proportions reminiscent of the small Palace of the Tsars at Livadia. Painted white and covered with vines, it was surrounded by a frieze of intricate lattice work under heavy, overhanging eaves. Below it, in the days of the Ferovs, had been elaborate gardens and a formal lawn running down to the large lake that all but encompassed the house.

But it is doubtful whether, had Princess Irina been returning to the family house instead of her grand-children, she would have recognized it. Everything else would have been familiar: the long trek from the port to the village, up a narrow railway track and by bullock cart along winding mountain roads in the old days. Now the journey was made swiftly in an hour in the black limousine, though even it laboured and panted up the narrow road through the forest of pines.

The house itself, though still painted white, still with its gables and lattice frieze, overlooking the lake, was merely the centre of a much larger complex of annexes, buildings, some attached to the original house and some surrounding it. These took up most of the space that had previously been the carefully tended emerald lawn between the old house and the lake.

Since 1921 Essenelli had been transformed first into a

refuge for those workers who had come from the hinterland to work in the south and couldn't find accommodation in the crowded port and then, latterly, into a holiday home for workers in the great factories in Kiev, Kharkov and places as far away as Moscow. Thus the profusion of largely jerry-built dwellings had sprung up with little regard for the architectural style and decorative touches initiated by the original architects in the nineteenth century.

But what there was, though spartan, was functional, clean and much appreciated by the masses, who had come from far worse dwellings in their crowded cities. Stefanie and Sasha were given a room overlooking the lake, one of a half-dozen usually kept for high party officials, or military or naval personnel on leave from Yalta or Odessa.

Stefanie and Sasha, tired from the rigours of the trip to Russia, the frenetic pace of Moscow and their primitive form of travel right across Russia, had been only too glad to have somewhere to rest for the week or two promised by Marshal Stalin before it was time to make their way to Odessa where they would join a ship to begin the voyage home.

The first two days they had spent mostly in their room sleeping, only emerging to take meals in the large communal dining-room or to go for short walks in the grounds.

It was May and it was holiday time, a beautiful season in the Caucasus and, gradually, the large complex was filling with sturdy farm and factory workers from the Ukraine or the Urals, most of them accompanied by large broods of children. For many of them it was the first time they had got away from cities decimated by the war, fought over by the German and Russian armies every bit as fiercely as the Red Army and White Russian troops had struggled against one another in the immediate years after the Revolution.

These people showed only polite interest in the strangers who inevitably stood apart as being not part of a group – maybe officials of the party, perhaps foreign. Though their command of the Russian language, spoken idiomatically and without accent, was perfect. This enabled Sasha and Stefanie not only to converse and to learn much at first hand of life in Russia, but to impart knowledge of the west which most people knew absolutely nothing about. The ignorance of the ordinary Russian was quite amazing unless one stopped to think that the average westerner's knowledge of Russia was pretty minimal as well.

'Except that we have newspapers,' Stefanie said, stepping back from the window from which she had been viewing the antics of a group of children on the lake, that deep beautiful lake still full of fat pink trout as it had been in her mother's day. She and Sasha had been talking about their latest conversation at lunch-time with an aggressive tractor driver, full of accusations about the west. Sasha was lying on the bed reading *Pravda*.

'They have papers, too,' Sasha waved his paper at her.

'Yes, but ours are free. They tell the truth.'

'Do they?' Sasha peered over the edge of his paper at his wife, then laid it on the bed and gazed at her. Stefanie's extremes of tiredness sometimes worried Sasha. She became pale and pinched-looking and her beauty faded altogether. Large black rings encircled her eyes. But in no time at all she was able to regain her vitality; her pallor vanished, to be replaced by an ethereal kind of beauty that invariably took his breath away, reminding him that he was as much in love with her as he had been when he'd married her.

Putting the paper aside, Sasha got up and went over to

stand behind her, putting his hands on her shoulders, nuzzling her cheek with his. Sometimes Stefanie would lean back in his arms as though welcoming the endearment, but today she remained stiff and unresponsive, her eyes fixed on the lake and then on the distant white-capped mountains towering over the pine forest which coated the slopes of the nearby hills.

'Penny for them?' Sasha enquired, following her gaze.

'I was thinking of my mother, wondering if she ever stood here looking out at the scene – children on the lake, maybe, her brothers and sisters, friends and cousins. Babushka looking out as I am now . . . I wonder where Mama is now, Sasha?'

Stefanie turned suddenly, burying her face in his thick jersey and Sasha stroked her hair, murmuring soothing words, grateful for these moments of closeness because they had very few.

'I think we must accept that both our parents are dead,' he said, his arms entwining themselves comfortably around her. 'Neither have been seen or heard of since the War. We must accept that, my darling, and also that neither of us is to blame. Please realize that.'

Sasha knew that Stefanie's main emotion about her lost mother was one of guilt. It was the guilt of a child who realizes too late that he or she has misunderstood a parent. For his part, Sasha's main feeling was of regret that his father was lost, not that he had failed him.

After a while Stefanie left the protection of his arms, and went and lay on the bed, her eyes heavy with weariness. Sasha sat beside her, taking her hand.

'Sorry,' she said, smiling at him. 'I'll never resolve it, will I? I'll always feel guilty about Mama.'

'Until you learn to realize there was *nothing* you could do. You were too young to understand what was happening. Why torment yourself now?'

Stefanie shook her head as if unable to fathom the mystery, but Sasha knew that it went very deep, to the very roots of the bond between mother and child.

After a while Sasha got on the bed and lay beside her, cradling her head in his arms as she slept. In many ways Stefanie was as much an enigma as her mother, almost as impossible to understand. Like her mother, she had a unique fascination, especially for men. Mother and daughter shared many of the same qualities and, withal, the same remoteness that made understanding them so difficult; they were both fallible, yet above the law, outside the reach of ordinary people. Often Sasha wondered if he would ever know his wife.

That night there was a dance in the hall that had been made out of the old Ferov stables. Once they had housed twenty fine trotting horses, in the days when trotters had been bred especially in the south for races and competitions. The newly-constructed hall was sparse and functional, and the music was provided by two fiddlers, a flute player and a balalaika player. It had very little to do with anything remotely like what was being played in the west. The gay tunes seemed to take one back to the old Russian heartland, folk memories of which remained buried deep in every Slav, however far from home.

Stefanie, well rested now after her third day at the camp still called Essenelli, came alive that night. Sasha was overjoyed to watch her as she danced with one lad after another, not jealous of the glances they gave her, the lingering touch of their hands as they let her go.

Sasha loved his wife and all he wanted in life was for her, Nicky and any children he and Stefanie might have. It was for their sakes he had agreed to work for Bobby, a job involving lots of paper and desk work that he still didn't find congenial. To come to Russia and visit the old family home was a holiday for both of them and, as he leaned against the wall watching Stefanie enjoying herself, listening to the unfamiliar sound of the music of their native land, he found himself wishing for the first time that they could stay; that the world of big business and the fortunes of the Lighterman empire, endless negotiations, meetings and dealings involving millions of pounds or dollars, could be left forever.

During a break in the dancing they went on to the wooden terrace surrounding the old stables and sat at a table sipping lemonade, alcohol being completely forbidden at the camp. The moonlight on the lake seemed like a glittering path leading through the forest until it burst once more, in all its radiance, on the snow-topped Main Caucasian Range in the far distance. Stefanie wore a Russian-style blouse with a round neck and puffed sleeves which, like the bodice, were heavily embroidered. With this, she wore a *dirndl* skirt, gathered at the waist, and on her feet were the pretty embroidered Turkish sandals which were in plentiful supply in the shops in Batum where a sly form of private enterprise apart from the State collectives still flourished.

'What would it be like to be a collective farm manager?' Sasha glanced at Stefanie who had her mouth over a straw, her eyes on the frothy mixture laced with lime in her glass. She took the straw out and held it in her hand.

'Are you serious?'

'I feel at home here. Don't you?'

'I feel peaceful here,' Stefanie said, tossing back her head and leaning against the bench. 'I don't know about "at home". Can you really envisage giving up everything we know in the west?'

'Don't you think there would be a kind of justice in that?'

'Justice?' Frowning, Stefanie put her head on one side.

'The family forsook Russia, now we've come back. Look what Russia went through during the war.'

'Look what *we* went through during the war,' Stefanie retorted, 'you especially. We were all victims of the Germans, not just the Russians. I feel no guilt on that score, I can assure you. I didn't know you were at all attracted to Communism.'

'I'm my father's son,' Sasha said. 'I think he never forsook the Cause, even though they imprisoned him for it. I often ask myself if that's the reason for his disappearance.'

'Does that mean you support it?' Stefanie looked astonished.

'Much of it I admire,' Sasha gestured round him. 'This may be our home but once upon a time this place existed for a handful of privileged people: the Ferovs. Now hundreds, maybe thousands, can enjoy it every year; fish and swim in the lake, go trekking in the forests, climb the mountains. Sleep well and comfortably at night. They are citizens, not slaves as they were in our grandparents' day. Yes, I do support the new order, rather than the old.'

'We have socialism in Britain.'

Sasha smiled. 'Hardly socialism, and not for much longer if you ask me. The socialists have failed in all their promises – we have neither socialism nor capitalism, but a mixture in between. In England we have the old inequalities that we had before the war. In Russia they are all gone. There are no inequalities now.'

Because they were in their homeland Stefanie and Sasha mostly spoke Russian; they had lapsed into it quite naturally.

As they sat on the terrace, surrounded by other couples and families out to enjoy the night air, they were unaware that much of their conversation had been overheard by a man who sat at the table next to them, on his own, smoking a pipe. He now leaned forward as if to introduce himself and Sasha recognized the manager of the complex who had welcomed them the first day, but who they hadn't seen since.

'It is interesting what you say, Comrades,' he said politely, moving along the bench towards them. 'I hope that you don't mind me listening. At first I was fascinated by your Russian, which is so good yet a little foreign, and then I remembered that you came here as honoured guests of the Party. You live in the west?'

'In England.' Sasha moved up so that their neighbour could squeeze in. 'But one side of our family is Russian. My wife's mother and my father were brother and sister; the Ferov family.'

'The Ferovs? Of course! I noticed the name at once. When I was a boy they were the owners of all this land, this very house.'

'You're a local man?' Stefanie said, interested. 'You might have known my mother.'

The man laughingly introduced himself as Boris Vassilevsky and they shook hands.

'If I knew your mother, Comrade, it could only be from afar. I was only a very small boy in the first war. My family were tenants of the Ferovs, as were most people in these parts. As I remember, they were well thought of though, of course, as peasants we knew no better in those days. Some still venerate them in this district.'

'There are people here who would know my family, remember them?' Stefanie looked up, excited. 'My mother, my grandmother?'

'Undoubtedly,' Boris nodded and raised a finger. 'There is old Nikolai Yvchenko who worked for the last Prince. He stayed on in the house well after the Revolution. He must have known your family well.'

'Oh, Sasha, did you hear,' Stefanie turned to him, eyes alight with hope. 'He may have known Mama.'

Nikolai Yvchenko lived in a small house that had been pointed out to them on the edge of the forest, well above the village. When they approached the house a young woman was working in the garden with a hoe and she stopped abruptly as they reached the gate. Shading her eyes against the sun, she asked what they wanted in the gentle courteous way of the Caucasian people who had lived all their lives in a temperate climate, enjoying the minimum of Party restrictions because of its inaccessibility, and mostly cut off from the war. She had on a long cotton dress, such as might have been worn at the turn of the century, and on her head a straw hat with a wide brim that protected her face. Her rolled-up sleeves showed strong brown arms.

Sasha explained that they were seeking Nikolai and the woman told them that he was her father-in-law and they would find him inside the house. Smilingly she put down the hoe and gestured them to follow her into the small wooden cottage with latticed shutters covering the windows to protect them from the heat.

Inside the cool front room were two small children playing and, in a corner, an elderly man sat gazing at them fondly through the smoke emanating from his pipe. Through a doorway Sasha could see an elderly woman peeling vegetables, and by her side a crib shaded from the sun in which undoubtedly there was a sleeping baby. It was a scene of such tranquillity and joy that Sasha's heart turned over and his eyes filled with tears. But the eyes of the old man went from the children to linger on Stefanie. Then, as Stefanie looked enquiringly at him, he tried to get on one knee as he reached for her hand, murmuring, as he kissed it, the Russian word for princess: *kniaginia*.

'They said you were here,' he murmured in a broken voice, 'but I didn't believe it.'

Stafanie, frowning, gazed first at the old man, as his lips touched the back of her hand; then at his daughter-in-law and his wife, who had come into the room wiping her hands on her apron. Finally her eyes returned to Nikolai.

'You knew who I was?' Stefanie said.

'Someone said they'd seen you. I couldn't believe it. I still can't. Surely even you would have aged in thirty years, *kniaginia,* yet here you are just as I remember you in the old days.' Once more he kissed her hand and the tears began to pour down his wrinkled cheeks.

'I think there's some mistake,' Sasha began and Nikolai's wife bustled up to him, gripped his shoulder and murmured something in his ear, shaking her head. Sasha caught the words, 'It cannot be.'

'She is much, much too young,' the old lady smiled anxiously at her guests and settled her husband once more in his chair. 'He thinks you are the *kniaginia* who lived here before the Revolution. I told him it was not possible.'

'I was told that you were seen weeks ago,' Nikolai pointed a trembling finger at Stefanie, who clutched Sasha's arm. 'Someone said the Princess was seen in the forest, close to her old home. On the edge of the lake . . .' As he faltered, his daughter-in-law went on.

'My father-in-law refers to the Ferov family who lived here until the Revolution, owning the house by the lake that is now a holiday home. Well, some time ago one or two people who claimed to remember them – and it is thirty years ago since they left – thought they saw one of the princesses. We said it was not possible; she would now be a woman of fifty or so and no one would recognize her. Still, it impressed Nikolai because he loved the family.' The young woman nervously licked her lips. 'That is not to say we are not better off now, but some older people like to remember the days when the Ferovs lived here.'

'We are Ferov,' Sasha said quietly. 'I am the son of Kyril and my wife, Stefanie, is the daughter of Hélène, one of the daughers of . . .'

'Hélène, Hélène,' the old man cried. 'They said it was Hélène, Princess Hélène . . . and you are her daughter. God is good.'

He crossed himself and was about to drop to his knees once more, but Sasha went forward to restrain him.

'My wife and I have only been here two or three days,' he said. 'Not weeks, or months. You must have seen someone, a visitor, perhaps, at the camp who resembled her. In fact my wife is not very much like her mother.' Gently Sasha removed the scarf that Stefanie had covering her head, to display the colour of her hair. 'Hélène was fair, Stefanie is dark. The features, yes, I see you might have misunderstood, but once you see the colour of the hair that's not possible. There is some mistake.' Quickly he went on. 'You may remember my father too, Kyril. Perhaps, if you lived on there after the Revolution, my mother as well who briefly visited here in 1921, the year they were married.'

'I was at the wedding,' Nikolai said, tears streaming down his face and this time he did succeed in falling on his knees again and, taking Sasha's hand, kissed it, murmuring as he did the Russian word for Prince – *kniaz* – over and over again.

That night Sasha and Stefanie lay in their large bed recalling the events of the day – the welcome, the explanations, the drinking of the *tomade*, a toast to the new arrivals in white Caucasian wine. They had been pressed to stay for lunch and food was prepared; plates of *zakuski,*

Russian delicacies consisting mostly of fish caught in the warm waters of the Black Sea, and kebabs roasted on a charcoal fire and eaten with *lavish,* crisp flat bread made of coarse wheat flour.

There was much talk and explanation, smiles when the mistake became obvious, the fact that Stefanie had been mistaken for her mother but, above all, joy; joy that the family had returned in the form of its youngest members. They were urged to stay but finally had to tear themselves away.

Stefanie pressed close to Sasha in the large, old-fashioned bed. 'I feel I belong here too, now. Fancy, Nikolai was at your parents' wedding! He used to take our parents fishing with Uncle Dima and Aunt Evgenia. He knew Aunt Varvara, who disappeared in the twenties and . . .' She stopped abruptly and clutched Sasha.

'Yes?'

'Suddenly I feel frightened,' she whispered, as though someone were outside the door listening to them. 'Supposing it *was* Mama they saw.'

'How could it be? We know your mother is dead.' He spoke as gently as he could. 'If she were alive we would have known.'

'Supposing she escaped here, to her old home, the home she loves? Supposing she *is* hidden somewhere just over there, unwilling to reveal herself? Sasha, remember she's alone in the world; maybe she has lost her memory.'

Stefanie began to sob so wildly that Sasha held her close to him, filled with pity.

'It is not possible, my darling. It is a fantasy. This is thousands of kilometres from Poland, from Auschwitz. After her experiences your mother would hardly be recognizable as she was before the Revolution. I doubt if she would be flitting through the woods near Essenelli. It is an illusion, a nightmare.'

87

Sasha did his best to calm Stefanie, murmuring to her and comforting her until she fell asleep. But long afterwards he lay in the dark feeling uneasy within himself, wondering what it all meant.

The next day Sasha and Stefanie joined a group that had arranged to go up into the mountains. They set off early in an old bus belonging to the camp that had been imported into the Soviet Union from England in the thirties and had seen far better days. It grunted and heaved its way up the winding mountain passes, stopping frequently for a rest and water for its overheated engine, like an old man. Finally, amid the spectacular mountain scenery, Sasha and Stefanie forgot their preoccupation with the past and, when they returned to the camp by the same circuitous route, the brakes of the old bus this time giving cause for concern, it was very late and they went straight to bed.

The following morning there was a sharp tap on their door and one of the women who cleaned the rooms told them that Boris wanted to see them urgently in his room. There was only ever cold water to wash with in the morning, so they splashed themselves as usual and dressed as quickly as they could before hurrying downstairs after the woman, who implied that something was amiss.

'Is there something wrong at home?' was Sasha's first question when they were shown into the sparsely furnished office at the back of the complex.

Boris rose, shaking his head, his expression a mixture of pain and regret. He took a paper from his desk and showed it to them.

'I regret to inform you that you are to go at once to Odessa. Your presence is no longer welcome here.' Boris looked at his watch. 'A car will arrived for you in an hour and will put you on a ship from the port straight for Odessa.'

'But what has happened? What have we done?' Sasha glanced at the paper, rapidly assimilating its formal message, which was as Boris had said: Immediate expulsion.

'You have been engaged in activities dangerous to the safety of the State. That is all I can say. Maybe more will be told you, I don't know.' Anxiously Boris rubbed his hands together, looking behind him at the door as if any minute it would spring open and the KGB appear. Sasha remembered a similar gesture two nights before when he had spoken to them on the balcony. Suddenly he recalled what that conversation had been about. Boris was a nervous, perhaps a frightened, man.

'Is it because we spoke to Nikolai?' he lowered his voice. 'Is it because we visited him the day before yesterday?'

'Whether it is that or something else I cannot tell you.' Boris uneasily caressed his chin.

'But it's incredible,' Stefanie burst out. 'We only spent a few hours with the old family servants. I can't believe that in such a short time . . .'

'Someone spied on us. Someone reported on all this,' Sasha said angrily. 'Maybe someone was looking after us all the time, making sure that we didn't betray the Revoluton. Damn it all, man,' Sasha thumped the table with his fist, 'we *support* the Revolution. I was only saying how much I admired the Soviet system, how attracted I was to it and how much I'd like to stay here. You heard me. Damn it all, I'm a supporter, not an enemy.'

Boris anxiously gestured with his hand towards the door, that unseen presence, maybe, behind it. His expression was terrified.

'Don't make it difficult for me, please. All I know is that you must go but,' he lowered his voice so that it was

89

scarcely audible, 'make sure that as long as you are in the Soviet Union, or if ever you are allowed to return, you never again allow yourself to be addressed as "prince".'

The last word was mouthed, rather than whispered, as though he didn't even dare allow himself to utter it: *k-n-i-a-z*.

CHAPTER 4

Bobby sat back in his large leather chair, the executive type reserved for chairmen of the board and other aspirants to great power, and gazed thoughtfully at the model of the car in front of him. The designer had completely eschewed the rather bulbous design currently in fashion, favoured by Rover and Vauxhall among others, for the lower, sleeker lines of the Triumph or Sunbeam. Like its predecessor – the Askham range of the twenties and thirties – it could be either a saloon model or coupé. As a model it was beautifully made, painted in the Askham colours of burgundy and cream. Bobby reached out a hand and fingered it, hardly able to conceal his delight.

'A birthday present for me?' He smiled up at his young cousin, aware of his glowing face. 'Charming, delightful.'

'Not a birthday present, Bobby,' Pascal said, stepping forward and glancing at Sasha. 'We actually hope to make it.'

Sasha took the model from Bobby and gazed at it from all angles. 'With your approval, of course.'

Bobby stood up and stuck his thumbs in the pockets of his waistcoat, impeccable accoutrement of a business-man's clothes; Bobby, member of the House of Lords and head of the Lighterman empire, was never less than perfectly turned out, whatever the occasion. He gazed for a while at the model, walking round it, leaning closer to inspect it in Sasha's hand. 'I see I am presented with a *fait accompli*. We go into the motor business again?'

'Why not?' Sasha's eyes were shining. 'You know I love

machines. I wanted to stay in the RAF. I'd love to develop the motor car business again.'

'Ford never marketed the Askham name,' Bobby mused, staring at the trees in Berkeley Square. 'The premises were only used for light machine tooling.'

'I think we can get them back again,' Sasha gave a discreet cough.

'You've done a bit of enquiring, have you?' Bobby smiled. 'Got it all worked out?'

'Subject to your approval, Uncle Bobby.'

Bobby sat again his chair and surveyed his two young relatives. Pascal was twenty-two and had graduated in engineering the previous summer from Durham. Since then he'd worked for BSM in Birmingham on the shop floor, an apprentice learning the ropes the hard way. But all the time he'd been designing, even at university, and his ambition was to be like his father: a racing driver. Pascal was a doer – a man practical with his hands, a lover of speed and danger.

'You'd better come into the company, Pascal,' Bobby said abruptly while the two younger men appeared to wait on his words with bated breath. 'As new projects manager.'

'Uncle Bobby!'

'Bobby.'

Impulsively the two converged on Bobby, clasping him by the shoulder.

'On one condition,' Bobby said smiling, gratified at this show of affection, even if it was cupboard love. 'No racing cars.' He gazed at Pascal who dropped his eyes to the ground.

'Oh.'

'Ah-ha, I thought you had that in mind, young man.' Bobby wagged a reproving finger at him but continued to smile. 'No racing cars.' His expression became severe.

'Besides, it would break your mother's heart.' Bobby put an avuncular hand on the young man's arm. 'She has had enough heartbreak in her life without adding to it unnecessarily, don't you think, Pascal? Cars, yes. I say, yes. But racing cars – no.'

'Not for the time being, anyway,' Sasha said *sotto voce,* but Bobby heard him.

'Not now, or ever. Is that clear, Sasha? I don't want you plotting against me. You have enough to do trying to make up to me for getting yourself expelled from the Soviet Union! I had to write a grovelling letter to Stalin to try and restore normal relations.'

'We didn't get ourselves expelled,' Sasha said defiantly. 'How were we to know that we were watched everywhere we went?'

'They expected you to be spies. According to them you behaved like spies. According to some you were lucky, in this atmosphere of cold war, not to follow the fate of your father.'

'Sometimes I wonder if it's because of my father we were expelled,' Sasha said, staring at the ground.

'But how could that be?'

'Well, we don't know what happened to him, do we? We don't know if he's alive or dead. Sometimes I wonder if Father was sent back to Siberia and they are frightened of us finding out.'

'Well, you've cut yourself off from the Soviet Union, at any rate for some time,' Bobby said. 'No more trips there for you. And I was hoping that, with your knowledge of Russian, you could be valuable to me. As it is . . . no racing cars, anyway.' He shrugged and began the preliminary ceremonials of lighting a large Havana cigar. 'Now, let's be positive and get down to business.'

* * *

93

It was now five years since the war had ended and preparations were in hand for a great festival on the anniversary of the Great Exhibition of 1851. Somehow or other many of the members of the Askham family had been drawn into its preparations. The Lighterman empire was going to take a corner of the pavilion devoted to industry; Em was writing enthusiastically about its preparations in her paper, and Anna Ferov got herself a job in the public relations department because of her linguistic abilities – fluent French, Italian and she was polishing up her Russian and learning German.

She looked and played the part perfectly of an ambassadress for England – an attractive girl who knew her way around, a cosmopolitan who was accomplished in many languages. Anna had never had the command of the Russian language of her brother and, certainly, not her Lighterman cousins who had lived with Prince Alexei and Princess Irina in Paris. But she had a gift for languages and found learning them easy.

Anna worked late hours in her office at Savoy Court, opposite the complex on the south bank of the river which was gradually being turned into the exhibition, the buildings to house the exhibits growing higher day by day. Sometimes she didn't leave her office before nine, sometimes she worked until midnight.

Anna was ambitious and the chance to be part of the organization for the Festival of Britain had been one not to be missed. She wanted to climb and she felt it could lead somewhere; be a stepping-stone to something better. Her talents not only for languages but for organization would be put to the test.

Before the war there had been few chances for women in executive positions, but Anna felt all that had changed. More women were going to university and, although the top echelons of power still eluded them, there were many like Anna gathering round the base, their eyes ever upwards.

One night in November 1950 Anna left the office, the last one to do so, and after locking up took a cab to Sasha's house in Hampstead where she'd been invited to dinner.

But when she got there, apologies on her lips for being so late, there were no signs of preparations for a feast. Instead Sasha and Pascal were squatting over plans which lay beside a large model of a motor car and Stefanie was sitting in a chair watching them, her feet up because she was pregnant.

The three hailed Anna excitedly as she came through the door, tugging off her hat and woolly scarf, throwing her briefcase and handbag on a chair. She stood beside the group, hands on hips.

'What goes on?' she said, looking around enquiringly. 'Isn't anyone hungry? I'm starving, or have you eaten?'

'Too excited to eat,' Stefanie smiled. 'On the brink of a great invention.'

As Anna raised her eyebrows Sasha said, without turning round, 'A new car.'

'They want to relaunch the "Askham".' Stefanie patted the chair next to her. 'Come and sit next to me.'

'I must have a drink,' Anna said, with a note of irritation in her voice.

'Let me, please.' Pascal sprang up and, losing his balance, almost fell over her. He steadied himself and then stared at her, as though seeing her for the first time. 'Oh. Sorry, Anna,' he said, looking startled. 'I say, do you know, you look absolutely smashing.'

'Weren't you aware of that before?' Sasha murmured from the floor.

'Even more smashing,' Pascal said. 'What can I get you?'

'Gin and T please.' Anna ran a hand through her short fashionably-cut hair, which immediately sprang back into place. She wore a russet-coloured jumper with a green tweed skirt and high heeled, highly polished boots the same colour as her jumper. Stefanie thought she looked like some creature of the sun and wind and gazed at her for a moment as she and Pascal, heads together, chatted by the drinks table.

Stefanie had never completely felt at ease with Anna. She disturbed her and it was difficult to think she was Sasha's sister. It was hard to establish a rapport with her, to find any areas of common ground. Stefanie gradually came to realize that she wasn't comfortable in the company of the younger woman, that she was always on her guard as though silently, secretly, Anna were constantly sitting in judgement upon her.

Stefanie, now feeling fat and unattractive, gazed with some envy at her sister-in-law. Somehow, one could never imagine Anna looking so ungainly. She hated being pregnant, but it had seemed a way of saying 'thank you' to Sasha for all he had done for her. To have a child of his own was his dearest wish. Yet ever since Stefanie had returned from Russia the previous spring she had suffered from nightmares, attacks of anxiety and moods of inexplicable dread. Even her pregnancy didn't take her mind off her mother, the thought that, somewhere in that forest near Essenelli, might be a woman who had take refuge from the authorities after escaping from Poland.

Sasha did his best to assure her that it was impossible; that the resemblance between mother and daughter had stuck in people's minds. That her mother would, by now, be in her late forties and totally unrecognizable from the young girl who had left so many years before. Stefanie knew all this, yet the possibility haunted her.

Maybe Stefanie would have been a melancholic

anyway. She had always been a grave, rather unsmiling girl, different from her sisters. Beautiful, yet with a detached, crystalline kind of beauty that women found enviable but forbidding.

The house that Bobby had bought for her and Sasha as a wedding present was in that pretty part of Hampstead, Downshire Hill, which runs down from Rosslyn Hill to Hampstead Heath. The house was eighteenth-century, painted white with black wrought-iron balconies under two of the elongated upstairs windows. It had a narrow garden that sloped to the road, with a verdant close-cut lawn, flame-coloured rhododendron bushes clustering up against the walls of the house and a pink magnolia tree leaning over the low garden wall.

Stefanie and Sasha lived there with only the help of a daily woman. Neither of them had been used to servants and Stefanie's life in Paris had made her very domesticated. She had had to take her share in cooking and cleaning, in shopping and making beds. She was a good cook and housewife but her periods of melancholy drove her often out on to the Heath, walking round the pond or through the woods as far as Kenwood; hands deep in her pockets, in these winter days, thinking, brooding, wishing so much that time could roll back to that point when she'd last seen her mother. Now, she knew, she would not have let her go, shutting the door after her, but would have called her back, barred her way, done anything to keep her with her. If only she had her time again, her chance to undo the faults of the past, how different things would be.

Stefanie came to from her reverie and found Sasha gazing down at her. Anna and Pascal were now squatting together on the floor, studying the plans.

'Like to go out for a bite? It's late.'

'That's a very good idea,' Pascal looked up. 'Anna's starving.'

'You go out,' Stefanie said. 'It's been a long day and I'm tired. I don't think I could even face walking up the hill.'

'I'll stay,' Sasha perched beside her. 'Pascal can take Anna for a meal.'

'It seems so terribly inhospitable,' Stefanie began, but Anna held up her hands.

'It's a fine idea, really. I can see how tired you are and how exciting it's all been about the car.'

'It seems so rude . . .'

'It isn't rude at all.' Pascal winked at them behind Anna's back. 'My cousin and I can get a better chance to know each other.'

'We really don't know each other, do we?' Pascal smiled at Anna from across the table of the small Italian restaurant in Flask Walk, to which they'd walked.

'Not really.' Anna watched him as he studied the menu.

All the way up to the restaurant he'd been explaining to her, like an excited boy, the ideas behind the new version of the Askham that had come to him even when he was at university. There were so many competitors in the same field cashing in on the post-war boom in motor cars; but the 'Askham' wasn't for the popular market. It would be a special car for special customers and the price would be special, too. Anna had a vision of Sasha and Pascal shutting themselves off for good while they developed the car.

Pascal ordered spaghetti. Anna said she'd join him. Over his wine he looked at her again.

'We really have a lot in common, particularly Italy.'

'Ah yes, Italy.'

'You must feel half-Italian?'

'Not really.' Anna tossed her head back. It was a mannerism of hers which he found attractive. 'Ten years in Italy doesn't make you Italian. You, of course, *are* half-Italian.'

'Yet I don't even speak the language.' Pascal shrugged his shoulders. 'Odd, really. I'll have to make up for that one day. Tell me, what do you make of the family? I thought you were just coming for a visit and now you're here to stay.'

'What a lot to answer all at once.' Anna laughed. 'What do I think of the family? Now let me see.' She put a fist under her chin, gazing at the cheerful check tablecloth. 'Well, it's a very discordant family, in many ways. Not quite what I imagined.'

'All families fall out. Are you thinking of Uncle Bobby and Hugo?'

'I'm thinking of Stefanie and Bobby, too.'

'Oh, they never got on. He was an awful father.'

Now Pascal stared at the cloth. When he raised his eyes they were solemn. 'He's an awful man, really. I can't say anyone loves Bobby except, perhaps, his mother. Gran is very good to him, too. She always makes excuses for him, as though he were deprived.'

'Aunt Rachel makes excuses for everyone.' Anna grimaced. 'She's almost too nice to be true.'

'Don't say you don't like my grandmother!' Pascal looked alarmed. 'Now, if that's the case, you and I can't get anywhere.'

'Oh, I like her, who wouldn't?' Anna said carefully. 'I didn't think she liked me very much. I don't think your mother likes me either, to be honest.'

'What on earth makes you say that?'

'She didn't like me taking Angelica away. She blames me for that.'

'But it's good for Angelica. I approve of it. She's come

99

out, grown up. Mother feels protective towards us all, to make up for what happened in the war.'

Pascal sat back and studied her. He'd never realized quite how alarmingly attractive she really was. It was alarming in the sense that it was rather unexpected. She was not conventionally pretty. In fact, there was nothing conventional about Anna at all.

'You're controversial, that's the thing,' he said at last.

'How?' She looked surprised.

'I don't know.'

'That sounds as though people don't approve of me.'

'I think they envy you, a little, always throwing stones into ponds, getting things done. I admire the way you've gone into this festival business.'

'Oh, but it's a wonderful job. I was lucky. It was the languages really. That was through Uncle Bobby.'

'Everything, invariably, is through Bobby.' Their food had come and for a while Pascal ate, rather jerkily, interspersed with mouthfuls of Chianti. 'I've only got the chance with the car through Bobby.'

'And you're serious? Really serious?'

'Very serious.'

'Then why don't you show it at the Festival Exhibition?'

'But that's in May, only five months away.'

'As a model. Couldn't you try?' Anna began to feel excited. 'Didn't you ever *think* of it, to try and get it launched?'

Pascal impulsively reached out and seized her wrist.

'Anna, I think you're a genius. Do you know, I love you.'

He squeezed her hand very tightly and then put it to his lips.

It was natural that, given her background, Flora Boling-broke should have chosen that classless bastion of further

100

education, the London School of Economics, in which to take her degree. Influenced by her Liberal father and her mother's brother, Spencer Foster, who had for many years been a Labour MP, she was attracted to that temple of twentieth-century learning – peculiarly twentieth-century in its curricula range – founded by Sidney and Beatrice Webb.

Flora had no Askham blood in her. Her father, Adam Bolingbroke, had had an Askham as his first wife; but his second, Margaret Foster, was a working-class girl from the north who had aspirations to better herself. For a time she had worked as a secretary in Adam's chambers.

In many ways, however, Flora resembled her aunt Rachel who, although the mother of Askhams, had no Askham blood in her either. Rachel had been a radical and so was Flora. Since she had become aware of these things as an adolescent, Flora had been an espouser of good, preferably lost, causes. She was left wing; she was vegetarian; she loved orphans, lost, stray, abandoned, and wild animals. She was anti-war, anti-vivisectionist, anti-pollution. She was for home-spun clothes, organically grown food, cosmetics without animal fats and homeopathic medicine.

Naturally the only place for Flora was the LSE. She had come up in October, the month of her eighteenth birthday, and lived in a hostel in Malet Street. The LSE had recently introduced a new degree; a BSc in Sociology, a vague subject that couldn't be better suited to Flora's disposition and she had entered into her studies, and all the activities of that large college, with her usual whole-hearted enthusiasm.

The LSE occupied an unprepossessing site in Houghton Street just off the Aldwych, opposite Bush House. It was a huge, modern building, with little architectural merit of character, set on five floors, with no grounds of its own.

101

It had a very fine library – the British Library of Political Science – and a room that was more for cultural gatherings and entertainment – the Shaw Library, named after that pioneering friend of the founders. It had two main amphi-theatre-style lecture halls known as the Old Theatre and the New Theatre, many classrooms and a large student refectory. However, some of the students preferred to foregather either at a café next to the LSE known as 'Joe's', or the Three Tuns, a converted pub in Houghton Street belonging to the students' union.

Flora enjoyed her first term at the School. She had no difficulty settling down and making friends, though she knew that a good many of the girls in her hall of residence considered her odd. She dressed oddly in that day of conventional skirts and jumpers, ropes of pearls, tidy hair, seamed nylon stockings and make-up, and she looked odd. Many years later no one would have given her a second glance but in the year 1950 she stood out for her lack of conformity, her bizarre appearance. She was a precursor of the beat generation.

Flora was small, only just over five feet two inches. She was very un-Askham-like in being small because most of the women of her family were above average height.

The only one who had been small in that family – and she was never very popular, but not because of her height – had been Flora's mother, Margaret. Flora was very like her mother – diminutive with a pale face, very blue eyes and black curly hair. But whereas Margaret Foster in the twenties, when she captured the love of Flora's father, had dressed suitably and demurely, her hair styled in the current neat fashion, short at the back and curling over the ears, Flora had let her naturally curly hair grow almost to her waist, so that it seemed all out of proportion, like an overgrown lawn, or vegetables gone to seed, and was a tangled mass of fuzz.

Flora, of course, would never have dreamt of wearing make-up and her pale face and pre-Raphaelite hair-style attracted glances and comments. She wore glasses. Unattractive frames, made of steel, as if purposely chosen for their lack of appeal. Yet she had her admirers, despite her attempts to discourage them.

One of these was a leading light in the Communist Society, a fellow eccentric called Dick Crosby. Dick was already a postgraduate student in political science when Flora came up to the School and he knew his way around. He was an attractive man, but unconventional, too – a wearer of corduroy suits and pullovers, sporting long hair before the style became fashionable. Most of the young men at the LSE had either been in the War or had done their national service. Short back and sides were fashionable with well-shaven cheeks, shirt with collar and tie, tweed jacket and pressed grey flannels. The student eccentric of the sixties was, in those days of post-war austerity, not even a gleam in anyone's eye and Flora, who came close to prefiguring her, was regarded as unusual. Dick too was a 'commie' and 'commies' were not expected to conform. Commies were meant to look absurd and behave absurdly. No one took any notice of them at all. All they produced were sniggers and, not surprisingly, those attracted to this form of outrageous political belief tended to stick together. Their view of life coincided with and embraced many of the other things, those peripheral matters of life and death, that Flora was interested in too.

Dick Crosby came from the small Lancashire town of Chorley, which was very near the home town of Flora's mother. That gave them a bond as a start. He was not very tall and the severity of a black beard, moustache and long black hair was offset by warm brown eyes and a gentle smile. Flora didn't fall for him as such; she was too

103

sexually unaware, too naïve, and his attraction, initially at any rate, was not overtly sexual; but she felt very lucky to have met him so soon and the crowd of people he went round with, all almost exclusively committed to left-wing and allied causes.

Flora told people very little about herself or her family background. The Askhams had always been Tory, but there was a good strong, radical tradition with her Aunt Rachel, her dead cousin Freddie and her namesake, Lady Flora Down, who had been Aunt Rachel's sister-in-law. Moreover, she didn't want anyone to know about her background or where she lived and since she had come to London she had seen no members of the family, except for Christmas time when there were the usual family gatherings at her father's home and at the Hall.

Back in London again for the spring term at the beginning of 1951, Flora threw herself once more into her extra-curricular activities, but she didn't neglect her studies. She was to be seen in the library until closing time; but then she would join her friends and go out for a meal, usually Schmidts in Charlotte Street or the Colombino d'Oro off Bloomsbury Square. At Schmidts one could get a very good meal for five shillings; for the Colombino one had to be a little more affluent.

Dick lived in digs in Charlotte Street so Schmidts was a popular haunt, especially on a Saturday night after a game of football, which he played for the School. Flora spent Saturday afternoons in the library and met Dick and some others in a Soho pub at about seven after she had gone back to the hall and changed. On Saturday evening she usually wore something a bit different from her customary uniform of long skirt, high boots and Russian jerkin that Sasha had brought back from Batum.

Flora would quite like to have seen more of Sasha and Stefanie, but that would have meant cultivating all the family. Charlotte was always inviting her round because she had promised Rachel she would, and Flora wanted to shake off all that hateful thing of being overprotected. So she saw none of the family except for an occasional, dutiful visit home to her father and Aunt Rachel.

One evening, shortly after the beginning of term, Flora was eating at Schmidts with Dick and the usual gang when, to her amazement, she saw the elegant form of her cousin Angelica eating at a nearby table with a man. His face was rather familiar but Flora couldn't put a name to it. She felt embarrassed and awkward at seeing the cousin she had so idolized as a young girl and tried to keep her face averted, hoping Angelica wouldn't see her.

She was quite surprised to see Angelica eating at a place like Schmidts, with its plain white tablecloths and general lack of ambience, which was popular with academics and people on low incomes. Angelica was now a model and all the young men she went out with were the kind of men one expected to see with models: City types, ex-Army, public school – just the sort, in fact, who was sitting opposite Angelica now chatting away. Flora ducked her head even further until Dick asked her if there was anything the matter and, as he turned round, Angelica looked up and saw Flora.

'Well, I don't know,' Angelica said in her loud, upper-class voice. 'Sandy, look who's *here*.'

Sandy Kitto was a cousin, one of the large clan of Kittos who had been introduced into the Askham family by Dulcie, Angelica's great-grandmother. The Kittos were very numerous, not particularly wealthy but indubitably upper-class. They went to the best schools and were seen in the best places. The moved easily about in society and usually found employment in property, the armed forces or the City. Sandy was an accountant for an old-established firm. He had on a tweed jacket with patched

105

elbows and an open-neck shirt. He, too, looked over his shoulder as Angelica spoke and said in a well bred, equally upper-class voice, 'Golly, it's Flora.'

Angelica was shrieking out 'Flora, Flora' by now, and Flora didn't know where to look.

'Do you *know* them?' a girl at her table asked, with some amazement. Flora nodded, mumbling and, to stop Angelica drawing any more attention to herself, rose awkwardly from the table, tripped over her foot and stumbled over to Angelica's table collapsing on to a chair. Angelica had thrown back her head and was laughing quite heartily by this time.

'Typical Flora,' she cried. 'How are you, dear? Keeping yourself to yourself?'

'I'll say,' Sandy said. 'Someone said you were dead.'

'Nonsense, *Sandy*.' Angelica dug him in the ribs. 'Mummy said that Flora wanted to find herself. Well, you found yourself, old thing.' Angelica leaned forward, eyes conspiratorially indicating the table beyond her. 'I have *never* seen such a weird bunch of people in my life. Are they *all* like that?'

'You're being quite *impossible*, Angelica!' Flora hissed, eyebrows furiously knotted in the middle of her forehead. 'I wish you'd shut up.'

'Yes, shut up, Angelica,' Sandy echoed. 'You're embarrassing the poor girl.'

'The last place I expected to see *you*!' Flora murmured.

'Don't you think it's rather smart?' Angelica smiled. 'I think it's a lot of fun and Sandy hasn't a bean, have you, Sandy?'

'Not a bean,' Sandy agreed. 'Angelica's paying, anyway.'

'Oh, you . . .'

'I wish you'd keep your voices down,' Flora said urgently.

106

'Your dinner's getting cold.' Flora looked up and saw that her worst fears had been realized. Dick was standing by the side of the table gazing at her. Awkwardly, Flora tried to get to her feet, but her leg became entangled with the table and she was stuck half-way between sitting and standing.

'Hell,' Flora said. 'This is my cousin, two cousins actually – Angelica and Sandy.'

'How *do* you do?' Angelica gave Dick her smile of practised charm and stuck out her hand. 'Do you know, we haven't seen Flora for ages? Sandy said he thought she was dead.' Angelica started laughing again and Dick sat down opposite her, joining his hands on the table.

'You're Flora's family?' he said, as if to himself.

'I imagine you think we're too awful and she's ashamed of us or something.'

'That's not true.' Flora felt close to tears. The one thing about trying to conceal one's origins was that, sooner or later, someone was bound to discover them. Angelica was not only beautiful: she was clearly top-drawer, the product of an upper-class home, and Sandy, with his casual tweeds, his well-cut neatly parted red hair, even the freckles on his face, looked just like Fettes and the Guards, which is what he was – Fettes and the Guards and a firm of accountants in the City. One day he was sure to be a partner. Flora, striving so hard to be a woman of the people, felt bitterly ashamed, as though she were guilty of gross deception.

Angelica was chatting quite animatedly to Dick, pointing to his friends, and finally Flora heard the dreaded words:

'Why don't we join tables? I'm sure they won't mind.'

Dick seemed to think this was a fine idea and summoned the waiter, who came bustling over and helped to push the tables next to one another. Everyone was introduced: Angelica, Sandy, Dick, Michael, Geraldine, Louise, Tom . . . and Flora. Yes, everyone knew Flora, but Flora suddenly felt forgotten. The encounter between her family and friends was too successful.

But then Angelica was a charmer and always had been. Flora herself had been half in love with her at school; she'd followed her around, hung on her words, tried to emulate her, been influenced by her. It was impossible to imitate her; they were too different, Angelica a goddess then. But when she was fourteen or so the crush had worn off. Flora had begun to discover other things of more interest in her life than an absurd admiration of a cousin to whom matters of the intellect were boring, and who used her good looks with a quite ruthless determination to succeed. Then Angelica and Flora ceased to have anything in common and Flora regretted all those years worshipping an idol whose feet were made of clay.

Flora liked Charlotte and the twins, but it was primarily her lack of anything in common with Angelica that made her keep away from the Crewe home. That and the fact that Anna and Angelica rather terrified Flora. They were a pair of flamboyant, daunting young women filled with an equal measure of ruthlessness and determination. Now, apparently, according to Aunt Rachel, Anna had Pascal Verdi following her around and Charlotte wasn't pleased. She had never welcomed Anna to the bosom of the family.

But this evening Angelica was proving popular. To them she was unusual. Sandy was chatting up Louise, the prettiest of the girls, who was shy and blushed a lot. Also her politics were suspect. Flora often thought she wasn't really dedicated to Marxism-Leninism but was keen on Tom. Flora despised women like that. Because of the purity of the relationship between Dick and herself, she felt she could. She hated people who used sex for political ends.

That night there was a hop on at the School; a dance organized by the students' union. Flora hated dancing and she hated hops. She could hardly believe her ears when she heard Dick suggesting that, after their meal, they should all go on to the School.

Naturally, Angelica said she'd love it and Sandy smiled at Louise.

Flora decided to go home. She was quite near her hall of residence and she wanted to work. She had an essay to do for Monday.

'You'll spoil *everything* if you go home,' Angelica whispered, while some people went to spend pennies and others got their coats. 'You'll make me feel awful.'

'There's no need for you to feel awful,' Flora gave her a derisive smile. 'I just never go to hops.'

'But they're *your* friends.'

'It doesn't matter. Now they're yours, too.'

Flora didn't know whether she was being childish or not as she gave a casual wave in Tottenham Court Road as they all made for the tube. Everyone stopped. Dick tried once more to persuade her, standing arguing on the pavement while Angelica looked bored. Sandy, by now, had his arm round Louise's waist.

'You know I don't like hops,' Flora said savagely.

'But we can't go without you.'

'Why not?'

'It doesn't seem fair.'

'Of course it's fair, silly. I didn't know you were going to go.'

'We weren't.'

'And yet you suggested it.'

'I thought . . .'

Flora patted his shoulder and said: 'See you.'

She remembered wondering at the time if she were doing something irrevocable.

Angelica looked round the scene with some astonishment, her first view of a students' hop – an informal evening with a band, flickering lights and tickets at two shillings and sixpence. It was held in the large students' refectory and when they'd got there it was nearly full. Angelica, used to débutante balls and much, much grander affairs, had never seen anything like it.

'What a lark,' she said, as Dick put his arm round her waist and led her into the measured glide of a foxtrot.

The whole evening had been a lark for Angelica. Dinner with her cousin, though she liked him, wasn't exactly the most inspiring event and, somehow, the evening had come alive when she's spotted Flora and her student companions. Flora had obviously been trying to hide. Now she felt a bit guilty about Flora. But it was too noisy to talk about her to Dick and, instead, she surrendered to the occasion, determined to enjoy herself.

Dick was solid and furry, like a bear. When he attempted to put his cheek against hers she backed away. Closely chaperoned by their mothers, the debs' dances and ones that followed hadn't been at all like this, even though Angelica had been presented in 1948 when she was seventeen. This year she would be twenty-one.

After the dance Dick took her by the hand and steered her to the bar. Angelica was thirsty and wanted lemonade. Dick had a beer and seized a table that had just been vacated by another couple. He wore an open-neck check shirt with his brown corduroys. With his bearded face, his intense eyes, he looked like her idea of a Canadian lumberjack, slightly unnerving.

'Enjoying yourself?' Dick said, sitting next to her, sipping his beer.

'Enormously. It was totally unexpected. I wonder what happened to Sandy?'

'I think he's quite happy.' Dick smiled. 'What do you do?'

'I'm a mannequin. Flora's the only intellectual one in the family, you know.'

'She's very clever,' Dick nodded. 'She never talks about her family. I often wondered what they did.'

'Her father's a judge.' Angelica looked surprised.

'Oh. Maybe that's why.'

'Why what?'

'She never talks about him. She's very committed to the CP.'

'What's that?'

'The Communist Party.' Now, Dick looked surprised.

'Flora's always been a little crazy.' Angelica touched her head.

'I'm a member of the CP, too.'

'Ah-ha, I *thought* you might be.' Angelica gave him a crooked smile. She felt she was on rather dangerous ground.

'Then do you think I'm crazy, too?' Dick's smile was quizzical. Angelica nodded.

'A little. I had an uncle who was a Communist. He was crazy, definitely. He disappeared in the war.'

'Oh really? How interesting. Flora didn't mention that either.' Dick sipped his beer again. He had froth on the edge of his moustache which he attempted to move with the back of his hand. Angelica thought there was no doubt that he was working-class. In fact she'd never met a man like him, certainly not to dance with.

'Part of our family is Russian. Didn't she even tell you that?'

'No.'

'My mother's cousin Bobby married a Russian princess. He had three daughters by her. She was called Hélène.

111

Her brother married Bobby's sister and they had a son and, later, a daughter. Both are here in London at the moment. That's the Russian connection.'

'And who is the Communist?'

'Kyril, the father of Sasha and Anna. Some people think he was a spy.'

'How exciting.' Dick, a little out of this depth, rubbed his moustache again, peering at his fingers.

'So you see, we really do think Communists are quite batty. But we love Flora.'

Dick studied her face.

'"We"? Are you a very large family?'

'Quite large.' Angelica paused. 'Didn't she *ever* talk about the family?'

Dick shook his head and Angelica went on,

'I must say I'm surprised. We're all very close; but since she's been in London she's never been to see my mother or any of the aunts or cousins. She's struck out on her own.'

'She's very independent.'

'I'm sorry she's not here tonight.' Angelica hesitated. 'Do you think she's angry?'

'Why should she be?'

'Because we all came away together.'

'She could have come here, too. Actually, we didn't know we were going to the hop.'

'What were you going to do?'

'Just talk. I think Louise liked your cousin, too. Anyway, I'm glad we came. But Flora won't be angry. That sort of thing doesn't interest her.'

'Won't she be angry with me?'

'Why should she be?'

'I thought I might have spoiled the evening.'

'If anything *she* spoiled the evening. She is a bit too serious, but she's young, a bit younger than you.'

112

'Perhaps.' Angelica gave him a smile of such sensual sophistication accompanied by a tilt of her head that Dick felt the ground move beneath him. He swallowed his beer and held out his hand.

'Feel like another dance?' he said.

Dick and Flora didn't meet for some days after the hop. They bumped into each other in the corridor outside the library and Flora was about to hurry on when Dick grabbed her arm.

'I say . . .'

Flora stopped and by the way she looked at him he knew something was wrong.

'Come for a coffee?' Dick said.

'I haven't got time.'

'Go on.'

'Oh all right.'

Dick hadn't got much time either and took her down the steps to Joe's next door which was, as always, full. They squeezed in and he ordered two coffees.

'Are you coming to the meeting on Tuesday?' he asked.

'Of course.'

Her mouth was pursed, lips tight.

'What *is* the matter, Flora?'

'Nothing's the matter.'

'Is it the other night?'

'What night?'

Dick was beginning to lose patience.

'Don't pretend. You know, Saturday night, when we went to the hop.'

'Why should it be?' She spooned sugar into her coffee. 'I felt tired and wanted to go home. I didn't mind at all.'

'Oh well, I'm glad, then. We liked your cousins and we had a good evening.'

'That's good.'

'There's nothing wrong, then?'

'Nothing. I was busy, too. They say the Korean war will soon involve us all. It might lead to another war. I'm trying to arrange a meeting on it.'

'Good idea.' Dick nodded his approval. Then he raised his head and looked at Flora. She was so unlike Angelica that it was difficult to think they could possibly be related. 'Angelica said you come from a very large family.'

'Not personally. I just have a brother, but there are many relations. My father married twice and has a grown-up family from his first marriage. They have children too, some of them are older than me.'

'I had the impression Angelica was very upper-class.'

'Did she give you that feeling?' Flora was aware of some quiet satisfaction.

'Very definitely. I've never met anyone like her.'

'I can't imagine you'd have anything in common,' Flora said. 'She was a débutante. Her stepfather is a *Tory* MP. He was elected in the last election.'

'Good Lord.' Dick felt shattered by the news and studied the bare table at Joe's.

'What's more,' Flora was beginning to enjoy herself, 'her mother is the daughter of an earl. Now, what do you think of *that*?'

Dick continued to gaze abjectly at the table. What price Marxism-Leninism now?

CHAPTER 5

As the crowd gathered around the sectioned replica of the new Askham motor car Anna Ferov stood just behind the King and Queen. Bobby Lighterman, having introduced his brilliant new designer Pascal Verdi, encouraged him to point out items of unusual interest to His Majesty – such as automatic transmission and a heat exchange to control fuel consumption – while the young Duke of Edinburgh peered closely into its interior. Princess Elizabeth was chatting to Charlotte, who was dressed in a Hartnell creation – a navy blue dress with large white revers – that reminded those nearest to her of her modelling days in the thirties. Arthur Crewe had been on one of the planning committees of the Festival of Britain while Bobby had been a member of the Council, thus ensuring that most of his products were prominently displayed in the many pavilions devoted to science and technology.

As the royal party passed on, the Duke of Edinburgh stayed behind for a moment to chat to Pascal, complimenting him on his youth and energy and forecasting for him a fine career. Bobby and Aileen continued with the royal party on their tour of inspection on this, the opening day, but the members of the Askham family stayed by the model car in the Transport Pavilion, and Rachel remarked to Em that it reminded her of the day the original 'Askham' was unveiled at Askham Hall in the summer of 1923, twenty-eight years before.

'You were all children playing on the lake,' she said. 'I remember. It was when Ralph gave Hugo a beating.' But

Em looked sad. Any attempt to recall those far-off days had this effect on her, because it had been such a happy childhood, despite the loss of their father in the War. All that they owed to Rachel.

'I thought the King looked ill,' Charlotte said, gazing after the party. 'This kind of things seems almost too much for him.'

'He's *very* frail,' Rachel nodded. 'Looking at the Princess and the Duke I wondered how much longer they have of this relatively carefree existence.'

'Oh, you don't *think* . . .'

'They say he has cancer. Who knows?' Rachel shook her head. 'Where's Anna?'

'Anna has continued with the royal party,' Angelica said. 'She is very well in there after all her work. And I must say she has worked. We hardly ever see her.'

Pascal, having donned overalls, was on the floor under the car tinkering with a spanner, because the whole thing had been thrown together in such a short time.

Soon after the departure of royalty Rachel went off to lunch with her daughters. Angelica had a modelling engagement and Pascal remained by his treasure waiting to be joined by Sasha, who had gone off to fetch a spare part.

For that week, and the many weeks during which the Festival lasted, Anna was to be seen all over the place, an indispensable adjunct to any official party welcoming foreign dignitaries. Many of them came from all over the world and, with her languages and her flair for making important people feel even more important, Anna was much sought after. She had a knack for communication.

There was so much to be shown and be seen, from the great Dome of Discovery in the centre, which tried to tell the story of British industrial initiative and invention over the centuries, to tiny arts and crafts which still flourished

116

in odd corners of the land. Anna always took care to see that as many distinguished visitors as possible should view the exhibits at the Festival site that threw credit on her family, especially the new 'Askham', now going into production at the re-acquired premises near Askham Hall.

One day, in the height of the summer – the Festival had been opened in May – Anna arrived at her desk at Savoy Court to find a message waiting for her: 'A Baron von Spee called. He is staying at the Savoy and asks you to telephone him.' There followed his room number.

Anna studied the message and frowned. As usual she was in a hurry. In an hour she was due to escort a delegation from Japan round the Festival and then take them out to dinner. However, von Spee . . .

She impulsively lifted the phone, asked for the Savoy Hotel and the Baron's room number. After a few seconds a cultured German voice answered in English and Anna gave her name.

'Ah yes, Miss Ferov. Thank you for calling,' the Baron said. 'I wondered if we could meet? You do not know me, but I knew your father. I wonder . . .'

'I could come at once,' Anna said, rather breathlessly. 'I'll be there in five minutes.'

The Baron had a room overlooking the river. It was really the best view in London of the Festival complex on the other side with the elongated skylon, seemingly suspended in space, riding above it all.

The Baron was in his forties. He had Aryan good looks: a rather pockmarked face with blond sleeked-back hair, bushy eyebrows and very blue eyes. He was about six foot two and wore a well-cut grey suit with a blue and silver tie that seemed to mark his membership of some club or the other.

The Baron had greeted her at the door, placed a drink

in her hand and now they were gazing out of the window remarking on the variety of buildings, their shapes and sizes, a strange collection. The Baron seemed impressed, especially with the huge Royal Festival Hall, which was to be the only permanent feature when the Exhibition closed.

'Do you like music?' the Baron asked, gazing down at Anna, and she nodded her head.

'Very much.' She looked up at him. 'You said you knew my father. How did you know I was here?'

'There is a list of people to help us,' the Baron pointed to a pile of brochures and booklets on the table beside his bed. 'I knew a Kyril Ferov a little in the thirties and I recollected he had a daughter, a small girl, I remember at the time, called Anna. I wondered what became of him. Am I right that you are his daughter?'

Anna felt a wave of disappointment sweep over her and looked round for a chair.

'You don't know what became of him, either?' She shook her head, sinking into the chair. Somehow his call had seemed full of promise. 'He disappeared during the war. No one has ever heard of him since.'

'I am sorry about that.' The Baron sat down beside her. 'How very distressing for you.'

'I thought maybe . . .'

'Yes, I see,' the Baron nodded. 'You must feel very disappointed.'

'The last people to see him were my grandparents, who lived in Paris all during the war. That was in the summer of 1943. He suddenly left Paris without saying goodbye. It was very strange. In 1945 my cousin Ralph Askham is supposed to have met him in Berlin, shortly after the liberation. But no one could verify that and Ralph is dead. If it *was* my father he was a Russian Colonel.'

'That *is* strange.' The Baron looked puzzled. 'I didn't

think he was of that persuasion. Just the opposite. In the thirties he, well,' the Baron studied his highly polished shoes, 'he seemed an admirer of Hitler, as many of us were, of course, in the early days. Not that there was anything political in our relationship then or at any other time. In those days my family had a castle in Silesia and he was one of a party that came to shoot. He was a Russian prince.'

'That's right.' For a moment both Anna and the Baron were silent, as if trying to summon up the past and those far-off days before the catastrophe of war.

'Of course, I was a relatively young man,' the Baron continued. 'Your father was a good bit older than I. He was friendly with my father, also called Gunther, who died just before the war. They were very friendly indeed.'

'So no one can help me find out what happened to my father?' Anna got up and the Baron rose, too, and gesticulated towards her sympathetically.

'I'm afraid not. Not at the moment, anyway. So much changed in the war. We had a house near Berlin but that has gone. However, maybe when I return I can try and find out something. I'd like to help if I could.'

'I'd be so grateful.' Anna held out her hand. 'It's quite a blight on one's life not to know what happened to a parent.'

'It must be.' As the Baron took her hand and held it, Anna could feel a surge of sympathy passing between them.

'I hope this isn't goodbye yet,' the Baron said. 'It would give me much pleasure if you could show me round the Festival. After all, that's why I'm here.'

It was two days before Anna could clear herself of appointments to escort the Baron and, by that time, he had already visited the Festival, but assured her he wanted to see it all again. They met in the hall of the Dome of Discovery at the entrance opposite the Transport Pavilion, which the Baron had said he particularly wanted to see, especially when he heard that Anna's cousins were exhibiting a car there. Among his many interests, the Baron explained, was motor cars. He was hoping to help build up the German motor car industry so famous before the war.

By the time Anna arrived he had already seen round the Dome, which featured exploration of the earth, its age, scientific discovery and technology, and the prospects for exploring outer space.

The Baron thought it would be very agreeable to come down to earth with the motor car.

'Right away?' Anna said.

'Right away,' he replied. 'I am anxious to meet your relations. Will they be there?'

'My cousin who developed the car might be,' Anna said. 'He practically lives in a white boiler suit.'

'He developed it himself?'

'We're quite proud of him. He has only just left university. He designed most of it while he was still there. In the twenties and the thirties my family were in the motor car business.'

'That's your mother's family?'

'Yes, on her mother's side, the Askhams.'

'And your father's family?'

'They left everything in Russia in 1920.' By now they were crossing the tree-lined court between the Dome and the Transport Pavilion. To their left was the river and to their right the entrance to the Festival site from Waterloo station. 'They remained in Paris for twenty years; but my grandfather was killed at the Liberation.'

'Killed? How?'

'He was a shot,' Anna said unemotionally, 'by the Communists. They thought he sided with the Germans.'

'And did he?' The Baron spoke gently. 'Forgive me if I intrude.'

'He certainly wouldn't side with the Communists,' Anna said shortly, as they entered the crowded pavilion. 'I think if we hurry up we might meet cousin.'

As usual, the first sight to be seen of Pascal was his feet appearing under the car. It was a life-sized model but it wasn't a real car. However, all the components had been specially tooled and, to all intents and purposes, it was real. The model Pascal had on display was a coupé with the roof rolled down, the gleaming leather interior open for all to see.

Anna bent down and tweaked his foot and slowly Pascal rolled out from underneath, wiping his hands on a rag.

'Anna!' he said with pleasure, and then looked beyond her. 'Have you brought us a purchaser?'

'Maybe:' The Baron stepped forward and leaned down to shake hands. 'It is a *very* impressive model. All your own work, I understand.'

'Only the design.' Pascal got up, still casually wiping his hands. 'Of course it isn't real. It couldn't go.'

'I can see that,' the Baron said knowledgeably, standing back. 'But it's very good.'

'This is Baron von Spee,' Anna said. 'He used to know my father.'

'Really?' Pascal looked at him with interest. 'Anna will be excited.'

'Not very well, I'm afraid.' The Baron pulled a rueful face. 'And it was a long time ago – almost twenty years.'

'Oh dear.' Pascal threw down the rag. 'Then you won't know what happened to him?'

'I'm afraid not.'

There was a thoughtful silence, then the Baron said in

121

a more cheerful tone of voice, 'However, I am here in the hope that we can do some business.' He reached into his breast pocket and produced a case from which he selected a card. This he gave to Pascal. 'I don't know if you've heard of the von Spee organization, but it is quite large. We were one of the first to get going after de-Nazification and we have been very lucky, supported by German and foreign banks. I have a range of interests, and cars . . .'

'These won't be mass-produced,' Pascal said firmly. 'Special cars, custom built. We haven't the facility for mass-production. The old "Askham" wasn't mass-produced either and only the death of my father in a racing model persuaded my cousin Bobby, now Lord Lighterman, to sell the business.'

'Of course, I've heard of Lord Lighterman.' The Baron sounded impressed. 'You cousin, you say. And who was your father, if I may ask?'

'Paolo Verdi.' It was quite easy now to say his name without emotion. Pascal's father had been killed almost twenty years ago to the month, in the first Grand Prix race at La Monza.

'Paolo Verdi, Paolo Verdi.' The Baron sounded really excited although, from his appearance, one would have imagined him an unemotional man. 'He was one of the great ones, along with Jimmy Murphy, Bradley, Caracciola, Robert Benoist.' The Baron extended his hand once again.

'I really am most proud to know you. I can see now that I must let you get on with your work, but I do hope we can meet again. Meanwhile . . .' he looked at Anna with a flourish of his hand, 'do we proceed?'

'*Sehr gut*,' Anna said in German and smiled at Pascal. 'See you later, perhaps.'

'Do fix a meeting with the Baron,' Pascal called after her. 'Invite him to mother's . . .'

122

Anna turned and casually waved her hand.

As she and the Baron walked between the rows of cars, most of them production models on display, replicas or sections – the Morris 'Oxford', the Hillman 'Minx', the Triumph 'Mayflower', the Standard 'Vanguard' and the Aston Martin DB2 – Pascal remained staring after them.

Anna was an enigma. He thought she liked him and then he thought she didn't. He had started to take her out quite seriously after she'd come up with the idea of putting the 'Askham' on display at the Exhibition. There had been a great air of excitement as Bobby enthused about the idea and exerted his considerable influence to get it going with only five months before the Exhibition opened. In fact, had it not been for Bobby and his drive and valuable contacts it wouldn't have been possible.

But Pascal had to spend a lot of time in the country; days and days over the drawing-board; late nights in the office. Anyway, it hadn't occurred to him that he was seriously courting Anna or that she was interested in him. It was difficult to see someone you'd known as a child in any romantic light.

But he had found that whenever he came up to town he gravitated towards his sister's flat, in the hope of finding Anna at home. Ten to one she wasn't and he'd found himself wondering what she did with her time. He knew she worked hard preparing for the Festival. Occasionally he'd found a curious bearded fellow having dinner with Angelica. Apparently he was too poor to take her out. Not Angelica's type at all. Pascal wondered if the bearded stranger kept Anna away but, on the few times he'd seen her, she assured him he didn't. He was amusing; a student at the LSE, a friend of Flora's. Once Pascal had found them all having dinner together.

But Pascal was too absorbed in his car and his vision of

the future. He was only twenty-two and not seriously interested in romance.

But now, as he watched his sophisticated cousin saunter off with a much older man, he wondered if he'd been too casual about her. She was extraordinarily attractive. She had a subtle kind of allure which was helped by her growing confidence and maturity. She wore clothes well. She had style, and looked much older than her twenty years. He became aware of a new sensation – a spasm of jealousy, and stifled an impulse to run after them, to suggest lunch, a meeting there and then. But he knew what they'd think. They'd say he was childish. One was in a very grown-up league indeed here. The Baron was twice his age – at least.

Pascal lit a cigarette and furiously sat down beside his car, feeling like someone cheated of a prize.

A short time later Anna and Gunther strolled back across Waterloo Bridge in the warm sunshine, looking up-river at the devastation caused by the war, the acres of bombed sites still visible by the docks and around St Paul's. He told her that in Germany reconstruction was proceeding very quickly. When they got to Simpson's in the Strand, beef – still rationed – was in short supply, so Anna volunteered to have a cheese salad.

'I prefer it, anyway. It's so hot.' She tossed off her jacket and slipped it over the back of her chair. She wore a cool green frock made of moygashel, fastened with a white belt, and white toeless sandals on her feet.

'In Germany the growth is phenomenal,' the Baron continued. 'Some cities are almost completely rebuilt. Tell me,' he broke off from studying the menu, 'your cousin has developed that car himself? Remarkable. And the backing was from Lord Lighterman?'

'It *is* Lord Lighterman's company. The Askham Motor

Corporation is part of the Lighterman empire, with Pascal and my brother Sasha as directors.'

'Sasha is interested in cars, too?'

'He was in the RAF in the war.' Anna paused, as if wishing to change the subject. 'How do you manage to speak English so well?'

'Ah,' the Baron acknowledged the very small piece of steak set before him. 'My mother was an Anglophile, but I didn't speak it with anything like proficiency until after the war, dealing with the English and American authorities.'

'Did my father speak German?'

'Very well.' The Baron looked surprised at her ignorance. 'He was a *very* accomplished man. I suppose you know very little about him?'

'Practically nothing.'

'Let me see what I can remember.'

Probably with the hope of engineering her attention, the Baron sat back and put a hand on his chin, brow puckered in concentration. Every time he mentioned her father Anna was aware of a quickening of the pace of her heart. It was so long since she had been able to talk to anyone about him. Her mother was unforgiving and seldom mentioned his name. She craned forward eagerly, watching every movement of her host's mobile face.

'He had an "air" about him,' the Baron said finally. 'What the French call *je ne sais quoi*. I remember him very well after all this time, the Russian prince. We called him "Prince", you know. He seemed to like it. He was a very good shot. I do remember that. When is the last time you saw him, actually?' The Baron hastily got on with his meal, which was getting cold. Anna as yet hadn't touched hers.

'It was about 1935.' Anna closed her eyes in the effort

of remembering. 'So you see I was very young, only five years old . . .'

'I was calculating,' the Baron smiled again. He had a number of gold fillings in his teeth, which caught the light. 'You haven't seen your father since you were *five*?'

'He was often away and then he disappeared completely. My mother said he was in Spain assisting the Nationalist Cause. She, meanwhile, had quarrelled with the Askham family, and took me to Venice where she had, and still has, a house. As the war clouds gathered she decided to stay there and we never saw my father again, though he did return to Paris. He left some time during the War, as I told you.'

'And turned up again in Berlin in 1945?'

'Supposedly. There is no corroboration.'

The Baron put his napkin to his lips, pressed it and nodded. 'I will do all I can,' he said, 'on my return, although it is still not very easy to find out what happened in Berlin in 1945. The Russians were the first to enter and they sealed everything up. You know what they are like – the Communists, I mean. Tell me more about your family.' For a moment he paused. 'I think your cousin likes you.'

'My cousin?' Anna looked nonplussed.

'The car designer.'

'We're like brother and sister.'

'Something more, I think, at least for him. You must be, let me see, about twenty-one?'

'Next month,' Anna smiled.

'And you see I'm forty-five. *I* could be your father.' The Baron looked rueful but brightened as he said, 'Tell me, what are you doing for dinner tonight?'

He was old enough to be her father, it was true; but in a way he was an important thread in her life. He had known

126

her real father, hunted with him and eaten with him many times. He could tell her lots of incidental things about Kyril, and Anna could never hear enough. Maybe he made some of them up. His memory was so extensive. She made many cancellations in her programme in order to keep herself free for him and, naturally, she introduced him as quickly as she could to the family, all of whom were agog to meet him because seemingly he, and only he, could fill in so many of those little details in Kyril's secretive life.

The news about the Baron travelled quickly and most of the family found themselves free to meet him at a party given by Charlotte. Arthur demurred at first and then agreed. He said that although he could never invite a Jap to his house one had to be forgiving about the Germans.

Bobby couldn't be at the party although he'd met the Baron privately. Sasha and Pascal had already taken him out to see the car in construction at the works; but everyone else was there, even Rachel, who had come up for the night specially. She and Em sat quietly studying him as he walked through the throng, which included a number of Members of Parliament and industrialists invited by Arthur.

'What do you think?' Rachel said. She raised an eyebrow. 'Do we know what he did in the War?'

'One is not supposed to ask. I do think, however, I must talk to him.'

The Baron had an ear cocked towards a Labour MP who was talking about the unions in Germany. The lack of them gave Germany an unfair advantage over the English. Baron von Spee coldly informed him that there was no lack of unions, but they were more disciplined than the English and thus likely to be more effective. Then he turned to greet a German diplomat whose wife was a distant cousin of his.

'I wonder if you could come and meet Em.' Anna tugged at his arm. 'She was in Germany in the thirties and would so like to meet you.'

Anna thought she saw an expression of alarm, even horror, pass over the Baron's face but decided she must have been mistaken, as immediately he was nodding and smiling again.

'Of course.' He kissed the hand of the diplomat's wife, said something to her in German and smiled coldly at the discomfited Labour MP. Then he followed Anna who introduced him.

'This is Lady Askham, Pascal's grandmother.'

'How do you do?' Gunther looked into her eyes and kissed her hand. 'What a *talented* grandson you have, Lady Askham.'

'Thank you.' Rachel found his aristocratic gaze a little unnerving.

'And this is Lady Emmeline Down. We call her Em.'

'How do you do, Lady Emmeline?' The Baron kissed her hand, too. Then he sat in a chair by her side after extracting a cigarette from a gold case. 'Anna said you particularly wanted to meet me. I believe you were in Germany in the thirties? Is it something to do with that?'

'Oh no, nothing at all.' Em observed a nerve twitching in his jaw. Then she saw him smile and relax suddenly as though she'd said something that pleased him. 'I just wondered, we all wondered, if you were in Berlin at the end of the war?'

'Thankfully, no.' The Baron studied his hands. 'Nowhere near, I'm glad to say.'

'My brother Ralph told me he'd seen Kyril. There is no reason to doubt him; but we have no proof.'

'I know.' The Baron gave a realistic sigh. 'Poor Anna has told me everything and my heart goes out to her and

128

Sasha. But how can I help them? I believe you have done everything. You were there. I was not.'

'It was just a chance,' Em said, thinking of Ralph's mysterious end, a lump in her throat. 'Because Anna said you had a house on the outskirts. I thought it was a possibility . . .'

'Believe me, my dear Lady Emmeline,' the Baron's hands flickered close to hers, 'when I return to Germany I will leave no stone unturned.'

At the far side of the room Pascal was watching the effect that the Baron had on his family, particularly Anna, who hovered constantly at his side even though he spoke excellent English.

'He seems to mesmerise everyone,' Pascal said with irritation to his brother Joe, who had come up specially from the country to meet the German guest. 'What *is* it about him?'

'That he knew Kyril,' Joe said. 'But apparently he knew him nearly twenty years ago and hasn't seen him since.'

'I must say he is quite knowledgeable about cars,' Pascal said grudgingly. 'Anna seems very taken by him.'

'I would have thought he was just Anna's style.' Joe's tone was malicious. Pascal looked at him sharply.

'What do you mean by that?'

'Well . . . can't you work it out for yourself?'

'Not really.'

'He is older, rich, a man of the world, probably a Nazi. Kyril was a Nazi too, at least that's what I have always believed, and Anna is his daughter.'

Pascal curled his fist to his side and imagined sending it into the soft flesh of his brother's nose. 'That is a perfectly foul thing to say,' he hissed. 'Quite uncalled for.'

'Is it? You don't mean to say you like her?'

'Why shouldn't I?'

'Because she's scheming, devious and ruthless. Mother is quite right not to trust her. When Anna is about all the family are at sixes and sevens.'

'I don't know why that should be.'

'Neither do I. But it is a fact.'

'I didn't know you hated her so much.' Pascal looked puzzled, slowly uncurling his fist.

'I don't hate her, but I avoid her. She's a schemer.' Joe looked anxiously at his brother. 'If I were you I'd avoid her, too.'

Sasha said: 'This is my wife, Stefanie. Kyril was her uncle.'

'How do you do?' the Baron said with his customary warmth. 'I hear I am to congratulate you as well. You have a new daughter.'

'Oh yes, thank you,' Stefanie smiled, but she looked strained.

'Her name is Galina,' Sasha said, 'after my father's mother – Princess Galina. She was a Gorchenko by birth.'

'I see you are very proud of the Russian connection.' The Baron laughingly put his hand on Sasha's shoulder. 'And why not?' He turned to Stefanie. 'I can see something of your Uncle Kyril in you. Something about the eyes, maybe.'

Stefanie appeared surprised. 'I'm supposed to look like my father; but I wanted to ask you something, Baron,' Stefanie's tongue flicked nervously across her lips. 'My mother disappeared in Auschwitz. I wondered . . .'

'My dear, dear girl.' The Baron's smile suddenly vanished, to be replaced, as though a mask had suddenly slipped, by a look of profound irritation. 'I assure you I had nothing to do with Auschwitz. Nothing at all. I was nowhere *near* the place.'

130

'I'm awfully sorry, Baron.' Sasha looked angrily at Stefanie. 'My wife really had no right . . .'

'No right at all!' Anna, who never left Gunther's side, echoed her brother. 'You must understand, Stefanie, that the Baron was merely a member of the Wehrmacht during the War. Called up to serve a Führer he, by that time, despised.'

'Just a serving officer,' the Baron said. 'Nothing to do with the SS, or the Nazis. Nothing.' He looked at his watch. 'As I have to leave tomorrow, Anna, I think I should be going.'

'But it's so early. Charlotte will be upset.'

The Baron passed a hand across his forehead. 'It has been a *very* tiring day. A tiring week. I must take leave of my hostess.'

'Oh, but you can't,' Charlotte began, as the Baron went over to her. 'Some people we have asked to meet you haven't yet arrived.'

'Alas, dear Lady Charlotte.' The Baron bowed low over her hand. 'So much paperwork to do, and there will be many other opportunities. *Please* forgive me.' He encased both her hands in his, a gesture which Charlotte suddenly found distasteful.

'Arthur will be *so* disappointed,' she said, looking round for him.

'Let me creep out before I cause a stir,' the Baron whispered, one hand to his lips. The other reached for Anna. 'I know you won't mind me borrowing Anna to show me the way home. We have a little more business to discuss.'

For some time they were silent as the taxi sped along Kensington High Street, past the Albert Hall towards Knightsbridge and, ultimately, the Strand.

131

'I'm frightfully sorry about that,' Anna said. 'I know it's why you left.'

The Baron turned to her.

'You know, one thinks: "What next?" I can't be responsible for *all* the people who disappeared in Germany during the War.'

'Of course you can't and I'm sorry. I'm very sorry indeed. I hope it won't alter the way you feel about me, or the car.'

'Oh, the Askham.' The Baron settled back and lit a fresh cigarette. 'Now that *has* possibilities and, believe me, I did like your family but, yes, the evening made me nervous. First Lady Emmeline. I wondered if she was going to question me about Hitler; and then your sister-in-law. Her mother disappeared in Auschwitz! I ask you. Should I say I personally pushed her into the gas ovens?'

'Please don't,' Anna said. 'I've already said I'm sorry. She had a baby not too long ago and she is pretty unstable anyway, a worry to Sasha. Please, put it out of your mind.'

The Baron didn't reply but sat there smoking his cigarette. Then he said suddenly:

'It's gone. I forget it completely. I am tired, you know.' He stubbed out his cigarette and leaned towards her. 'Of course it won't alter the way I feel about you. For you I would do anything. Do you know that?' Impulsively his hand closed over hers. 'Anything.'

Then he bent over and kissed her lightly on the lips.

The party at Charlotte's, which was meant as a gesture of goodwill towards the representative of a former enemy, had an unsettling effect on the whole family. It helped to bring back memories, to expose old sores. It also divided the family once more into two camps: the Askhams and the Ferovs. It reminded them that to be Russian wasn't to be English.

What was more, our wartime allies were now our enemies. The Berlin Blockade was still fresh in everyone's memories. The Russians were obdurate, intractable, devious. It was easy to forget that originally the Ferovs had fled from their homeland – to think of them as still part of modern-day Russia.

Of course it *was* very unfair. But Anna's attitude hadn't helped and she wasn't even born in Russia. However, there was also the fact that, during the war, Ralph had implicated Kyril in the death of Freddie in 1937. But there was no proof.

Nevertheless, the feeling against Anna hardened imperceptibly and it was with reluctance that Charlotte agreed to hold a joint birthday party for the two girls to celebrate their twenty-first.

'You can't be so *unreasonable* about Anna,' Pascal said, aware of his mother's disapproval. 'She isn't responsible for the sins, real or imagined, of her father.'

'No, she's not.' Charlotte was addressing invitations. 'It is something that Anna brings with her which I can't explain.'

'I think *that's* prejudice,' Pascal said angrily. 'The family always make her feel uncomfortable. She says so.'

'I'm sorry about that.' Charlotte paused in her addressing of envelopes, feeling guilty. 'I really am. It makes me feel bad. After all she's Susan's daughter too, not just Kyril's.'

'You never think of Sasha as Kyril's son, but always of Anna as his daughter. It's not fair.'

Pascal lounged against the fireplace, hands in his trouser pockets, lock of black hair falling over his forehead. Charlotte thought he looked pale and interesting, but she also always vaguely worried about his health. Yet few

133

young men could be more robust. She didn't worry half as much about Joe. Maybe she felt he was better able, as the elder twin by half an hour or so, to look after himself.

There was a lot to worry about in the family, she thought. Yet compared to what it was like in the War there was little really to concern one. Yet one always seemed able to find something to worry about. It was as though one looked around for things to make one anxious when none seemed to exist already.

Had she, in her middle age, turned into a fusser?

'I don't know what you see in Anna.' Charlotte bent her head to resume her invitations, glancing at the list. 'You're always *defending* her.'

'I feel sorry for her.'

'Sorry for Anna!' Charlotte looked up, removing her reading glasses. 'I'm amazed. I would think her perfectly able to look after herself.'

'How would *you* like it if no one liked you?'

'But she's got plenty of friends. Angelica likes her well enough.'

'Yes, but there are other people who matter. Joe can't stand her, for some reason. He avoids her and it's obvious. She knows you don't like her and now Stefanie won't speak to her after the incident here with the Baron. Anna does feel very isolated.'

'Well, I'm doing all I can,' Charlotte said between clenched teeth, 'by giving a joint party for her and Angelica. Let's hope she appreciates that.'

Stefanie opened the envelope, glanced at the invitation inside and then let it drop on the table. Little as she wanted to go she supposed she would have to. Anna was Sasha's sister. Stefanie put her elbows on the table and stared at the grain of the plain, unvarnished deal wood. Sometimes moments of unbearable tension welled up inside her without warning and then she would cup her hands to her ears to try to drown the drumming sound though, in reality, such a gesture intensified it.

When Sasha went off to work she realized that the day lay before her in which she had nothing to do but care for a young baby, do some household chores, think, read or sleep. But when she was depressed, reading or thinking was the last thing she wanted to do. She wanted to be occupied and none of these things was enough, certainly not looking after a small baby.

Sometimes Sasha stayed at Askham to be near to the works while Pascal was testing something to do with the car, and then she was alone for twenty-four hours except for the visit of the daily woman.

Stefanie briefly had had a career modelling woollens but, indirectly, it led to disaster though no one could say it was the cause of it. She'd met a man much older than herself called Jack Blackstock and she'd become obsessed with him. He wasn't a nice man and he'd treated her badly. Once he nearly killed her and Sasha saved her and the baby she was carrying by Jack.

Sasha took her away and married her and ever since he'd looked after her; but sometimes she thought it was rather as a parent watched over a baby, the way she watched over Nicky and Galina.

Stefanie wasn't trained for anything; she was not academic like her sister Olga; nor had she the dramatic talents of Natasha, who wanted to go on the stage. Bobby had never wanted any of his daughters to work: they were 'honourables', he told them, they had money and they should find husbands when the time came, settle down, and be happy. Well, Stefanie had done what her father wanted. She had found a husband, someone her father approved of, and she had two children; but she wasn't happy.

135

Here in this pretty little house, a stone's throw from the house the poet John Keats had once lived in, she wasn't happy at all. She felt that her life was fragmented; sometimes she had the sensation that literally she was splintering, and that it would take something quite powerful to put her together again.

Taking her elbows off the table, unblocking her ears, Stefanie looked around. It was a sunny September day and the stillness was perfect. Why couldn't she be happy? Why was everything so black? It was only nine o'clock yet already she felt tired. She longed to go to bed again.

Taking a tray, she cleared the breakfast things to the sink and stacked them carefully, going back to wipe the table. She didn't mind housework; she'd done a lot of it as the eldest granddaughter helping her grandmother in Paris. She rather liked it, in fact. She put the salt and pepper on the dresser and the clean plates next to the condiment set. Just by her hand were a few bottles that she and Sasha kept in the kitchen where they ate their evening meal if they were alone. There was gin, sherry, whisky, a half-empty bottle of Chianti.

Stefanie thought that maybe if she had a glass of sherry she would feel better about the day. Gin and whisky, wine, were too bitter; but sherry was a nice drink. She knew that if one drank in the morning it was a bad sign; but this would just be one tiny drink to get her through this difficult patch. Swiftly she reached up to the cupboard, produced a sherry glass and, filling it to the brim, put it to her lips.

It really did taste good. She had another and, as she drank, she felt the strength flow through her again, what had been black was now a kind of dullish grey.

She felt quite cheerful as she swiftly washed up and then went upstairs to get Galina ready for her walk with the girl who lived two houses away. She took Galina in her pram through the Heath at the same time as she exercised her dogs.

There was no doubt at all that, whatever anyone said, a glass or two of sherry put a little lift into anyone depressed by the beginning of the day. She wouldn't do it again, but it was there if she wanted it.

Nicky was already at Robertswood with Irina. He spent a great deal of time with his great-grandmother, especially now that Stefanie had a much younger baby to take care of.

Stefanie found motherhood difficult. She was not a natural mother and concluded that she didn't like small babies. Yet as she stood by Galina's cot this morning she was aware of a stirring in her breast that was possibly the beginning of love.

Galina had the Ferov looks: she was fair, blue-eyed, with the very dark, rather thick eyebrows, even at this early age, of her grandmother, Hélène.

Suddenly Stefanie could see her mother in her baby's face and she dropped on her knees by the crib and peered into those immature yet knowing blue eyes. She touched the baby's soft hair with a finger and in her mind's eye she saw her mother that day as she walked out of Charlotte's apartment in Paris, carrying her case – a rather battered case with a leather strap around it because the key was lost – smoking a cigarette, trying to be brave.

What had been the thoughts in her heart as she walked slowly away, out of the lives of her daughters and her parents, although no one knew it then, forever?

Stefanie reached for Galina and drew her into her arms, burying her face in those soft, fragrant cheeks. The tears poured down her face, wetting the top of the baby's head like another baptism: a baptism of sorrow.

'Oh, Mother,' Stefanie sobbed, going to the window,

Galina in her arms. She could see down the road, which led straight on to the leafy Heath, but it seemed like a long, narrow path leading upwards to eternity. The baby whimpered in her arms as if she, too, understood and turned those wondering, blue eyes to the tortured face of her mother.

'Oh, Mother,' Stefanie sobbed again. 'Did you ever forgive me?'

CHAPTER 6

The birthday party was delayed because, until the end of September, Anna had been busy in the press office. The Festival closed on September 30, having been judged a great success, but there was a lot to do afterwards. Anna knew she would feel very flat again, looking for a job.

On the actual day of her twenty-first birthday Pascal had taken her out to dinner and she thought that, really, he was the nicest one of the whole family. There was a warm sympathy about him that none of the others, even Rachel, seemed to have. She hadn't deliberately offended any one of them, but she knew they didn't like her.

But Anna's mind was constantly on the Baron, Gunther. He never wrote to her but occasionally he rang her, and just to hear his voice was to bring him vividly to mind again. She felt she was tantalizingly on the verge of an affair that was already out of control. But he was old enough to be her father, much, much too old. Now it was time to think of her birthday party which was being held at Robertswood instead of the Hall, the traditional place for Askham parties.

Anna had wondered if this was because the family didn't consider her a proper Askham, despite her mother who was the granddaughter of the ninth earl. On the other hand, Angelica was much more of an Askham than she was and they hadn't had a party at the Hall for her.

Someone said they hadn't had a proper party at the Hall since before the war, in the heyday of Dulcie. That was when the last real parties that everyone talked about were held.

Yet perhaps the truth was that Hugo and Jenny found entertaining made too much work, especially on the large scale expected by the family. They regarded themselves as hardworking farmers, market gardeners who really, in Askham Hall, had taken on something that was too much for them, too big. Its sentimental associations for Hugo were understandable, but now seen to be misplaced. Askham Hall had become a large, rather empty shell where the family stayed for odd weekends, or when they visited the growing Askham motor works ten miles away. Pascal had a permanent room there; but then Pascal was a man without pretension, one who was glad to muck in.

Robertswood, on the other hand, grew finer, more grand with every day that passed. Bobby had plenty of money and Irina, who reigned there like a dowager queen, was glad, more than glad, to spend it for him. It had a kindly vengeance for her; and revenge was sweet. Bobby was responsible for so much ill that had fallen on her family.

Had she not been chatelaine in her time of two magnificent palaces in Moscow and St Petersburg, of Essenelli in the hills above Batum? Was it not a marvellous opportunity for a woman who, though seventy-eight years of age, still enjoyed remarkable health and vigour, to make up for all the years of deprivation that cruel fate had allotted her?

Theoretically Robertswood was the country home of Sasha and Stefanie, which had been given to them to avoid death duties. But it was still Bobby's money that maintained it, refurbished it to its pre-1914 standard after it had been used for six years as a convalescent home during the last war.

Gradually it was restored, room by room, painstakingly, artistically, accurately. All the furniture that had been stored was renovated, recovered if necessary, revarnished and restored to its original place in the house, maybe, moved somewhere different if Irina thought it more suitable.

For the Princess, whose family had been even older than the Romanovs, had impeccable taste, if a little dated. To her, velvet, satin and damask were the materials with which to make curtains, line walls, upholster chairs and sofas. There was velvet everywhere and strong primary colours of red, blue and green. There was polished wood and marble, onyx and jade, and from the ceilings hung crystal chandeliers, every piece of which had been washed and polished until they sparkled like diamonds. Some of them were priceless.

In many ways Robertswood, on the banks of the Thames, in such a gracious setting surrounded by trees, looked very much as it had when Sir Robert first built it, somewhere around the year 1880. Except that it had modern central heating and plumbing it was very much the house it was then: cosy, even though full of antiques like an opulent museum, the brainchild of an eccentric millionaire.

Looking out of her bedroom window over the river Susan Ferov, the mother of Anna and Sasha, could recall very little of that pre-1914 war scene, though she was eleven when the war began. Those years had mostly been spent at Askham Hall; they were the splendid years, ones that lingered in the memory. They seemed not only peaceful but full of fun and laughter. And indeed they were full of sunshine and joy, Susan thought, carefully putting her long emerald earrings through the lobe of each ear as she stood watching the leaden clouds scurry by at the end of another grey English day.

She was glad she had left England. The sunshine of Venice suited her much better, as that of the south of France had suited her mother when she had decided to live there after her third marriage in the twenties. Even in those days divorce among the aristocracy was scandalous enough for the ones involved to consider voluntary exile, and Melanie and Denton had taken themselves off to Cannes and not returned.

Susan seldom came back to England now. Her last visit was in 1946 to sign some papers to do with various family business and attend the memorial service for Ralph. In fact, she reflected, she didn't like England and was glad she no longer lived there. Which made it all the more strange that Anna . . . As she thought about her daughter there was a gentle knock on the door and Anna poked her head round.

'Mummy, you do look glamorous!'

'Oh, I don't think one would associate glamour with *me,* darling,' Susan said, smiling at herself in the mirror, but pleased with the compliment. 'I was always the ugly duckling, forced into second, or possibly third or fourth place, by a beautiful mother and pretty cousins. Charlotte, especially, always stole the show, though as she was much younger than I it didn't really matter.'

Carefully, precisely, slowly, Susan finished her toilet. She seldom hurried. There was never the need. A woman who had lost her husband twice, but who had comfort and plenty of money to sustain her, plenty of interests and a successful antiques business – more a hobby than a business but, inevitably, it did well – seldom needed to hurry.

Now aged forty-eight, Susan was a handsome woman who had put on a few extra inches round the waist in the last twenty years but dressed smartly and fashionably so that this extra upholstery was well disguised. She spent a lot of money on her clothes but, like her mother-in-law Irina, she had good taste. She was rich, elegant and

142

attractive and in her long evening gown, with the green emeralds, she looked almost beautiful.

Anna sat on the edge of the bed, a huge, canopied copy of one of the works of the sixteenth century Flemish designer and architect Hans Vredeman de Vries which, nevertheless, Susan approved of. De Vries had been a classicist who applied Gothic designs to furniture and his beds were adorned with classical nudes, masques, garlands and sculpted niches in the great decorative bedheads. Susan, after carefully examining this, thought it might be an original de Vries, but there were certain telltale signs that it might have been some artist of a later period imitating him.

Anna sat watching her mother, the slow graceful way she dressed, the care with which she selected her jewellery and put the finishing touches to her face with a soft camel brush.

Susan was one of the few people, perhaps the only person apart from Irina, that Anna really loved. Her father she loved in the way that one loves God – a mysterious being worshipped from afar, and she loved Sasha but only out of duty. She scarcely knew him either, and his reappearance in her life had curiosity value rather than the cementation of a permanent bond of affection. Sasha was eight years her senior and already at prep school in England when she was born. For years during the war they hadn't seen each other at all.

Anna watched Susan moving quietly about the room, disappearing into the adjoining bathroom, reappearing to smile at Anna. The two women were used to shared silences. In many ways they enjoyed them; partly they communicated through them.

'I've scarcely seen you since I came,' Susan murmured, surveying the back of her hair in the three-cornered mirror. 'We've hardly had a moment to ourselves, darling.

I miss you, you know. I wish you'd come home more – now the aeroplane makes it so much easier. Compared to the old days it's a dream. I might even get Granny to come one of these days.'

'I think Granny's stuck in Venice, Mummy. She's too old to change.'

'In many ways you're right,' Susan nodded. 'I never thought the day would come when my mother showed and felt her age, but it has.' Susan turned to Anna, her eyes raised in surprise. 'She is a year younger than Rachel, you know, but seems much older. She is so set in her ways. The war frightened her. I agree with you, darling. She won't leave Venice – ever.'

It was sad to think of a woman who, in her heyday, had enjoyed life so much, spending what was left of it in the dark, though beautiful, recesses of an ancient Venetian palazzo with only her old husband and dotty son for close companionship. Susan was away a great deal. In middle age she was beginning to find life much more enjoyable, almost, than at any other time in her life.

'I'm thinking of opening the Paris apartment again,' Susan said. 'I thought I might spend six months of the year there, at least. Why don't you come and join me, darling, after this is all over?'

Anna toyed with the fringe of her damask bedspread, heavily interwoven with a medieval hunting scene.

'I might,' she said, and something in her tone of voice made her mother pause and look at her.

'What is it, Anna?'

'This and that,' Anna said.

'You're frightfully mysterious.' Susan didn't like problems, either her own or those of anybody else. She had spent most of her life avoiding them, using her money to cushion herself against them as far as possible. Susan went over to the drawer of her dressing-table and began rooting through it. 'I would have thought you would be happy on your birthday. You don't seem very happy to me.'

'I liked my work at the Festival office. That's finished. I've nothing to do, Mummy, no qualifications.'

'You're a wonderful linguist.' Susan looked at her in surprise. 'Everyone says that. Why don't you go and study at the Interpreters' School in Geneva? It's world famous.'

'I thought I might go to Germany.'

'*Germany*?' Susan stared at her. 'Why Germany?'

'Did you ever know the von Spee family? They were friends of father's.'

'Von Spee.' Susan found what she was looking for in her drawer and sat still for a moment. 'Von Spee? I think I do remember the name, though, you know, your father and I seldom travelled about together.'

'Well, Gunther von Spee, the son of father's friend, also called Gunther, was over here recently. He remembered my father well and spoke of him.'

'That's nice,' Susan said shortly, meaning that she didn't think it was nice at all.

Anna rose with an exclamation and began to pace around the room. 'Mummy, I don't think you know . . .'

'Spare me, Anna, *please*,' Susan put out a hand. 'I don't know how much you miss your father, etcetera. I've heard it all before, haven't I? What am I to do about it? I haven't seen him *or* heard from him. Think what a situation it puts me in. I don't know if I'm a widow or merely abandoned. It's very inconvenient, but *very* like Kyril, always full of mysteries. Why you want to go chasing after him I don't know but if you did find out the truth I, for one, would be glad. Can this Mr von Spee help you, do you think?'

'Baron. Baron von Spee. He says he might be able to.'

145

'Go to Germany, then,' Susan said, thankful that that problem was solved. 'If you think it will help.'

'Anyway, the family don't like me,' Anna burst out. 'I'm not popular here.'

'Whyever not?' Susan looked not only amazed but annoyed that another problem had asserted itself. 'You must be mistaken.'

'They've never liked me. They resent me.'

'Who is "they", may I ask?'

'All of them, especially Charlotte.'

'But you share a flat with Angelica!'

'That's why Charlotte resents me. She wanted to hang on to Angelica.'

'Charlotte *is* a bit like that,' Susan admitted, glancing at the *diamanté* watch on her wrist. 'I think she feels she neglected her children, which she did, and now she won't let them go. Curious psychology, Charlotte.' Susan shook her head. 'I did think, actually, that in the brief time I've been here, Pascal had eyes for you.' Slyly Susan glanced at her daughter.

'He's too young,' Anna said dismissively. 'Anyway, I should never want to have anything to do with someone content to be a mechanic.'

Susan sighed, rose and ran her hands over her bottom, straightening the elegant evening dress Balenciaga had made for her for the occasion of her daughter's twenty-first.

'I wasn't trying to marry you off, silly! He seems a nice person. I thought he might be a friend. That's all.'

Just then the gong sounded and they both went down for dinner.

Fourteen of the family sat down to dinner. The oldest was Irina and the youngest Paul Askham, the thirteenth earl and still a schoolboy at Eton. Paul was the son of Freddie and his tragic, tubercular wife Marian, whose death had made him decide to go and fight in Spain. Paul had been brought up by Rachel and Adam and at sixteen was a dark, rather frail-looking boy of medium height, not a bit like an Askham. His delicate good looks, his tendency to colds, had for many years made Rachel dread he would inherit his mother's disease, but so far he never had. Rachel loved him dearly.

Paul rarely appeared at family functions. He was probably the most scholarly earl the Askham family had ever produced, taking after his mother's side of the family. He wore glasses in thin steel frames and spent most of his time somewhere out of sight with a book. Paul was the titular head of the whole family, but the accepted head was Adam, who sat next to Aileen presiding at one end of the long dining-room table while a jovial Bobby sat at the other.

The only stranger at the dinner-party was a young man called Dick Crosby whom all the family were excessively polite to without really being able to place. Then someone said he was at the LSE and a friend of Flora's, and Pascal told his mother that Angelica knew him, too.

In fact Angelica had invited him to her party, but passed him off as a boyfriend of Flora's to save herself the embarrassment of being thought to have invited someone so odd.

For Dick was odd. He was odd, yet he was fascinating, and she felt he was the most unconventional man she had ever met.

Flora knew she was being used by Angelica but she didn't mind. Dick knew all about her family now, anyway, and didn't appear to think any the less of her for it. Flora knew that Angelica, occasionally, asked Dick for a meal alone, and sometimes she came with him. She was quite sure that there was nothing physical in the relationship between Dick and her cousin, because Angelica had assured her that he wasn't the type she fancied, but she found him interesting. Flora wasn't supposed to care, anyway. She had spent a whole year telling herself that Dick meant nothing to her except as a friend and comrade.

Angelica, after her evening at the LSE hop, rather liked the idea of cultivating the intelligentsia, even if it was only on the side. She liked smart gatherings and good restaurants and the LSE crowd wasn't the sort for this aspect of her life, which was important to her.

Angelica would never admit even to herself that she was sexually drawn to Dick and she, Flora and even, perhaps, Dick, were supposed to be firmly of the opinion that what attraction there was was cerebral.

Dick Crosby was the only man round the table not wearing a black jacket. He had on a navy-blue suit, a white shirt and an awkwardly knotted tie. He had looked so out of place when he had come nervously into Bobby's splendid drawing-room with Flora that, with one accord, the family swooped on him to try and make him feel at home. Now he sat between Rachel and Flora, toying with his food, the plethora of knives, forks and glasses, the unaccustomed number of courses with minute quantities on each plate.

Rachel was a good person to put Dick next to and it had been deliberately arranged. Always an active social-ist, in her younger days she had been known as the 'Red Countess' and barred from many London drawing-rooms on account of it. She had been a working journalist and a seasoned political campaigner. Moreover, Rachel was a natural democrat and found talking to all kinds of people congenial. She quickly put Dick at his ease by asking him questions about the LSE.

'I did my finals a year ago,' Dick said. 'I'm doing research into political parties.'

'Do you want to go into Parliament?'

'Maybe.' Dick looked grim. He very seldom smiled. 'The trouble is Parliament changes people. It makes them all stuck-up.'

Rachel though of Flora's uncle, Spencer Foster, her old love, and was about to mention him when Flora, who had been nervously monitoring the conversation, leaned across Dick and said:

'Please don't mention Uncle Spencer, Aunt Rachel. Dick hates him.'

'Hates Spencer Foster!' Rachel said indignantly. 'He is the nicest of men, the least spoilt.'

'But a *Tory*, Lady Askham,' Dick said firmly.

'He is certainly not a Tory!'

'Well, he is a Tory, the way I hear it. He certainly doesn't believe what I believe in.'

'That's not surprising,' Rachel said mildly. 'If, like Flora, you're a member of the CP.'

Flora's communism was taken in good part by the family, as though it were something amusing like vegetarianism or being an anti-vivisectionist. Anything the family didn't understand it laughed at. No one felt at all threatened by it. In fact they were glad that poor Flora had an interest and now, apparently, a young man. Her first year at the LSE seemed to have suited her. They felt with relief they could forget about Young Flora being a problem and think about other things instead.

'Spencer Foster is certainly not one of us,' Arthur, who had been listening, butted in. 'I'm a Tory Member of Parliament. Believe me, I know.'

'I thought you knew that all my family were Tories,' Flora said to Dick, with exaggerated patience. 'I told you to keep off politics.'

149

'*I'm* not a Tory,' Rachel said cheerfully. 'Never have been, though Dick might well think I'm one. To change the subject, Dick, or rather to sidetrack a bit, do you know that Lord Lighterman,' she glanced in Bobby's direction, 'once met Lenin?'

'*Did* he?' The surly, truculent expression on Dick's face became transformed into one of intense interest.

'I did indeed,' Bobby said. 'And I've met Marshal Stalin, too. I have always kept in with the Russians, my boy. Believe me, they're very good businessmen, very shrewd.'

'You amaze me,' Dick said, nonplussed.

'I thought I might,' Bobby chuckled. 'Come and have a cigar with me later and I'll tell you about Lenin. He was a remarkable man.'

'Even if he did send my father to prison,' Anna glanced at her mother opposite her.

Bobby shook his head as if the memory still pained him. 'How were we to know . . .'

'Stalin nearly sent me to prison, too,' Sasha said. 'We got out of Russia last year by the skin of our teeth.'

'*That's* an exaggeration.' Stefanie shot him a warning glance.

'But it was on the cards. We were very lucky.'

'I didn't know you all knew so much about Russia,' Dick said and, for the first time that evening, he appeared to relax.

The guests started to arrive from nine-thirty onwards, climbing the huge marble staircase to be greeted by Bobby and his family at the top – the two birthday girls and their mothers and Angelica's stepfather, Arthur. Sasha also stood in line and Angelica's brothers Pascal and Joe.

By the time the last guest had been received and the

150

family started to circulate, a band playing in the corner of the huge salon, it was nearly ten o'clock.

'All that time in that line,' Anna said, shaking her hand. 'My fingers are sore.'

'Let me get you champagne,' Pascal had been hovering around her all evening.

'I may have had enough,' Anna said, 'at that ghastly dinner-party.'

'I thought it was quite good.' Pascal looked surprised.

'Then you weren't sitting at our end. Did Angelica have to ask that dreadful man? He's a Communist!'

As Pascal smiled Anna continued, 'She has him at our flat! I can't stand him. He would have us all in chains and in the tumbrils. Doesn't Flora *know* what communism did to our family?'

'Yes, but no one takes Flora's communism very seriously.' Pascal seized her hands. 'Come on, let's dance.'

Reluctantly Anna allowed herself to be led on to the floor where they were soon swallowed up in the crowd, dancing to the music of a fashionable band that had come down from London.

Bobby had been in a very good mood for most of the evening. He loved to show off, to have his family about him and to have people admire them and the appurtenances of wealth that went with them. Bobby's fiftieth birthday ball the previous year had really marked the opening of the house after its wartime transformation into a convalescent home.

Yet, Bobby felt, with some justification, that he had to take everything upon his shoulders. Sasha was more fanatically keen on one aspect of the business than immersing himself in its totality. He spent a lot of time closeted with Pascal under the prototype of the new 'Askham' rapidly taking shape for its presentation,

151

hopefully in 1952. Sasha in a way was a disappointment. He should have been made chief engineer, not managing director of the whole enterprise under Bobby's presidency.

After standing for half an hour in the reception line shaking hands, Bobby felt the need of a quiet whisky and a cigar and, nodding amiably to people as he passed through the throng, he made his way slowly towards his study on the ground floor which had once been occupied by his grandfather, Sir Robert. Hearing footsteps behind him as he approached the door he stopped, looked back and saw his youngest daughter, Natasha, hurrying after him.

'Father,' Natasha called, as Bobby reached the door.

'What is it, Natasha?' he said, his hand on the door knob.

'I just wanted a word.' Natasha smiled at him and slid past him into the study, stood back for him to enter and closed the door. Natasha was nineteen. She wore a simple evening dress of midnight-blue silk cut on the bias and swathed across her well-developed bosom. Her long fair hair, in the peekaboo style favoured by the film star, Veronia Lake, hung on her shoulders and her face, almost totally without make-up except for eye-shadow and lipstick, made her appear older than she was.

Natasha was a girl anxious to please. She only slowly became aware of her outstanding good looks and how to use them to the best advantage. Hitherto she had concentrated on being sweet, compliant, in order to get her own way. She reckoned that if you were very nice to people they couldn't help but be nice to you.

None of the Lighterman girls who had lived in Paris in the thirties and during the war could have other than feelings of resentment towards their father, the man who had abandoned them. Even Bobby's attempts to make up

152

to them afterwards were not very successful. Stefanie clearly hated him and Olga cultivated indifference, but Natasha continued to try and please, to be self-effacing, not to give offence. She had just returned from a year at a finishing-school in Switzerland, which had made her more sure of herself, not quite so diffident, and more determined to make a mark on the world other than being some rich man's wife.

Bobby poured himself a whisky, lit a cigar and settled in his chair by the fire.

'What is it, Natasha?' he said again, expelling a stream of smoke.

'I wanted to talk to you, Father.'

'What about?' Bobby eyed her. 'Not enough money?'

'Not enough to do, Father.' Docilely, as of old, Natasha sat on a stool at his feet.

'My dear, you have only just come home. What do you expect to do?'

'I'd like to go to drama school, Father.'

'Oh no,' Bobby said immediately, shaking his head. 'Drama and modelling are out as far as I'm concerned. Charlotte may not mind but, personally, I don't like what it's done to Angelica. It's made her look old; old and hard. I don't like the kind of people you meet in that kind of world. Take a secretarial course, work in a library if you must, something like that; but not drama school.'

'I've already been accepted at RADA, Father.'

'What?' Bobby stared cholerically at her over the tip of his cigar.

'The Royal Acadamy of Dramatic Art.'

'What do you mean, you've already been "accepted"?' Bobby demanded.

'I had an interview, an audition. They offered me a place. It's not easy to get in.' Natasha sounded quite proud of herself.

153

'You did this without my persmission?'

'Yes, Father.'

'Then they had no right to see you. I shall write to the Principal tomorrow.'

'Oh, Father, how *can* you say that? How can you destroy my life, just like that?'

'Because I can,' Bobby said. 'I'm sick of the way all my children disobey me, oppose my wishes. David goes off to America; Stefanie, well the less said about Stefanie . . . Olga becomes a bluestocking, and you . . . an actress? Over my dead body.'

'That's what I'm going to be though, Father, an actress,' Natasha said defiantly, colour showing in each cheek. 'I'm sorry I told you tonight. I thought you would be in a good mood; you looked in a good mood . . .'

'Well, I'm not now,' Bobby said truculently. 'You've put me in a very bad mood. Go away.'

'Not until you've agreed.'

'I don't agree. You've got too much of your mother in you, my girl,' he looked at her thoughtfully for a moment. 'She was a "show-off" too; also she couldn't take advice. In the very end she lost everything.'

'You've never really liked me, Father, have you?' Natasha stood up and walked to the fire, gazing sadly into it. 'I wanted you to love me but I don't feel I've ever had your love. I don't think that any of us have really been loved by you, except perhaps David . . .'

'At least I knew David was my son,' Bobby said suddenly.

Natasha stared at him. 'What do you mean by that?'

Bobby wriggled in his chair. 'Oh nothing . . . silly thing to say . . . didn't mean . . .'

'You hardly ever say anything you don't mean, Father.'

'Well, your mother had a lover, you know that,' Bobby pointed an accusing finger at her. 'That's why I don't want

154

you to be an actress. You're too like her. You're not like me . . . at all,' Bobby took a sip of his whisky. 'You are less like me than the other two. Your physical resemblance to your mother is uncanny and, like her, you're wayward and wilful . . .'

'But I've always tried to *please* you, love you . . .' Natasha began to shout. 'What are you saying? I'm not your daughter?'

'How do we know?' Bobby looked ruminatively into the fire. 'How can we ever know? He's dead, she's dead . . .' Bobby looked up, placed his glass on the table beside him and joined his hands over his stomach. 'To be honest, I've always been convinced you were Jamie Kitto's child. You were the youngest, born when she had resumed her affair with him.

'I've looked after you, acknowledged you because I had no proof. I've been far too good to you, in fact, good to you girls who might be bastards, except for Stefanie. She *does* look like me . . .'

'And she behaves like you!' Natasha burst out. 'She's selfish. Like you, she thinks only of herself, doesn't care who she hurts. Now that you've told me I say thank God if I'm *not* your daughter because, from this moment on, I will never take any notice of you again or do anything you say!'

Natasha rushed out of the door, cannoning into her grandmother who was cautiously approaching on the other side, having heard raised voices. She threw herself into her arms, laid her head on that welcoming bosom and wept.

'Oh God, Bobby,' Irina murmured in Russian, patting her granddaughter on her back, 'what have you said, what have you done?'

* * *

155

It was quite cool in the garden, too cool. Because it had been so hot indoors Anna had been quite agreeable to a stroll in the early October evening. But now she shivered and Pascal put his arm protectively around her.

'We needn't get married just yet,' he said. 'I'm just talking about being engaged. Getting to know each other.'

'That is absolutely crazy,' Anna said, 'to be engaged and not intend to get married.'

'But I do intend to get married . . .'

'Well, you can't get married without having someone to marry.'

'But Anna,' Pascal said. 'Don't you care anything for me at *all*?'

'What made you think I did?'

'I thought you always seemed pleased to see me.'

'You can be pleased to see someone without wanting to *marry* them. Anyway, you're too young. I don't know how you could even *think* of it. You completely misread the signs, I'm afraid. I thought all you cared about was cars.' Anna had felt quite shocked by his proposal. Now she was annoyed. A horrible day had been followed by a horrible evening. 'Besides,' she went on, 'don't you know your mother can't stand me? Have you told her what you intended?'

'Of course not.'

'Well, you should.'

'I would never ask my mother who I may, or may not, marry.'

'I'm glad of that, at any rate.' Anna gazed at him for a few moments. 'I suppose I should be flattered. Pascal, you're still a *boy*.'

'I am *twenty-three*,' Pascal exclaimed. 'Quite old enough to fall in love.'

'Well, I'm sorry. Not with me. I am sorry, really. I don't want to hurt you, but that is how I feel. Anyway, I discussed the future with my mother this evening and told her I wanted to go to Germany.'

'I suppose you're after the Baron,' Pascal said bitterly.

'I don't know what you mean by "after the Baron".' Anna looked stung. 'But that is *certainly* not the case. He's old enough to be my father.'

'So I noticed,' Pascal replied then, without thinking, his judgement warped by jealously. '*And* a Nazi to boot. So Joe says.'

'Well, Joe is a fairy,' Anna said heatedly. 'Trust a fairy to call a real man a Nazi.'

She began to laugh so loudly, so cruelly that, without knowing what he was doing, Pascal reached out and hit her right in the face.

Charlotte's mother and Susan's father, Rachel and Adam, were brother and sister. The cousins were close though there was five years' difference in their ages. When they were young that made quite a difference. Charlotte was only fourteen when Susan made her spectacular trip to Russia and returned home not only married, but pregnant. Even now Charlotte could recall the fuss that had caused in the family – the awe and veneration she felt for the older girl.

For Susan had been a girl, a rather naïve and impressionable girl, when she went to Russia; but when she returned a few months later she was a woman seared by an experience she never got over.

In the years when they both lived in Paris Charlotte and Susan had drawn closer together and, even though they had seen very little of each other since, their rapport remained.

With so many friends and family to see, some for the first time for years, Charlotte and Susan had scarcely had a chance to talk until the evening was in full swing, the newly-renovated ballroom full of dancing couples.

Charlotte's lissom figure had scarcely changed since the thirties, and she wore a Schiaparelli sheath evening gown with a split on one side, calf high. The eyes of most of the men in the room at some time or the other drifted towards her.

Seeing Susan coming over, Charlotte put both hands to her ears and shook her head. 'Isn't it terrible?' she shouted, cocking her head in the direction of the band of enthusiastic jazzmen who had joined the party. 'I've got to get something from my bedroom. Come with me?'

'Why not?' Susan took her arm. 'At least we'll have a bit of peace.'

'I believe I saw you dancing with my husband,' Charlotte laughed as they crossed the hall and began to climb to the second floor. 'It doesn't take much to get him going.'

'Arthur's very charming,' Susan said, admiring to herself Charlotte's elegant legs, her almost unbelievably slim waistline, as she followed her up the stairs. 'He seems much more charming than I remember him before the war.'

'Doesn't he?' Charlotte looked behind her and nodded as they reached the floor on which all the main bedrooms were. 'Dear old Arthur was a bit dreary and pompous as an airman, but business and, especially, being an MP, seems to suit him down to the ground. He's hoping for office if the Tories get in and we're sure they will.'

The country was in the throes of an energetically-fought election campaign announced by the Labour Government to try and improve its tiny majority in the House of Commons. This was one of the few nights that Arthur had allowed himself off from campaigning, usually accompanied by Charlotte, a considerable asset as she sat on the platform beside him looking cool, controlled and supremely, incredibly elegant.

The cousins walked past the empty rooms to the suite occupied by Charlotte and Arthur at the end of the corridor, with a two-way view on to the grounds and the river. Charlotte hurried over to close them and as she began to pull the curtain she hesitated, looked through the windows, opened them again and stepped out on to the balcony. She stood there for a minute looking into the grounds and then she came back and, glancing at Susan, went over to her dressing-table and opened her jewel-box.

'The clasp on this earring is killing me,' she said, taking off the offending object. 'I couldn't stand another moment's pain.'

'Agonizing,' Susan agreed. 'Why didn't you have your ears pierced?'

'Couldn't stand the thought of it.' Charlotte fitted another clasp to her left ear and stepped back to pat them into place and look at herself. Susan thought it was amusing to hear that a woman who'd suffered so much, so bravely, in the War, couldn't stand having her ears pierced. It seemed to tell her something she didn't know about Charlotte.

'There.' Charlotte turned to look at Susan. 'I saw Anna and Pascal in the garden just now.'

'Oh?' Susan went over to the French window, undoing the catch that Charlotte had fastened.

'Taking a stroll. It's rather cold, I would have thought. They looked to me as though they were talking in great earnest.' Charlotte sighed. 'I supposed you know Pascal is quite keen on Anna?'

'Oh dear.' Quickly Susan shut the door again. 'I thought I noticed an interest in the brief time I've been here,' she said carefully, 'but Anna dismissed it. She's awfully restless.'

Charlotte's eyes were on her own face in the mirror. 'Well, she had such a big job for the Festival. She did it very well. I can understand that.'

'She said something tonight about going to Germany.'

'Oh?' Charlotte turned round, earring in place, eyes on her cousin. 'Maybe it's the Baron.'

'Did you meet the Baron?'

'Yes. He was over here for the Festival. He say's he's interested in importing Pascal's car to Germany.'

'Did Anna see a lot of him?'

Charlotte looked cautious.

'Go on, you can tell me.'

'Well, I don't really know for sure, but I *think* so. He knew Kyril in the thirties.'

'So she said. She gave me to understand that was the attraction.'

'Then it might have been.' Charlotte had grown up in a world where tact was synonymous with godliness.

'She said you didn't like her.'

'Oh dear.' Charlotte felt the remark as though it had been a blow to her head. 'It isn't that I don't like Anna . . . But, how can one put it?' Charlotte put her finger on her cheek, alluring, casual, model-like.

'She thought you were a bit possessive over Angelica.'

'People do think that.' Charlotte inclined her head. 'I certainly don't dislike Anna. She misunderstands if she thinks I do.'

'She says none of the family like her.'

'That's rubbish. Shall we go down?' Charlotte was beginning to feel embarrassed.

'I must know, Charlotte.' Susan, instead of walking to the door, sat purposefully on the bed. 'I must know what's been going on with my daughter.'

160

'Nothing has been going on.' Charlotte reluctantly sat beside her. 'But Anna is very cool, you know. She doesn't give a lot. She's difficult to fathom.'

'Mother finds her difficult,' Susan nodded. 'Mother always calls her "Kyril's daughter", and she doesn't mean to be complimentary That's part of the reason I wasn't sorry when Anna came over here. They didn't really get on. So, you see, it saddens me to think that the family feel as mother does. She may be Kyril's daughter, but she's mine, too. I must count.'

'Of *course* you do,' Charlotte said, impulsively reaching for her hand.

'I'll confess Anna does worry me,' Susan went on. 'She's such a difficult girl to understand. She never confides. She never let on at all about the Baron. That's typical. I hoped she'd settle down, but how can she settle down with a boy like Pascal?'

'Pascal is really *much* too young for her,' Charlotte said firmly. 'I'm afraid the Baron was more suitable, but rather old and . . . probably married?'

She gazed at Susan, who lowered her eyes to the floor. More problems, which she so hated.

Dick Crosby stood on the edge of the crowd watching the dancers. In a way it was a bit like a Saturday hop at the LSE or one of the other colleges, except that everyone was much better dressed and he'd never seen so much champagne. It seemed that upper-class people knew how to enjoy themselves, too, and someone had lowered the lights.

Flora had, with difficulty, persuaded Dick to stay with her family for the weekend and attend the birthday-party to please Angelica. To him, Flora was part of committee rooms, addressing envelopes and attending street-corner rallies on behalf of the Party. He liked her as a comrade and not for anything else. But Angelica was intriguing. Her attention flattered him. She attracted him and, grudgingly, he gave in so that he could be with her. Apart from her and Flora he heartily despised her family, Lord Lighterman, his house, his works and, especially, his pomps.

Flora didn't like to dance and she didn't dance well. She was too self-conscius and her best clothes ill became her as if she had reluctantly squeezed herself into them in order to please the family. Whatever she said Dick knew that the family were very important to Flora. He didn't know that, apart from them, Dick's approval was what mattered most to her.

Dick had been busy talking to Flora and her father, an elderly man who had been over fifty when she was born. Now he knew a lot about the circumstances of the birth of Flora and her brother; of her father's second marriage to a working-class woman from the north, whose brother had been the Labour MP he rather despised, too. Dick tended to despise most people whose views contradicted his own.

Despite the family, Flora had always felt rather isolated and alone, cut off from her cousins by age, by temperament and by the fact that they seemed by implication to condone and support a way of life she hated.

Flora hated the concept of class and class distinctions. She felt ill at ease tonight with Dick, torn between two worlds, and was sorry she'd asked him just to please Angelica.

'Bring your friend,' Angelica had said, with a funny expression on her face, and Flora had known at once whom she meant. And she did; though now she realized she shouldn't have.

Flora stood by Dick's side, watching the dancers.

'Go on, ask someone if you like,' she said.

'How about you?' Dick said turning to her.

'I'm hopeless, honestly.' Flora pushed her glasses up her nose.

'I'm not much good, either,' Dick said and at that moment the throng cleared and he saw Angelica momentarily standing by herself. 'Oh, there's your cousin.'

'Go on, ask her to dance,' Flora said. 'She's a good dancer. I'm not.'

Dick felt awkward and looked at Flora as if really trying to fathom what she wanted.

'I don't mind at all,' Flora said. 'I want to talk to Aunt Rachel, anyway.'

Then, rather dispiritedly she watched Dick eagerly cross the floor and wandered off to find her aunt.

Rachel had never been much of a dancer either. It was certain that age had nothing to do with it, nor could she use it as an excuse because there was Irina, at the age of seventy-eight, merrily bopping up and down on the floor with a man young enough to be her grandson. Adam, too, had made one or two stately turns of the floor; but he was bronchitic and his chest was bad.

Rachel, however, liked to watch and, with a drink in her hand, she would take one of the comfortable chairs at each end of the room which were reserved for dowagers or wallflowers. She looked up with pleasure as Flora came towards her and moved her chair up to make space for one for her niece.

'Hello, darling,' she said. 'Where's your young man?'

'He's not my "young man", Aunt Rachel,' Flora said, flushing. 'He's just a friend. He's gone off to dance with Angelica. You know I don't like dancing.'

'I don't either.' Rachel put her niece's hand in hers. She loved Flora as she'd loved her namesake. She could never forget how, as Margaret lay dying after Flora's birth, the presence of that older Flora had seemed to permeate the room. It had been one of the few uncanny, almost paranormal experiences of Rachel's life, the vivid sense that her departed friend was in the room at the bedside of the woman who had supplanted her.

So she had always watched over Flora with particular care, though she had many other claims on her affection, too. She had Paul, Luis and Jonathan, her grandsons, one of whom was an orphan, and the other had lost a father. Shy, awkward little Flora with her lack of looks, mainly because she didn't pay any attention to them, had a character that none of the others had. Rachel had always feared she would find life difficult because she would help to make it hard for herself; she would not equivocate or compromise. It was not at all surprising that she shone at school and her choice of the LSE was followed by membership of the CP.

She knew that Flora's eager little eyes had been raking the dance-floor until she found Dick and Angelica dancing together, rather closely entwined. She knew that Flora would feel a pang of jealousy, of envy even, but that she would make the best of it. Her hand tightened over Flora's.

'I don't mind, honestly, Aunt.' Flora, whose rapport with her aunt was so complete, knew that her eyes, too, were on Dick and Angelica and what she was thinking. Flora tossed her hair back and smiled, a rare instance of beauty based on character. With her intelligent, mobile features, her eyes sparkling behind her unbecoming glasses, Young Flora reminded Rachel of many of the suffragettes she had been involved with before the First War: women who put cause before marriage, spiritual before homely comforts; women dedicated to an ideal in the way that she, Rachel, could never have been.

'Angelica, anyway, wouldn't have any time for Dick,' Rachel said. 'She's too ambitious.'

'Dick's ambitious, too.' Stoutly Flora rushed to his defence.

'Yes, but in a different way. Angelica wants to be seen to be successful. No tub-thumping or street corners for her.'

'I think Dick finds her fascinating,' Flora said and sighed.

She knew, in a way, that it was masochistic, a self-inflicted death wish to bring him to the party.

PART 2

Golden Days

February 1952–July 1955

CHAPTER 7

The King was dead.

On a dull February day Dick and Flora found themselves among scores of their fellow citizens, huddled together for warmth as the line moved slowly over Lambeth Bridge towards the Houses of Parliament and St Stephen's Hall where George VI lay in state. It was odd that two Marxists should find themselves in that situation at all; but Flora knew Dick was lured there by the prospect of seeing Angelica and she herself by curiosity, more than anything else. And, also, there was pity, even grief, at the departure of that man who had never wanted to be King; a shy, retiring man worn out by the cares of State but, particularly, by the War.

It had all rather amused Dick, the emotion shown by Flora when the King died suddenly in his sleep. They'd had a good many arguments about it as they sat around talking, planning meetings, rallies, anything that would whip up the apathetic British in favour of class revolution.

But the British were unlikely to revolt, they both knew that. The British were too comfortable, too conventional, too set in their ways, like the Royal Family, to change. Things which had gone on for a hundred years would go on for a hundred years more, unlike the continent of Europe where numerous coups and *putschs* had ravaged nations for generations, and were doing so again as an invisible iron curtain rose between East and West.

But appreciation of reality did not affect devotion to an ideal. Both Dick and Flora, for various reasons, clung to the dream of a new world dominated by the dictatorship of the proletariat and nothing would shift them from it.

In the end they had agreed that viewing the catafalque of the dead monarch would be a useful lesson in the behaviour of the bourgeoisie. When Flora had said that her three cousins would be there, that clinched the matter for Dick.

The procession seemed to go extremely slowly and of the Verdis there was no sign.

'Perhaps they can't find us in the crowd,' Flora suggested.

'Sure they weren't having you on?' Dick looked at her suspiciously.

'Angelica said she, Pascal and Joe would meet me by the bridge. The first one there would start to queue.'

They had been up and down the long queue, stretching as far as Lambeth Palace, twice and there was no sign of the Verdis. It was very cold. A mist rose from the river, whose upper reaches were completely shrouded. Flora tucked her arm through Dick's for warmth and he smiled at her, understanding. It was then that she understood the real meaning of 'comrade' because this was a comradely gesture, coming together for mutual warmth and protection.

There was no sex between them, no romance. But theirs was a marriage of minds, Flora often thought. Theirs was a deeper, finer relationship free of the bonds of the flesh. Flora sometimes thought that her lack of concern for her appearance, her almost deliberate defiance of canons of beauty and good taste, were deliberate efforts to protect herself from the necessity of having to attract men. It went on around her all the time and she thought it demeaning.

People should know and like her for what she was and not for what artifice made her. By ignoring the way she looked, what she wore, she was being manifestly herself: Flora.

Dick's rugged, bearded face was impassive, his eyes ranging over the crowd assembled round them. He was doing an MSc in the Sociology of Political Parties and here was his raw material. He chatted to them, but would like to have interviewed some of them in depth to find out why they were here; what the monarchy meant to them.

Everyone around them loved the Royal Family, admired and respected the late King. That much was clear enough. They felt warmth and sympathy towards his daughter, now Queen Elizabeth II, and grief for his wife.

'This devotion to people who didn't care a whit for them is absolutely absurd,' Dick muttered. 'They could all drop dead tomorrow for all royalty care about them.'

'I don't think that's true,' Flora said. 'My family . . . well, I have *reason* to think the late King did care an awful lot about his subjects . . .'

'I hate the word "subjects",' Dick said. 'I'm not a "subject" of anyone. What you meant to say was that your family know them pretty well.'

'My family once knew them. In the old days. Not me.'

'Didn't they know the King and Queen though, I mean the one who's just died?'

'Maybe a little,' Flora acknowledged guardedly. 'But not as closely as King George V and Queen Mary. My great-aunt . . .' Flora stopped. She had been about to tell him how Dulcie had been Lady-in-Waiting to Queen Alexandra, but decided not to.

'I think you're a little capitalist at heart,' Dick said, but he pressed her arm closer to him.

'I'm not,' Flora said stoutly. 'I am not and I never will be. My mother's family came from Preston . . .'

'Oh, the *Tory* . . .' but now she knew he was making fun of her.

Altogether it took five hours to reach St Stephen's Hall where the late King lay in state in his coffin, covered by a flag and flanked by four guards standing with bowed heads. Various other people who had gained privileged access to the hall without having to queue – visiting royalty, heads of state, members of both Houses of Parliament and other dignitaries – stood around in little clusters as the endless stream of ordinary people who had queued in the cold for many hours filed past. It took only a few seconds. Before they knew it Flora and Dick were on their way out, scarcely having taken it all in, towards the exit at the far end of the hall.

'Flora!' A dark-coated figure detached itself from a small group near the entrance to the House of Commons and Angelica seized her cousin by the hand.

'Angelica! Where did you get to?'

Looking behind her Flora saw that the group she had passed unseeingly consisted of many of her relations – her father, Aunt Rachel, Charlotte, Arthur, Joe Verdi and Em. Flora flushed, and gave a gasp.

'You cheated! You didn't queue.'

Arthur put his finger on his lips and silently the various members of the small group bowed once more in the direction of the coffin and then made their own way towards the exit, where they gathered on the pavement outside.

'I tried to get hold of you but I couldn't,' Angelica said apologetically. 'Arthur managed to get passes for us.' She looked at Dick and smiled. 'You, too. How nice to see you again.'

Dick nodded and mumbled something, stamping his feet in the cold.

'I'll be going, then,' he said, tying his muffler more securely round his neck.

'Do come back and have a snack with us.' Charlotte

172

rubbed her gloved hands one against the other. 'It's frightfully cold.'

'I . . .' Dick started, but Angelica gave him a nudge, while Flora gazed impassively at them, blinking like an owl.

'Come on,' Angelica said and Dick fell into step beside her.

They were all in black, all correctly attired except for Dick and Flora, classless representatives of the proletariat. The Askhams always wore mourning for any member of the Royal family for whom Court mourning was decreed. Charlotte even wore black stockings, sheer nylon with very high-heeled shoes, so that the effect was to make her look chic rather than sorrowful. Her black woollen dress had a high collar and the thin gold band round it was undoubtedly 18 carat. Gold clips in her ears added to the overall effect of *haute couture*.

No one could quite match up to Charlotte. Em certainly didn't try and Angelica was too young to wear mourning well. It made her look drab. Rachel's black dress had seen many mournings and over it she wore a black cardigan to keep out the cold. Rachel had never had any pretentions to being fashion-conscious.

Gathered in the drawing-room at the house in Holland Park – Adam and Arthur in morning dress, Joe in a black suit with black tie – they could have been any group of mourners lately returned from a funeral. Only Flora and Dick were the odd ones out. Flora even had a scarlet jersey on, never expecting it to be seen under her duffle coat, and her black, yellow and purple LSE scarf. Her frizzy hair was screwed back into a bunch and her face had a well-scrubbed look, free of make-up, unlike Angelica, who had quickly learned how to use artifice to enhance her natural good looks. Angelica's black dress had not been used for countless family funerals, though

173

there had been a good many of those in her lifetime, but had been newly acquired. It was plain and made of wool like her mother's, but with a pleated skirt and scalloped neckline, round which she wore the double string of pearls Charlotte and Arthur had given her for her twenty-first birthday. Angelica's dark hair was short and fashionably styled and, like her mother, she too wore black stockings and very high heels.

Dick stood there smoking, looking nervously at the family. He wore brown cords, a tweed jacket, check shirt and brown knotted tie. Arthur towered over him but was courtesy and friendliness itself as he put a drink in his hand and commented on the weather.

'Perfectly shocking,' Dick agreed. He felt uncomfortable in these surroundings, of a splendour and opulence utterly unfamiliar to him, and put his glass first in one hand then the other. Through Flora and her family he felt completely out of his depth.

Arthur had never spoken to Dick alone. He had met him at the birthday party, but that night he had been far too busy acting host to take any notice of this rather unusual, odd-looking young man; not the kind in City suits or hacking-jackets, before going riding with Angelica in The Row, that the family were used to seeing. Arthur had always loved riding and kept horses for the family stabled in a nearby mews. It was not easy to ride in London but it was possible and they enjoyed it.

'Do you ride?' Arthur didn't know what to say to Dick. He understood that Dick was a professed Marxist and he really didn't know how to talk to one. It was a little like knowing that someone had an obscure, unmentionable disease. Dick obviously lacked the civilities one expected of the men surrounding Angelica, who would know exactly what to say.

'Ride?' Dick screwed up his face.

174

'Ride. Horseride?'

'Oh,' Dick smiled, 'I thought you meant a bike. I don't even ride a bike. I certainly don't ride a horse.'

Arthur, a polished performer at the hustings and in people's doorways, just now seemed lost for words. Flora, sensing the dilemma both men were in, sidled up to them.

'Arthur and Angelica ride in the Park,' she explained. 'Charlotte does, sometimes, too.'

'Do you?' Dick looked at her.

'Of course not!'

'You *can* ride, Flora,' Arthur said accusingly, thinking she was intent on letting the side down. She was showing off in front of this peasant.

'I can, but I don't ride in London, Arthur.'

'Not easy,' Arthur nodded. 'Too much traffic. Would you excuse me a second?'

With the practised smile of one used to making diplomatic exits, Arthur moved over to Rachel and Adam, who were sitting together on the sofa drinking whisky.

'Everything all right?' Arthur bent towards them.

'Lovely, thank you, Arthur,' Rachel smiled up at him. 'I felt so sorry for Flora and that nice young man with her. Five hours they queued to see the catafalque. I would have done it myself at their age; but I feel sorry for them nevertheless.'

Arthur sat down in the place that Rachel and Adam had made for him, whisking the tails of his morning coat to one side as he did.

'Did you say "nice young man"?' he asked, keeping his voice low.

'Don't you like him?' Rachel looked amused.

'I find I can't talk to him. I don't know what to say.'

'Well he *is* a bit shy perhaps. I sat next to him at the dinner for Angelica's party and found him delightful. Very well read. He is doing an MSc at the LSE.'

'*Is* he Flora's boyfriend?' Arthur whispered.

Rachel shrugged her shoulders. 'I think she'd like it if he were. I'm not sure what the situation is now.'

Charlotte came in from the kitchen where she had been supervising the preparations for a buffet supper, which she declared was now ready in the dining-room. She invited everyone to bring their drinks and then stood back holding the door open while they filed out.

'Just help yourself and bring your food back if you wish,' she called, 'there's plenty of room.' She smiled brightly at Dick, who was about to precede Flora from the room when Rachel called her back.

'It's terribly informal,' Charlotte said to Dick. 'I hope you don't mind.'

'It's very kind of you to invite me, Mrs Verdi,' he said politely as Angelica caught up with him, coming from a side-door and nudging him in a rather familiar fashion towards the dining-room.

'*Lady* Charlotte,' she hissed in his ear.

'I beg your pardon?' Dick looked at her.

'My mother is known as Lady Charlotte, not Mrs Verdi. That's the right way to address her.'

'Bollocks,' Dick said under his brath.

'*I* beg your pardon?' Angelica smiled wickedly at him.

'I said what a lot of rot.'

'Not at all.' Angelica passed him a plate with the expertise of one used to *al fresco* entertaining. 'My mother is not Mrs Verdi, in any case. If she were "Mrs" anything she'd be Mrs Crewe. Arthur is my stepfather.'

Dick stuck his fork into a huge slice of ham and awkwardly put it on his plate.

'*Do* let me help you!' Angelica took his plate and began with ease to fill it with lamb, chicken and salads, all from Hugo's farm.

'All this comes from an uncle's farm,' she said. 'All home-grown to help the War effort.'

'The War's over,' Dick said, enjoying the game he knew they were playing, his role of disgruntled, monosyllabic revolutionary.

'Well, we still have rationing, don't we? We still have austerity. My uncle has made a wonderful market garden to serve the people from the ancestral family home. *You* should approve of that – all muck where once roses bloomed.'

'I would approve of that,' Dick smiled. 'It sounds just like Russia.'

'Don't you let my stepfather hear you.' Conspiratorially Angelica smiled over her shoulder. 'He *hates* the commies. He'd be absolutely livid if he heard you.'

'What does he think of Flora, then?' Dick said, as Angelica poured red wine into a glass and handed it to him.

'Oh, he doesn't take Flora seriously. None of us do, I'm afraid.' Angelica glanced over her shoulder. 'Flora's a bit of a joke in the family. Never quite belonged. You can understand it, can't you? Though we do adore her, of course.'

They moved from the dining-room through the hall into the drawing-room, where Flora was standing, still talking to Rachel.

'I'm just getting Aunt Rachel some supper,' Flora abruptly broke off and hurried past Dick and Angelica when she saw them together.

'Isn't she kind?' Rachel looked after her anxiously, knowing that Flora felt awkward, perhaps a little jealous.

'Granny,' Angelica admonished her playfully with her fork, as though she were showing off in front of Dick. 'You remember Dick Crosby, don't you?'

'Of course,' Rachel said with her warm smile. 'How nice to see you again, Dick.'

'And you – er – um . . .' Dick went red.

'*Lady* Askham,' Angelica chanted in a clear voice. 'Dick hates titles,' she told her grandmother and Rachel nodded understandingly.

'I do too, to tell you the truth, Dick. Unfortunately I was landed with one.'

'Which you got to like. Go on,' Angelica enjoyed chiding her grandmother. 'Mummy said you wouldn't give it up.'

'That is not true,' Rachel looked severely at her grand-daughter. 'If you mean because of Flora's Uncle Spencer, you're wrong. We didn't marry because we decided not to, that's all there was to it.'

'*You* were going to marry Flora's uncle?' At last Dick looked interested.

'No, I was not,' Rachel said firmly, laughing. 'I found I still loved my husband, Charlotte's father, who was killed in the First World War, too much. I also didn't want to lose my independence. My children and grandchildren, when they feel mischievous, like to say I didn't marry Spencer because I didn't want to lose my title. It's not true.'

'I believe you,' Dick said. So far she was the only one of the family he felt at all comfortable with. His feelings about Angelica were more complex.

'My origins were *very* ordinary,' Rachel assured him. 'It was just my misfortune, or fortune, to fall in love with the man who was to become Earl of Askham.'

'It's terribly romantic,' Angelica said. 'Tell him all about it, Gran. About Omdurman and everything.'

Omdurman, was it really possible that a battle fought with swords and spears had happened in one's lifetime? Was it possible, when the last War had ended with a nuclear explosion which killed thousands of people? If technology could advance so much in less than fifty years what would happen in the next fifty? In 1898 it had take Bosco and Adam two weeks to go from Cairo to the battle site near Omdurman. Today one could fly there in an hour or so from Cairo. In those days Cairo had been full of horse-drawn vehicles, and not only Cairo: the streets of London, too.

'You must get my brother to tell you about Omdurman if you really want to know.' Rachel looked round for Adam. 'He was there, too, and so was Winston Churchill.'

Flora reappeared with a plate of food and a glass of wine neatly set out on a tray which she placed before her aunt.

'Thank you, dear,' Rachel said. 'Where's yours?'

'I'm going to eat with Daddy,' Flora glanced at Dick and Angelica sitting together on the sofa. 'He likes sitting up at a table.'

'So he does,' Rachel smiled after her niece as she hurried away. Then she looked at Dick.

'Do you and Flora have any classes together?'

'No, Lady Askham,' Dick shook his head. 'We're doing completely different subjects.'

'How did you meet, then?'

'We're both members of the Communist Party.'

'Of course you are. You told me and I told you about my visit to Russia. It all comes back now.'

'I'm hoping to go to Russia in the summer,' Dick said. 'On a student exchange. I may stay a year.'

'Oh dear, will they let you back?' Angelica pretended to look alarmed. 'I'm sure that if Mr Churchill is Prime Minister you won't be allowed in.'

'What makes you think he will be?' Dick stuck his fork in the air. He really had no manners, Rachel thought, immediately despising herself. She'd been an Askham so

179

long that she'd adopted their stereotypes and prejudices. She knew she was being especially kind to Dick not so much because she liked him as because she knew he felt out of place. Yet in a way she did like him. His pleasant north country accent reminded her of Spencer.

'The CP won't get in, that's for sure,' Angelica said. '*And* Labour won't. My stepfather might be a member of the Government. He's working very hard at it. We had Mr and Mrs Churchill and the Amorys to dinner here the other night. Mr Churchill said Mummy was a wonderful political hostess and a great asset to Arthur. We hope Mr Churchill will put Arthur in the Cabinet.'

'Darling, don't talk like that.' For once Rachel felt embarrassed. 'Arthur's never held any kind of office. He can't go straight into the Cabinet.'

'Are you knowledgeable about politics, Lady Askham?' Dick enquired politely just as Em came up to them, also with a plate in her hand, with Joe closely behind.

'I'll say she's knowledgeable,' Em squatted by Rachel on the floor. 'Didn't you know my mother wrote leaders for *The Sentinel* for twenty-five years? I thought Flora might have told you. She's met Hitler, rescued me from his clutches no less, and practically directed the war, whispering daily into Churchill's ear.'

'That's not at all true,' Rachel said, laughing. 'I doubt if I spoke to him more than twice in the whole five years, and once was trying to find out where Charlotte was.'

As Em began to argue with her Dick realized what an extraordinary family he had unwittingly become involved with. It had begun with a few kind remarks to a rather plain young girl addressing envelopes at Party Headquarters. The sort one liked to encourage. Now he was talking to people who were at the seat of power itself, at its very heart.

He wanted to dislike the family, to disapprove of them

with their titles and snobbish little ways, their servants and their obvious familiarity with gracious living, their pedantic phraseology and upper-class accents; but he found it increasingly hard. They were attractive, they were vital, alive, knowledgeable. They were human, just as he was.

But, in particular, there was Angelica. She comformed to no stereotype he had of the upper classes. She had a vitality that was all her own, a way of getting under his skin that was unique.

Dick was twenty-four. He had been eighteen when the War ended and still at Chorley Grammar School. In a way he had led a privileged life of his own – the first boy to go to university, admired by a family circle from whom he'd set himself apart.

For him Angelica's animal high spirits made her sexual attraction overpowering, regardless of her class. Even if she were a Tory he would follow her wherever she led. He had known her for over a year; fantasized about her, thought about her, angled in his awkward way for a sight of her. Yet he had never asked her out.

When they'd finished eating, they sat chatting, inhibitions falling away under the influence of wine, cigarette smoke and a sense of comradeship that was quite different from Dick's feelings for Flora.

'Would you like to come out one night?' he said, aware that, beneath his beard, he was blushing.

'I thought you'd never ask,' Angelica looked into his eyes, not even smiling.

Anna Ferov stepped carefully off the plane at Frankfurt airport, looking anxiously around her at the crowd of people waiting to greet arrivals. As the passengers exited from the plane the ranks of the onlookers broke as friends were welcomed, reunions took place; there were hand-shakes, kisses, tears interspersed with shrieks of welcome.

After ten minutes or so had elapsed Anna saw no sign of the Baron and, giving instructions to the porter, she decided to give him half an hour and took a seat on a bench. As she did a man in chauffeur's uniform stepped over to her, saying in German, 'Fräulein Ferov?'

'Yes,' Anna replied in the same language.

'The Baron von Spee sends his regrets that he is unable to meet you personally for business reasons. Instead he has sent me to meet you and take you to your hotel.'

'Thank you,' Anna raised an eyebrow but said nothing more.

The chauffeur then instructed the porter, who preceded them with the two suitcases Anna had brought, to a highly polished Mercedes-Benz waiting outside.

Anna had travelled light. The cases were quickly stowed away, she took her seat in the back of the car, the chauffeur climbed in in front and they were driving through the outskirts of Frankfurt towards the newly constructed centre of the city.

Anna lit a cigarette, drawing thoughtfully upon it as they travelled swiftly through the flattened plain. She asked some desultory questions about the bombing of Frankfurt and the chauffeur replied in an equally desultory way, as though it were not a subject he much cared to discuss.

Finally he drew up in front of a new hotel, directed the porters where to take the luggage, opened the door for Anna, after informing her that the Baron would contact her as soon as he could, and drove away, leaving her standing on the steps of the hotel.

But she was expected. A room was booked in her name, to which she was swiftly escorted. Her cases were put inside the door, the key was kept in the lock, the young porter bowed and took his tip and she was on her own. Alone in Frankfurt. Not even a vase of flowers greeted her. This was not what she had expected.

Anna very rarely felt frightened or alone; all her life she had been protected by someone, even if it was only her mother, and it was towards her mother she felt like turning now. A call to Paris would put a swift end to this misery, this feeling of rejection. An invitation to stay with the Baron had been interpreted by her as an invitation to stay at his home, wherever that might be. Even Susan hadn't a qualm about the fact that Anna would be chaperoned, well looked after, even though neither of them knew the Baron very well, or much about him.

But a hotel built swiftly after the war to accommodate those who were striving desperately to put Frankfurt on its feet again? A shining modern hotel in the middle of nowhere. Not even a note.

Anna smoked another cigarette. She had no intention of unpacking. She lifted the telephone and asked for coffee. Room service was swift and efficient. To telephone her mother would be acting like a baby; a cry for help would be to emphasize a dependence on her that she didn't like. Three months in Paris with her mother had made her feel like a little girl again. However much she loved her mother she had no wish to be that.

Anna had left for Paris with her mother shortly after her twenty-first birthday. She wanted something to do and the opening of her mother's elegant gallery on the Rue de Rivoli, simply called FEROV, gave her the opportunity.

Fresh from her experience with the Festival she lost no time in establishing contacts with the influential people in France: the curators of museums, the antiquarians and members of academies, the journalists who covered the sale-rooms and many of those wealthy and acquisitive people who had made their fortune in the War, the *nouveaux riches,* who were likely to become clients and buy for their refurbished châteaux or innovative, architecturally designed houses on the Riviera.

Ann was so good at her job, the opening was so successful, that Susan offered to employ Anna full time in her fledgling organization. But Anna was restless and the image of the Baron haunted her. Besides she didn't feel an equal with her mother, and Susan, for all her good intentions, would always keep her daughter under her thumb.

When Gunther at last suggested a visit it was to Germany that Anna flew as soon as she could arrange a plane ticket.

As she finished her coffee and another cigarette Anna decided to take a walk round Frankfurt, when there was a knock on the door. It opened very slightly and a bunch of flowers appeared round it. Then the door was flung open and Gunther stood there, face beaming, arms outstretched.

But if he thought Anna would fly into them he was wrong. Anna looked at him unsmilingly and immediately the smile vanished to be replaced by a look of concern.

'Anna?' He moved forward holding out the flowers.

'This wasn't the way I expected to be received,' Anna said coldly. 'I waited half an hour at the airport.'

'Kurt was a fool. He mistook the time, forgot the flowers.' Gunther went up to her, took her hand and bent low over it. 'A thousand apologies, my dearest Anna. It has all been most unfortunate.'

'I was about to return to Paris,' Ann said, feeling it was too soon to thaw. 'I also understood I was to be your guest, not put up in a hotel.'

'But you *are* my guest, my dear,' the Baron replied smoothly. 'Temporarily accommodated in this hotel.

184

Some repairs have unfortunately had to be done at my house which has had to be temporarily closed. I couldn't welcome you to my flat in Frankfurt. I'm sure *you* or your mother wouldn't have thought that proper at all and, as I didn't want to put you off, I did what I thought the next best thing. Please forgive me if I have offended you.' This time he lightly kissed her hand and Anna felt a thaw, a sense of acquiescence, gently steal through her body.

'Tonight I'm going to take you out to dinner,' Gunther concluded, 'and then we shall plan all kinds of treats.'

'Including, I hope, at least a peep at your house,' Anna said and Gunther nodded, promising that that would be soon.

Anna decided that now was the moment to forgive him; he had tried to make amends. She put up her mouth to be kissed.

Those first weeks in Frankfurt in the spring of 1952 were remembered by Anna as among the golden days. A relationship that had begun the year before was not only cemented but eventually consummated. She had known that she and the Baron would become lovers when she accepted his invitation to visit him. It seemed to her right that both she and he should wait a long time for something that turned out to be so perfect. It even crossed her mind that she might become his wife.

The trouble with Pascal Verdi was that he had been too young. His proposal on her birthday was absurd and quickly forgotten. Even his show of temper was forgotten, for which he had made extensive and prolonged reparation – flowers, letters, telephone calls – all ignored. Anna, feeling honour was satisfied, had left the country without seeing him again.

Anna was one of those people who appear to have been born older than they are; she matured very early. The

Verdi brothers with their half-Italian background had proved, at first, attractive, and then the attraction waned as it became apparent how naïve they were, how inexperienced and gauche compared to a man like the Baron.

Yet the Baron was a puzzle. The more she knew him the less she knew about him. His enigmatic character seemed an inevitable part of his attraction. After a month of intimacy she knew little more about him than she'd known at the beginning. He never repeated the mistake of letting her feel neglected again, even for a moment, but she still didn't feel part of him, even when they became lovers. He remained considerate, courteous, punctual, a tender and even passionate lover, but still a mystery.

But to the Baron, Anna was a mystery, too. He had never met so cool and composed a woman in his life, especially one so young. When he'd first met her in London he'd assumed she was twenty-five or -six rather than twenty. She had the poise, grace and *savoir faire* of someone much older, yet not old. He didn't know that she got this quality from her mother who, at about the same age as Anna, maybe even younger, had cultivated a certain detachment, a barrier against being hurt any more than she had already been hurt in her life.

Anna had not suffered the youthful traumas of her mother, yet she seemed to have inherited much of her mother's wariness. It was really a very good thing to be cushioned against life's imperfections – the only drawback was that one wasn't guaranteed foresight.

Anna and Gunther von Spee suited each other. It was like a symphony composed by two people who worked together in harmony, allowing no discordant notes in the even tenor of their lives.

But was it real?

* * *

Pascal crawled out from under the prototype 'Askham', his white overalls covered in grease. He sat for a moment by the side of the car wiping his hands on a rag and looked up, frowning.

'I can't for the life of me see what's wrong,' he said to Sasha. 'If it wasn't Sunday I'd get Jimmy Lockhart out – as it is he works a 72-hour-week, sometimes more.'

The car was due to have a splendid unveiling just before the motor show in October, only three months away, yet trouble gnawed at it as it had dogged the famous 'Askham' racing car twenty years before – the car in which his father had been killed.

It was July and there was a small gathering of the clan at Askham Hall. Sasha and Pascal had driven over to the works after attending morning service to try and resolve the latest hiccough which was slowing down production of this special-bodied car destined for the luxury market.

The car industry world-wide was recovering with difficulty from the war. In Europe many plants had been destroyed or damaged by bombing. There was a shortage of steel and tyres. It was a difficult market. Many new marques of car faded away, unable to compete with the giants, the established, well-known names: Renault, Fiat, Ford, Chrysler, General Motors and, in England, Austin and Morris, which had lately merged to become the British Motor Corporation and, of course, Ford and Vauxhall.

The intention of Pascal and Sasha was not to attempt to compete in this market but join the select band of *carrossiers* producing specially-built cars for those who could afford them.

Sasha was an ideas man rather than a mechanic. He sat on an upturned box in the yard and lit a cigarette. When he looked at the car his eyes shone. These little teething troubles would soon be ironed out. The design was beautiful, not unlike the pre-war *Askham de luxe*, which had been wildly successful among the better-off members of the European nobility who had their individual family crests embossed on the side, with the compliments of the management, with each model delivered. Some of these cars were now in motor museums and, as collectors' items, fetched fantastic prices, especially in the United States.

The Askham colours of cream and burgundy were here in evidence too, inside and out, with a walnut fascia, leather-covered steering-wheel and seats upholstered in burgundy leather.

Sasha exhaled and sighed with satisfaction. It had all been done in an incredibly short space of time, not quite two years from initial ideas to a production model ready to show in the London Motor Show.

'Let's pop over to the Hall in it,' he said suddenly. 'The family would love to see it.'

'But the exhaust . . .'

'The exhaust won't fall off,' Sasha said. 'You're getting obsessional about this, Pascal. Every little detail . . .'

'You're right,' Pascal smiled and peeled off his overalls. 'It's just the day for a spin.'

It was. The Wiltshire countryside looked at its best, the low-lying land covered in that lush, fragrant greenery that is peculiarly English. The works were about ten miles from the Hall in one direction and equidistant from Darley Manor, home of Rachel and Adam, and Littlestone Hall, the country house of the Crewes. All were foregathering at Askham for lunch. It would be a wonderful opportunity to show off the almost completed car to the family.

Sasha took the wheel so that Pascal could sit beside him studying details, listening to the engine for any faults. Sasha drove very slowly out of the works and along the country lanes and, finally, he sensed that Pascal was relaxing as he drew out his cigarette case, leaned back and inhaled.

'Happy?' Sasha turned to him.

'It's only a little fault. I don't know why I made such a fuss about it,' Pascal grinned.

'It's one of the many penalties of parenthood. All new parents worry about the least thing,' Sasha said, then wished he hadn't drawn that particular analogy, as Pascal turned to him, eyebrows raised.

'Don't you enjoy being a parent?' Pascal enquired. 'I thought you were all set into the domestic scene.'

'Oh, I enjoy being a parent very much,' Sasha assured him. 'If I could have more time . . .'

'Did you hear anything from Anna?' Pascal enquired, glad the wobble in his voice was disguised by the sound of the car.

'Anna's very happy,' Sasha said. 'At least I *think* she is. Who knows with Anna? She has found a job with the British Military Commission. She's trying to find out what happened to our father through contacts with the Military. I don't think she's getting very far.'

'It really does obsess Anna and you, doesn't it?' Pascal said, as the lane narrowed and Sasha changed into low gear to take it more carefully and avoid scratching the surface of the car.

'It matters more to Anna than to me, I think,' Sasha said. 'I'm sure Father is dead – killed either by the Russians or by the Germans during the fall of Berlin.'

'But he was seen . . .'

'We only *think* he was seen. Em didn't see him.'

'But Ralph did.'

'Can one be *sure*?' Sasha gazed at him. 'Who can be certain about anything in that terrible time? I think it affects women more, anyway. I often think that the real

189

trouble with Stefanie is that she doesn't know what happened to Hélène. It haunts her. Going to Russia, instead of being a good thing, unsettled her more. She thinks her mother is there, near the family home of Essenelli. It's quite nonsense but she is convinced that's why we were expelled.' Sasha sighed and braked as they came to the end of the lane on the approach to the main Winchester Road. 'I, of course, have my work, my interest in the business . . . Stefanie does nothing but brood. It's not good for her.'

'Does Anna mention the Baron?' Pascal enquired. 'That's really why she went to Germany, isn't it?'

'I wouldn't really know,' Sasha said, his eyes on the road. 'Anna *is* restless. Mother found her hard to put up with. If she's at all interested in the Baron, or he in her, maybe she's found her match. Who knows? Personally, I think she went to Germany to try and find her father. A hopeless task, but let her try.'

Pascal started to whistle as if deliberately to try and create the impression he didn't care.

Rachel was doing a little weeding in one of the herbaceous beds to the side of the front entrance when she saw the beautiful car being driven slowly up the drive. For a minute her heart lurched and, as she straightened up, clutching her hat, she felt a little lightheaded. It was as though she had slipped back thirty years, and they were all gathered round the 'Askham' here at the summer party at the Hall when the car was first launched.

Em, weeding another part of the flower bed, heard her mother gasp, saw her lurch slightly and ran anxiously towards her.

'Mother, are you all right?'

'Perfectly all right,' Rachel said, watching the progress of the car as it slowed down and came to a stop in front

190

of them. 'Just seeing ghosts. You never really remembered the old "Askham" did you?'

'Of course I remember it. I'm not as young as all that.' Affectionately Em took her arm. 'It gave you a shock, didn't it?'

'It always reminds me of the summer party that year – the first one that the Ferovs ever attended. Ralph and Freddie . . . and Hugo.'

'Hugo getting a beating on the lawn,' Hugo said, coming up behind them. 'Don't think *I* don't remember it either . . . but how good it would be to have those days back, Mother.'

Sometimes he called her Rachel and sometimes he called her Mother. Hugo remained confused in his mind about her, even though now he was a man of nearly forty. Once he'd been the little orphan abandoned by his mother whom Rachel adopted and grew to love almost more than her own children. Hugo had two large glasses of lemonade in his hands, one for each worker. Em and Rachel, staying the weekend at the Hall, had been hard at it since ten o'clock, before the sun got too hot.

'Time to call a halt, you girls,' Hugo said. 'Can't have you keeling over with the heat.'

'It *wasn't* the heat,' Rachel said, taking the glass from Hugo. 'It was the car.'

Sasha and Pascal had now got out and were still deep in conversation as they did a circular tour of it, discussing its performance over the ten miles. 'I was reminding Em that the old "Askham" was launched the year that Ralph . . .'

'I was a naughty little so-and-so,' Hugo said, taking her by the arm and pressing it. 'Don't blame him, blame me. I deliberately upset the boat.'

'Those far-off days, instead of making me sad, make me happy,' Rachel murmured, as the two men left the car

191

and slowly started to walk towards them. 'I can recall all our loved ones who are no longer with us: Bosco, Dulcie, Flora, Marian, Freddie, Ralph, Hélène, as vividly as if they were here now. I wish they were.'

'Amen,' Em said, taking the other arm. 'But my, it is a magnificent car.'

'The Shah of Persia has ordered one, and King Farouk,' Sasha said, when they were within earshot. 'The interest of King Farouk is directly attributable to Nimet, I believe, Hugo. I do hope you'll thank her for us.'

'I hope you'll thank her yourself,' Hugo said. 'She's coming over soon.'

'Oh, is she?'

Even after the passage of so many years Rachel knew that it was hard to keep the jealousy she felt about Nimet out of her voice. Her husband had been dead for thirty-seven years and Hugo's mother was his one-time mistress. Nimet, who was always secretive about her age, was probably a few years younger than Rachel, but still well into her sixties by now – no longer the nubile young dancer with whom Bosco had fallen so much in love.

Hugo seemed not to have heard Rachel, but was strolling towards the car with the two men who had driven it over. The sun shone on his bronze curly hair, just the colour of Bosco's. There was unrest in Egypt and Rachel knew Hugo was worried about his mother.

She finished her lemonade and gave a deep sigh. Em, taking the glass from her, gazed into her eyes.

'Still unhappy about Nimet?'

'Not really. It's childish, isn't it?' Rachel grasped the hoe with which she was attacking the hard soil of the herbaceous border, stabbing the earth with more violence than was necessary. 'Here I am, an old woman, and she's an old woman, too. Who would admit to jealousy at my age?'

'Perfectly natural, Mum. But look what a lot you've got from Hugo.'

'So much,' Rachel mumured, looking at his back. 'The only son I have left . . . So much and so precious.'

'I'm not at all your type,' Dick said.

Comfortably ensconced behind one of the laurels by the side of the lake, Angelica was quite sure no one could see them through the high grass and the protective covering of the trees.

'If you go on about this again I shan't kiss you,' Angelica said, gazing down at him. He was on his back and she, lying on her stomach beside him, dangled a long blade of grass over his face, tickling his nose. Dick smiled lazily and brushed it away. 'You're always on about class,' Angelica continued, moving the grass to his ears. 'You've got a bee in your bonnet about it.'

'It *is* important.' Dick brushed at the grass behind his ear. 'When I see all your family together here, I am reminded of it more than ever.'

'Then why come?'

Dick opened his eyes.

'I feel like a common frog who has fallen for a princess,' he said, dragging her down beside him, searching for her lips.

They spent hours like this, kissing and cuddling and hugging, whenever they got the chance – his room, her flat, now the garden of the family home. It never went any further because Angelica was afraid: she was afraid of the consequences and of what her mother would say.

In 1952 contraceptives were still hard to come by and the various techniques, at least for women, not widely known. It was the year the contraceptive pill first appeared, yet many women were nervous about taking it and it was not widely prescribed in England.

Dick was sexually demanding; but Angelica was strong enough for him. She had no fear of losing him if she resisted him.

Unfulfilled passion could go on for hours and hours and, invariably, theirs did. The noonday sun was high in the sky when Angelica pulled her blouse down and decided enough was enough. They were both red in the face, hot and perspiring.

She and Dick had come down on Friday with Charlotte and Arthur, who had left them at the Hall before going on to their home. It was Dick's first visit to the Hall since the previous February at the lying in state of King George VI, and he was now reluctantly accepted by the family as Angelica's boyfriend rather than Flora's. It was known they saw a lot of each other and Dick's attraction and qualities were not denied. Flora, needless to say, said she didn't mind.

Charlotte, however, hoped that familiarity would open the eyes of one or other of them before it was too late. She knew they argued a lot and disagreed and she hoped it would continue until there was a great, unsurpassable gulf between them.

'Mummy will be coming,' Angelica murmured in Dick's ear.

'Always Mummy,' he mimicked her voice. 'Mummy, Mummy, Mummy. Mummy matters, doesn't she?'

'Of course she matters.' Angelica sat up, tucking her blouse in her skirt and scraping back her hair with her hands.

'They'll know,' Dick said, smiling.

'Know what?' In the middle of tying a ponytail she looked at him.

'That we've been snogging. Your clothes are all creased.'

'You're terribly crude,' Angelica jumped up and shook herself.

'Working class.'

'Class again.' Angelica glared at him.

'I was only joking,' he took her hand. 'Can't you see I enjoy getting a rise from you?'

'I don't know why, though,' Angelica said. 'Why should you enjoy annoying me?'

'I don't, silly.' He put his arm round her waist as they emerged from the bushes and joined the path that ran round the lake. 'I suppose it's part of our chemistry, don't you?' He looked at her.

'What is?'

'Our scraps.'

'I think you overdo it,' Angelica glanced at her watch, then the house, wondering if she'd have time to change. 'You're always digging up my family, my class, the differences between us. Why *do* you have to go on and on about it?'

'Maybe it does bother me,' Dick said. 'It bothers me because . . .' he stopped.

'Yes?' Angelica prompted.

'Well, you know. You must know that I am very involved with you. I . . . well I hardly dare say it, but you know how I feel about you.'

'Are you talking about . . . something permanent?' Angelica, too, appeared to be groping for words.

'Yes.' He still held her hand and they faced each other.

'Really permanent?' She raised her eyebrow.

Dick nodded. There was a peculiar sensation in his throat.

'Do you want us to get married?' she said at last. 'If so it's the funniest proposal I've ever had.'

'Have you had many?' Dick's voice was a croak.

195

'You know I haven't, silly.' She put her hand on his neck, her cheek rubbed against his. 'Yes, if you want to.'

'But do *you* want to?' Gently he pushed her away, studying her eyes. 'You're only twenty-one. I'm still a student. There's not much I can give you. Frankly . . .' Again he stopped, searching for the right words. 'I wouldn't have dared ask. Your mother might think I'm gold-digging.'

Angelica was shocked.

'Mummy would never think that! She's rather democratic, despite appearances. She seems like a snob, but she isn't.' Angelica ran on ahead, Dick following. Still he wasn't sure. It was hard to feel at ease with his beloved's mother.

Dick had known that he was in love with Angelica Verdi for months. Her attraction was one of opposites – they were opposite in everything, but physically very close. It was hard to fight such an obsession and, when he realized it was mutual, he no longer tried. Sometimes, though, he felt he was falling into an abyss.

'*POOR BOY WEDS COUSIN OF THE EARL OF ASKHAM.*' He could see it now. But it was much too late to try and start to climb out of the abyss unless Angelica threw him a rope: she would never do that. Like him, she wanted to complete their immature attempts at love-making.

For too long, also, Angelica had felt oppressed by the overpowering influence of her mother – that perfect creature, somehow too aloof and unknowable to be really human, but paradoxically warm and loving, too. To be married would be to be free of the bondage of youth which inevitably always went with a certain dependence on one's parents.

Angelica was physically in love with Dick but, like her father, whom she so resembled, she was almost too detached to lose herself in total emotional involvement. She wanted to marry Dick because it was another stage in her life, a decisive step towards freedom and maturity. It was an exciting thing to do that would make her the envy of her friends.

'Besides we can't go on with the business, anyway.' Angelica turned to wait for him. 'One day I'm sure I'll go "pop", and you will too.'

'Marriage is a big step.' As they got nearer the terrace where the family were sitting he still looked scared.

Angelica seemed surprised. 'It is a tradition in our family to marry young. My mother was just twenty, Aunt Melanie nineteen. Anna's mother was eighteen, I think. Stefanie not much older. I think we would have a glorious, wonderful life . . .' She seized his hand and started to pull him up the hill.

Wondering what they'd done, Dick followed her.

Charlotte saw them emerge from the bushes as she was greeting her mother on the terrace. Rachel and Em had downed tools and changed just before Charlotte, Arthur and Joe arrived, and now they all sat on the terrace having pre-lunch drinks. The men were in flannels and open-necked shirts, the women in colourful frocks. It was very hot.

Rachel saw Charlotte's eyes and followed the direction they were taking.

'He *is* very attractive,' she said. 'One can understand how Angelica feels.'

'He's not the least bit suitable.' Charlotte sat down and took the gin and tonic Arthur was holding out. Jenny, who had no help, was busy in the kitchen. Luis was expected for lunch, too, and his mother was nervously looking out for him. She always felt nervous when she waited for Luis. It was quite ridiculous, most unnatural, to feel this way about one's own son. Yet in many ways they were like strangers – polite, slightly awkward strangers. Em was beside Charlotte, looking beyond the lake to the path that led down from the Grange where Luis lived with his father. She now, too, turned her attention to the two walking up the path and saw them stop and talk earnestly. Then Angelica broke into a little dance and scampered in front of Dick who was laughing, looking shy and embarrassed.

'I'm surprised to hear *you* of all people use the word unsuitable,' Em said to her sister. 'Paolo wasn't very "suitable", was he?'

'Mother didn't think so at the time.' Charlotte went slightly pink and laughed, glancing at her mother, who looked knowing.

'I was right in a sense,' Rachel leaned forward and clasped her hands.

'In what sense?'

'I don't mean to hurt you, darling,' Rachel touched her arm. 'But Paolo was reckless, and he did die very soon, leaving you a widow.'

'Paolo was not reckless,' Charlotte said angrily. 'Everyone knows there was something wrong with that ruddy car.'

Rachel felt her blood run cold as suddenly the three men – Hugo, Pascal and Sasha – appeared round the corner of the house, hands in their pockets, talking earnestly about the car. Yes, there had been something wrong with that old Askham, a flaw in design, many papers said. Now they were doing it again. But not for racing – Bobby had forbidden that.

Em jumped up and began to pace the terrace. She could see Arthur and Adam, who had gone inside the house, ensconcing themselves in deep chairs out of the sun to read the Sunday papers and drink their whisky.

'Oh, for God's sake don't let's rake over what happened twenty years ago,' she cried. 'This is a new age altogether – how can we compare now with twenty years ago, or even ten? Charlotte doesn't like Dick because his father is a miner or something, and his mother takes in washing. He says he is a Communist and has a north country accent. Yet he's a highly educated, intelligent young man and I, for one, like him a lot . . .'

'It isn't that!' Charlotte, stung by her sister's words, rose too. 'How *can* you say that, Em! You know me.'

'I thought I knew you,' Em said, eyes blazing. 'But ever since you married Arthur you've become an awful prig. You tried to stop poor old Angie modelling and she's making a huge success of it. Now you're going to try and stop her marrying . . .'

'*Marrying*!' Charlotte gasped. 'Who said anything about marriage? They scarcely know each other.'

'They know each other well enough, if you ask me,' Em said meaningfully, shading her eyes. 'There's Luis! I'm going down to meet him.' She jumped over the small balustrade that ran around the terrace and began to run across the meadow towards the lake.

'Em's *very* prickly.' Charlotte distractedly entwined her hands one inside the other. 'I can't understand what's the matter with her. I have not got priggish since I married Arthur, have I, Mother?'

Rachel remained silent, watching Em as she ran across the grass, trying to recall that young tomboyish girl again.

'Have I, Mother?' Charlotte said again.

'We all change, don't we, with the passing of the years?' Rachel replied tactfully.

'Yes, but I'm *not* a prig. Are you saying you think I am?'

'Not at all, dear.' Rachel took her eyes off Em. 'But Arthur *is* a Private Secretary, maybe *en route* for the

199

Cabinet. You can't lark around as you did. Besides, you're older. We *all* change. None of us stays the same.'

Now Em and Luis had met, embraced and, linking hands, began to climb back the way she had come. Of Angelica and Dick there was no sign.

'You're saying I'm the stuffy old wife of an up-and-coming MP,' Charlotte persisted. 'Not the woman who parachuted into France and had an affair with Marc . . .'

'No, darling, of course you're not,' Rachel chided gently. 'And I'm not the woman who campaigned for women's rights and threw stones at the window of my own home. I'm a very staid old grandmother, growing plants and interfering in the affairs of others.'

Still, Charlotte had changed. She was rather unbending, even severe when it came to seeing that her children did the right thing; that appointments were kept on time and that the house ran like clockwork. Charlotte organized everyone like a thoroughly disciplined Staff Sergeant – nothing was ever wrong, late or out of place. Arthur needed it, she said and, in a way, Arthur did.

The Tories had regained power in the October elections the previous year. Churchill was again Prime Minister, though many people thought he was too old for it and should yield place to someone like Butler or Eden. Arthur had been made a PPS and it was true his day was filled with appointments, parliamentary and business, from early morning until very late at night. He travelled a great deal. He was a successful, well-organized person growing in importance and he relied heavily on the smooth management of his life by his wife and his secretary, a woman of about thirty called Jill.

Arthur frequently brought Jill home for late supper, or she was invited to Littlestone for the weekend. Jill was down with them this weekend, but had remained behind to work on a speech Arthur was delivering on the balance of payments in his constituency the following week. Jill travelled around a lot with Arthur but Charlotte didn't mind. She liked her. Jill was one of those self-effacing people who were always glad to make up a number: a fourth at bridge, a sixth or eighth at table. She was very useful and had become part of the family.

Just before Jenny came out to say lunch was ready Angelica and Dick appeared on the terrace, hands linked. They had both changed so that their clothes were immaculate – her cotton dress, his flannels and white shirt. His beard was neatly clipped and seemed to hug his face. His hair was smooth and shining.

'We've got an announcement,' Angelica said without preliminaries. 'Where's Arthur?'

Charlotte shot up and then sat down again.

'He's inside with Uncle Adam. Maybe they should *both* hear?' Charlotte knew the inevitable had happened. A great calm seemed to descend on her.

Angelica nodded and, releasing Dick's hand, hurried indoors. Soon the men were seen preceding her, hastily getting into blazers, Adam moving rather slowly because, although he liked the heat, it was not good for his chest.

Pascal, Sasha and Hugo were sitting on the terrace wall sipping beer, the talk still about gear-shifts and camshafts and the like. Hugo wasn't a mechanic but he liked cars. They, too, looked up as Angelica came back with Adam and Arthur and there was suddenly a feeling of expectation in the air.

'Em . . .' Charlotte began looking round, but Em and Luis had disappeared from sight, gone for a walk on their own.

'Em can hear it later,' Angelica said. She thought her heart would burst out of her chest and go bounding over the paving stones if she didn't speak. 'We're engaged. It's frightfully bourgeois, but we are.'

Immediately the air seemed hot and thundery, the silence broken only by the many sounds of birds flitting in and out of the trees in the park. All eyes were on Angelica and no one seemed to like to look at Dick. It was not a spontaneous outbreak of joy. Rachel, as usual, came to the rescue and, hastily getting up, went over to her granddaughter and embraced her, kissing her warmly on each cheek. Then, an arm linked through Angelica's, she reached out for Dick and drew him towards her, too.

'We're *very* pleased,' she said. 'It's not altogether a surprise, is it?' She looked at Charlotte, who suddenly seemed voiceless, her mouth slightly open as she gazed at her son-in-law to be.

Arthur went to his step-daughter's side and took her hand. 'But we're all delighted, as your grandmother said. Congratulations, Dick.'

Arthur, the perfect diplomant, always knew what to do. He shook Dick by the hand, and kissed Angelica.

'I think I've got some champagne,' Hugo said. 'I'll go and tell Jen. She'll be delighted, I know.'

Doing the right thing, being seen to do the right thing, having the right reaction, presenting a united front, was very important to the Askham family. It drew together and, as Hugo went out, the atmosphere became charged with cries and kisses, smiles, a babble of voices, the sound of laughter.

Then Em came up with Luis and threw her arms round Angelica.

When, a moment later, Jenny emerged with Hugo, each with a bucket of champagne in their hands, she went immediately over to Dick and was the first of the family actually to kiss him. Then she held on to his shoulders, gazing smilingly into his eyes.

'It really *is* thrilling news. I know you and Angelica will be very, very happy.'

Then, again, everyone started talking at once. Only Charlotte remained rather withdrawn and silent, as though imprinting the scene on her memory, standing to one side of the terrace, as if everyone had forgotten she was there.

CHAPTER 8

The throng that gathered round the newly unveiled 'Askham' was totally different from the crowd who had admired it before the motor show in London. One could see here that there remained plenty of wealth in Germany or, maybe, most of it had been freshly created by the re-emergence of German industry after the war. Here there were no restrictive trade union practices to bedevil progress, or rules and regulations to interfere with every aspect of free enterprise, such as had happened in England under the Labour government. Or, at least, that had been Gunther's argument, explained very loquaciously and convincingly over dinner at the preview the evening before.

Now, as Sasha and Anna watched from a corner of the showroom, Gunter appeared through a side door and put an arm round Anna's shoulders.

'A success, I think. My secretary says it will be six months before we can fulfil orders. We could shut the door this minute and have no further problems. It is a tribute to Anna almost as much as to you and Pascal, my dear Sasha.'

Sasha nodded and watched as Anna, abruptly excusing herself, went up to a man wearing a coat with a fur collar and smoking a large cigar, and began to talk to him animatedly.

'Manfred Arnoldi,' Gunther whispered in Sasha's ear. 'They say he has made millions since the war ended. His mother was German and his father Italian . . . not bad to survive with such a pedigree, eh?'

'It depends what he did,' Sasha said, but the Baron merely shrugged and gave his charming smile.

The 'Askham' was a success, the groundwork carefully prepared by Anna since the spring, when she had foresaken the Control Commission to work full-time on publicity for Gunther and the new car.

At the end of the war the German motor industry had been practically defunct, most of the production being concentrated on the 'Bizone', the area occupied by the British and American forces. In the Russian zone only the BMW works at Eisenach were still in operation. In the French zone, only the Daimler-Benz factory at Gaggenen was in production. The Volkswagen, which was to become one of the most popular cars of all time, had been producd in limited numbers from 1945.

By 1952 the German recovery was well on its way and those with money in their pockets were anxious to spend it on something that set them apart from everyone else. The old 'Askham' had fulfilled a similar function in Britain and on the Continent in the twenties, and the new model was to do the same in the post World War II world – a touch of ostentation and luxury to replace years of crippling gloom and austerity. For Gunther and his growing von Spee organization the timing was just right.

Gunter had negotiated the exclusive agency for the whole of the Continent and to the opening in Frankfurt came representatives from Spain, France, Austria and Italy, as well as those members of the German plutocracy who had been convinced by subtle persuasion, lavish, carefully placed advertisements that their lives would not be complete until they were in possession of an Askham motor car.

Initially, the presentation was simple. 'The Askham' were the words on an otherwise totally blank piece of paper. That and the Askham crest did the rest and, in its first year of production, the Askham custom-built, individually tailored motor car would outsell any of its rivals in the exclusive market of the *carrossiers*.

Sasha had come over for the launch, staying with his sister in the flat to which she had moved when her stay in Germany looked like becoming permanent. Anna had just celebrated her twenty-second birthday and Sasha could see she was in her element. The fluency of her German was remarkable.

'You look as though you've found yourself, at last,' he told her that night as they had a drink together before bedtime. Gunther had left and they were alone.

'I think PR is definitely my line,' Anna said thoughtfully. 'Whether here or elsewhere I don't know. It depends.'

'On what?'

'What do you think!' Anna smiled at him as she held out her glass. 'On Gunther, of course.'

'It *is* serious, then? I wondered.'

'It is serious for me. For him?' Anna shrugged, her eyes narrowing. 'I'm not so sure.' Sitting down next to her brother she neatly crossed her legs. 'I never thought, you know, Sasha, that I would find myself in a ridiculous situation.'

'Why is it ridiculous?'

'Gunther says he is too old for me.'

'I thought maybe he had a wife.'

'He had a wife,' Anna looked surprised. 'I thought I told you. They're divorced.'

'Any children?'

Anna shook her head. 'However, I don't let myself think too much about it. I shan't hang around forever waiting for Gunther, you can be sure of that.'

* * *

Sasha had the chance to find out a good deal more about Gunther in the days that followed. They were frequently in his company, entertained to lunch, dinner and, sometimes, breakfast, as people wanted to meet the promoter of the Askham car and hoped to increase their chances of improving their position on the waiting-list. Only one thing was missing: the designer. Pascal was too busy, Gunther explained, too tired, after the terrifying weeks before the first production model was finished in time for the motor show, to make the journey.

The designer must be a man of great gifts, it was supposed, a younger Issigonis. Certainly there were many features of the car that were well in advance of their time.

Although the new 'Askham' was one of the most expensive cars in the world there was no shortage of buyers. Its appeal went straight to the hearts of the status-conscious *nouveaux riches* with the legend created by Anna, and presented in the same stark manner on the almost blank expanse of paper:

'CAN YOU AFFORD THE MOST EXPENSIVE CAR IN THE WORLD?'

It was a challenge of a kind.

Sasha thought that Gunther and Anna did make a good pair. They complemented each other. Gunther, the older man, seemed to be the steadying influence that Anna needed, that was good for her. Anna was certainly good for Gunther, an adornment in every sense of the word. They were frequently pictured together in the columns of the society papers – Baron von Spee and his red-headed publicist, a member of the distinguished Askham family.

By Christmas Anna had been in Germany for nearly nine months and the 'Askham' was well established. It was time to think of something new.

'Go away?' Gunther was aghast, threw down his paper on the bed. 'For a holiday?'

'For good.' Anna blew a jet of smoke straight into the air. 'I feel I've done my bit here, Gunther.'

'But what about us? Doesn't that mean anything to you?'

'Of course it does, but where does it get us?'

Gunther propped his head on his hands, leaning comfortably back on the pillow.

'What is it you want, Anna? Marriage?'

'I don't just want to be known as your red-headed girlfriend.'

'I can understand that.'

'I feel I know so little about you,' she looked at him earnestly. 'It's as though there were so many secrets in your life.'

'What kind of secrets?' The expression on his smiling face was bland.

'Just secrets. No one really knows much about you.'

'I've always valued privacy but,' he reached out his hand and took hers, 'I don't want to lose you. There are certain things I can't deal with just yet, but I will attend to them. Please don't go away. You can be sure that by the summer everything will have changed.'

Flora Bolingbroke had been very carefully brought up. She had gone to a good girls' school, a boarding-school where, as well as scholarship, one learned how to control one's emotions, not to show jealously, pettiness or spite. In adition, she belonged to a family where emotions were kept tightly under control, too; was not her Aunt Rachel the epitome of the noble matriarch who kept going despite the loss of a husband and two sons, who ran and organized a large household, a family newspaper, without ever for a moment breaking down? Flora's father, Adam, had scarcely ever showed any emotion at all, whether pleasure or pain, that wasn't subdued, controlled. Even when he was suffering intensely people scarcely knew it.

Flora had known that she would lose Dick Crosby to her cousin the day she introduced them. With a kind of fatalistic certainty she knew it would happen, even though for her he was the only man in the world. She admired his strength of character, his dedication to the cause of Communism, his outspokenness, his fearlessness. She never dared ask herself what else appealed to her about him. Flora had always eschewed sex, as though her lack of attraction were to be for evermore a bar to physical fulfilment. She also felt, in a strange, primeval way, that Angelica's stunning looks gave her the right to choose whom she liked for a mate. In a sense it was as though the law of the jungle had invaded the human world; that beauty and fitness took precedence over the claims of the intellect or nobility of soul.

Flora remained content to hover in Dick's shadow; to address envelopes, lick stamps, lick boots, if necessary, to show him that her emotions were under control. She would never, ever make a spectacle, a fool of herself on account of him, or anyone.

Dick and Angelica were married in January 1953 and afterwards Flora went about her business as she always had, studying hard for her final exams but not neglecting the Party, the discussions, conferences, street-corner addresses to the faithful few, the pathetic few who stopped to listen. Dick was there as before, doing the things he had always done, depending on her. Nothing seemed to change Dick, not even marriage to a beautiful woman, the granddaughter of an earl.

Flora became a secretary of the Party and there was even more work for her to do. She thus became more indispensable to Dick, even though she knew that she was only on the periphery of his interests, the perennial 'good sort', and that his emotional life was deeply involved with someone else.

Dick and Angelica were considered an incongruous couple, even by modern standards. Some compared them to Beauty and the Beast, though most women considered Dick to be attractive. But it was with difficulty that he had been got into a morning suit for his wedding at St Paul's, Knightsbridge, although he was happy enough to have the reception at the House of Commons afterwards.

Dick, however, didn't mean to lose his ideals, despite the gift of a house in Knightsbridge from Charlotte and Arthur as a wedding present. He wanted Angelica to work because it was what she wanted; Dick was a passionate believer in equal rights for women. He felt they were a truly enlightened, modern couple and, for many months, that he was the luckiest as well as the happiest of men.

The press had a bit of a dig at Dick because of his political beliefs and Arthur got some chaffing from his colleagues at the House, but on the whole everyone approved of the alliance of these representatives from opposing, contradictory cultures and in a way the publicity did them both good: Angelica increased the number of her modelling contracts and the Party felt it benefited from its benign image. Indeed, many of his colleagues were at the reception in the House of Commons in their best clothes, enjoying the good things of life denied to the masses.

Flora was everywhere, being helpful, organizing, arranging, though she drew the line at being a bridesmaid. This honour went to the two Lighterman sisters, Olga and Natasha, with little Elizabeth Down carrying the bride's bouquet.

Soon after the wedding Flora went to live in the East End of London with a group of people who had a similar outlook on life and shared her views. She was helped in this by the decision of the British government to conduct its first atomic tests at the Montebello Islands in the Pacific. There was a hue and cry about this, and Churchill's subsequent remark that 'it went off beautifully', so a group of people began to campaign to stop all nuclear weapons. Naturally Flora was in the forefront – planning, organizing, activating. 'Ban the bomb' was an urgent cause, shared by the party, even though Russia was quietly developing an atomic bomb of its own.

Flora found fulfilment and happiness in the course her life was taking. She felt she had a very clear idea about what she wanted to do and where to go.

Yet Dick always came first, and when he became chairman of the local party she was at his right hand.

It was not only her father whom she reminded of his long-lost love: that other Flora who had drowned herself in the waters of the Nile just after he married Young Flora's mother. It seemed, in many ways, as if he were seeing her reincarnation in his daughter. But this was a modern, emancipated Flora – who would never have dreamt of killing herself for a man.

Anna enjoyed business. She was good at it. She could be ruthless and dispassionate like any man and she made a good bargain. After the launch of the 'Askham' she travelled quite widely around Europe, visiting her grandmother in Venice on her way to Rome to open an office there. She went to Paris in the spring of 1953 for the opening of another showroom and on to Madrid for negotiations with a new sub-agent.

Anna also enjoyed her life. She felt she was a woman of the world – detached, poised, sophisticated, with a clever, handsome German lover, the quintessential cosmopolitan.

211

Anna wondered how long this state of affairs could continue for. She was still young, she knew that, and Gunther was quite old. Possibly, too, her status, her potential for success, might be enhanced even further by the title of Baroness. Even in these post-war days titles mattered; in business they were a positive asset.

Yet Anna had her pride. She had nudged Gunther once or twice about the matter but she didn't intend to turn into a shrew, someone who nagged him night and day. Besides, she wanted to be sought. If he didn't want to marry her willingly, she didn't want to marry him. She wasn't one of those tiresome women who would do anything to get a man. She wasn't going to make any ultimatum. One day she would just depart from the scene.

Anna was very confident of herself and one day, as she was driving home through the Black Forest from Austria, an idea came into her head. How often had Gunther not enthused about his ancient home in the Schwartzwald, surrounded by trees, a place of legend and mystery? One day he would take her there, but not before it was ready.

Anna knew exactly where the house was and how to get there. Acting, untypically, on impulse, she spent the night in Freiburg, consulted a map, and the following morning set out in the 'Askham' – a car that always made people stop by the wayside and gawp as it glided by – and drove south of that attractive old Black Forest town with its medieval buildings and ancient clocks, its famous Bear Inn, to Lake Titisee. This was a beautiful expanse of blue water surrounded by the thick, literally 'black' – because it was so dark – forest with, in the distance, a view of the romantic Feld Berg still capped with ice.

Anna paused by the lake to have a cup of coffee at a café right by the lakeside and to consult her map again. It was a very hot summer's day, a beautiful day, and the water was covered by a haze which caused some delight and confusion among the many oarsmen, sailors in tiny yachts, and swimmers enjoying themselves in the water. It was a carefree, bustling scene with picnickers sitting on the grass surround of the lake and the smell of sizzling Bratwurst coming from the confines of the café.

After making a few false starts, and an unnecessary detour, Anna found herself on a road that wound up towards Feld Berg and then she came to a clearing in the forest, an expanse of open ground at the end of which there was a large house: *Rheingarten*.

Anna sat for some time in the car staring at the house, not quite sure why she had been so anxious to see the von Spee family home. Had she been reluctant to face up to those whispered insinuations that she'd heard in more quarters than one? And, if so, how untypically Anna, how unlike her not to want to know the truth.

Resolutely she drove slowly up the drive towards a house which had no sign of scaffolding or repairs in progress but, in a oasis of peace, basked in the summer sunshine.

The house looked very English in design and quite modern, as though it were not more than fifteen or twenty years old. It was a long, low, two-storeyed house, and a continental touch was added by the shutters in the windows, some of which were now closed against the noonday sun. Flowers grew everywhere in profusion, there were window-boxes filled with geraniums at every window and hanging baskets trailing petunias and lobelia. It was a pretty, well-kept house with a neatly-raked pebbled drive in front, whose white stones glistened in the almost tropical heat of the day.

Anna rang two or three times and finally the door was opened by a neatly-uniformed maid, who bobbed and courteously asked Anna how she could help her.

Anna removed her large sunglasses and replied in German.

'I'm terribly sorry, I seem to have lost my way; but I think I know the people who live here. Is the Baron at home, by any chance?'

The well-trained maid frowned and shook her head.

'I regret not, Madam. Only the Baroness.'

'Would it be possible to see her?'

The maid hesitated and said, 'Who shall I say, Madam?'

'Fräulein Ferov. Anna Ferov.'

The maid politely stood aside to let Anna into the large airy hall with bowls of marigolds on a great ebony chest which stood to one side on the highly-polished parquet floor. The sun streamed in through the windows and the sound of birdsong through the open door was almost deafening in its sweetness, its sharpness.

Anna sat perfectly composed in the seat she had been shown to and realized, somewhat to her surprise, that her heart was beating quite slowly, its normal, regular, steady pace.

For some time the insinuating whispers had been that Gunther was not divorced from his wife, whom he hid away; but for as long as she heard them she had been reluctant to believe them. But the detour to the Schwarzwald on her homeward route had proved irresistible. Maybe she had, either consciously or subconsciously, devised it that way.

After a while the maid returned, this time with a smile on her face, and asked Anna to follow her. She took her along a straight corridor to the back of the house and led her into a sunny room, again filled with strong-scented flowers. The ebony parquet floor was strewn with rugs, there were low chintz-covered chairs and sofas, family portraits and hunting scenes on the wall and, over by the French windows leading on to a terrace, sat a woman in a wheelchair. She was a pretty, youthful woman, not much older than forty, and she held her face in the way that was unmistakably characteristic of people who were blind. Her fair hair was curled round her face and her sightless eyes were an almost breathtaking colour of delphiniums. She was dressed in a pretty summer frock and had bare legs and sandals on her feet.

'Fräulein Ferov,' she said in cultured German, holding out her hand.'How very kind of you to call. I have so wanted to meet you; but Gunther says you have always been too busy.'

Anna crossed the room and took the hand of Gunther's wife, clasping it firmly and holding on to it for a moment.

'I have so wanted to meet you, too,' she said, aware of the irony of what she was saying. 'And this has been my first opportunity.'

'Of course you'll stay for lunch.' The Baroness rang a bell by her side before Anna had time to reply. It couldn't possibily be the case, because Gunter had no idea of her intentions, but it was almost as if she'd been expected. As the maid re-entered the Baroness gave a command and then said to Anna:

'I thought we'd eat outside on the terrrace. It's such a lovely day. Would you mind?' She indicated her chair with a smile which indicated intimacy and released the brake and Anna, taking her cue, pushed the chair on to the terrace, which already contained tables and chairs overshadowed by a large striped umbrella. The Baroness seemed genuinely delighted by her surroundings and excitedly sniffed the air.

'Isn't it such a beautiful day? You can see I love flowers.' She paused for a moment and gazed unseeingly at Anna. 'I would love to see you too, Fräulein Ferov, for I hear you are very beautiful.' The Baroness gave a shy smile and held out her slim, white, beringed fingers. 'Of

215

course, I am a little jealous, who in my position wouldn't be? But Gunther has been so good to me, so how can I deny him the pleasure of female companionship when he works so hard?'

'I'm not exactly a "female companion", Baroness,' Anna said, with some acerbity. 'I am a full partner in the business, only now on my way back from a trip to Vienna promoting the new car. I hope you haven't got the wrong idea about me.'

The pretty Baroness looked, for a moment, stricken with remorse.

'Please don't misunderstand me, Fräulein. Gunther has been completely frank with me about you. I understand entirely that the relationship is solely to do with business and that your father was a friend of the family. It is just that,' the Baroness smiled rather shyly, 'my maid reads me the papers with the bits of gossip about my husband and the attractive red-head he is seen with so frequently. How *very* vexing for you it must be! And he would hardly have sent you to see me, would he, had there been anything untoward between you?'

'Hardly,' Anna said, glad, for that moment, that the woman beside her was sightless.

In her life Anna Ferov had played many parts but the one she played that day when she met Gunther's invalid wife for the very first time was among her finest. An excellent luncheon was served on the terrace by the maid and a manservant while Anna and her hostess chatted about the Askham car, the countryside, the fate of the German nation after the war and its remarkable recovery. The Baroness was knowledgeable and articulate, an educated woman and, Anna guessed, one who was wealthy in her own right. Everything she did seemed effortless, a sign of good breeding, despite her disability.

Anna almost regretted she had to go, but was quite

adamant in refusing the Baroness's invitation to stay the night. She had her hotel room booked in the Bear Inn in Freiburg and wanted to be in Frankfurt by early in the afternoon the following day.

The Baroness wheeled herself to the main door to bid her guest goodbye. She was astonishingly mobile within the limitations of a wheelchair, amazingly free of self-pity. Never once in the two-hour conversation, during which she learned all about the Askham and Ferov families, had she ever mentioned her situation or uttered a word of complaint against it.

In a way it was an extraordinarily impersonal encounter. Very little was given away and, when Anna left, she knew little more than when she'd come, except that Gunther and his wife were not divorced but very much a couple in the locality, and she was only prevented by her disability and distaste for the town from sharing his life in Frankfurt.

'Gunther must bring you when he comes again,' the Baroness said, pressing Anna's hand warmly and putting up her cheek to be kissed. 'I will chastise him for not introducing you to me before. No wonder I was jealous, but no longer. I can tell you are a fine woman, a good companion for my husband . . . in business.'

The Baroness held up a hand to wave as Anna ran down the steps of the house towards the car whose door was held open by the smiling manservant. Behind the wheel Anna adjusted the mirror and put on her gloves. Then she leaned out of the window and gazed serchingly into those sightless eyes that, yet, seemed to have such an uncanny facility for watching her.

The following night when Anna reached Frankfurt she started to bleed. Hastily summoned, the doctor examined her, shook his head and ordered her removal to hospital if she wanted to keep the baby. She said she didn't. The doctor asked her to call him if it got any worse and left her after she assured him she would call a friend.

But she called no friend and the bleeding stopped of its own accord. She stayed in bed for two days until she felt better then rang Gunther. He was not expected back from a visit to Italy until the following day.

Anna had had quite a lot of time for reflection between leaving Gunther's home and arriving in Frankfurt. She was only just pregnant, and going away had been partly to think about this, too. She hadn't wanted to use what was an accident as a lever to move Gunther towards marriage, and now she knew she couldn't.

It was very strange how things had a habit in life of working out quite differently from what one had planned and anticipated.

Gunther knew there was something amiss the moment he saw her the following day, having driven straight from the airport to be with her. Anna, remaining seated, watched him coming through the door of the elegant flat they'd often made love in but never shared as a couple. In a curious way, Gunther had almost prepared her for the inevitable by keeping her at a distance.

He went up to her and kissed her, at once sensing her lack of response.

'What is it?' he said, sitting down and taking her hand. 'I can tell it's bad news.'

'It's about Maria, your wife,' Anna said in a bantering tone. 'I am extremely sorry to see the extent of her disabilities. One can't be angry in the circumstances, can one?'

'I'm glad you see it that way.' Gunther released her hand, slowly took a cigarette from his case and lit it. 'It was very wrong of me not to tell you. Naturally, it's been on my mind.' He glanced at her before continuing. 'Maria had undetected diabetes. You can see what it's done to her, some of it quite recently. She only went blind during the war. You can see how I couldn't leave a woman like that. I . . . I never pretended to you about marriage.'

Anna rose and walked towards the window, looking down on to the busy street from her fifth floor modern apartment block built after the War.

'I would still have expected you to be honest.'

'Would you have become my mistress if I had?'

'That might have depended,' Anna said, with an unexpected choke in her voice. 'I would certainly have taken good care *not* to become pregnant.'

Gunther sat back and closed his eyes. The smoke from the cigarette in his loosely-clasped hand stained his fingers so noticeably that it was a wonder he didn't feel the burning.

'I thought you did take care.'

'Not as much as I should. Carelessness, I believe they call it.'

'Maria can't have children,' Gunther said. 'That's another thing. She's only my wife in name; but you can see I can't leave her.'

'Oh, I can see that!' Anna gave a bitter little laugh. 'I can see that quite well, and how clever you've been disguising our relationship. She knows about me, maybe she suspects something, but she is grateful to you, too. Just as you are grateful to her.'

'What do you mean?' Gunther raised his head sharply.

'I gathered from the conversation she and I had at lunch that your money comes from her family; that you lost all yours before and during the war. It is *Maria* who has enabled you to start up again with such success. Maria who trusts you and believes in you.'

'I'm surprised she told you,' Gunther said stiffly. 'She comes from a very old, noble German family.'

'She didn't tell me in so many words. I could see she was a woman used to money and I guessed the rest. It also seemed to me that the house was hers because she loved it so much. She told me her father built it when she was a little girl. Quite ecstatic, she was, about her childhood. Your family home, indeed!'

'My homes were bombed in the war,' Gunther said, holding out his hands. '*Please* try and understand, Anna. In a way, you know, you frighten me a little. Everything is so straightforward as far as you're concerned; even difficulties don't seem to bother you.'

'Lies bother me a great deal,' Anna said, 'and the myth about your divorce was a lie, whatever else you call it. You can be quite sure that I shall go into a clinic as soon as I possibly can and get rid of this thing, this memory of you, that I certainly have no desire to bear.'

The clinic was outside Frankfurt, a large house in extensive grounds in the Taunus mountains. Whether it was used for anything other than abortions Anna didn't know. Gunther sent her there by car from Frankfurt and, within twenty-four hours, she was operated on and recovering in a white antiseptic room with a view of the hills.

It was a very impersonal kind of place with quiet, long corridors and few people to be seen. Many of the windows had drawn blinds and everyone spoke in whispers.

Two days after the operation a car came to pick her up again and take her back to the flat. There she found a large bunch of flowers and a little note from Gunther saying he was in America.

Anna thought that, emotionally, she had dismissed him but even then she felt devastated by his remoteness. A terrible sense of vulnerability overtook her. She felt that she was alone in a large city, far from home. But where was home? Was it Venice, London, Paris? Hadn't she lived this kind of peripatetic existence, not quite belonging, all her life? Had anyone really ever cared about her very much? And wasn't Gunther just the sort of dispassionate, disinterested person she would get involved with?

Anna had been told to rest but she didn't realize how tired she would feel – as though life had literally been drained out of her. When she got up she could scarcely crawl to the kitchen to make herself a drink. Food was out of the question. A daily woman came to clean but Anna asked nothing of her and no favours were offered.

Anna bled a great deal but the doctor came and said she was all right. He prescribed iron – iron and plenty of rest. Anna Ferov, alone in her antiseptic, modern apartment day after day that summer of 1953 felt that, indeed, the iron had penetrated her body and entered her soul.

Then one day Pascal Verdi came and everything changed. First he rang and within an hour he was at the apartment, sitting by her bedside, concerned to see her looking so ill. She didn't tell him she'd had an abortion but a bad dose of influenza. But Pascal wasn't deceived. He thought she was too sick for influenza and sent for the doctor again who had Anna removed to a private clinic where they gave her massive transfusions of blood.

Pascal probably saved her life.

CHAPTER 9

'Anna certainly *looks* very ill,' Jenny observed to Rachel, who sat in Jenny's little sitting-room clutching a large bunch of flowers.

'But what happened? Do we know?'

Jenny had been trained as a nurse, and nurses were supposed to keep their patients' confidences.

'I do know, as a matter of fact, Rachel, but I don't feel I should be the one to tell you. Can't you guess?'

'Very well,' Rachel said immediately. 'I only hope the man in question wasn't Pascal.'

Jenny smiled. She had known Hugo's adoptive mother for nearly ten years and this remark was characteristic. No Askham, or relative of an Askham, should be known to have wittingly done the wrong thing. It may have been wishful thinking, but that's how it was.

'Oh no, it certainly wasn't Pascal! He found her in time and, according to her, saved her life. She was bleeding to death.'

'Oh, my God.' Rachel put a hand on her breast. 'And where was Susan?'

Jenny paused then said: 'Well, I may as well tell you the rest. Naturally, Anna didn't want her mother to know . . . or Charlotte.' Jenny looked at Rachel. 'You know how Charlotte feels about Anna.'

Rachel nodded. 'I know, and I know, or rather guess, how Pascal feels about her, too. He is in love with her.'

'A knight in shining armour, if ever there was one. Arrived in the nick of time. Poor girl. The Baron had taken off for America and left her on her own. Even Anna cracked.'

'Even Anna,' Rachel nodded. No one would expect Anna to break down, give in, collapse. Anna always seemed to have life perfectly under control. What had gone wrong this time?

'It's the new contraceptive pill,' Jenny explained awkwardly. 'No one quite knows how it works yet. Personally, I wouldn't take it for anything.'

Rachel found Anna sitting in the garden, feet up, a blanket over her lap. She did still look very pale and Rachel felt a sense of anxiety, even shock, as she sat down in the chair that Jenny had brought out for her. Anna's pallor reminded her of Marian and her death from TB in 1936.

Anna took the flowers and held them up to her nose.

'It's extremely good of you to come, Aunt Rachel.'

'Nonsense, it isn't far away.' Rachel smiled warmly at her. 'I'm glad Pascal thought of bringing you here.'

'Jenny's a nurse,' Anna said wanly. 'He thought I'd be in good hands. I was glad to get out of Germany.' She looked speculatively for a moment at Rachel. 'Did Jenny say . . . anything?'

'No,' Rachel said, in all honesty. Anna thought how infinitely wise and compassionate she looked; her gentle, rather lined face mellow under a wide straw-brimmed hat. 'I guessed,' Rachel said at last, anxious to escape Anna's scrutiny. 'I have lived a very long time, you know.'

'Pascal saved my life.' Anna leaned back in her chair. 'I think if he hadn't come I would be dead now. I didn't know he could be so firm and decisive. I left what was happening far too long.'

'Haemorrhages are not unusual in this kind of thing.'

'It was a proper clinic, a proper operation.' Anna still

avoided Rachel's eyes. 'Not a nasty back-street abortion or that kind of thing. That was perfectly all right. It was afterwards that things went wrong.'

'Anyway, it's all over now.' Rachel leaned forward as if trying to find some words of comfort, advice – maybe a little speech. But Anna, as though wary of such good intentions, suddenly leaned back and closed her eyes. Instead, Rachel patted her hand, saving her words of wisdom for another day. She doubted very much, anyway, if Anna would be in a mood to listen. In time Anna would justify what had happened and continue as before.

Just now Anna was desperately tired; she was unwell and she needed the kind of quiet support that only family could give. Rachel, too, sat back and realized how happy she was to be in the sunshine once more, in that dear, familiar place within sight of her old home, the Grange. Summer was always a happy time for Rachel, full of nostalgic memories – of parties, boating on the lake, candlelit suppers on the terrace, walks home around the lake with her husband and the children.

She looked once more at the sleeping Anna and wondered what it was that motivated this curious girl. Even when she was so ill she still seemed to be detached, controlled, determined to show no weakness. There was something unknowable about Anna, a lack of emotion that seemed almost sinister. Even now she appeared neither vulnerable nor truly grateful, despite what she said.

Rachel shivered slightly and, rising, quietly crept away to seek once again the company of Jenny.

Hugo was in the kitchen with her, drinking coffee. The new baby, Anthony, was in his crib outside the kitchen door. Rachel came in and sat down at the table, reaching for the coffee pot.

'Strange girl,' she observed, to no one in particular, shaking her head. 'Could never make her out.'

'Did she offend you, Rachel?' Jenny lowered her cup.

'Oh no, not at all. I just find her strange. I mean all this has happened and . . .'

'Detached,' Jenny nodded. 'Takes everything for granted. It *is* unnerving sometimes. It's as though she has no feelings.'

'Kyril didn't have any feelings, either,' Rachel said, frowning into her cup. 'That's what wories me. Anna is too like him. She seeks perfection. This time she made a mistake and can't forgive herself. I don't think she can trust anyone, you know. Kyril didn't either.'

'She's certainly very complicated,' Hugo glanced towards the door where Anthony slept. 'But I see nothing sinister in her. She's grateful to be here and a very good guest. No trouble at all. You always did have likes and dislikes, Rachel. Don't be too critical of poor Anna.'

Rachel felt momentarily rebuffed, rather hurt, and sat gazing for some moments at Hugo. Slowly her own good sense made her realize that it was not for her to sow doubts in his mind about the guest to whom he had been so good. Indeed, her own complex emotions about Anna induced in her a profound sense of guilt – as though she were visiting on Anna the presumed sins of her father, which was unfair. Rachel despised such atavism in herself and atoned for it by trying to concentrate on Anna's good points – after all, she was part Bolingbroke, like herself, and Adam's granddaughter. Instead she said:

'How's Johnny?'

'Jenny thinks he's not being well-enough educated at the local school.'

'I think he should go to prep school and follow Ralph,' Jenny said after a moment, avoiding looking at Hugo.

'Well, he's still down for Eton,' Rachel said. 'But if he

225

wants to get Common Entrance he'll have to go to prep school straight away. No time to lose. They won't take him if he doesn't pass, even if his father and grandfather were there. But I do think you should remember how much Paul hated Eton, how glad he was to leave. I think Johnny is in the same mould as Paul. I have my suspicion that public schools are rapidly becoming antiquated institutions. And a good thing, too, if you ask my opinion.'

'I think you really believe that.' Hugo poured more coffee.

'I do,' Rachel said, accepting a fresh cup. 'In my opinion a good grammar school and home life takes a lot of beating. I'm sorry I didn't see that with Paul, but I do think it will be best for Johnny. But you must do as you think best, of course.' Rachel always added this kind of remark when she wanted someone to do her bidding, as if exonerating herself from the charge of being too dictatorial. It always made members of her family smile, as Hugo and Jenny did now, to each other.

'Does Paul know what he wants to do?' Hugo started to light his pipe.

'He talks about business,' Rachel's tone was non-committal.

'Another Bobby,' Jenny laughed.

'Yes, he's very keen on business, he tells me. But he doesn't want to go into the Lighterman empire. He says he's going to steer well clear of that. Well, he should sort things out at Manchester. I must say he has a mind of his own. I do approve of him going there.'

Rachel smiled with satisfaction. She had brought Paul up entirely. His mother and father had both died when he was a baby. He had been more like a younger son to her than a grandson. In her life she had brought up four boys – her two sons, Hugo and her grandson Paul, none of them alike, all the usual mixture of joy and vexation. Yet

226

Paul, Freddie's son, currently hitch-hiking with two friends on the Continent, was very different from the other three. For one thing he was much more scholarly. She would never have been surprised to hear that he wanted to be an academic. Despite himself he'd carried off many prizes at his school. Yet his goal was business.

Rachel was always happy in the company of Jenny and Hugo at the Hall. It was a home she'd never lived in, through force of circumstances. Her mother-in-law had lived there until she died, outliving her eldest son by many years. Rachel had missed being chatelaine of the family seat of the earls of Askham but she had never minded. She was happy enough with Adam and their more modest home ten miles away across country. At the thought of her brother she frowned.

'I must get back. Adam isn't feeling too well. That emphysema has taken a nasty grip of him. I was quite worried about him yesterday.'

'Oh dear,' Jenny swallowed her coffee and got up. 'Hugo's got some veg for you from the greenhouse, and some butter. Don't worry about Anna, leave that to me, but do take care of her grandfather.'

'I'll do that.' Rachel prepared to follow Hugo out of the back door towards the greenhouse. She kissed Jenny, who accompanied her to the door where Anthony slumbered in the sun.

'Isn't he *perfect?*' Rachel bent down and planted a kiss on the chubby cheeks. 'I could eat him.'

Jenny laughed, uncovered him and picked him up, making a face as she did. 'Too late,' she said, as the baby opened his eyes, and looked ruefully at the damp patch on her skirt.

Rachel collected the produce from Hugo, who offered to carry it round for her to her car parked in the front. They ambled companionably together round the great house, Hugo with his arms full of produce, all in neat bags carrying the legend 'Askham Hall – the mark of quality'. Just as they got within sight of the drive one of the new Askham motor cars swept up and Pascal jumped out. He was about to hurry inside when he saw his grandmother.

'Gran, how very nice!' he said, giving her a smacking kiss on the cheeks. She could immediately see how happy he was, and her heart filled with foreboding, because she felt she knew the reason why.

'I came to see Anna,' Rachel said, 'and give a report to her grandfather.'

'Well, that's *very* kind of you, Gran.' Pascal fell into step beside her, leading her to her car. 'How is Uncle Adam?'

'Not too good,' Rachel sighed. 'But I hear Anna is much better.'

'Oh, *much*,' Pascal said. 'Thanks to Jenny and Doctor. She was practically *dead* when I got there.'

'So I hear. What a good thing you went. *Why* did you go?' Rachel enquired. 'I forgot to ask.'

'Well, you know she runs the German agency for the car. I had to see that bastard von Spee,' Pascal's face clouded. 'I never really liked that man, or trusted him, and I hate him now. If I ever see that swine again I think I'll kill him.'

Suddenly alarmed, Rachel put a hand on his cheek, looking earnestly into his eyes.

'Don't be too hasty, Pascal. Please. It's never worth it. Anna is back here now. Let bygones be bygones.'

Pascal took her hand and brought it to his lips. He held it for a moment and then gently lowered it. 'Anna's different now, Gran. She doesn't know it yet but I'm going to marry her just as soon as I can. Don't you see?

Fate sent me to Germany just at that moment, Gran. Fate. I'm convinced of it. Just you wait and see.'

Angelica sat rather awkwardly across the table from Dick's mother. They'd been married nearly a year yet she'd never met his family. For various reasons none of them had come to the wedding. There had been a distant cousin, who was a senior civil servant and thus able to mix quite comfortably with the Askhams.

It had been just as well because Angelica knew that Dick's family would have felt out of place in those exalted surroundings; unhappy among that vast clan embracing some of the noblest names in the country. She hadn't minded very much then; too excited about her marriage to question any aspect of the behaviour of her groom.

Now they were motoring up to the Lakes, dropping Flora off at Preston to stay with her mother's brother, Spencer Foster, and picking her up on the way back. En route, too, they'd stopped at Chorley to be introduced to Dick's family.

Shyly, Dick's mother reached out for a plate of cake, which she handed to Angelica.

'Try some parkin,' she said. 'This is a Northern speciality.'

'Thanks, no,' Angelica said politely. 'I have to watch my figure.'

Dick's mother turned dejectedly to Dick, her eyes expressing rejection. She'd been cooking for days, ever since the visit was announced.

'Angelica's a model, Mother. She can't put on weight.'

'Oh, I see.'

Angelica tried to atone by thrusting forward her cup. 'But I would *love* another cup of tea.'

This was poured awkwardly by Dick's father, a thin

wizened man who looked much older than he was. Instead of a left hand he had a hook, which he wielded skilfully to position the cup against the spout. He was clearly rigid with nerves at the appearance of his daughter-in-law, cousin of an earl, daughter of a 'lady' who had somehow, in this extraordinary way, married their Dick. His father, Len, couldn't take his eyes off Angelica, never having seen anything like her outside the pages of a magazine.

Chorley was a small industrial town, not far from Preston. Like Preston, it survived by means of the cotton industry, and it had rows and rows of terraced houses with no gardens and little back-yards. Sometimes there was an alley between them where children played and housewives gathered for a gossip. In the mornings the street resounded with the heavy tread of clogs as people went to work. Chorley had a flourishing market and, just outside, a beautiful park around Astley Hall, which had once been a stately home. It was surrounded by moors and, though some thought it a grim place, it had its own peculiar Lancashire charm. It was well abreast of the times with a Woolworth's on the main street and an Odeon Cinema in the centre of the town. It also had a good grammar school.

Angelica remained unimpressed by her first visit to Chorley, or any of the towns they'd passed, an endless line of ugly streets, since leaving Manchester. It was also the first time in her life she'd entered such a small humble dwelling in a narrow street where all the others were just like it.

She was not, however, the daughter of Charlotte for nothing and at one set out to try and charm her in-laws, a task she found comparatively easy. They were completely bowled over by her and soon the news of their arrival grew, and neighbours started surreptitiously to pass by the front of the house, hoping for a peep in.

Also there was Dick's sister, Teresa, her husband Norman and their two children, both of whom happened to have runny noses. His other brother, Geoffrey, was there and his mother's sister Freda with her daughter Kath, who had brought her baby, Jimmy. All had on their best clothes and on the table was his mother's best cloth and the Sunday crockery filled with cakes and sandwiches on doilies, and paper napkins.

As a contrast, however, to Angelica, Flora at once felt at home. She had no need to set out to charm because she knew she had none. All she could do was be herself – clad in a chunky sweater and skirt, hair flying down her back, glasses on the end of her nose. No one knew at first who she was. Teresa, knowledgeably, decided she was the nanny, though there were no children. It was a mystery until Dick introduced her more fully than he had at first.

Flora immediately fitted in. She stayed with the children and put the baby on her knee. The baby immediately started to bawl and reached out sticky fingers for the glamorous Angelica, who fastidiously drew back. Flora stuck her finger in Jimmy's mouth, at the same time giving one of the children a piece of parkin which he smeared all over his face. She said 'never mind' and brushed the crumbs off the tablecloth on to the floor. Angelica looked appalled.

But Dick was grateful to Flora. Her simplicity and naturalness saved the day. He'd known it would be a nightmare, but some time he had to show Angelica to his family and them to her.

The conversation was desultory, no one quite knew what to say. Dick's mother felt his wife would want to hear about his childhood, his prowess at school, on the football field. He was a King's Scout.

'How frightfully good,' Angelica said, nodding at Dick approvingly.

But it was impossible. The torrent soon dried up; there was no area in common, no meeting point. What exactly did one talk to the granddaughter of an earl *about*? No one, even Teresa, seemed to know, though they all tried hard. Dick started looking at his watch, shaking his head as if with regret. 'We really must go now.'

All the family got up, shrugging. Time went too quickly, they seemed to be saying. Dick's father was eyeing his new television set, now firmly turned off. Dick's mother drew him into the kitchen, pressed a five-pound note in his hand.

'No, Mother, no.'

'Go on. You're still a student.'

'I can't, Mother.'

'You've got a wife to support . . .' his mother's voice trailed off. 'How *do* you support her, Dick?'

'She works, Mother. She supports me.'

'I don't agree with that, Dick. Your father doesn't like it, either.' His mother looked at him anxiously. 'What made you *do* it, Dick? She's not like us.'

'Oh, Mother, don't be so old fashioned.' Angrily Dick pushed his mother away. 'This isn't the twenties, Mother, or the thirties. It's the fifties . . .'

'Still, a man should support a woman, and people should stick to their own class. Those are my views and my views they'll stay. I was proud of you at the grammar school, Dick, but you made a mistake when you went to London. You've got beyond yourself and I don't think you look happy.' For a moment she studied his face. 'You don't look happy at all. You've taken on too much; her father a lord, indeed!'

'Grandfather, Mother.'

'Well, grandfather then, what's the difference?'

'Her father was a racing driver. Times change.'

'Well, she looks like the daughter of an earl to me,' his

mother said, stepping back, arms akimbo. '*That's* all I can say. She looks too upper-class and I know she can't help it but, if you ask me, she's wrong for you.'

Dick pushed past her out of the tiny kitchen before she could speak again. Angelica and Flora were standing on the pavement outside the front door. Angelica had on a Pringle twin-set, a tweed skirt and a matching coat hung over her shoulders. Her dark hair was cut short about her head and as usual she was heavily made-up. She always wore make-up, never left her bedroom in the morning without 'her face', as she put it. She was very conscious of her appearance. It showed in everything she did and the way, now, she stood on the pavement swinging her body, stamping her feet, as if anxious to be off. She and Dick's father seemed to be aware they should be saying something to each other, having at last met, but now could find nothing to say. Len smoked his pipe and coughed. Flora, on the other hand, was talking animatedly to Kath, the baby still in her arms, now laughing at her, touching her face with wet fingers, running them down her jersey. Flora didn't mind.

'Oh, *there* you are!' Angelica said with some irritation, as Dick appeared in the narrow hallway. 'Whatever were you doing?'

'Mother just wanted a word with me.'

Dick's mother remained in the kitchen, but everyone else flocked round as Dick opened the door of the car for Angelica, while Flora gave the baby back to Kath and got in the back by herself. The baby screamed with rage and Flora leaned out of the window, waving.

'You've got a way with you,' Freda said admiringly. 'I'll say that. You can come any time.'

'I'd *love* to.' Flora blew kisses as Dick turned on the ignition and the engine sprang to life.

233

'Where's Mum?' Geoff said, looking round. 'Don't go without saying goodbye.'

'I said goodbye,' Dick replied with forced cheerfulness, smiling. 'See you soon.'

'Stop on your way back,' Teresa called animatedly, pushing her head through the window. Teresa, a bright, cheerful girl, lived in hopes of bettering herself. 'Traa, love.'

'Traa, traa,' they all called and the car went slowly down the tiny street towards the main road into town. As Flora looked back she could see this tiny group all frantically waving, all probably still saying: 'traaa.'

They were almost passing Astley Park on the way to Preston, before anyone spoke.

'This is our local park,' Dick said, looking to his left. 'The Astley family home. No Astleys there now. It's a museum.'

'I don't know what you're trying to say,' Angelica retorted.

'I'm not trying to say anything, darling,' Dick looked at her.

'Well, why refer to it?'

'Something to say,' Dick added lamely.

'I thought you might be making references to the Askhams. Astley-Askhams, see?'

'Not at all.'

'Astley *is* like Askham.'

'It is a bit. I never thought of it, I can assure you.'

Angelica settled back into her seat, hands in her pockets, pursing her lips.

'I thought you were trying to suggest that as the Astley family home was a museum . . .'

'Angelica, I was *trying* to suggest nothing. Nothing at all.'

Dick's voice rose and Flora, listening in the back, knew

that a row was imminent. Dick, it was true, was a nervous man with a quick temper. Angelica was volatile and unpredictable – all smiles one moment, moody and mono-syllabic the next. It was difficult in many ways to think she was the daughter of the impassive, controlled Charlotte, used to concealing emotion, but people said it was the Italian influence that made Angelica so volatile.

'I don't know why you ever brought up the Astleys then . . .' Angelica began, but Flora intervened.

'I loved your family, Dick.'

'Thank you. They liked you,' Dick said warmly.

'And me?'

'They loved you,' Dick smiled at his wife. 'They've never seen anyone so glamorous in their lives.'

'What did your mother want, then?'

'When?' Dick pretended to consult his memory.

'When she took you into the kitchen.'

Dick looked in the driving mirror. 'She wanted to give me some money.'

'Money? Whatever for?'

'She said I was still a student.'

'I don't suppose you told her that I kept you?'

'Yes, I did,' Dick glanced at her.

'And what did she say to that?' Angelica sounded smug.

'She said the man should support the woman, so I said times have changed.'

'Have they, though?' Angelica snuggled down into her thick, comfortable tweed coat.

'I hope you'll stop for a drink with Uncle Spencer,' Flora said. 'He'd like to meet Dick.'

'I've heard about you,' Spencer Foster said half an hour later, warmly shaking Dick by the hand.

'And I've heard a lot about *you*,' Dick replied. 'Flora's always talking about you.'

Dick, looking at this tall, upright old Socialist, recalled with a feeling of shame that he had once referred to him as 'the Tory'. He was one of the old guard and Dick was a modern radical, a putative revolutionary despite the comfort of his circumstances. One could still be radical even with a rich wife and a house in Knightsbridge. Spencer Foster looked like a rather watered-down, older version of Stalin, with a thick greying moustache and white hair. His eyes crinkled like those of the leader of Russia, but anyone knowing them both would have said the lesser-known man's expression was kindly.

Spencer had been waiting for them in the porch of his detached house near Moor Park in Preston, which he had bought after his retirement from Parliament. Spencer was a Prestonian and his roots were there, though the tiny family house where he'd been born behind the mill where his father worked at the top of Lark Hill had been torn down for development.

Spencer's house was red brick with a gable and quite a large garden surrounding it. It had probably belonged to a mill owner, or one of the more affluent of Preston's citizens – say a professional man or an entrepreneur – in the nineteenth century. It was, by any standards, a substantial house for a single man. Spencer had never married and now he found he had not many friends left in the north and he missed London. He'd not realized that he could be quite so lonely despite all his interests, so he gladly welcomed visitors, especially his sister's daughter, Flora.

Spencer had shaken hands with Angelica, his eyes lingering on her features, trying to detect some trace of her grandmother whom he'd loved for so many years. Indeed did so still. He had held on to her hand for several moments as he gazed at that beautiful face, murmuring how pleased he was to see her. But there was very little of Rachel's soft English features in Angelica's Italianate face with its hooded, brooding eyes and full, sensual lips. Still, Rachel's blood was there, inside, and he hung on to Angelica as though trying to establish contact with his old love.

Angelica, only a little puzzled, kept smiling at him. She knew enough about him – though she scarcely remembered him – not to be alarmed by his scrutiny.

Eventually Spencer led them into a large book-lined room overlooking the park, commenting that it was cold for the time of year and he had lit a fire for them.

'What brings you up here?' he said, as he went over to a side-table to pour drinks.

'We're just having a few days in the Lakes before I go back to college. Term starts on Tuesday.'

'You're still a student, then?'

'It's my last year,' Dick nodded. 'But I hope I'll be offered a job on the staff.'

'*Dr* Crosby, then,' Flora said, with a proudly proprietorial air not lost on Spencer. 'PhD.'

'You're a political economist?' Spencer said, offering him his drink.

'Practice and theory of Marxism,' Flora said, as though she were Dick's spokesman.

'Did Angelica's grandmother ever tell you about our visit to Russia in 1921?' Spencer kept his eyes on Dick, but he was aware of Flora's interventions, her seeming desire to be associated with Dick, while Angelica's attitude remained one of distance.

'She did,' Dick smiled at his wife. 'And I've heard about Lenin and Stalin from Lord Lighterman. He's surprisingly broadminded in his views.'

'It's because of business.' Spencer put his glass of beer to his lips. 'Bobby always put business before politics.'

'Jolly good job too, I think,' Angelica sat down, crossing her elegant legs, and sipped her drink.

'You're awfully like your father.' Spencer smiled kindly at her.

'Oh, did you know Daddy, too?' Angelica responded to him immediately. '*Do* tell me what he was like.'

'He was a very charming man.' Spencer took a seat beside her. 'A good man. He was just right for Charlotte and it's a tragedy they had so little time together. He wanted to retire, too. You were just a baby when he died.'

'Nine months,' Angelica said. 'But Arthur's very good. Not quite the same, though, as one's own father.'

'I wish you'd stay for dinner,' Spencer said to them as he saw Dick glance at his watch. 'I hardly ever have guests.'

''Fraid we can't.' Dick stood up and put his glass on the chimney-piece. 'We're expected at the hotel for dinner. That's in just over two hours.'

'Keswick? You'll make it.' Spencer was not a man to try and persuade people against their will. 'And are you going to call back for Flora?'

'I said I'd let them know, Uncle,' Flora took his hand. 'If we're having a good time I'll stay.'

'Splendid,' Spencer said, smiling at her. 'I can see I'll have to be good.'

Flora loved the starkness of the Lancashire countryside. It was almost an unfriendly area, with little appeal except to those who knew it. It was not as celebrated as the Yorkshire dales, or the fells and lakes of Lakeland, but for those with an eye to see and discover it was beautiful. The hills and valleys, interspersed between the industrial

238

towns that flanked the sides of the Pennine Range, had their own magic for the discerning. The clouds, trapped by the hills, made the area a wet one, ideal for cotton spinning, which had made the burghers of Preston rich. But now the industry was on the decline, thanks to imported materials from the East. Preston was rapidly and not too successfully trying to find new industries as the mills gradually began to close. But what could replace cotton – for over a hundred years the main source of livelihood for the citizens of Lancashire?

Preston was a historical town set on a hill. As well as being a centre of the cotton trade it was known mainly as a place on the way to the Lake District, or Blackpool, Morecambe and the Lancashire coast. It had narrow cobbled streets full of back-to-back houses set in straight lines, and some of its architecture was quite distinctive.

Flora loved pottering with Uncle Spencer round the house or in the garden, talking about her mother, about the old days when her uncle was an influential MP bent on righting the world. Those days had come and gone. A Labour government, returned by the people with a huge majority, had failed to make its mark and the Tories were now back in power. It made Uncle Spencer sick to his very soul to have all those opportunities thrown away. It would be a long time, in his opinion, before Labour got another. Flora agreed. The only solution to their difficulties was the discipline of Communism, which interwove prosperity with proletarian welfare. Spencer, once a friend of Keir Hardie, wasn't so sure.

Flora could sense that her uncle's loneliness had increased since the last time she'd seen him. He had brothers and sisters, all of whom lived locally, but he'd grown away from them.

'They think I'm different,' he said one day, as they sat by the fire having tea.

'Like Dick,' Flora looked sadly at the embers in the grate.

Spencer nodded. 'I could see he had a problem.'

Flora thought it was funny they hadn't discussed Dick and Angelica at all until now, three days after they'd gone. They'd be on their way back to London by now. She was enjoying herself, after all.

'In what way did you think Dick had a problem?' Flora looked at her uncle.

'Well, in my opinion he has two problems. One is Angelica, and the other is probably his alienation from his family. I didn't see him for long but he reminded me very much of myself as a young man, though I was a bit older than him, I suppose, when I met the Countess of Askham, and she was older than me. Our problem was of a different kind.'

'Did you actually *love* Aunt Rachel?' Flora's mind boggled at the thought of those two elderly people going through that traumatic upheaval that so interfered with the emotions. One never associated tall, austere Aunt Rachel with something so rash and undisciplined as sexual love.

'I loved her very much indeed.' As Spencer put down his cup and saucer Flora saw that his hand shook. 'I don't think she ever really loved me in the same way, though we were together for a long time.'

'Together . . . do you mean . . .?' Flora felt too shy to complete the question.

'Yes, I mean that.' Spencer raised his eyebrows and nodded, confirming her worst suspicions. 'For many years. I wanted to marry Rachel, but she had too many other things in her life – especially her family, her paper. Then she had the name of Askham. It was a very formidable name in those days. The great Hall was still fully operational, with a staff of about fifty servants.

240

There was the house in St James's Square, a great town house with its staff of servants, too. There were the doings of her children – Angelica's mother widowed so early, Em and her problems and so on. Rachel couldn't take me abroad as well, so she thought, though I'd have helped her. In fact,' Spencer rubbed his chin ruefully, 'she couldn't take me abroad, if the truth be known, for the same reasons Angelica shouldn't have married Dick: the difference in our lifestyles, in our backgrounds, was too great. I see it now and that Rachel, in her wisdom, was right. One day, I fear, Dick and Angelica may see it, too.'

'Oh, you can't *possibly* say that nowadays.' Flora, frowning, knelt on the floor and put some coal on the fire. 'Things are *very* different than they were in your day, Uncle Spencer.'

'That's true enough,' Spencer said, lighting his pipe, 'and I do hope they'll be happy; but she looked a discontented girl to me. Hard to satisfy. It seems to me, now, that *you* like Dick very much,' Spencer said softly, leaning forward to look into her face. It was that pleasant hour of twilight which, like midnight, seems conducive to confidences.

'I do like Dick very much.' Flora tossed back her head and looked at him. 'But not in *that* way. Don't think I'm jealous of Angelica. I've known Dick a long time, ever since I went to the LSE, and we have been close; but in the sense that our activities and beliefs brought us together. Dick was never interested in me in any other way.'

'And you him?' Spencer raised an eyebrow.

'Oh no. Oh no,' Flora shook her head vigorously, too vigorously, Spencer thought. 'Never in the way you think. Nothing like that, at all.'

* * *

On another day, just before she left, Flora and Spencer climbed the steep streets of the town to where Spencer and Margaret had been born. All they could look at was the site, because the house was gone. Near to it was the large convent building where Margaret's nieces had gone to school, an opportunity Margaret never had to have a better education. Lark Hill Convent stood in its own extensive grounds and provided an excellent education for those whose parents could afford it. A chance as well to acquire good manners and a polish that would, hopefully, last its pupils through life. On Saturdays and Sundays crocodiles of brown-uniformed boarders, with their neat little round hats and blue badges, would parade through the town, or individual members would be seen with their parents having tea at the Royal Oak Hotel. Preston had a large Catholic community; there was another convent for girls in Winkley Square and the Catholic College for boys.

Yet despite their own Council school education, Margaret and Spencer had broken out from the mould that they had been reared in. They were bright and ambitious. Spencer had become a trades union official and then an MP. Margaret had trained as a shorthand typist and eventually married a High Court judge. She'd died Lady Bolingbroke. Both, in their ways had succeeded yet, in other ways, both had failed. Spencer had remained a bachelor and Margaret's marriage had not been happy. Often he tried to explain the reason to Flora.

'You see, your mother could never replace the affection Adam had for Aunt Flora, the one you were named after. The two were as different as chalk and cheese.' Spencer, puffing a little from the climb up the hill, took her arm and looked into her eyes. 'They were as different as you and Angelica and yet your case is very similar in many ways. Flora, you see, was earnest and Melanie, her sister,

242

whom Adam first married, was a beauty, a flirt. Adam married the beauty and regretted it. That's what I mean when I say . . .' Spencer took her arm and urged her on along the street past the high red brick walls of the convent which sheltered the girls from too close a contact with the world. 'That's what I mean when I say,' Spencer gripped her arm, 'I think Dick married the wrong woman. I knew it instinctively. He should have married you.'

Flora stopped, her expression shocked. 'That's an *awful* thing to say, Uncle Spencer. You see, it's too late.'

'It *is* too late,' Spencer shook his head. 'But Dick couldn't see the wood for the trees. He and Angelica haven't a thing in common. I knew that from the start. But you and he have plenty.'

'I haven't Angelica's looks,' Flora said sadly. 'Dick was never attracted to me. I'm plain. How could I compete with Angelica – even if I'd wanted to?'

'Adam wasn't attracted to Flora either until it was too late,' Spencer said, resuming their walk. 'But these days things are different, attitudes have changed. Divorce is much more common.' He paused again and shook his finger at his niece. 'Seize your advantage, my dear, if you ever get it. Don't let what happened to poor Flora happen to you.'

CHAPTER 10

Anna looked radiant at her wedding, everyone agreed
about that. Brides, of course, are traditionally radiant; it
is a rather common, hackneyed sort of term. But it really
was the only word to describe Anna, dressed in a white
wedding gown by Hartnell with a full-length veil and train
carried by Jonathan Down and Jeremy Crewe. Elizabeth
Down and Anthea Kitto were the two younger brides-
maids and Natasha and Olga Lighterman the elder ones.
Three-year-old Galina, small and beautiful, carried a
posy, part of the procession.

It was a spring wedding in the church where Pascal's
parents had been married twenty-seven years before.
Religion was of little importance alike to Pascal and
Anna, one baptized a Roman Catholic, the other into the
Russian Orthodox Church. Thus they were used to show
and incense and the fashionable ambience of the Jesuit
Church in Farm Street decided the matter as much as
anything else. Its Pugin gothic architecture and glittering
Byzantine sacristy, pictured against massive arrangements
of gold and white flowers and a dressy fashionable congregation, looked marvellous.

As Anna wasn't a Catholic there wasn't a full nuptial
mass, as Charlotte had had. But the brief service, as
though the church disapproved of mixed marriages, which
it did, was fluffed out by a full choir and a compliant
priest who preached a long sermon glorifying both families. The main thing that day was to be among the list of
invited guests, to see and be seen.

Rachel felt out of place in the church as she had when

Charlotte and Paolo were married all those years before. Roman Catholicism was very alien to her brand of low-church Protestantism. She found it vaguely repellent, though there was no doubt that they did things well even when they disapproved. One could always rely on the Jesuits to be accommodating.

Everyone had their memories. Stefanie had been married in Paris in the Russian Orthodox Church, but there had been no ceremony and only two witnesses taken in from the street. Susan recalled that day in the village above Batum when the priest had taken his vestments from hiding to marry her and Kyril in a marriage later alleged to be illegal under new Russian law.

It was hard for Charlotte, standing next to her mother and Susan – Arthur was one of the ushers – to recall that day when she and Paolo had plighted a troth that was to last for such a short time. It was, indeed, a lifetime away and as Pascal walked down the aisle with Anna as his wife on his arm, briefly she saw his father again, as she never had since his death. But everyone thought her tears were tears of joy.

Pascal had wooed Anna from the day he brought her back from Germany. Gradually recovering, with the help of Jenny's expert care, she had had a chance to reappraise her life and from her aspect then it had looked bleak indeed. She was not old, only twenty-three, yet she was rootless. The peripatetic cosmopolitan life of her mother provided no anchor. She had no father; her brother was busy with his business and family, the problems of his marriage to Stefanie. In a different mood she saw Pascal differently. He was two years older than she was and he had matured. He had always been handsome, but now those dark good looks had seemed to her more imposing, impressive. Also he was successful.

He had made such a good job of designing, making and marketing the new 'Askham' that she knew Bobby looked on him favourably, more favourably, in many ways, than Sasha.

Sasha was bogged down in difficulties of all kinds, professional and emotional, but Pascal was in the ascendant. People came from all over the world to see him.

Besides, reluctant as she was to admit it even to herself, Anna had sustained a serious wound – both physically and emotionally. An abortion that had gone wrong was a dangerous business and the doctors had warned her she might be sterile. To be jettisoned and betrayed by a man one loved was an even greater trauma, were that possible, than the assault on one's physical well-being.

To replace such a man by someone younger, more caring, and who clearly venerated her was not difficult for Anna, who needed a boost to her self-esteem. Abandoned in Frankfurt and rescued by Pascal seemed like a miracle, just when one needed one.

It made her grateful to her saviour even if she didn't love him in the way she'd loved Gunther. She felt she could never love that way again; indeed she hoped she never would. She would purposely control her emotions; never let her defences down so far.

When Anna agreed to marry her second cousin she felt she was making a bargain – though she took good care not to explain it to him. In exchange for security and harmony she would be a good wife – for a time. Then she would see. But as she made her vows at the altar this reservation never occurred to her, nor did it show in her demeanour as they walked hand in hand towards the great south door.

It was a beautiful day in May for the wedding and the garden at Charlotte's house in Holland Park seemed to give promise of an equally beautiful summer. It had been a hard year with a lot of unrest, national and international, and it was good to be able to find something to celebrate. The Four-power Conference in Berlin in January, which Arthur had attended as a representative of the government, was considered a failure and the attitude of the Kremlin was little different from that of Stalin, who had died the previous year. There was talk of war, yet again.

Thus it was with relief that people turned to the chance to enjoy themselves, and what was more enjoyable than a wedding? Food rationing had finally ended, and caterers at last came into their own. A sumptuous buffet had been prepared in a marquee erected on the lawn.

Rachel and Hugo had wanted the wedding to be near Askham so that the Hall could once again be used for a joyful occasion, but Anna and Pascal insisted on London so that their fashionable friends could attend. Besides, the Hall was not what it had been, and the Crewe country home, Littlestone Hall, too far away.

Cars were driving up to the house for a least an hour after the ceremony, depositing the guests and driving away again. Those who reported on the scene afterwards said that it was the wedding of the year, and there were many articles on the Askham family and how it had broadened its base by intermarriage with the Lightermans, the Ferovs and the Bolingbrokes. Charlotte's heroism in the war and Ralph's mysterious death were much reported on.

There was the usual gathering of people that were always present for events connected with the Askhams, old friends whose association with the family went back, in their many ramifications, for more than a century: the Bulstrodes, the Forresters, Plomley-Pembertons, the Pardoes, Lawfords and Rigbys seemed as strongly represented as ever whereas some, like the Pooles, the Copley-Hendersons, the Savages and the Tufts had somehow, perhaps due to death, or family feuds, faded away. The Kittos, of course, always a strong contingent, were there in full force and many of the young Lighterman and Bolingbroke representatives, whom few people had ever met; great-grandchildren and great-great-grandchildren of Bobby's grandfather, Sir Robert, or nieces and nephews of Rachel and Adam. Missing from the assembly gathered for her granddaughter's wedding was Princess Irina, stricken with an unseasonal bout of influenza which kept her in bed at the family home at Robertswood. Irina loved nothing better than a party but, perhaps, it was just as well that she was spared an encounter with Lady Melanie, with whom she had never seen eye to eye. Or maybe it was Lady Melanie, that arch-snob, who had never seen eye to eye with her mother's former companion and thought that her influence over her had been excessive. Irina was also the mother of Bobby's first wife, Hélène, and it was no secret that Melanie had had little time for *her*.

But by many Irina *was* missed, talked about but soon forgotten. The eyes of everyone were on Lady Melanie who had come over specially for the occasion. It was her first appearance in London since before the war, her first reunion with Rachel, and her second husband, Adam. Like Rachel, Melanie had weathered well and, indeed, both women remained much the same, retaining those characteristics, habits of dress and so on, they'd had when they were young. Rachel had never been concerned much with appearance, but to Melanie fashion had been almost as important as the breath of life, and still was. She managed, by the way she dressed and carried herself, to lose about ten years and her skin was as firm as that of a much younger woman.

Melanie had had her trials in life, many of them self-induced. Yet, in her seventies, she seemed to have transcended them, and was pleased to be back among her family and her family's friends, her long aristocratic nose quivering as she surveyed the scene. Melanie was still beautiful, exuding the kind of warmth that drew people to her, both those who had known her before the War and the younger element of the family to whom she was a legend.

'It is so difficult,' Melanie was saying in a loud voice, 'not to have a proper *town*house.'

'But Auntie, this *is* a proper town house,' Charlotte leaned towards her. 'You must consider it your home while you're here.'

'It's not as big as Askham House,' Melanie sniffed around. 'Quite tiny, in fact.'

'Tiny in comparison, Mother,' Susan chided her gently. 'And all that was a long time ago.'

'We should never have let it go,' Melanie said firmly. Her one concession to frailty was a stick, a large ebony cane with a gold top, because of an arthritic hip, and this she thumped vigorously on the floor.

'Never. I shall always blame Cheryl for that . . . *and* for much else.'

'Melanie, you can't blame Cheryl for *that*,' Rachel protested. 'I wish you had known Cheryl as she became during the War. She changed completely and really thought of others. She adopted two war orphans and took them to Africa.'

'I always said Cheryl killed my mother,' Melanie said in such a loud voice that those standing on the periphery of the privileged circle seated in the shade on the terrace, turned to stare.

'Nonsense, Melanie,' Rachel whispered. 'What an *awful* thing to say.'

249

'I don't mean directly,' Melanie grudgingly corrected herself, 'but by her behaviour. Mother *detested* her and Cheryl wore her down, in her own home, too. She made everyone she came in contact with unhappy and good riddance to her. She ran down the Hall and she ran down the House. She has a lot to answer for.' Melanie shook her finger as if at a departing ghost.

Except for that rather faded look that age invariably brings unmercifully to all, Melanie would have been recognizable to those who had known her in her twenties and thirties. Her hair was still a striking dark auburn (her hairdresser uncannily captured just the right shade) and her aquamarine eyes blazed from that almost perfectly moulded face, delicately and expertly made up so that small lines and blemishes were disguised. Her figure was trim and taut, her bust firm, only the creases under her chin gave a clue to advanced age. But she tended to wear dresses or blouses with high collars and these were a good disguise.

Many of the younger members of the family were in awe of Lady Melanie and some had to be forcibly rounded up and presented to her because she insisted on meeting everyone. There were lots of young great-nieces and nephews on the Kitto side, of whose existence she was hardly aware, and they were led before her, rather like sacrificial goats, by anxious parents for her inspection and approval. Lady Melanie sat in her chair rather as though it had been a throne, the palm of her left hand firmly clutching her stick, her right hand poised for a blessing.

'I can't remember half the names,' she said, smiling at Rachel as the latest offering drew humbly away from her.

'Gordon and Elsie Kitto, your mother's brother's grandchildren.'

'Oh yes, of course.' Melanie looked towards them and gave a friendly wave. '*Now* I know.'

No one had observed the first meeting between Melanie and Adam, for it took place in private in Arthur's study the night she arrived. She had only come because she was anxious to go in an aeroplane. Despite good health, she daily expected to die. One could never be sure. She and Susan, who accompanied her, had been met at the airport by Arthur's chauffeur, Arthur and Charlotte being in the north on constituency business, and when she and Susan had reached the house Adam was already there waiting for them. For Susan and her brother Christopher, who had brought his father up from the country, it was a very poignant moment to see their parents together after such a long time, about thirty years, and after they gave them time to have a private greeting there was a quiet family dinner together with Anna and Pascal.

That had been two days ago. Now Adam and Melanie appeared as familiars – something which would have been impossible in the twenties – on good terms, and Adam sat on her other side, commenting as members of the family were brought up for inspection and blessing.

'This is my Flora,' Adam said as Flora came nervously up to the woman who was her mother's predecessor. Melanie put down her stick and held out both hands in a gesture of special welcome.

'Flora. My dear. Kiss me.' She drew Flora towards her and Flora was aware of that faint smell of roses that she associated with babies and elderly ladies. Then, as Flora drew away, Melanie looked at her critically, still holding on to her hand.

'I know who *you* take after,' she said. 'My sister. You even look a bit like her. Doesn't she, Adam?'

Adam nodded but, really, he thought the resemblance was more in the mind than in actuality. Flora had been very tall: Young Flora was unusually small.

'She's very like her in nature. Scholarly.'

251

'I knew it,' Melanie said, and suddenly and completely unexpectedly her brilliant eyes brimmed over. 'I loved my sister, you know, so much but, maybe, I didn't realize how much until after she was dead. This is always the way, isn't it?' Her head turned from Rachel to Adam. 'We never appreciate what we have. If Flora had married Adam, as she should, how very different life would have been.'

'Well, I wouldn't be here for a start, Mother,' Susan said with her usual practicality, 'and nor would Anna, so there would be no wedding.'

Melanie laughed and put a hand on her daughter's arm.

'It's a silly game, isn't it, saying what would have happened if something had been different? As you say, none of us would be here had our parents not married each other, or whatever. But Flora, my sister, did love Adam and he her . . .'

'You were very beautiful, Melanie, my dear,' Adam said, leaning towards her, 'and still are. I would do the same again whatever the consequences. You left me, remember. I would always have stayed with you. Always.'

As he gazed at Melanie, Rachel thought how skilfully her brother had avoided an embarrassing situation from developing. Flora, though, seemed spellbound by her father's first wife and didn't leave the circle with the others, but lingered.

'I've always been fascinated by Aunt Flora, what I know of her,' she said. 'I have quite a lot of her things which Daddy kept – her books, pictures and so on. Except that she was very tall and I am not, I think I am a little like her, though antiquities are not my subject.'

'And what *is* your subject, you dear little thing?' Leaning forward Melanie patted Flora, as though she were a family pet and not a grown woman. Indeed, something about Flora did, and probably would, remain child-like. 'I must say, I'm *very* taken by you.'

'I'm a sociologist, Lady Melanie.'

'And what is a sociologist?' Melanie enquired of those around her. 'I never heard of one before.'

'It's the study of society, Lady Melanie,' Flora said, with uncharacteristic docility.

'She got a first class degree,' Rachel said proudly, 'and is now doing research. By the way, you must meet Angelica's husband Dick. He and Flora work together at the LSE.'

'What *is* the LSE?' Lady Melanie said tetchily. 'I do hate this modern use of letters instead of names.'

Rachel told her what it meant and couldn't help smiling to herself at the same time. In her later years Melanie had grown almost imperceptibly to resemble her mother. She had Dulcie's imperious manner as well as Dulcie's looks. Who would ever have thought of Melanie growing old?

'I'll go and get Dick,' Flora said eagerly. 'He wanted to meet Lady Melanie.'

'And bring Angelica to me, too,' Melanie called in a loud voice. 'I hear she's *enceinte*.'

Pregnancy was not a nice word, not quite a nice condition for someone of Melanie's generation. Yet she was a mother of four. Her eldest child, Bobby, was now steering a course towards her, flanked by the usual sycophantic members of the family who hoped that some crumbs would fall on them from the rich man's table.

In many ways Bobby, though he was in his mid-fifties, looked not much younger than his mother, nineteen years older. Melanie commented on it *sotto voce* as she espied him at the edge of the terrace, greeting an old acquaintance.

'Bobby looks *old*,' she said. 'I hardly recognized him.

Has he got some disease?' She looked sharply at Rachel, who shook her head.

'Not as far as I know, Melanie. Bobby has had his troubles, of course, but he suddenly aged when David went to America. He loved David very much.'

'Mmm,' Melanie grunted, 'and his daughters not enough. Stefanie looks *awful*.'

'Stefanie's not very well,' Rachel concurred, looking anxiously to where Stefanie was wandering on the edge of the crowd, appearing a little unsteady on her feet, followed about by Sasha. Rachel was afraid she knew why.

Rachel had heard it from Charlotte, who knew it from Pascal to whom Anna had confided. But so far very few others in the family were aware of the secret only recently prised out of an unwilling Sasha: that Stefanie too often had too much to drink. No one knew quite for how long it had been going on, or how serious it was: was it an illness or a temporary aberration?

Naturally it had badly affected Sasha and his work, and at public functions like this he tended to watch his wife, which irritated her. She could frequently be seen turning to snap at him.

Both Stefanie's sisters were here – Olga with her new fiancé, Max, and Natasha, who had recently finished her course at RADA and was in rep in the provinces. She had the actress's instinct for drawing a crowd and a number of people, mostly men, were now gathering round her. It was noticable that Natasha and Bobby avoided each other.

'Ah, there *is* Angelica,' Melanie said, doing her great-niece the compliment of rising to greet her. Angelica had always been fond of her great-aunt, and as Melanie leaned towards her she ran forward and fell into her arms.

'Oh Auntie, how *good* to see you!'

'You said you would come and visit me again in Venice, darling,' Melanie chided. 'You promised.'

'I know, Aunt Melanie, but what with the wedding, my work and,' ruefully, Angelica pointed at her stomach, 'now *this*, I haven't had the time.'

'I'm delighted about the baby, dear,' Melanie looked at her approvingly, 'but come and sit down. I didn't realize it was so near. Fancy, Charlotte to be a grandmother. *That* I can't believe.'

Angelica blamed her unplanned pregnancy on the bad weather in the Lake District the previous October, carelessness on her part in the matter of contraception and a somewhat erratic and infrequent desire to be nice to Dick. She was so horrified when she discovered she was pregnant, concerned at the risk to her career, that she wanted to have an abortion. For once Dick put his foot down and wouldn't hear of it. He wanted a baby and Angelica, for once, gave in to him. By now she'd got used to the idea of being a mother and even reconciled to it. It was the sort of thing a woman had to do and the family, she knew, worried about her marriage to Dick, were relieved and pleased.

In fact her pregnancy hardly interfered with her life at all. Nothing showed for months and then her agency got her work modelling maternity wear; now she was almost more in demand than ever. 'Fashionable young Mrs Crosby, who is married to Dr Richard Crosby, a lecturer at the London School of Economics, is expecting their first child.'

Somehow, 'Dr' Richard Crosby sounded all right, looked good in print. He was also earning some money of his own. But no one could have called them a happy couple; misfits from the beginning. Now that the initial passion had gone both realized how little they had in common. Dick worked every night, either in his room at the School or in his study at home. As a junior lecturer he was on probation; encouraged to publish and only successful if he did. But Angelica always wanted to go out. She was a healthy young woman and had a trouble-free pregnancy. She liked entertainment: clubs, theatres, good restaurants and the cinema. Gradually former boy-friends turned up to take her out, to 'escort' her merely, but Charlotte had lately become concerned about it.

Melanie, however, greeted Dick warmly when he was presented, drawing him to her and kisssing him.

'I can see you've got brains,' she said. 'I've always admired brains, you know, even though in the opinion of some people I'm possessed of very few myself.'

'On the contrary, Melanie,' Adam said wryly, 'you've got your fair share, believe me.'

'Yes, but I was never *scholarly*, Adam,' Melanie pro-tested coquettishly, fishing for compliments. '*Not* a stupid woman, by any means, I grant you that, but not a scholar. Angelica's a very lucky girl.'

'You're quite legendary, Lady Melanie,' Dick said, taking a seat next to her. 'I've been longing to meet you. *Everyone* talks about you with the greatest admiration.'

'Oh, do they?' Melanie was clearly delighted. 'But Flora had a brain you know, my sister, one of the first women to get a Cambridge degree . . . unawarded even though they were to women in those days. She was considered an expert on Egypt, wasn't she, Adam?' She turned to Adam for confirmation and he nodded. It was thirty-seven years since Flora had died and, really, he couldn't recall her all that vividly now, to his shame, whereas to Melanie her memory seemed very vivid indeed.

'Flora talks a lot about her aunt,' Dick said, looking at her. 'Flora, this Flora I mean, is also a very clever girl. She got a first class degree.'

'So did you,' Angelica said, 'don't be patronizing. Why shouldn't a *woman* get a first class degree?'

'I'm not saying . . .' Dick began and then he shrugged, knowing it was hopeless. Angelica questioned almost anything he said, examining him for class bias, family prejudice and any number of real or imagined misdemeanours.

'And what is Flora doing, *now*?' Melanie asked, clearly delighted with her young relations.

'I'm doing research, Aunt Melanie,' Flora replied, 'into the problems of the urban poor.'

'Most interesting,' Melanie said. 'You must come and have tea as soon as all this is over and tell me all about it.'

Flora felt she was being dismissed along with the others as Susan approached her mother, her arm linked to that of a tall young man with fair hair and a suntanned complexion, who had just arrived. The young man stopped, inclined his head and put out his hand as Melanie stared at him, waiting for him to be placed in her memory.

'Mother, *who* do you think this is?' Susan was almost overcome with delight.

'I've no idea.' Melanie shook the newcomer's hand.

'This is your great-nephew, Mother, Ross Glencarran,' Susan declared triumphantly. 'Your brother Arthur's grandson.'

'My brother's grandson,' Melanie said disbelievingly, while Charlotte, who had come within earshot, paused, surprised.

'Oh, my God!' Melanie dramatically clasped her chest. 'Oh, my poor brother Arthur.'

'This is his daughter Dorothea's son,' Susan went on quickly. 'He has just come over from Australia and, of course, looked us up. I told Ross to come to the wedding if he could. I wanted it to be a surprise for you all.'

'A surprise,' Melanie said, as the tears welled in her eyes. '*That's* an understatement. Frances never kept in touch. Arthur's grandson. I can't believe it.'

The young man sat beside his great-aunt, his arm round her shoulder.

'I can see you've had a bit of a shock, Aunt Melanie,' Ross said in a broad Australian accent. 'We should have warned you.'

'A shock, but nice,' Melanie said in a strange voice. 'But it brought back memories of dear, dear Arthur . . . though you're not a bit like him. He died in America of poliomyelitis in 1904 and then Frances, his wife, went to Australia with the two girls and we never saw any of them again . . . except for cards at Christmas, we haven't really kept in touch at all, and I don't think there have been any of those since the War.'

'Mother said you'd lost touch,' Ross said. 'But she said to be sure to look you up. I had no idea I had so many relations.'

'And close ones, too,' Melanie said, gazing at him. 'Little Dorothea – always such a plain child – to think you're her son. Dear, dear. Miracles will never cease.'

Suddenly there was a rustle among the crowd surrounding Melanie and the bride, still dressed in her wedding gown, made her way through the throng and leaned over Melanie.

'Granny,' she said sharply, 'what on earth is the matter? Someone said you were crying.' Behind her, anxiously, hovered Pascal.

'Oh, my dear,' Melanie clutched her hand. 'It's like someone back from the dead.' She pointed to Ross, who was staring shyly around him. 'This, *this* is a relation of yours whom no one knew about – my brother's grandson, Ross, come all the way from Australia.'

Awkwardly Ross, who was the only guest not to wear morning dress, shook hands with Anna and Pascal.

'Congratulations,' he said. 'Sorry I missed the ceremony. I'm the son of Aunt Melanie's niece, Dorothea, who came to Australia before the First War. I'd no idea I would create such an impact.'

'This is *my* granddaughter,' Melanie said, feeling more emotional than ever. 'Isn't she beautiful? Isn't she a lovely, talented girl?'

'She sure is, Aunt Melanie,' Ross said, looking lost.

Anna reached up and kissed his cheek. 'Hello, Ross. Welcome to the family. It's a very large one . . . much larger then when Aunt Frances left for Australia. When Pascal and I come back from honeymoon be sure to come and see us. We're cousins, you know.'

'I hope you'll be very, very happy.' Ross shook hands with the groom.

'I expect to be,' Pascal said, gazing at his bride. 'We must go now, darling, or we'll miss the plane.'

As they saw off the bridal pair it seemed to Charlotte that this sort of scene had been acted and re-acted in her family for as long as she could remember; this familiar scene of the bride and groom leaving for the honeymoon – the changing into going-away clothes, the appearance on the staircase, the throwing of the bridal bouquet, the almost hysterical scenes as they made their way to the car, the waves, shouts and cries as they drove off.

Always tears and laughter.

Eventually, she was aware of Susan standing just behind her in the drive and of Susan's arm pressing hers tightly as the car disappeared from sight.

'It's over,' she said. 'They've gone.'

Charlotte turned and bent to kiss Susan's cheek, taking her hand as she did so.

'It's obvious she's very much in love with Pascal,' Susan whispered.

'She learned her lesson in Germany. It was a hard one, but she learned it. I'm glad for both their sakes that it came out so well. A beautiful day, really beautiful.' Together the two women linked arms and, turning, walked up the drive back to the house.

But had Anna learned her lesson, really? Charlotte couldn't help asking herself this question as the family gradually regrouped itself on the terrace and indoors, saying goodbye to guests who were not expected to stay on. Arthur was taking close family out to dinner at the Café Royal and Charlotte rather regretted agreeing to it. It had been a very strenuous day and she had a headache. She would much rather have had a quiet evening at home.

People were already in the hall saying goodbye when Charlotte heard a crash from the drawing-room, followed by one or two loud screams. She just got to the door when she saw Sasha bending over someone on the ground, and, on the far side, Melanie looked on in shocked amazement, her hand to her mouth.

Sasha stooped to pick up the person who had fallen and when he stood up Charlotte saw the limp body of Stefanie in his arms. White-faced he began to edge through the crowd, begging for space.

'Is she all right?' Charlotte said, meeting him at the door. 'I'll get a doctor.'

'She's only passed out, Aunt Charlotte. She'll be all right,' Sasha said bitterly. 'She's had too much to drink.'

'Oh, no, Sasha!'

'Oh, *yes*, Aunt Charlotte.' Sasha grimly headed for the stairs.

Charlotte looked anxiously about her before leaving the room to follow Sasha. But she needn't have worried. The family, those who remained, were adept at covering traces, whoever they were and wherever they might be. Everyone immediately regrouped and diverted the unwelcome attentions of those present.

Now even Melanie, aware of her responsibilities, was deeply engaged in conversation with the Australian great-nephew, and Angelica was shepherding a small crowd of bewildered onlookers through the French doors into the garden. Susan had beckoned to a bemused couple and was offering them a drink and Arthur had put on the gramophone. There were very few people left. Hopefully a potential family scandal would once again be hushed up.

Sadly Charlotte made her way across the hall, pausing to peer at her face in the elongated mirror. Sadly because she had always felt close to Stefanie, always tried to be a friend to her and she knew she had never been entirely successful. Charlotte had been very close to Hélène; she had been the last member of the family to see her alive, and she had loved her. She loved Hélène's daughter and always tried to encourage her confidences.

But she had been one of the last to find out that Stefanie had developed a drinking problem; or rather she hadn't found out from Stefanie but from her son. As Stefanie had begun to drink she'd closed up, become secretive, refused to face her problem. Now, today, it had come face to face with her, for everyone to see.

Charlotte was about to go upstairs when she faced Joe on his way down. It had been a hard day for Joe, being his brother's best man, and it showed.

Charlotte often wondered why Joe disliked Anna so much, but it was a secret which he kept, as Stefanie had hung on to hers. Maybe Charlotte wasn't the person she thought she was – a good listener, someone to whom people responded, a second Rachel. She liked this image of herself but, really, few of those close to her confided in her. Angelica never talked about her marriage and it was left to everyone to guess. Like drowning people clutching at straws they all desperately hoped now that the baby would bring Dick and Angelica together.

'Is she all right?' Charlotte asked.

'She's out for the count, but Sasha seems to be used to it. I'd no idea it was as bad as this, Mother.'

'I think few of us had,' Charlotte put a hand on his arm. 'I'm sorry it had to happen today and in publc. I'm *glad*, though, Anna and your brother got off first.' She searched Joe's impassive face.

'Always trying to keep up appearances, Mother,' Joe said.

'Well, they *are* important.' Charlotte felt hurt, but brushed aside this slur from her son as she had others. Joe often confused fact with hypocrisy. Bravely she smiled. 'It all went well today, don't you think?'

'Very well,' Joe's voice was expressionless. 'I promised Sasha I'd get some iced water. Please excuse me, Mother.'

As Joe went to the kitchen Charlotte abruptly sat on the stairs and put her head in her hands, succumbing to a rare moment of weakness. Then, terrified that anyone might see her, she rose and hastily ran up the rest of the flight to her room.

Upstairs, Sasha sat by the side of his sleeping wife, head in his hands. It was not the first time she'd passed out and he knew it would not be the last. It was only gradually, and reluctantly, he had begun to face Stefanie's drink problem, because it was only in the last year that it had become at all noticeable.

Sasha and Stefanie had been married for more than six years. During this time he had remained in love with his wife, but it was an emotion he knew was not reciprocal. He realized that Stefanie had never loved him but had been grateful to him for rescuing her from Jack, for giving her respectability and a name to her baby. He was family and when she needed him he'd been there.

Sasha had embarked on marriage with high hopes, and the birth of Galina had made him hope still more. But now an idealistic view of what a marriage could be had faded and also, with it, the possibility that they would have more children.

Once upon a time Sasha, who had grown up as a rather lonely boy in need of love, had fantasised about one of those story-book marriages to a beautiful, loving woman with a family growing up around them. He was married to a beautiful woman, but Stefanie had never been loving except, maybe, just at the beginning and even, perhaps, in Russia where Galina had been conceived.

After her birth, Stefanie had seemed to retreat into a world of her own in which very few other people had a part. She scarcely ever saw her son Nicky, who seemed to make her feel worse and reminded her of those days with Jack. One night she woke from a nightmare and said that Galina was the reincarnation of her mother and she couldn't bear to look at her because of the guilt it made her feel. For a time Galina had been removed to Roberts-wood to be with Nicky, in the care of the ageing but willing Irina. But Sasha realized that being on her own was no good for Stefanie, either, especially as he was often away. It was then that he started to notice that she drank and, soon, that she had to have alcohol to start the day. No amount of his love and protectiveness could convince her that this was unnecessary.

But this was the first time she'd passed out in public; she had steadily drunk from the start of the reception, unconcerned by the presence of the family. This was the first time that he really felt he was losing control and the ability to help her, or restrain her from the path she was resolutely taking towards self-destruction.

Sasha's heart was heavy as he raised his head to look at the woman – still so young – who represented his shattered dream. He felt they had so much that could make them happy – a lovely house, two children, each other. They had the family for support and he had his growing interest in the development of the new car. There was no shortage of money. But it wasn't enough so long as Stefanie remained haunted by memories.

There was a tap on the door and, getting up, he rapidly went over to it before anyone could come in. To his surprise Natasha put her head round the door and with her was the new Australian cousin.

'This man says he's a doctor,' Natasha said, pointing to Ross. 'He says he's a cousin.'

'He is. Come in.' Sasha let them both in, then shut the door carefully behind them, locking it. 'I'm sorry you should find my wife like this. I think she's OK.'

'Maybe a little over-excited,' Ross said, bending over her and studying her face. 'Or does she do it often?' Straightening up, he looked at Sasha as carefully as he had his patient.

'She does do it rather often, I'm afraid,' Sasha said.

'Is she having treatment?' Ross glanced from Stefanie to Natasha, who was standing with folded arms leaning against the wall.

'No, but now I think she must.'

'She must,' Ross said, feeling her pulse. 'She's much too young to be an alcoholic. How old is she?'

'Twenty-six,' Natasha said. 'Not very old, is it?'

'Too young.' Ross sat beside her and, with a pencil torch he took from his pocket, he flicked back Stefanie's eyelids and studied her pupils. Then he pulled the blanket over her and gazed at her for a few moments before looking at Sasha.

'Alcoholism isn't my speciality, but you must do something. I'll do all I can to help while I'm over here.'

'Thanks.' Sasha sat dejectedly in the chair next to the bed. 'I don't think she'll agree to treatment. She doesn't admit she's got a problem. She says she can give it up whenever she likes. She chooses not to. Maybe now that you are here, and family, she might listen to you.'

'I sure hope so,' Ross said slowly. 'I sure do. She's a lovely girl.' Slowly he looked from Stefanie to her sister. 'You're both lovely girls.'

'*I* haven't got a drink problem, don't worry,' Natasha said and, suddenly, as she smiled at him, Ross felt as though a new and important dimension had entered his life.

'What a day,' Charlotte said, kicking off a shoe. 'Thank heaven we had an excuse not to go to the party. Thank heavens for Jill. She always steps in when she's needed. She's a marvellous organizer.'

Arthur had been upset that Charlotte wouldn't go out to dine, using Stefanie as the pretext; but Jill, as always, took over, rearranged the party and agreed, at Arthur's insistence, to come herself, even though she hadn't been at the wedding. Jill was nothing if not unobtrusive and would never have dreamt of attending a family occasion – though she was quite willing to arrange them and ensure all went well.

Melanie loved a party but, though she had no concern about looking after her granddaughter, even she was too tired. It had been non-stop all day, greeting relatives and friends, jawing endlessly over old times. Melanie sat there with a glass of whisky in her hands, gazing thoughtfully at Charlotte.

'You shouldn't let a man's secretary take over, you know.'

'Why on earth not?' Charlotte kicked off the other shoe and smiled. Earlier in the year Chanel had reopened her salon after fifteen years of silence and Charlotte had been one of her first patrons – a blue suit lined in white silk with a plain white blouse for the wedding. 'There's nothing to be jealous of about *Jill*. She's been with Arthur for *years*.'

'She's not exactly an oil painting,' Rachel interjected. 'Arthur finds her indispensable. Jill is really rather plain, though a real sweetie.'

'Oh, you couldn't possibly be jealous of Jill,' Charlotte agreed.

'Remember Aileen,' Melanie said ominously, taking a sip of her whisky. 'She scarcely held a candle to Hélène.'

'But that was different,' Rachel said, glancing at Adam to see if he was listening. 'Charlotte and Arthur are *very* happily married. Bobby and Hélène never were.'

Still, Rachel felt there was a thoughtful air about Charlotte as she leaned her head back in the chair and closed her eyes. Maybe she was just very, very tired.

Rachel felt very close to her daughter, two of whose children were now married. She was about to become a grandmother. Yet to Rachel her children had always remained as they were aged about seventeen when they seemed suddenly to grow up and, really, looks didn't change all that much after that age. Ralph and Freddie would remain eternally youthful, immured in death. Em, who had never cared about appearances, really did look middle-aged but Charlotte, forty-seven this year, looked ageless: a beautiful, mature woman, graceful, elegant – the last word in poise and sophistication.

'How did you find Mademoiselle Chanel?' Melanie tactfully changed the subject as Charlotte removed her jacket and put it over her lap. 'She must be well into her seventies.'

'She's incredible. She's by no means finished, I assure you. She means to succeed even though the critics were so unkind about her first show. She realizes she's rusty but says she has a lot to show the men – Dior, Balenciaga, Fath. She says men can't dress women. I'm not sure I agree with her.'

'She can certainly dress *you*,' Melanie said in admiration, then: 'Is Sasha still with Stefanie?'

'I think Flora's there, too.' Charlotte looked towards the door. 'She's such a sweet child, wouldn't go out but wanted to stay with Sasha.'

'Wouldn't go because there's too much competition,' Melanie said shrewdly.

'How do you mean?' Rachel frowned at the implied criticism of her favourite.

'All these young people, good looking, light-hearted. You can tell Flora has her mind on higher things. Besides, is she not smitten with that Marxist husband of Angelica? It looks like it to me.'

Charlotte opened her eyes and struggled up from a recumbent position.

'Aunt Melanie, much as I love you, I think you're talking rubbish tonight. You're seeing plots where none exist. Flora has *never* been at all interested physically in Dick, who always made his love for Angelica clear from the beginning. And as for Jill and my husband, the idea is quite preposterous!'

Charlotte got to her feet, the jacket of her suit over her arm. 'I think I'll go and put on a housecoat, if nobody minds, and then organize some supper.'

As she passed her aunt, Melanie put out a hand to stop her. Melanie was still so beautiful, her eyes still so arresting, her face so expressive and her features so malleable that only the hardest heart could fail to be moved by her.

'*Dearest* Charlotte,' Melanie said gently, taking her hand. 'Forgive me. I can see I've annoyed you. I'm a silly old woman, you know, a bit lonely in Venice all day on my own without Susan and Anna. Denton is no companion to me. The casino is his mistress. I have nothing but fantasies and memories. Please, please forgive me.'

For answer Charlotte bent down and kissed her on the cheek, but she still felt angry – angry and tired.

Watching her go, Melanie tossed her head back and finished her whisky.

'I never was discreet, was I, Rachel?'

'Maybe a little tactless.' Rachel smiled.

'It's that I'm upset about Stefanie, really,' Melanie said, gazing into the depths of her glass. 'I can't believe my granddaughter's an alcoholic.'

'Well, maybe not *quite* an alcoholic,' Rachel felt unable to conceal her own anxiety, 'but she does drink too much, and has done for some time. Poor Sasha desperately wants a happy normal home, but maybe he's tried too hard. He's spoilt Stefanie a great deal, given her everything she asks for, satisfied every whim. Made life, perhaps, a bit too easy for her. Stefanie has become a very selfish girl. Much as we all love her I have to say that; but then I don't know how much is caused by this disease . . .'

'What disease?' Melanie said sharply.

'Alcoholism is a disease.'

'*If* she has it.' Melanie shivered.

'That nice young Ross is a doctor,' Rachel said. 'He went up to see Stefanie.'

'Keeping it in the family. That's good,' Melanie nodded. 'We don't want it to get out, *if* she is . . . We've *never* had alcoholism in the family, have we, Rachel? A good deal of heavy drinking, but never an out-and-out *alcoholic*.' Melanie sighed and refilled her glass from the bottle on the table beside her, as if to take her mind off the contemplation of such an awful thing. 'Now *I* like a drink. I always have, but no one would ever call *me* an alcoholic. Mind you, one never knows; these Russsians are an odd people. I should think it came from the Russian side, if it came from anywhere. *Certainly* not the Askhams. I don't believe she is, myself.' Melanie lifted her glass and surveyed the amber liquid as if studying its potency. 'She'll get over it. You'll see. Just send her to old Granny in Venice and she'll be as right as rain.'

Dear Melanie, Rachel thought, getting up to see if she could help Charlotte, she never would and never could face up to any problem in her life. She ran, letting other people do it for her. Maybe in this she had her own special wisdom.

In the kitchen everything was in surprisingly good order. The expert team of caterers had left, taking everything with them that was not needed by the family. They had brought all cutlery and crockery, table adornments, napkins and so on, and everything had been painlessly and, apparently, effortlessly removed. It was difficult, really, to think there had ever been such a large number of people there. Not only was the kitchen clear of everything except items of food left over for the family but the terrace and garden, the inside reception rooms, looked just as they had in the morning before anyone had arrived.

On the large kitchen table was enough for supper: smoked salmon, fresh Scotch salmon, beef, ham, more than enough for the eight people who had not gone out to dinner.

In the kitchen Paul and Flora sat at the table, helping

themselves to food, and Charlotte was making a sarcastic comment about some people never having enough to eat.

'You can say *that* again, Aunt Charlotte,' Paul said, unceremoniously stuffing a huge piece of fresh salmon into his mouth. '*I* hardly ate a thing, I was so busy helping.'

'You were very good, darling.' Rachel, coming behind him, ruffled his hair. 'Quite the host. What time's your train?'

'I have to be at Euston at midnight.' Paul looked at his watch.

'Pity you have to go back.'

'I have a lecture at nine tomorrow, Gran.'

'I'm glad you're taking your work seriously, anyway.'

'I'm always serious,' Paul said, winking at Flora.

Flora and Paul were close. Not only had they grown up together but they were very alike: studious, dedicated, political. Paul had hated his public school, he hated class distinctions and privilege as much as Flora, and he loved the life at a provincial university, where no one knew he was the Earl of Askham. Paul thought he would never use his title but remain plain Mr Askham. In this he took after his grandmother who, at times in her life, had preferred to be kown as Mrs Askham. In fact Rachel, who had brought them up, was very much responsible for the egalitarian ideals that influenced her niece and grandson.

Paul lived in a students' hall of residence, which he hated because it reminded him of school; but Rachel insisted until at least his second year. Rachel, his legal guardian, was also a very strong and abiding influence on Paul. She was the only mother he had known, and Flora, too, had been motherless. It gave them a bond.

'Flora's coming up next weekend,' Paul said. 'Harry Pollitt's coming to address the Party faithful.'

'I *do* hope you're not one, too,' Charlotte said, turning from a cupboard and looking at him with horror.

'Of course I'm not, Aunt Charlotte!' Paul glanced at his grandmother. 'You know that I'm going to be a wicked capitalist. The Party will have my head whatever happens.'

'I wish you wouldn't be silly about the Party,' Flora said crossly. 'You may not take it seriously but I do. You know I hate you making fun of it.'

'They say the Party is penetrating the unions,' Paul said slyly. 'That it's going to undermine the opposition by stealth. It was in *The Economist*.'

'That's rubbish, too.' Flora was spreading butter on a large piece of French bread. 'The Party is completely open, compassionate, caring. I wish . . .'

'I wish you two wouldn't argue,' Charlotte clasped her head. 'I just want a nice, peaceful evening.'

Rachel looked at Charlotte in bewilderment. The two young people were only having a friendly squabble, hardly an argument. Charlotte did look exceptionally pale, even though she was one of those women with a natural pallor. She wondered if Charlotte had something on her mind other than worry about Stefanie, exhaustion after the wedding. Quite natural, really. She thought that, at last, Charlotte had become reconciled to Anna, even liked her. In the last few months Anna had certainly done her best to please.

However, she had other things on her mind: Angelica and Dick, who had quite noticeably had little to do with each other at the reception; Arthur's ambition and a conflict of loyalties. To be by his side, a good wife, she had to be too often away from her family. Then Joe – what about Joe? He was unsettled. But was there some underlying reason for Charlotte's pallor – a feeling, perhaps, that only in the excitement of war and dangerous love had she felt really fulfilled?

Sasha strolled into the kitchen, hands in his pockets. He had taken off his tie and in his white shirt and black trousers he looked somehow incongruous. He merely nodded when Rachel asked if Stefanie were all right and made himself a ham sandwich, poured himself wine, with a preoccupied air.

Rachel sat next to Flora and started nibbling at a piece of cheese. 'Why didn't you go to the dinner, darling?'

'You know I don't like that kind of thing, Aunt Rachel – dancing, fussing, dressing up. I hate it. In fact I hated the whole day. What *awful* people we seem to know.'

'Flora, you mustn't say that!' Charlotte looked shocked. 'We know some *very* nice people, as a matter of fact.'

'Well, I think they're all awful. Bastions of the Tory Party. It's a wonder Mr Churchill wasn't here.'

'He might have been, he was asked, but he's really not well.' Charlotte looked anxious. 'Arthur thinks he ought to go.'

'Isn't he all there?' Paul enquired, touching his head and taking another piece of salmon with his fingers, while Rachel looked at him disapprovingly. He, too, had changed out of his morning suit into flannels and a jersey.

'Of course he's "all there"!' Charlotte sounded affronted. 'Don't be horrid, Paul.'

'I heard he wasn't.'

'Well, you hear wrong. He is a *very* old man. Eden has been waiting in the wings for so long. Arthur hopes that if Eden gets in he might join the Cabinet.'

'Should you like that?' Flora asked.

'Why shouldn't I?'

'It just seems to me, to be truthful, you aren't all that enamoured of politics. I mean, all these people here today were so stuffy. When you think you were in the war parachuting on dangerous missions,' Flora raised her eyes to the ceiling and her hands in the air, 'well, frankly, I can't believe it.'

'You mean I'm stuffy, too?' Charlotte smiled wanly and looked at her mother.

'Not exactly, but . . .'

'She means you're "establishment".' Paul licked his fingers. 'I know what Flora means. All these people *are* a bit stuffy. They're all wealthy and well connected. Where were the intelligentsia? The artists? The writers? The scholars?'

'Well . . .' Charlotte looked to her mother for help. Rachel, to her surprise, was actually smiling.

'I *like* to hear young people being radical,' she said, approvingly. 'Whereas it's all right for Arthur to be a Tory, I'd hate it if Flora and Paul were. Paul *may* say he's a capitalist, but I know his heart is in the right place. The thing is, you see, darling, that many of these people have known our various families for years and years. But I thought Dick got on well with most people – and he's a Marxist.'

'He isn't really a Marxist,' Flora said. 'Not any longer. Angelica's been getting at him.'

'But isn't he Chairman of the Party?'

Flora shook her head. 'Not for a year. He doesn't even pay his subscriptions any more. He's been corrupted by glamour and money.' She looked close to tears. 'I never thought it would happen to Dick, but it has. He's lost all his ideals. He's betrayed his comrades.'

To everyone's astonishment Flora suddenly burst into tears and ran from the room.

Rachel, looking after her, thought, 'So Melanie *was* right, after all.'

Instead she said aloud: '*What* a day! You can never tell with families,' and she put her arm round Charlotte and gave her a gentle hug.

273

CHAPTER 11

The big white house along the Sussex coast west of Hove, surrounded by a large garden, could have been a hotel or a rich man's country home. It was approached by a circular drive and, around the back, it could be seen that the house had been substantially extended with red brick buildings that gave some sort of clue to its identity as a private hospital.

Charlotte left her car in its usual place in the visitors' car park to the rear of the house and entered through the side entrance. In her hand she had the usual bunch of flowers, the usual fruit, chocolates and magazines that people take to the sick.

The receptionist at the desk knew her well by now because, apart from Sasha, Charlotte was the only person allowed to visit Stefanie regularly and some weeks Stefanie didn't even want to see her husband. She was quite capricious about it and he would travel all the way to be told that she wouldn't see him. But she never refused Charlotte. As soon as the receptionist saw her she lifted the phone and spoke rapidly into it, her smiling, welcoming eyes on Charlotte. Unlike some medical establishments the receptionist in this case had been chosen for her efficiency, courtesy and charm. The clinic was an expensive one and, as those who visited were usually paying, the management took good care to see they were properly received.

As Charlotte came up to the desk the receptionist replaced the phone.

'Dr Grant would like to have a word with you, Lady Charlotte, before you see Mrs Ferov. Would you mind?'

'Of course not,' Charlotte said, feeling mystified. 'Is she all right?'

'I'm sure Dr Grant will put your mind at rest,' the receptionist said tactfully. 'Please follow me, Lady Charlotte.'

Leaving her flowers in the reception, Charlotte followed the woman along a corridor to the side of the large house and stood while she knocked at the door and a voice told them to enter.

'Lady Charlotte,' Dr Grant said, hand extended, a welcoming smile on his face. 'How good of you to see me.'

One couldn't fault the Bellevue Clinic, Charlotte thought. If only their treatment was up to their PR, Stefanie should make a good recovery.

The medical director, Dr Grant, and Charlotte had met several times since Stefanie's admittance shortly after Pascal and Anna were married. Stefanie had entered as a voluntary patient on the advice of Ross Glencarran, to whom the Bellevue had been recommended. For a time, however, Stefanie remained very much the same, except that she wasn't drinking. This made her even more depressed and for days she wouldn't get out of bed.

It was easy to say that Stefanie was spoilt, that she should pull herself together, but until one had seen the depths to which depression could reduce a person one couldn't begin to comprehend the problem of mental illness. Charlotte had seen many terrrible things in her life inside and outside the concentration camps and nothing could compare with these; but to see a healthy woman reduced, as Stefanie had been, by drink and guilt was another lesson altogether: peace had its perils, too. Who knew what would have happened had Hélène survived the war – rootless and without the love of the man who had died before her, with whom she had worked, to help her?

Charlotte never used phrases like 'pull yourself together' now, after what had happened to Stefanie, and doubted whether she ever would again.

Recently Stefanie had seemed better but now Charlotte wondered what the director wanted to see her about.

She took a cigarette from the box Dr Grant offered her and thanked him as he lit it for her. 'They say they're bad for one,' Dr Grant said, lighting a pipe.

'Cigarettes, too?' Charlotte raised an eyebrow.

'A report is to be issued soon, I believe, showing the association of tobacco and lung cancer. It's based, I'm told, on reliable medical statistics.'

'Oh dear,' Charlotte pretended to look concerned. 'I'm afraid most of my family smoke, except my mother. I don't think I have ever seen her smoking. Too late for me to give it up, I'm afraid. Is Stefanie all right, Dr Grant?'

Dr Grant made a great fuss of his pipe, inspecting the bowl and prodding it with an unlit match. Then he took a puff at it again, saw it was drawing satisfactorily and sat back.

'Mrs Ferov is perfectly all right, Lady Charlotte, physically anyway. She is certainly in better shape than when she came to us. She no longer drinks . . .' The doctor paused and examined the bowl of his pipe again as if looking for cracks. Charlotte began to find him mildly irritating. 'That's a good thing.' Charlotte nodded in agreement and must have shown her sense of impatience because Dr Grant hurried on.

'However, I'm not satisfied that Stefanie is making the progress we would have hoped to achieve by this time. She has been, from a psychological point of view, almost stationary. We use drugs on her but, of course, we would

276

like gradually to eliminate these. She is curiously unresponsive to therapeutical forms of treatment: reluctant to talk. Indeed, she is capable of sitting for an hour and saying nothing. It's very frustrating for those who are trying to help her.' Dr Grant put down his pipe, which had gone out, and joined his hands. 'I wonder if you can help me, Lady Charlotte?'

'If I can,' Charlotte said.

'You, of course, knew Stefanie's mother?'

'I knew her very well.'

'What sort of woman was she?'

'Very charming. Beautiful, attractive to men . . .' Charlotte paused.

Hélène raised her thin skeletal arms from the pitiful pile of rags upon which she lay on the floor of one of the medical blocks in Auschwitz which Charlotte ran. She had been hiding her for days. Usually the very sick were taken immediately to the gas chambers. But now the Russians were advancing on the camp and the Germans were preparing to flee, marching their healthy prisoners in front of them in order to prevent them telling tales.

'Charlotte,' Hélène cried, 'don't leave me. Stay here with me.'

Charlotte knelt on the floor beside her.

'Darling, I can't. You can't travel and if I stay we'll both be shot. You will be all right.'

'I'm afraid of the Russians as much as the Germans. Charlotte . . .'

Charlotte got up, turned her back on the woman she had spent the last two years with and fled. She didn't even look behind . . .

'Lady Charlotte . . .' Dr Grant's voice seemed to come from very far away and Charlotte avoided his eyes as she wiped a tear from her own.

277

'You must forgive me,' she said, blowing her nose. 'I knew Stefanie's mother very well and I loved her. To start trying to think of her objectively is impossible for me. Beautiful, charming, and so on. They're meaningless words to me now. You see, I had to leave her in Auschwitz and she was never seen again . . .'

'Ah.' Dr Grant nodded wisely. 'So *you* feel guilt, too?'

'Of course I feel guilt! It has never left me.'

'She hounds you as she does the daughter?'

'Yes,' Charlotte said emotionally. 'She had that effect on people.'

'Because Stefanie thinks she killed her mother. By rejecting her she made her mother end up in Auschwitz.'

'That's certainly not true! It had *nothing* to do with Stefanie.'

'I know, Lady Charlotte.' Dr Grant leaned forward appealingly. '*I* know it and *you* know it; but how do we convince her daughter if, even after all these years and knowing you could not help what you did, you feel guilt, too?'

Some time later Charlotte collected her flowers from the reception and slowly walked upstairs to the bright front room that Stefanie occupied, overlooking the sea. Stefanie invariably sat by the window, looking out, scarcely ever joining the others who sat downstairs in the various sitting-rooms or walked in the garden on warm days. Some even played tennis, or croquet that was set up on a far lawn. In many ways Bellevue was like a gracious country home rather than a psychiatric clinic.

Charlotte knocked, opened the door, and there was Stefanie, gazing as usual out over the sea, looking so pretty in a yellow cotton frock which made her seem like a young girl. She turned from the window, her eyes

278

shining with pleasure and, getting up, she rushed over to Charlotte and kissed her.

Charlotte dropped the flowers and chocolates on the bed and, putting both arms around Stefanie, hugged her.

'There, what a lovely welcome,' she said, brushing back her hair and looking into her eyes.

'Didn't you expect it?' Stefanie stepped back. 'You went to see Dr Grant, didn't you?'

'How do you know?' Charlotte sat on the bed and began to take off her hat, removing the pin at the back that fastened it to her hair.

'I saw your car come, such a long time ago. I know that Dr Grant must have wanted to see you. He's not very pleased with me.'

Charlotte got up and went over to the window to where Stefanie had resumed her seat.

'He doesn't think you've made a lot of progress.'

'I know.'

'He wondered if I could help him.'

'Why you?'

As Stefanie stared at her Charlotte drew over a chair and sat by her side.

'Because I knew your mother. I loved her, too.'

'I didn't love her enough,' Stefanie said in an apathetic voice. 'Otherwise she would never have left us. If I'd kept her back she wouldn't have gone. She would be alive now.'

'Stefanie, that's *absolutely* wrong,' Charlotte said in a firm voice, taking her hand. 'Your mother left because she had work to do, important work in the war as I had. I had to leave, too, because I felt I must do what I could to rid Europe of the Nazis. Your mother felt the same. It had nothing to do with you. She was a patriot, a heroine. She hated the Boche. For her sake, darling Stefanie, please remember that and don't reproach yourself.

Please. It is the key to your health. If I, who knew your mother and why she did it, can't convince you, who can?'

On the journey south across Europe in the dying throes of a catastrophic war, Charlotte thought about Hélène as she'd left her, lying on the floor on the rags. The march had started almost as soon as she came away from the hut, closing the door after her. The kapo had asked her if it was empty and she said it was. It was the only possible way to save Hélène. And yet . . .?

She kept on looking back, but the further and further away she got she knew it was useless. Even then she knew she would never know the truth, never know if Hélène were dead or alive.

If only she'd stayed . . . she might have saved her.

Charlotte returned from her reverie to find Stefanie gazing at her.

'Are you all right, Charlotte?'

'Perfectly all right,' Charlotte said, fumbling in her bag for a cigarette, hoping that Stefanie wouldn't see the tears in her eyes.

'You were remembering Mummy, weren't you?'

'Yes.' Charlotte found her pack and rapidly extracted a cigarette, tapping it vigorously on the outside. 'Yes, I was. I was thinking – and I often do if you want to know the truth – that if I'd remained behind *I* might have helped your mother. At least I could have comforted her. As it is we would probably both be dead. But who is to say that I had the right to live? How can I know? Oh, Stefanie,' and, to her horror, Charlotte found herself engulfed in tears, leaning her head against the shoulders of the already stricken young woman, weeping helplessly.

* * *

280

Later they walked in the garden together, arms round each other's waist.

'I'm glad you told me,' Stefanie said. 'It helps me to know that you feel guilty, too.'

'But we mustn't.'

'I know.'

'We both mustn't,' Charlotte said, then, with added urgency, 'If you continue to feel guilty you will never get out of here. It's preventing you from getting well, and there is so much to live for.'

'Is there?' Stefanie sounded sceptical.

'Oh, *yes*, and,' Charlotte's hand flew to her mouth, 'I have completely forgotten the reason for my visit. It was to tell you I'm a granny.'

'Oh, a *granny*! Charlotte.' Stefanie seized her as if delighted and kissed her on the cheek. 'Boy or girl?'

'Boy,' Charlotte said. 'They've called him Myles. Isn't that a nice name?'

Flora stood by the font of Askham Church, gazing at Dick's baby, the infant Myles, held tightly in her arms. He was a large baby and looked almost too big for the diminutive Flora, but she clung on to him for dear might as if fearful that she would drop him. Half-way through the ceremony Pascal, one of the godfathers, offered to take over as Flora seemed to be wilting, but she looked at him angrily and moved the baby out of reach. Flora wore a hat for the occasion, something that no one could remember. Her loose tangled locks always flowed freely as part of her personality. But today they were constrained beneath a wide-brimmed hat and she wore a neat tailored suit and a white blouse, so that she looked like a respectable member of the bourgeoisie. For Flora it was extremely incongruous, and she felt odd, too.

Not that she wasn't outshone by most of the women

present, some gathered round the font, others scattered throughout the church. In the midst of these tall, elegant, languid ladies, model friends of Angelica's, she looked a bit of a freak; but Flora always had been individualistic. None of the family would have dreamt of calling it bizarre.

A truly fashionable crowd had assembled for the christening, in September 1954, of Angelica Verdi's baby.

For Angelica was still known by her family name. There seemed no end to her celebrity and now Gérard, the celebrated French couturier, had engaged her for the opening of his salon in Bond Street in the New year.

Myles Neville Crosby had eight godparents, none of them from his father's side of the family, and most of them either noble or related to the nobility. Dick's mother and father had been invited to their grandson's christening but sent apologies and regrets, and a large blue teddy bear which Angelica thought too vulgar for words and put aside to give one day, discreetly, to the poor. Dick's sister, Teresa, she of the ambition to better herself, badly wanted to come but wasn't asked. She was told there was insufficient room. Dick played down the social aspect of the ceremony and, indeed, he had been very much against having his son baptized at all.

As usual, Angelica got her way and she stood beside him now by the font looking very proud and happy, and also rather anxious as Flora juggled the heavy baby about in her arms. Both had been unanimous about Flora as chief godparent and she, suitably flattered, had agreed even though it was odd for an atheist to promise to protect the baby against the devil and all his pomps. For these occasions Flora became a member of the family, of the Established Church into which she had been baptized. For occasions like this she forgot about being a radical member of society and became an Askham.

Askham Parish Church, with its square Norman tower, was one of those familiar sights in the English countryside nestling, as it did, in the heart of the village which clustered beneath the walls of the great house. The Rector, by tradition, was appointed by the Earl, but this privilege had long ago been gracefully yielded to church authorities.

Now the current Rector, in his white surplice, stood in the traditional place for baptisms at the great stone font by the west door of the ancient church. The sun shone through the stained glass of the west window which like all the glass in the church had been the gift of members of the family over the years – a commemoration of this event or that. It shone on the great brass urns of delphiniums, antirrhinums, peonies and hollyhocks, on the slender silver ewers of chaste white Arum lilies, which had been arranged with loving care by the Askham Ladies Guild. The congregation, turned towards the font and grouped round it, contained many distinguished names; but mostly it consisted of members of the family, that extensive web of relationships that stretched all over England, and relatives of the retainers who in days past had, like the Rector, owed their livelihoods to the Askham family.

Charlotte and Arthur stood behind Pascal and Angelica, and beside them were Anna and Joe and the other godparents – three of four were abroad. In the front row were Rachel and Adam, Em and Luis, Paul, Hugo, Jonathan, Natasha and Olga Lighterman, Sasha, Bobby, Aileen – a full complement. Jenny had stayed at the Hall to prepare the christening tea with the help of Arthur's secretary, Jill, who was an acknowledged genius at organization.

Rachel was now a great-grandmother – another milestone in a long line. As always on these solemn occasions in the family church, she thought about her dead husband, who had perished nearly forty years before. At his memorial service in this same church, on a bright summer's day in 1915 had stood the young girl only eight years old, Charlotte, who was now a grandmother, if a very young one. How strange it was to look at the generations, Rachel thought, as if she had suddenly become detached, fixed at a precise moment in time and suspended in space – looking down on herself, Charlotte, Angelica and now Myles, the latest member of the family, and Bosco's great-grandson, too.

Beside her Adam coughed and abruptly sat down. Rachel glanced at him anxiously but he smiled and shook his head, pointing at his leg. He was tired of standing, he seemed to be saying, and she felt a moment of relief, but only a moment. Adam's health had deteriorated during the winter; his bouts of emphysema were more frequent and the times when she got up to him in the night came more often.

She reached down and took his hand, holding it for the rest of the ceremony.

Back at the Hall Jenny and Jill, in between supervising a large number of women who had come back from the village to help, were busy buttering scones at the kitchen table. Jenny always liked to do her own baking for these occasions, although Hugo was quite willing to employ a firm of caterers. Jenny made work for herself; but she liked it. She wanted to show the family that she, too, had talents, if only modest, yet sufficient to make her worthy of a place in their midst.

Despite having been married to Hugo for seven years and borne him two children Jenny had the same inferiority complex about her husband's family that she had when she, as the lover of Ralph Askham, became aware that he was an earl, the owner of one of the great country homes of England. Even then it had been too late to give him up even had she wished. He wouldn't let her.

But Rachel had no more approved of Jenny then than she had when Ralph had been the object of her affections. It was only gradually, and fairly recently, that Rachel's attitude had changed and she had not only acepted her but begun to feel real affection for her; it was too soon to call it love.

Jenny had worked very hard for Rachel's approval and, with it, that of all the family; yet when at last it came it didn't seem as important as it would have some years before. It had seemed to her, then, that she had a natural right to her place in the sun beside Hugo; that she should have had it all the time and that this habit of the Askham family of distancing itself from people they considered inferior, though it was largely unconscious, should stop. It was high time it stopped in this post-war world with its egalitarian values.

She knew why it was: inherent snobbery. They'd had it towards Cheryl, her and now she saw it at work again with Dick; subtle, but there. She'd seen Dick change, too. He'd shaved off his beard, he wore clothes Angelica had had made for him in Savile Row, he'd begun to talk in a different way, his attractive Lancashire accent less and less noticeable. Gradually the Askhams were taking over; once again, they were winning.

Jill and Jenny had only met a few times but they got on. Jill Langley had been in the WAAF in the war, in charge of NAAFI supplies, and she was extremely good at managing other people's lives. She was a woman of pleasing but nondescript appearance that one easily forgot. Few people meeting her casually would have looked at her twice. She'd worked for Arthur since he first started in the City, after they were both demobbed, though she hadn't known him before. She'd got her job, however, because of RAF recommendations and Arthur had been a good and generous employer.

Jill was one of those people always used to being second best, or even third or fourth best. She knew that she was someone whose role in life was to serve others. She was here, there and everywhere, the kind of woman no successful man feels able to do without. She lived in a semi-detached house in Surbiton with an aged aunt and the company of two cats. She seemed, to all intents and purposes, a woman who, all her life, would take a back seat and wouldn't mind. She was the very antithesis of Charlotte Crewe.

Jill glanced at the clock on the kitchen wall and observed to Jenny that the ceremony would be nearly over.

'Do you wish you'd gone?' she added.

'Not a bit,' Jenny said, popping her head into the oven to look at the latest batch of cakes. 'I absolutely loathe these family occasions.'

'You surprise me.' Jill deftly split a dozen scones and spread them with butter just as quickly, piling them neatly on to plates. 'I would have thought you enjoyed them.'

'They always make me realize I'm not an Askham,' Jenny held up her head and smiled, wiping the sweat from her brow with the back of her arm and leaving in its place a white floury smudge. 'You know what I mean, in the sense that anyone belonging to the family is an Askham.'

'But you are,' Jill looked puzzled. 'You're Hugo's wife. He's an Askham.'

'Only half. You know, of course, that Hugo was Charlotte's father's natural son?'

Jill nodded, tactfully bending her head to her task.

'But they've always accepted him, especially the girls, and Rachel has always been quite potty about Hugo. Not me, though.'

'Oh?' Jill had been trained not to gossip. As the personal secretary to an MP and possibly a future Cabinet Minister, one had to be very careful about listening to tittle-tattle, but in this instance she decided one couldn't just say nothing. It would be rude. One had at least to say 'oh?' as she had.

'Rachel never thought I was quite good enough. Rachel is "the" Lady Askham, you know, the matriarch, the cat's whiskers, however much she pretends otherwise.' Jenny turned around and opened the oven door again. 'Having said all that, it may surprise you to know that I'm very fond of her.'

Jill, used to the nuances of human emotions, had detected a hostility that did, indeed, surprise her. But she said, loyally, 'Oh, I'm sure everyone is. Mr Crewe is absolutely devoted to his mother-in-law.'

'And you're absolutely devoted to him.' Jenny looked across the table at Jill, who immediately became flustered.

'Me? Devoted? Not at all. I am an *employee* of Mr Crewe . . .'

'That's just what I meant.' Jenny, flustered herself, firmly shut the oven door. 'Please, *don't* misunderstand me. From what I hear I think the family is extremely lucky to have you . . .'

'Oh? Oh, I see. Yes.' Jill felt almost numb. Sometimes she wondered if the heart she felt she wore on her sleeve showed.

'There must have been about a hundred for tea,' Pascal said much later that day as he and Anna were preparing for bed.

'As many as that?' Anna sat in front of the dressing table mirror, examining her face very carefully, as she habitually did last thing at night before she cleansed it and after, looking for signs of age.

287

'Oh, easily,' Pascal removed his tie and shirt and came and stood behind her, one hand caressing her cheek.

'You're still as lovely, and as young.'

'Quite old,' Anna said. 'Nearly twenty-four.'

'Time . . .' Pascal began, but stopped. They'd only been married four months. It was too soon to start talking about a baby, a subject that Anna, because of experiences only a year before, always avoided. As an engaged and then married couple they'd discussed few of the important things in life.

Pascal was a rather shy new bridegroom, as if scarcely able to believe his luck. But in the church that day, holding young Myles in his arms, once Flora had finally relinquished him, he had felt a longing for paternity that was something quite new. He also realized he wanted something more: a home of his own, dogs, cats, the sort of things that made families. Lacking a domestic upbringing, he found he pined for it.

He and Anna had travelled most of the time since their marriage – the actual honeymoon was spent in Venice seeing Anna's grandmother and cruising on the Adriatic. After that they'd visited all the capitals of Europe, combining business with pleasure, interviewing the Askham agents. Now they'd gone back to the flat he had at the Hall so that his trip to work every day was a pleasant ten-mile drive through some of the prettiest rural scenery in England.

'Time to move,' Pascal said, gripping her shoulders. 'Time to get our own place. Don't you agree?'

'Oh, I do. *Darling!*' Anna spun round on her stool and clasped his hands. 'Oh, I'd love a place of our own. Can I go up and start looking?'

'Up?' Pascal gazed at her in surprise. 'Up where?'

'To town, of course. We don't want to live here, do we, Pascal?'

'I thought of moving out of the Hall, certainly, but not too far away. I saw a house . . .'

Anna gave a deep sigh and, putting her long fingers in a jar of cream scooped some out and lathered it on her face.

'Pascal, please don't talk about living in the *country*. I have no intention of living in the country, I can assure you.'

'But, darling . . .'

'No intention at all.' Anna carefully rubbed the cream into her skin and smoothed it over the surface, massaging it in. 'I'm not going to be a little country mouse, if that's what you think.'

'I never dreamt . . .'

'Well, what did you think?' She reached for a tissue and slowly began to wipe the thick greasy cream away. Then she would apply astringent to close up the pores.

'I thought, darling, that you knew I worked almost full-time down here, and that we should live near my place of work.'

'And, no doubt, that I should have a baby and keep dogs and cats, maybe a chicken or two?'

'Yes.' Pascal felt shy, now that his secret fantasy had been so transparent. 'That, too.'

'Well, put it out of your mind, Pascal, please. Just for now, anyway. I have *no* intention of living in the country or of having babies. I suppose all that business today put it into your head. Do you know what Angelica's going to do?'

Pascal nodded dumbly.

'She's going to stick it right in the arms of a nanny, forget about it and go back to work. And do *you* know what being a mother has done to Stefanie? Put her in a mental home. Did you see my poor brother's face today?

289

He's aged about a hundred years, with all the cares that marriage has brought on him.

'No, thank you. Not for me.'

'It needn't be like that, Anna darling.' Pascal sat dejectedly on the bed, still half-undressed, and stuck his hands in his pockets.

'It certainly needn't,' Anna patted the astringent on her face, looked again at it critically then applied a thin layer of moisturiser. 'And for me it's not going to be. I want to go back to work and I want a house in town.' She stood up and, coming over to him, draped herself on the bed beside him. She smelt delicious. Her clear, fair skin gleamed with a renewed vitality because of the rigorous cleansing it had had, and her thin nightie revealed more than it concealed by draping its folds over her bosom and disappearing into the cleavage between her legs. 'We make a perfect couple, Pascal,' she murmured. 'I could see people today looking at us and whispering, and oh, I had such dreams about us darling. Things we could do together, where we could go. And do you know, as I stood there looking at you by the font, I saw that picture of your father where he's standing by the Askham racing car, his helmet in his hand. Know the one I mean?' As Pascal nodded she put an arm round his neck. 'I thought, darling, why not let's go into business designing a Grand Prix Formula 1 car? You know you have the know-how and you'd love to. You could be the first driver, an ambition you've always had.'

'But Mother . . .'

'Would hate it. Don't I know it! She's *always* kept you back. Don't say it. But, Pascal, it's absurd, don't you see, to live in the past? The Askham saloon and coupé are perfect. They'll sell for years. There's nothing more you can do with that aspect now. I talked to Sasha about it and he says "yes". So, let's go for a racing car! Let's go

290

for a house in Kensington or St John's Wood. Let's go for
life and excitement before we're too old.'

'But Bobby forbade it.'

'Who's talking about Bobby being involved?'

'He'd have to be involved if we used the Askham name.
He'd have to know.'

'Let's design the car, raise some finance and then see
Bobby. He'll come round, you'll see.'

As she slid a hand suggestively round his waist he
melted. He knew that soon there would be the ultimate
in pleasure and satisfaction as he made love to her; and
tonight would be special because she wanted something.
She wanted to please him.

With that thought in mind everything else was suspended. It was no time to think of country cottages and
dogs and small babies at a moment like this.

Looking at her brother lying in his bed completely still,
deathly pale, Rachel thought back to the christening party
a few weeks before when, though she was happy, she had
been aware of a sense of foreboding that she couldn't
account for. The family had all been there, numerous,
happy except for poor Stefanie, but the news about her
was better and Sasha was expecting her home. With such
a large family everything could never be *completely* all
right. There was always something wrong somewhere but,
on the whole, things had been good. The newly-weds
seemed happy, and Angelica and Dick with their baby
were thought to be looking more relaxed together than
for some time.

Adam, with his favourite place in the sun on the terrace
at the Hall, had seemed the happiest of all. A kind of
glow of content emanated from him that quite a few
people remarked on.

But now he was ill, very ill indeed. A heart attack

complicated by his bad chest, the emphysema that had marred his later years.

Adam had always been a heavy smoker and, too late now, came the official statistics emphasizing the relationship between lung cancer, diseases of the chest and smoking. It was now thought to have been the cause of the death of George VI. Adam, at least, had lasted until he was seventy-eight, not a bad age to go by any standards.

But would he rally? He had before, ever since his chest had become a chronic problem. Was it possible to envisage life without a brother with whom she had been so closely involved and had shared so much? What would happen now if, once more, Rachel found herself alone? Anxiously Rachel leaned over him.

'Adam?' she said.

Adam's eyes flickered and he managed a wan smile.

'Still here, Rachel.'

'Don't be silly. You're going to get better.'

Adam drew in a deep breath and his lungs rattled like a set of rusty tin cans.

'That's what you think.'

'You have before.'

Adam grimaced, and as he spoke his voice grew stronger.

'Do you know, I was dreaming about Mel? We did have some happy years.'

'Of course you did, darling.' Rachel smoothed his bedclothes. This was the way dying people spoke. They knew.

'I was dreaming of Omdurman and the charge. Harry's death. Harry has been dead for over fifty years. Perhaps I'll see him soon. Did you ever think of that, Rachel? And think of the life we've had? The children? The pleasures? And the pain: Bosco, Flora, Freddie,

292

Ralph . . .' There was a catch in his voice and Rachel, feeling near to tears herself, gripped his hand.

'Don't, Adam, think only of the good things.'

'I did, I do. I was dreaming of the time when Mel and I were happy. I loved her very much.'

'I know.'

'For a long time.'

'I know that.'

'Longer than you think. I think I always remained a bit in love with Mel and that's why I made Margaret such a bad husband.' Adam sighed, and again his tubes played a cacophony in his chest.

'I thought that was because of Flora,' Rachel said gently, thinking he was improving a bit. Maybe there *was* hope.

'No, I loved Flora in a very different way. I don't think we ever would have married, you know, even if we could. I never felt at all carnal about Flora, not really. She never excited me; but I always felt a little something for Mel when I saw her. I even felt it at Anna and Pascal's wedding.'

'Did you really?' Rachel smiled. 'You old goat.'

'Oh, not like *that*. But she was a devilish fine woman, wasn't she, eh? At seventy-six, eh? I'm glad I saw her again.'

'Yes, she was devilish fine,' Rachel said lightly. 'Would you like to see her now?'

'Oh, no. That makes it sound too final.' Adam sighed. 'It's too far to come. I don't *want* to die, you know.'

'You won't die,' Rachel said, but that night she called Adam's childen – Susan in Paris, Christopher in Winchester, Giles in London and Flora, who was in Manchester, to come as quickly as they could.

Christopher Bolingbroke had never been a very inspiring figure: solid, worthy, these and other adjectives were applied to him but, in fact, he was a stereotype of the middle-class to which he belonged; the affluent middle-class who were supposed to be the bedrock of English society. Naturally, he and his half-sister, Flora, had never got on.

Christopher, part of Adam's first family, was now approaching his fiftieth birthday. His wife, Sylvia, was a pillar of the local community, an inveterate do-gooder, a magistrate and chairman of the Tory ladies, now that their two children had grown up.

That side of the Bolingbroke family had never mixed much with the rest of the clan, except for Sylvia, who had once longed to be part of it and was briefly befriended by Ralph's wife, Cheryl.

Sylvia was there with Christopher, looking suitably grave, as he demanded explicit details about his father's health. Why hadn't he been sent for before?

'I didn't think it necessary,' Rachel said. 'You can be sure I would have had I thought it was. But today, suddenly, I felt he wouldn't last long and I knew you would want to see him.'

By the next day Flora, Giles and Susan had arrived and Rachel was glad to see them. Christopher was heavy company. He was possibly the least favourite of her nephews and nieces and she had a good many. She had never really found anything in common with Christopher at all.

Giles Bolingbroke, now Dr Bolingbroke, got on with his half-brother quite well. They were a little alike, not only physically but in temperament. Giles had qualified as a doctor in Edinburgh and was now twenty-six. But there was not, and never had been, any altruistic motive about his decision to study medicine. He wanted to be a rich, respected man and medicine seemed as good a way as any of doing it. He hadn't liked the law and at school he excelled in sciences, so his career was carved out for him at an early age.

Giles knew it would be a long time before he reached the top, but he was working at it. He got posts in the best hospitals and cultivated the people who would help him. He used his family, especially the Askham side of it, as much as he could, doctors being notoriously snobbish. Thus he got posts in Thomas's, Guy's, St Mary's. He studied hard and he was doing well. He had his career planned until he was forty, when he expected to have achieved a full consultancy, rooms in Harley Street and, somewhere on the way, he would acquire a wife.

Giles had a look at his father from a professional point of view and he was able to confirm Rachel's prognosis: not good. He, too, wondered why they hadn't been called earlier and he and Christopher quizzed her as though she was trying to conceal a crime.

'I tell you I had no idea,' she said, 'the deterioration was very sudden.'

'Going slowly downhill, if you ask me.' Christopher's tone was reproachful. 'You might have let us know.'

Rachel looked at these two pompous, self-satisfied men with their accusatory eyes and felt like bursting into tears.

'Adam's my brother, you know,' she said. 'If you think you love him, well, let me tell you, I love him, too. I don't want him to die . . .'

Susan, who had been upstairs with her father, hearing raised voices as she was coming downstairs, rushed into the drawing-room just as Rachel buried her head in her hands.

'What on earth are you all squabbling about?' she cried. 'When Father . . .'

Rachel finally burst into tears and was about to rush from the room, but Susan stopped her, took her in her arms.

295

'I might have known it was them, Aunt Rachel. Forgive me?' She held her aunt back and, looking into her eyes, smilingly tried to wipe away the tears with a finger. For moment Rachel leaned her head on her breast and then she pressed the palms of her hands in her eyes, sniffed and looked up.

'They think I should have called you all before. I didn't *know* Adam was dying. I swear I didn't. I was telling them I loved him, too . . .'

'There's something we might have wanted to say to Father,' Christopher said accusingly.

'Say what, for instance?' Susan demanded.

Christopher shrugged. 'Anything. Who knows?'

'Did you actually want to tell Father he was dying?' Susan enquired.

'Of course not,' Christopher retorted crossly. 'But I haven't seen Father for a long time.'

'That's just the point, isn't it?' Susan said. 'You *never* visit him and then you have a go at Aunt Rachel. Too late for remorse, my man, which is what this is all about. You've neglected Father, Christopher, *and* you know it.'

'That's *not* true,' Christopher began. 'I . . .'

'When did you last see him?' Susan demanded, and Giles said:

'Oh, for heaven's sake, Susan, let's stop this. Father is dying and let's at least be civilized about it. Let's, for God's sake, have a drink.'

Flora wanted to say 'Daddy, don't die' but she knew it was useless. He was slipping away from her, on a journey that she knew now was irreversible. She, too, had been shocked at the change in her father since she'd seen him at the weekend but, unlike her brothers, she didn't blame Rachel.

Flora was glad to be alone for a few moments with the

man whom she had sometimes, in the past, regretted was her father – a man who was over fifty when she was born. When she was young and he was in his sixties she had rebelliously thought that people had no right to have children when they were old. She envied her friends with young parents who seemed little older than themselves. Fathers who played tennis and cricket, who swam and hunted. Adam had already been a High Court judge when she was born; well past those frivolities of youth. She and Giles were always told to be quiet so that their father could work, or read, or sleep. No wonder he was resented.

But, as she had got older, Flora had come to appreciate the qualities of her father; his great qualities of love, and wisdom. Sensing that Flora was different, a bookish, intellectual girl not blessed with the good looks of her cousins, he had given her more love, understanding and advice than maybe the average parent would be capable of. In these last years he had been so proud of her idealism, intellectual dedication and academic achievements that they had become very close indeed, and he would often reminisce with her about her namesake, Aunt Flora, who had been one of the first women to qualify for a degree at Cambridge.

The iniquity of those years, when women took the examinations of Oxford and Cambridge but were not awarded degrees; of the days of early feminism and the suffrage movement, had filled Flora with a desire to know more and, now that she was able to, to do something to avenge what Aunt Flora and Aunt Rachel went through. She became a student of feminism, an early adherent of the women's liberation movement.

Flora reached for his hand, which lay limply on the sheet slightly curled up, though powerless. Now that dear friend, the closest person to her on earth, would no longer

297

be able to help and counsel her, moderate her headstrong views, encourage her when she wanted to make a stand. Even her Communism he had understood because he knew that, for her, it arose not from devotion to party dogma but out of compassion and concern for those who were less fortunate in life; the two-thirds of the world who didn't have enough to eat and drink, the ill-educated, unenlightened masses. She knew that, in her father's day, he had been a rebel, too, had helped the poor and defended the weak.

Dear friend, dear father . . . Flora leaned her head on his palm and wet it with her tears; but still there came no response, no glimmer of life.

After a while she felt a hand on her shoulder and, instinctively, her own hand reached to close over it. Rachel, Aunt Rachel – mother and father to her now.

'Oh, Aunt Rachel,' she said and, as Rachel knelt beside her she threw her arms around her while her aunt did her best to comfort her, needing comfort herself.

Then together they kept a vigil by his bed and, a few hours later, with his family gathered round him, Adam Bolingbroke died.

CHAPTER 12

Joy and sorrow always seemed to follow each other throughout her long life, Rachel thought as she rode behind the coffin to the church. Adam was to be buried at Darley and the church was only a short way from the manor. It was, in a way, a relief for her that his interment was not to take place at that church so long associated with the Askhams though, inevitably, they would not lie together in death. But Adam had been quite specific in his will. He was not an Askham and he didn't want to lie in the family vault. He wanted his own plot of earth near the house where he'd lived some of the best, most tranquil years of his life, and what he'd wanted he got.

All the villagers gathered on either side of the main street, heads bowed in sympathy, some in tears, as long as the funeral procession passed by. They were then to drive ten miles to Askham to a reception at the Hall.

Only a month ago they had all gathered for the christening of Myles Crosby, great-grandson of Dulcie, and it was of Dulcie that Rachel thought as the coffin halted before the church and the vicar came out to greet it.

A month before Dulcie had died there had been a jolly celebration at Christmas. Before Bosco had been killed it had been Christmas, too; before Adam's second wedding, Flora's death, before Ralph met his end, the birth of Johnny.

Adam's children were the chief mourners, led by Susan and Christopher, who went into the church immediately after the coffin. Rachel followed with Flora leaning heavily on her arm. Flora had taken her father's death very

299

badly and Rachel knew it was because she felt she was alone in the world. Adam had been a very good friend to her as well as a father in these last few years while Flora had wrestled, with much difficulty, with life. Some people aways found things easy but Flora always seemed to find them hard. Adam understood her and loved her just because she was that little bit different, a little unusual even in a family accustomed to eccentricity.

Rachel would have to be father as well as mother to her now. Sometimes she felt responsibilities weighing heavily on one who, by her time of life, would have hoped to have shed most of them.

Adam was buried in the grounds of the church beside Margaret, his wife, who had died twenty-two years before. Only the family gathered round the grave and they included Spencer Foster, Margaret's brother, who had not seen Rachel since he'd gone to live in Preston. He scarcely ever came south.

After the interment Giles drove Spencer, Rachel and Flora over to the Hall and Rachel thought how strange it was to be sitting again next to the man who so nearly became her husband. Would it have made a lot of difference to her life if he had? Yes, she would have had that support which married people give to each other in a way that other people couldn't. That understanding born of mutual, intimate love. She and Spencer had drifted apart; there had been no dramatic break-up, no violent rows. They stopped sleeping together and then they stopped seeing each other, but over a long period of time. Each just faded out of the other's life. It was better that way. Now to her he was a dear familiar, part of the family, someone she knew and understood; who knew and understood her. In fact in many ways Spencer felt a disappointed man. Despite his political ambition, he had never achieved high office, he had never married or had children. He was a man of moderate means who lived on his own, his life haunted by memories, one of the most poignant of which was Rachel.

Rachel on the other hand, had led a crowded life, and did so still; one bursting, full to overflowing with achievements. She had been one of the first women in the country to own a newspaper; she had been a leader of the suffragette movement; she had known and influenced many of the leading politicians of the times, including all the prime ministers between the wars. Her personal life had been full, too. She had had four children, adopted a fifth, brought up an orphaned grandson and her brother's two motherless children. She had fought, coped and carried the day.

'You really look marvellous, Rachel,' Spencer said, as they sat on the terrace outside the Hall. It was October, but an Indian summer and still warm enough to sit out of doors. Spencer's hand enclosed hers. For a moment she let it rest and then gently she moved hers away, not rudely but as though it were a natural thing to do, and joined hers together on her lap.

'I feel I've aged recently,' she said, touching her hair and flicking a stray wisp in with the rest.

'Adam's death wasn't such a shock, surely? You kept him alive.'

'It was a shock at the end. Death, in my experience, always is. I thought he was going to recover and then he rapidly declined and lapsed into a coma. The doctor said it was his heart. For so long it had had to strain, coping with his lungs. I shall miss Adam, you know, Spencer. We have been very close all our lives. We grew up and we've grown old together. There was only a year between us. I don't think a brother and sister could ever have been as close as we were.'

'He owed you a lot,' Spencer nodded.

'And I owed *him*! He gave me stability, a home . . .'

Rachel stopped and, as Spencer looked her, her brow furrowed and she looked troubled.

'What is it?'

'Well,' Rachel nervously touched her hair again, sighed and leaned back. 'It's Adam's will, as a matter of fact. He has left everything to Christopher, including the manor. I must say *that* was quite a shock. I didn't want any money, of course. I didn't need any. But Darley has been my home for over twenty years.'

'But Christopher wouldn't kick you out. He can't possibly *want* it, can he? He has a home of his own.'

'Exactly. That's what Em and Charlotte say. But we have never really got on, you know. We even had a row the other night. Christopher accused me of not calling Adam's children to his bedside early enough. He was most unpleasant about it. You see, Adam hadn't made a will since Margaret's death. His first action when she died was to ensure the future of his two young children, Flora only a baby. That was before I agreed to go and live with him. It wasn't even thought of. For a year or so Adam coped with nannies and such like. Then, of course, I had to leave Askham House because of Cheryl and Ralph, so it all fitted in. Adam had by that time made his will, leaving everything to Christopher in trust for his younger children. Susan, of course, was well provided for. Adam was never a wealthy man and the manor was his main asset. He gave it to Chistopher to make a home for his younger children until they should be twenty-one. Of course they're both over twenty-one now and have no need of a home.'

'What an extraordinary will.'

'The odd thing was that he never made another. For a lawyer it does seem extraordinary . . .'

'But didn't you ever think of it?'

'Why should *I*?' Rachel looked at him wryly. 'It never occurred to *me*. He was a lawyer. I think it did occur to Christopher, who knew the contents of the will but, not unnaturally, he had no desire to change them.'

'What a swine.'

'I think many solicitors are slightly dishonest,' Rachel said. 'They can't help it, especially if they have a vested interest. They have such power. Adam was a barrister, not a solicitor, and he was never a man who thought much about himself. But Christopher *is* greedy and Christopher worries me.' She turned to Spencer and, even after all this time, his heart turned over at that clear, penetrating, thoughtful gaze. 'You see, Spencer, without the manor I have no home.'

Ross Glencarran had rapidly become absorbed by and in the family to which he was only tenuously related by blood. Since Anna's wedding he had been a pretty regular attender at family functions. His main interest in the family was his cousin, Natasha Lighterman, who was the same age as Flora, twenty-two; but as unlike her as it was possible to be. Natasha was not only extremely beautiful but her looks were of a kind so rare that, as soon as she finished at drama school, she was offered parts. She had the fair hair, blue eyes, dark brows of her mother, Hélène, and the air of tragedy of that poor woman seemed to have been inherited by her youngest daughter, who turned it to to good advantage. She was quickly given major parts, especially the doomed heroines of plays by Russian and Scandinavian masters. She had a very faint foreign accent because of her years in France, her use of the Russian tongue, that was very alluring, and Ross quickly fell under her spell and sought her out wherever he could. But she was not easy to find, or easy to get. She had inherited her father's shrewdness and was too

303

ambitious to fall for a young doctor from the Antipodes who had grown up on a farm.

But though it was easy to dismiss Ross in this way it was also wrong. He was thirty and had studied in Vienna as well as America. He was not going to be an ordinary run-of-the-mill doctor, but he had set his sights high. He was a neurologist and, like a famous neurologist before him, he was thinking of changing his discipline. Sigmund Freud had turned from neurology to psychiatry after his experiences at the Salpêtrière hospital in Paris, and Ross had an inclination to do the same and transfer from the Hammersmith to the Maudsley in London, the Institute of Psychiatry.

He was fascinated by deviant personalities, which was why he took such an interest in Natasha's sister, Stefanie and, because of Stefanie, Natasha came to see a lot of Ross and liked him.

Natasha, though sympathetic, had managed to detach herself from the predicament of her eldest sister. Although artistic and imaginative, Natasha was a rather tough, sensible young woman, who neither suffered from guilt about their mother, nor chagrin for the past.

Ross and Natasha naturally gravitated towards each other whenever there were family gatherings, and there were many.

Now he was standing on the terrace recently vacated by Spencer and Rachel, looking at the landscape, when Natasha joined him. He smiled at her as she emerged from the French windows, a bewitching figure in a black silk dress, rather décolleté, and black stockings. On her, mourning became high fashion. Although they were not intimate Ross reached out to take her arm; and they sat together on one of the old ornate iron benches that the perfectionist Hugo had rescued from the shed, where he had found them, and done them up, scraping and revarnishing them himself. Hugo was an industrious man, who never sat still, though he had a hard job making a dent in what still needed to be done at the Hall.

'I was thinking,' Ross said once they were seated, 'that, had things been different, my grandfather would have inherited all this and I might not be here. My grandmother was always very bitter about it.'

'Didn't he die young?' Natasha enquired, wrinkling her nose.

'Yes, he died of polio in the States in 1904. He was Bosco's elder brother. Bosco then inherited the title and married Rachel. He might not have married *her* if Arthur hadn't died. Who knows?'

'Who knows anything,' Natasha agreed in that low vibrant voice, tuned to mellow perfection after her years at RADA. 'My own life is witness to that. Did I tell you I might have a part in the West End?'

'That's marvellous,' Ross said, turning excitedly to her. 'How did that happen?'

'A producer I know has been asked to do a play. Like me, he's only worked in the provinces. If he is successful he wants to cast me, not in the lead, but with a very good role. It's a play about the war, about the Resistance, and I should be playing a character not unlike my mother or Charlotte.'

'Would you like that?'

'Yes.' Natasha nodded. As the youngest she had assimilated what had happened to her mother, to her family, more easily than her sisters. That early upbringing greatly influenced her adult life in an opposite way to Stefanie, as she was seldom permanently upset by anything.

Ross was very interested in the reactions of the sisters to the experiences of the war and before, when their lives changed after their father divorced their mother. Natasha's imperturbability was remarkable. He felt that

305

she sublimated her experiences through her love of the theatre, her ability to lose herself in her roles.

Ross knew that, more and more, he was being inextricably involved in the fate of Natasha and her family. He welcomed it. He was glad she might be coming to London.

Rachel left the Hall early with Spencer, Flora and Charlotte. Arthur had to go north on urgent business and Jill was meeting him at Paddington to put him on the right train at Euston.

'Marvellous to have Jill,' Charlotte said, 'she takes care of everything.'

Rachel felt, rather like Melanie, that Jill took care of a good deal too much, that Arthur was very dependent upon her; but she supposed she and Melanie were old-fashioned, maybe narrow-minded. No one could suppose that Arthur would ever look at another woman when he had a wife like Charlotte whom he had adored for so many years.

Still, Rachel thought as she sat at the back of Charlotte's car, she and Arthur *were* drifting apart. They never seemed to be in the same place together and Charlotte was beginning to develop her own life, her own interests, while Arthur was more and more submerged in being a junior member of the government. Watching Charlotte's profile from her seat at the back as she skilfully manoeuvred the large family 'Askham' along the narrow roads, Rachel thought that Charlotte was more beautiful than ever, maturity giving her a poise and serenity she hadn't had as a young woman.

'I'm so glad we came away,' Rachel said. 'I didn't feel like the family party, for once. I would just like to have slipped back to the manor on our own.'

'I wish Em could have come,' Charlotte murmured. 'Then we should have been truly together.'

Ever since the death of Ralph Charlotte knew that she and Em were her mother's mainstay. The three of them seemed somehow invincible.

'Em has got to sort something out with Felipe about Luis.' Rachel sounded worried. 'That boy is becoming a recluse there all the time with his father. It can't be healthy. I think Em should put her foot down and I told her we would support her.'

'How *can* she put her foot down?' Charlotte was worried, too. 'Adam used to say she could take Felipe to court; but she was against it. Oh, what *shall* we do without him? His wise counsel?'

And his companionship. But Rachel didn't say it. Adam had been the man in her life since the death of Bosco: a husband in name only. She had lived with him since Margaret had died. She had never lived with Spencer; shared a bed but not a home and, in a way, Spencer had been jealous of Adam.

Still, it was good to have Spencer next to her now, his solid, reassuring presence. As Flora's uncle, Adam's brother-in-law, he was family; as her ex-lover something more. Yet Spencer had come for the sake of Flora more than her, she knew. He had told her how worried he was about Flora alone in the world; but Rachel had assured him her niece wasn't alone; she had a huge protective family round her.

How good it was to be back at the manor, she thought, as Charlotte turned through the wrought-iron gates and up the short round drive to the house. It was part Tudor, part Jacobean, nestling in a valley formed by two hills which gently sloped on either side, greenswards, one of them covered with trees.

The manor now had been the place where she'd lived longest, except for her parents' home in Bath which, officially, she hadn't abandoned until her marriage, though she had hardly ever lived there after her girlhood.

The manor was a dear, familiar place, an enduring link with Adam, and there on the doorstep were the small staff dressed in mourning, like her, waiting to greet her.

'Welcome home, Lady Askham.' Mrs Berridge, the housekeeper, and the two maids each gave a small bob and Berridge the butler bowed low. Rachel was followed by Charlotte and then Flora and Spencer, all of whom shook hands with the staff. Berridge said he had taken the liberty of putting sherry in the drawing-room and asked what time her ladyship would like dinner, and would Lady Charlotte and Mr Foster be staying? It was all very comforting, timeless, enduring, all the things that were considered out of fashion but which the Askhams stood for.

Flora didn't join them in the drawing-room but went up to her room, saying she wanted to be alone. Rachel understood this need for privacy in grief. She knew how alone Flora felt, even though she had the love and support of the family. Nothing ever replaced a parent, ever.

Charlotte stayed for a few days with her mother. Em came over on the second day having got nowhere with Felipe over Luis. Luis had stood silent and withdrawn to one side as they'd argued, she said, saying nothing, showing no emotion. It was very worrying. She, too, felt it was like a bereavement, as though she had finally lost her son. She, too, felt alone in the world. That tall, grave young man, now sixteen years old, had seemed to her no longer her son but a stranger.

On the third day Spencer took Flora back to London on his way north. The family was dispersing, splitting up. Things were returning to normal except that for Rachel, without Adam, as without Bosco, they would never be normal again.

Charlotte was reluctant to leave her mother. Although she was a grandmother she sometimes felt like a small girl in need of a mother's love and advice. She felt anxious about Angelica, worried about Pascal, concerned about Joe. Rachel had an analytical gift that seemed to enable her to separate problems into their component parts, so that when one fitted them all together again one saw them differently. It helped Rachel to return to normality, this talk about her grandchildren. Once removed she was able to see them more objectively than Charlotte. They discussed the problems in the drawing-room after dinner.

'But Angelica and Dick seemed delighted with Myles. I think you worry too much about them, their differences. That is sometimes the mainspring of passion, you know.'

'Oh, I think they're still in love,' Charlotte said. 'They're still sexually attracted; but Dick has started to hit out at Angelica. He wants her to change her life, be more domestic. He says he'd like to apply for a job at Oxford or Cambridge and settle down.'

'Seems like a good idea!'

'It's anathema to Angelica. Gérard wants her to work exclusively for him. It's a tremendous honour. She wants to resume her career full-time.'

'I'm sure they'll sort something out. I like Dick. He's sensible.'

But still, they were an incongruous couple, there was no doubt of that – Dick withdrawn, scholarly, grave; Angelica rather superficial, bubbling over with laughter, conversation, ideas, every bit as beautiful as her mother and, somehow, more so now that she was a mother, too.

'I hope they'll have more children,' Rachel said. 'Children are a bond.'

She gazed for a few moments at Charlotte, sensing she, too, was not happy.

But would she talk about the real cause of her unhappiness or would she go on pretending it was the children? Children who were all over twenty-one and well able to look after themselves. Rachel felt that Charlotte used them as a cloak for her real worries about Arthur. 'And why on *earth* should you worry about Pascal?' Rachel continued after a moment. 'I understood that he and Anna . . .'

'Pascal wants to concentrate on the car,' Charlotte said anxiously, 'expand the works here. Bobby is trying to draw him into a larger managerial role.'

'But surely, that's Sasha's job?' Rachel seemed surprised.

'Exactly.' Charlotte looked grim. 'Pascal thinks Bobby has lost confidence in Sasha. All this worry over Stefanie had drained Sasha. Bobby now says he never was a businessman and had to be cajoled into the job.'

'That's true,' Rachel murmured. 'Another person who is doing something he didn't really want to do. Like Pascal, he'd rather be with cars or aeroplanes, preferably the latter.'

'Sasha *is* Pascal's brother-in-law. Pascal would never be disloyal to him. Anyway, he's not interested in the wider aspects of the business. On the other hand, Anna would like him to be. She is anything but happy to settle down in the country. She and Angelica are rather alike.'

'They shared a flat. They got on well,' Rachel said. 'Joe now . . .'

'Joe feels that Em isn't giving him enough to do. She's keeping him down.'

'She doesn't want to *seem* to favour him,' Rachel said. 'That I do approve of.'

'Yes, but you favoured *her*, didn't you, Mother? I mean you gave her preferment. Be honest.'

'But she was very good at what she did,' Rachel said defensively. 'She was a first-class correspondent. Look

310

what she did in Germany. Even Hilter was frightened of her.'

'But Joe is first-class, too. Em is always saying how pleased she is with him, yet all he is is a reporter.'

'He writes a few leaders.'

'He would like to be deputy editor.' Charlotte looked defiantly at her mother, knowing that if anyone had control over Em it was she. Yet Rachel could be pig-headed too, like Em. Maybe Rachel thought that Joe should be kept down.

'I am against nepotism,' Rachel said. 'In the thirties it was different. The paper was smaller. Now, since the War, we have become a national paper with national responsibilities. Em is a first-class editor, well known, well respected and well thought of. If she appoints her nephew as her *deputy* you can imagine what people will say, however capable Joe is. Personally, darling, I think Joe should leave the paper for a while and get experience elsewhere, say in America. His is only twenty-five. Then, when he returns, he will be better qualified to be Em's deputy.' Rachel looked at her daughter, who was only doing what she had done many times in her life, interven-ing on behalf of her offspring. Yet this time she knew she was right; she was trying to be impartial. In this way she would help Joe better than putting pressure on Em to do something she didn't want to do.

In a way, Charlotte also knew that her mother was right. But she knew Joe was unhappy and she didn't want to lose him now that her two elder children had fled the nest and Jeremy was at boarding-school. On the many nights that Arthur wasn't at home Charlotte enjoyed a quiet dinner and natter with Joe, whose views on every-thing were so balanced and informed. Had he not been related to the Askhams he *would* have been a very good deputy on *The Sentinel* regardless of age. On the other hand, it didn't seem to prevent Bobby offering his twin advancement to a very senior level in the Lighterman empire.

Charlotte was still thinking how to reply to Rachel when Berridge came in and, with a discreet cough, announced that Christopher had come to see his aunt.

'Mr Bolingbroke?' Rachel jumped up. 'Do show him in.'

Rachel hardly had a chance to glance at Charlotte, never mind convey any of her foreboding, as Christopher followed Berridge in, going over perfunctorily to kiss his aunt, then Charlotte. This in itself was unusual. Christopher wasn't a kisser.

'What a nice surprise,' Rachel tried to sound sincere. 'Have you eaten?'

'Yes thanks, Aunt.' Christopher looked at his watch. 'I apologize for the hour, but I felt I had to come and see you.'

Rachel felt disturbed. It was nine o'clock in the evening and it was rather late for a visit. 'Is it something about the will?'

'In a way, it is.' Christopher waited for Berridge to leave the room, gently closing the double doors of the drawing-room behind him. 'Sylvia and I have come to a decision and we feel you ought to know it as soon as possible.'

'You want me to leave the manor,' Rachel said, standing where she had stood since Christopher came into the room. She hadn't moved.

'Well,' Christopher looked taken back. 'Not immediately, not now, but when you can, yes. How did you know?'

'I guessed. Something told me, as soon as I knew Adam had left it to you, that you would want to come and live here.'

'But you have no *right*!' Charlotte burst out. 'This is *Mother's* home. It has been for years.'

'I'm afraid, legally, it's mine, Charlotte,' Christopher said in his pompous solicitor's manner, not even trying to look apologetic.

'You *know* that your father would have meant Mother to live here. He couldn't *possibly* have wished otherwise!'

'Nevertheless, he didn't say so. He didn't make another will, so that must have been his wish: that the will he had made when Margaret died stood. I did want to ask father if he had made another will or wished to make one, but I never got the chance. Your mother never indicated how ill he was.'

Charlotte gave what, to Rachel, sounded like a very rude and uncharacteristic laugh of pure derision.

'Oh, that *is* funny, Christopher. Do you expect *anyone* to believe that? Your father has been a sick man for a long time; for years. Now you say you never had the chance. I call that *most* amusing!'

'Charlotte, *please*.' Rachel felt rather shocked at her daughter voicing what could only be interpreted as an implication of deliberate malice on Christopher's part. Yet what else could one think?

'Mother, don't be naïve,' Charlotte retorted. 'Christopher was Uncle Adam's lawyer. He knew quite well the contents of the will and that there was no other. Why did he have to wait until Uncle's death-bed to ask if he wanted to change it?'

'Because *I* didn't know if he was going to die.' Christopher's voice, too, had risen. 'I'm not omniscient. I didn't want to alarm him. Anyway, that's not the point. I resent Charlotte's implication that I deliberately . . .'

'Well, I think you did *deliberately*, if you want my opinion,' Charlotte put her hand on her hip and leaned slightly forward. 'You wanted this place whatever the consequences to Mother.'

'I did *not* want this place.' Christopher had begun to shout. 'It never entered my mind.'

'Well, I *don't* believe you,' Charlotte shouted back, advancing towards her cousin.

'Please, please, *please*,' Rachel kept her voice very low, a contrast to the other two. 'This must not develop into a brawl.' Slowly she sat down and put her feet neatly together, her head on one side. Suddenly she seemed like an old lady, but her voice was firm. 'Whatever the rights or wrongs, and I am quite prepared to believe Christopher acted from the best motives, this *is* his house. He has every right to ask me to leave and I shall, whenever he wants.'

'It's just that it would be very convenient, Aunt Rachel,' Christopher's tone was conciliatory. 'It is a nice house, larger than we have now and only ten miles from town. My practice is expanding and it would do my image good.'

'Your *image!*' Charlotte spat out, but Rachel raised a hand.

'No insinuations, please, Charlotte. You can only make matters worse, not better. Whatever you say, do you think I would continue to stay here for a moment longer, knowing that Christopher wants his home?'

'But it's *your* home.'

'Technically it is his.' Rachel paused and, almost immediately, the old-lady look vanished and she became her usual self: brisk and matter-of-fact. 'When would you like me to vacate Darley, Christopher?'

Arthur peered into the mirror of Charlotte's dressing-table as he undid his tie. He had flown from Paris and looked, and felt, tired. Charlotte, lying in bed, watched

314

him. He would take his tie and jacket off in her room then go through into his dressing-room and remove the rest of his clothes. Often at nights when he came home they had a little chat about the day, then they said good night. Since Pascal's marriage they had had separate bedrooms. There was so much space in the house it seemed pointless not to, as Arthur said. He also hated waking Charlotte up after late-night sittings. Ever since the war Charlotte had been a poor sleeper and this could be construed as considerate of him. Anyway, upper-class people were accustomed, by tradition, to their separate bedrooms and Arthur and Charlotte were indubitably upper-class.

Or was it politic? Charlotte never knew. She had slept alone for so much of her life that she didn't really mind. In many ways she was thankful.

Charlotte had never considered herself in love with Arthur. She had seldom enjoyed sex with him, except on some occasions during the war when they were lovers and danger added zest and excitement, as it had with Marc, her wartime lover, with Paolo, her racing-driver husband. She thought she was the sort of woman who needed danger and excitement to add spice to a rather basic distaste she had for sex, something she had never really wanted to analyse or discuss. She had only ever slept with three men in her life: her two husbands and Marc, though she knew her mother thought she'd had affairs before her marriage. But she hadn't.

Paolo and Marc had reconciled her to sex, but a peacetime marriage to Arthur had confirmed her lack of interest in it and she'd repulsed him as often as she could. Since he'd been in the House, Arthur had seemed to lose his desire for it, too. It was very rarely he returned to her room and asked if he could come to bed with her. He always asked. Arthur was so nice, so correct that it would have seemed churlish to refuse, and they went through the ritual of intercourse, the most intimate act men and women were capable of, more or less out of politeness.

But after nine years of marriage Charlotte was used to Arthur. In her way she loved him. He was a very nice man. The family had always said that. He was considerate, thoughtful and he worshipped Charlotte. He had wooed her for years before she married him. Now he had made something of himself: a life in the City, in the House of Commons. He was a very worthy man to be the husband of an Askham, and the family relied on Arthur a good deal, and knew they would more than ever now that Adam was dead.

Arthur wandered around Charlotte's room before sitting on her bed, his tie in his hand.

'That's an absolutely fiendish thing Christopher has done to your mother,' he said. 'Can't we fight it, do anything about it?'

'She doesn't want us to.' Charlotte looked at him gravely.

'Would she like me to talk to him?'

'No, I don't think so. Thanks all the same.' Charlotte touched his arm. Yes, she was fond of Arthur, who could not be?

'Then what's she going to do?'

'Well, Hugo wants to have her, of course. But she feels rootless. I think I can understand it. She's always been pushed out of places. Granny never wanted her at the Hall.'

'*And* she had a right to be there,' Arthur murmured. 'It was her home.'

'Exactly. Rather the situation you would think Christopher would feel he was in. Mother wouldn't have *dreamt* of asking Gran to leave the Hall. I only wish she could get back the Grange.' Charlotte pursed her lips. 'Now that's something I *do* feel strongly about. Felipe has lived there like a pariah for *seventeen* years. In that time we have hardly ever seen him, although we keep him. What's more, he has kept Em's son from her. The whole family has supported him when we ourselves were short of a bob or two. I really do detest Felipe.'

Arthur got up and began pacing the room again.

'Perhaps I should speak to Felipe?'

'What could you say?'

'Might threaten?'

'Yes, but what could you actually *do*? I mean, would we take him to court? No, we would not. We wouldn't want the stink, to remind everyone that Em and Felipe were never married. Em would hate it and so would I.'

'You're right,' Arthur said, sitting down again on her bed. 'Your mother will have to go to the Hall. She likes Jenny and Hugo.'

'She loves them.'

'Well, then?'

As Charlotte gazed enigmatically at him Arthur thought how ethereally beautiful she was, her white nightie lending her an air of wax-like purity; untouchable, curiously asexual. Sometimes intercourse with Charlotte seemed like an act of violence; like rape.

'I wondered if she could come to us?' Charlotte said eventually. 'We have plenty of room.'

Charlotte realized then that she wanted her mother more than her husband.

But her suggestion appeared to upset Arthur and he got up to resume his pacing. He would never deny Charlotte anything, never criticize her mother or her family, but Charlotte could see from the expression on his face that he wasn't pleased.

'Oh, well,' she said, 'it was just an idea.'

'You see Charlotte, I . . . I like Rachel. I love her; but

317

on the whole I am against parents living with their children, unless it's absolutely necessary, and in this case it isn't. The Hall is huge; Hugo adores your mother. She loves the country. She's near the Grange. It seems absolutely ideal.'

'Yes, I suppose it does,' Charlotte said slowly. 'I think perhaps you're right, Arthur. It was only a suggestion. I never discussed it with Mother.'

'Believe me, dear, the Hall *is* the best idea.'

'Perhaps you're right.'

Charlotte watched Arthur pick up his coat from the back of one of the chairs and his tie which he'd slung over it.

'Arthur, there's just one thing,' she said tentatively, feeling inexplicably nervous. After all, she wasn't afraid of Arthur.

'What's that, Charlotte?' Arthur said, looking at her kindly.

'Would you mind awfully if I took a job?'

'A job?' Arthur said in the tone of voice that indicated he had very little idea what she was talking about.

'I thought I'd be rather good as a vendeuse in a frightfully smart couturier showroom. Gérard is to open up in Bond Street. He'd like me to work for him, too. It would be very smart.'

'*Vendeuse*,' Arthur said, savouring the word. '*Vendeuse?* Isn't that a saleswoman?'

'A very pukka saleswoman,' Charlotte said, with a faint blush, 'and only to the most exclusive clientele. Gérard worked for Chanel before the War. I know him quite well.'

'No,' Arthur said, firmly. 'No, definitely not. You don't need the money and he just wants your name.'

'But I'd enjoy it . . .' Charlotte's voice trailed off. She knew when she had lost a case with Arthur.

'If you want to do something there are many good causes which need a person like you, on a voluntary basis, your name on the letter heading, that kind of thing. But a saleswoman . . .' Arthur raised an eyebrow. 'I'm *most* surprised at you, Charlotte.'

'Very well, dear,' Charlotte nodded, the obedient wife, and Arthur knew that would be the end of the matter. He leaned forward and kissed her on the brow of her head.

'Good night, dear.'

'Good night, Arthur.'

Charlotte waited until he had left the room and then leaned over and switched off the light.

She knew he would not be back that night.

CHAPTER 13

All winter Pascal and Sasha worked secretly on the design of the new Formula 1 Askham 'Phoenix', which name was added to denote a car, famous in the twenties and thirties, rising from the ashes. It may have seemed inspired but perhaps it was not a very good idea to name it after that mythical bird and, had they talked about it, they might have been dissuaded; but for many months the new car was top secret. Only three people – Sasha, Pascal and Anna – knew of its existence apart from a few of the most trusted workers at the factory, who had been sworn to secrecy.

Motor racing had perhaps reached its zenith in the twenties and thirties with great names such as Tazio Nuvolari, Hermann Lang, Prince Bira, Jules Goux and, at the very beginning until his death in 1931, Paolo Verdi.

Before the war the Grand Prix racing car had been a formidable product, a combination of speed and efficiency, its acceleration very fast. Such machines had, however, been costly and Hitler and Mussolini, anxious to foster national prestige by means of motor racing, had made available to a number of manufacturers large sums of money to build up and operate such powerful cars.

After the war racing was revived by the French in September.1945 in the Bois de Boulogne. A new Grand Prix formula was announced in 1946 specially to cater for the prevailing depressed post-war situation. Impoverished Europe was having a hard time even getting ordinary motor cars into production.

The new controlling body, the FIA, arranged for two

very different types of car to compete together; a car of not over 1½ litres supercharged, or not over 4½ litres without supercharger. It meant that expensive super-charged engines could be paced against the big capacity power units and Britain was extremely interested in this formula, having been concentrating on *voiturette* racing from 1934 onwards. It had produced innovators of genius like Geoffrey Taylor, who produced the Alta from a small factory similar to the Askham works, and millionaire Tony Vandervell, who hired Colin Chapman to design the Vanwall which was to win several Grand Prix races.

Pascal Verdi was in this small, exclusive entrepreneurial company of classy designers who were not limited to England. Maserati had been set up just to make racing cars; Lancia came in in 1954 and the famous firm of Bugatti was preparing to re-enter Grand Prix racing. Men who designed racing cars had to be technicians, engineers and innovators of great talent and they also had to have that overwhelming drive and ambition to succeed in a very competitive market.

Pascal had wanted to race cars ever since he was a small boy, and that famous photo of his father with his racing helmet in one hand, a cigarette nonchalantly in the other, had remained by the side of his bed. But this ambition was something that one never dared mention. It was a subject that was absolutely taboo in the family, so much so that even Bobby, who realized the value of inter-national motor racing to bring publicity and big sales to an already existing marque, had dared not broach the subject. 'No racing cars,' he had warned. And he'd meant it.

But for years even while he was at school Pascal had been sketching his dream racing car, a futuristic ideal which, by 1954 when he began to put his plans into practice, was not so unrealistic. The line was much sleeker than the bulbous motor car which his father and others

321

had driven over twenty years before. The tubular chassis was constructed of metal sheeting on 0.030 inches thick, to reduce the weight and enhance speeds which were calculated to reach 190 mph.

There were various other technical refinements which Pascal and his Scots mechanic, Aidan Macpherson, introduced which were to revolutionize British motor racing for years to come, outclassing anything produced by his competitors, including the endlessly expensive and largely fruitless development of the BRM.

It was amazing, really, that the 'Phoenix' took shape and reached the stage of prototype for testing by the spring of 1955 without any of the family discovering the secret, although rumours were beginning to circulate among the racing fraternity. Sasha, especially, had some private means and Pascal made quite legitimate economies on the conventional models which enabled him to channel funds elsewhere. He was not being paid for his own designs which were carried out in his time and not that of the firm, nor for the considerable amount of draughtsmanship and paperwork that went with them.

Anna and Pascal moved into a large rambling cottage which they agreed to rent for six months or a year while Anna searched for something suitable in London. Anna was excited about the venture and made elaborate plans for launching the car, which they hoped to do later in the summer, with a tentative try-out in the European Grand Prix races for 1956. It was very hard being a publicist and not being able to talk about the product one was intending to promote. But, as well as being a publicist, Anna had that certain Russian relish for secrecy. She could be devious, even evasive, and when people asked what she did with her time she smiled mysteriously so that some innocents thought she was planning, if not already expecting, a family.

322

To Anna, the thought of a racing car was far more exciting than a baby.

The cottage was only three miles from the works and often late at night Pascal would wheel the far-from-finished model out of its shed and coast along the road between the works and his home, taking care not to be seen. The three-mile stretch there and back, a fairly straight run, was ideal for giving him a work-out and, as it was in the heart of the countryside, it provided him with much-needed privacy as well. Often Anna rode behind him in her Askham coupé to time him and the enterprise became a shared experience which they intended to turn into a shared triumph. They seemed very much in love with each other, as well as with the car, in those days.

Anna would house-hunt all day in London, or work at her desk in the cottage on plans for the future, and then she might take a picnic over to the works where the lights often burned all night after the ordinary sheds had been closed down and the main work force had gone home. Then the secret operation began, with the chosen few hurrying to the special shed with its bolts and security locks where no one was allowed. Naturally, there was some talk among the workforce and frequent visitors, but no one suspected a racing car, merely a more streamlined version of the current saloon, for which there was a waiting list of two years.

One day early in the spring there was a scary moment when Bobby made an unscheduled visit and asked what was in the shed, but he was easily deflected by Sasha, who murmured something about spare parts which had to be locked up for fear of theft.

But the best part of that time was the togetherness the three shared: they thought only of the car. It became an obsession all the more treasured for being so secret. Sometimes it was dawn before they extinguished the lights

323

and left the shed, driving home happily to the sound of blackbirds. Anna would cook for Pascal and Sasha, if he were with them, and usually on nights like that he was, a huge breakfast, fulfilling a domestic role that was strange to her but which she enjoyed; then the men would shave, shower and drive back to the works to resume a normal day, just as if they'd all had a good night's sleep.

They were kept going by the adrenalin of excitement and anticipation; of great hopes and expectations such as people have when a momentous discovery is about to be made.

Rachel was used to waking to the sound of birdsong. It seemed many years now since she'd lived in the city, in fact in the heart of the city, but even then the birds in St James's Square had their own dawn chorus, supplemented by the sounds from St James's Park, that noted bird sanctuary which was a short walk away. In the large front room she'd shared with her husband she always used to wake early, as though in answer to the first cry of greeting from the blackbirds who announced the new morning in that high, excited, distinctive way of theirs. It was often in the morning, too, just as she opened her eyes, that she thought of the husband who had lain beside her for a very short time in the span of her life. For forty years now he had lain alone in his grave, and she had slept alone far more often than she had slept with another person; she was used to it.

It was, however, surprising how often Rachel did think about the man who had so changed her life; by whom she had had four children. *Dulce et decorum est pro patria mori:* it is sweet and fitting to die for one's country. If that were the case the Askham family had done it more times than most. Rachel had been thirty-eight when Bosco was killed. He had been a year older. One of the nice things about her memories was that always, in retrospect, they remained the same age.

Yet, as the earth took, it gave, and this had happened in her family, too . . . fresh sprigs growing from the seeds that had been watered by blood – Paul, Johnny, and all the generations that would follow them.

It was no time to be sad, though it was a temptation in these early mornings when one thought of the life that one had lived as Bosco's wife. To be a widow for forty years was a very long time; and now to be homeless as well, rehoused on the goodwill of others. But Rachel had always been a philosopher, always fatalistic, and she concentrated when she could on the blessings of life rather than its misfortunes.

When Rachel woke she usually lay quietly for a time, reviewing what was currently going on in her life. It was strange, too, that now she no longer had to take Adam into account; worry about his breathing, his heart, whether he was overtaxing himself. That worry had, literally, been laid to rest forever and was the reason why she was where she was now, back at Askham Hall.

Rachel had stayed at the Hall many times in the past years but it had never belonged to her, it had never been her home. She was always there as a guest or had been until now. Now it was home; home maybe for the rest of her life. And Hugo and Jenny had done their best to help her to settle down. She had selected the rooms she wanted, at the end of the wing, with views both of the lake and the ornamental gardens on the west side. Or rather they had *once* been the ornamental gardens, a special pride of Dulcie's, with a magnificent collection of standard and half-standard rose trees; but during the War they had been divided into several allotments for the growing of vegetables to feed the village. Now, gradually, the ornamental nature of the garden was being reverted to again and Rachel had made it her special task; she who had always loved gardening and had for many years been President of the local District Horticultural Society.

Rachel had an interconnecting bedroom and sitting-room, both furnished with much of her own furniture, which had been brought over from Darley very soon after Christopher asked her to go. When the time came she had gone quite willingly. Something always drew her back to Askham emotionally, and from her bedroom – which was one of the reasons she had chosen it – she could see the sandstone house known as the Grange, which had always been the dower house until the present century, always associated with the mother of the current earl. And it was the Grange that had been her real home for so many years, until she had gone to live with Adam. At the end of the thirties Em had moved into it with Felipe and Luis – it had seemed a perfect home for them – but now Em was no longer there and, somehow, despite the presence of Luis, it no longer seemed part of the family. It was as though strangers lived there now.

Had Rachel been able to go back to the Grange she would have had a feeling of homecoming. As it was, here at the Hall, despite the welcome of Jenny and Hugo, the concern of her family, she would always feel something of a stranger.

Rachel was usually the first into the kitchen in the morning. Having had her morning tea, made from a kettle in her room, she made herself busy setting the table for breakfast, stoking the Aga and doing such minute household tasks that, before the war, were done by myriad servants, each of whom had their place. The kitchen at this time would be buzzing with activity as various members of the staff got on with their appointed tasks; preparing breakfast, taking shaving-water or trays up to the rooms of those who wished to breakfast in bed, setting

the places in the dining-room for members of the family –
a full set of silver and plate for each – and for the staff in
the servants' hall.

Only twenty years ago such activity would have been
quite normal. Now there were no live-in staff at all,
except for two gardeners who lived over one of the old
stables near the paddock, and the huge place was looked
after by a number of women who came in from the village
and surrounding countryside and divided the chores
between them.

But, above all, the place was looked after by Hugo and
Jenny – Jenny in charge of the domestic side, Hugo
maintenance, repairs, the external parts of the Hall and
the developing business.

And what a task it was! As Rachel finished laying the
table she put on the kettle to make herself a fresh cup of
tea and then went to the back door to complete her early
morning tasks by feeding the hens, who would be gathering at the back wing for her. Sometimes that scamp
Elizabeth joined her early and helped her, but this
morning she had slept in. In a way Rachel was glad,
because Elizabeth was a chatterer and the peace of the
morning, the tranquillity of the house and garden, was
somehow vital for her soul.

Hugo and Jenny worked every day and most nights on
tasks that were necessary for the upkeep of the Hall. They
seldom went to bed before midnight and they were always
down by seven-thirty. Yet, for all their hard work, it was
a never-ending battle, a task often compared with the
painting of the Forth Bridge: once one came to the end it
was time to go back to the beginning again. Only, in this
large place with its hundreds of rooms, its interminable
corridors and numerous outbuildings, one never came to
the end at all. The trouble was, it looked it. Despite what
anyone could do, the efforts Hugo and Jenny made, the

Hall was beginning to look ramshackle. It had too many leaks, draughts, too much faulty plumbing. It needed, maybe, millions, not thousands, spent on it and who, in these days, would there be forthcoming to put up such a sum?

Not Bobby, Rachel thought, as she went to the back door, flinging it open to the warm sunshine. Bobby would say he had given them their chance and they had lost it. If Bobby had taken it over when he wanted to in 1948, by now it would be a luxurious hotel.

Rachel walked over to the outbuilding which housed the feed for the hens who, as she knew they would, had gathered expectantly round the kitchen door, pecking and muttering. Two grey tabby cats lay stretched in the sun reminding her of Lenin, the family pet who had died just before the war. Hugo had always loved animals and he encouraged the children to have a lot of them. There were rabbit hutches and cages for gerbils and hamsters, and two glorious red setters who slept in one of the buildings and were let out even earlier by the gardeners who took them for a walk in the woods.

It was a simple, charming scene of country life and domesticity and Rachel, having procured the corn for the hens, was contentedly scattering it about her when she heard the sound of a heavy engine chugging up the drive and curiously, looked in the direction of the noise.

What she saw made her put down the bucket and rub her eyes. But when she looked again the oddly-shaped car was nearer and, at the same time as she discerned that it was painted in the Askham racing colours of burgundy and cream, she saw Pascal at the wheel, giving her a cheery wave. Behind him in an Askham coupé with the roof down was Anna, wearing a large pair of black sunglasses. She waved, too.

The two cars came slowly round the house and stopped

just out of sight as Rachel, forgetting about the kettle boiling on the hob, ran as fast as her legs could carry her to the front of the house. There she saw that Anna had emerged from her own car and was standing beside Pascal with a work sheet in her hand as though, heads together, they were checking details. Pascal's expression as he gazed up at his wife was clearly one of delight and Anna appeared to be excitedly adding some figures together and, at the end, she gave a loud whoop and stooped to kiss him.

They *were* a charming couple, Rachel thought, as she slowed down. One was dark and one fair. Daily Pascal seemed to get more like his father, but Anna, with her reddish hair and Slav looks, was like no one in the family. She was a Ferov, Kyril's daughter; there was no mistaking that. Yet she and Pascal were happy; the marriage, just a year old, was to everyone's surprise, a good one. Anna, if not popular, was tolerated and, anyway, very little was seen of either of them; Pascal immersed in his work, Anna busy hunting for a suitable town-house. She seemed hard to please because it was taking a very long time. Anna wore a short leather coat over slacks. She had pushed her sunglasses over her hair.She had a red bandana round her neck and looked attractive and very sporty.

Both looked up at Rachel as, arms akimbo, she slowly approached the car.

'What is this?' she said, looking first at the huge streamlined bonnet of the car with its protruding gleaming tubes, then at the man behind the wheel.

'A car, Gran.'

'I can see that. What sort of car?'

Pascal leapt out of the cockpit behind the wheel. He was dressed in white dungarees and his hands were black with grease. Rachel swiftly sidestepped as he tried to kiss her. Like the red setters, he seemed large and clumsy, a rather overpowering animal for first thing in the morning.

'It's a secret,' Anna said, walking slowly round the car to join them. 'You are the first to know about it.'

'It's a racer,' Rachel said, sighing. Somehow, a cloud seemed to have passed over the morning sun.

By the time Hugo and Jenny descended with Elizabeth and Anthony, bathed, dressed and ready for the day, Anna and Pascal were consuming large plates of bacon, eggs and toast. They had been up all night, preparing to put the car through its paces at dawn, the best and quietest time on the road. The results made them feel triumphant. Anna had planned the trials and manned every check point with her stop watch.

'We could touch over 200 miles an hour,' she was saying to Rachel as Elizabeth bounded into the kitchen and ran up to her grandmother, giving her a wet, sticky kiss.

'We?' Rachel turned from the frying-pan to catch Elizabeth in her arms before the whole thing upset on the stove. Six-year-old Elizabeth was an energetic, rumbustious tomboy who had a genius for making messes. Anthony had only just started to crawl and now he gazed about him contentedly from his father's arms as they stood rather bewilderedly contemplating the scene.

Hugo carefully put Anthony on the floor, where he crawled rapidly in the direction of the Aga, gathering up as much dirt as his mother had managed to wash away the night before. Added to her duties in the house, the children were an extra burden for Jenny, but one she welcomed. Ralph's son, Jonathan, had been reluctantly despatched to boarding-school as, in the winters, the journey to the local grammar was often impossible. Jenny and Rachel sometime disagreed about Johnny's upbringing but, in these cases, Hugo always sided with his wife and Johnny had been sent away to school where, as Rachel knew he would be, he was unhappy. The English winters were not so terrible, she had argued, that it was necessary to send someone to boarding-school who didn't want to go. It was not as though they lived in the Scottish Highlands; but her arguments went unheeded.

'I thought I heard a car,' Hugo said, smiling cheerfully at the visitors.

'Two cars,' Rachel said, anxiously deflecting Anthony from the beeline he was making for trouble. 'There's a racer as well.'

'A what?' Jenny scooped Anthony up in her arms and unceremoniously plonked him in the playpen by the window. He spent most of his time there as he was too inquisitive to be left anywhere without an eye constantly being kept on him.

'A racing car,' Pascal said, in a tone of glee, 'at the moment, potentially one of the fastest racers in England, if not the world. This morning at dawn I let it out at full throttle on the main road for a measured mile and it clocked up 199.7 miles an hour.'

'You *what?* My God, on the main road . . .' Hugo put a hand to his head.

'How is it that this is the first time we've heard about it?' Jenny looked at Rachel, who had started to crack more eggs in the large family-sized frying-pan.

'It has been a carefully-kept secret,' Anna explained. 'We knew Bobby wouldn't approve.'

'Not only Bobby! Charlotte certainly won't approve,' Rachel said, rapidly basting the eggs. 'I'm not sure I do.'

'Oh, Gran.' Pascal got up and nuzzled her neck, towering over her.

'No, I don't, Pascal.' Rachel turned round sharply, pushing him away. 'You both seem to be terribly pleased, but I'm rather upset, to tell you the truth.'

331

'Just because my father . . .'

'Well you can't blame your mother, can you? I mean to say, your entire lives were changed by what happened to your father. Charlotte would be most unnatural if she'd wanted you to race. You don't remember the crash but I do. It was horrific.'

'That was *years* ago, Gran. Things have changed. Cars are much safer, so are conditions on the tracks.'

'But not on the main road at five in the morning. Anyway, isn't speeding like that illegal?'

'Very.'

'And dangerous . . .'

There was silence for a moment as the extent of Rachel's disapproval sank in. Jenny and Hugo didn't seem quite to know how to react and looked at each other in some bewilderment. Anna carefully put her knife and fork together and dabbed at her lips. Then she got up and, joining her arms, walked slowly over to Rachel by the stove.

'Aunt Rachel,' she said, 'you and Charlotte and all the family between you have made Pascal grow up in fear, in the shadow of his father. He has wanted to be a racing driver all his life yet because of what happened to his father he has never *dared* mention it. He has drawn racing cars since he was eleven or twelve. Designed lots and lots of them on paper. He has some really marvellous ideas; he is an inventor of genius, yet because of a silly family superstition . . .'

'It is *not* a superstition,' Rachel said frostily. 'It is a *fact*. The one thing, the only thing, that none of us wanted was for Pascal or Joe to follow their father. You would quite understand it, if you had any sensitivity or sense which, frankly, I don't think you have as you seem to have encouraged Pascal for all you're worth. All right, Pascal loves cars and wanted to design them, we know

332

that; but we hoped that he would sublimate that energy into ordinary cars and he seemed quite happy with that . . . until he married you. Trust you, Anna, to put a spanner in the works.'

Rachel turned her back on Anna and hastily lifted the eggs out of the pan, arranging them on plates.

Hugo had gone to the door and stood looking at the car, which had been moved out of the drive so as to be out of sight from the road. It stood looking rather forlorn, but proud, in the morning sunlight.

'It's a very fine car,' he said, scratching his head. 'Maybe . . .'

'Maybe you *are* being rather fatalistic, Rachel,' Jenny said gently, putting an arm round her waist. 'After all, Pascal isn't the first son to want to follow in the footsteps of his father. Maybe you're being *too* pessimistic, and unfair to Anna. If Pascal has had these ideas all these years . . .'

'Years and years,' Anna said, quite unrepentantly. 'And it took *me* to fish them out. To get Pascal to do what he really wanted to do all the time . . .'

'*And* destroy the happiness of all his family. Once again, Anna, we have you to thank for *that*!' And untying her apron strings Rachel, clearly distraught, flung it on a chair and hurried out of the kitchen.

Hugo looked anxiously after her and seemed about to follow when Jenny stopped him.

'Don't go after her,' she appealed. 'Anna and Pascal are perfectly old enough to lead the kind of life they want. I side with them, not with Rachel. I think she's being absurd.'

'That's a bit harsh.' Hugo frowned and, looking uncertain and uncomfortable, sat at the table next to Pascal, who hadn't said a word.

'But it's true.' Jenny, finishing off the task started by

Rachel, put a plate with his breakfast in front of him. 'They have *always* tried to interfere. Rachel interfered about Johnny's education. She didn't speak to me for a week after we decided to send him away to school . . .'

'She was thinking about Ralph . . .'

'But he's my son, too! Ralph never even saw him and if Johnny grows up wanting to be a soldier I shan't stop him, even though his father and uncle and grandfather have *all* been killed in war. Now then, Hugo, what do you say to *that*?'

Hugo picked up his knife and fork and began to eat, scowling.

'Thanks a lot, Jenny,' Anna said warmly, lighting a cigarette. 'I was beginning to feel like the arch bitch. It's good to have *one* friend in this family.'

'Oh, come on, Anna,' Hugo said. 'You've got more than one friend. You've got a lot of admirers.'

'That's not true,' Anna replied silkily. 'I've always felt the family hated me, as a matter of fact. I've never felt I fitted in. Everything I do is wrong. If someone else had encouraged Pascal to develop his natural abilities and race, they'd have got a medal. Not me, yet I'm just trying to bring out my husband's talent, that's all. Not stifle it.'

'If the family really think that about Anna,' Pascal said angrily, speaking for the first time since Rachel left, 'I'll emigrate. She is the best support a man could have. Anna encouraged me all the way with this car. She suggested it. She saw something in me that no one else saw. I tell you, without her I would be half the man I am.'

Anna went over to him and draped herself behind him, leaning on his shoulder and planting a kiss on his cheek.

'Thank you, darling,' she said. Then she raised her head and looked at Jenny as though seeing in her her only ally. 'The point it, we haven't come over here just to show you the car. We want to keep it here for a while and work on it. It is too public at the works. It is much too big now for the shed. We'd like, if we may, to hide it here for a while until we are ready to announce it.'

Subtly, Anna's voice changed from a wheedling tone to a brisk announcement. 'It's a real shame about Rachel, but it's just too bad. As you own the Hall she'll have to accept it, won't she, Hugo, and just keep her mouth shut?'

As she spoke even Jenny, momentarily her champion, felt a spasm of alarm about what she'd done.

Aileen Lighterman was very little known by members of the family. She had always kept herself to herself as if remembering the days when she was Bobby's mistress, living in a detached house in Harrow, bringing up a child on her own. They were days she had never forgotten; or that Bobby had eventually married her for David, not for herself. Bobby had at one time wanted to take David from her, give him a home and pension her off. She could go round the world, he had said, anywhere she liked. But that had not been Aileen's style. She had put her foot down and she had never looked back. Now she was Lady Lighterman.

In the years since their marriage Aileen had become an important figure in her own right, not merely Bobby's wife. She had come into her own during the War when, as an active energetic woman of a patriotic disposition, she was much sought after to sit on committees and organizations which proliferated to aid this cause and that – soldiers, sailors, airmen – in the welfare of their families. After it, of course, there were refugees.

Bobby and Aileen were very seldom together. Since the days of their passion in the early thirties, relations between them had cooled to the point where either would have considered divorce had it been expedient.

Bobby and Aileen didn't row, they didn't argue, they saw as little of each other as they could. Since David had gone they had no bond at all. But in a sense they depended on each other to maintain the *status quo* – and each went their separate ways. Bobby got richer and Aileen developed her own special brand of power that gave her independence: she was a formidable committee woman, a much-sought-after speaker.

Aileen was a tall, grey-haired woman, rather thin and angular, who dressed smartly and chose plain expensive clothes well. She was two years older than her husband and very few would have recognized in this rather severe, imposing matron the uncertain young woman Bobby had taken as a mistress twenty years before. Aileen was fond of Robertswood, especially in the spring and early summer. She liked to have a few days' break there for a time. She enjoyed the company of Princess Irina, to whom she had always been a good friend, and she was very fond of Irina's eldest granddaughter, Stefanie. In her work for refugees she had done her best to find out for the Ferovs the fate of Hélène but it had proved impossible.

It was perhaps strange that this rather severe lady, this busy committee woman, should have so much time for a young woman who had taken to drink to try and console herself for the disappointments of her life, but she did. To her, Stefanie, like her mother, was a tragic figure and Aileen had done much to help rehabilitate her. She had visited her at Bellevue and, when Stefanie was eventually pronounced well enough to leave, it was Aileen who suggested that she should make Robertswood her home, at least until she felt really strong enough to go back to town.

At Robertswood Stefanie could enjoy peace and security and also the company of her two children in conditions that made it safe for them all. Because no one was in any doubt that Nicky and Galina were a problem to their mother of almost frightening dimensions. They terrified her and she was terrified of what she might do to them. She was seldom happy alone in their company, and at Robertswood there were always maids and nannies or Princess Irina to take charge and see that the children were seldom alone with their mother.

These murderous impulses that Stefanie suffered were not uncommon both in numerous normal mothers with small children, and in women suffering from that acute sort of depression that made them wish to leave the world and take those they loved with them. Stefanie didn't hate her children or wish them harm. Even she could see that Nicky wasn't responsible for his father. Her feeling towards her son was one of resentment rather than hatred and for Galina she felt only remorse – that someone so like her mother still haunted her.

One day Aileen arrived at Robertswood unannounced. She had decided on an impulse to take a few days' holiday and was met by the staff with some confusion because her rooms were not ready. Aileen dismissed this as a matter of no importance – she was an easy woman to work for – and she went up to her suite on the first floor to leave her overnight bag and change into fresh clothes. Her rooms were not ready in the sense that the bed was not aired; but everything else was in pristine, apple-pie order and she smiled at the thought of what the servants would say were they to see some of the conditions in which displaced people still lived in Europe.

Glancing out of the window of her room Aileen saw a solitary figure sitting in the garden under the laburnum that Bobby's grandmother, Mabel, had sentimentally planted on his twelfth birthday. Near her, Princess Irina knelt by one of the herbaceous borders, energetically digging with a small trowel, teaching her four-year-old great-granddaughter, Galina, the fundamentals of gardening. Galina was an enchanting child and every now and then she would seize the trowel from her grandmother and tenderly plant one of the flowers that lay spread in a tempting array on the ground beside them.

Aileen paused for some moments at the window and then changed out of her travelling costume into a blue linen dress, one of a number she kept in the house, passed a comb through her hair and hurried downstairs.

It was very quiet in the big house, the sunshine coming through numerous open windows, shining on the polished floors, on the priceless pieces of antique furniture that Bobby's grandfather had accumulated over the years and which had been added to with skill and taste by Bobby and Princess Irina. She ran lightly down the stairs, across the vast hall with its baronial bearings and through the open front door, where one of the maids was polishing the great brass handles which adorned it. Aileen stood on the steps and then slowly, almost casually, started across the lawn, appearing to see Stefanie by chance. She stopped as slowly Stefanie raised her head from her book and, shading her eyes, gazed at her.

'Why, hello!' Aileen said. 'What a nice surprise to see you here. Isn't it a lovely day?'

'Lovely,' Stefanie nodded. 'I didn't know you were coming.'

'I just decided on the spur of the moment. It's such lovely weather and I seem to have had so little time off this year. Do you mind if I sit with you?'

'Of course not!' Stefanie gestured towards a deck-chair which Aileen pulled to her side, her back to the river. Then she placed a pair of sunglasses on her nose, joined her hands against her chest and closed her eyes.

'Quite blissful,' she said. After a few minutes she

338

opened her eyes again. 'Galina is *so* pretty. She loves Irina, doesn't she?'

'Babushka is marvellous with her. When you think that she's over eighty, and yet she has all this energy. I'm so lucky.'

'And how are you?' Aileen leaned forward. 'You look very much better.'

'I am,' Stefanie said, trying to smile. 'I am much better; but I rely on drugs, you know. Without them I can't cope.' At last she managed a wan smile. 'It's not much of a life, is it, being dependent on drugs and other people? On my grandmother, my husband, to some extent my sisters, on my father, who despises me . . .'

'Oh, Bobby doesn't despise you,' Aileen protested.

'Oh, yes, he does. He hates weakness and he thinks I'm weak. I shouldn't give in. I should fight. As far as my father is concerned I'm a terrible failure.'

'Well, I wouldn't worry too much about him.' Aileen sat back again in her chair, pursing her lips. 'I think you've made a wonderful fight and you've overcome many things your father never had to overcome, surrounded all his life by luxury and care. He lived in a different age.'

'Father's coming down tonight,' Stefanie sounded depressed at the very idea.

'Oh, is he? I didn't know.'

'You never really know what he does, do you?'

'Not really. We lead separate lives.'

'You're lucky.'

'How do you mean?'

'That you can do that. My mother couldn't.'

Aileen leaned forward again and reached for Stefanie's hand.

'Stefanie,' she said, 'you know I really am very fond of you?'

'I know that.' Stefanie returned the pressure on her hand.

'And what I'm saying is because I *am* fond of you but, please, dear, after all you've been through, try and forget about the past, what happened between your father and mother, and afterwards. A lot of people, you know, suffered in the War. You should see the dreadful cases I come across in wretched camps all over Europe. The problem is still a huge one even though the War has been over for years. I know you lost your mother, and Anna and Sasha lost a father. Rachel lost Ralph, and Johnny lost a father, too. I feel that if you could understand and accept that what happened was no one's fault; neither yours nor your father's nor your mother's, you would feel happier; you would depend perhaps a little less on the medicines that keep you going and, maybe, do without them altogether and enjoy your husband and the beautiful children you have.'

Stefanie leaned back, her hand still in Aileen's.

'I try,' she said, 'believe me, I try, and I know I disappoint everyone; but I do try.'

Coming back across the lawn, her great-grandaughter's hand in hers, Irina waved at Aileen and quickened her pace, arriving at last by her side, puffing a little.

'I didn't know you were coming,' she said in consternation. 'Your bed isn't aired.'

Aileen smiled and, nimbly getting up, embraced the older woman, then stooped to kiss Galina, who had suddenly gone shy. Then she pointed to Irina's high wicker chair, which the Princess needed because of her bad back, and waited until she had sat down.

'I was saying,' Aileen said, encouraging Galina to come and sit on her knee, 'that I see so many terrible sights still in Europe, so much deprivation, that an unaired bed means luxury to me.'

'You're very good.' Irina gave a deep sigh and held her hand out to Aileen. 'You're a good woman. All your family have been good to us. Stefanie doesn't realize it, but they have. One day she will. She'll thank her father, and you and the Askhams for all they've done.'

'Done what?' Stefanie said bitterly, flinging back her head. 'Done *what*, I ask you, Babushka? You are always so grateful to people, for what?'

'Much of my life I spent without anything,' Irina said soulfully. 'I was born into great wealth and I lost everything, so I know what it is to be without. Believe me, I know. I have lost a husband, a daughter and a son.' Irina groped for the handkerchief in the pocket of her copious pinafore dress, and stuffed it into her eyes with a chubby, well-manicured hand.

'Believe me, I know what it is to have nothing. And so do you, my dear Stefanie; yet now you have everything you cannot be happy. I ask myself, sometimes, what does it take to make someone happy, and you know?' she gazed mournfully at Aileen, 'I don't know the answer.'

Galina wriggled off Aileen's knee and ran over to her mother, trying to struggle up on her lap. People often most want those who reject them and Galina was no exception. She sensed that when she was around her mother froze up and she sought, by her childish ploys and charms, to melt that solid, unbending mass. She would have done anything to please her mother.

Stefanie apathetically reached out for Galina and helped her up; but the child wouldn't sit still and tried to put an arm round her neck and kiss her. Aware of two pairs of eyes watching her, Aileen's and her grand-mother's, Stefanie tried desperately to calm the rising tide of panic that threatened to engulf her; the knowledge that she was a bad, even wicked mother who couldn't love her child. As little Galina gazed into her eyes begging for her

341

love, Stefanie suddenly saw her mother's eyes that day she'd looked at her before she left forever. Her mother seemed to say; 'Please tell me not to go, let me stay with you,' but Stefanie, hanging on to the door, had no pity in her own eyes and shut it in her mother's face. That way she sent her to her death.

Suddenly Stefanie gave a cry and tried to rise from her chair, heedless of Galina, who tumbled helplessly to the ground. Quickly Irina rose and helped the distressed child from the grass and led her towards the house, while Aileen knelt by Stefanie's chair and, by talking to her quietly and gently for a long time, tried to adminster what comfort she could.

Bobby listened to Aileen with some impatience later on that day between tea and dinner, when opening letters in his study. Though, technically, the house was Sasha's, Bobby maintained a presence there and, as patron of a number of local causes, had mail sent there.

Bobby kept on reading while Aileen told him about what had happened in the garden in the morning, looking at her from time to time with an expression of irritation on his face.

'I wish you wouldn't interfere,' he said at last, throwing used envelopes into the wastepaper basket. 'I can't see what business it is of yours.'

'It *is* my business,' Aileen said. 'Stefanie may not be my daughter but I care about her and I care about Sasha and the children. She thinks you don't care about her enough. That you're indifferent to her. It doesn't help with her illness.'

Bobby went over to the window and sat down on the long sofa that ran alongside it, his arm resting on the back.

'It's a pity *you* didn't care more about David, your own son and mine, but lost to me now.'

'Bobby,' Aileen said heatedly, 'you know very well that nothing I could have done would have stopped David. What happened was your fault and only yours. I refuse to accept any responsibility for it at all. You have never been responsible for your children, Bobby, and look what has happened to them: they are all alienated from you. They only use you and get what they can get out of you and I don't blame them. Sasha is the sweetest, noblest, most generous of men and look what you do to him. He is beside himself with worry and you give him so little support.'

Bobby didn't reply for a moment, but continued to sit sideways on the sofa, gazing out of the window and tapping his fingers on the leather-covered back.

'Sasha *may* be very sweet and noble, he has had a lot to put up with, but he's no good at business,' he said at last. 'And this weekend I'm going to tell him. It's one of the reasons I came down here.'

'*What* are you going to do?' Aileen looked at him, aghast.

'I'm going to say that he doesn't show the promise I hoped for. He hasn't got it in him. He said he hadn't and he was right. Of course I shan't throw him out, but I'll move him sideways. Pascal is the man I want to succeed me, not Sasha. Pascal has guts, and since he married Anna he's got even more. Even Anna has a better command of the business than Sasha, more dedication. She'd drop anything for a business deal.'

'I'm sure she would,' Aileen said dryly.

'I just want to restructure my company.' Bobby gave her a bleak smile. 'Don't worry, I shan't be ruthless and I shan't be cruel. Just practical. You'll see. You'll be there; you'll hear me.'

* * *

343

Bobby, as usual, misunderstood the reactions of his family when, over dinner a day later when Pascal and Anna had arrived for the weekend, he outlined plans to them for the development of Lighterman Ltd. He explained that it had got too big, too unwieldly, and he was breaking it down into parts. Sasha would be in charge of product development, particularly the Askham car and, now that Pascal had made such a success of that, he could move on to other things. For a start he would move into Bobby's office as his right-hand man and learn the ropes.

To Bobby it was all very simple but to those gathered round the table with its glittering candles, Crown Derby plate and Georgian silver, it seemed incredibly complicated. He was listened to with some incomprehension. One thing however was obvious: Sasha was being moved sideways and Pascal was being moved up. That much was clear enough.

After Bobby finished speaking, at a prearranged signal his butler entered to instruct the staff to move the plates and serve the next course. This was an attempt to forestall the criticism he knew would come, but it did nothing to stop the outburst that followed as the servants withdrew, and the chief criticism came from Pascal.

'You can't do this without consulting us, Bobby.'

'I *am* consulting you,' Bobby said unctuously. 'All together. I thought it fairest that way. I'm telling you now.'

'Yes, *telling*, not consulting. What does Sasha say to all this, for instance? Does he know about it?'

'I think Sasha knows how I feel,' Bobby said, glaring at Stefanie. 'Not to put too fine a point on it, Stefanie's health has been of concern to us all, but particularly Sasha. I think it would be easier for him if he had less responsibility.'

Suddenly Stefanie, who had said little during the

344

dinner, spoke nervously, moving the silver about by the side of her plate.

'If you have done this for my sake, Father, please think again. I am very much better. I want to help Sasha, not hinder him. Please don't demote Sasha because of me.'

'Sasha is *not* being demoted,' Bobby said angrily. 'He is just . . .'

'It *sounded* like demotion to me, Father,' Stefanie said, with some heat. 'It is just the sort of thing you'd do, the way you work. You're flinging Sasha to one side then you'll try Pascal. When he . . .'

'Oh, for heaven's sake,' Bobby said, banging the table. 'I wanted a friendly discussion, not a war.'

'What does Sasha say?' Anna said, looking at him. She had been listening very carefully, almost aghast at what had happened because of the consequences to the car. Pascal in London would mean no racing. It couldn't happen. 'Sasha must have an opinion.'

'I'm not surprised,' Sasha said suddenly. 'Uncle Bobby's right.'

'Father is *not* right,' Stefanie cried. 'I will not have you sacrificed on account of me.'

'For goodness sake, *I'm* not sacrificing *anyone*,' Bobby burst out.

Pascal said: 'I'm not even interested in running the business, so you can count me out, Bobby. I'm perfectly happy as I am. I've other fish to fry. I'm a car designer, not a tycoon.'

'But you have the qualities.' Bobby was clearly non-plussed by this turn of events.

'I'm not interested. I have my cars, my home and,' he looked lovingly at Anna, 'my wife. We are a very good team.'

'I am actually quite interested in the business,' Anna said suddenly. 'Why not try me?'

For a moment there was a pause. Aileen, at the head of the table opposite Bobby, looked down and smiled as if to herself and Stefanie gazed at her husband, while Pascal gazed at Anna.

'You?' Bobby said at last.

'I'm frightfully interested in the business as a whole,' Anna said, almost casually. 'Seeing none of the men seem able to agree, try me.'

'You couldn't go into the business!' Pascal said heatedly.

'But, darling, I already am.' Anna looked slyly at him. 'Don't I represent Askham Motors abroad? Don't I do the PR? Aren't I good at it?'

'Yes, but that's only a tiny bit of the business.'

'Well, then, I'd be interested in it all. I'm looking for a house in London. I'm ambitious.'

'I'll certainly think about it, Anna,' Bobby said, pompously brushing crumbs of cheese off his white shirt-front. 'But I do agree with Pascal. This isn't a woman's world.'

'I didn't say anything about it not being a woman's world, Bobby,' Pascal said. 'But Anna is my wife. We have our life together. I don't want her to turn into another you.'

This time the silence was more prolonged. Even Aileen looked concerned, and it was difficult to tell whether Bobby was going to bluster through or throw a tantrum. In the event, unusually for him, he decided on tact, avuncular understanding.

'You may think me a harsh man, Pascal,' he said, after a while, 'but I can assure you I am not. Aileen knows how much I have sacrificed for this family, not only family, but all of us, Askhams and Bolingbrokes as well as Ferovs and Lightermans. I have worked non-stop since I left school, like any working-class boy, and I have fulfilled my stewardship. I am not ashamed of what I've

346

done. My company means a lot to me. It is my life. I want it well run.' Bobby leaned over the table and rang the bell. 'I just wanted to tell you the way my mind is working. No need to quarrel, after all this is a happy occasion. Stefanie is so much better. You're all here together.' Bobby smiled expansively. 'Let's have some more champagne.'

Stefanie said: 'I can't understand you letting go so easily.'

'I'm not letting go,' Sasha stared moodily into the mirror. 'Bobby's right.'

'You didn't have to tell him.'

'Why not? I'll never be a tycoon.'

'You don't have to be a tycoon, but you can run the business.'

'I don't think I want to.' Sasha stretched and began to unbutton his shirt as though he were a weary man.

Stefanie sat upright on the bed still fully clothed, her arms akimbo. It was a long time since she had felt so angry and so determined and, suddenly, so well. All those fears and fantasies which had afflicted her mind for so long were, temporarily at any rate, at bay. Maybe she had relied on Sasha too much, had let go. Now he needed her.

'What *do* you want?' Stefanie asked.

'I want you to be well, for us to live a life together with the children. We have so much to live for.' He looked at her sadly.

'We have nothing to live for if you let my father kick us to one side as he kicked my mother,' Stefanie said, and Sasha looked up, aware of the new strength in her voice. 'My father must be fought at all costs. If *you* fight, Sasha, I'll fight with you.'

'Will you?' Sasha looked at her incredulously.

'Yes, I will and I can.' Stefanie sat back on the bed, more relaxed now. 'The doctors have for a long time been

347

telling me I didn't need drugs, that I was well. But I refused to see it. What did the future have? I thought.'

'It had me and the children.'

'Yes, but isn't that what brought about my illness in the first place? Maybe I didn't want to be a housewife and mother? That's what Dr Grant said.'

'What did you want to be?'

'Something different. It was no use yearning for Mother because she had gone. It was deluding myself to think she'd come back, to think she was still there somewhere in Russia. I think I got ill then. It was stupid to think Mother could be there, looking as she did when she was a girl.'

'I told you,' Sasha said.

'I know, but I so wanted to believe it was Mother.' Stefanie crossed her arms again and, just then, despite the difference in their colouring, Sasha saw Hélène as she had been in France when they last met. Stefanie had that same look of resolution in her eyes that Hélène had acquired from her wartime experiences. Mother and daughter *were* starting to resemble each other. 'Look, Sasha,' Stefanie went on, 'I'm sorry. I'll do my best. I'll try and be what you want me to be. I'll try and help you beat Father. But you must promise me to fight.'

'But why should we fight?' Sasha looked bewildered and ran his hands through his tight brown curls. 'We have enough money, if we live modestly. We can sell up and go and live abroad.'

'I don't want to go and live abroad.' Stefanie pursed her mouth in a thin, grim line. 'We have the children to think of. Why should we be a poor branch of a family that has so much? My mother's family, our family, the Ferovs, were used to such riches in Russia. Why cannot we be rich again? Why should we always be content to be poor?'

'We're not *poor*,' Sasha protested, 'not in the least.'

'We will be poor if you stop working for Father, compared to what we could be. Father is a fabulously wealthy man. Do you want Pascal to get all the wealth that should come to us?'

Sasha sat wearily on a chair by the side of the bed. It was nearly two o'clock and he was tired. The evening had gone on much longer than anyone thought. The last thing Sasha wanted was a conversation like this. On the other hand, to know that Stefanie was thinking more positively was worth staying up all night for.

'I didn't know you cared so much,' he said. 'You really astound me.'

'I astound myself,' Stefanie said, with a note of satisfaction in her voice. 'I really am surprised I feel so intensely; but just seeing Father sitting there like a smug beetle, the source of all our miseries, Mother's death, made me so mad. It even made Anna mad because she surely doesn't think she can run the business.'

'Why not?' Now Sasha looked surprised.

'Because she couldn't. Father would never allow that, even if she were capable of it.'

'She's very capable.'

'Why don't you and Anna run it, then? Pascal is a mechanical genius. He doesn't want to sit behind a desk. Why don't the three of you make Lighterman twice the size it is now – and send Father to some distant island for retirement, like Napoleon was banished to St Helena?'

Looking at Stefanie revitalised, a new light in her eyes, suddenly for Sasha the world seemed alive once more and he realized that for him, as for her, in many ways it had for too long been a dead place. Now, with so much to live for, perhaps he would fight. There was only one thing to be got out of the way: they must come clean about the racer and then once again everything would fit into place.

* * *

349

Anna always felt uncomfortable at Robertswood. The presence of the family in any large numbers always made her uneasy – though the worst time was when Charlotte was there. Even her presence was enough to indicate, somehow, subtly, disapproval of Anna marrying her son.

But Anna had felt even more uncomfortable tonight, at dinner, because what Bobby said increased the sense of guilt she had about encouraging Pascal to design the racer – to design and test it all in secret. It had been a massive undertaking and both Pascal and Sasha were tired. Yet she was very fresh, stimulated and excited by what had happened and was about to happen.

Whatever the outcome she, personally, was on the crest of a wave.

Now it was necessary to try and placate Pascal. He felt bruised, angry, tired. She had spoken out too vigorously at dinner and, almost as soon as she had, she regretted it. Later, as they got undressed, Pascal was silent; he slipped into bed and looked as though he were going to go straight to sleep. Anna, still in her clothes, lit a cigarette and sat beside him; even in repose his face looked tense.

'I'm sorry,' she said.

'What about?' Pascal opened an eye.

'I shouldn't have said what I said.'

'Well, if it's what you wanted. The whole thing was a mess. I thought you cared most about the racer.'

'I do. Bobby was beastly to Sasha. He took us by surprise.'

'That was his intention. Maybe he's heard about the "Phoenix".'

'I don't see how he could.'

'Maybe Rachel said something. We can't keep it a secret forever. I was almost on the verge of telling him tonight.'

Anna stubbed out her cigarette and bit her lip.

350

'Soon, soon,' she said. 'We must test it under proper practice conditions first. We can't go running it on the roads. As Rachel said, it's dangerous. But if Bobby does accept it, and I think he will, what happened tonight will be irrelevant. You want to be a racing driver, not a tycoon; but what do I do then? I don't want to spend my life following you around in the pits. I will be there, of course, but I can do other things, too. I wanted to put the idea of me working into Bobby's head . . . sow the seeds.'

Pascal, wide awake again, lay on his back and gazed at the ceiling.

'Don't you want kids?'

'Some time. Not yet.' Nervously Anna got up and began to undress.

'I'd *love* to be a father. I'm getting on.'

Impulsively Anna threw herself on the bed beside him, grasping his face between her hands.

'Don't be so impatient, darling. We have our lives in front of us. Everything is wide open: children, fame as a racing driver, success in business.'

Her green eyes gleamed and, as he reached up to her to kiss her, Anna threw back her head and cried, 'Life is in front of us – the past is only experience. Don't worry, you'll see. Things will be very good indeed. I think, I'm sure, we're on the verge of great things.'

CHAPTER 14

Flora Bolingbroke looked round the tiny, sparsely-furnished room at the top of the hostel. She put down her small suitcase and turned to smile at the warden, a woman of about fifty, slightly overweight and dressed in a cotton skirt, with a round-necked sleeveless cotton T-shirt which stretched tightly across her large bust. She was a bright cheerful woman whom Flora had met at her interview and personal appearances seemed to mean as little to her as they did to Flora. Flora knew they would get on.

'Maybe you'll come and have a cup of tea with me when you're settled in?' The warden, Mrs Foulsham, was slightly intrigued by her new deputy, a woman with as mysterious a past as any of her inmates – obviously what was called a lady, and yet . . .

'Thank you, Mrs Foulsham,' Flora said politely. 'I'd love that just as soon as I've unpacked.'

After the warden had left the room Flora sat gingerly on her bed to test it. From underneath came the twanging of a spring but otherwise it seemed solid enough. The wisp of curtain at the window was hardly sufficient to keep out the light and the tallboy, wardrobe and dressing-table had seen many years of good service; the latter, especially, was stained with innumerable cigarette marks. The lino on the floor was bare, in the interests of hygiene, except for two rugs, one by the side of her bed, the other in the middle of the floor. As the curtains stirred, wafted by a breeze that came through the cracked window, Flora was overcome by a mood of such dejection that she could have wept. She sat on the bed, her arms on her knees, and she said aloud: 'What have I done?'

Two years of post-graduate research at the LSE had left Flora dissatisfied. She had decided after her father's death to try and lose herself in work, but she hadn't altogether been successful. The loss of a parent was always traumatic, needing time to readjust, but when Rachel moved out of the manor Flora felt homeless – that she had lost father, mother and home as well. Flora became more isolated than ever from her family, remote and withdrawn, unresponsive to kindly-meant overtures on the part of those of her friends. She was only close to one person and that was Dick. It was to Dick's room in Clare Market that she went in School hours, Dick to whom she talked, who tried to help her and offer her not only consolation but a meaning to the puzzle of existence.

Not that Dick had much of a clue, either. His own marriage was unsatisfactory and he sometimes felt that he and Flora were like two empty coracles tossed about on the sea of life.

Gradually Flora realized that she was becoming too dependent on Dick; not only dependent but involved with him. She needed him. She counted the hours until she could find some pretence to see him. She felt very guilty about her feelings for him and when she saw the advertisement for deputy warden at a women's hostel in Mile End she decided to try and get away from him, to remove herself from danger.

But was their relationship dangerous? She had known Dick for over five years. How could she possibly be dangerous to him? How could he possibly threaten her?

Flora was aware of her lack of attraction for men; but just because she was plain it didn't mean that she didn't have feelings, that she wasn't drawn to the opposite sex. But the opposite sex was seldom drawn to her. At twenty-

353

three she had never had an affair; never really had a boyfriend, just a lot of mates and comrades connected with the Party and, now, the growing number of people opposed to the Bomb.

Flora found her greatest satisfaction in opposing cruelty and helping others. Her studies in sociology had begun to seem so theoretical compared to the suffering not only of the poor, but the sick, the unwanted, the lonely. Maybe she saw, in all these people, some part of herself. She was attracted to the destitute, the lost, the insecure. It was a logical step to the hostel off the Mile End Road which gave refuge to such women – ex-prisoners, alcoholics, unmarried mothers, those whom society, for one reason or another, had rejected. She found it very easy to identify with stricken humanity.

But Flora was Flora, heir to a great tradition of service, sacrifice, denial of self. She opened her suitcase and unpacked the picture of her father, which she placed on the dressing-table, and then her brush and comb beside it and the pot of the Ponds cold cream she put on her face at night.

Her two nightdresses and underthings went quickly into the two drawers in the dressing-table and her dresses, skirts and blouses hardly took up any space in the wardrobe. Some of her books, together with an alarm clock, were put by the side of her bed. She then washed her hands in the basin in the corner of the room – quite a luxury this – combed her hair, peered at her unmade-up face in the mirror and began to descend the stairs.

From every corner, as she passed, came sounds: voices, occasional laughter, a baby's cry. It didn't seem a gloomy place. It was a joint university settlement and, while funds were sparse, they were carefully controlled and there was no lack of supervision. The warden and deputy warden worked closely with the relevant authorities, for most of these women came from one authority or another – probation, health and various welfare agencies.

The hall was painted yellow, and yellow curtains with bright red, blue and green flowers flapped at the windows. There was a notice-board filled with posters, particularly of clinics, playgroups, voluntary agencies of various kinds, and appeals for attendance at local churches.

Next to the notice-board was the warden's room and, after tapping at the door, Flora made her way inside. Mrs Foulsham sat at a desk going through papers, a large pair of blue-framed glasses on her nose, and put out a hand.

'Do take a pew,' she said. 'Shan't be a tick.'

Mrs Foulsham's room was functional, being both an office and a kind of confessional where the souls of many of those entrusted to her care were laid bare, willingly and sometimes unwillingly, when Mrs Foulsham threatened to send them back to where they'd come from if they didn't improve their ways. She was a firm, friendly woman, not lacking understanding or compassion for her charges; but she had been in her job for a long time, not always at the same hostel but at the same kind of work, and she had little time for those who stepped outside a closely controlled system.

As Flora took a seat and looked round, Mrs Foulsham finished what she was doing, then she got up and pressed a bell by her desk while she straightened some papers on her table. After a few moments a girl in an overall popped her head round the door.

'Tea, please, Jean, for two.'

Jean nodded without saying anything and closed the door.

'Jean is one of our "good" girls,' Mrs Foulsham said approvingly. 'She came here four years ago after being imprisoned for soliciting and now she is one of my most trusted helpers.'

'Four years is a long time,' Flora said, in some surprise. 'I thought people came and went.'

'Oh, they do,' Mrs Foulsham shook a cigarette from a packet towards Flora.

'No thanks,' Flora said, as Mrs Foulsham lit hers and sat down.

'But Jean had nowhere to go, many of them don't, but I try and send them home or get them placed. Jean was a war orphan and the circumstances were particularly trying. She came home one day from a school in the country she'd been evacuated to and found her home razed to the ground and her entire family killed. She was the only one left. Wasn't that awful?'

'Terrible,' Flora agreed.

'She was sixteen, now she is twenty-six, and in those ten years she has lived a lifetime. I . . .'

Mrs Foulsham stopped as the door opened and Jean came in, skilfully balancing a tray on her arm. Flora got up to help her and Jean smiled.

'S'all right, Miss.'

'This is my new deputy warden, Miss Bolingbroke,' Mrs Foulsham said. 'She's joining us from today.'

'D'je do,' Jean said with a pleasant smile. 'Shall I pour, Mrs Foulsham?' Jean was clearly a woman of few words, but Mrs Foulsham smiled and Jean was about to go when she said:

'I've been telling Miss Bolingbroke how invaluable to me you are, about what happened in the War . . .'

Jean looked on impassively as though the story of her deprivation had long ago lost its power to move her.

'A relative of mine ran a school in the country in the war,' Flora said, without thinking. 'Where were you?'

'Askham 'all,' Jean said. 'Near Salisbury, Miss. Is that all, Mrs Foulsham?'

'But that's the school my cousin ran,' Flora said

356

excitedly. 'You must have known her. Lady A . . .' she suddenly stopped, without completing the name, and looked at Jean, feeling foolish. She'd only been in the place half an hour and her intention to remain strictly anonymous had already foundered.

'Lady Askham,' Jean finished for her. 'Was she a relative of *yours*, Miss?'

'Only by marriage,' Flora said contritely, sneaking a glance at Mrs Foulsham.

'She was ever so nice, Lady Askham,' Jean continued, thoughtfully, 'a bit snobbish, but that was her way. She was good to me and wanted me to come back to the school after I found out about my family. She came to London to see me, but I wouldn't go back. I often wondered what happened to Lady Askham. Her husband was in the war.'

Flora was suddenly solemn. 'He was killed right at the end. Cheryl, Lady Askham, went back to Kenya with two war orphans she'd adopted.'

'Johnny and Clare.' Jean nodded. 'They was the lucky ones.'

'What a remarkable coincidence,' Mrs Foulsham said, when Jean had gone. 'Fancy Jean and . . . your cousin.'

'I didn't mean to let all that out,' Flora burst out awkwardly. 'I didn't want you to think I was different.'

'Oh, but I could tell you were different at once, my dear.' Mrs Foulsham sipped her tea, cigarette still burning between her fingers. 'Even if you do try and disguise it. But you need have no fears. There are no class differences here.'

'I've lived apart from my family for a long time,' Flora said. 'My mother was a working-class girl from Preston; she was my father's second wife. It was through his first wife that he was related to the Askhams. So I'm not

357

related to them at all, really. But in a sense we're so close through my aunt, the dowager Lady Askham.'

Mrs Foulsham nodded approvingly. 'Very laudable that you choose work like this. Very laudable indeed. And I do hope you'll be happy with us, Miss Bolingbroke.'

Myles Crosby was a year old when Angelica decided that maybe they should have another child. She didn't particularly like children, but she particularly disliked *only* children. She thought that if children were to exist at all they were best in pairs.

She put the idea of another child to Dick as if they were having another pet – another puppy to add to the one they had. For Angelica had found that one could work and be a mother quite easily, providing one had a nanny, of course, and plenty of help in the home. She also felt that she should have her family while she was young, if she was going to go on modelling for Gérard and the top couturiers. Two children and then she could concentrate on her figure and her career. A year and it would all be over. It was almost as easy as buying a dog from Harrods.

'If you'd *really* like another child,' Dick eyed her doubtfully.

'I would, wouldn't you?'

'I would.'

'Well, then. I don't like this pill thing anyway. Some people say they haven't been sufficiently well tested. If we have another baby I can be sterilized.'

'Supposing you wanted another baby after that?' Dick smiled.

'Don't worry, I won't,' Angelica said, glancing at herself in the mirror before she got into bed.

Dick put down his paper and watched. He always desired her and he always would. He reached for her as she slipped into bed and pulled her nightdress right over her thighs.

'You do want it? Don't you?' Angelica said, cupping his face in her hands.

'Of course I want it,' he said gruffly.

'The baby I mean, silly. I know you always want *this*.'

Afterwards they rested contentedly in each other's arms. Their sexual chemistry was as good as it had been at the beginning when they were first drawn together, and when they made love she could forget all the other things that vaguely displeased her about Dick.

For one thing he was unambitious. He was content to work at a university for the rest of his days, writing rather dreary books which had a small circulation and quickly went out of date. Then he didn't like her friends and she didn't like his. They seldom met equally on social grounds. She felt they lived in a different world but, sometimes, she thought it was a good thing. That way, if she wanted to, she could have the discreet boyfriend or two, when the breeding days were over.

She was progressing well in her career, they had a nice home and the relations were always around if needed. Dick liked the relations, there was no doubt about that. He got on particularly well with her grandmother, though he and Arthur hated each other. In the recent election the Conservatives increased their majority, the first government to do so in peacetime conditions for ninety years. Eden had succeeded Churchill as Prime Minister just before the election and Harold Macmillan, the Foreign Secretary and, naturally, a friend of the Askhams, through his own noble connections, had promoted Arthur to a Minister of State in the Foreign Office.

Arthur and Dick argued continuously when they met. Charlotte said it gave her a headache and tried to invite them when Arthur was away. She would invite Rachel with Dick or Flora and Em and the four of them would discuss politics and world affairs until the small hours. Discussions one didn't mind. Argument was hateful.

Flora was a good companion as far as Dick was concerned. They went together to meetings and discussed banning the bomb and the eventual demise of the Conservative Party. Not that this was likely in the near future but it was nice to dream about. Angelica thought they were all dreamers and she and her mother smiled and let them get on with it, knowing that nothing would really change.

Flora was there when Dick and Angelica gave the family the news about the baby during one of the gatherings at Askham. It was July and they were about to go to the Continent on their summer holiday, motoring through France, to stay with Melanie and Susan in Venice. Dick and Angelica looked very happy and the family sitting around the dinner table were delighted. Arthur was there too because, for once, it couldn't be avoided.

It was a fine, warm summer and Charlotte was looking forward to going to the country too. She and Arthur liked to potter for their holidays. Angelica was leaving Myles with them and Stefanie was going to come and stay with Nicky and Galina. There would be trips to Askham and the seaside. Charlotte loved it.

To think of Dick and Angelica being parents again made her very happy. It seemed an indication they wanted to stay together, which people sometimes doubted.

'I'm so delighted, darling,' Charlotte reached out and clasped Angelica's hand. Her daughter smiled back, knowing that Charlotte was just as relieved that she and Dick still got on as she was pleased about the baby.

Afterwards she said to her mother, when they had gone up to her bedroom to powder their noses after dinner:

'Dick and I will never divorce, you know, Mummy. We suit each other.'

'I'm glad.' Charlotte looked at herself in the studied way that beautiful women do, as she patted her face. 'I do worry at times. You scrap so much.'

'But we make love well.'

'That's good. It's not the only thing, but it's good. Love can't go on forever though, you know, in marriage.'

'Yes, but Dick and I will keep going. We may have nothing in common but we'll stay together. To me marriage is an institution and Dick knows that. It is to him, too. He likes institutions.'

Both women smiled, sharing a joke. Mother and daughter felt very close at that moment and, as they came into the drawing-room together, Rachel noticed the *rapport* and she had one of those moments of sheer pleasure that sometimes came upon her.

To the far side of the room Dick and Arthur had started an argument. Ruth Ellis had been recently hanged and Dick was an ardent abolitionist. Arthur, old-fashioned Tory, favoured the retention of capital punishment. Rachel did wish that Dick and Arthur would keep out of each other's way and she shook a finger at Charlotte.

'I told you you shouldn't have brought them together.'

'Mother, I can't *always* keep them apart. He's my son-in-law and Arthur is my husband. Besides, Angelica and I are so close lately I don't want to spoil it.'

Rachel agreed. 'I can't remember ever having seen you so close.'

'We haven't been. I think she's happy and she has matured. I worry about her and Dick, but this baby makes it seem that everything's all right, doesn't it?'

'Well, we certainly hope so.' Rachel found it hard to be insincere. She didn't actually think that Angelica and Dick got on at all, even now, but then she didn't see them as much as Charlotte. When she did see them they usually had a squabble. They had come down to the Hall one weekend and Angelica had actually left before Dick, taking the car and leaving him to go back by train. That was only in May and this was July.

'It's so hot,' Rachel raised her hand in front of her face. 'When are you going to Littlestone?'

'Next week, with any luck. Stefanie and Sasha are bringing the children down on Saturday. I do hope you'll come over and stay, Mother.'

Rachel nodded but she wasn't sure. She was extremely nervous about Pascal driving his car around at high speeds on summer mornings and was terrified of anyone finding out. While the family were here it was under lock and key.

The car made Rachel anxious and she'd begged Pascal to tell Bobby and bring it into the open. He'd promised that as soon as he could he would; there had been some snags that were difficult to iron out. In truth he and Anna liked the atmosphere of secrecy in which they worked. It gave spice to their lives – shared trysts with a stop-watch involving the 'Phoenix' which was like a third person in their lives, or a baby.

'Oh Charlotte, I *do* wish you'd separate Dick and Arthur,' Rachel said suddenly. 'They're making me nervous.'

'I'll go and suggest bridge,' Charlotte said brightly. 'That *always* draws Arthur.'

It was very quiet on the terrace lit by the mellow light from the drawing-room, where the silence of the four playing bridge inside was occasionally interrupted by laughter, congratulations or recriminations. Angelica lay in a swinging hammock that had been part of the terrace furnishings since anyone could remember although the canvas, due to its popularity with the younger children, had been renewed from time to time. It was a long, comfortable hammock, suspended from an iron rail and surmounted by an awning of the same material. Angelica swung gently from side to side, her hands behind her head, and Anna sat by her side, sipping coffee.

'Do you ever play bridge now?' Angelica enquired.

'Very seldom these days. I like it, but we're too busy.'

'Doing what?' Angelica gave an incredulous laugh, 'stuck down here in the country.'

'Oh, we're anything but stuck, I assure you. Pascal is extremely busy on the car . . .'

'What car?' Angelica looked sharply in her direction.

'It's a secret at the moment. It's something quite special that we're about to announce to the family, and the world, very soon.'

'Is that where Pascal is now?'

'Probably,' Anna smiled mysteriously. 'He's more married to the car than me.'

Angelica's gaze remained on her sister-in-law, this curious, enigmatic woman whom she thought she knew but never did. New aspects of Anna were always revealing themselves, some likeable and some not. Anna had certainly taken Pascal out of the close family group he had flourished in. The relationship with Charlotte wasn't easy and, whereas Angelica had grown closer to her mother, Pascal had drifted further away. People said it was inevitable, especially with a woman as strong-minded as Anna. But strong-minded about what? Pascal, indifferent to the advancement offered by Bobby, continued to work on his cars and Anna seemed quite happy to stay at home in the rented country cottage, only making occasional forays to London. Some of the family even wondered if she was actually serious about finding a house there.

Angelica was one of the those closest to Anna and she felt able, now, to ask her something which no one else would dare. Anna was intimidating, however close one got to her, and she had a private, withdrawn side to her that few were able to penetrate. She and Pascal were close, that much was obvious, but how close really? What forged the conjugal bond between them, if it was not the usual thing of family and home? Ambition? Quite a few members of the family thought it was that. Certainly, since Bobby had made his offer to Pascal, seeming to push Sasha to one side, there had been yet another rift in the family which appeared to leave Sasha out on a limb and Stefanie battling with her father on his behalf.

'Don't you want a family?' Angelica asked at last.

Anna, who had been gazing thoughtfully into the dark, seemed jolted from a reverie and gave Angelica a cool stare.

'Nothing is further from my mind.'

'Sorry.'

'Why are people always on about babies? I find it tasteless, myself.'

In the dark even Angelica blushed. 'I suppose it's because I'm pregnant. It's on my mind. You must forgive me.'

'There's absolutely nothing to forgive,' Anna said with a pleasant smile. 'Where's Dick? He doesn't play bridge, does he?'

'Oh, goodness, no.' Angelica threw back her head and laughed. 'Nothing so frivolous. He's probably closeted somewhere with Flora having a good earnest talk. He should have married her.'

'One can quite see why he didn't,' Anna said, putting her empty cup on the table beside her. 'I absolutely adore Flora, but she is horribly plain.'

'That's not quite true, you know,' Angelica squinted up

364

at the awning above her head. 'She likes to look a mess; but if she tried, she could be quite pretty. The trouble is she'll never try. Sometimes I wonder what will become of our dear Flora. Probably an old maid like the last one.'

It was a tendency in the family to treat Flora like a beloved pet. They were all so fond of her, but they were not quite sure why. It is true that they gathered round her to protect and defend her, but they actually regarded her as eccentric; different, not quite an Askham, despite her distinguished connections.

Most of them disagreed with Flora – whether to try and change her, or leave her alone to get on with the odd sort of life she had chosen. Her motivations escaped most of the family except, perhaps, her Aunt Rachel and Dick.

Anna, who had been trying to suppress a feeling of excitement all evening, looked at her watch and slowly got out of her chair. She went over to Angelica and gazed down at her, a half-smile on her face.

'You shouldn't draw parallels. I think Flora's happy in the life she leads. Marriage isn't everything. Is it?'

'It certainly isn't.' Angelica sighed and closed her eyes, swaying to the motion of the swing. 'Sometimes I wonder why we think it is. It's expected of us, that's all.' She opened her eyes and stared straight into Anna's. 'Are *you* sorry you married Pascal?'

'Not a bit,' Anna said, aware of the excitement starting up again. 'Not a bit.'

'I'm glad of that. I'm sometimes sorry I married Dick. I could hardly have made a less suitable choice. We'll stick together, I expect. I promised Mummy we would. It would so upset the family if we split up.'

In the library Flora turned over the pages of the manuscript Dick had just given her.

'Thank you,' she said, a little breathlessly. 'Thank you very much.'

'You're the first to see it and I'm going to dedicate it to you because of the help you've given me.' Now that the act was done Dick felt shy. 'Although you know a lot of what's in it, having helped me so much.' He leaned forward and kissed Flora on the cheek and she seemed slightly taken aback and went rather red. Kisses didn't really seem to go with a learned treatise on the politics of capitalism.

Writing would never make Dick rich. His first book had been commissioned by a small, prestigious academic publisher which considered that it was doing him an honour by printing 500 copies and selling them for a fortune, out of which he got nothing.

'I really want to know what you think,' Dick went on, 'before it's typed. Your opinion is very important to me, Flora.'

Flora put the pages neatly together and, still a little flushed, pushed back her chair and walked over to the fireplace, which was closed off for the summer by a huge bronze urn full of flowers. She turned and faced Dick, who was still sitting in his chair by the table gazing at his massive manuscript, the result of five years of research and brain fatigue.

'I feel very privileged, Dick. I can't tell you how thrilled I am to be the first one to read your book.'

Dick looked up at her, feeling pleased himself. She'd plaited her untidy hair and coiled it neatly on top of her head. This gave her an inch or two of added height, and she wore a rather pretty, and most un-Flora-like, summer dress of navy blue with red spots, blue sandals on her feet. The dress had a low neckline and a red belt and the colours seemed to enhance her white skin and dark hair, her almost black brows over very blue eyes. Flora rarely made the best of herself, but why should she if she didn't want to? It wasn't her philosophy to try and please other people by her appearance. What mattered was what went on inside a person, not irrelevant externals like dress and appearance. Yet today she'd tried. Why? To please the family, as she had for Myles's christening, or to try and please Dick?

'We make a good team.' Casually Dick got up and went to stand next to her. 'How would you like to co-operate on a book with me, joint names? I'd like to trace the whole history of Socialism and its deviance from Marxism. You could deal, most valuably, with the feminist angle.'

'I'll have to think about it,' Flora said, after a pause. 'I really am terribly busy at the hostel. I feel I do very good work there, you know, practical work. I like to think that I'm actually doing something that is of value; that I can physically help other people. I feel I've led a very privileged life when I see how some people live and have lived all their lives.' Flora threw up her arms as if in exasperation. 'When I'm tired and in need of a little luxury, some good food, I can come here, or go over to Charlotte's or Anna's. Some people in the East End never get to the country in their lives. I'm going to ask Jenny if I can bring some of our girls down here from time to time for a few days of country air. I'm sure she'd say "yes".'

'I'm sure she would,' Dick said. 'But don't let your good works detract from the other important work you can do, which is using your brain. A lot of people can help those less fortunate than we are; but a good, analytical brain is priceless.'

Flora looked at him and, bowing her head, smiled.

Later, in bed, turning over the pages of Dick's manuscript, deciphering with difficulty his large uneven handwriting, she thought of him and Angelica asleep, just down the corridor from where she was now. Her feelings about Dick were very confused and she was not unaware of the parallel with Aunt Flora and her father. So many people had warned her about it, so it must be obvious now. She knew that Aunt Flora had always refused to be her father's mistress, even though they had shared a house and many people assumed they were lovers.

That evening, as she'd heard Angelica tell the family about the new baby, she'd had a feeling of jealousy that was quite new to her.

Flora was very careful about concealing emotion, even from herself, and, for many years, she had concealed the true nature of her feelings about Dick. She knew that now. She'd realized that tonight as she took the manuscript from him, the gift to herself of his most priceless possession and to be dedicated to her, not his wife.

Maybe now was the time to try and detach herself from him, rather than working more closely together. What was the point, now she knew that she was jealous of him, of Angelica, of what went on between them? What was the point of tormenting herself, of allowing herself any hope when they had deliberately decided to have a second child which did away with any idea that Myles was a mistake? Sometimes she wondered if Dick told her the truth.

Two children were definitely not a mistake. It seemed to mean that a couple intended to stay together; that they saw a lifetime before them, if not of connubial bliss, then at least of stability.

Resolutely Flora pushed her glasses up her nose, had a drink of water and turned over the pages of Dick's thesis on the politics of capitalism which was, undoubtedly, a work of genius.

* * *

Charlotte woke suddenly and lay in the dark, listening. Beside her Arthur stirred, too, and she said:

'Did you hear anything?'

'No,' Arthur mumbled from the depths of sleep. 'Hear what?'

'I thought I heard a car.'

'A car?' Arthur struggled to sit up, rubbing the sleep from his eyes. 'What time is it?'

'It's after three,' Charlotte said. 'I'm sure I was awoken by a kind of roar like a car. Who could it be?'

'I'm sure it wasn't a car,' Arthur said. 'No one was leaving tonight and no one would come at this hour.'

'I am wondering about Pascal,' Charlotte said, turning anxiously to the packet by her bedside and shaking out a cigarette. Arthur groaned.

'My dear Charlotte, Pascal is a grown-up, married man.'

'We've hardly seen him all weekend. He's fiddling away with something in that large old garage which is kept locked. Something's going on, Arthur.' Charlotte lit her cigarette with a slightly unsteady hand. 'I'm not sure what, but something. Mother knows.'

'Your mother knows what, Charlotte?' Arthur was wide awake now, sitting bolt upright and looking cross. The following day he was due to travel north before joining Charlotte for the holiday. Happily, Jill had arranged everything, but still it was a chore. In a busy life Arthur valued his sleep.

'I'm sure Mother's unhappy about something. Every time I mention Pascal a funny look comes into her eyes. I'm jolly well going to find out tomorrow what's up; what's going on in that garage.'

'Darling,' Arthur said, lying down again. '*Whatever* it is, I'm sure that it is something to do with cars and that can't possibly be dangerous, well, no more dangerous than usual. He's not making bombs, for instance. He has probably got some new project he's fiddling away on. You know you're the mother of a mechanical genius. Why bother?'

'They've both been acting peculiarly this weekend,' Charlotte went on, as though she hadn't heard him. 'Pascal *and* Anna. I tell you, there's something going on that's not quite right. Something they're trying to keep from me.'

'Then maybe you should be pleased,' Arthur said with a smile, his head deep in the pillow. 'Maybe you're going to be a grandmother again.'

'People seem to have babies on the brain,' Charlotte said mildly, but she did cheer up a bit. After all, Anna and Angelica had been having a long chat on the terrace while the others had been indoors playing bridge. The two young women, their heads together, had seemed very serious. Maybe it was women's talk; Anna, perhaps, confiding in Angelica, asking advice of the more experienced girl.

Yet, somehow, it didn't seem like Anna. And, also, what would Pascal be doing all weekend in the garage? And why didn't anyone know or, at least, ask?

Tomorrow she'd find out the truth.

Charlotte settled down and tried to go to sleep. Arthur began to snore gently beside her. She wished she had Arthur's capacity for putting aside all worries and getting a good night's sleep. For Charlotte worries came alive at night; like spectres assuming almost human dimensions. When, finally, her heavy-lidded eyes closed she abruptly came awake again, thinking she heard a car; but when she did fall into an uneasy sleep she dreamed about the day that Paolo had been killed in Italy, when she'd remained at home near Paris with the children, dreading, fearing the worst.

Sometimes one's worst fears did come true.

* * *

Pascal looked up, his eyes shining, as Anna crept into the garage, muffled in her coat.

'All ready?' he asked.

'Yes.' She nodded. 'I drove my car very slowly to leave it near the gate while everyone was playing bridge.'

'This is our big risk,' Pascal said, emerging from the bonnet of the car and rubbing his hands on a rag. 'Getting this out without anyone hearing. But the engine is much more silent than it was. It's time, anyway, that people knew. Shall we announce it to the family tomorrow?'

'We can announce it at breakfast,' Anna said, '*if* we get going now. I'm sure your mother thinks something's up.'

'Open the door, then,' Pascal commanded. He held up a hand and she stopped. 'Let's just recap once more. When I get past the church and on to the straight I'll stop and line up, as if for the start of a real race. I'll flash my lights and you will begin timing me the moment you hear the engine start up. I shall go just flat out until I get to the main road. Then, if all goes well, we shall come jubilantly back and break the news to the family.'

Pascal bent and kissed her, but Anna's lips were cold.

'Frightened?' he asked, breaking away and looking at her.

She nodded. 'Very. It's a terribly fast speed on a minor road. A terrible hazard if anything's about.'

'But nothing *will* be, darling. Nothing ever has at that time. That's why we chose to come here. You will have gone ahead to see. It will all be over almost in seconds but, I promise you, no more racing on the road. Next time it's Silverstone.'

Anna, ashamed of her display of nerves, held the door wide open and very slowly, Pascal rolled out the heavy car, pushing with all his might from behind. Then she closed the door, locked it and, between them, they pushed as far as they could until they were out of breath, not

371

wishing to disturb those in the house with the roar of its powerful engine. But it was very hard work and, at the beginning of the drive, Pascal started up and drove slowly and as quietly as he could to the gates, while Anna ran behind him, aware of a constricting pain in her chest which, she knew, was due to nerves. Thank heaven the gate-house was unoccupied. When she got to the gates Pascal was already out and opening them and, the engine once more silent, they pushed the 'Phoenix' through the remaining few yards to the road.

It was nearly four o'clock and soon it would be daylight. The countryside was alive with birdsong and the air smelt marvellous. A new, splendid day was in front of them. All weekend Pascal had been working on the engine, fine-tuning it to try and break that vital barrier of 200 mph.

From the entrance to Askham Hall the road wound for about a mile, skirting the village until, by Askham Parish Church, there was a junction and then a long straight road that ran for about five miles until it met the main trunk road from London to Southampton. This road, resembling as it did a race track, was ideal for Pascal to try and get the kind of speed he was aiming at before making his announcement to the world, thus stifling the criticism that would inevitably come from Bobby and the family if he could announce that he had achieved a real breakthrough. Before that he could be stopped, after that he couldn't. No one could stop him if, on a race of 197 miles or so, he could average over 120 mph. In the 1954 French Grand Prix at Reims the Mercedes driven by Hans Hermann had set the fastest lap of 117 mph before blowing up. It was a dangerous, experimental time in Formula-One racing and too many drivers were being killed – recently Marimon and Ascari.

The distance Pascal was to race from the church to the

road was a measured mile over two laps and Anna's timing would give him the average.

Pascal saw Anna into her car, closing the door and then leaning through the window, his eyes sparkling with excitement. His whole body seemed vibrant with emotion and expectation. Anna, still feeling cold and nervous, looked at him with some anxiety.

'Please be careful.'

'All *I* have to do is press the accelerator,' Pascal said. 'You have much more to do; clear the way and ensure the stop-watch is accurate to the milli-second.'

'Don't worry.' Anna, aware that her teeth were beginning to chatter, blamed it on the cold. 'I have it under control.' Lightly Pascal bent forward and kissed her on the lips, which were still as hard as marble. He stepped back, his smile gone.

'You really are terribly nervous, aren't you?'

'I'm terribly cold,' Anna said, pushing him back and attempting a brave smile. 'Now get going.'

'You get going,' Pascal said and, giving her a casual wave, loped back to the car which was hidden by a tree. Then he got into the cockpit and sat watching her drive off until she was out of sight.

Anna drove rapidly along the straight road. She was worried about the light. But there was no one around. A few sleepy cottages, well off the road, were silhouetted against the skyline, and one or two farmhouses still slumbered in the distance. Only the birds moved, swooping around in their morning search for food. She drove until she reached the trunk road and then she turned back until she came to the spot they had selected where she would hear Pascal, observe his lights flash and set the stop-watch for the measured mile. By the time he passed her he would be already into it.

At 4.15 A.M. she heard the car roar into life, saw the

373

lights and, ignoring the pounding of her heart, the pain in her chest, pressed the button to start the watch.

Peter Martin looked with satisfaction at the newly-cut hay which lay where it had fallen the day before to dry out. This season, with any luck, due to the fine bright summer, they would have two harvests. He had promised to lend his tractor to a fellow farmer, whose own had broken down, to help him bring in the hay. The farm was seven miles away and Peter had wanted to be off at dawn before the traffic began to build up on the major roads.

Just as Anna went by, Peter Martin came to the edge of the field and opened the gate. He thought, maybe, that someone was coming from the Hall, going up to London early. All his life Peter Martin and his family had been associated with the Askhams, living on a tenant farm, and his younger son had gone to school with Johnny before he went to boarding-school.

Eventually Peter Martin drove his tractor through the gate and, leaving it in the middle of the empty, silent road, jumped down like a good farmer to close the gate after him at the same time as Pascal Verdi started his measured mile.

In the Hall three miles away Charlotte woke up from her nightmare, her heart pounding, her face drenched with sweat. Arthur slumbered beside her and throughout the park she could hear the birds singing.

She got out of bed and went to the window, drawing back the curtain and opening it a little to peer out. This beautiful scene, familiar to her since childhood, was so serene, so peaceful, it made her catch her breath. It instilled in her a feeling of great, pervasive calm. Below her the lake shone like a mirror, broken here and there by a swan venturing down the grassy slopes of the bank

374

for a morning swim. Ahead of her the uneven conifers, of varying shapes and sizes, of the forest of Askham seemed to brush the opalescent sky into the colours of a new, sun-filled day.

It was a scene of such harmony and tranquillity that, reassured, she got back into bed, thankful that what had been was only a dream.

PART 3

The Sins of the Father

January 1956–August 1957

CHAPTER 15

'The Askham constitution has, as a rule, been considered so strong,' Lady Melanie said, with some irritation. 'I can't think what went wrong.'

'Mother, you *are* seventy-nine,' Bobby said in a gentler tone of voice than people, even his mother, were accustomed to hearing.

'Seventy-eight,' Melanie said sharply. 'Don't make me older than I am.'

Propped up in bed on white pillows Lady Melanie who, in the twenties, had caused so many scandals, so many hearts to flutter, looked like some ethereally pale ghost, her face faintly lit by the translucency of death. The previous month she'd been shopping in the Merceria when she'd fainted and came to in the Ospedale Civile surrounded by grave-faced doctors. After investigation and several weeks in hospital they had let her go home, without telling her the verdict. She had advanced cancer and would not have long to live.

Trying not to alarm her – and Denton was almost paralysed with shock – Bobby and Susan were sent for, and Sasha and Anna came too. Stefanie stayed behind with the children, and Christopher sent word he must be kept informed. Christopher and Sylvia had alienated themselves completely from the rest of the family, including Melanie, by their treatment of Rachel. Besides, Melanie had never had much time for her middle son who, to her, had always lacked charm; an unforgivable sin in her books.

Bobby sat on his mother's bed and contemplated the

reflection of the pale wintry sun on the polished parquet floor. One of the servants spent his entire time polishing the floors just as, in the old days, one servant was responsible for nothing else at Askham Hall but lighting the fires. He had gone all day back and forwards with wood and coal, keeping them blazing and, in the winter time, his task was hardly ever done.

All the floors in the Palazzo Quinducale on the Rio de Fava, round the corner from the Merceria which linked the Piazza of San Marco with the Rialto Bridge, were polished parquet. Some were sprinkled with rugs and some were covered with carpet. Some, like the corridors, were unadorned. There seemed to be miles and miles of highly-polished parquet and it was the task of one man to keep them in a high state of gloss, winter and summer, year after year.

'Mother, even the Askham constitution can tire . . . you're merely tired.'

'Rubbish,' Melanie said.

'It was thought I had a minor heart attack myself, a spasm, after David left to go to America.'

Melanie clicked her tongue in apparent sympathy. It was seldom she thought of others than herself but, just occasionally, the miseries of a member of her family might affect her and Bobby was her eldest son.

'You're quite *old* yourself, Bobby,' she said severely. 'Fifty-seven. Don't forget how young I was when you were born. You're no longer a young man and you must take care. You should delegate more; let that wretched business of yours run itself.'

'No business can run itself, Mother. I am incapable of delegation.'

'So I hear.'

'Anna has been talking to you?'

'Anna *and* Sasha were in my room last night. They

380

talked for a long time about you and the business. How you won't delegate, how you won't let her be a director.'

'But Mother, she's a woman . . .'

'Very competent,' Melanie sniffed. 'A granddaughter of mine and a daughter of Susan, who is also a very competent businesswoman. Susan is very competent indeed; galleries in the main capitals of Europe and all doing well.'

'Then Anna should go and work for her mother if she thinks she has the time. I don't want any petticoats running my company.'

At times, Melanie thought, Bobby showed his worst side. After Pascal's terrible accident one would have thought that he would have more sympathy for a woman whose husband, having escaped death, had become a paraplegic. For nearly six months Pascal had been a patient at the hospital for spinal injuries at Stoke Mandeville. Yet even now everyone knew that he, who should never had driven his car at such a speed on a public road, would never walk again.

'Anna has a lot of spunk,' Melanie said, eyeing Bobby with some dislike. 'I admire her enormously for what she has done for Pascal, and if she wants to work now I don't blame her.'

'In time Pascal will be able to do work, of a kind,' Bobby frowned, 'if only from a wheelchair. The doctors say his mental attitude is remarkable, thanks, too, to Anna. The whole thing should never have happened. It was a ghastly scandal which badly dented our image, yet again. Millions were lost from Lighterman shares on the stock market. Of course, I'm sorry for Pascal but he has only himself to blame – and Anna.'

'Well, I know I can't do anything to change your mind. I'm too old, I'm afraid. I've realized that, at last. Never thought I would, but now I have. I shan't bother about my family, not that I ever did much. I'll let you all get on with it.' Melanie paused for a moment and looked towards the window where she could see a patch of blue Venetian sky, the birds hovering overhead, pigeons cooing on the window sill. She realized that, in Bobby's opinion, the real harm had been done to his reputation, never mind the human sacrifice. She gave a deep sigh. 'I know people thought me selfish, very. I wasn't a heroine like Rachel, slaving for my family. How she did it I'll never know, running that paper, losing all the Askham money.'

'Rachel didn't lose all the Askham money,' Bobby said, in surprise.

'I know she didn't. You took it. But she lost it all the same.'

'I didn't *take* it, Mother!' Bobby angrily got off the bed and began to pace the room. 'I got them off the hook, if you want to know. I actually helped them.'

'That's not what I heard.'

'Then you heard wrong, Mother, with all respect. I gave them a good price for what they had. Most of their money went in the Wall Street crash. None of them ever had a clue about money. Ralph least of all.'

'Poor, dear Ralph,' momentarily Melanie's eyes clouded. 'What a tragedy . . .' she shook her head. 'And now to have a little Jew as Earl of Askham. I don't know what my father would have said.'

Bobby glanced nervously at the door.

'Mother, you can't talk like that!'

'Why not? It's my own home. The doors are closed. I shan't hide it from you, you above all. I don't like the Jews. That's why I supported Germany. You don't remember before the war, Bobby – the First World War, I'm talking about – how much the Jews dominated London society. They had too much influence over King Edward. Poor Teddy; he was in hock to the Jewish money-lenders. Now we have an Earl of Askham who is half-Jewish. And he's very Jewish-looking, too. As least he was when I last saw him.'

'He was baptized in the Church of England, Mother. Don't be so silly.'

'Ah, but his *mother* was Jewish,' Melanie said, lowering her voice. 'That's the thing. That's where the Jews get it from, the mother. Marian was thoroughly Jewish and so is Paul. There's nothing of Freddie in him at all . . .'

'Well . . .' Bobby looked uncomfortable. 'Paul *is* very shrewd. Now, I wouldn't mind him in the business. He's very different from his father, that irresponsible Freddie. I can tell you that.' Bobby nodded with satisfaction as though, somehow, the credit for it was due to him, which decidedly it wasn't.

'Children are very different from their parents,' Melanie said. 'That's well known. Thank heaven, I say, sometimes, anyway. You're not a bit like your father, who was dashing and debonair. I can never see Harry handling money the way you have. You're like *his* father, Sir Robert. I don't know what Harry would have done in life, I'm sure.' Melanie's blue eyes, still unfaded, looked vaguely puzzled. 'Do you know poor Harry has been dead *fifty-eight* years? I was working it out the other night. I find that absolutely incredible. To think of his white bones by the side of the Nile . . .'

Bobby shuddered, though it was difficult to feel anything real about the bones of a man he had never known, even if he was his father.

'Bobby.' Melanie put out a hand and took his. 'Come and sit beside me. I have something to tell you.'

His mother's face worried Bobby. Ashen as she was she looked very close to death, yet her blue eyes seemed to blaze like aquamarines, still hard and brilliant despite her years. Compulsively he clasped her hand and sat on the bed again.

'Lord Lighterman,' she said. 'How proud Harry would have been of you. And Sir Robert, dear old man, he always wanted a peerage. I don't think he paid Lloyd George quite enough. He was a very greedy man, Lloyd George. Did you have to pay anything for your peerage, Bobby?'

'Mother, how *could* you?' Bobby said angrily, hastily dropping her hand. 'I certainly *didn't*. I can't see the late King consenting to the sale of peerages. Mine was recommended by Winston himself. I practically won the War for the Allies.'

'I'm sure you did, dear. I'm so sorry.' Melanie stroked his arm placatingly. 'Could you give me a sip of water, dear, because I have something to tell you.'

Anxiously Bobby passed her the glass, looking at her face. His mother seldom worried him, but now he was very worried indeed.

'Maybe you should rest, Mother, and I'll come back later.'

'No, I want to tell you now. I want to get it off my chest.' Melanie paused. 'Bobby, what I want to tell you is this. Come close now.' Nervously Bobby bent his head until her lips were nearly touching his ear.

'Your brother Jordan is alive.'

'Jordan is *what*?' Bobby said loudly, starting away from her.

Melanie put her finger to her lips, vigorously shaking her head. 'Jordan *is* alive. In this house. He has lived here since the end of the War. No one knows, or very few.'

'Oh, my God,' Bobby said, rocking backwards and forwards, his face in his hands. 'Oh, dear God. I hoped he was dead.'

'Bobby! He's your half-brother.'

384

'I know, but still, what a liability. Supposing it gets out? The shares in my firm would plunge immediately. I wouldn't be invited to the Royal Enclosure at Ascot. I . . .'

'Bobby, *stop* thinking of yourself,' Melanie said sharply, 'and think of Jordan. I'm very worried about Jordan in case I die . . .'

'Well, don't expect me to do anything for him. Look, Mother,' Bobby sat up straight, '*Denton* is his father. Let *Denton* be responsible for him.'

'Denton couldn't be responsible for himself,' Melanie said scornfully. 'You know he's been half-senile for years. He doesn't even play at the tables now, but sits in a chair at his club all day, nodding over a brandy and soda.'

'Does Denton know he's here?'

'Of course Denton knows he's here. Jordan turned up one day in 1945. It was a terrible shock, I can tell you, even if he is my son. Jordan is a little crazy, too, to tell you the truth.'

'He always was, Mother. He is truly Denton's son.'

'Don't be cruel, Bobby.' Melanie adopted an uncharacteristically wheedling tone to her voice. 'Jordan is a sick man.'

'Then you must get rid of him. Put him in a home.'

'He's not that sick, Bobby. He's just slightly odd. I agree he's given us enormous problems, but one can't simply just get rid of him, however much one would like to. He is very happy in a flat at the top of the house and never comes down. He hasn't been on the streets for eleven years. Occasionally he wanders through the house at night, but otherwise he never leaves his room. Poor Jordan. His hair is quite white. He looks about seventy, even older than you.'

'Why are you telling me this, Mother?' Bobby said.

'Because *if* I die I want you and Susan to look after

385

Jordan, as a last favour to me, your mother. Jordan and you share the same blood, the same mother, however much you may regret it. In my memory I want you to look after your half-brother and see that he's taken care of.'

Jordan said: 'I'd never have recognized you, Bobby.'

'Nor I you,' Bobby said, taking the seat indicated by his half-brother, who had remained seated with his back to the window, though it was still possible to see how much he had aged. That once luxurious black hair was completely white and, due to the many years he had spent in this state of voluntary incarceration indoors, his white skin looked thin and fragile, like parchment.

There was ten years' difference between Jordan and Bobby but it could have been a generation. They had grown up apart and had never liked each other. During Jordan's 'difficult years' – and they had been prolonged and, in the thirties, included adherence to the Nazi party – Bobby had frequently been despatched by his mother, who shared responsibility, to 'talk' to Jordan. The talks had rarely been successful. Bobby hadn't seen Jordan for nearly twenty years, since he had visited his mother in Cannes after Jordan had escaped from Germany because he had fallen foul of Hitler.

Bobby shivered. He was sorry he had to see him now.

'Are you cold up here, Bobby?' Jordan said affably, as Bobby wriggled in his chair. 'Or frightened?' Jordan's black eyes widened and it was possible to see the handsome youth he had once been. Bobby and Jordan resembled each other though they had different fathers: they were both dark and each, in his youth, had been called beautiful. Now they were both middle-aged and Bobby knew that there were many instances when Jordan strayed over the bounds of rationality.

'Why should I be frightened?' Bobby said, finally finding a comfortable position in the high-backed Renaissance-style chair.

'I'm a wanted man.'

'I know that.'

'I wonder Mother told you. She's terrified I'll be betrayed. That *would* bring shame on the family, wouldn't it, Bobby?'

'You already did that,' Bobby said, 'during the war. The things you said were terrible, but I'm not here about that.'

'Why are you here, Bobby?' Jordan looked at him with the curious, darting eyes of a rabbit.

Bobby realized his attitude was unfriendly, but he liked Jordan no better than he had years before. He felt no pity for him now and no sorrow for his condition. Of all the members of the family who had been 'lost' during the War – Hélène, Charlotte, Ralph, Kyril – no one had ever bothered, after it was over, to look for Jordan. They were only glad he was gone. He was an embarrassment; a blot on the family scutcheon.

Clearly everyone, except those in the know, hoped he was dead.

'Because Mother's dying.'

'Mother's *dying*?' Suddenly terror came into Jordan's eyes. 'But she hasn't been ill for long.'

'Well, she was ill and she didn't know it. She has inoperable cancer. Gradually it's penetrating all the parts of her body. I felt you should know that, Jordan, and also that our mother has charged me with your care. After she is gone you will be looked after. I have promised her that.'

'Here? As I am?'

'I think so. I can't see where else you could go, unless Susan disposes of this palazzo. Then we'd have to find

387

you somewhere else.' Seeing the panic on Jordan's face even Bobby felt pity. He knew he was dealing with a sick man who had reverted, almost, to his childhood. If that point was reached they would have to put him in a home. Hopefully by that time the Allies would have stopped caring about him. Wasn't there a time limit to the hunt for war criminals?

Jordan looked at the floor, his body hunched up, his hands like little talons on his lap. The tears were trickling down his face.

'Without Mother I'll have no one,' he said. 'No one cares. Susan hates me. Anna . . . Anna I liked. Anna has always been good to me. Terrible about Pascal but, maybe, if he dies, she will come back and live with me. She says she loves it here.'

'Pascal won't die,' Bobby said. 'He is being too well looked after.'

'You sound as though you regret it, Bobby.'

'Not at all,' Bobby replied sharply. 'Please don't provoke me, Jordan.'

Somewhere there was a stench in the room which reminded Bobby of death, though his mother's room was kept fragrant and sweet-smelling. It was decay, it was putrefaction. The man in front of him had undoubtedly caused many deaths by his treachery in the War.

Jordan gave a deep sigh and seemed to return to some inner form of contemplation that perhaps comforted him.

Bobby got up and abruptly left the room. He couldn't stand any more of it. It was incredible to think that Askham blood ran in Jordan's veins as well as his – the blood of heroes coursed through the veins of a traitor.

To Anna, Venice was home. She had spent her formative years there and, although she loved England, the time-lessness about Venice that spoke to so many people spoke to her too. It spoke to her inner ear and gave her a kind of peace she seldom enjoyed.

Susan and Anna sat inside at Florians looking on to a windy, rain-swept St Mark's Square. They often had their morning coffee or afternoon tea there. In the spring and summer, the warm days of autumn, the café's patrons liked to sit outside and watch the drifting population: but inside, in winter, it was very cosy and full of people they knew, acquaintances to whom they nodded and passed the time of day.

Since Pascal's accident Anna and Susan, who had come over as soon as it happened, had become very close. Susan had remained with Anna all the time during which Pascal was on the critical list in hospital, and without the wise counsel and comfort of her mother Anna didn't know how she herself would have survived. Anna was a fighter, but fighting to keep Pascal alive and her own spirits up was an almost insurmountable task and, if the family tried to comfort her as well, some of them were half-hearted about it.

Many of them blamed Anna for what had happened to her husband.

By Christmas Pascal had improved, and then came news of Melanie's illness, much more serious than was at first supposed. It was only when Melanie was pronounced to be dying that Anna and Susan took the chance of leaving Pascal, still undergoing tests to establish his true condition, to fly to Venice.

'It really *is* lovely to be here,' Susan said with a sigh, looking at Anna, 'despite everything.'

'I know what you mean,' she said, after a while. 'Just to be in Venice *is* to lift the spirits. I wish we could stay here forever. I wish,' Anna paused and looked at her mother, 'I'd never left.'

389

'Do you really?' Susan's hand closed over Anna's, who violently nodded her head.

'I do. Pascal would still be perfectly all right if I hadn't married him. He would never have dreamt of defying the family to build a racing car.'

'He may have done. I don't believe in Fate.'

'I do, unless fate and chance are incompatible. You may say I was fated to meet Pascal and yet . . .'

'You *were* cousins, after all. There was a very good chance that, knowing each other anyway, you would eventually fall in love and marry. Also Pascal, with the blood of his father in him, might have developed the car on his own.'

Anna gazed at the black dregs of coffee in the bottom of her tiny cup as though trying to tell her own fortune. Slowly she shook her head.

Susan felt that, in a way, Anna's fate was worse than Pascal's. She was imprisoned by guilt, by the unspoken recriminations of the family. No one knew the exact truth because neither Anna nor Pascal had told anyone, but it was suspected that Anna had encouraged him to defy Bobby and work away on the car in secret. There was also a criminal element in much of what he appeared to have done: using the firm's funds to finance parts of the car and driving at dangerous speeds upon a minor road. If Peter Martin had been in his tractor when Pascal hit it he would have been killed outright. As it was, his prompt action in dragging Pascal from the car before it burst into flames was not only an act of heroism but saved his life.

The heavy fine that had been fixed on Pascal was, however, academic. Nothing could fix his broken back.

Soon it would be time to go back to England and face it all again. Now, just for a while, despite the gravity of Melanie's illness, there was a little respite, a little peace.

390

They were preparing to leave when a voice behind them said, in faultless English:

'Anna Ferov!'

Anna turned round at the sound of the voice as though someone had stuck a knife with a sharp point in the small of her back. Her pale face took on the faintest blush of colour and her mother turned her head to see the cause of the disturbance. Behind them stood a tall, distinguished-looking man with sparse greying hair, a florid, Teutonic face, a cigarette in his hand. As he bent towards her Anna said: 'Gunther' in a voice so faint that Susan hardly caught the name.

'My dear Anna, how lovely to see you.' Gunther stooped to plant an elaborate kiss on the back of her hand.

'This is my mother,' Anna pointed to Susan. 'Princess Ferova.'

'Dear Princess,' the Baron said, gallantly kissing her hand as well, 'how delightful to meet you at last. Anna used to tell me so much about you during those happy days in Frankfurt.'

Happy? Anna looked at him. Happy? Well, maybe they were happy, in the beginning. In the beginning, but not at the end. But did Gunther know how unhappy she had been since? Probably not.

'This is Baron von Spee, Mummy,' Anna said, trying to regain her composure.

Susan looked at him frostily. It was the Askham way to smile, though, even when one was disapproving and even when one remembered with awful clarity just who the Baron was and what he had done to her daughter.

Susan extended a strong shapely hand, manicured nails lacquered a brilliant red. She wore a red woollen dress with plenty of chunky jewellery on her arms and round her neck, her brown hair was stylishly cut and becomingly

391

streaked with white. She was an attractive, but not a pretty woman, whose handsome looks had scarcely changed since her twenties.

'How do you do, Baron?' she said. 'We are just about to leave. Good-day.'

'Please wait a moment,' the Baron said urgently and, crossing the room, talked rapidly to three male companions, obviously all Italian, whom, evidently, he'd been sitting with. They all stood up and politely shook hands with him, looking curiously in the direction of Anna and Susan. The Baron came back across the room and took a seat between Anna and Susan who, out of politeness, had sat down again.

'I'm just here on a business visit,' he said breathlessly. 'What a bit of luck I bumped into you.' Searchingly he studied Anna's face. 'Are you all right?'

Susan thought that he seemed bewildered by her appearance and quickly answered for her daughter.

'Anna's husband has been seriously injured in a car crash.'

Gunther nodded.

'I was very *sorry* to hear that. How exactly did it happen?'

'He was testing a racer he had built,' Anna said in a clear unemotional voice. 'He was trying it out on a local road and went straight into a tractor that had just come out of a field.'

'At four o'clock in the morning,' Susan said, icily. 'Not the time one expects tractors to be out and about on country roads. Pascal was dragged from the wreck which catapulted right over the tractor, but his back was broken. He had the most dreadful injuries.'

'I really am very shocked,' Gunter said, beckoning to the waiter. 'Please allow me to buy you a cognac.'

'No, thank you,' Anna said. 'It's too early for us, but

392

please do have one yourself. You see, it's exactly the sort of thing that happened to his father. He was killed in a crash, as you know. Unfortunately, now we are all over here together because my grandmother is dying.'

'How sorry I am to hear all this,' Gunther said sympathetically. 'And is Pascal . . . is there any hope . . .'

'He has made a really remarkable recovery,' Susan said.'He is very strong-willed and Anna has been marvellous; but the doctors still think that there is no chance he will ever walk again, or even be very mobile. His movements may be very restricted even in a wheelchair. They are doing tests at this very moment. His spirit, though, is absolutely fantastic.'

'I was in South America in the summer,' Gunther said, as though racking his memory. 'That's how I must have missed it and, of course, the "Askham", continues to sell well.'

Susan felt better disposed towards the Baron as the meeting continued. He was a man of a good deal of charm, as well as tact and sympathy, and she could see why he had once attracted her daughter. Indeed he was most paternal in his concern; he was so much older than her daughter.

'I do hope you will allow me to visit you while you're in Venice,' the Baron said as the two women made movements to suggest that they must go.

'We shall only be here a day or two longer,' Anna replied. 'But thank you for thinking of it.'

As she rose Gunther rose, too, and she held out her hand. For a moment as she looked into his deeply sympathetic eyes she remembered the good things about their relationship. There were many. As they clasped hands she was aware of his strength and, for an instant, she longed, just momentarily perhaps, to lean on him.

393

'My wife died last year,' Gunther said, lowering his voice. 'When you met her she had not long to live.'

Anna thought she saw a suggestion of tears in his eyes and her grasp on his hand involuntarily tightened.

'I'm so sorry,' she said and, in that moment of mutual bereavement, the glances that passed between them, Anna felt that, in some explicable way, a new bond had been formed.

'I found the Baron rather charming,' Susan said after dinner, when Bobby had gone up to sit with Melanie.

'Didn't you expect it, Mother?'

'I suppose I did,' Susan smiled. 'Knowing what good taste you have. A man of experience, very attractive to women.'

'His wife is dead,' Anna said, looking impassively into the fire.

'Really?' A nerve flickered in Susan's cheek. 'Well, no point thinking what might have been. You must put him out of your mind, Anna.'

'Oh, don't worry, I already have,' Anna said, pushing her hair back.

'I can see, darling, that the future doesn't look too rosy,' Susan said, realizing that she was guilty of massive understatement. 'But remember that you have duties, and obligations.'

'Of course I have and, don't worry, I shall do whatever is expected of me.' Anna gazed for a long while into the fire and Susan imagined that what her daughter saw in the flames contained little cheer. Maybe there was a forbidden but quite natural thought that Pascal would have been better dead. In a way his tremendous spirit made it even worse.

But still there was the guilt. She knew how guilty Anna felt.

'Do you think Uncle Bobby has finished talking to Granny?' Anna said. 'I would like to have an early night. I feel terribly tired.'

'Why don't you go up and listen outside the door? If he's there I'll explain to her that you were tired.' Anna leaned down for a kiss and Susan's hand lingered on her cheek. 'Good-night, my darling. Try and put all the bad thoughts out of your mind. You never know, there may be a miracle.'

Anna smiled but said nothing. Scooping one of the Palazzo's languorous Siamese cats off its comfortable chair by the fire, she draped it over her shoulder and, cooing to it, left the room.

When she had gone Susan put down her needlework and went over to poke the fire. The Palazzo was a cold place in winter, despite central heating. The rooms were high and some of the windows didn't fit well as, over the years, the foundations of the Palazzo had shifted on the marshy ground in the Venetian lagoon on which it was constructed.

Susan had bought the Palazzo in the thirties, well before the war. There was no thought of escape in her mind then but it had been a refuge: for her, for her mother, for Jordan. Sometimes it was difficult to remember that Jordan still lived there. Days went by without one seeing him. Had it not been for Melanie, Susan certainly would never have taken him in, but left him to find his fate with other hunted war criminals. When her mother was dead that sense of obligation would die, too. Decisions, lots of decisions would be necessary.

Susan shivered and pulled the cashmere shawl she'd put on over her red dress. They seldom changed for dinner now, unlike the days before the war when it was *de rigueur*. Many, many things had changed and she had changed too; from a rather insecure girl, living in the shadow of a legendary beauty for a mother, to a successful, accomplished woman who, like her half-brother Bobby, had made a fortune in her own right.

But Anna worried her and the expression on her face when she first saw the Baron was more worrying still. It was perfectly obvious to her that the Baron still had the power to charm her daughter.

From outside the heavy door Anna could hear her grandmother's strong voice quite clearly:

'It's useless to go on blaming Anna, Bobby. You must blame yourself for not exercising more control. You should have known exactly what was going on. It's *your* business.'

'But, Mother, I trusted them.' Anna could sense the irritation in Bobby's voice. 'Is it so wrong to trust? There was Sasha, too.'

'Sasha had far too much to worry about,' Melanie said tersely. 'Sometimes I think this family *does* have a curse on it. Has Stefanie stopped drinking?'

'Sasha says she has; but she is not a very happy young woman. Pascal's accident devastated her. Sasha is very responsible for what happened, too.'

'Blame, blame, blame, Bobby,' Melanie said, and Anna could imagine one of those long bony fingers thrust at him. 'There's nothing you can do about it now. If Anna wants you to give her some position in your company, do so. She is very capable. It will give her something to do.'

'Out of the question,' Bobby said. 'I once quite liked Anna – when she first came, supposedly, on a visit. But now I have little time for her.'

There was a long silence and Anna thought they had begun to whisper to each other, maybe sensing her presence. Fearing that Bobby might be tiptoeing to the door she was about to move away when she heard him say in a loud, clear voice:

'I have always thought there was something rather evil about Anna, Mother, as though she'd inherited the mantle of her father. You know that Em and Ralph were quite convinced Kyril killed Freddie.'

'A story I dismissed immediately,' Melanie said, with emphasis. 'Utter rubbish. What was he doing siding with the Republicans in Spain?'

'He was a double spy.'

'Nonsense, these things don't happen in real life. The notion inflamed Em's journalistic imagination. I only hope to God Anna never gets to hear such a fabrication. You must take care never to repeat it again outside these walls, Bobby.' Melanie paused and Anna was sure that her loud heartbeat could be heard on the other side of the door. 'Anna *may* have a touch of evil, and I grant you she is an odd girl, but all the Ferovs were most peculiar. Even after his excellent war Sasha has proved rather weak; Stefanie has taken to drink. What are we going to make of them? I was always against first cousins marrying. I tell you, my dear, it was a very bad day for us when those Russians entered out lives. Personally, I'm extremely sorry that the Askham family ever had anything to do with them.'

Anna fled along the polished corridor on tiptoe, more fearful than ever now that she might be detected.

In the course of the next week Melanie seemed to rally a little and Anna and Susan left for home. But Bobby found it hard to tear himself away from his mother, in case he should never see her again. Bobby's response to the fact of his mother's impending death had surprised him. He had long felt that most of the emotion had been drained from his life; but the thought of Melanie leaving it was too much for him. He had rushed to be with her and now he couldn't bear to go.

Bobby stood at the window of his mother's room, gazing down into the dark, shiny waters of the canal which wove its way through Venice between two opposite sides of the Grand Canal. The Quinducale Palazzo in its little backwater was undisturbed by the noise of the traffic that flowed ceaselessly up and down the Grand Canal: the *vaporetti*, the water buses, the motor boats, gondolas and private craft that made it one of the busiest thoroughfares in the world.

Up the Rio Fava chugged, a few times a day, motor boats delivering goods, or passengers, to various other houses up or down stream; gondolas with tourists in high season and barges full of produce being taken to or from the various street markets; or building materials used in mending or constructing some building along the way. The canal was very narrow and on the other side was one of the municipal buildings that had once been a private palace of an illustrious family, long since extinct. The only lights that illuminated the waterway were those from the Quinducale.

Very soon the Lightermans would be extinct, Bobby thought, pressing his head against the latticed window as if to try and expunge a kind of agony. David, his heir, had deserted him. Maybe he would never be found again, never inherit his title upon Bobby's death. There would be no Lighterman dynasty which Bobby had so wanted. He thought a lot about death these days; it seemed to pervade his life. There had been so much of it in the war, which had affected him and his immediate family; there had been the terrible tragedy of Pascal and now that anchor between him and the past was dying, too: his mother.

He swiftly crossed the room and took the hand of his

mother, who had been watching him with bright, knowing eyes.

'Penny for them, dearest boy?'

'I was thinking of David.'

'I thought that was it. Always David. Have you any idea where he is?'

'Somewhere in the South, maybe New Orleans. He had, or has, a jazz band there. We send money to the New York bank and he draws on it.'

'Stop the money.'

'I can't.' Bobby shook his head. 'It is the only way I can ever hope to see him again. I was also thinking about the Lightermans, Mother, and what a short period of glory we've had.'

'All *your* glory, Bobby. Yours alone.'

'And Grandfather's.'

'Ah, yes, dear old Sir Robert. And Mabel,' Melanie put her head back on the pillow and sighed. 'I loved Mabel better than my own mother.'

'I know you did.'

'And Harry . . . your father.' Melanie looked at him. 'He was my first love, my first man. You are very like him, Bobby, and Harry would have been proud of you.' Her hand tightened on his. 'Now, dear, I think you should consider returning to London. We have had many happy days together and I know you have work to do. You know what I want and I am sure you will do it. I have given you my instructions and they are clear, Bobby.'

'Very clear, Mother; but I'll soon be back.'

Melanie studied his face for a moment, as if seeing every feature for the last time. Then she smiled and shook her head.

'I do not intend to die, Bobby, inch by inch, wasting away as I am wasting now, putrefying, decaying while they try and keep me alive. Oh yes, don't worry, I know that I am dying. I'm no fool, you know. I'm a realist. My heart is strong and my brain good, but what use are they to a woman whose body was once her chief asset?'

Melanie shook her head.

'When my dear sister Flora felt she was no longer necessary she knew what to do.' Melanie kissed his forehead as he bent down, tears beginning to well in his eyes. 'She knew what to do, and so shall I.'

Kneeling beside her, Bobby buried his head in his mother's lap and she stroked it, crooning a little tune as she had when he was a tiny baby – as helpless as she was now.

CHAPTER 16

Rachel sat studying the letter that Hugo had handed her. He stood anxiously watching her as she read it, turning the pages slowly before going back to the beginning again. Then she put it down and carefully removed her half-moon spectacles.

'Of course you must give your mother a home.'

'Oh, Rachel.' Hugo sat by her side and took her hand. 'I really think you're perfect.'

'Nonsense, boy,' Rachel burst out laughing. 'Didn't you give *me* a home when I needed one? I could quite easily have gone to Charlotte or moved in with Em. I daresay quite a few people might have been kind enough to offer me shelter. Yet your mother has no one but you and now she has no money left. Of course you must have her. What a good thing, incidentally, she made over half her fortune to you when she did, otherwise you would have had nothing.'

Rachel had been aware that for some time Hugo had been worried about Nimet who, after the exile of the King in 1952, had moved to her villa in France leaving, however, most of her fortune behind in Cairo. The revolutionary government of General Neguib had seized the assets of many of the wealthy Cairenes who had been unwise enough not to have moved them out of the country already, and Nimet was left only with the money she had deposited abroad and her house in St Tropez bought before the war. The irony was that, during the war, the vast fortune left her by her late husband had been brought back to Egypt for safe keeping. Now only the return of the monarchy could restore it to her, and that seemed very unlikely.

For the last four years Nimet had lived in increasing discomfort in St Tropez forced, by her standards, to save and scrimp and make do in a way that had not been necessary since before the first war when, as a very young, uneducated girl, she had been forced into prostitution to make a living.

Yet Nimet was a woman who refused to abandon her dignity and it had been with some difficulty that she brought herself to write to her son telling him that, in order to make ends meet, she would have to sell her home and live on the proceeds in some cheap hotel. But the cry was there, in every page of the letter. Nimet seemed to be saying to Hugo: give me a home.

Hugo, comfortably seated, was studying the letter again. Finally he said:

'She may not come, but I feel I have to offer.'

'Of course you have, and this place is big enough for both of us.'

But was it? Em didn't think so. She thought it was quite preposterous that Hugo should consider giving Nimet a roof over the same head as her mother: two women who had once been rivals for the affection of the same man.

'But it was donkeys' years ago, darling,' Rachel said. 'We're both old ladies. I am eighty next year. There is no sexual jealousy, or any other kind of jealousy left as far as I am concerned.'

'Nevertheless, Mother, it is a difficult situation. You never particularly liked Nimet, even though, when you've met, you've been civil to her. I think to share a house with her would be intolerable.'

'It's a very large house.' But even Rachel's self-confidence was waning. It *was* a large house but there

402

were meeting places, communal quarters where they ate and congregated. There was the garden which she tended and the terrace which she considered almost her exclusive sphere, sheltered from sun and wind and with its lovely views of the lake and grounds.

Here, now, as she was, Rachel felt privileged, important and wanted. What difference would the presence of Nimet make to all this?

'You could move in with me, Mum,' Em said. 'But it wouldn't do, would it?'

'I'd hate London again,' Rachel said. 'Maybe Bobby would lend me the money to buy a house.'

'It is quite awful,' Em said, jumping up and lighting a cigarette, furiously throwing away the match, 'that we, the Askhams, have to go to Bobby begging for money.'

'That's how it is, darling.' Rachel resignedly folded her hands on her lap. 'I'm quite used to it now.'

'Bobby took it all from us in the first place.'

Rachel reached out for Em's hand and pulled her over.

'Don't go over that again, Em. That *is* water under the bridge. I'm sure Bobby would lend me the money, but I don't like to ask him and I do love it here.' Rachel looked round at her pretty chintzy sitting-room with its corner views of the grounds, the Grange, with its chimney smoking, tucked in the woods on the other side of the lake. Next door was her bedroom, and Hugo had made a private bathroom and lavatory for her so that she was quite independent from the rest of the house. If she liked she could stay in her flat for days on end. There was a house telephone as well as an external one.

'Really, I could wall up here against Nimet if I wished,' Rachel said. 'It might not be for long.'

'What do you mean?' Em looked at her sharply, but all she got was an enigmatic smile.

* * *

403

Walking through the grounds towards the lake later in the day Em recalled that smile of her mother's, a smile without joy, and realized that she had been thinking of Melanie, dying in Venice. Melanie was a year younger than Rachel, and that sudden sapping of vitality must have both saddened and alarmed a woman who had very rarely been ill. Now Rachel suffered a bit from shortness of breath and occasional palpitations. The doctor said that she had a very slight heart condition which was nothing unusual for a woman of her age. Otherwise she was as robust as someone twenty years younger. It was no longer possible to garden quite so vigorously, one had to potter instead.

Thoughtful Hugo had immediately put her in charge of some of the greenhouses where he was cultivating rare plants to mass-produce for market gardens. The age of the garden centre was about to dawn in England, encouraging a flurry of activity on the part of those who, before the war, used to make do with a few packets of seeds. Rachel was thus able to sit, or stand if she wished, cultivating her embryonic plants, experimenting with cuttings and creating a private botanical world which she supplemented with wide reading and catalogues from rival establishments.

She should also rest more and not cavort with the small grandchildren as though she were one of them. In other words she hadn't to stop but slow down and, being Rachel, a woman renowned for her activity, it had been difficult.

Now how would she react to a woman ten years younger in the house who had once been her husband's mistress, be it ever so long ago? Nimet and Rachel were very different; one the practical Englishwoman, used to hard work, doing good and putting others before herself; the other a highly volatile, temperamental oriental whose only work in her life had been to use her body to do the kind of thing she knew best how to do: pleasing men. In the end she had been fortunate in pleasing one who not only fell in love with her but was very rich, the Turk Theo Igolopuscu. It was he who had made a respectable woman of Nimet el Said, the Cairene prostitute who had so ensnared the eleventh Earl of Askham, Rachel's husband Bosco.

Rachel had brought up Hugo after Bosco's death when his mother abandoned him. How ironical, now, that the wheel had come full circle.

Em involuntarily squared her shoulders as she neared the Grange, puffing a little as she got to the top of the hill because it was still March and the weather was cold. She stood in front of the garden gate and then, pushing it open, went in, down the path and stood knocking at the door. She was aware that the quick beating of her heart meant that she was afraid as well as out of breath, but still she knocked again and when the door opened an inch she pushed it right open and said:

'Hello, Felipe. Might I have a word?'

Felipe, surprised, stood back and watched her as she walked into the hall of the house that had been Rachel's favourite home, the house where she, her sister and brothers were born. Dear, familiar home. Em took a deep breath and faced Luis's father.

'Do you think we could go and sit down?'

'Luis isn't here,' Felipe said, standing his ground. 'I don't know when he'll be back.'

'I didn't come to see Luis, but you.'

Felipe, glasses on the end of his nose, slippers on his feet, frowned. He clutched a book in his hand and she had obviously interrupted him reading. She saw Felipe about twice a year when she came for Luis and they scarcely ever spoke. There was very little for ex-lovers, who now hated each other, to say. The best thing was to say nothing.

But Em had decided she could let this go on no longer. The time had come to speak. She didn't wait for him to open the door to the lounge but went in herself, noting the smell of must and decay that seemed to permeate the house where Felipe had lived for eighteen years. From time to time it was redecorated at family expense; a woman came from the village to clean it but, otherwise, Felipe was left alone.

Em was aware of Felipe shuffling after her as she lit a cigarette and pulled her coat round her for warmth. Her hands were blue with cold. Felipe had obviously been crouching over some fire, for the one in this room wasn't lit. It looked, in fact, as though it were hardly ever used and suddenly, vividly, Em recalled what fun they had had as children in this large gracious room, with the view of the Hall, standing in its neo-classical elegance, at the top of the hill opposite Askham forest.

Yet it was still a friendly house, her mother's house. She gave a deep sigh.

'I want this house back, Felipe. My mother needs it.'

Felipe pushed his glasses up his nose again and stared at her. More extraordinary than anything else was the fact that she had ever loved him, she thought. Difficult, no, impossible now, to recall those passionate years in Spain and England, nearly twenty years before. Difficult to remember that hard, tough fighter, Felipe Barrio, commander of the Madrid garrison that held out against the Nationalists until they were overcome in 1938 and forced to flee. What dreams and hopes they had then.

Felipe was ten years older than she, which made him now fifty-eight. He looked another ten years older than that with a grey fringe surrounding a bald dome and loose, wrinkled skin over a thin cadaverous frame. Like

406

her, he smoked incessantly, a habit nurtured by the tensions of the thirties but, unlike her, he looked ill and had a rasping cough.

Yet in his way he had been a good father to Luis. Whenever he mentioned his name his voice grew softer and the expression in his eyes changed.

Felipe had sat down when she began to explain what had happened about Nimet and the predicament Rachel now found herself in. It was unfair, in Em's opinion, that Rachel should have to share a home with her father's mistress. Besides, Rachel had always loved the house where she had lived in their early married years with her husband, where all her children were born. It was the family home and it was theirs. Not his. Luis was now eighteen and about to become independent. She was, she explained, appealing to Felipe's better nature.

'In other words I'm being flung out,' Felipe said, his tone almost the snarl of a wounded animal.

'No, I'm not flinging you out,' Em replied. 'I've thought about it very carefully. I'm not going to do what my family have refused to do all these years, make you homeless. It's what you deserve, Felipe, for you are nothing but a parasite, but we wouldn't do it. We didn't do it mainly because of Luis, but now Luis is old enough to understand.

'For nearly twenty years my family, which lost all its money and could scarcely make do for itself, has kept you, body and soul, fed you, clothed you, housed you.'

'Very inadequately,' Felipe sniffed.

'I'd dispute that,' Em said. 'I think you did quite well. At first we were subsidizing you until you had produced a great, authoritative work on the Revolution but it has never materialized.'

'Marx . . .' Felipe began in tones of indignation, but

407

Em knew what he was going to say. It had often been rehearsed before her.

'Marx, I know, lived in poverty and his great work didn't appear in its entirety until after his death. But Engels had money and we haven't. If my mother moves elsewhere she has to borrow the money from Bobby and we don't want that. It's humiliating. Besides, why should we if we have a home that is rightly my mother's? She is eighty next year. Her heart's not at all good. Why can't she live here in peace for the remaining years left to her?'

'Because it's my home,' Felipe said, tapping a cigarette out of the yellow Gold Flake packet. 'I shan't let you have it. I shall fight you.'

'With what? You have to have money to fight in a Court of Law.'

'I shall use Luis to fight you. You and all the Askhams who have treated him, and me, like pariahs.'

'Never Luis.' Em had begun to tremble. 'Never him. Luis was always loved, always wanted, always loyal to you. And my family wanted to love you, too, until you became so objectionable, so rude, so intolerable.'

'I hated your class, your people. The more I saw them the more I detested them.'

Somewhere inside the house a door clicked but, in their mounting anger, neither of them heard it.

'Your mother with her fake socialist views. How they made me laugh. The Red Countess, what a joke! La Pasionaria would have made mincemeat of Rachel. You are all products of your class, all of you, especially you, Em, and for that I despise you.'

'Then how can *you* continue to take charity from us?'

'Quite easily.' Felipe lit a fresh cigarette from the stub of the old one. 'It is not charity, it is my due. I have made my contribution to society. I am one of the few original thinkers the Revolution has produced and, one day, I will be recognized. You, you miserable Askhams, should feel privileged that you can in any way support and help me. I'd rather your old mother walked the streets than that I give up this house to her.'

As Em, goaded beyond endurance, moved over to strike him he seized her hand and, with his eyes blazing with hatred, began to twist it behind her back. At the same time he started to beat her with the clenched fist of his left hand and Em's cry of pain almost became a scream.

All this happened within seconds so that when Luis intervened between his warring parents it was almost too late to prevent Felipe breaking her arm. As Felipe saw Luis he jumped back, letting her arm fall, and Em lost her balance and fell heavily into Luis's open arms.

'What in God's name is going on?' Luis cried. 'Mother! Father!'

Em was trembling so much that Luis led her to the sofa and anxiously examined her arm which seemed to hang rather oddly at the side of her body. To Em it was quite numb, but she began slowly to waggle her fingers and at last said with a rueful smile:

'No bones broken. I'm frightfully sorry about this, old thing.'

Em still spoke in the accent, and with many of the mannerisms, of the thirties, as though stuck forever in the memory of her happiest, most rewarding years. She had a rather dumpy figure and wore her hair in a style reminiscent of the pre-war years too, cut very short at the back with a wave falling over her forehead. Em favoured tweeds or jerseys, slacks and skirts and sensible shoes. She could hardly have been more of an antithesis to her fashionable but much beloved sister Charlotte.

Felipe stood in the middle of the floor, angrily studying his feet and biting the nails of his right hand.

'Father!' Luis said. 'How *could* you attack my mother?'

409

'Don't blame him,' Em said shakily. 'Well, not too much. We both lost our tempers.'

'I'm afraid I heard what it was about,' Luis said. 'I heard a lot of things I didn't like; lots of things about the family that are untrue, Father. I think the Askhams have done everything for you, and me. I don't know how you can speak about them like that.'

Felipe attempted to address his son in Spanish but Luis would have none of it.

'Let's talk English, please, Father, in front of Mother. I don't want you to think I am ungrateful, but I am slightly disgusted to find *you* so ungrateful. Mother, I'm sorry.' Luis turned to her. 'Are you sure you're all right?'

'I'm fine.' Em attempted to stand right up. 'Perhaps you could call the Hall and ask Hugo to come and fetch me.'

'And what about Gran?' Luis stood where he was, staring at his father. 'What about my grandmother, Father?'

'What about her?' Felipe said.

'Where is she going to live?'

'Not here, certainly.'

'But it's her home.' Felipe stared back at his son as if not comprehending what he had said. 'It's her home, Father,' Luis repeated.

'Then where is *my* home?' Felipe said. 'Am I to be put into the street? Is this my reward for so many years of looking after you?'

'Depriving *me* of the chance of seeing my family, Father, of being with my mother, my cousins, my grandmother. Making things as difficult as you could as often as you could; making *me* feel guilty.'

'You're an ungrateful . . .' Felipe began with a roar, but Luis held up his hand.

'I'm grateful to you for many things, but not for that. It

410

is only as I've become older I realized what I've missed; the company of my cousins, friends of my own, my mother's love. Did you know how I hated those "duty" visits? How I resented knowing the rest of my family were gathering at the Hall and I couldn't visit them? Did you know, Father, that I used to slink into the grounds and get as near to the Hall as I could to see what was going on?'

'Oh, Luis!' Em burst out, holding out her good hand to him; but Luis ignored her. This was between him and Felipe.

'I know you loved me, Father, but you terrified me, too. Hearing the way you talked to Mother today has released me from the obligation I felt towards you. I love you, Father, and I always will; but I will never be subject to you again. As for this house, you must get out of it and give it to Gran.'

Felipe sank on to a chair and buried his face in his hands. Momentarily even Em felt a spasm of sorrow for him.

'What is to become of me?' Felipe murmured. 'I am not well . . .'

'You are not being abandoned, Felipe,' Em said, aware of the lightening of her heart. 'You never gave me the chance to say that I am prepared to go on supporting you out of my own income. I have never had the expenses that other members of my family have. I am prepared to buy you a flat or a small house wherever you wish, to go on supporting you. But I want this house, Mother's house, for her.'

Rachel held on to Em's good hand; the other arm was in a sling. In front of them the newly emancipated Luis walked up and down, his hands in his pockets.

Luis took after Em. He was of medium height and

sturdy, with Em's nondescript colour hair, blue eyes and firm chin. He was a boy whom none of the family felt they knew very well. Even his mother didn't feel that she knew him and the day's outburst had been both a shock and a surprise. Luis had got a place at Oxford from the local grammar school and was to study Spanish, in which he was naturally fluent. It was as if it had been his first language rather than his second. He didn't look particularly English but rather continental.

Rachel said:

'I couldn't possibly do what you say. Thank you, though.'

'But Mother, it *is* your home.' Em's eyes filled with tears. The doctor had left an hour before and there had been some pain in treating her arm, not broken but twisted slightly by her shoulder and very, very painful.

'It is my home, darling, but it is Felipe's, too. He has lived there much longer than I ever did. Your father and I only had a relatively short marriage, you know, ten years. The ten years following I moved about a good deal. The Grange was a weekend retreat, you were all dispersed. I think Felipe has a right to it, too. I would never, never ask him to give it up. Poor man, from what you say he is in rather a bad way.' Rachel smiled up at Luis.

'The thing that would make me happiest, Luis, apart from having you to ourselves again, is if your father could feel more kindly towards us. He is a lonely man, very isolated with few friends, if any. No wonder he is unwell. You are to leave home and he must feel unbearably lonely. I would never dream of taking his home from him as well! I know what it is to lose a home – it's a terrible experience. If I'd known what Em had in mind I'd have stopped it. I would never have allowed her to go, and I shall make sure that Felipe's mind is put at rest as soon as

412

I can. Maybe you, Luis, would tell him and ask if, in time, I might come and see him. I only want to be his friend.'

Knowing what his father had said about his grandmother, Luis's heart filled with tenderness towards this venerable old lady who was the matriarch, the mother of the family.

'You are a wonder, Gran,' he said, bending down to kiss her. 'I do admire you.'

And that, for Rachel, was the miracle that had come out of all this trouble and misunderstanding; the very best thing of all: the return of the prodigal to the fold.

During the winter and spring of 1956 almost all of Melanie's immediate family came to Venice to take leave of her. She received them all regally, propped up on her white pillows in her canopied bed, her hair freshly done daily by her maid Agnès, who had been with her since she exiled herself to France in the twenties after her third marriage. Agnès was thought not to have a tongue or a mind of her own, which was as well. For over thirty years Melanie had been her tongue and her brain, her direction, her very life. Now Agnès looked after her with the tenderness of a mother, a nurse, a slave. Without Her Ladyship, Agnès did not know what would happen to her. So every day she washed Melanie and clothed her in a fresh nightdress, each one with a variety of pretty, lacy jackets. She applied Melanie's make-up and perfume and, when she was ready to receive her first guests, she guided them to the bedside like a votary to the goddess that, over the years, Melanie had become to her.

Melanie rather enjoyed the process of dying. She enjoyed the long-drawn-out affair it had become; receiving her sorrowing relatives, observing how brave they tried to be. She felt she could detach herself quite easily from it all. She enjoyed the little homilies she delivered

413

to them, rather as a confessor does to a penitent: pointing out their faults and emphasizing their virtues. They were not allowed to answer back. She was quite stern to some; indulgent to others. For some she deeply cared and, with them, she became sorrowful, too. Charlotte was one.

Charlotte came with Arthur for a week and she and Melanie spent many hours together.

Charlotte, a woman of fashion and elegance, had always got on with her aunt, who had once been the toast of London. She admired how, even towards the end of her life, Melanie had maintained standards: the hennaed hair, the perfect grooming, the immaculately made-up face – a face that grew increasingly skeletal as her illness progressed; those once-splendid features disappearing in mounds and crevices, areas of hanging, wasted flesh that plummeted on to her neck and bosom. The garishness of the make-up enhanced the impression that one was watching a play, and that the death of Melanie wasn't real at all.

Melanie and Charlotte had not met since the accident and as soon as she had arrived Melanie had asked to see her, to be left alone with her. Somehow Melanie who, throughout her life, had been a selfish self-centred woman, felt she had a contribution to make to help Charlotte, and she had. In those many talks, sitting together hand in hand, Melanie had helped her.

'You're such a rock, Aunt Melanie,' Charlotte said, pressing the almost withered hand in hers. 'I don't know what I will do without you.'

'Oh, I'm not going yet,' Melanie said brightly. 'Not until I'm ready. But you have your mother, Charlotte, and, of all the women I have known in a long life – I hope I too shall live to see eighty – your mother is one of the finest.'

'I know.'

'She is the best mother you, or anyone else, could have. The best friend. She is a rock. All I would have wanted for Rachel in her old age is happiness and peace of mind and this she has not got. I know how she loves Pascal . . .'

'I thought it would kill Mother,' Charlotte said. 'But she was there with us, the first there at the hospital to see him. For weeks we thought he might die – he didn't recover consciousness, you know, for a fortnight. We thought he had brain damage and his speech still is a little affected. It was the most frightful time in my life; but, oh, how grateful I was then for my family – Mother, Angelica, Joe, Arthur, Em. Even Jeremy knew what I was going through. And Anna . . . well,' Charlotte blew her nose. 'Anna was splendid.'

'She would be.' Melanie patted her arm.

'But it was *her* fault, Aunt Melanie.' Charlotte's voice rose a little hysterically. 'It was her fault. Sasha said it was she who encouraged Pascal to build the car, defy Bobby, who had specifically forbidden him to do it. They thought I was a silly superstitious woman because of Paolo and, oh, the night it happened I had such dreams . . . I remember waking up and it was so calm and peaceful at Askham, you know how it can be early on a summer's morning?'

'Oh, I know,' Melanie sighed. 'How I know.'

'And that was about the time it happened, and I went back to bed and slept until they woke me up. I still can't believe it.'

'Will he never recover?' Melanie looked searchingly at her niece. 'He is so young.'

'He *has* recovered a lot; but the spinal nerve is completely severed. Nothing that is at present known to modern surgery can be done. Even now he has limited use of his hands and arms. The best we have been told to hope for is that *one day* he may be able to propel himself along in his wheelchair unaided. But walk? Never. Never walk, never have a proper married life, never have children . . .'

'It is a terrible price to pay for a prank.' Melanie, close to tears herself, shook her head and began to stroke Charlotte's burnished curls, neatly coiffured about her head. 'But don't blame poor Anna. It must have been something he wanted to do, too. She was ambitious for him. I can see that they, mere children, could regard it as a challenge.'

'I *do* blame Anna,' Charlotte said, with emphasis. 'I do blame her. Without her, Pascal would be walking today, perhaps here to see you. I blame her and I shan't forgive her. Ever. The moment I saw Anna I knew she was bad news. There *is* something about her, Auntie, something wrong. Everything she touches goes bad. Her influence on my family has been awful. Angelica changed completely after she met Anna. Pascal became enslaved. Even Joe can't stand her, and I've never known why.' Charlotte paused. 'In a way I fear her.'

Slowly Melanie nodded her head, her hand still resting in Charlotte's.

'Kyril's daughter,' she said.

The one person who didn't come to see her old friend and former sister-in-law was Rachel. She disliked the idea of flying and felt she was too old to begin. In many ways, perhaps, she was glad that she was spared the spectacle of seeing someone so vital and attractive deteriorate. In other ways she felt she couldn't face any more tragedy. Pascal's accident had weakened her.

There was a time when she had not particularly liked Melanie, and, while she was married to Adam, she had occasionally hated her. But there was always that admiration that one has for beautiful, self-absorbed, powerful women and Rachel had been no less a victim of envy than others. She wrote many loving letters to Melanie in these last months and, towards the end, she thought of her constantly, as though Melanie's death were somehow, inevitably, a prelude to her own.

Olga and Natasha Lighterman came; Joe Verdi flew over with Angelica; Paul Askham and Luis came hitch-hiking across Europe; Em came by car to see her aunt and drive the boys back, and finally, in the late spring, there were two important last visitors from England: Sasha and Stefanie, the latter looking much better, though her grandmother didn't think so.

'Terribly, terribly drawn, dear,' she said. 'For a young girl with looks like yours it's a scandal. Your mother would have been ashamed of you.'

Stefanie sat down by her grandmother, reaching for the hand that lay on the bed, so thin and skeletal that it was as though death had already paid its last visit.

'I can't expect you to understand, Granny. You've always been so strong.'

'I know you drink, dear, or drank. Now I've always been fond of alcohol; champagne and occasionally a little whisky, but to drink too much is ridiculous. It solves nothing. It sent you to hospital.'

'It *is* in the past, Gran.' Stefanie, conscious of her weakness, attempted a smile. 'We have had such a terrible year that my sufferings seemed nothing. Sasha felt so responsible for what happened to Pascal I thought he might kill himself. It was up to *me* to be strong then, to help him. My father blamed him, too. People blame everyone rather than Pascal, and it was *his* fault. He made the car and *he* insisted on testing it secretly on the roads long after Anna and Sasha had begged him to go to a proper race track. Sometimes I hate my family, Gran.

417

They are so unfair. They make Sasha and Anna feel they don't belong.'

'Hatred isn't good for the looks, either,' Melanie said reflectively, 'and a woman's best, most effective weapon is her face.' For a moment she studied Stefanie's carefully. 'You have a very beautiful face, or you had. You are now, let me see, how old?'

'Twenty-eight, Granny.'

'Twenty-eight is nothing. In my day it *was* quite old, but today it isn't. Now, I want to tell you this, my dear Stefanie, because I have always had a weak spot for you. You had a tragic life. I never forgave your father for what he did to you girls, and he knows it. But he is my son and I love him, though I know just what he's like. Your mother was not what she should have been: she was vain, unfaithful and ambitious, but in the end she was a heroine. She was a brave woman. She redeemed herself. Why don't you, in memory of your dear, brave mother, take a little more care?' Melanie's fingers fluttered in and out of Stefanie's thick dark locks. 'Bring a little joy to your husband for all he has endured? We all had such hopes of Sasha and, now that Pascal will never walk again, we have hopes again. Bobby is determined to make Sasha succeed in the business. If anyone benefited from poor Pascal's accident it was Sasha. *You* must be the woman behind him. *You* must push him and make him strong. I was always a strong woman, and the only one who was too strong for me was poor Adam. I left him and married a weakling who has spent my money gambling, and drunk too much. Let Denton be an example to you.' Melanie began visibly to tire and drew Stefanie towards her. 'I have a lot of hope and faith in you, my dear. I shan't see you again after you go back.' She lifted a finger as if pointing to heaven and her face was illuminated by an almost ethereal smile of great beauty. 'But I shall be watching.'

Stefanie waited until she was outside her grandmother's door and then, uncontrollably, she broke down and wept.

Sasha and Stefanie went back and then Melanie knew that she had seen all her family, given her advice and benediction. How wise Melanie had become in those last few days, as if making up for a lifetime devoted to herself. Few left her who did not feel better for what she'd said to them. Only Susan and those who lived at the Palazzo now remained.

Melanie had good days and bad days, many indifferent ones and some when she was full of pain. At the beginning of summer, when Venice began to get so hot and Susan had used to take her to the house on the Lido or, latterly, a hotel on the mainland, she found she was unable to move. In the summer an odour rose from the canal that gradually permeated the Palazzo; the heavy walls seemed to attract and retain the heat and the only respite came at night or early in the dawn.

Melanie knew then that her time had come.

She sent for Jordan towards eight in the evening when it was still twilight. The windows were tightly closed against the pervasive stench and a fan gently whirled beside her bed. Agnès had bathed and dressed her for the night and, as she left to fetch her mistress's youngest son, Melanie's hand lingered in hers.

'Thank you, dear friend,' she said in French, the language in which she always addressed her maid. 'Come, let me kiss you.'

Agnès, trembling, stepped forward and the tears rolled down her cheeks as her mistress's lips brushed her brow.

'*Adieu, mon amie*,' Melanie said, 'you are well provided

for,' and then she put a finger to her lips, gently pushing her old servant away.

After she had gone Melanie lay for a while turning over the pages of the Bible that her mother had given her as a confirmation present. The date written in her mother's neat hand was 23 July 1891. She had been thirteen years old.

Melanie couldn't see very well now and it was no use trying to find some comforting words from those yellowed, little-read pages. But as she let her fingers run through the leaves she could see in her mind her mother and father, her brothers, Arthur and Bosco, her sister Flora and herself all tripping into the family pew at Askham Church, while the congregation rose and remained standing until the gentry had said their brief prayers and taken their seats. Soon she would be there again.

It really was another age. It had lasted for centuries – people knowing their places, an established hierarchy in an established order; but it could never come again. It ended with the First World War and it would never return. In a way she was glad to be going. As she placed her Bible by the side of her bed the door opened and Jordan softly stole in. He only ever moved around at night, like a ghost, and often he sat by his mother's bed in companionable silence until she was asleep. In a way Melanie was the only one who had ever understood him.

Melanie put out a hand for him, slowly, painfully, and drew him to her. She looked at his tired prematurely old face and something told her that Jordan might not be long behind her. She loved Bobby, but as a whole human being. To her, from a very early age, Jordan had always been a cripple, an invalid, someone to be protected from the world. Someone not as other people were. She had been told she was over-protective, and that it was all her fault. But she loved Jordan with an irrational passion that only a mother can know.

Jordan looked anxiously at her and then drew up the chair he was accustomed to sitting in and leaned forward.

'Why did you send for me so early?'

'I feel tired tonight,' Melanie whispered. 'I feel like a long sleep. I wanted to talk to you first, my dear, because one day I may not wake up . . .' She felt Jordan's hand tighten over hers and an expression of blind panic flitted across his face.

'Not yet. Not yet,' he pleaded.

'It *has* to come, my darling.' Melanie knew that her strength was ebbing, but she tried to keep her voice strong. 'And I want you to be prepared for it.' She felt very weak now and wondered if the medicine the doctor had given her would not be necessary, if she would pass into eternal sleep without its aid. But he had promised, Melanie had made him promise, that the end would be swift and painless.

She could see a little phial of liquid just out of arm's reach because, somehow, she had never intended to make that final act herself. As a well-brought-up girl, of the upper-classes, it offended against all those good Protestant instincts she had been nurtured in; and maybe Flora too, when she let herself over the side of the ship on the Nile, had not been quite sure whether or not she would see the other side.

'Just open that little bottle, would you, my dear?' Melanie said, pointing with a shaking finger, 'and pour the contents into a glass? It will help me sleep. And Jordan, my dear boy,' she kissed him on the forehead as she had Agnés and the rest, that final gesture of benediction, 'I do believe in eternal life and that we shall meet again.'

421

'Don't talk about that just yet,' Jordan said, rising slowly to his feet. 'I'll see you tomorrow.'

'Tomorrow,' Melanie nodded, watching him go to the far side of the bed. First of all he didn't see the bottle in the gloom and then he nearly knocked it over. But, finally, he unscrewed the top and poured some of it into the glass that had stood by its side. Melanie watched him keenly, wanting everything to be right.

'All of it,' she said impatiently. 'I had a lot of pain today and I need a long, deep sleep . . . a very long, deep sleep. Thank you, darling.'

Reaching up, she took the glass from him, swallowed the contents and settled back on her bed, sighing deeply, her hands already resting on her breast. Jordan saw her close her eyes and then, moments later, he crept from the room, not knowing what he'd done.

CHAPTER 17

Maybe Melanie's spirit had settled over Askham the day in September that they buried her in the family vault, where so many of her ancestors lay, their coffins piled one upon another on slats, like the catacombs. She rested over her mother, whose oaken coffin lay over her husband's.

Ironically, Melanie was the only child of Dulcie and Frederick, the tenth Earl, to be buried with her parents. After so many years of exile, she had come to rest in her father's house.

There was almost an air of levity as the congregation emerged into the sunshine and got into cars, to be transported back to the Hall. There had been no resounding choruses as at the memorial services for Freddie and Ralph, no calls to the faint-hearted to be warriors like them. The hymns to shepherd the soul of Lady Melanie into the Eternal Presence had been gentle, nostalgic. A kindly light had been invited to lead her home.

And she had come home, in the fullness of her years. It seemed a reasonable thing to do and, some thought, she was lucky to have achieved it.

For Rachel it was a day of intense nostalgia. She had been at Melanie's first wedding in Cairo fifty-eight years before; at her second in London to Adam in 1901, was aunt to Melanie's two children by Adam, Christopher and Susan. Christopher was pall-bearer at his mother's funeral, together with her grandchildren Sasha Ferov and Mark Bolingbroke, Christopher's eldest son, Paul Askham and Joe Verdi. Except for passing visits to

423

London and Askham, Melanie had ceased to be part of the social scene after she went to live in France with Denton, when Royal Ascot was barred to her and her name was crossed off the list of those acceptable at court. Melanie was sybaritic and she loved the heat – not the heat of Venice in the summer, but the heat of the south of France when the mistral blew. Now she was at rest and soon, inevitably she, Rachel, must join her.

Back at the Hall the ever-busy Jenny had, as usual, organized the kind of party most people remembered before the War, except that then mourners partook of refreshments in a very different setting, waited on by footmen in full livery. Now the grand reception rooms were almost empty of furniture and the Aubusson carpets threadbare. The walls needed a coat of paint, and the chandeliers swinging from the ceiling looked none too safe.

Many, of course, went into the garden, on to the terrace or wandered along that well-worn path that led to the lake. The young people helped out, the men in rolled-up sleeves, the girls in cotton frocks, and there was an army of volunteers from the village, whose ancestors had almost all worked at one time or other at the Hall. Now they did it out of respect to the memory of one of the last of the real Askhams, for it was difficult to think of the young Earl, who ran in and out of the crowd like the rest of them, trays balanced in each hand, as a member of the family like Frederick or Bosco or Ralph, his predecessors.

Paul was twenty-one, had just left Manchester University and was hoping to hear he had obtained a first class degree in law. If successful he was to join an engineering firm near Stockport as a management trainee. No one knew he was the thirteenth Earl of Askham and, if he had his way, no one would.

Flora had come down with Angelica, now the mother

of a baby daughter Emily, and Dick. Flora was a regular appendage to the couple, rather as Aunt Flora had been with Adam and Melanie. She loved looking after the children, or travelling around with them, ostensibly editing Dick's new book. It was extraordinary how history repeated itself. Angelica felt free to get on with her career, as once Lady Melanie had considered herself at liberty to conduct a life of outrageous flirtatiousness apart from Adam. Aunt Flora had helped Adam with speeches and accompanied him to meetings, and Young Flora did the same, even driving Dick to various parts of the country where he was lecturing or conducting seminars so that he could get on with his work in the back of the car. Angelica hated serious music, so Flora and Dick went to concerts together, or to the avant-garde plays that were being put on in provincial towns and the back streets of London.

One or two journalists with cameras followed Natasha Lighterman who, from her first triumph in *The Three Sisters* on the West End stage, had landed a major part in a Hollywood film.

Neither Irina nor Olga had come to the funeral. The Princess had been a little afraid of Melanie and was glad to remain at Robertswood with Nicky and Galina.

The Crewes and Verdis were there, Charlotte probably the most genuinely sad one among them. She could put her hand on her heart and say she had truly loved Melanie. She loved her and she would miss her. She mourned her.

Susan and Bobby also genuinely mourned their mother. Christopher too, probably, though he didn't go back to the Hall but drove straight home after the funeral. Since his ejection of Rachel from the manor the rest of the family hadn't even attempted to try and heal the breach. Christopher had put himself beyond the pale and, as far as everyone was concerned, he would remain there. He could never atone for what he had done.

Em was there with Luis, who was at Oxford, but had moved in with her for weekends and holidays. He now visited his father as he had once visited his mother. There was no sign of Felipe, with whom the hoped-for reconciliation had not taken place. He mourned his son as if he were dead.

Perhaps the strangest of the mourners, if a mourner she could be called, was Nimet, now in her seventies and, despite pleading poverty, still a patron of the couture houses of London and Paris. This was quite welcome to Rachel because it meant Nimet was often away. She had not sold her St Tropez villa and occasionally visited it to spend some days gambling at the casino in Monte Carlo. She loved flying and in many ways had found a new lease of life now that the worry of her future was over. Nimet had certainly found her place in the sun which, due to skilful manoeuvring, now shone for her 365 days a year. Her only problem was arthritis, but her rather slow walk had a quality of stateliness which made the couturiers welcome her and give her a discount at their houses.

It would be difficult to think of people more unalike than hard-working Hugo, with his brawny arms and yeoman qualities, and his delicate fragile mother, who reminded some people of the Duchess of Windsor. Nimet shared that infinitely misleading quality with the Duchess of appearing to resemble a fragile figurine into whom one of the gods had blown life, as God is depicted blowing life in the creation of Adam in Michelangelo's masterpiece on the roof of the Sistine Chapel.

Nimet dressed beautifully and looked after herself. She encouraged others to look after her so well that it was not unreal to speculate she would live for ever. She spent all morning in bed and Jenny brought her a tray at about noon. Rachel got up at seven and was in one of her greenhouses by nine; had done a day's work by lunchtime. It had been very difficult to accept Nimet but, somehow, they had established a *modus vivendi,* merely because Rachel made adaptations, not Nimet.

Nimet, petite and exquisitely dressed, lacquered hair and make-up immaculate, was in the middle of a crowd on the terrace, drinking whisky. She got on quite well with Bobby, who had known her late husband the Bey, and they liked to discuss horses. Bobby sometimes took her to Longchamps. Bobby had once owned horses in both countries but now only trained them in France. The Labour government after the war had driven him out with its threat to soak the rich. Now, with the Tories back in power, one felt more confident and he was trying to talk Hugo into reopening a stable. Hugo said he preferred the smaller rewards but certainty of market gardening.

Hugo was busy with his growing family, his market gardening, his losing battle to refurbish the Hall and a host of activities. He was chairman of the local magistrates and, in many ways, performed the functions of previous earls of Askham, a position he would now hold had he been his father's lawful son.

Anna stood at the back of the throng on the terrace, as she had stood at the back of the church, her hands firmly on Pascal's chair. Her knuckles shone like alabaster and her face was very pale but the rest of her was black; drab black with a little black hat sitting unsuitably on her head. These days they always had to take a back seat and the people who gave way to them, or rushed forward trying to be helpful, seemed to emphasize their predicament, their apartness.

Gradually, over the months since his accident, Pascal had regained the use of his limbs except his legs. From complete paralysis he now had reasonable movement in his arms and fingers, he could turn his head quite freely and the upper part of his body was flexible. This was due partly to his youth and stubbornness, partly to skilled medical and nursing care, partly to the encouragement of his family, above all his wife.

But it was still a frustrating life for an active young man and he suffered from terrible moods – feelings of anger, inadequacy and despair. Sometimes he was so depressed he didn't want to get out of bed and, when he did, it was thanks to Anna and Cecily, his nurse.

The last time he'd seen Melanie had been at his wedding when he'd married her granddaughter, and he had insisted on going to her funeral. But then there had been all the business about getting him into the car and out again; in and out, backwards and forwards, Anna always standing behind, the loving wife, everyone feeling sorry for her, but particularly for him. What a life for a young man.

Anna's mourning weeds expressed exactly how she felt; her disgust with the lot she had inherited just over a year ago when Pascal crashed into Peter Martin's tractor. They had even had to pay to replace it. But nothing had replaced the racer. The 'Phoenix', that particular bird, would never rise again. It was forbidden even to mention it. Anna wanted to *do* something again, but no one would listen. Her place, they seemed to say, was at Pascal's side. That was her job from now on.

Pascal said something and Anna quickly bent forward to listen. The nurse they now employed had stayed at home that day. Pascal was a difficult patient to nurse and Cecily was frequently exhausted. Jenny had offered to have Pascal at the Hall, to convert a suite for him and Anna, but Anna valued her independence. Besides, she didn't want to be with the family. She knew what they said about her: Kyril's daughter. Kyril, who was supposed

428

to have killed Freddie in Spain; that calumny that her mother had told her was a wicked fabrication, a lie, a slur for which Kyril would be able to take them to court were he alive. But no one knew if he were alive or dead. And now it was Kyril's daughter who had nearly killed Pascal.

These were very bitter days and there seemed no end to them. There was no end in sight as Pascal fought to move just a tiny bit more of his body and she sought to control her misery, *her* frustration and *her* despair.

Pascal showed tremendous spirit in public, but at home he was temperamental. He took it out on Anna. She knew he, too, blamed her for encouraging him to race, as if he'd had no will of his own. She felt terribly indignant at everyone blaming her. It was Pascal who made the car, and Pascal who wanted to run it on the road. Pascal, not Anna. Yet what sort of life was there now for Anna Verdi, only twenty-six years old? It seemed that her life was over, too.

Near her Susan hovered protectively and Charlotte was never very far away. Sasha came up to talk and Stefanie asked her if she wanted a drink. She gave people drinks quite happily, but she never drank herself. The atmosphere was tense and uneasy because it was the first time Pascal had appeared in public at a family function and most people pretended not to look.

Anna knew that Pascal felt awkward, too.

'Let's go home,' he said.

'I thought you wanted to come?'

'I did. I think I thought it was the old days.'

'You can say that again.' Anna sighed. 'But you'd better get used to it now we're here.'

It was very easy to be short-tempered with Pascal. He was so trying. She knew it was hard for him, but disability made people selfish. If only the family knew the truth, maybe they'd think he was less of a martyr.

429

'Shall I take over, Anna?' Joe said, smiling at her. 'Why don't you go and relax?'

'He said he wants to go home.'

'I do want to go home,' Pascal said, the veins of frustration standing out on his forehead. 'Why can't anyone ever believe what I say? They treat me like a baby.'

'Look, old fellow,' Joe said, leaning over him. 'I *know* it's bloody hard, but make an effort just for today.' Joe was very good with his brother, there was no doubt about that. He was very loving and patient. He was even nice to Anna, as if he knew what she was going through. Joe had given up his job in London to be near Pascal after his accident, and was working as a freelance reporter for a number of agencies.

Effort, effort, effort. That's all one ever had to do. Make an effort. Anna decided to go upstairs and remove her hat, anything to get away and out of these weeds. To live again.

In the hall she bumped into Jenny.

'Is everything all right?' Jenny was always so normal and bright. 'How's Pascal?'

'Himself,' Anna said abruptly, trying to brush past Jenny. 'I thought I'd take this hideous hat off.'

'Do use our room. Anna . . .' Jenny took her arm to prevent her hurrying away. 'I do know what it's like. I nursed these cases in the war, you know. So many of our soldiers had spinal injuries. If they've been very fit men it's almost unendurable. It will take a very long time . . .'

'Oh, *please*,' Anna said, brushing her hand away. '*Please* don't talk about time. We've plenty of *that*.'

Jenny watched her rushing up the stairs and, in a way, she felt almost as sorry for Anna as she did for Pascal. Sometimes she felt even more sorry for her because Pascal had the family's sympathy whereas Anna hadn't.

Wrongfully, in Jenny's opinion, they all blamed Anna for what had happened to her husband. But Jenny wasn't an Askham and she knew how partisan, how unfair, really, they all could be.

Ross and Natasha had wandered away from the crowd in the drawing room of the Hall or on the terrace, and now they sat on the prow of one of the boats in the boathouse. Ross wanted badly to marry Natasha, yet he also knew that he couldn't trail round the world after her. She was a strong, independent woman and she would despise him if he became a poodle following her wherever she went. Besides, he couldn't achieve eminence in his career if he did.

If she would be happy with anyone, Natasha knew she would be happy with Ross. But did she want to *marry* him? It was a terrible tie. It was a bond that she was not sure she could handle. Her sister Olga was very settled and domesticated and Stefanie had, recently, seemed to come to terms with her lot. But Natasha wanted something different. She wanted to be a star – to outshine her father, the Askhams, all those people on whom her family had once been dependent.

Ross talked a lot about marriage and now, the day of her grandmother's funeral – a woman she hardly knew, but still her grandmother – he was at it again. He wanted to go back to Australia.

'We could get married here before we part, if you like. Then after Hollywood you meet up with me in Sydney.'

Natasha turned to him, smiling as gently as she could, to try and soften the blow.

'It won't work, Ross.'

'What won't work?' Already he felt a sense of despair.

'That kind of marriage. One of us will have to give in and neither of us wants to. Besides I *may* want to stay on in Hollywood.'

'What you're really saying,' Ross swallowed, 'is that we can't get married at all.'

'Not yet, anyway.' Natasha was a great equivocator. She wanted to please everyone. Yet when it came to it she realized she could be quite ruthless. She really had to take the risk of losing Ross.

In the last few months, she had realized that gradually Ross was being superseded – not only in her affections, but in the protection he gave her. She was now protected by a lot of people, surrounded by love and the kind of admiration that success, particularly on the stage, gave. The photographers outside the church at the funeral, tipped off by her agent, had irritated Ross. Of all days and places, he'd said sternly, at her grandmother's funeral! The family clearly hadn't approved, either. This was supposed to be Melanie's day, not hers.

But Melanie had meant very little to Natasha. Of all the Lighterman girls she knew her least well because she had been the youngest and scarcely remembered her. The following day there would be a photograph of her, in the *Daily Mail* or the *Express*. 'Miss Natasha Ferov, the famous film and stage star, at the funeral of her grandmother, Lady Melanie Rigby, at the family home, Askham Hall, Askham.' Ironically Melanie would have liked that sort of thing and her granddaughter liked it too; publicity, attention, whatever the occasion.

Ross got up and walked to the end of the boathouse. From here one got a wonderful view of the lake, of the path through the trees leading to the Grange and, to the right at the top of the hill, the back view of the Hall itself.

In the distance he had spotted a pair of figures running down the path from the Hall to the lake. The path snaked in and out of the bushes, the rhododendrons and azaleas on either side, that shielded people on it from the gaze of those sitting or standing on the terrace. The path was favoured by young people keen on getting to know each other better, and over the generations many furtive kisses had been snatched on it.

As the pair came into view, laughing and out of breath, Ross realized with a shock that they were Flora and Angelica's husband, Dick. Unaware that anyone had seen them they continued to run as though propelled by sheer spirits, maybe fuelled by something else.

As he stood watching them, realizing he was unseen, Ross was joined by Natasha who slyly, comfortingly, slid her hand into his.

At that moment Flora saw them and her pace slowed as she looked behind for Dick, who had seen them, too. The animation suddenly went out of both their faces and a kind of guilt took its place. Ross put up a hand to hail them.

'Hi.'

'Hi.'

'We wanted to get away from that stuffy lot,' Dick said. 'Funerals are stifling.'

'I don't blame you,' Natasha smiled at Dick. 'We did, too.'

'It really *is* glorious down here,' Flora held out her arms to the sun and Ross realized that really she was an overgrown child, retaining something of the innocence of a small girl. Or was it because of the man she was with? Dick, standing behind her, looked grave.

Flora sat on one of the upturned boats and Dick perched beside her.

'Angelica has gone back to town,' Flora explained. 'I'm sort of Dick's minder to see that he behaves himself. Angelica trusts me.'

'I'm sure she does.' Ross smiled. Yet he felt a bit awkward in this company, as though he were an interloper.

He said suddenly: 'Why don't we take a stroll round the lake while the girls chat?'

'Good idea,' Dick said, rather surprised. Neither he nor Angelica knew Ross or Natasha very well and, although the Australian was supposed to be part of the family, Dick always saw him as an outsider, like himself.

Flora watched them go, hands in their pockets, heads raised as though savouring the air. She was a bit nonplussed to find herself alone with Natasha. She had always been a little awed by the Lighterman girls; had never known them very well. Natasha was exactly her contemporary, yet it was as though they were separated by years. Flora felt rather gauche beside this woman who was a film star; whose experience spanned a life she knew nothing about.

Yet she knew Natasha was nice; the family all liked her and that accolade went for something. She said:

'I like Ross awfully. Are you going to be married?'

Natasha was watching Ross too; but her eyes were grave and thoughtful.

'I don't think so.'

Flora looked abashed. 'I'm sorry, it's none of my business, but I do think you make such a good pair. Though people say that, don't they, when they don't really know?'

'Oh, we make a good pair,' Natasha said, carefully shifting on the upturned boat in case she creased her black silk suit. 'But there is more to it than that. We have our careers. Ross wants to go back to Australia and I'm going to Hollywood. I don't think one should sacrifice everything for a man, do you?'

'Certainly not,' Flora said, looking at Dick's broad back as he strolled away from her round the lake. '*Nor* should a man sacrifice everything for a woman.'

'You sound very sure about that.'

434

'I am,' Flora said, pursing her mouth. 'Dick has been offered a wonderful job at Cambridge and Angelica won't go and live there.'

'Well it's not very far, Cambridge. One could commute.'

'Dick would like to buy a house there. He hates London.'

Natasha smiled at her in a rather insinuating way.

Flora saw her look and her colour subtly changed. 'There's nothing between me and Dick, you know, except friendship. We *are* very friendly, and have been for years. But Dick loves Angelica. How could he possibly love someone like me?'

Natasha's arm went impulsively round the slight, rather girlish form beside her.

'Why do you say that?' she enquired.

'Because I'm not beautiful, like Angelica. No man has ever loved me. You know that?' Nervously, Flora put her hand to her hair, aware of Natasha's clasp. 'I don't mind, really. I have my work and I love it. Dick and I are soulmates, and I love him too, but not in the way people think.'

'Wouldn't you like to go to bed with him?' Natasha said, in some bewilderment.

'I wouldn't even *think* of it,' Flora vigorously shook her head, her colour by now very high. 'I assure you, I don't love him in that way at all.'

Charlotte stood on the terrace beside her mother, watching the small group in the boathouse. It was possible to see right inside because of the lack of doors. Rachel was talking to Admiral Bulstrode, whose father had once been a lover, or an admirer at any rate, no one was quite sure which, of Melanie. The Bulstrodes were very old friends of the Askham family and hadn't missed a function, whether grave or gay, in all the years Rachel had been a member.

Admiral Bulstrode had had a distinguished war and was now connected with Arthur in the City. He was a tall, rather choleric man with a bald head and a red face and he stood with his hands behind his back as though still barking orders to the fleet from the quarter deck.

Arthur had gone to fetch another whisky for the Admiral, who was reminiscing about old friends with Rachel.

'All dead now,' the Admiral said, almost with satisfaction. 'My father was extremely fond of the family and, as you know, a great admirer of Lady Melanie. He couldn't bear to come to her funeral.'

'How old is he now?' Rachel wondered.

'He was eighty-five last year.' The Admiral had a note of pride in his voice as though to emphasize the fact that Bulstrodes were a tough, long-surviving breed. '*Eighty-five*, but he walks three miles every day or occasionally goes by bicycle.'

'Amazing.' Rachel turned to Arthur as he appeared with a tray of drinks.

'Waiting staff not too good, I'm afraid,' Arthur said. 'Not like the old days.'

'Times have changed, Arthur,' Rachel replied. 'I think Hugo and Jenny do a marvellous job. Helped by Jill, of course.' The ubiquitous Jill had been there since dawn, but had tactfully slipped away before the mourners arrived back from the church.

'Marvellous,' the Admiral echoed. 'This place should rightly be a ruin by now.'

Out of the corner of her eye Rachel could see Nimet, swathed from head to foot in deep mourning, approaching, inclining to right and left in acknowledgement of the people, she either knew or didn't know, greeting her.

436

Instinctively Rachel bridled. There was no doubt that Nimet had taken over the role previously held by her in the household. It was as though Nimet had become the Queen Mother and her own function was reduced to that of lady-in-waiting. Very few people at this gathering knew Nimet but they knew who she was. Even after all these years Rachel could still feel the sting of humiliation at the presence in the house of her husband's one-time mistress. She often wondered what Bosco would have said had he known; but memories of Bosco were very few and far between now, and dim after the passage of forty years.

Below her Charlotte saw the men split from the women and start to walk around the lake. Natasha and Flora remained in the boathouse, heads close together.

'It's almost as though they were a couple,' she murmured to her mother, who turned away from the Admiral and Arthur, now chatting about share prices.

'Who, darling?' Rachel peered in the direction of the lake.

'Flora and Dick. They came down the path together. If I didn't know better I'd swear they'd been holding hands.'

'I think you're very wrong about those two.' Rachel lowered her voice too. 'Dick is very much in love with Angelica. Anyone can see it when he looks at her.'

'I think he's *in* love with her, in other words he's still sexually attracted; but that's all it is. He gets a lot of comfort from Flora. Angelica's going to America next week to model there.'

'Is that why she left early?'

'Yes, she had a lot to do to get ready.'

'I see.' Rachel paused. 'The younger generation don't seem to miss Melanie very much,' she looked sad. 'I don't suppose they will miss me . . .'

'Oh, *Mum.*'

'It's true. Once you get beyond a certain age people think you should die.'

Charlotte tucked her arm in her mother's as Bertie Bulstrode said:

'I must be going or my wife will be annoyed with me. She made me promise not to stay all day.'

Maisie Bulstrode was inside with her own small clique – the Partingtons, Wellbeloveds, Gore-Whites and Anstruther-Greys – who also had been part of the coterie that gathered about the Askhams on solemn occasions for many years past. Maisie would not really want to go, and the Admiral fastened the coat of his morning suit and complained of the heat.

'Can I give anyone a lift?' he said, looking round. 'Going up to town, are you, Arthur?'

'Yes, but my secretary's calling for me,' Arthur glanced at his watch. 'Charlotte's going to stay in the country.'

'I didn't know *Jill* was coming for you, darling,' Charlotte said, rather sharply. 'I thought you were staying down here, too? The House isn't sitting.'

'Can't,' Arthur looked regretful. 'There is so much to do.'

'Is Jill coming down specially?' Rachel asked. 'I thought she'd just left?'

'She was picking up some papers from Littlestone.' Arthur looked deliberately vague. 'I'll come in with you, Bertie. I want a word with Maisie about that gala for Korean War orphans. It's a very good idea to be *seen* to be charitable, you know.'

'Can't do any harm.' Bertie laughed and extended his hand to Rachel.

'My dear Rachel, look after yourself. I know this is a loss for you.'

Rachel inclined her head just as Nimet reached them.

'You're not *going*, are you, Admiral? I was coming to talk especially to you.'

'My dear lady,' the Admiral dropped Rachel's hand and seized that of Nimet. 'I wish you had come earlier. Now, when are you coming to dine with us in town? Come and meet my wife.'

He tucked her arm through his and, with Arthur in the lead, walked off the terrace chattering away to Nimet.

'She does have an effect on men,' Rachel shook her head. 'Even after all this time.'

Charlotte knew how her mother felt about Nimet and took her arm.

'I wish to God Hugo hadn't asked her.'

'He had to.'

'Jenny doesn't like her, either.'

'She *is* difficult.' Rachel spoke reluctantly. She felt she had to be very careful not to be heard criticizing Nimet. For a woman of nearly eighty to display jealousy was absurd. 'Whenever she's here we're all unsettled. Besides, she and I have so little in common.'

'I think I'd better go after Arthur,' Charlotte said. 'I'd no idea he was going back. He may need something.'

She looked at her mother but Rachel shook her head. In a way she knew that Charlotte was beginning to feel threatened.

Over on the parapet, with his back to the lake, Joe was sitting talking to Pascal, who had become quite animated about something and was waving his arms about while Joe, and Paul next to him, in shirtsleeves, were laughing. It seemed quite extraordinary to think that Pascal would never leave that chair again, except for his bed; that he wouldn't suddenly rise out of it and walk away like anyone else. The family had had to learn to be very careful not to show Pascal too much sympathy or he resented it. They had to try and treat him as they always had, and this was difficult.

But it was, in a way, very strange how quickly they had become adjusted to his disability; how easily one took over his chair from another, unlike the days when he had to be fed and nursed almost like an infant. At that moment, as Rachel walked towards him, Paul got up after saying something that made Pascal laugh again. It was quite a jolly scene.

'Bobby wants to see me,' Paul grimaced at his grandmother. 'I'm being summoned to "the presence".'

'Bobby seems to have been conducting interviews all afternoon,' Rachel said. 'Quite an extraordinary way to behave on the day of his mother's funeral.'

But to Bobby business was business and when all the family, daughters and assorted friends and colleagues were gathered together there was much to be done. He was standing at the window of Hugo's study when Paul came in, gave him a cheery greeting and dropped casually into a chair. Bobby remained standing, looking at Paul with a frown of disapproval. Paul caught his gaze and his smile vanished. He straightened up in the chair.

'Is there something wrong, Bobby?'

'There certainly is,' Bobby said. 'Have you any idea *who* you are, young man?'

'Paul Askham,' Paul replied, knowing there was a trap.

'The *Earl* of Askham. Thirteenth Earl of Askham, Viscount Gore. Heir to a great tradition, yet you would never think it.'

'That's good,' Paul said, lighting a cigarette. 'I didn't want to be an earl.'

Bobby carefully crossed the room and, flicking up the tails of his morning coat, sat on the chair behind Hugo's desk as though emphasizing his distance from the younger man.

'Nevertheless, you are an earl. *The* Earl. You have inherited, through the death of your uncle, a very old, famous name. Sometimes I think you're a disgrace to it, Paul. Today, for instance, was there any need for you to strip to your shirtsleeves and go around with a tray of drinks?'

'I think I did it rather well, Bobby.' Paul gave him a cheeky smile. 'I was helping out.'

'Someone asked me who you were. I was ashamed to say you were my cousin, Paul Askham. The person I told seemed so incredulous he couldn't find the words to answer me.' Bobby leaned forward and gave Paul a forced, avuncular smile. 'Now, Paul, I know you have had an unconventional upbringing. You lost both your parents tragically. But you went to the best schools. You have a good education; a steady home. You're a clever, personable young man. It is time you did something about yourself, Paul, your image. You are much too informal, too free. I didn't like you going to Manchester University and, in my opinion, it hasn't been good for you. Your Uncle Ralph, for all his faults, had a lot of style. He was a very stylish chap. As an older member of the family I feel I should point all this out to you. You've got no dignity; no style. I don't like this job you've taken. I don't like your lifestyle and you are doing the family no good. Now, Paul,' Bobby flicked his cuffs as if preparing for a fight, 'I want to make a proposition to you. I want you to come into the business, with me. I want to train you to take over from me. I think you have the right instinct. The cut and thrust of business will suit you.'

Paul looked at his cousin in amazement.

'But I thought that Sasha was taking over from you, or that, if he was better, Pascal . . .'

Bobby shook his head impatiently. 'No, no. Sasha has forfeited my confidence completely. The crash finished him. He deceived me; he tricked me. He and Pascal may even have stolen from me . . .'

'What a beastly thing to say . . .' Angrily Paul rose to his feet, fist clenched, but Bobby made a soothing gesture with his hands.

'Don't get so wound up, young man. I'm not saying "deliberate dishonesty", but some work *was* done in my firm's time . . .'

'*For* the firm. Their object was to publicize the "Askham".'

'Yes, but I had forbidden racing cars. I had expressly forbidden them. Don't you see? I knew what I was talking about. They were doing something I had forbidden and it went disastrously wrong. Terribly wrong. It was extremely bad for the image of the firm. Besides, Sasha has no head for business. He is weak in a way I didn't expect. As for Pascal, well,' Bobby shrugged, attempting a half-smile. 'Who wants a cripple at the head of a huge empire? Now, you, as Earl of Askham . . .'

Paul advanced on Bobby, his eyes glinting dangerously. He curled his fist into a ball and shook it under Bobby's nose. Then he made a lightning gesture as if to punch him and Bobby jumped back.

'See this, Bobby?' Paul snarled. 'It is my fist. Another word from you about "cripples" and it goes right into the squashy, fleshy part of your nose.'

'How dare . . .'

'I *dare*,' Paul said. 'I dare and I will. Look, Bobby, older than me as you are, I'm going to tell you something you might not know.' Paul uncurled his fist and thrust it against his hip. 'No one likes you very much. I hear your daughters can't stand you. Even your wife is never with

442

you. Where is she today, on the day of your mother's funeral?'

'You know she's in America.'

'She didn't come rushing back, did she?'

'My mother never liked Aileen. She thought she was beneath us. She and my mother never got on.'

'But *no one* gets on with you, Bobby. One person who did like you was Sasha; and Pascal, I know, admired you. Yet both of these men you now spurn.'

'For good reason . . .'

'Nevertheless, they liked you, admired you. Frankly I don't know why or how anyone likes you. You are a most despicable man. You diddled my uncle, your own family. Even on the day you bury your own mother you can't stop plotting. You seem to have no decent feelings of any kind, Bobby. I think you're lucky to have any friends at all. As for your offer to me, you can stick it.'

And Paul, before turning sharply on his heels, made a rude two-finger sign whose meaning not even Bobby could mistake.

After his young cousin had left he sat down heavily and began to mop his brow.

Charlotte embraced her mother, hugging her with both arms.

'I'm running up to London, after all. Joe's giving me a lift.'

'But *why*?' Rachel appeared taken aback.

'I changed my mind, that's all. Arthur may need something.'

'I'm sure *Arthur* will be all right.'

'I explained to Anna.' Charlotte looked round with a preoccupied air. 'She'll bring Pascal over to Littlestone in a day or two. She understands.'

443

'I'm sure she does, if that's what you want, dear. You're *sure* you're right?'

For a moment mother and daughter gazed at each other, and then Charlotte nodded.

'Quite sure. I'll just go and say goodbye to Em, Susan and Pascal.'

It was almost as though Pascal sensed the presence of his mother because, as she approached, he turned round. His eyes always shone when he saw her and he raised an eager, loving face for her to kiss. It was a very touching and tender moment to see them together, Rachel thought, as if in his infirmity they had found a perfect harmony and understanding. Charlotte, always fearing the worst, had found, when it happened, that life was endurable after all.

Charlotte had been much more relaxed since Pascal had come out of hospital. For one thing there were so many things to see to. Anna and Pascal couldn't live forever in the small cottage near the Askham works, especially with a nurse. Anna wanted to go back to town, but Pascal to remain in the country. He was determined that very soon he would be able to go back to work.

Rachel waited while Charlotte and Pascal made their fond goodbyes and then she accompanied her daughter to the door, after she had also taken her farewells of Hugo, Jenny, Nimet and some of the funeral guests who were having too good a time to leave. Melanie's funeral had turned into a bit of a party. But it was quite certain she would have approved.

'I do hope everything *will* be all right,' Rachel said once more, looking searchingly at Charlotte.

'Of course it will be *all right*, Mother,' Charlotte said heartily, bending to kiss her on the cheek. 'I think you've got hold of the wrong end of the stick, darling.'

Joe got out of the car to kiss his grandmother, saw his

mother to her seat and, with a cheery wave, started up the engine. Rachel, arms akimbo, watched them until the car was out of sight.

She didn't feel as though she had got hold of the wrong end of the stick at all and, as she walked back into the house, she realized she had a sense of deep foreboding about the state of her daughter's marriage to Arthur.

Em was waiting for her inside the Hall.

'Why did Charlotte fly off?' she said.

'She wants to look after Arthur.'

Em grunted. 'I shouldn't think he needs much looking after. He has too much already, if you ask me.'

'Oh, Em, don't say that.' Rachel felt distressed. 'What a day it's been. Are you going back tonight?'

'I was going on with Charlotte but I think we'll pop over to Robertswood with Sasha and Stefanie. I hear Irina's not too good. Luis just went over to say "hello" to Felipe.'

'I'll say goodbye then, dear.' Rachel leaned forward to kiss her daughter. 'It has been a heavy day and there's still a party going on on the terrace. Kiss Luis for me.'

'I will, Mum, and *don't* worry.'

Em stood at the foot of the staircase, watching Rachel as she slowly mounted it. At last, she thought, her mother was beginning to show her age.

In her room, to her surprise, Rachel found Jenny rocking herself in the rocking-chair but looking hot and flustered. Rachel shut the door and went quickly over to her.

'Jenny, darling. Is anything wrong?'

'Everything's wrong,' Jenny said, rocking furiously. 'Either Hugo's mother goes, or I go.'

Or I go, Rachel thought, but didn't say it. She sat by Jenny and put a hand on her knee, watching it rock up and down in time with the chair.

445

'Is it as bad as that?'

'She not only made a pest of herself all afternoon; she criticized the food, the serving of it, all the arrangements generally. "Not like in the old days" she had the cheek to say. I couldn't even go to the funeral.'

Rachel said nothing but, by the pressure of her hand, tried to convey her sympathy to Jenny.

'Nimet has put us all out, hasn't she, Rachel? Be honest.' Jenny looked at her earnestly. 'She criticizes me the whole time either by word, looks or implication. She talks to Hugo for hours about me. I'm not good enough for him, another man's mistress and so on.'

'*She* can talk about being another man's mistress.' Rachel gave a sarcastic smile. 'Maybe she's forgotten how she came to know *us*.'

'I hate her,' Jenny said suddenly. 'How can I tell Hugo I hate his mother?'

'I shouldn't actually tell Hugo you hate her,' Rachel said gently. 'Try and put up with her. Hugo, I know, is very attached to Nimet. He feels guilty about her.'

'But she doesn't *need* to be here,' Jenny said angrily. 'All that business about not having enough money was sheer fabrication. She has kept her house in St Tropez, she travels about as she pleases, stays in the best hotels. She had that dress today run up especially for the funeral and she hardly knew Melanie. It must have cost her a fortune.'

'She has to show off,' Rachel agreed.

'But you don't like her either, do you, Rachel?' Jenny pleaded. 'Be honest.'

'I don't really like her,' Rachel removed her hand from Jenny's knee. 'How could I? Even if what happened happened over forty years ago the hurt remains. It's that we've never been able to get rid of the woman. She keeps on turning up. If it had all been over in 1915, and we had

446

never seen her again, I wouldn't have worried. But just when you think she's gone, there she is again. Damn General Neguib.'

Rachel leaned forward. 'There's nothing much we can do, dear. Hugo cannot possibly ask her to leave. In a way I think she enjoys annoying us. It gives her power. Sometimes I think she's getting her own back for the way Bosco abandoned her all those years ago.'

After they left the Hall Joe and Charlotte remained for some time in companionable silence as though each were closeted with their own thoughts. Melanie? Angelica? Pascal? Maybe a little of each as they reflected on the day. The aftermath of such gatherings was always a certain kind of sobriety, mourning the dead, moments of solemn reflection. Everyone there had to some extent been fond of Melanie, although some, like Nimet, had scarcely known her. For the family, even in Venice she had been part of their lives and her going had left a gap it would be hard to fill.

'Mother thinks that Flora and Dick are too much together.' Charlotte was the first to break the silence.

'Haven't *you* ever thought that, Mum?' Joe looked at her.

'Have you?'

'Oh yes. I wonder that Angelica puts up with it.'

'But there's nothing in it!' Charlotte protested.

'Isn't there? Maybe she encourages it.'

Joe came to the main road and waited as the London-bound traffic flashed by before he joined it. He could never come to this part of the route without thinking of Pascal and the crash. Were there another way to the London road he would have taken it.

'Why *should* Angelica encourage it?'

'Because she knows it's innocent. I'm sure it is; and she

447

can have a good time without feeling guilty. You know they're hopelessly incompatible, Mum, she and Dick.'

'She promised me they wouldn't get divorced.'

'They should never have married.'

'*Why* did they have Emily? That was a deliberate choice. I know; Angelica told me.'

'Maybe they do mean to stay together. Sometimes I don't understand people.'

With one hand Joe started fiddling with the radio.

As they fell silent again Charlotte wanted to tell her son that quite often she didn't understand him. But she didn't dare ask him the kind of probing questions which, sometimes, she felt she'd like to.

As far as she knew Joe had never been interested in any woman; never had a special girl, as Pascal had, as other men had. Joe was now twenty-seven. Wasn't it a long time to go without love or affection in one's life? By the time she was his age she was a widow with three young children.

What emotional satisfaction did Joe have in his life, or was he one of those people who didn't need any? No, that was impossible.

The family never talked about Joe or queried his lifestyle. Even Rachel never asked questions, which was unusual for her. Somehow it didn't seem one's business to question a grown man about his love life. Maybe Joe was one of those asexual people who sublimated in their work; a bit like Em, a bit like Charlotte herself perhaps, who only fulfilled her marital obligations to Arthur out of a sense of duty. Her mother, too, had certainly not slept with a man since her relationship with Spencer finished in the early thirties.

Maybe as a family they were all rather like that, undersexed, and perhaps, in a way, it was a good thing.

But Angelica certainly wsn't undersexed. Charlotte

knew that this was what Joe meant about having a good time.

Joe drove for several miles before he spoke again. 'Why are you going up to London? Don't you trust Arthur?'

'Don't be silly. Why shouldn't I trust him?' Charlotte sounded affronted. She produced her compact from her bag to hide her confusion, studying her face in the mirror.

She still wore black and she knew it suited her; suited her pallor. She knew she was still an attractive woman and, had she cared to, she could have had any number of lovers, or even mere admirers – 'Walkers' the Americans called them – men who took one out to dinner or the theatre when one's husband was busy.

'You say Flora and Dick are an odd couple,' Joe said. 'I say Arthur relies too much on Jill.'

'Maybe that's the way it is.' Charlotte affected an air of casualness. 'She's the perfect secretary and Flora, in her way, is the perfect amanuensis, too. She's practically rewriting Dick's book. She learned to drive just to take him to meetings.'

'For a feminist she seems extraordinarily subordinate.'

'Do you think so?' Charlotte pondered the question. 'I never thought of it like that. I don't think she does, either. She'd be horrified. Your grandmother always says she behaves towards Dick the way Aunt Flora behaved towards Uncle Adam. Mother thinks it's something in the genes.'

Charlotte laughed and Joe smiled as he leaned forward over the wheel, his eyes on the road. It was that dangerous time for traffic, gathering dusk just before lights on.

They passed a hotel which stood at the side of the road, a familiar landmark which catered mainly for the passing motor trade. It had a large car park in front and a garish neon sign that had just come on. Charlotte stared idly at the cars parked in front of it and then suddenly she said to Joe:

'Do you think we could stop and turn back?'

'Go back to the Hall?' Joe braked sharply.

'No, into that hotel there, the one we just passed.'

'But that's a dump. What do you want to go there for, Mother?'

'I'll tell you when we get there,' Charlotte said. 'Please drive back.'

Joe put the car into gear again and went on until he came to a turning where he could reverse and go back the way they had come. Then he turned in to the drive of the hotel and whistled, seeing what his mother had seen: a large maroon 'Askham'.

'Arthur's car. Is *that* why you turned back, Mother?'

'Wait here,' Charlotte said briskly. She got out and went across the gravel of the parking bay, walking slowly round the car and then peering in the back. On the seat was Arthur's brown homburg hat and his briefcase with the initials A.G.C. on it – Arthur George Crewe.

Joe signalled an enquiry to his mother but she shook her head, indicating she wouldn't be long. Swiftly she went through the main door of the hotel to the foyer, where the reception clerk looked up at her, smiling.

'Madam?' he said.

'Have you a Mr Crewe staying here?' Charlotte came at once to the point. Through the open door of the dining-room she could see a few people sitting at the tables. 'Crewe with an "e".'

'Crewe, Crewe,' the receptionist pulled the register towards him and looked down it. 'Crewe, Crewe. I'm afraid there is no Mr Crewe registered here, Madam.'

'Oh, maybe he's in the dining-room,' Charlotte said then, as if as an afterthought: 'Might I just glance at the register to be sure?'

450

The clerk hesitated but, under the spell of that brilliant, fascinating smile of hers that was capable of moving mountains, he allowed her deftly to turn it towards her. Quickly she scanned the signatures on the page.

There was no Crewe registered but there were a Mr and Mrs Carstairs and the address alongside it was Jill's: Ennismore Gardens, W8. The handwriting was in Arthur's familiar, rather neat schoolboyish hand.

Charlotte thanked the clerk and said he was right. There was no Mr Crewe there. She was terribly sorry to trouble him. Slowly she went out of the hotel down the drive to where Joe was waiting for her, impatiently tapping his fingers on the wheel of his red sports car.

'What was all that about?' he said, as Charlotte carefully got in beside him. 'Is he there?'

For answer Charlotte shook her head, gave a deep sigh and lit a cigarette. Later she would answer questions.

Mr and Mrs Carstairs . . . her father-in-law had been the Earl of Crewe and Carstairs. No doubt Arthur thought that quite a good joke.

CHAPTER 18

Now there was an autumnal air about the place, unlike when Anna had last seen it in the summertime. The conifers and. trees of the Black Forest were a dark, brilliant green, but the trees that·shed their leaves in winter were turning into rich, volcanic-coloured reds and browns. The distant hills were more thickly covered with their caps of snow, but nothing else had changed. The house still lay in the shadow of the Feld Berg, reached via the long winding road through the Black Forest from Lake Titisee; the polished furniture shone; the sunshine streamed through the windows, upon the clever arrangements of winter twigs and shrubs in the large urns and ewers. Only missing was the wheelchair and the pretty woman who had once sat in it.

Gunther had met Anna in Mannheim and together they had driven to his house, deserted now except for a housekeeper who received them impassively and served them with hot chocolate after the cold day's drive.

'Does your husband know you're here?' Gunther said, gazing at Anna over the rim of his cup.

'Here or in Germany?'

'Here, with me.'

'Of course not. Since his accident I hardly ever get away at all; but he knows I am coming to Germany and that, inevitably perhaps, I'd see you. After all, you still have the Agency.'

Gunther politely passed her a plate of home-made biscuits. It was the charm of Gunther's exquisite manners, combined with everything else, that made such an impression, Anna thought. Good manners and good breeding. 'Despite everything, the "Askham" sells. Will there be other models?'

'Pascal already goes every day to the works. He is remarkable. It is as though he has put his accident away from him entirely – to outward appearances, that is.'

Gunther didn't miss the heavy sigh.

'And "inner appearances", if one can say such a thing?'

'Ah, that's different. Naturally Pascal is very frustrated; he has had a lot of pain. He has no feeling below the waist. He will be very bright all day and then sinks into a great gloom at night.' Anna crossed her legs, sat back more comfortably in her deep, upholstered armchair and flicked back a lock of her thick hair. 'Unfortunately, I am not in the mould to play Florence Nightingale. I really haven't the patience for an invalid. I wish I had.' Anna leaned forward, briskly brushing a few of the biscuit crumbs off her lap. 'You see, our life before was very active. We were always doing things, planning things. Now we have been thrown back on our own resources only to find that we have very few. Sometimes I think the boredom will drive me mad.'

'Do you still love him?'

'Oh, *course* I love him . . .' Anna faltered. 'It would be very cruel to say I didn't.'

'But would it be true?'

Anna was aware of the enquiry in Gunther's eyes, the insinuation in his voice.

'I don't think I ever stopped loving you,' Anna said abruptly and, simultaneously, Gunther sighed and, rising from his chair, swiftly came over to her; but she held up a hand.

'Please don't . . . do anything. You ask me, so I'll tell you. You treated me very badly. I was heartbroken. Naturally, I turned to someone who was sympathetic.'

'On the rebound?'

Anna nodded and suddenly, to her chagrin, her eyes filled with tears.

'It *is* a terrible thing to say, but I was always thinking of you. I acted hastily. I was shocked about your wife, the baby. Your apparent unconcern. I thought you were too old . . .'

'Of course, my dear,' Gunther said gently, letting his hand rest lightly on the dome of her head. 'Of course you were and of course I did behave badly; but you see . . .' he removed his hand and sat beside her. 'I simply didn't know what to do. You saw how it was with Maria; you know I couldn't have left her. Yet I never ever imagined you and I could have so much as had an affair if I'd told you about her.' He paused. 'And I wanted you so much, believe me. It was *very* selfish of me, and I paid for it. Meeting you in Venice . . . I was so shocked to learn about the accident, but even then it occurred to me you still cared a little for me.'

'Very much.' Anna's voice was still shaking. 'It was obvious to me too, and my mother. I couldn't leave Venice quickly enough. Now, as you were, I am stuck with a cripple for the rest of my life . . .'

'Perhaps he, too . . .' Gunther began, looking rather guiltily at her. But he didn't finish his words.

Then he continued: 'Things change so much in a few years, don't they? Tragedy seems to enhance life, make it more vivid and precious. I don't believe we've ever been closer.'

The bed was that of a voluptuary. She wondered if he'd slept there with his wife, but he assured her they never had.

'My wife and I had separate bedrooms. This was mine but she never visited me here. As an invalid she needed

454

her own room. I daresay you have separate bedrooms, too.'

Yes, they had separate bedrooms, separate thoughts, separate lives. Anna turned on her stomach and contemplated the exquisite richelieu work of the pillow, undoubtedly embroidered by his mother, or his wife. The inheritance of linen was such an important thing in families.

'I never actually thought you'd forgive me,' Gunther touched her timidly, 'or that I'd ever sleep with you again, especially here.'

'I didn't think I'd forgive you, either,' Anna said. 'I'm not sure I have. But for you I wouldn't have married Pascal and I haven't made him happy. But for me he wouldn't have had his accident. I am not right for him and I don't think I ever was.'

'Can't you undo a bad marriage quite easily?' the Baron said. 'Your family are no strangers to divorce.'

'It's not quite as easy as that,' she said. 'I can't just drop everything to marry you. What would the family say if I left Pascal? They would say I was cruel, ruthless. You could never leave Maria.'

'But Maria had no family, nowhere to go. You have a large family – Pascal's mother, his grandmother, brother and sister. I'm sure they must all love him.'

'It isn't *that*,' Anna said. 'And you know it. Maybe, in a few years, they may even find a way of mending spinal injuries. They say several years ago he would never have made the recovery that he has. But it's not only that, it's what the family would say if I divorced him. What they'd think.'

'They *do* mean a lot to you, don't they?' Gunther stroked her arm with his finger.

'Yes, a lot. What they think about me matters a great deal, you see, because of my father.'

* * *

455

Dressing in his dressing-room while he had a bath some hours later, Anna took her time inspecting ornaments, looking at the pictures hanging on the walls, largely personal pictures, photographs and snaps chronicling Gunther's life and that of his family. There were some of him with his wife before she was confined to a wheelchair. He'd been married when he was twenty-one in 1932 and they'd gone to Kenya on safari. She'd been very beautiful then, lithe and athletic, and she seemed always to be smiling.

There were pictures of them at shooting parties, race meetings and visiting various baronial residences. There were pictures of his grandparents, mother, father, sister Hilda and brother Kurt who'd been killed on the Eastern front in the war. Suddenly Anna leaned forward peering at a small one tucked in a corner a little apart from the rest. A group of men in hunting gear were standing with their arms round one another, smiling jovially to the camera. One of them was undoubtedly . . .

'Is that *Hitler*?' Anna said, pointing to the photo when Gunther emerged from the bathroom with a big towel round his waist.

'Probably,' he said off-handedly, inspecting his shaven cheeks in the mirror.

'Were you *friendly* with Hitler?'

'At that time, yes. Many were. It was before he became Reichschancellor. After that it wasn't so easy to be photographed with him.'

Anna had a feeling of shock, that peculiar desire to say: 'But what *did* you do in the war?' She never had. In Germany it was the forbidden question. Judging by the familiarity of her lover with Hitler in about 1933, arms round each other's shoulders, she wasn't sure she wanted to know the answer.

'I didn't think it mattered so much to your Askhams,'

Gunther said at dinner, just the two of them waited on by the housekeeper, facing each other across the long carved table. 'About the war, I mean. They were well-known supporters of Hitler.'

Thinking of Jordan, Anna started guiltily. 'Not all of them.'

'There was the famous Jordan Bolingbroke. Lady Melanie, I believe you said . . .'

'Yes, yes,' impatiently Anna crumbled her bread roll into fragments. 'There was my grandfather Alexei and, perhaps, my father too. In the war my Russian grandparents preferred the Germans to the Russians. I didn't say I was terribly anti-Nazi. But most of the Askham family were.'

'I'm glad about you,' Gunther said, 'because I was a member of the Party and I want you to know it. I don't want there to be any misunderstandings between us again. I joined the Party shortly after Hitler came to power and, like millions of other good Germans, I remained in it until the end. However, as a member of the Wehrmacht, I was never involved in any of the activities of the SS. I was simply a soldier fighting at the front. I was only formally called for de-Nazification, so you can see that the Allies accepted my story. After the war I was able to start up the business again without the blemish on my name that haunted so many others.'

'I don't know why you're telling me all this,' Anna said. 'Anyone would think we were getting married.'

'One day, I hope, we shall,' Gunther leaned towards her, 'and then they'll want to know, your family. You can be sure of that, and I know you care about what they think.'

'By then it won't make any difference.' Anna blew him a kiss. 'What I want I get.'

* * *

The baby was a tiny dark little thing, with black wispy hair like its mother. Flora leaned over and kissed its downy little head smelling of powder and baby oil. She adored babies and she felt a surge of affection for the unwanted child that surprised herself.

'It *is* a lovely baby,' she said, straightening up and gazing at the mother lying in the bed, her face as white as the hospital counterpane. 'I'm glad you want to keep it.'

Ruth looked as though the very idea of not keeping it was offensive to her.

'I'm sorry,' Flora said, seeing the look, and sat down gingerly on the side of the bed. 'Of course I knew you wanted to keep it. You do now, anyway.'

'She,' Ruth said. 'The baby's a girl. She isn't an "it".'

Inwardly Flora sighed. Ruth Earnshaw was not an easy girl. Whatever one did to try and please her, whatever one said was usually wrong; whatever words one chose, however carefully, were inept. Ruth had come to the hostel when she was six months pregnant, referred to them through the Salvation Army, who had found her at King's Cross Station. She'd been sitting there on a bench for two days, wondering where to go and what to do after being thrown out of her home by her disapproving parents when she revealed to them her condition.

Ruth came from Blackburn in Lancashire but, maybe, she thought London a kinder place, even the bleak confines of the busy station. People would actually stop and give her food, as though she were one of the pigeons that stalked along the platform, before the police took her in and handed her over to the Salvation Army.

Ruth Earnshaw was a difficult case from the start because, instead of agreeing to have her baby adopted and make it easy for everyone all round, including herself it was argued, she insisted from the start on keeping it. Her mother might even have had her back if she had agreed to do the proper thing and give it away. Selfish, people called it; thinking of herself and not the poor, fatherless baby. Not much of a chance in life, they said.

Flora took to Ruth almost as soon as she came to the hostel, barbed and bristling with complexes, ready to defend herself against all comers, to take on anyone who attacked her or offered her advice. Indeed it was Flora who proved the only one who could approach Ruth with any confidence and the reason was that Flora genuinely loved people and also that, with her working-class northern accent and dark, pretty looks, Ruth reminded Flora of her mother, whom she only knew by pictures, whose voice she had only ever imagined.

Ruth Earnshaw was so slight that her large stomach had made her look almost deformed, and the other girls had laughed at her behind her back and called her names. But Ruth didn't care or try and defend herself. She just avoided people who hurt her and had spent a lot of time alone in her room.

Gradually Flora had befriended her and, once, she had taken her to Askham Hall to meet her aunt. Rachel liked Ruth, too, and had confirmed that Ruth did indeed bear a distinct resemblance to Flora's mother and, from then on, Flora knew that their destinies were to be linked.

'What did you think of for a name?' Flora asked.

'Joan,' Ruth said without hesitation.

'Joan Earnshaw.' Flora wrinkled her nose. 'Well, it's rather plain.'

'I like it,' Ruth said with her habitual stubbornness.

'How about Felicity or Florence?' Flora said hopefully.

'Joan,' Ruth said. And Joan it was.

But what was to happen to Ruth and Joan? They couldn't stay at the hostel for ever, as Mrs Foulsham was always saying. Ruth would have to find a job and a home for Joan as she had insisted on keeping her. The new contraceptive pill had increased the number of people seeking to adopt babies because live births had now diminished, and there were long queues in the adoption agencies. Ruth was nothing if not inconsiderate, depriving all these suitable parents of the chance of a child; the child of a loving, maybe affluent home.

Ruth was a problem. Even Flora agreed on that. She found her days in the hostel being increasingly taken up with what to do about Ruth, and Mrs Foulsham lost no time in pointing this out to her.

'You must be very careful not to have favourites, Flora,' Mrs Foulsham said one day in the warden's room, where morning coffee was habitually taken with the other helpers, including the psychiatric social worker, Miss Dean, and Mrs Grace who liaised with various authoritative bodies. They had been discussing what to do about Ruth and Mrs Grace was all for giving her notice, an ultimatum to make her stand on her own two feet as she put it. One had to be cruel to be kind.

Flora had rushed to defend Ruth. She pointed out that she *had* shown evidence of being able to stand on her own two feet by her courage in coming to London, insisting on keeping the baby and so on. It was then that Mrs Foulsham embarked on what was a kind of tirade against Flora for not pulling her weight. What with her preoccupation with Ruth, her cousin's husband's book *and* the Communist Party, she gave, in Mrs Foulsham's humble opinion – and the opinion of those present if the nodding heads were anything to go by – insufficient time to her work and the other inhabitants of the hostel.

'That's not fair,' Flora said with indignation. 'You know we've *all* been worried about Ruth.'

'But not as much as *you*,' Miss Dean said suggestively. 'We have had *many* girls in that position before and they have all found satisfactory ways to work things out. No reason why Ruth shouldn't either.' Miss Dean, who was a rather intense young woman, a stickler for facts and rules and regulations, consulted a sheet of paper. 'Ruth had an offer of work as a domestic at . . .'

'Ruth doesn't *want* to be a domestic,' Flora said, as if she were an agent discussing the contract for a film star.

'But she has no qualifications.'

'She can type,' Flora said. 'She can . . .' Flora put a hand to her mouth, as if a sudden thought had crossed her mind. 'Come to think, *I* may be able to find her work.'

'I'm sure you can,' Mrs Foulsham raised her eyes to the ceiling and gave Flora a funny look, which she wasn't meant to see but the others were. The implication was that Flora's relationship with Ruth was slightly unnatural. Flora knew what they thought, but she ignored them. In her own way she was just as pig-headed as Ruth.

'Even if you can find her work,' Mrs Grace said in a more kindly tone, now that there was a prospect of getting rid of Ruth at last, 'there *is* the baby. We can't keep the baby here for ever.'

'I'm not talking about "for ever",' Flora said brusquely. 'Meanwhile you all have a statutory duty; don't forget it, please.' With that warning she gave them all a dark look and abruptly left the room.

Mrs Foulsham shook her head.

'She thinks she can say what she likes, being from the upper classes. They have a certain arrogance no one can equal.'

'Yet I would *never* have thought she uses her family connections,' Mrs Grace said unexpectedly. 'She has a very kindly nature. She just wants . . .'

'She just wants her own way,' Miss Dean said. Jennifer Dean couldn't stand Flora at all. She voted Conservative and Flora's loud and oft-expounded views were anathema

461

to her. Flora didn't care who she offended in defence of her own beliefs. 'I don't really think there's a place for her here, Mrs Foulsham.' Miss Dean coughed and turned back the pages of her notes. 'I regret this is not the first young woman Miss Bolingbroke has shown excessive attachment to. There was . . .'

'Jessica Armitage,' Mrs Foulsham said. 'In fact I think Flora was directly responsible for Jessica being sent back to prison. Her example encouraged her to steal. "Everything belongs to everyone" Flora said. Jessica took her at her word.'

Flora continued to be a matter of controversy and discussion until the end of break and Mrs Foulsham thought, reluctantly, she would have to write to the area authority about Flora and ask for her resignation.

Flora was still steaming about Ruth when she got to Party headquarters just off Islington High Street. It occupied the first and second floors of a narrow house that stood in one of the passageways round the corner from the Angel. Officially Flora was events organizer but, unofficially, she was one of the key Party workers, a member of the executive, close to the leaders at national as well as local level.

Don Macmillan was a Scot who had no connection at all with either the publishing house or the politician of that name, currently Minister of Housing. Don had been born in the Gorbals and his strong class bias was reinforced by early experience. As far as Don knew, Flora's mother had been a working-class woman from the north and her father was dead. He knew nothing about the Askhams or the social ramifications of her family. Don was not, by nature, inquisitive. Flora lived in a hostel off the Mile End Road and from his point of view she was all right.

When Flora got to the office in the afternoon of her talk with her colleagues at the hostel Don had his head close to the war-time wireless in his office, busily fiddling with the controls. As Flora started to speak Don held his hand up and said 'Sshhh.' Flora mouthed 'What is it?' But Don continued to shake his head. Flora could hear the words 'Hungary' and 'fighting in the streets.'

Flora sat at her desk and started to sort through the papers that had accumulated for her attention. This is where she thought Ruth would play a useful role. She was a neat, meticulous girl and she could type. They badly needed help in the office. The noise on the wireless became a confusing crackle and, finally, Don shrugged and switched off.

'I was trying to get "Voice of America",' he said. 'There is fighting in the streets of Budapest. The Soviet Army has invaded with tanks.'

'Oh, no!' Flora put down her papers and ran over to the wireless, turning it on again. 'Oh, *no*.'

'It was time they came in,' Don said. 'Nagy was trying to restore political parties even in the name of Communism.'

'Well, what was wrong with that?' Flora furiously fiddled with the buttons, but all she got was a cacophony of sound.

'It couldn't work. It would have disrupted the State,' Don said icily, as one obeying a diktat. 'Nagy threatened the ideological stability of the whole of the Eastern bloc. The Czechs and the East Germans are supporting the Russians. Maybe others.'

'That is absolutely terrible.' Flora walked back over the carpetless floor and sank into the chair. She pushed her steel glasses up her nose. Don's face registered disapproval.

'I don't agree with you at all, Comrade.' He only called

463

her comrade when they fell out and, indeed, there were and always had been ideological differences between them. Don was a hard-line member, pro-Russian through and through. Flora had supported the attempt of Imre Nagy to take a line independent of the Soviet Union and had cheered when troops, called in by the Party Secretary, Kadar, withdrew after a cease-fire negotiated by Nagy. But Nagy's triumph was very short-lived and, by 4 November, the Soviet troops were back, reinforced now by tanks. Don was explaining that without the Russians the Party in Hungary was under threat and Flora told him, in some heat, not to be absurd.

They were still rowing an hour later when Dick walked in and joined in the argument on Flora's side. This immediately exacerbated the situation even further. Don had little love for Dick because of his defection from the Party, although Dick had not done anything dramatic to draw attention to it. He had simply ceased to pay his subscription. Don thought it was rather a cowardly way of doing things and despised Dick accordingly.

Don Macmillan was a strict follower of the Party line as dictated by Moscow whether it was pro-Stalin, anti-Stalin or whatever. He took people as they were and asked no questions. Flora was devoted to him because he never tried to probe her family background; but he did know about Dick's. At the time of his marriage to Angelica their wedding picture had been on the front pages of all the newspapers because it was such a good story: working-class man weds aristocrat. It was after that, in Don's opinion, that Dick had started to lose faith in the working-class and the working-class movement.

So the argument about Hungary grew even more fierce and it looked as though missiles might be thrown, or a fight ensue, when Lorna Miller, who was one of Flora's co-workers, came in and interrupted by shouting even louder than the other three. Don immediately cooled down but Dick, his face aflame, was still leaning over Flora's desk, thumping it for all he was worth, denouncing the Russians for intervention in a sovereign state.

'*With* the Czechs and the Poles,' Don said, but his anger had gone off the boil. As a veteran, a man used to Hyde Park Corner and meetings in streets and draughty halls all over the country, he quickly got over an argument, was seldom heated for long.

'I think you'd better get out and cool off,' Don said to Dick, 'and, please, don't show your face in here for a long time. You're no longer a member, anyway.'

'He doesn't *have* to be a member to come and see me,' Flora said hotly. 'He can come when he likes . . . *if* I'm still here.'

The two men looked at Flora, and Lorna, who was taking off her coat before starting to address envelopes, said:

'What do you mean "if you're still here"?' Lorna was a pretty girl who favoured a severe hairstyle and long pre-Raphaelite dresses that made her look much older than she was. She was studying social psychology at the Regent Street Polytechnic.

'*If* I'm still a member of the Party,' Flora pointed to the wireless, now muted, 'after Hungary.'

'Many will feel like you,' Dick said an hour or two later, when they were sitting at a table in Schmidts, which they still patronized. It was there he'd first met Angelica, but she never came here now.

Dick tucked into his jaeger schnitzel served with red cabbage. 'A lot will leave the Party.'

'I couldn't *think* of leaving the Party,' Flora said, aghast.

'Then what did you mean?'

'Well, I spoke rashly, I suppose. I am *far* too devoted to the Party to consider leaving it.'

'"My Party right or wrong",' Dick frowned. 'That really is a very narrow-minded attitude, Flora. Why do you think I left it?'

'Because you were married to Angelica, I supposed,' Flora managed a sweet smile.

'It was *nothing* to do with that.' But Dick looked uncomfortable. It was not long after his marriage that he had let his membership lapse. In a way it had everything to do with it.

'What *really* made me leave the Party,' Dick continued, 'was the insidious way Communism has taken over Eastern European countries. How can you continue to be part of a movement which can take so little account of the sufferings of individual people?'

'Because the State is bigger than they are.'

'Yes, but is it any *better*?'

It was then that Flora began to wonder. She suddenly had no appetite and pushed her plate away. For so long the Party had been like a family to her. In a way it had taken its place, representing security, the *status quo*. Father had died and Christopher like a medieval tyrant had told Aunt Rachel to move. Aunt Rachel no longer really felt at home in the Hall since Nimet had been there. Everything fragmented and became disrupted, and so it was with the Party. One clung to a belief but, finally, one had to accept that much of what Dick was saying was true.

'I was hoping to get a job at HQ for one of the girls at the hostel,' Flora said thoughtfully. 'She is really my protégée, a nice girl from Blackburn. She's called Ruth.'

'Blackburn?' Dick said with interest, Blackburn being virtually the next town of any size to Chorley.

'Surely I mentioned Ruth? She's just had a baby,' Flora

466

coloured slightly. 'She's not married and she won't say who the father was, but I do admire her. She's keeping the baby, although everyone has been on at her to have it adopted. It's a dear little thing. She's called it Joan. Joan Earnshaw.'

'That's a rather plain name,' Dick said, smiling.

'She's very down to earth, the mother,' Flora continued. 'You'd like her. She needs work because they want her to leave the hostel. I thought she could work part-time at HQ but now, after that row with Don, I'm not so sure.'

'Don will come round,' Dick tried to reassure her. 'Basically he's a very nice fellow.'

'Don *might* come round,' Flora's tone grew more positive. 'But I really don't know that I shall. I feel rather as St Paul did on the way to Damascus. The scales have fallen from my eyes, and now I see.' She smiled at him. 'I *was* educated on the Bible, you know.'

Dick was silent, studying the tablecloth.

'Maybe I could find something for Ruth, if it would help. Can she type?'

'Yes, but no shorthand.'

'I need someone to type my book. She could go over to the house.'

'Oh, Dick,' Flora joined her hands together, eyes shining. 'What a marvellous idea. She could take the baby.'

'Why not?' Dick said. 'There's plenty of room.'

'Oh Dick, you really are a saint, and . . .' ecstatically Flora leaned towards him. She wanted to add 'and I love you,' but something about his expression stopped her.

'Of course I'm not having this woman to live here with her baby!' Angelica, late home after work, was in time to hear the end of the enthusiastic discussion between Dick

467

and Flora about Ruth's future. They'd arranged everything, having progressed quite naturally from the conversation at Schmidts the week before. Dick had met Ruth, they had got on well. Dick had admired the baby, agreed that conditions at the hostel were getting intolerable and Ruth had been more than enthusiastic about the job she was to do, even though Dick's handwriting would pose problems.

Dick and Flora met constantly in that week while the news in Hungary confirmed both their fears. There were barricades and fighting in the streets and, in a very short time, Nagy fell and the revolt was over.

Charlotte had called in on her way back from Askham and had been quite enthusiastic about the plan until she heard her daughter's reaction.

'But, darling, there's *plenty* of room,' she said. 'She would be ideal to babysit for the children as you do often have difficulty finding someone on Nanny's nights out.'

'On Nanny's nights out, Dick stays in,' Angelica said firmly then, as an afterthought, 'that's if I'm not here.'

Angelica seldom was there. In the past year her career had taken off to the extent that, like her mother in Paris twenty years before her, she was one of the top models in London, the quintessence of elegance and chic; her face familiar to half the population, not only from journals and newspapers, the covers of magazines but, increasingly, from television. Angelica, Gérard's top model, was seen here, there and everywhere, usually on the arm of some celebrity like herself, seldom on Dick's.

Angelica had come in from a first night, but instead of going on to a party afterwards she came home because she had a headache. Everyone else was informally dressed, Charlotte in her customary country outfit of tweeds and cashmere, and Angelica looked rather incongruous in their company dressed in a Norman Hartnell evening gown slit up to the knee with her fox fur still over her shoulders. She had been the guest of Munroe Goldblatt, the American film mogul, who had delivered her to the door in his studio limousine.

At the age of twenty-six – though she was careful not to reveal her age – Angelica Crosby was one of the most acclaimed, sought-after women in London. Married to an academic, the mother of two beautiful children, with whom she was frequently photographed, allied to the noble Askham family, niece of the millionaire industrialist Lord Lighterman, she was thought to have everything that birth, money, talent and natural good looks could give. Few saw the discontent underneath. Sometimes it showed in her eyes in studio photographs, but it was mistaken for natural aristocratic hauteur, a sign of birth and good breeding. She was seldom photographed smiling and that air of disdain was unsuccessfully imitated by many who modelled themselves after her, wanting nothing more than to be like her.

In a way Angelica had become even more famous than Charlotte had been before her. Charlotte always remained a working model; Angelica had become something of an institution, known rather for her good looks, for herself, than what she did. She was celebrated for being celebrated – a new race that television was largely responsible for. The most untalented people could become celebrities simply by appearing on the box often enough.

Angelica was picking at items on the kitchen table, where they'd been having a late snack. Flora, wearing trousers and a turtle-neck sweater, had her hand curled round a mug of hot chocolate. Charlotte and Dick were drinking wine. It was ten o'clock and Angelica was tired and bad-tempered after spending a whole evening trying to be not only pleasant but gracious and beautiful with a

469

horrible man who kept on making suggestive remarks. She'd only tolerated him because of his power, despising herself for it. The sheer frustration and boredom of an artificial life lived largely in the public eye made her particularly difficult at home, and Charlotte took to dropping in more and more, because she was worried about what was going on in the Kensington house, the rift between her daughter and her husband.

'It just *seemed* a good idea,' Dick said equably, aware of his wife's mood. 'She needs somewhere to live; she can do a job for me, help generally in the house and . . .'

'I'm not having her here, that's all.' Angelica glanced at her watch and poured herself half a glass of wine, smiling wanly at her mother and adding: 'I've a frightful head.' Charlotte smiled in sympathy. Her life had never been as taxing as her daughter's, but she knew where to look for the lines of tiredness – by the side of the mouth, at the corners of the eyes.

Charlotte glanced at the clock on the kitchen wall. Arthur had been in Wales. He should be home by now. She felt a familiar knot form just under the ribs, the pain of tension; an indication of the strain that life with Arthur had now become. A life of pretence and deceit. How much longer it could continue she didn't know, but it was every bit as wearing as the life of her daughter and son-in-law, maybe more so.

'It's none of my business, of course,' she said. 'You must work it out for yourselves. I just think it is nice, darling, where one can, to help less fortunate people.'

'Why don't *you* help her, then?' Angelica took a sip from her glass. 'You have more than enough room, a huge house just for you and Arthur, occasionally Joe.'

'That's not the real point,' Charlotte sighed. 'Is it? Dick needs this girl to work for him and it would seem to me ideal . . .'

'Seem to *you*, Mother, but you're not here. I do wish you would keep out of our affairs.'

Charlotte got up, took her bag from the floor and went over to kiss Dick. He was an affectionate man of whom she had grown very fond. As she bent to kiss him he rose and took her arm. Then she walked over to Angelica and put her hands on both her shoulders.

'You look lovely tonight, Angelica. Try and get more rest.'

She kissed Flora who got up awkwardly and followed her and Dick out of the kitchen, leaving Angelica staring moodily into her glass.

'I'm *awfully* sorry about that, Charlotte.' Dick hovered in the hall, helping her on with her coat. 'I'd better drop it, I think.'

'Why?' Charlotte looked at him with raised eyebrows. 'Why let her get her own way over *everything*? You're not doing her, or yourself, a favour, you know.'

Dick shrugged again and, telling Flora to keep out of the cold, opened the door for his mother-in-law and saw her to her car standing in the drive.

'Will you be all right?' he said, after she had seated herself in front of the wheel.

'Will *you*?' Charlotte looked at him keenly. 'I think you and Angelica should have a good talk.'

'We've had so many,' Dick sounded sad. 'Maybe too many.'

'Then maybe you should take some action.' Charlotte adjusted the mirror and turned on the ignition. 'My daughter is *very* spoilt. That's my fault to begin with, I'm afraid, and one we're both paying for.' She kissed him again as he leaned down and then she wound up the window and waved again before easing the car slowly away from the kerb.

Sometimes Charlotte wondered if life had dealt her a

471

particularly bad set of cards. She was fifty in May and she had never known real peace. Her father had died when she was a small child and she had grown up in an atmosphere of stress and change, despite the calm and capability of her mother who could hardly have been better, and remained an anchor in her life.

Every time Arthur went away Charlotte knew he slept with Jill. Maybe he slept with her at other times, too. Yet she had never told him what she'd discovered on her way back to London after Aunt Melanie's funeral. She kept on meaning to say something, but she never did; she didn't know what to say, or how to say it or what would happen if she did. If she did, if there was an explosion, that could mean the break-up of her marriage, and Charlotte had decided that she didn't want to be alone. She wouldn't give Arthur a divorce easily, nor did she want the scandal that a messy case inevitably would bring. Whenever there was the threat of publicity in a court of law the family drew back, closed ranks, agreed to settle rather than risk unwelcome publicity which had once so damaged them.

But not only that. She needed Arthur; she wanted to be married. She wanted to have position and her place in society. Jill was not the first mistress the men in her family had had. Maybe the women just accepted them – rather like nineteenth-century wives. Maybe things hadn't changed so much, after all.

Anyway life with Arthur, even sharing him, was better than life alone. She was quite sure of that. Only Joe disagreed; but Joe, sworn to secrecy, loved his mother too much to betray her. All he wanted was for her to be happy, at whatever cost.

It was a short drive from the Boltons to Holland Park, a drive through tree-lined streets with pretty houses, many of them still undergoing refurbishment and repainting in

472

the long aftermath of war. Charlotte crossed Kensington High Street, still marvelling at the plethora of lights though it was eleven years since they'd come on again. Changing gear to enter the narrow street near her home she thought that, somehow, she had become stuck in those war years. Even though they were grim, there was much that was glorious, exciting, noble. In her present state of uncertainty and misery, of aimlessness, sometimes she found herself wishing they were back, that the lights would go off again. She was a casualty of peace.

When she got home all the lights were on in the house, which rather surprised her. Or, at least, they were on downstairs and one or two upstairs, so that the whole place appeared brightly lit up. She wondered if Joe had come home. They hardly ever seemed to see him these days and, as he was a devoted son, she missed him.

But he was so good to his brother and, with mounting tension between Pascal and Anna more and more apparent, he was needed in that divided household, where he did much to keep the peace.

It was no use just getting angry at Anna. Pascal was very difficult and, in Joe's opinion, Anna did her best. But the life had gone out of the marriage, and many wondered how long it could possibly last.

As she stopped her car in front of the house Arthur opened the door and came out to greet her which, again, was unusual. His own 'Askham' was parked in the drive without having been put in the garage; strange again.

'Is everything all right?' she said, as Arthur opened her door.

'I wondered where you were.' Arthur looked worried as he helped her out.

'It's not so very late, is it?' Charlotte glanced at her watch in the light over the porch. 'I'd been to see Mother and then I stopped in at Angelica. I . . .'

Arthur hurried her in. It was very cold. When she got into the hall she looked around, peeping into the brightly-lit drawing-room.

'Is Joe here?' she said. 'Is Pascal all right?'

Arthur took her fur and put in into the vestibule off the hall.

'So you don't know,' he said, coming over to her and holding out his arms.

'Know what, for God's sake?' Charlotte, seriously alarmed, took both his arms and shook him. 'Know *what*, Arthur? Has something happened to Pascal?'

Arthur drew her into the drawing-room, his arms round her waist. There was a fire burning brightly in the grate and a plate of sandwiches and some coffee, a half-drunk glass of whisky on one of the small tables near the hearth. On the chair in which Arthur had obviously been sitting there was a newspaper lying open where he'd left it.

'Arthur, I *must* know,' Charlotte felt close to panic and gazed wildly at him. He handed the paper to her.

'I'm frightfully sorry, darling,' he said. 'But I think the best thing you can do is to read it yourself.'

Arthur went over to the table to pour Charlotte a whisky as, slumping into the chair vacated by him, she slowly read the paragraph he'd indicated in the middle of the page:

COUSIN OF A PEER ARRESTED

Mr Joseph Verdi
held on serious charges

Mr Joseph Verdi, cousin of the Earl of Askham, was arrested this afternoon on a charge that he conspired with other persons to commit acts of gross indecency on male persons in the months of August and September last year and, again, in October at the country home of his stepfather the Honourable Arthur Crewe MP, Minister of State at the Foreign Office. Mr Verdi and two

474

companions, Mr Marcus Trew and Captain Jasper Lester RA, will appear at the magistrates' court in Winchester tomorrow.

Mr Verdi is the twin son of Lady Charlotte Crewe, daughter of the eleventh Earl of Askham who was killed in the Great War. Lady Charlotte herself had a distinguished war career and was awarded the *Croix de Guerre avec Palmes* for her work in Occupied France. Mr Verdi's brother, Pascal, was seriously injured in a car crash eighteen months ago. He . . .

The print began to blur and Charlotte blinked as she looked at Arthur. She didn't know how long he had been standing before her but, mechanically, she put out her hand and took the glass he held out.

'Poor Joe,' she said. 'We must go to him at once.'

'I've phoned, but there's no answer.' Arthur pulled up a stool and sat at her feet. 'We can't see him now until after the court appearance. I've briefed Jeremy Pettigrew and he's going down first thing in the morning.' Jeremy Pettigrew QC was their son Jeremy's godfather.

Charlotte nodded. Everything seemed mechanical now.

'I'd better ring Mother,' she said.

'Your mother knows, Charlotte.' Arthur took her hand. 'I rang to speak to you but you'd left. I told Hugo and he was going to tell your mother. I'm frightfully sorry, darling. Had you . . .' he screwed up his nose and looked at her, 'had you any idea?'

'None at all.' Charlotte drank some of the amber liquid in the glass. 'I wondered many times, because Joe has never shown much interest in girls. But some men are like that, aren't they? Without being . . .' It was still a word one didn't like to use in connection with one's own son. 'I didn't dream that . . . Oh Arthur,' she bent forward and leaned her head against his chest. 'Why did he have to do it? *Why?*'

475

CHAPTER 19

The trial of Joe Verdi and his companions lasted a full week at Winchester Assizes and occupied the maximum amount of space in the popular press. In the end all the accused were found guilty of acts of gross indecency against a number of male persons, mostly young army recruits who had been on manoeuvres near the Crewe country home at the time the alleged events took place. Joe and Captain Lester were sent to prison for eighteen months. Marcus Trew, who was only twenty and who was held to have been corrupted by the elder men, got a suspended sentence.

Joe had wanted to plead guilty and so shorten the proceedings because of the harm he knew the publicity would do to the family. But Jasper Lester wanted to try and save his Army career so both men were defended by leading counsel.

Joe's fears were justified. The family got more publicity than they had ever dreamt of in their worst nightmares, far worse than anything that had happened in 1913, though that had been bad enough. But there hadn't been television then, and every night the population of Britain saw on the screens pictures of the accused accompanied to the court always by his mother and, sometimes, by others of his family who thus voluntarily threw themselves into the limelight. They'd had a foretaste of this kind of exposure after Pascal's accident, when the press and television cameras besieged the gates of the Hall and the village of Askham for days.

One day it was Rachel, another Arthur, and Pascal

insisted on being wheeled in his chair. Angelica showed support with Dick. Flora was there every day and Paul Askham made a point of being seen going into the court beside his cousin.

For those who could admire the Askhams, and there were many, it was a brave scene, but typical for those who knew the family, and the history of a family which invariably united together against a common enemy, in this case Regina who prosecuted one of their number in the name of the law.

There were, however, exceptions: Bobby Lighterman decided to go on a world cruise as soon as his cousin was committed for trial and missed the entire event. He was there in spirit, however, because the papers with their varying accounts of the sensational trial were sent to him by his private secretary at every port of call and he would retire to his stateroom to search for one thing. Happily it only occasionally occurred; the name of Lighterman was seldom mentioned.

The publicity concentrated on the Askham family, and he hoped his own would escape association with that pervert who had blotted a proud family scutcheon. Adultery and falsehood were one thing: buggery was something quite other. Bobby sailed away to the sunset in order to forget.

Joe didn't appeal. He was sent to prison which, hopefully, with remission for good behaviour, he would leave in about a year's time.

The public, it is true, had short memories and one scandal was soon followed by another. But for the Askhams the mark would remain for a very long time. With some of them for ever.

Anna read the final reports of the trial in Frankfurt. Like Bobby, she chose to be out of the country, ostensibly on business, while her brother-in-law was tried. After all, she had the same name.

'I always thought he was a fag,' she said. 'I once made a pass at him and he turned me down.'

'That must have been humiliating.' Gunther stood up and poured more brandy for himself and Anna. They were sitting in the lounge in his flat after dining alone.

'I'd had too much to drink. I'd forgotten all about it – until this.'

'Did Pascal have any idea?'

'Joe kept himself very much to himself. He's a very quiet and controlled person, you know. You wouldn't dream of asking him a personal question. But he did venerate his mother, much more than Pascal. Pascal and Angelica blamed Charlotte for doing dangerous work in the war, but Joe didn't. He idolized his mother and he talked a lot about her. It's Charlotte I feel sorry for most. She had such intolerably high standards herself. The crash for Charlotte and Arthur, with his political ambitions, must be dreadful . . .' Anna paused because Gunther, who had been sitting opposite, returned to the sofa beside her, putting both their glasses on the low table in front of them. Anna sensed that Gunther had something other than the trials of her family on his mind and she looked at him.

'Anna,' Gunther said, placing his hand on her shoulder, 'when are we going to do something about us?'

'How do you mean?'

'You know what I mean. When are you going to ask Pascal for a divorce?'

'I can hardly do it *now*. He's been through a terrible time.'

'Yes, but it's not your fault his brother is a pervert.'

'They'd think it something to do with it if I asked for a divorce now.'

'Well? Does it matter?' Gunther seemed surprised by her response.

'Yes, it does. They're my family, too, unfortunately. I'm beginning to wish I'd never left Venice.'

'In that case I wouldn't have met you.'

'True.' Anna smiled as he kissed her.

'You do want to, don't you?'

'One day.' Anna's eyes opened wide. 'But I tell you, now is not the time. I care enough for Pascal not to want to wound him any more. He's not the one who's been on trial and I've hardly been much support to him.'

'I still don't see . . .'

'Gunther,' Anna's tone changed and she put a hand on his knee. 'Will you tell me something truthfully?'

'If I can.' He smiled at her a little nervously.

'Will you tell me if you just want me to be a wife, possibly a mother, living in the Black Forest all by myself while you fornicate in Frankfurt, or wherever . . .'

'*Anna*, you know . . .'

'Or,' Anna went on as though she hadn't been interrupted. '*Or* whether I can play a full part in your life and the business.'

'The business?' Gunther looked at her, surprised.

'Ah, I see by your look you didn't expect that.' Anna stubbed out the cigarette she'd been smoking in a large glass ashtray.

'You never suggested it before.'

'But you *know* that I'm ambitious and that that ambition has been constantly thwarted by my family. They still blame me for Pascal's accident. They're vindictive.'

'But, to be fair, I don't think Bobby wanted a brother and sister running the business.'

'Whatever the truth is, that's not the point. I would like to have some part in the business. My German and Italian are fluent. I could be an asset to you. I could develop the motor car side and not just as an agency. I am very knowledgeable. I feel frustrated in the role that my family fob off on me. I have doubled the sale of custom-built "Askhams" despite the bad publicity caused by the crash; yet they never think I'm very important. Now, if you were to offer me a full partnership in the Spee group, I might consider being your wife, eventually, if I can do it without upsetting too many people. But business first. How about it?'

'You drive a hard bargain.' Gunther settled back in his chair. 'But one not without advantages.'

'If you offer me a partnership now it makes it easier for me to wrench myself away from the family. They will know what to expect in a year or two . . .'

'A year or two!'

'Or more, even. When they've got over the shock of the trial. Then, if the time is suitable . . . well, how about it?'

Gunther heard a little warning bell inside his head. He knew if he agreed to what she wanted he would be taking on a very formidable companion.

Flora held the baby in her arms watching her as she sucked at her bottle, aware of her comforting, protective arm so important to the helpless defenceless baby. These tiny little creatures . . . really, one had to do everything for them. As if divining her thoughts, the baby stopped sucking and gazed at Flora and, in that instant, Flora felt a complete and utter love for tiny Joan that bewildered her so much it made the hand holding the bottle shake.

Flora knew that, for most of her adult life, she had suppressed her normal instincts; the desire for love and affection that were common to men and women. Brought up by an ageing father and aunt, shy and awkward at school, she had developed bookishness, academic industry to compensate for the lack of good looks common to her family.

Unexpectedly the trial of Joe had brought the family closer together as they supported Joe as well as one another. She now wondered if it was the resurgence of family love that had inspired this altogether unexpected maternal love for Joan. Or was it that she simply grew closer to her because now she was almost totally responsible for her upbringing?

The dilemma about where Ruth and her baby could live had been solved shortly before Christmas when Flora decided to move into a flat not far from the hostel, where she was increasingly unhappy anyway, and make a home there for Joan and Ruth. Flora could stay at home, while Ruth went to work, and work and look after the baby. On the days she had to go into the LSE she got a local woman to help out. It was a very good arrangement and both Ruth and Dick were grateful for it. Ruth had her dignity too, and now a comfortable home for herself and the baby.

Flora felt full of goodwill and happiness as she took the teat out of Joan's mouth, sat her up on her lap and winded her.

'Who's a good girl, then?' Joan smiled and reached out with her tiny hands which Flora seized and kissed.

She had never felt like this before about a baby, never about her little cousins, nieces or nephews. In fact, up to now, she would never have considered herself as one who was particularly fond of children; but now she was besotted.

After the feed Flora changed Joan and put her into her crib to sleep. Then, drawing it away from the sunlight, she drew up her chair and began to read. But, too frequently, she kept turning to the cot and gazing at Joan; or going to the window and looking out across the roofs of the pretty houses that had once been an elegant street before the inner city decay of the thirties and forties, and the increasing influx of post-war immigrants dissatisfied with conditions in their own countries.

Flora was widening her interests and black immigration was one of them. West Indians were pouring into the country without adequate housing and were forming ghettos.

But the most important thing in her life was the emergence of a serious group of people against the nuclear bomb: the growing campaign for nuclear disarmament. A number of eminent people, among them the philosopher Bertrand Russell and the writer J. B. Priestley, were showing interest in the formation of such a movement; and Flora had got Rachel to add her name to those willing to sponsor the formation of a proper organization. Rachel said she was too old, but so was Russell! Age didn't matter when the future of the human race was at stake. Currently there were nuclear tests being held in the Pacific and the volume of international concern was increasing. These tests were terribly worrying for the future of the human race. No one, not even scientists, knew the consequences. Once more Flora looked at Joan and, instinctively, went over to plant a kiss on her chubby cheeks.

Ruth usually got home about seven but, that night, she rang to say she would be late and would Flora mind feeding Joan? Flora reassured Ruth she wouldn't mind, then began to prepare the baby's food, solids which she was now taking with her bottle. Flora was not interested in food for herself. She knew that the family considered her painfully thin, almost scraggy, and somewhat abnormal, because there were a number of gourmets among them and, as a group, they liked their food. Flora made do with anything that was in the small fridge or the kitchen cupboard and, if there was little or nothing, she did without.

That night, after she had given Joan her bath, fed her and tucked her up for the night, she had a boiled egg, thinking that maybe she'd have something else when Ruth came in.

But by midnight Ruth was not in. She hadn't said where she was going, or who with, and it hadn't occurred to Flora to ask. She wasn't curious about what Ruth did and thought that, anyway, it was none of her business. Certainly Ruth had taken on a new lease of life since she'd moved into the flat with Flora, shortly after Christmas. She'd blossomed. It was only then that Flora had realized how very attractive Ruth really was – with her healthy glowing skin, and velvety brown eyes framed by thick black lashes.

At one o'clock Flora telephoned Dick's house. The phone rang for a long time before it was sleepily answered by the nanny, who curtly informed Flora that neither Mrs nor Dr Crosby were at home and she hadn't seen Miss Earnshaw all day.

'Wasn't she in at all?' Flora said with some bewilderment thinking, naturally, that Ruth had been telephoning from Dick's house.

'No, miss,' the nanny said. 'Mrs Crosby is in America on a modelling engagement and Dr Crosby and Miss Earnshaw haven't been here all day. Now it is late, miss, *if* you don't mind.' The receiver was sharply replaced, leaving only the burring sound lingering in Flora's ear.

But the whole episode unsettled her. Worse, in the dark, in the security of her own bed within sound of Joan, should she cry, she began to imagine dark and mysterious things, possibilities that had never crossed her mind before.

She began to imagine that Dick and Ruth might be involved, and the very idea seemed shocking.

The next day was a Saturday, when Ruth wouldn't have been working anyway and she came home at about eleven in the morning just as Flora, after a very bad night, was going over her reading, having settled Joan. She started as she heard a key in the door and then realized that it was Ruth depositing her bag on the sideboard, some books and her coat on a chair. Ruth shook out her hair and smiled a shade nervously at Flora as she came in.

'Sorry,' she said. 'I hope I didn't worry you.'

'Where were you?' Flora rubbed her eyes, feeling suddenly angry.

'I stayed the night with a friend. We went to a film. It was very late.'

'What friend?' Flora enquired suspiciously.

'You don't know her,' Ruth said casually. 'Someone I knew at home.'

'What's her name? Where does she live?' Flora's tone surprised herself. 'I mean, I *do* think I have a right to know. I was *very* worried when you didn't come home. I thought of all sorts of things . . .' she trailed off and her eyes met Ruth's. 'I rang Dick. He wasn't at home, either.'

'That's nothing to do with me, is it?' Ruth said in an offhand way, going to the kitchen sink to fill the kettle.

'Didn't you go into work yesterday?'

'Of course I did.' Ruth paused, then turned to look at her.

'The nanny said you didn't.' Flora felt empty. 'The nanny said neither you nor Dick were there all day and Angelica was in America.'

'Well, I can't help what that silly nanny said.' Ruth spun round in sudden fury. 'And perhaps *you* can tell me why *you're* so busy snooping when . . .'

'I'm *not* snooping!' Flora felt outraged. 'I was just very

worried. It never occurred to me . . .' She stopped and, as Ruth stared back, she knew that her thoughts were transparent. 'It never occurred to me that you and Dick . . .' she said slowly, and slumped in a chair. 'It simply never occurred to me at all that you and he . . .'

Ruth suddenly sat down, too, as if deflated, her face worried, a nervous little tic starting at the corner of her eye.

'I don't know how it started,' she said. 'It never occurred to me either. He's very lonely, you know, and his wife doesn't love him.'

'Oh, he told you that, did he?' Flora's voice was shaky. 'The old story. Doesn't understand him either, I expect.'

'No, she doesn't. You should know that. I see them together. Don't forget I'm there every day. They have nothing in common. She despises him, everyone can see that. The nanny knows it, too, and talks about them; the cleaning lady knows it and talks with me and the nanny about them. They think I'm one of them, you see. Staff. I like Dick. I liked him at the beginning and I admire the work he does. His book *is* brilliant and he's been teaching me a lot. We . . .'

'How long has it been going on for?' It dawned on Flora that now she was being called on to make a bigger sacrifice than ever; to be noble when the man she loved loved another. It was a terrible irony.

She and Dick had a lot in common, too. What was more, she had known him for years. She had introduced him to Angelica and now she had done it again: she had introduced him to Ruth.

'We haven't slept together often,' Ruth said, as if the number of times mattered; as if she were still not certain whether to feel joy or guilt. 'Angelica's been away all week in America and it was a chance to go away. On Thursday Dick said we could go into the country the next

485

day, as the weather was good. He'd booked a room in a
hotel on the river, not far from Robertswood. It's so nice
to be able to spend a whole night together. It was a place
he knew and he said he hoped that no one saw us
there . . .' Ruth raised her head, her eyes shining now
with an assurance that Flora could only recognize and
envy. 'No one did.'

'Will it go on then, as an affair . . .' Flora tried to make
her voice sound practical, as if she didn't care very much.

'I expect so. I don't know. We don't discuss it. I don't
know what will happen. Do you?'

Ruth's voice was appealing, her pretty face had the
trusting expression on it of a little girl.

'Could she *possibly* not have known,' Flora thought,
'that I cared?' But all she did was shake her head and say
she didn't know, either. But she could guess; she could
guess.

'It's Mother's eightieth birthday soon,' Charlotte said
across the breakfast table to Arthur. 'We must have a
party.'

'Of course.' Arthur was eating his toast and reading
The Times folded on to the political page.

In January the Prime Minister, Anthony Eden, had
resigned on the grounds of ill health though, really, he
was a broken man after the Suez fiasco which had
coincided with the revolution in Hungary. But Harold
Macmillan, who succeeded him, was also a good friend of
Arthur's, as he and his wife, Lady Dorothy, were of the
whole family. Arthur had reason to hope for preferment,
maybe a Cabinet position at last; but in the reshuffle he
was passed over. It coincided with the announcement that
Joe had been arrested on a charge of indecency. Harold
had told him that it had nothing to do with it, but it was
hard to believe him.

It was therefore very brave, but quite typical, of Arthur to attend the trial and be seen with Charlotte and Joe going into court. Everyone admired him for it, inside and outside the family. His political colleagues and rivals, especially, admired him for it and were grateful to him, too; they felt that he had sunk his chances of promotion in the government for good.

Arthur George Crewe had been born in 1905, and this year he would be fifty-two. It was not old for a man, as a politician or anything else; but to continue for many more years in the wilderness with only a junior government job might mean that he would never reach the Cabinet. Macmillan and the government were popular, but how long would it take the fickle British public to lurch, as it so often did, towards the opposition of whatever party was in office?

Arthur stirred his coffee thoughtfully and continued to read the paper. But his mind wasn't on it. Just before Joe was arrested he'd promised Jill he would ask Charlotte for a divorce. Jill was young enough to have children and she wanted them. She didn't feel she had many more child-bearing years left and she wouldn't consider either a baby without matrimony, or leaving Arthur. It was an awful choice to have to make.

He didn't want to leave Charlotte to marry Jill, but Jill could make things awkward if she tried. Besides, he had become very dependent on her.

Maybe it mattered less now, but a divorce would hardly advance his career. Charlotte was an Askham and, despite the scandals that rocked it from time to time, she and her family were well thought of. Often at night Arthur lay awake sweating, tormented by indecision. Sometimes he just felt he'd like to get away from it all: vanish, throw up the whole thing.

But he couldn't. He was a Crewe and, through his association with that family, an Askham.

He was only half-heartedly listening to Charlotte talk about the plans for Rachel's eightieth birthday, just as he only half-heartedly did most things these days. He supposed he might be going through some kind of mid-life crisis that he heard men went through as well as women. He didn't know if Charlotte was going through it because it was the sort of thing they would never discuss. She was never very enthusiastic when they made love, but then she never had been. She went through it as a duty to him and he went through it as a duty to her. It was a very rum situation; both of them pretending. If he left her and went to live with Jill they could give it up altogether; discontinue the farce that had largely marred their married life. Jill was an enthusiastic, willing lover; he didn't need another.

But there was Jeremy, too. The effect on Jeremy of the divorce of his parents . . .

'You don't seem to be listening, Arthur,' Charlotte said rather sharply. 'Is there something on your mind?'

Arthur looked out of the breakfast-room window into the garden. All the trees were in leaf, the herbaceous borders bright with flowers. One could almost hear the bees, it was so tranquil. Joe's trial had been over for weeks. There came a time in the life of every man, and woman, when decisions had to be made. Jill might ask him today and, if she didn't, tomorrow, and the day after tomorrow. She would nag at him until he did something. Maybe Charlotte would understand.

'Charlotte,' he said, removing his reading-glasses and folding them beside his paper. 'I have something quite serious to tell you.'

'Oh?' Now it was coming.

Arthur cleared his throat.

'Charlotte,' he said again, and stopped.

'Yes?'

How could he tell her? 'Charlotte,' he said, for the third time. His voice was trembling and he saw Charlotte rise, go to the window and take a deep breath as if sniffing the air, to give her courage, too. Then she turned to him.

'Arthur,' she said. 'If you're trying to tell me something personal, maybe I know already.'

'Personal?' Arthur stumbled over the word.

'If it's about Jill, I know, and have for some time.'

'You know about *Jill*?' Arthur felt so relieved, so ridiculously pleased, that he sat back, his arms dangling by the sides of his chair.

'Yes. I've known for about,' Charlotte looked at the ceiling as though doing a calculation, 'I've known since Aunt Melanie's funeral.' She then told him about the car in front of the hotel. 'So *silly* of you to leave the car outside the hotel,' she said, as if reprimanding a naughty child. 'It was asking for trouble. As though you *wanted* to be discovered, Arthur.' Charlotte sat down again and poured herself coffee, a look of annoyance on her face. She rang the bell to ask for a fresh pot.

'But why did you never say?'

'Because I didn't want to. I didn't want to present you with an ultimatum, to lose you. I didn't want a divorce and I don't now, if that's what you are thinking of.'

But all Arthur could think of was the fact that she'd known. It was so unlike Charlotte. All the time she'd known. And how *could* a woman like Charlotte tolerate the knowledge of a mistress? She so proud, so intolerant of others. How *could* she knowingly share his body with someone else?

'I didn't know you, Charlotte,' Arthur said at last, almost to himself. 'I never thought you would tolerate a situation like that. I never dreamt you knew.'

He reached into his breast pocket and drew out the silver cigarette case she'd given him as an anniversary present.

'You *thought* I would never tolerate it, didn't you, Arthur? I must say I surprised myself. I was furious, of course, and angry and upset. Jill was a menial, the secretary; rather like sleeping with the housemaid.'

'That's a horrible thing to say,' Arthur interrupted her angrily.

'True, though. At times like this one is reminded of who one is. I'm surprised at you, *too*, Arthur. You surely could have found a better-bred girl for a mistress? I can understand why she should fall for you, but not why you should fall for her, if it's an affair you wanted.'

'It's *not* just that with Jill. It's . . .'

'Please spare me the sordid little details, Arthur.'

'Jill is thirty-six, hardly a girl.'

'Quite. She doesn't look a girl. I don't know what you see in her at all. Not pretty, not anything, no personality, a nothing. You see, I didn't feel, at my age, that I wanted to be alone; that I wanted to be divorced, forced to live the life of a single woman.'

'You would have *many* admirers. You might marry again.'

'But would I, Arthur? That's just it. Would I? I'm fifty. Not all that number of suitable single men around. I realized that I was used to the stabilizing influence of marriage. You were very persistent about marrying me when I was quite happy to remain single. You owe me, Arthur. You owe me that independence I lost; the job you wouldn't let me take. Why should I lose, now, what you insisted I have? So, if it's a divorce you're after, by any chance, the answer was and is "No". No divorce, not on any terms.'

Arthur stubbed out his cigarette and got up, walking to the open French windows.

'I find this *very* hard to understand, Charlotte. I'm surprised at you. I thought you had more pride.'

'It's *because* of my pride that I'm saying what I am, Arthur. Besides, I feel we should stick together, if only because of Joe's trial. The mud has stuck and will cling for a very long time.'

'I know.' Arthur hung his head. 'I know it's a bad time. For that much, I am sorry.'

Charlotte smiled at him. 'No need to be sorry, Arthur. No divorce, not now or ever. I made up my mind about that. I've talked to Mother about it and she agrees.'

'Your *mother* knows?' Arthur choked on his words. 'I *am* astounded.'

'I confide in Mother. I always have. She's my best friend. She likes you, but she also knows that I gave up someone else for you, Arthur, a man I met in the war and loved very much. His name was Marc and we were lovers. But I felt I could never let you down, having promised to marry you. And I didn't. I married you, Arthur, and you're stuck with me. You mustn't let me down, either. I'm pretty sure, too, that you won't want to walk out and live with Jill because Harold will boot you right out of the government. He'll see to that, don't worry. In fact, if you ask me, it was because he knew about Jill he didn't put you in his new Cabinet. It had nothing to do with Joe. Sleeping with the hired help, Arthur! Shame on you.'

'On the contrary, I think it had *everything* to do with Joe,' Arthur said spiritedly. 'Having a pervert in the family is hardly a good recommendation for a Cabinet Minister.'

'That *is* unworthy of you, Arthur. I'm surprised.'

'Still, it's true. I thought I'd been very good about it,

491

Charlotte, because I knew how much it made you suffer . . .'

'You were good, and about Pascal. You're part of the family, Jeremy's father, and you're stuck with it.' Charlotte, pale-faced, looked up from the fresh coffee she had poured, the maid having hastily sidled in and sidled out again. God knew what she'd heard. But Charlotte didn't care. They probably knew everything already. Maybe, when she was away, Arthur and Jill made love in the house. She was only relieved that she and Arthur didn't share a bed. 'I am not divorcing you, whatever you do. You can beg and you can steal, but I won't divorce you, and that's it.' Charlotte crossed her arms on the table and looked at him.

She was very beautiful, very young-looking. Many men, he knew, would envy him; but, at the moment, Arthur hated her. He would have liked to hit her across the face with his paper. He wanted to violate her crudely. Arthur firmly put his baser thoughts out of his mind. One wasn't brought up as a gentleman to relinquish that training so easily. His hands firmly clasping the folded copy of his paper, he stood up and left the breakfast-room.

He didn't even slam the door behind him.

CHAPTER 20

In a way it was like old times, as Pascal sat there excitedly sketching and Sasha leaned over his shoulder making suggestions. Only this time it was not Anna, but Stefanie in the background providing coffee and sandwiches and making encouraging noises.

Pascal was staying with the Ferovs in Downshire Hill while he had more tests at the Hospital for Nervous Diseases in Queen's Square. There was just the chance that an operation might restore some more movement, but it might be too risky to take a chance. In a way Pascal had become very adjusted to his life in a wheelchair. He sometimes claimed that it had improved his creative drive and that the ideas tumbling through his head kept him awake at night.

But this time the drive was focused on something quite different. Ever since the war Sasha had nursed an ambition to fly again and he had joined a flying club not far from Robertswood. During his protracted convalescence Pascal took to going to the club with Sasha and watching the planes taking off and landing. Maybe it accentuated the feeling of freedom he longed for; stimulated his imagination – the thought of taking off and soaring above the ground. Soon after that he began to study the principles of aerodynamics which, after all, were not so very different from the principles that made supercharged cars hurtle along the ground at nearly two hundred miles an hour.

After that it became a sort of hobby; designing light aircraft that businesses could use for transporting their executive personnel swiftly about the world. He indulged in wild flights of fancy in his drawings, but in his model-making he was more down to earth, and some of them were very good.

Of course, again there were many competitors in the field, as there had been with the 'Askham'. Yet that custom-built car had established a place now in markets all over the world and there was very little more that needed to be done about the basic design. Since the accident Bobby had largely lost interest in the car and talked once again of selling the works, much to the chagrin of the two men who had worked so hard to build it up: Sasha and Pascal.

There was also an additional factor: Sasha hated working for Bobby. He knew he was there on sufferance in place of Pascal and that Bobby had already made over-tures to young Paul behind his back. Paul had been very rude to him and Bobby had not yet forgiven him, but there was much to admire about the Earl of Askham. He was dynamic, he was keen, and he was talented. He had a 'nose' for business, a talent that was remarkably like the young Bobby Lighterman's, and even at university had made a number of casual profitable deals on the side which helped him finance himself through his studies. For Askham finances were still minimal. The only money around belonged to Bobby, and Paul had declared he had no intention of touching it.

Sasha and Pascal felt that way, too; but there could be no aeroplanes without money, quite a lot of it.

'We shall just have to ask Bobby at Rachel's birthday party,' Sasha said, standing back from Pascal's latest design and scratching his head. 'There's no other way we can get the money, and we can't get going without it.'

'You know he'll say "no",' Pascal turned to the table

and sipped his coffee. 'We will humiliate ourselves yet again.'

Stefanie was busy in the background. She had surprised herself and her doctors at the clinic by discovering a talent for painting and during these long summer evenings, while the men worked, she set up some still-life subjects in the corner of the drawing-room and painted them; or sketched the men while they concentrated on their task. She was having lessons at St Martin's School of Art, where her teachers were astonished that she hadn't tried to develop this gift before.

Stefanie looked up from the bowl of fruit she'd set against a backdrop of a folded green cloth and a basket, sat back and sucked her brush. In the background the men went on chattering.

'I have money,' she said, without turning round. 'Remember, when I was twenty-five I inherited most of my fortune.'

'But it's all in Lighterman shares,' Sasha looked at her busily studying her artistic creation.

'I can sell them, can't I? There was no stipulation as to what I had to do with them.'

'Your father will be absolutely furious if you do that. Five per cent of Lighterman shares is worth a fortune.'

'Well, then, enough for the aeroplane if Father won't help out. I'm sure Natasha would want to help, too. It's her birthday this year.'

'Ten per cent of the Lighterman shares on the market.' Pascal began to cackle. 'Bobby will have a fit.'

'Serve him right,' Stefanie dabbed at the canvas with her brush. 'Do you boys know it's one o'clock?'

Sasha began to clear away while Stefanie cleaned her brushes and put away her paints. Pascal was very mobile in his wheelchair and often positioned it by the sink to wash up. He could have stayed with his mother, who

wanted him. But Charlotte was a fusser and he liked his
independence. Charlotte treated him as a cripple and,
except for carrying him up and downstairs and helping
him dress and undress, Sasha and Stefanie treated him
like an ordinary person who they expected to do ordinary
things and help in the house. In fact he loved staying with
Sasha and Stefanie because life *was* so normal, unhurried
and domesticated with little Galina, who was so full of
mischief. It resembled the sort of home life he had wanted
for himself, and now would never have.

Sasha was very skilful at assisting Pascal to go to bed.
He carried him up the stairs and helped him to wash and
undress with loving care. Pascal and Sasha were very fond
of each other, thrown together more than ever by the
tragedy for which Sasha still partly blamed himself. Had
he been there he would never have allowed it. He wasn't,
but he still blamed himself for keeping it a secret from the
family.

Ever since the accident Bobby and Sasha had not got
on. It had soon become common knowledge after
Melanie's funeral that Paul had stuck two fingers at Bobby
when he asked him to come into the firm. This was a most
un-Askham-like thing to do and the older generation were
very shocked when they heard about it. But the younger
ones approved; they thought two fingers, preferably hot
pokers, were just what Bobby needed.

Sasha had struggled on at his desk in the Lighterman
empire Berkeley Square offices, seeing as little of Bobby
as he could, but hating every minute. Two things, however, had transformed his life, as well as his flying:
Pascal's recovery, and the great change in Stefanie since
things had started to go wrong. It was as though disaster
had managed to do what no medicines, psychiatrists or
doctors were able to achieve: throw her out of her
depression, give her the ability to enjoy life again. She

found in Sasha's misery, in the painstaking efforts of Pascal to lead a normal life, the kind of spur she needed to get well herself in order to give them the will to recover.

Her painting had helped, too. It was marvellous to find that what one had always considered a natural, fairly unimportant gift could be developed, improved upon and extended. It was also a job, a vocation, and she diligently gave part of each day to the practice and study of her art, as much as a writer gives to writing or a musician to his or her musical instrument. She was very carefully, and painstakingly, building up the idea of one day having her own exhibition. In the meantime she worked very hard, to make up for all those lost years.

And they were lost years, Stefanie thought, as she lay in bed waiting for Sasha to finish with Pascal and join her. They were terrible futile years of misery and wretchedness, introspection and self-hate. And for what? How could one explain self-destruction of this kind? How could one justify an almost deliberate wish to destroy self and family, to hurt those nearest to her?

She still didn't know the answer. There had been no blinding light, no miraculous cure. It had simply come gradually, improving a little bit day by day. But, in many ways, she thought she owed it all to her father: perhaps for making her ill in the first place by his treatment of her as a child and then, by his harshness to her husband, helping her to get better.

Sasha crept into the darkened bedroom thinking she was asleep, but she said:

'What kept you so long?'

'He wanted to talk.' She heard the sounds of Sasha moving around the room in the dark as he swiftly undressed, having washed and brushed his teeth in the bathroom next door.

497

'About the aeroplane?'

Sasha got into the bed beside her and sat up, his knees huddled to his chin.

'A bit. About the future, really. Mostly about Anna.'

'What about Anna?' Stefanie asked softly.

'He feels he should let her go.'

'Well, he lets her go quite a lot. She's hardly ever at home.'

'She needs it, you see,' Sasha explained patiently. 'She can't stand being tied down. She didn't know that Pascal was going to be disabled.'

'It's hardly the reason to chuck a husband up, is it? I'm sorry, Sasha, I know she's your sister, but if that is *really* how Anna feels I think she's very selfish.'

'No, we don't know that it is how she feels,' Sasha said defensively. 'It's just that she *is* very restless and her anxiety about leaving Pascal makes her tense while she's at home. He knows she feels very guilty about it and he feels he should offer her a divorce.'

'But *is* that what she wants? I thought that she really looked after him with a lot of devotion when she is around.'

'He says they have a lot of rows. They both feel miserable most of the time. I feel, in a way, it's what he'd like, too. He'd like to make a fresh start. He'd like to design things to help other disabled people. Of course he loves Anna and he does want her, but he's too noble to keep her against her will. He says he's not the man she married. He feels, you see, that as he can't be a proper husband to her he has no right to keep her.'

'Do you think she's gone back to the Baron?' Stefanie, at last giving vent to a deep suspicion in her heart, kept her voice low because Pascal was only next door.

'Why do you say that?'

'She's always abroad.'

498

'I don't think she'd ever go back to him after the way he treated her. Pascal certainly doesn't suspect anything; but you never know.'

One never knew, Stefanie thought, snuggling up to him as he lay down, stretching his large frame in the bed with a deep sigh. One never knew the outcome of anything in life.

She had never guessed, for instance, that she would fall in love with her husband so many years after marrying him and, as he tenderly put his arms round her, she clung desperately to that which she had so nearly lost.

'I do love you,' he whispered, 'and I know, now, that you love me, too.'

She was about to protest but he leaned towards her and gently closed her mouth with his.

Rachel woke up early on the morning of her eightieth birthday, 17 August 1957, and lay for a long time listening to the songs of the birds in the park. Some rare and unusual varieties were attracted by the peace and safety of the spot. She knew it was not much later than five-thirty and she had a couple of precious hours to herself before the rest of the household awoke. Maybe her younger great-nieces and nephews would start banging on the door, and Galina, she knew, and her grandson Jonathan would have been almost too excited to sleep if their excitement the night before had been anything to go by.

Rachel sighed and slipped her legs over the side of the bed to draw the curtains and make her morning tea from the kettle which, together with a tray, was on a table at the far side of her room.

She flung back the curtains and saw it was, indeed, a lovely day: the sort England was justifiably famous for as its temperate weather seemed, occasionally, to yield such perfect days. Below her was the meadow running down to the lake which mirrored the swans serenely taking a morning swim. The ducks with their growing brood were much more busy and active about the calm surface of the water, hustling about, heads popping in and out in search of food.

The tall oaks and heavy chestnut trees surrounding the lake dipped their fronds towards it and, just visible from where she stood, was the green wooden bench where Bosco had first proposed to her flanked on either side then, as it was now, by rhododendron bushes, their red, pink, and white flowers making a dazzling show. On the far side of the lake the path widened, and a turning off it led up through the thick coniferous forest of Askham to the Grange, which was out of sight in the summer, occasionally glimpsed through the trees when the wind was strong. When she and Bosco were young one could see the Grange quite easily at all times of the year, which was a measure of how high and thick the trees had grown in nearly sixty years.

Rachel spooned her favourite blend of tea into the brown teapot she had brought with her from Darley Manor, poured the boiling water over it and busied herself with the cups and milk while it brewed. She always had extra cups when people were staying in the house because young people, up early like her, sometimes popped in to see her. She liked these morning visits, though not until she had had time to drink her tea and wake up properly.

When the tea had brewed she poured it into a large porcelain cup which again had a history, as things tended to do when one was very old, and walked slowly back to her bed. Slowly but not awkwardly, clumsily or with difficulty. Slowly so as not to spill any of the tea, not because she had to.

At eighty years of age Rachel, Countess of Askham, was in good shape, as she was the first to admit. She looked twenty years younger than she was and, on her good days, she felt young, too.

Rachel chuckled to herself as she lay on top of the bed, stirring her tea. One could never see oneself as old. For her, time had stopped when she had first become aware of herself as a young woman and, unchaperoned – very daring for those days – had set out by herself to see the world. But it was the world that had stopped in Cairo and her encounter with the Askham family sealed her fate. She knew that most of her family thought she would live to be a hundred, and some days she thought she would. On others she felt she would be glad to go; but didn't everyone have days like this? On the good days she was happy to be alive; happy to be part of this large family which she and her husband were largely responsible for: Freddie and his son Paul, now Earl of Askham; Charlotte and her four children; Em and Luis, and dearest Jonathan – that apple of her eye. Now, through Angelica, she was a great-grandmother with Myles and Emily Crosby. The great sorrow was what had happened to Pascal and, now, poor Joe.

Rachel's heart always felt heavy when she thought of Joe, a victim of unacceptable desires, and tormented by them. She knew he was tormented, not only by the shame he'd brought on the family; but because he wasn't what his family expected him to be: a strong heterosexual male, an Askham. Even Rachel shuddered when she thought of what Bosco would have said about a grandson who had offended against society in this way.

Joe talked to her very little about it, but he talked to Charlotte and Charlotte talked to her, about her worries concerning Joe, and herself.

Rachel sighed. The happy day full of treats and nostalgic memories had clouded. But there were always lots of clouds about. Charlotte had refused Arthur a divorce and Arthur had left home for a few weeks to stay in a hotel. Not, he had assured Charlotte, to be with Jill, but to have time to think. Charlotte let him have all the time he wanted and, in the end, Arthur returned home, just as if he'd only left for the office that morning, in time for dinner at eight. No one knew what he'd said to Jill.

Charlotte and Arthur, in fact, had very little to say to each other. Arthur had his bedroom and Charlotte had hers and when they came to stay at the Hall they had separate but interconnecting rooms. No one questioned the right of Arthur and Charlotte to sleep as they liked and the estrangement between them was apparent only to a very few, or people in the know, like Em and Jenny.

Rachel knew that whatever the state of things between Charlotte and Arthur, however far they had grown apart (or had they really ever come together?) they would do the right thing in public; there would be no sign of estrangement to embarrass family or friends. But she knew how much Charlotte was suffering because after all these years she, an old lady of eighty, still felt the pain of that betrayal of Bosco with Nimet.

It was, perhaps, unusually tactful of Nimet to decide to go abroad for Rachel's birthday, when the Hall would be packed with family. No one knew whether Nimet did it from tact or convenience, probably the latter as she seldom thought of others than herself. It was known that, although she liked to show off, she didn't like large crowds; she liked smart dinner parties with sophisticated, accomplished men who would admire her, flatter her and pay her compliments. There were still enough of them about, married and unmarried, widowed and divorced.

Rachel had her second cup of tea and turned on the radio to hear the news and the weather forecast. Postage had increased from 2½d to 3d but there was nothing much else to stir the conscience of the nation as Parliament went into recess. Charlotte and Arthur had already taken up residence in their country house where Arthur liked to entertain his political friends throughout the holiday, though Charlotte felt that he had at last abandoned hope of high office and would probably go back to business.

Finally there was the tap on the door Rachel was expecting and, her face already wreathed in smiles, she called:

'Come in.'

The door opened and Elizabeth and Galina entered shyly, each with a hand in one of Flora's, who was also trying at the same time to carry a large bunch of flowers, while in the hand of each little girl was a posy.

'Darlings,' Rachel extended her arms. 'Come in. Come in.' But first of all, at a signal from Flora, they all stood in the threshold, the door open behind them, and sang 'Happy birthday, dear Aunt Rachel.'

This seemed the signal for pandemonium to break out in the house as the younger members, roused from sleep by the sound of singing, slithered out of bed and raced up or downstairs to join in the chorus. Or they would make fresh choruses of their own, substituting for 'Aunt', 'Granny' – a term much beloved by Rachel. It was very precious to be a grandmother.

Anthony and Myles wriggled their way past the others to throw themselves on her bed. There was a mêlée as everyone else joined in until Rachel began to fear that the bed would break under the combined weight.

Em, whose room was next to Rachel's, was the first to come to her help, hauling off panting youngsters and, where appropriate, administering a reproving tap on an exposed bottom.

'That is enough!' she chided Jeremy, Charlotte's youngest son, who was too big to cavort safely with the smaller ones. 'Your grandmother will be black and blue.'

'Won't have a breath in her body.' Flora laughingly caught Nicholas Ferov by the ankles and dragged him down to the floor. 'Happy birthday, *darling* Aunt Rachel. I thought I was going to be the first. I couldn't get a word in.'

'You were.' Rachel took the flowers and held them to her nose with an expression of ecstasy. 'Only you were not quick enough.'

Angelica poked her head round the door, eyes still encrusted with sleep. Few people ever saw Angelica so exposed, completely devoid of make-up. She looked almost naked but, in the bosom of her family, Angelica felt secure. There was no need to pretend she was something she was not and, even with no make-up on at all, she was still very beautiful. Her own children pretended to hide under Granny's eiderdown when they saw their mother, but she, too, pretended not to notice them and, bending over, kissed Rachel warmly on both cheeks.

'Happy birthday, darling Granny.'

'Thank you, Angelica,' Rachel responded with another kiss and a hug and drew Angelica on the bed beside her. These children she had brought up as her own were very precious to her; precious in a special way. Yet every single one meant an awful lot to her – grandchildren and great-grandchildren, nieces and nephews alike.

Angelica looked pale, Rachel thought, and she said so.

'No make-up on, Granny!' Angelica smoothed her hand over her face. 'Completely exposed to the world.'

'Darling, *I* know what you look like, with make-up on and without, but you are still too pale. Are you eating enough?'

'*Plenty* to eat, Granny,' Angelica said, laughing and getting up. 'Now I'm going to take my two away and see that they are at breakfast on time. Where are they?'

Angelica pretended to roar like a monster and her two

504

very young ones squealed with pleasure and ducked for cover again, to be dragged out by Jonathan, who had stolen into the room fully dressed and stood watching the proceedings with detachment.

As Angelica dragged her two youngsters, protesting loudly, out of the room, Rachel reached out her arms for Jonathan, who shyly handed her a small wrapped gift.

'For you, Gran,' he said.

The others gathered round as Rachel unwrapped it to reveal an exquisitely made square box. It had ornamental hand-carving on it and a small silver plate on the top on which were inscribed the words:

> For my grandmother Rachel Askham
> with love on her eightieth birthday from
> Johnny, August 17 1957.

'Oh Johnny, *darling*.' Tears filled Rachel's eyes as she hugged him. 'It's beautiful. You made it yourself, didn't you?'

Shyly Jonathan nodded, his face flushing, just as Ralph's used to in times of emotion. 'I also wrote the words,' he said. 'Dad helped me a bit, but it was mostly me.'

The word 'Dad', used to mean Hugo, still tugged at Rachel's heart; but it was good that Hugo, who had so loved Ralph, had stood in as a father to his son. If only Ralph were here now . . . but then Ralph would be married to Jenny. Or would he? Time had stopped still at the point of his death and one would never know what might have been.

Johnny saw the tears in Rachel's eyes and, thinking they were tears of happiness, leaned over to wipe them tenderly away.

'Don't cry, Gran,' he said. 'This is a happy day.'

* * *

Breakfast had been divided into two rooms, the youngsters under ten in the nursery rooms and older children and grown-ups breakfasted in the family dining-room helping themselves, as in the old days, to dishes on the sideboard of bacon and eggs, kedgeree, sausages, kidneys, smoked haddock, with plenty of toast, a variety of jams and tea or coffee to drink. Jenny had been up since dawn preparing it. When one considered that she also had the preparation of the other two meals to be taken during the day, plus the party at night, it really was a formidable proposition. There was no Jill to help out now.

Yet there was Jenny at one end of the table neatly, even prettily dressed, not a hair out of place, smiling at Hugo, who sat at the other end. Rachel was on his right. The only two people who were not members of the family were Jenny's sister, Beth, and Peregrine Eckburgh, known as 'Perry', an old friend of Bobby's who had recently been widowed and was always at a loose end. Lord Eckburgh was one of the wealthiest men in the country and farmed several thousand acres in Wales. He also owned a vast shooting estate in Scotland where one of his many homes occupied a commanding position overlooking the Tweed. Perry was a great friend of the Kitto family and most of those round the table had known him for years.

Perry was sitting next to Angelica, who was quite transformed from the pale young woman who grandmother had worried about two hours before. She was beautifully, and exactly, made-up with a bloom on her cheeks and a sparkle in her eyes, and she wore a silk dress in the palest and most unfunctional shade of pink. In the course of a working day Angelica would change several times and the same would happen today. If she went riding later it would be jodhpurs or, if walking, tailored slacks and a shirt. The pink silk dress was just for breakfast, to display herself to the world.

Perry Eckburgh was older than Angelica's mother and had known her since she was a little girl but he was looking at her with a good deal of admiration, listening most attentively to her, as they sat at the breakfast table swapping sporting stories and joking a lot over their grilled kidneys and bacon. Dick had been up much earlier and was already at work with Flora on the revision of his manuscript in the library. Perry was a well-preserved man, attractive to women, with a world-weary air that was a puzzle to many people because he had lived extremely comfortably most of his life, having married money as well as inherited it. However, this apparent lassitude, perhaps, explained much of his charm. It was certainly most appealing to someone like Angelica who liked breeding as well as old money, and was married to a husband who always had his nose in a book and had neither. Perry and Angelica agreed to go riding later and Hugo advised them on the best horses to take.

Rachel could not help noticing how well Perry was getting on with her granddaughter but felt no alarm. Everyone had known Perry for years. Angelica responded to admiration and flattery as a flower does to the sun and, in this, she was most unlike her mother, who sat opposite her and who, as far as Rachel knew, had never used her beauty to manipulate people as Angelica did.

The door opened and Paul, looking rather sheepish and sleepy, sidled in. Going up to his grandmother, he put a small parcel by her plate.

'Just a token, Gran,' he said, giving her a kiss, 'of my great love for you.'

'Thank you, dear.' Rachel hugged him. 'But maybe the best present of all is that you have managed to get up in time for breakfast.'

'That *was* an effort, Gran.' Paul slid into the chair next to her, after smiling in a general way at those seated round the table. Paul was well known for his unorthodox hours, very late nights and very late mornings, so that he was coming alive as others felt it was time to go to bed. Paul had acquired these habits at university, preferring to study at night and take his pleasure late at night too, although there had been very little to do in Manchester after ten o'clock. Paul was naturally pale and his face looked almost haggard, a fact his grandmother attributed to these late nights as well as the fact that he had hitch-hiked down from his job near Stockport where he did shift work.

She rumpled Paul's wiry black hair and shook a finger at him: 'Too many late nights. They must stop.'

'Yes, Gran,' Paul smiled at her and, after eating his grapefruit, got up to help himself from the array of plates on the sideboard. 'My, what a spread.'

'Like Askham in the old days,' Bobby said, watching his young cousin with a mixture of approval and disapproval. One couldn't disapprove of Paul forever. It had been disgraceful to get the two-fingered sign – on that day of his mother's funeral of all days – from a member of the aristocracy, and it was not something that he'd forget or let the family forget. But it was quite true that young people were not what they were in his youth – not respectful, deferential or reverent enough towards their elders. Yet the fact was that, after all, Paul *was* the Earl and one day would take his seat in the House of Lords. Bobby also admired Paul's spirit and the way that he was making a career of his own.

'How's the engineering industry?'

'Fine.' Paul nodded in a friendly way at Bobby and took his seat again at the table after piling his plate high with food. 'Where we are it's flourishing – machine tools, small parts for aeroplanes, TV sets and so on.'

'Aeroplanes?' Sasha said, raising his head.

'We have a lot of small aeroplane factories round us,' Paul said. 'A.V. Roe, near Wilmslow – we do a lot for them.'

'Do you think there's a future in small aeroplanes?'

'I do,' Paul nodded. 'There's a future in entrepreneurial skills for everyone, especially in the north.'

'Where's Stefanie?' Rachel asked Sasha.

'She'll be down soon, Aunt Rachel,' Sasha said. 'She's very busy wrapping something mysterious.'

Rachel smiled to herself. Already she could guess what it was.

Once again the door opened and Anna came in, followed by Pascal propelling himself in his chair. They had arrived late from London and no one had seen them. There was a chorus of welcome as they came straight over to Rachel. Anna kissed her first and gave her a beautifully-wrapped gift.

'Something I bought you in Germany, Auntie.'

'Thank you, darling.' Rachel returned the kiss and then embraced Pascal who whispered to her:

'I haven't wrapped mine up, yet. Happy birthday, Granny.'

Rachel's arm remained a little while longer round Pascal, to whom she had always felt close. She knew that what had happened to Joe had affected him, too. He missed him and what he did for him. He missed his counsel and, above all, his friendship. As twins they had not been inseparable but there was a deep bond between them and what affected one affected the other. Their grandmother wondered how much Pascal had known about Joe before.

Bobby had just been about to get up when Pascal and

Anna came in and now he rose, asking Jenny if he could be excused as he had work to do.

'*Work*, Bobby?' Jenny said. 'On a day like this?'

'There is always work to be done, Jenny, my dear.' Bobby smiled at her and looked at Aileen who was steadily eating her bacon and eggs, saying little, as usual, but taking everything in.

She had given Rachel a practical present of a warm housecoat for the cold house. Aileen would never give anyone anything frivolous if she could help it.

'Do you mind if I go, my dear?' Bobby enquired of her.

'Obviously not,' Aileen said, breaking her toast in two, 'as you have decided to go.'

'Bad manners, Bobby,' Susan shook her finger at him.

'I'm sure Aunt Rachel doesn't mind,' Bobby said.

'I don't mind in the least,' Rachel smiled. 'Breakfast is always an easy meal. It's so nice to have it as it was, though. It takes me back to the old days and it was *very* good of Jenny to go to so much trouble.'

'It was no trouble at all,' Jenny said.

Paul swung back in his chair.

'Can you *really* remember the days, Gran, when they had butlers and footmen in livery?'

'Of course I can!' Rachel looked at him in astonishment. 'Serving every meal, and there were a lot of them. Breakfast was taken at about this time and coffee in the drawing-room at eleven-thirty. Luncheon was always at half-past one and that was a big meal, too. Tea, with sandwiches and cakes, at four-thirty and dinner at eight-thirty. The amazing thing was that none of the Askham women were fat, though your great-grandfather, Frederick, my father-in-law, was portly.'

'I can dimly remember Grandfather,' Bobby said, pausing at the door, his hand on the knob. 'In fact, I can remember him very well. I was about twelve when he

died. Every *inch* the gentleman, wasn't he, Rachel?'
Pointedly he looked at Paul.

'Every inch,' Rachel said, '*and* fearsome, too. He
almost paralyzed me when I first came to the house. In
fact, I was overwhelmed by everything.' She sat back and
the expression of nostalgia in her eyes was familiar to
those who sat around her for, as she got older, she loved
to talk about the past. Everyone else loved to listen. They
encouraged her to tell them stories about Egypt or the
suffragettes, or the great balls and parties at Askham Hall
or the house in London before the First War.

'Not that *I* was a partygoer,' she would add, though she
had enjoyed dancing with her handsome husband, and
knowing how many women envied her.

Thus everyone leaned forward in expectation as she
began to reminisce about Frederick and Dulcie, the
extravagant entertaining, the hunts and supper-parties for
politicians, for both Frederick and Bosco were active
politically. Frederick had been a member of Lord
Salisbury's last administration and Bosco had been active
in the House of Lords after he succeeded his father.
Before his death Arthur Gore, heir to the earldom, had
been a member of the House of Commons. Someone now
asked her about Arthur, Ross Glencarran's grandfather.

Rachel looked round, catching the eyes of Charlotte's
husband.

'I remember Arthur Gore quite well though, of course,
I wasn't married to his brother until after he died. Some
people said Bosco would never have married me if Arthur
hadn't died and sometimes I think it's true.'

'Oh, go on, Auntie!' Flora loved the family reminis-
cences and her eyes gleamed like a delighted child's. 'I'm
sure *that's* not true.'

'Well, Bosco *was* quite a one with the ladies. He was a
dashing subaltern in the Lancers and Arthur's death

changed all that, though,' Rachel smiled, 'it *is* true he proposed to me before Arthur died.'

'And Mother didn't accept him because she didn't approve of the aristocracy,' Em butted in. 'She never realized she'd become a countess.'

'Would you have married grandpa if you knew that, Granny?' Paul, knowing the radical instincts of his grandmother, was curious.

'Well, I knew it when I married him, darling, of course, that one day he would succeed his father. Arthur died in 1904 and we were married in 1905 and *your* daddy,' she looked at Jonathan, 'was born the year after. I wish you had known your daddy, Johnny. You would have loved him so much.'

This was not the mood they wanted for the day, Charlotte thought, seeing the expression on Jenny's face. For she had loved Ralph, too. Hastily she intervened, perceiving that Rachel's eyes had moistened. She leaned over and clasped her mother's hand.

'Be *happy* this day, Mummy, not sad. Ralph wouldn't have wanted it.'

'Or Freddie,' Em said. Even after twenty years hardly a day passed when she didn't think even momentarily of her twin, Paul's father.

Rachel quickly recovered and, blowing her nose, said, 'You must understand that I am an old lady and this is a day for tears as well as laughter. So many have gone before me and yet I have been spared to live this very long, very full and, on the whole, happy life. My dear Bosco was under forty when he was killed. Who would have thought I would have lived on another forty years? At the time, I know, I never did. But, yes, we have all suffered,' she glanced round the table at the company, now silent, watching her, 'most of you here have had your lives touched by tragedy of some kind. So maybe we are,

512

after all, fortunate to be gathered as a family round this table and, do you know, now that breakfast is nearly over, I feel like saying as a kind of thanksgiving the grace we used to say as a matter of course at every meal in the time of my father-in-law.' Rachel closed her eyes and bowed her head and most people, though surprised by her action, obediently imitated her. 'For what we have received, may the Lord make us truly thankful. Amen.'

Rachel opened her eyes and, this time, they were brimming with tears of gratitude and happiness.

As Rachel sat on the terrace after breakfast she was reminded of all the parties that had been held at Askham Hall since her first association with it in the year 1899.

Askham Hall was synonymous with celebration, as well as with less happy occasions – the many funeral parties that had been held here, too; Pascal's tragic accident, which had taken place only a mile or two away.

Rachel felt a little guilty as she was swept out on to the terrace after breakfast while Jenny disappeared into the kitchen with an army of willing helpers; but Pascal came with her and for a time they sat in the sun awaiting the arrival of Irina, whose own eightieth birthday had been celebrated four years before. Sasha and Stefanie had gone over to fetch her.

Pascal did everything in his wheelchair except walk. Watching him manoeuvre it so skilfully, it was hard to believe that he couldn't leap out of it at will. Pascal resembled a suppressed dynamo and even as he sat beside his grandmother he couldn't keep still, but kept energetically bustling about, his hands on the wheels of his chair.

'*I* should be in that chair, not you,' Rachel said. 'You can't keep still.'

'*Mustn't* keep still, Gran,' Pascal said with an air of seriousness. He did a little spin which all but toppled the chair. But after a while he did settle down and produced his sketch pad while Rachel got on with her embroidery. It was a big help to Jenny to re-cover all the dining-room chairs, and Rachel had become a skilled restorer with her intricate tapestry, in itself a modern work of art. She had only two more chairs to go.

'That looks like an aeroplane,' she said, glancing sideways at the pad on Pascal's lap.

'It *is* an aeroplane, Gran.'

'Surely you're not designing aeroplanes now?'

'Why not?'

'I thought we had enough speed.'

'That's what Bobby will say.'

Rachel put down her tapestry and removed her pince-nez.

'You're not *serious*?'

'Perfectly. As a matter of fact I thought you knew. This isn't a secret. Sasha and I want to go into aeroplanes. There is, we feel, a huge potential market for light, executive-type aircraft.'

'But what about the "Askham"?'

'There's nothing much we can do to that, Gran. There are no new challenges. It's just improving it a bit, or changing it stylistically, as they do with the Rolls. I can do that quite easily, when necessary. But we don't make too many changes because of the re-tooling that's needed and that *is* expensive. We keep the basic body design. Anyway, today we're going to ask Bobby to turn a little money our way and invest in a new business.'

'He'll never do it,' Rachel said and she wished that, today of all days, her birthday, the matter had never arisen. In many ways she wished Bobby hadn't come; but he had a great sense of family and Rachel's eightieth birthday was an important family occasion at which Bobby felt he had to be present.

* * *

Bobby said:

'I have never heard such an absurd, riciculous idea in the whole of my life.'

'But you haven't heard us out, Uncle,' Sasha pleaded, spreading his hands over the plans they had carefully been working on for weeks; the neat portfolio with capital requirement, cashflow forecasts and so on signed by a chartered accountant. And the drawings were to scale and had been checked and approved by an aircraft designer, John Neri, who acted as consultant. Now Bobby, with scarcely a glance at them, was throwing them out.

'I've heard quite enough to say "no",' Bobby said, 'and that is my last word on the subject.'

Anna had known he would react like this. She sat in a chair by the window gazing out at the grounds. It was now mid-afternoon and some of the younger children were playing in the tall grass, the sight of which made her a little nostalgic for what she and Pascal would never have. She hadn't realized, until it was no longer possible, that she had wanted to be a mother. Or rather, it was still possible, but not with Pascal. The irony was that he'd wanted children most when she hadn't. But ostensibly she seemed to play no part in the proceedings taking place in the room. She had only just heard the full extent of the plans herself and had been horrified.

'Move to *Manchester*?' she had said to Pascal the night before. 'Never!'

So now she wasn't sorry to hear Bobby throw them out. A lifetime here with a crippled husband was bad enough; but exile in the north of England, with no trips abroad? No visits to Gunther? The idea was insupportable.

'I do think you're a *bit* rash, Bobby,' Susan, who was also there, said. 'I've only recently been made aware of these plans but the boys have worked very hard on them for months.'

'They worked on the racing car for months,' Bobby said, 'and look what happened. Anyway, I'm not interested in aeroplanes. It's a field we know nothing about. It will take millions to develop. I've burnt my fingers twice on racing cars, and speed of any kind no longer interests me. Askham Motors, in fact, is beginning to interest me less. The turnover on capital is very small now. There are too many competitors – Lagonda, Ferrari, Alfa Romeo and Mercedes have too many expensive, elegant cars which they mass-produce. I'm thinking of selling Askham Motors, but I certainly don't want to go into aeroplanes!' Bobby cupped his ears as though they had deceived him.

'You *can't* just do that,' Anna said, alert now to a new danger, rising from her chair and coming to stand by the side of Pascal. He had said very little and sat there, white-faced, clutching the arms of his chair. 'You can't just throw a thing up, like Askham Motors, without consulting the people who work for it.'

'Who said I can't? I haven't come to any decision yet, anyway.' Bobby looked at her with irritation.

'Yes, but you haven't even consulted *us*. We thought the thing was going well.'

'Well, it isn't. It's going well, but not well enough. I can make more money by putting my money elsewhere.'

'Haven't you made enough, Bobby?' Susan had been sitting on the side of Sasha's chair, her arms crossed, her mouth pursed, during Bobby's entire diatribe. The proposal to make aeroplanes had shocked her quite a lot. It seemed to her as foolhardy as racing cars; but she knew that behind Sasha and Pascal's plans was idealism, whereas behind Bobby's was greed. If anything didn't pay well enough, pull out.

'My dear Susan,' Bobby, hands in his pockets, leaned towards her. '*You* should know all about maximising

516

profits. If that stuff you sold didn't pay handsomely you wouldn't stock it.'

'I'm in it as much for pleasure as for business. That's what you don't seem to understand.' Susan found it hard to keep her contempt for her half-brother out of her voice.

'Yes, but *if* it didn't pay, Susan . . .'

'Some of it doesn't pay, it may interest you to know,' Susan said. 'Some is very profitable. I have one or two antique bookshops that don't make enough profit yet they give me immense pleasure and, incidentally, prestige. From the "Askham" you get an *enormous* amount of prestige. From guns and ball bearings you only get mere money.'

'Mother's absolutely right, Uncle Bobby,' Sasha said. 'Pascal and I never, in our wildest dreams, imagined abandoning the "Askham". This is just an extension. There *is* a small aircraft company near Manchester badly in need of capital. We planned to buy it and develop our own ideas. The man who owns it is very enthusiastic about coming in with us.'

'Then let him come in with you by all means, and find the money,' Bobby said in a deceptively silky voice. 'It sounds perfectly simple to me.'

'You know it isn't simple at all,' Pascal said angrily. 'It's the money we need. Money he hasn't got.'

'Ah, isn't that always the problem?' Bobby smiled and selected a cigar from his case. 'No money, no aeroplane.'

'I think you're being perfectly foul about this.' Pascal edged his chair forward. 'That thoroughly nasty streak of yours is coming out again.'

'The less you talk about "thoroughly nasty streaks" the better,' Bobby said haughtily. 'You have enough nasty streaks in your own family to be careful what you say.'

'And what do you mean by that?' Pascal thundered.

517

'A thoroughly nasty perverted streak,' Bobby shouted back. 'If *I* had a brother who was a homosexual and a jailbird I'd talk less about . . .'

Bobby shot back against the fireplace as, with all his force, Pascal propelled his chair hard against the desk behind which Bobby had been standing. For a moment Bobby looked as though he'd be squeezed to death but Sasha leapt forward and released his imprisoned and very angry uncle, whose face had gone puce, his cigar crushed in his hand.

'How *dare* . . .'

'I'd do it again,' Pascal snarled, but Anna and Susan kept a firm grip on the chair, holding him back.

'That was a terrible thing to say, Bobby,' Susan chided.

'Yet true, true,' Bobby cried. 'None of you can face up to the truth. None of you realize the effect it has had on *my* family, and the business, to be associated with something so distasteful as pederasty. And then you have the nerve to come asking me for money.' Bobby, courage restored, advanced round the side of the desk, shaking a finger at Pascal. 'You have the nerve to ask *me* for money when you wasted thousands of pounds designing and making a useless car, which you then crashed into a tractor on a public road at four in the morning. A year later your brother is sent to prison for buggery. I really . . .'

Pascal tried to edge his chair forward again but Susan, suddenly taking command, turned to Anna:

'Please take Pascal out of here, Anna.'

'I will *not* go,' Pascal shouted, banging his arms against the side of the chair. 'I will *not* go. I will . . .'

Anna, with Susan's help, seized the chair and, turning it round, wheeled it quickly out of the door which Susan held open.

'Go with them too please, Sasha,' she said, pushing

them all out into the corridor. Then she shut the door on them, locked it and confronted her brother.

'You really overdid it today, Bobby. You really exceeded yourself.'

'I was very provoked, Susan.' Bobby sank into a chair and mopped his brow. 'I'm not a young man, you know, and I've just about had all I can take from these impertinent young people who seem to think I am a bottomless pit, and then, when I refuse their latest and excessive demands, insult me. No one these days has *any* respect for their elders. Neither Sasha nor Pascal has done a single thing that hasn't depended on my money.'

'Sasha had a very good career in the war. He has always loved planes. He flies them very well.'

'And I admired him,' Bobby nodded his head approvingly. 'I really did; but then I thought because he could fly a plane he could run a business and he can't. He's quite hopeless at business and yet here I am, still kind enough to employ him at a fat salary for doing what . . .? Kicking his heels, designing aeroplanes, I ask you! It's like having a couple of delinquents on my hands. I've had enough, I can tell you, also of their insults.' Bobby looked with apoplectic rage at his sister. 'Susan, you and I have always been close. I have seen you through many bad moments and you have always given me good and wise counsel. There was a time when we didn't get on, when I divorced Hélène, but that is all over now. I'm fond of you and I admire you for what you have made of your life despite that worthless husband of yours. But support your son any longer for doing nothing I cannot and, after what has happened in this room today, the same applies to Pascal.

'Neither of them, from henceforward, can be considered to work for me. They're out of a job.'

'Bobby, you can't do that.' Susan, horrified, agitatedly

ferreted in her bag for a cigarette and Bobby moved swiftly from his chair to light it for her. She observed that his hand still shook. Her brother, at fifty-eight, was ageing very quickly. In his way he was a lonely, unhappy, but also very stubborn man. She knew it was useless to plead with him. She accepted his light graciously and then shook her head.

'You *have* been provoked, Bobby, but you were extremely harsh to Pascal. He loves Joe, and what has happened to Joe happens in a lot of families. We're all sad about that and sorry for Charlotte. You know if you reject Sasha and Pascal they'll find the money elsewhere.'

'Let them,' Bobby said with a note of triumph in his voice. 'And jolly good luck to them.'

Rachel gazed at the picture and she knew that if she didn't stop the tears coming people would say she was a silly old woman who cried all day. But it was a beautiful portrait of her done from a photograph and embellished with those special touches that only Stefanie with her art knew how to achieve. It was a half-portrait of her sitting on the bench by the lake where Bosco had proposed, her straw hat on her knee and a far-away look in her eyes. There seemed to be a little breeze blowing that caught at her hair. In the background, high on the hill, was the Hall.

'It *is* absolutely marvellous,' Rachel rose to embrace Stefanie, who had shyly placed the framed portrait on an easel while Aunt Rachel was talking to her grandmother. She and Sasha had brought the portrait from Roberts-wood when they went to pick up Irina because it had only been completed the week before, and had been sent to be framed.

Rachel and Irina were alone on the terrace when Stefanie came out with the picture, the easel carried by

520

Paul, who set it up. Pascal and Sasha, Susan and Anna were having some mysterious meeting with Bobby and from time to time raised voices could be heard from the study window.

'It is the best present I could have,' Rachel said, kissing Stefanie. 'Nothing could have given me more pleasure.'

'It is pretty terrific,' Paul agreed and Irina, viewing it with the pince-nez which hung on a gold chain round her neck, nodded her head vigorously.

'Of course I have seen it before and I knew you'd be pleased, Rachel dear. My granddaughter has great talent.'

'This is her best, and a marvellous present for me. Thank you so much, dear.'

Rachel kissed Stefanie again and then went up to the painting, inspecting it closely. Then she moved back to look at it from a little distance.

'Do you know, I have never had my portrait painted before? I began to feel a little hurt about it. All the previous Countesses of Askham were painted several times, but I arrived just a little too late. I coincided with the art of the photographer. I think Ralph had Cheryl painted, but me, never. Now, dear Stefanie, you have made up for it, and this is the best of all.'

As Rachel inspected the picture Irina dabbed at her eyes and, as usual, streaks of mascara began to form in the crevices of her wrinkled cheeks. She was very arthritic now and moved about with difficulty so that she had got rather fat. The dresses that she'd worn in the last days of the Tsar were now too old for further alteration and even Dulcie's creations, which had been passed on to Irina in the thirties, couldn't be let out any more. But Irina had found an émigrée dressmaker whose own creative ideas had stopped somewhere about the time of the fall of the last Tsar, and her style suited her patroness very well. So what Irina wore today, a frilly dress in pink georgette, with a slight bustle at the back, recalled the years of the First World War and so did the choker of pearls round her neck which Dulcie had left her in her will. So far, incredibly, Irina had never needed to pawn them; though she had got very close to disposing of them altogether in some of the dark days in Paris during the war where there was no shortage of buyers among the occupation troops.

Rachel was just about to resume her seat when there was the sound of a crash, raised voices and a general commotion from the direction of the study round the corner from the terrace. Paul looked at them and then, getting up, ran into the house, cannoning into Charlotte who was emerging with the tea things on a trolley.

Just as Paul reached the hall the door to the study flew open and Pascal came out muttering and swearing, banging the arms of his chair, which was pushed by Sasha and Anna. They all looked very cross and Pascal seemed to be shaking with rage.

'What on earth . . .' Paul began.

'Tea, everyone?' Charlotte sang out in a clear voice.

'I'm *not* . . .' Pascal shouted, but Anna bent down and whispered something to him and Sasha took hold of the chair and began to push it firmly in the direction of the drawing-room, towards the terrace.

When the rather disjointed party arrived, with Charlotte and her trolley in the lead, everyone on the terrace had risen. Arthur had been asleep on the hammock at the back and sat up, rubbing his eyes and mumbling, 'What's going on? What's going on?'

Rachel saw Pascal's angry face and sat down again murmuring to Irina:

'I *knew* Bobby would spoil it. He always does. I wish he hadn't come.'

'What on earth happened?' Charlotte said in a voice of resignation as though she knew what was coming. No family occasion was complete without a row. 'There's always *some* sort of rumpus when we have a family party.'

'We should bar all meetings on birthdays,' Em followed with a tray full of sandwiches and cakes and, behind her, came Hugo with a large teapot.

'I wish Jenny wouldn't work so hard,' Rachel murmured, but her words were lost in the clamour as everyone demanded an explanation.

As quickly and succinctly as she could Anna told them, her hands still on the back of Pascal's chair.

'Personally, I think they were very unwise to ask him,' she concluded. 'I could have told them that Uncle Bobby would say "no".'

'Did you know about the plan?' Charlotte looked at her curiously as she passed her a cup of tea.

Anna made sure the brake on Pascal's chair was fixed and perched on the hammock with Arthur, who was still rubbing his eyes, looking bemused.

'Not really,' Anna stirred her tea. 'I knew they were thinking about aeroplanes, but not how far they had got. Nor that they were talking seriously with John Neri in Manchester about taking over his company. He's half-Italian, by the way, so there *is* a connection. What shocked me more than anything is Bobby's plan to ditch the Askham Motor Company without asking any of us. I've travelled all over Europe this year just promoting the damn car. I feel as personally involved and annoyed as Pascal and Sasha. We're all, in fact, thrown out of a job.'

'You could get another backer,' Arthur said, scratching his head. 'I'm not quite sure who.'

'With your contacts in the City . . .' Charlotte began, but Arthur shook his head.

'It is a very unwise investment by any standards. I can't help half-agreeing with Bobby. Pascal, for all his talent, knows nothing about aeroplanes and after the accident

523

with the "Phoenix" . . .' Arthur threw his hands in the air as Charlotte thrust a cup of tea at him, a look of scorn on her face.

'Trust you to be so negative, Arthur. Always looking for a safe investment.'

'Everyone is, my dear,' Arthur said placatingly. 'No one wants to throw money away.'

Arthur had only been prevailed upon to come because it was Rachel's birthday. He and Charlotte now seldom went anywhere together; but family parties were sacrosanct.

Charlotte finished pouring the tea and counted the cups.

'I know how many are in the kitchen,' she said, looking up. 'Beth, Jenny, me, Em and a host of good ladies from the village, but where are Angelica and Perry?' She looked around as if counting heads.

'They went for a drive,' Rachel replied. 'Perry had a friend staying near here and he asked them to tea. Sorry, I should have told you.'

Charlotte nodded, but didn't comment. It was quite typical of her daughter to find something more pleasant to do when there was work to be done. Maybe she felt she had a duty to entertain Perry while Bobby was engaged. Maybe: maybe not. Angelica was not the sort who helped in the house, or mucked in, and, in her mother's opinion, she wouldn't change.

'Flora and Dick are in the library,' Paul said, getting up. 'If you give me a tray I'll take them something.' Charlotte smiled at Paul and thanked him, while not commenting on the whereabouts of her daughter. Charlotte was always very good on these occasions, used to years and years of running village fêtes and Conservative tea-parties.

Meanwhile the younger members of the party started

to arrive on the terrace, most of them having made their way up from boating on the lake, a perennial sport of young members of the family. The conversation became more generalized and more relaxed.

A raid was made on lemonade and cakes and, for safety's sake, the portrait, after being admired once again, was taken indoors.

Galina sat contentedly at her father's feet, licking her fingers which were covered with cream. Next to Galina was her great friend Elizabeth, Hugo and Jenny's girl, who was older than she was and rather bossy. The even smaller ones, Anthony and Emily, were remorselessly pushed around by the older girls who also, however, looked after them very carefully and responsibly.

It was quite uncanny, Rachel thought, contentedly sipping her tea, how much Galina did resemble her grandmother Hélène, and how difficult, too, it was to think that that wild, undisciplined beauty, had she been alive, would now be a grandmother. There had been something very fey and wilful about Hélène, a quality of youthfulness that she had never lost. And now, at last, Stefanie had become reconciled to the fact of her daughter's existence. She seemed to take comfort from the fact that Galina resembled her mother and rejoiced in it rather than be obsessed with a sense of guilt. The tables had indeed been turned.

In her new-found happiness and contentment, particularly helped by her painting, Stefanie had also begun to look on her blameless son, Nicky, with new eyes, as being, in fact, her son and not Jack's. Jack had no part of him, except genes; had never seen him since he was born. Jack, in fact, didn't even know of his existence.

Yet, maybe, the change had come a little too late for Nicky, who was a rather serious, withdrawn boy of eight, had a slight stammer and who made friends with difficulty.

He had largely been brought up by his great-grandmother and, however hard she tried, an elderly woman was no substitute for a young mother and father. Nicky was younger than Jeremy and Jonathan and older than the others, which placed him somewhere in the middle so he was out of step there. But he'd enjoyed himself on the boats and, watching them play down there and scamper down again as soon as tea was over, Rachel could not help but think again of the past. As everyone drifted away – Charlotte and Em back to the kitchen to help Jenny, Beth and Hugo, who were hard at work on preparations for the party in the evening, Stefanie and Sasha to the meadow with the younger children – she turned to her friend Irina, who had shut her eyes and now lay back contentedly with her head against the back of the chair.

'Are you asleep, Irina?'

'No, dear, of course not.' Irina opened her eyes and held out her hand. 'What a lovely day this is, Rachel. How glad I am to be alive to share it with you.'

'And I'm glad to have you here,' Rachel clasped the proffered hand.

'I shan't live much longer, you know,' Irina said.

'You've been saying that for years.' Rachel's clasp tightened.

'But now I feel it in my bones. I feel that I shall soon be joining Alexei, Hélène, Kyril. It is terrible, you know, Rachel, to lose two children and not know what has become of them. One never gets used to it, always expecting to hear. It is terrible to lose any child, indeed, as you did; but not to know . . .' The tears started to trickle down Irina's cheeks, as Rachel knew they would. Over the years tears had beaten a familiar path across Irina's once beautiful, but now rather ravaged visage, as though they knew by now exactly which path to take, as a stream does through well-worn crevices that time has carved for it.

'At least, dearest Irina,' she said, trying to comfort her, 'things have turned out well with Hélène and Kyril's children, especially dearest Stefanie who has almost returned to us from the grave. It is wonderful to see her so well and happy in a way that I think she never was before, since she was a girl. I don't think she was in love with Sasha when she married him; but he has been so good to her that she has grown in love with him. And that love has extended now to her children and in turn embraces us all. I can't help thinking that Stefanie, who has overcome so many difficulties, is the one that Hélène would have been most happy for and proud of.'

'I suppose one *must* be very thankful for those good things that are left,' Irina sounded doubtful. 'After the devastation we all went through, the suffering, it is a wonder that anyone or anything survived.' She wriggled in her chair and looked behind her to see if anyone were listening. But Pascal and Arthur were deep in conversation, maybe about a possible source of finance for the new project.

'What they don't realize, those people who have rows and disagree, is how lucky they are to be alive. Even Pascal is lucky, and Sasha is lucky, because he was shot down twice. Stefanie tried to kill herself with drink and she is lucky, too. I don't know if she realizes it. I don't understand, Rachel, why people can't be happy instead of quarrelling all the time. Can you?' She glanced at Rachel, who was gazing at the small children in the meadow surrounding Stefanie, who had her eyes bound in a game of blind man's buff. Quickly she nodded in agreement, as Irina repeated as if to herself:

'I can't understand why people can't count their blessings and be glad they're still alive when others, who also should be, are dead.'

Chapter 21

The heat of the afternoon didn't permeate the library which, at the side of the house, was dark and cool. It faced a row of huge elms which, some said, went back to the eighteenth century when the house was rebuilt. Quite probably they did.

The library was a long room, not unlike the library of an ancient college or school. It had shelves full of bound volumes from floor to ceiling on one side, and a more modern collection of books on the other. Some of the works were very valuable as Phyllida Askham, great-great-grandmother of the present Earl, had been a knowledgeable bibliophile as well as a connoisseur of antiques.

In the centre of the library was a long table surrounded by hard-backed chairs, the seats upholstered in leather. There were three alcoves along the room, each containing easy chairs, and a large sofa dominated the picture window, where it was not unknown for those weary of their labours to take a short nap. It was an imposing but attractive room imbuing most of those who read or worked there with a sense of peace.

Lady Flora Down had added much to the harmony of the room by arranging an attractive colour scheme of *eau de nil* and white. She had also substantially added to the library's collection of works of archaeological or historical significance.

Had she seen her namesake, head bent, working at the table in the library, there is no doubt she would have approved of her. They both shared the same scholarly interests, they were both altruistic and free from personal vanity, and they had both fallen in love with men who did not return their love, or not in the way they might have wished.

It might have been that the elder Flora would have warned her young kinswoman about the perils of illicit love. Yet maybe she would have been more concerned about the unhappiness that came with it rather than the morality of the situation. The older Flora, however, had achieved a measure of serenity in her regard for Adam; the comfort she was able to give him through the money she'd inherited and, when she felt superfluous to his life, she gracefully, and literally, sank out of it. It was true that she was mourned acutely only for a short while, as people without children or spouses inevitably are; but her memory lingered for much, much longer, not only in those who had known her but those who had not. Flora Bolingbroke, for example, had become quite obsessed by the woman who had died five years before she was born.

There was a large oil painting of Flora Down on the wall. Her father had been proud of his bluestocking daughter, though a little alarmed by her, and had it painted by Sargent when she was awarded honours, but not a degree because she was a woman, in the Cambridge Tripos examinations in 1896 at the age of twenty-one. Two years later she met Adam and her life changed forever. Young Flora had thus some idea of what the person who had played such a large part in her own life looked like. She saw someone who was much taller than she was, rather a gaunt woman with prominent features and, certainly, comely rather than beautiful; but there was an undeniable resemblance as people who knew them both often remarked. Maybe it showed in strength of character: the set of the chin, a stubbornness about the eyes and similar colouring though Lady Flora's hair was a rich auburn and Young Flora's was most definitely black.

Dick saw her eyes straying to the portrait from time to time as they sat at the large library table working.

'Who was she?' he asked.

'Lady Flora Down, daughter of the tenth Earl. She was the sister of my father's first wife, Melanie, and of Bosco, Aunt Rachel's husband. She was very clever.'

'She looks clever.' Dick sat back, hands in his pockets, and contemplated the striking portrait. 'Rather severe though.'

'We're supposed to be alike,' Flora smiled. 'She was a militant feminist, a noted scholar. She was also very much in love with my father and remained so until her death.'

'How did she die?'

'Some people say she killed herself when he married my mother. She had lived with my father after his wife left him; but I believe not in the Biblical sense.' Flora paused awkwardly. 'Just as "friends".'

'That sounds unlikely.'

'But it was true. My father wanted to marry her, but the thought of marriage to her sister's husband was repugnant to her. I think I know how she feels. In a way her love was greater, more perfect . . .' Flora's voice trailed off as she transferred her gaze from the portrait to Dick.

Dick met her eyes and smiled.

'Why is love more perfect that isn't carnal?' he enquired.

'Because it's selfless, don't you think? You love a person just for what they are; not for physical pleasure or any material gain.'

Flora abruptly turned her head to the manuscript, aware of his quizzical gaze. She had gone to the library immediately after breakfast to start checking his book with him painstakingly page by page, reference by reference. Each section, double checked, would then be forwarded to the publisher's copy-editor, who knew how accurate it would be.

Ruth had finished typing the manuscript only weeks before and it lay piled up on the table before them. They were both contemplating it now, silence having fallen between them, as though locked in their own thoughts. Perhaps Dick knew what she was thinking and his own silence was caused by embarrassment as much as anything else.

Whenever Flora saw Dick with Angelica she thought about Ruth and the clandestine meetings she had with Dick: meetings that Flora disapproved of. She felt that it was rather sordid and contemptible to indulge in an extra-marital affair, and gradually it had changed her feelings about Dick. Flora had high standards and she expected Dick to have them, too. But Dick *was* weak. He had abandoned the Party after his marriage to the step-daughter of a Tory MP and all during his marriage there was a gradual erosion of standards that Flora tried not to notice.

For, like many another flawed personality, she was convinced that Dick Crosby was an acute political observer who produced some remarkable work. His grasp of facts, the way he marshalled and presented them, was completed by his psychological insight into the human motivation of those who jostled for political power. His new work was one of great perception and integrity, one that she deeply respected him for.

Dick picked up his pen, sighed and studied the neatly typewritten page in front of him. Flora did the same and for several minutes they worked quietly together; but each was aware of an undercurrent, possibly caused by something that had nothing to do with the manuscript on the table.

'Ruth made a wonderful job of this,' Flora said at last, and the tension seemed to ease. Her name, that unspoken name between them, had finally been mentioned. It was an excuse. Dick knew it. He reached in his pocket and drew out a packet of cigarettes. Then, rather guiltily, he looked at the picture of Lady Flora staring haughtily down at him from high up on the wall.

'Would *she* have approved? Is it all right if I smoke?'

'I believe she was quite a raver in her way,' Flora laughed. 'Very unconventional. She went to Cambridge and travelled abroad on her own, studied archaeology. She was a suffragette too, though I don't think she ever went to prison.'

'In fact it's just the way that I'd expect decadent aristocracy to behave.' Dick lit his cigarette and puffed out his smoke before him, making small circles that evaporated towards the open window. Flora waved it away from her face.

'What a horrible thing to say!'

'But they did that, didn't they? Because they could. I daresay my aunt, at that time, was sweating in some mill while yours was going to Cambridge and globe-trotting.'

'You can be a swine at times, Dick.' Flora threw down her pencil and got up. She stretched and went across the room to peer out of the window. She could see the corner of the terrace and the path that led down to the lake. Sounds of childish voices penetrated the silence. Among them, well looked after, privileged in their way, would be Myles and Emily Crosby.

'Only at times, I hope,' Dick said, coming up behind her. She was aware suddenly of his overwhelming masculinity and, at that moment, a hand rested lightly on her shoulder. 'I thought you liked me a bit . . . a bit as Flora liked Adam.'

'I liked you a bit more than that,' Flora said, her voice shaking. 'How long have you known about it?'

'A long time, I expect. And I like you, too.'

'But not in that way,' Flora slowly turned towards him, her face flushed. 'Not in the way you like Ruth . . .'

'Ruth . . .' Dick let go of her shoulder and strolled back into the room. She sank on to the sofa feeling rather light-headed. 'I was silly to think Ruth would keep it from you.'

'Did you ask her to?'

'No. I thought she would use her own good sense, as Angelica is your cousin. Angelica doesn't love me, anyway. I suppose you know that.'

'That's why I think you should separate, if you're honest,' Flora said. 'I don't think cheating on a marriage is fair.'

'But she cheats on me.'

'Does she?' Flora felt surprised.

'Of course she does! Did you see her with the apoplectic old lord?'

'Oh, Perry's not "old" and he's not apoplectic,' Flora said huffily. 'At least, not that I know of. He's a friend of the family. He comes here quite often. Do you seriously think he's interested in Angelica? He's known her for years and years. It would be ridiculous if he were.'

'I don't see why. He can still be interested in her, however long he's known her.'

'Oh, I don't think it's in the least like that! She regards him as a sort of uncle. Anyway, it doesn't excuse *you* cheating.'

'You have got very old-fashioned standards, haven't you, my love?'

Dick sat on the sofa beside her.

'I'm not ashamed of them,' Flora felt he was uncomfortably close. 'I do think married couples should either stay together or part. Not cheat.'

'You want me to tell Angelica I want a divorce?'

'I don't *want* you to,' Flora said. 'But don't you think you ought? Don't you want to marry Ruth?'

Dick laughed. 'Oh, my dear, you really are old-fashioned. If you'd ever had an affair you'd know it was quite unimportant in many ways.'

'But don't you *like* Ruth?' Flora felt shocked at such cynicism.

'Of course I like her! But I don't particularly want to marry her. She is attractive and she attracts me. I'm quite happy with Angelica.'

'You're happy with her money!'

Flora shocked herself by her words and immediately put a hand to her mouth. 'Sorry, Dick. I shouldn't have said that.'

Dick had stopped smiling. 'No you shouldn't, because you know it's not true. Is that what your family say?'

'I don't know, because I don't talk to them about you. I shouldn't have said it and I apologize.'

'Freud would probably say you said it because you meant it.' Dick got up again and began to pace about. 'Yes, I am comfortable with Angelica but I do have money of my own, a good salary as a lecturer, an income from my books. I'm not dependent on Angelica as I was when I was a student. I pay my way – though not hers; she earns too much money. I could keep Ruth if I wanted to marry her, although I doubt if I could keep Angelica, too.'

'I think that business about "keeping" women is out-dated and old-fashioned,' Flora said. 'It's a way of subjugating them.'

'Of course, I agree,' Dick said. 'But some women do

534

need to be looked after, if they're having children and so on.'

'And what about Ruth,' Flora persisted, 'is it fair to her?'

'I think Ruth knows what she's about.' Dick looked at Flora quite kindly. 'She's not as innocent as you, my dear. What you need, Flora, is a man.'

'That is another *hateful* thing to say.' Flora got up furiously from the sofa and leaned out of the window to try capturing a rare gust of breeze to fan her cheeks. Then she turned and looked at him again. 'It is the sort of hateful, patronizing thing that men say to try and make a girl feel awkward. Well, I can tell you, Dick Crosby, that I am not ashamed of being the way I am, or of waiting for the sort of man I want – and the sort of man I most definitely don't want is *you*!'

Almost without knowing what she was doing Flora clambered awkwardly over the open window-sill and cannoned straight into a tall figure who had just finished toiling up the path from the lake.

'Oh!' she said to the stranger.

'Oh,' the stranger replied, and Flora looked at him suspiciously, glad that Dick was within earshot, probably leaning out of the window looking at her.

'Do you want something?' Flora asked politely.

'Is Lady Askham here?'

'Yes, she's here. Can I tell her who it is?'

'You don't know me, Flora, do you?' The man smiled at her kindly and suddenly his broken accent gave her the clue she'd been searching for. 'Mr Barrio!' she said, shaking his hand. 'I'm sorry. I haven't seen you for years.'

'Never mind, Flora. I hardly recognized you, either,' Felipe said. 'You've grown up. It has been a very long time since we were all together. But I would like to see your Aunt Rachel and wish her a happy birthday.' Felipe

535

clutched a brown paper parcel in his hand. 'I have a present for her.'

'Oh, how very kind of you,' Flora said. 'I'm sure she'll be absolutely delighted. I think she's on the terrace with some of the children. Aren't we lucky to have such a lovely day?'

'Very lucky,' Felipe replied politely, standing aside for her to lead the way.

Rachel, sitting in a shaded part of the terrace, had observed the man walking round the side of the lake before he was lost in the bushes which enclosed the steep path leading to the house. He was grey-bearded and he had on a hat and it was only now as he approached her with Flora chatting animatedly at his side that she realized who he was.

Since Luis had ceased to live at the Grange Rachel hadn't seen her grandson's father; she doubted if she'd seen him a dozen times in as many years. There had once been a furious row after which Felipe refused to come to the Hall, and those calling for Luis at the Grange were never invited in. Now here he was, apparently affably chatting with Flora.

Rachel had Anthony, Hugo's youngest child, on her lap and, rather awkwardly, she passed him to Irina as Felipe stopped before her and, removing his hat, gave an elaborate bow as he handed over a brown paper parcel.

'Happy birthday, Lady Askham. May I felicitate with you on reaching such an impressive number of years.'

'Why, *thank* you, Felipe.' Rachel was almost lost for words as she took the parcel he held out. 'How very sweet of you.' She felt quite flustered. 'Do, *please*, sit down,' she indicated the chair next to her which Jonathan hurriedly vacated. Rachel smiled her thanks to her grandson and Felipe, after taking off his jacket and rather nervously looking round, sat down.

'You have quite a crowd here. I didn't know. I hope I am welcome, Lady Askham?'

'Of *course* you're welcome,' Rachel said warmly. 'And always have been. Your exile was your own choice, Felipe. As Luis's father you have always had a welcome here.'

'That is not what I thought some years ago, Lady Askham, I must tell you.' Felipe frowned. 'Mr Down was once extremely rude to me.'

'I think he was provoked.' Rachel remembered the incident which happened years ago and involved an argument about politics. 'But let's not discuss it now. Let's not dwell on the past. It's my eightieth birthday and a lovely day for reconciliation. Em is here and Luis will be down for the party tonight. I hope you'll come?'

Felipe looked taken aback. He folded his arms and appeared to lose himself in thought, his beard sunk on his chest. Rachel would scarcely have recognized him had she not realized where he'd come from: the Grange. Nor did she realize that he had aged so much. He was ten years older then Em, who was now forty-nine, so that would make Felipe nearly sixty. No great age by Rachel's standards.

'Yes.' Felipe abruptly raised his head, giving her the smile that she knew had long ago trapped her daughter. 'Yes, I would like that. At what time?'

'About eight, I think.' Rachel held out her hand. 'But please don't go now. Have some tea and let me open your present.' She eagerly turned to Flora, 'Dear, would you go and see if you can get a pot of tea for us in the kitchen? I know it's a bit late and Jenny *is* terribly busy and, maybe, you'd ask Hugo to come out, if you can find him, and see Felipe.'

Quickly Felipe held up a hand. 'Not just now, if you don't mind, Lady Askham. I think later would be better. He might object and I would very much like to see my son.'

'I assure you Hugo won't object,' Rachel said with vigour. 'He will be very pleased; but if you prefer it, later.'

As Flora ran off in search of tea Rachel removed the paper that covered Felipe's present, letting it fall on to the flagstones on the terrace. Inside was a large book with a striking red cover and, on it, the twin flags of Nationalist and Republican Spain.

'"A History of the Spanish War by Felipe Barrio",' she read aloud. '"Part 1: The beginnings of the conflict". Oh, *Felipe*,' Rachel cried, with genuine warmth, 'I'd no idea it had got so far. *Published*.'

'And without anyone's help, Lady Askham,' Felipe said proudly. 'Not you, or Em or anyone connected with publishing.'

'You did it all yourself?' Rachel stared at him. 'Well done.'

'I did it through an agent,' Felipe explained. 'One I just picked out of a book I found in the library: the *Writers' Handbook*. He found me a publisher almost immediately in America, and there is the book.'

'It is very handsome. Thank you. A lovely present.' Rachel began to turn the pages of the densely printed book, exclaiming with admiration. 'It is a wonderful achievement, Felipe. Only Part 1, too, and you have been working on it for twenty years.'

'Part 2 is completed and being printed,' Felipe said. 'Yes, I am very pleased.' He sat back and sighed with contentment as Flora appeared with a tray and, after her, came Hugo with another tray on which there were plates and small cakes.

Flora and Hugo put the plates on a table hastily drawn up by Jonathan, and Hugo bent down to shake Felipe's hand.

'I'm very glad you came, Felipe. Please believe me, I mean it sincerely.'

'Thank you, Hugo.' As Felipe reached up to take Hugo's hand Rachel saw, or imagined she saw, tears in his eyes and her heart immediately contracted with sympathy. Poor man. He was a victim of his own pride, but he must have felt so very isolated for the seventeen years or so since the row with Hugo which had taken place not long after the beginning of the war. It had been a very long break indeed.

As Hugo and Felipe shook hands Em appeared suddenly on the terrace, as if someone had alerted her about the arrival of her one-time common-law husband.

'Oh dear,' Em halted suddenly as she saw him. 'It is true, then.'

'It is indeed true,' Rachel said quickly. 'Come and sit down, Em, and have a cup of tea.' She held out the volume Felipe had given her. 'Have you seen Felipe's book?'

Em also gazed at it with some amazement, then at Felipe. Finally she took it in her hands and began to run through the pages as if she couldn't believe her eyes. 'Then it exists, at last,' she stared unbelievingly at Felipe, who threw back his head and laughed.

'I have proved myself, Em, have I not? At last I am no longer a parasite.'

'Please, Felipe,' Hugo said earnestly. 'No more reproaches and recriminations.'

But Felipe seemed determined to continue, sagaciously nodding his head.

'Oh, I know what I am called by you all – Em has told

539

me often enough. But I had to do what I had to do, you know? I knew I could write a great book and I have.'

'But you must have finished it *years* ago to have had it translated *and* published,' Em said reproachfully, 'and you never said a thing.'

'I never said a thing,' Felipe replied, obviously with some satisfaction. 'Not a thing. I wanted it translated, printed and ready to hand to your mother on her eightieth birthday. I wanted her to know that all these years I have been kept by Askham hospitality and Askham money have been worthwhile.'

'They have,' Rachel said. 'They have indeed, and, had you let us, Felipe, we would have loved you and looked upon you as one of the family.'

'I know it now.' Felipe bowed his head, his smile of self-satisfaction momentarily vanishing. 'Believe me, I know it. I was a victim of my own stubbornness. Moreover, I have made Em and Luis very unhappy. But success has changed me now. I feel it, and I am here to make amends.' He leaned forward and grasped Rachel by the arm. 'Believe me, Lady Askham, I really am grateful, and I am sorry, too, for I know I have deprived you of your home.' Felipe paused and put his finger to his head. 'But you see, I knew that, inside here, I had a great work, maybe a masterpiece, and it had to come out; it had to be finished and to that end I had to be selfish and self-centred. And I was. And I do not regret it because, if I had not been, my masterwork might never have been completed. For some things, Lady Askham, you have to sacrifice family and friends.'

'I believe you do,' Rachel said quietly, conscious that this was a very important moment for them all.

'But,' Felipe quickly recovered his *bonhomie*, 'I have another birthday surprise for you. Perhaps an even better one.' He turned round and stretched out a finger towards the clump of trees which, in high summer, obscured the Grange from the view of the Hall. 'The Grange is yours. I know you want to live there and you can. I have been offered a professorship in Spanish studies at an American university from this fall and I am going to go there very soon.'

'For good?' Em gasped, and Rachel wondered if it was with relief or, perhaps, regret.

'For good, my dear Em.' Felipe inclined his head. 'I am moving there as I came here: without anything, no possessions, few encumbrances. Yet I am to have rooms, I believe, on the university campus and that will be sufficient for my needs as I proceed with Volumes three and four of the Spanish War.'

'How many volumes will there be?' Rachel said.

'Endless,' Felipe smiled. 'As many as I can make them. It will be my life's work. So from next month,' getting up he stretched his arms, 'it is your home, and thank you for the use of it.'

Going up the stairs after Felipe had gone it was difficult to analyze her feelings, Rachel thought, clinging to the banisters as she paused for breath. There was joy mixed with sorrow for all the wasted years; years when Em and Felipe could have been happy together with their son. Years that would have given Em the emotional security she had always envied in others, always lacked. There was no spark of love now between Em and Felipe but, perhaps, friendship would return and Luis, at least, would be able to communicate freely with both parents and have them communicate with each other. How thrilled Luis would be when he arrived that evening to see his father back at the Hall.

Rachel got to the first landing and walked slowly along

it towards her room, where she wanted to take a short nap before changing for the party.

It was the quiet time between daylight and nightfall and everyone had gradually dispersed from the terrace. Irina, who was also staying the night, had gone up to her room to rest. Stefanie and Flora were helping to put the younger children to bed and Sasha, Paul, Jonathan and Jeremy had gone to have a game of tennis before changing. Angelica and Perry had still not returned from the excursion: Jenny, Beth, Charlotte and Em had scarcely left the kitchen all day. Dick and Flora had spent most of it together in the library. Rachel had popped her head into the kitchen to thank everyone for giving her such a happy day and to apologize for being so lazy. There were smiles from many of the older women who had known her for years and she stopped and had a chat with each of them.

She realized how much the Hall was part of her life. It was life; it was an artery that flowed through so many branches of the family and now part of it would lead to that old home: the Grange. She was very thankful that, at last, on her eightieth birthday she had learned that there was a chance that she would die in the house where all her children had been born.

To be surrounded by the family despite discords was, Rachel thought as she slipped out of her dress into her robe, one of the greatest satisfactions in her life. It was the sure knowledge that, whatever happened, there was someone there. Of course there was always sadness and dissension; and there was always Bobby who, somehow, invited trouble, and always had; but the family seemed not only to survive, but to overcome all these vicissitudes, to grow even stronger. Rachel leaned on the sill of her window, drinking in the perfumed air of early evening, and felt for a moment that she had never been so happy: to have lived, to have suffered, to have achieved all this;

to have survived. Over on the far side, by Hugo's new greenhouses, the four young men were running about the courts and, just below her, Anna had appeared with Pascal on the terrace, pushing his chair in front of her as if taking a baby for a walk.

In a way Pascal was her baby and he leaned forward excitedly like an eager, overactive toddler, pointing something out to her. Anna bent over his shoulder to listen and smiled.

Maybe she did love him. It was hard to tell. She was away a lot, but when she was with him she appeared devoted. He certainly loved her; but what was all this about moving to Manchester and how would he cope if she didn't go with him?

Stefanie and Sasha were determined to go because, Sasha had explained to her over tea on the terrace, he wanted to work with John Neri, who was one of the foremost aircraft designers in the country. Rachel wished she had the money to give him. Susan had a lot of money but not enough to invest on such a scale; she needed what she had for her own business. But Sasha and Pascal had said they would never approach Bobby again. They would only speak to him on family occasions, as family, and that was all.

Rachel sighed. Sadness descended again, but it wouldn't last. She watched Anna carefully manoeuvre Pascal's chair off the terrace on to the path that ran along the top of the hill overlooking the lake, and then she turned back the coverlet and got on to her bed. She had woken early in the morning and it would be a late night.

As she closed her eyes her thoughts were once more of the Grange as it had been in the old days with Bosco, the children playing on boats on the lake. It always seemed to be summertime, then, but was it? But the Grange remained the same, covered with wistaria, clematis, roses and honeysuckle – like some forest house in a fairy-tale.

She felt a great calm steal over her as she thought of the comforting, womb-like ambience of its interior, where she had lived her married life in such happiness. It was as though Bosco, her beloved, on this day had given it to her as a present; as though he were looking down at her, as he so often did, smiling at her, waiting for her, now perhaps with some impatience, to join him.

The lake was like glass; sometimes it was ruffled by a breeze or, in the autumn, obscured by a carpet of fallen leaves. But at this time, in high summer, it was perfection. Except for the sounds of ball on racket and the calls of the men they seemed surrounded by silence.

'Isn't it uncanny,' Pascal said, 'how it can be very noisy and then suddenly silent as if everyone were engulfed by the vastness of the Hall?'

'The children make the noise,' Anna began. 'I wish . . .' She stopped the chair and Pascal half-turned to look at her.

'Yes?'

'That we had had children when you wanted. I feel very sorry about that.'

'I wish it, too,' Pascal said, groping for her hand. 'I would have wished for nothing better. I feel so devastated that I can't be a proper husband to you. Anna . . .' Pascal fell silent as Anna started gently to push the chair along the path again.

'Yes?' .

'I would never stand in your way if you wished to leave me.'

Anna's heart gave a bound and once more she stopped the chair.

'Why should I do that?'

'Because you are a lovely young woman and it's not fair.'

'But I love you,' Anna heard herself saying.

'Really?' Pascal sounded surprised.

'Of course I do,' Anna started vigorously to push again. 'What makes you think I don't?'

'I feel you get very impatient with me.'

'And *you* get impatient with yourself. It hasn't been easy, Pascal, for me or you. But you do see, don't you, that we couldn't possibly go and live in Manchester?'

'No, I don't see. Why?'

'Because . . . it's such a horrible place.'

'How do you know?'

'The climate is awful. It's surrounded by dingy towns and bleak moors. What would we do?'

'I'm sure there'd be a lot to do, with your genius for organization. We could find a nice little place in Cheshire near Sasha and Stefanie. Paul is up there, too. It would be a colony of the family.'

'But I'd hate it,' Anna said, grimly resuming their walk.

'Anna,' Pascal looked for her hand again, 'I don't want to lose you. You are everything to me.'

'I know that,' Anna said and, as she did, it was as though a great weight had attached itself to her heart, anchoring her in perpetuity as the companion of a crippled man; forced to lead the life of fetching and carrying, pushing chairs and lifting. Pascal was wonderful but he was almost completely helpless; his basic functions frequently needed to be attended to. It was humiliating for him, and for her it was not a labour of love; it was something she would much prefer to leave to the nurse; but the nurse wasn't always around.

'What about the money?' Anna said. 'We'd be absolutely skint.'

'Money *is* a problem,' Pascal admitted.

They had come to the end of the path and Anna asked him if he wanted to go round the lake. He shook his head, telling her it would be too much of a chore to push him up. Anna was about to turn the chair when she found her eyes riveted on the steep incline of the path that disappeared among the bushes straight down to the lake. It was a fairly precipitous path and, on foot, one had to tread quite carefully, sometimes clutching on to bushes, especially when it was wet, or icy underfoot. Many people avoided the path on this side, but preferred to take the path on the other side which sloped much more gradually, winding like a snake between the rhododendrons.

Anna thought 'If I just give the chair a *tiny* push Pascal will go hurtling straight into the lake and no one will be able to stop him. By the time anyone gets to him . . . if I just pushed it very gently . . .'

The sweat broke out on her forehead and she felt so nauseous that the path seemed to hit her; she could see herself spreadeagled along it, sliding inexorably to the bottom. It was a horrible, fatalistic vision and through it she could hear Pascal asking if she were all right, and her heart started to pound. Gingerly she pushed the chair past the turning and then she stopped, firmly put on the brake, and sat down on one of the benches lining the path.

'I think it must have been the heat,' she said. 'I felt momentarily overcome.'

'I think it's the thought of moving to Manchester,' Pascal smiled, 'or shall we say Cheshire?'

'We say nothing,' Anna replied. 'You told me you wanted me; but I really don't want to live there. You'll have to make a choice. We have no money and until we have the idea is idiotic.'

'Thank you for siding with us against Bobby,' Pascal said gently.

'Of course I had to side with you against Bobby! The man is a monster.' Anna clutched herself, aware that she was still trembling with apprehension, with the fear of what might have been. 'Pascal, there *is* someone else who might invest.'

'Who's that?' Pascal lit a cigarette and his eyes followed the direction of the smoke vanishing into the air.

'Gunther von Spee. He's terribly rich.'

'I don't want his money,' Pascal's tone changed immediately. 'Do you?'

'Why not?' Anna avoided his gaze. 'We don't have to have much to do with him.'

'If we borrowed a few millions from Gunther we'd have to have quite a lot to do with him, don't you worry. He agents our cars; but business is business. That runs itself. I certainly don't want to see any more of the person who treated you so badly.'

'But that was a long time ago and now I'm married to you.'

'I don't want him to crow over me for being a cripple.'

'He would *never* do that!'

Pascal looked over the lake and tossed his cigarette angrily on the gravelled path.

'Anna, I want to have nothing to do with him, now is that clear? Him or his money. I think we'd better go in and change.'

Peremptorily he pointed in front of him and Anna, resignedly, got up from the bench and put her hands on the back of his chair, as one steeling herself for a life of service and fortitude.

The evening party was a great success. Charlotte was a perfectionist and had left nothing to chance. She was the commander and Jenny obediently and correctly carried out her orders, assisted by her sister and a squad of helpers. Charlotte had found that by being very busy all the time she could blot out so many painful reminders of the unsatisfactory personal side of her life: of Pascal's disability, of Joe's disgrace and Arthur's infidelity. By being continually on the go she was so tired by bedtime that all she wished for was sleep and oblivion. When she awoke in the morning it was time to leap out of bed and start all over again.

There was dinner for the family at eight, when everyone excelled themselves in affability, especially Bobby, who had given Rachel a diamond bracelet, quite the most valuable, if not the most precious, of her presents.

It was hard to tell whether that was the portrait from Stefanie or the book from Felipe. The former was more personal but the latter had been the key to a much greater prize: her freedom.

There was no discord at dinner; even Bobby discussed trivialities and paid compliments where he could. He was gracious and affable, the kind of man he could so easily have been were he not so greedy, not so consumed by ruthless ambition. Bobby's ambition may have made him a lord and a millionaire several times over, but it had destroyed his family life. It had never made him a happy man.

Aileen, of course, was there, seated between Lord Eckburgh and Hugo, a gracious if somewhat remote and unsmiling presence. Aileen always contrived to signify acquiescence to and, at the same time, disapproval of the Askham family. If they never quite accepted her, she had never quite accepted them or forgiven them for patronizing her.

Irina was enjoying herself enormously. She loved parties – pretty, well dressed women and handsome, elegant men. Inevitably it reminded her of St Petersburg in the days of the last of the Tsars, the beloved Nicholas, and she spent a good deal of time reminiscing and a little of it in tears.

Felipe didn't wear evening dress. As a republican and a Communist he didn't believe in it, but he looked quite smart, if a little funereal, in his best black suit with a black tie, and he seemed happy with his place between Em and Jenny's sister Beth.

Charlotte sparkled, tired but not yet exhausted, and showing neither. Charlotte had been trained from her earliest days not to give in, and now no amount of stress or exertion would let her. She had deliberately not placed Perry Eckburgh next to her daughter. Perry could be most entertaining and their part of the table was quite frequently shaken with mirth. Nor were Flora and Dick put next to each other. Charlotte considered they had spent enough time in each other's company and Dick, in evening dress, sat between Em and Stefanie, while Flora was on the other side of Perry, who occasionally addressed her as though she were still a small child.

On Em's left hand side was Luis, who was studying Spanish at Oxford but wanted to be a photographer. He was overjoyed to find his father once again at the family table. Johnny was attending his first grown-up dinner party. Aged thirteen he was the youngest and sat between his mother and Angelica.

Hugo made a speech and so did Bobby, to which Rachel gave a brief, gracious reply. Champagne was drunk; there was a toast to the Queen, and the sounds of 'Happy Birthday' rang out as the first guests started to arrive for the reception.

Hastily the family exited and took their stations at the top of the staircase; the small orchestra, hired from Salisbury, tuned its instruments and the help, hired from the village and surrounding countryside, began to circulate among the new arrivals.

It was not quite as it had been in the old days, but what was? There was an absence of luxury though both food and wine were plentiful. There were few of the old paintings on the walls, none of the old decorative plaster-work on the ceilings, and candlelight obscured the flaking paint work and the frayed, slightly dingy curtains at the windows.

But the company drawn from near and far was, on the whole, as it used to be: the old aristocracy and squirear-chy, the backbone of the nation. Yet there were many new elements too – an injection of talent, meritocracy and the post-war *nouveaux riches*. There were a number of young people from the rural universities, and there were several local wealthy tradesmen and farmers with their wives who would never have expected to receive an invitation before the War.

Then the band finished tuning and struck up the strains of the Anniversary Waltz. Bobby led Rachel on to the floor to a volume of applause and another happy, success-ful party in the old Askham tradition had begun.

PART 4

A Proud Tradition

Easter 1958–October 1966

CHAPTER 22

Sasha crept downstairs in the dark, chafing his hands against the cold. On these dark winter mornings he tumbled out of bed straight into his clothes without bothering to wash. Once downstairs he brushed his teeth in the kitchen sink, and then laid the fire and put a match to it so that by the time Stefanie and the children came down there would be a little warmth in the place.

Stefanie always made his sandwiches the night before and left them in a box in the fridge. This was one of the few modern luxuries they had; there was no central heating, no television and the plumbing left much to be desired.

Sasha had his morning routine worked out to a fine art by now and soon it would be warmer. They had endured the worst of the winter in this old house by the side of the main railway-line to London in a suburb of outer Manchester.

Yet Sasha and Stefanie had in their lives both known deprivation, want and fear – she during the thirties and forties in Paris and he in the war, when, for many months, he had been on the run from the Boche. Their experience was good training for what they had had to put up with since they had moved north the previous October. Although it could hardly be compared to former experiences – it was hardly comparable to fear of the Nazis, for instance – yet it was certainly not like living in Downshire Hill or Robertswood.

But, as a family, they loved it. For the first time they felt like a conventional family: father going to work, mother staying at home doing the cooking and the children going to the local school. Nicky had been taken away from his expensive preparatory school and removed from the list for Eton where he had been since birth. Galina started to go to the same school as Nicky and as it was just across the railway-line Stefanie walked them there and back each day.

Sasha had been working nearly six months for John Neri at his works on the other side of Bramhall. It was about twenty minutes' drive by car and Sasha was expected to clock on with the work force at seven thirty and off again at five. He was learning about the aeroplane industry not from a leather-topped desk in an executive office, as he had unsuccessfully tried to learn about Bobby's business, but from the shop floor. He was a worker; but he was also a director, and after normal hours he spent a further period either studying or discussing policy with John and Pascal when he came up from London.

The problem was still money and the Ferov family had had to budget very carefully during those winter months. It was not exactly scraping for a living to make ends meet, but it was an exercise in self-discipline. Stefanie was quite used to taking care; before the War and during it even stale cabbage leaves could be used for making soup. Stale pieces of bread soaked in it were delicious. For many years coffee was made from acorns. She had learned how to cook and clean to help her grandmother; and how to do it well. She knew all about turning collars and cuffs so that the frayed part was on the inside and a garment looked like new.

As a housewife reduced to a small budget she found she was in her element; pivotal to the wellbeing of the family. In consequence of giving up so much they were now mutually interdependent and very happy.

554

Of course there was money; lots of it tied up in valuable Lighterman shares. Sasha wanted to try and raise money without Stefanie having to sell her shares; but so far what the company had raised was a pittance.

While Sasha cleaned out the grate and lit the fire he drank two cups of black coffee and ate some slices of bread. His continental training and his discipline in the War had made him content with a light breakfast. At six forty-five he took his sandwiches from the fridge, wrapped in greaseproof paper, and put them in the kind of luncheon box that all the workmen had. Then he slipped quietly out of the house, backed his car out of the garage and drove down the lane along by the side of the railway and past the children's school. He turned right under the railway-bridge and drove through the silent village until he came to the Bramhall road.

Cheadle Hulme had probably once been a pretty village in Cheshire, one of a number with attractive names like Didsbury, Bramhall, Wilmslow. But by 1958 Cheadle Hulme was part of the sprawling suburb of greater Manchester, linked to that metropolis by an extensively built-up area, only here and there interspersed with fields and areas of woodland.

There were parts of Cheadle Hulme that reminded one of its village origins, some quaint corners and old houses with inglenooks and beams. But now its main street was bisected by the Manchester to London railway and it seemed to sprawl, like suburbia, with orderly rows of semi-detached houses with neat pockets of gardens back and front.

Cheadle Hulme was still a leafy place and attracted some affluent members of society who had businesses in the area, as well as a good number of commuters who worked in Stockport or Manchester and lived in the semi-detached houses with neat gardens. It had a very good school which was a foundation formed by the Manchester Warehousemen and Clerks in the 19th century for the education of their orphan children. It still accepted foundation scholars, though not necessarily the orphan children of warehousemen and clerks, who were educated free. They were not discriminated against in any way but joined the general body of scholars, who came from a wide catchment area owing to the excellent reputation of the school.

This was a large neo-Victorian building which looked quite imposing from the front, but, inside, it was a ramshackle collection of corridors, classrooms and dormitories rather like one of the older English public-schools; and in the grounds were a strange assortment of modern buildings and Nissen huts which had been added to the school.

Cheadle Hulme School accepted both boys and girls. It had both an infants and a senior section so Galina and Nicky Ferov were able to be educated together.

Sasha drove past the school on his way to work and on his way back. He liked to feel that this little dormitory suburb, which really lacked any cohesive identity outside its parish church and its school, contained his small family.

Sasha realized that he was rapidly becoming the sort of man he had always, instinctively, wanted to be: a member of the bourgeoisie with the nuclear family of two children, a wife and some pets. He had forgotten that his father was a prince and his mother a princess, that his uncles, aunts and cousins were lords and ladies and that his wife's mother had been a war heroine. He thought that, at last, in this amorphous Manchester suburb, within easy distance of his work, he had found the kind of domestic life he had always craved. A peaceful family life and the drama of flying aeroplanes seemed, to him, an unbeatable combination.

Stefanie lay in bed, listening as the sound of Sasha's car grew fainter until it disappeared. When they had first moved into the house by the bridge the sound of the main-line expresses thundering along the line had kept her awake. But now she hardly ever heard them. The house literally rocked with the impact of the massive express trains; but after a hard day's work came a good night's sleep and now she remained undisturbed until Sasha's alarm went off at six and he quickly stifled it before she woke up.

She lay in a state of semi-somnolence for as long as she could, until the sounds of his car faded away and it was time to get up. In that time between waking and rising Stefanie thought a lot about the past, about the days when such a kind of life as this would have been unthinkable. But it was unthinkable now to return to them and she thought that then she had been an altogether different person, wrapped up in herself and, ultimately, remote from reality. She had nearly lost reality altogether.

Stefanie knew that it was to Sasha she owed her salvation. He had saved her from Jack and then he had saved her from herself. He had been patient, compassionate, understanding. Some people said he had been too soft for her but, in her estimation, being wise after the event, he had been about right.

She knew he had sacrificed his work and her father's regard for her sake, but a more dominating Sasha would have destroyed her altogether.

Stefanie got quickly out of bed and, as Sasha had before her, dived into her clothes to try and keep warm. There was no heating in the top part of the house; but during those cold winters in Paris during the war there had been no fuel of any kind to be had for the asking, even to friends of the Germans as her grandparents had been, and she had perfected the art of dressing under the bedclothes.

Finally, in slacks and a jersey, she ran downstairs and put on the kettle again for her morning tea. It was still warm from being used by Sasha half an hour before. Sometimes the fire had gone out and had to be relit, but usually it just needed a poke and some more coal and by the time she had set up the breakfast things and gone up to call the children it was roaring up the chimney.

Nicky was so pleased to be at home with his parents, particularly his mother, that he was almost an unnaturally docile and obedient boy. He never needed telling twice, but Galina was just the opposite: she needed telling all the time. She had to be cajoled and scolded and sometimes finally smacked before she would get out of bed or wash her face or put her school uniform on or come down to breakfast.

Stefanie often used to lose her patience with Galina and the mornings on her own were a trial. The best part was when she walked slowly back along the cinder path towards the house after depositing them at school and then she had her breakfast, a nice warm over the fire and read the daily paper.

Even her painting and drawing, which had helped to restore her after her breakdown, took second place to this pleasing domestic routine. But when her work was done and the weather was fine she might wander along the track, away from the school and towards the unbroken fields and hedgerows which led into the countryside, with a pencil and sketchpad, to recapture some moment of natural life which caught her fancy. Above all, she loved sketching the family and there were many studies, solo or in groups, of the children and Sasha, with the family pets, indoors or outdoors, in all seasons and all moods.

This ordered peaceful life suited Stefanie after the

turmoil of the life she had led both as a child and in her early adulthood. The ordinariness of being a housewife after the torment of being an invalid represented for her the quintessence of happiness. Now she had no ambition to be anything else, because she had been through the valley of despair and had emerged on the other side.

When she got back, Stefanie was surprised to see an unfamiliar car outside the door. She was no longer a nervous person and strangers didn't worry her; but it was obviously someone who was no longer in the car, and thus probably in the house, and she went cautiously around the car peering through the windows.

Then she heard a voice calling her and, looking up, saw Anna tapping on the inside of the sitting-room window. Stefanie cried out, waved frantically and ran up the front path towards the door.

Stefanie and her sister-in-law had not always got on. Stefanie was two years older than Anna and when they met again after the War she was married to Sasha and expecting a baby. She was only nineteen and yet to Anna, then, she seemed already to have reached the pinnacle of achievement and sophistication. In those days young women yearned to be married; it was a way not only of escaping from parental bondage but also of the 'knowing' that was essential to adult life, the mysteries of sex and procreation. When Stefanie, married and pregnant, had arrived in Venice, Anna felt that her nose had been put out of joint and she was jealous.

When, later, she came to London, she was much more in command of herself, and it was Stefanie who had begun to have problems. She was unhappy and she drank too much and, finally, she spent nearly nine months in a clinic. Anna didn't like illness; she didn't know how to cope with it. But after Anna had married Pascal and they began to see more of each other their relationship grew closer. Meeting together and planning the new 'Askham' had been fun, and even more fun was the secrecy surrounding the 'Phoenix' at the planning stages. Late-night foursomes after work turned into parties, not drinking-parties because Stefanie never drank; but good times, laughter and fun. Then came the tragedy, but, when Bobby rounded on Sasha, Stefanie defended him. She had always opposed her father; it had seemed to give her pleasure. As Stefanie grew in strength and resolution Anna began not only to admire her more, but to seek her friendship.

After greeting her, Stefanie wanted to know if she'd eaten. Anna said she'd breakfasted in the hotel where she and Pascal were staying near the Neri works. Now she was on her way back to London. Companionably they curled up round the fire with coffee and at first brought each other up to date with family news. Anna talked quite animatedly but Stefanie thought she looked unwell; something which Anna never seemed to be. Even in the worst, darkest days after Pascal's accident she had always looked like someone who had enough sleep, who had time to give attention to her appearance and her clothes.

Anna protested that she was well and had been sleeping. They'd had a late night in discussion with John Neri and she had got up early to take Pascal over to the works and prepare to drive back to London. Pascal was staying with the Neris and would travel back by train in a few days. Anna sighed and looked into the fire.

'Then I don't know what will happen.'

'How do you mean?'

'Pascal is quite determined to move up here. He thinks the project will work and it will take off. He says we should find a house here and move up. The journey is very tiring for him.'

'I love it up here,' Stefanie said, getting up to pour fresh coffee. 'The life is so peaceful.'

'That's what I couldn't stand,' Anna glanced around like an animal feeling itself ensnared. 'It *is* peaceful, I can see that, but it would stifle me to death.'

'But you've lived for a long time in the country.'

'And I hated it.' Anna nervously lit about her fifth cigarette since she'd arrived. 'I hate it. I stayed there for Pascal. I knew I could escape to the Continent whenever I wanted to. You know before the accident we were looking for a house in London. You see I love travel and . . .'

Stefanie's clear blue eyes were full of sympathy.

'It's not your style of life, is it, Anna?'

'Not at all. Not the teeniest little bit. At least the cottage is near Askham and London, not too far from Littlestone. There's always something going on, but . . .' she threaded her fingers together until she nearly burnt herself with her cigarette.

'I do actually, positively hate the north of England. It's bleak and it's cold.'

'But it's pretty round here,' Stefanie protested.

'It's pretty, relative to Manchester and Stockport. Oh, there are nice places but do you realize we'd live here *all* our lives and . . .' Anna paused while Stefanie gave her an encouraging smile. 'And I can't stand the thought. You see, Stefanie, there is . . . I don't know how to say this, but you're the only one I can confide in.'

'Of *course* you can confide in me.' Stefanie leaned closer as if to imbue her with a sense of confidence.

'It's a dreadful thing I'm going to tell you.' Anna lit a fresh cigarette from the stub of the old one. Then she looked up at Stefanie. 'There *is* another man.'

'I thought there might be,' Stefanie's voice was gentle. 'It's not surprising, is it?'

561

'I feel wicked. I feel so wicked . . .' Anna put her face in her hands. When she raised it again it was streaked with tears. 'The man is Gunther von Spee. I never got over him, you know. I married Pascal on the rebound just to try and show Gunther what I could do. Then, in Venice, just before Grandma Melanie died, I bumped into him by chance. We didn't meet after that for a long time, but I knew we would. Eventually we did and . . .'

Anna threw up her hands and then let them lie on her lap in an attitude of resignation and defeat. Stefanie had never seen her look so abject.

'I couldn't help it,' Anna went on. 'I fought against it; but the pull was so strong. Gunther *is* so strong . . .'

'I never felt you completely loved Pascal,' Stefanie intervened, 'if it helps. I never thought you were a couple. In the beginning Sasha and I weren't a couple, but now we are. That's how I know. I knew that you felt about Pascal the way I felt about Sasha when we were first married. He rescued me, too, as Pascal rescued you. He rescued me from Jack Blackstock and Pascal rescued you from Gunther. We were both grateful . . .'

'Oh, you *understand*,' Anna clasped her hands and reached out for her sister-in-law, who got up and knelt by her side.

'Of course I understand. I think, like with Sasha and me, you and Pascal might have grown together too.'

'There was so much to admire about him . . . and *is*,' Anna lamented. 'I feel so wicked for not loving him more when he has suffered so much. But, you see, no one knows how much I hate illness. It makes me afraid. I was never meant to marry a man who couldn't walk, who needed constant help. I'm not patient enough, and that's why I feel so awful, so trapped.' Anna put her head in her hands again and Stefanie's arm tightened round her waist. 'I felt like killing him one day last summer.'

'I think one has these feelings,' Stefanie said softly.

'Yes, but I nearly did,' Anna began to tremble. 'You know the steep path leading down to the lake at Askham? Well, I felt like pushing Pascal's chair into the lake. Wasn't that terrible? I nearly did . . .'

'But you didn't. *That's* the thing.'

Anna stared wildly at Stefanie. 'But supposing I had? Don't you know what they say about my father, that he killed Freddie? Kyril's daughter, they would have said, a madness in the family . . .' Anna started to sob again and tenderly Stefanie reached out to wipe the tears from her cheeks. Then she got up and poured a little brandy from a bottle on the sideboard into a glass. She gave it to Anna and said:

'Drink this. No one in the family seriously believes Uncle Kyril killed Freddie – Charlotte told me so. Even Em no longer believes it, and she was with Ralph in Cairo during the war when they met the man who thought he did. It was so fantastic, and unlikely, and, if it happened, it happened over twenty years ago so no one can ever possibly know. You must never torment yourself with this any more than I must torment myself about my mother; a guilty burden I carried, ridiculously, for years.

'As for madness in the family, that's nonsense, too. Neither the Ferovs nor the Askhams are mad; the Boling-brokes are much too sane ever to be considered mad. But many people do have murderous impulses.' Stefanie sat down by Anna's side again. 'Do you know that I used to fear I'd kill my children? It was the most awful sensation and would reduce me to rubble. That drove me to drink more than anything. I didn't dare remain alone with them. I think you wanted to push Pascal out of your life and it was an impulse. In a way your feeling of revulsion was understandable; but the main thing is that you didn't kill him and you won't. But I do think you should tell him and I think if you do you'll find he won't mind too much.'

'Tell him what?' Anna reached for a handkerchief in the pocket of her tailored jacket and dabbed at her eyes. 'Tell him I wanted to kill him?'

'No, no, not that! I think you should tell him about Gunther. That you love someone else. That you want a divorce. I suppose you do want a divorce? Hasn't Gunther a wife?'

'She died. She was also in a wheelchair but because of diabetes. Gunther knows what I'm going through. The terrible guilt. He's awfully sweet and concerned. He would invest in the business, you know, but Pascal won't hear of it. He'd give us all we need but Pascal wouldn't take it. Now to tell Pascal that I want to *marry* him. It's unthinkable.'

'A year ago he told Sasha and me that he wouldn't stand in your way if you wanted a divorce. He knew it was hard for you and he has found such strength in himself that he can face it.'

'But he told me he needed me and loved me . . . that day I wanted to push him in the lake. I think that's why I wanted to. I felt so trapped.'

'He does need you and your love, but not at all costs. He knows you don't want to live up here; that you aren't interested in the planes as you were in the car. He understands all that absolutely. I think if you did tell him you'd find he wasn't surprised. He might be upset that it's Gunther but he will let you go.' Stefanie abruptly stood up and began to walk around.

'We would willingly have Pascal here with us. There is plenty of room and it would be ideal. Sasha loves Pascal and I do, too. It would be no chore for us, no burden to have him and help look after him. The children adore him and I think he would be happy with us. Happier, perhaps, than with you, knowing how restless you were. In time, if the deal works, we will buy a larger house, maybe somewhere near Alderley. We would always look after Pascal. This is only a rented house, as you know, but it is near the school and for the time being it suits us. You must free yourself, Anna, before it is too late. Pascal, I know, will understand and we'll help him.'

Stefanie bent down and put both hands on Anna's shoulders. Anna impulsively reached up and grasped her wrists.

'You know what they say about your mother: how remarkable she was in adversity, in the war? How wonderful she was in the camps with people who were worse off than she was, and conditions for everyone were terrible. Charlotte says Hélène was a heroine many times over. I think you've inherited her mantle, Stefanie. I can see in you today the kind of nobility that made your mother a heroine. I think her mantle has fallen on you and her spirit lives on.'

The motley collection of people struggling along in the damp, many with inadequate footwear, had drawn a fair amount of derision not only from the press but from onlookers. The first day there were many cruel and unkind remarks hurled at them by the inhabitants of the towns and villages through which they passed, and Flora was reminded of the passage of Christ through the hostile mob assembled in Jerusalem that first Easter two thousand years before. But she and her fellow marchers, the founding members of the Campaign for Nuclear Disarmament, were undeterred. The weather had included snow and the roads were like bogs; but she had come prepared for the weather and it was no platitude to say that the warmth in her heart on this first march to Aldermaston made up for the discomforts of the three-day event.

And she was not alone. Dick and Ruth had come along with Joan and the three of them took turns to push the pram. The police were very concerned about the children on the march but they were well taken care of. Even the NSPCC was on hand and the younger participants only walked or rode part of the journey. Dick had brought his car along and he and Flora shared the driving. At night he went off with Ruth and Joan to stay in the comfort of a hotel while Flora dossed down with her companions, who included many of her former Party colleagues.

Flora had formally left the Communist Party after the ruthless suppression by the Russians of the revolution in Hungary. She had done all the things Dick hadn't dared to do: she had not only made a speech denouncing Russia but tore her party membership card up on the platform and scattered it in fragments among the audience. One or two had got up in a threatening manner, but many had sat back as if in tacit approval and quite a few followed her.

As far as Flora was concerned it was very convenient that the foundation of the Campaign for Nuclear Disarmament coincided with her departure from the Party. In November 1957 the writer J. B. Priestley had written an article on Britain and the nuclear bomb and this was the beginning of the movement whose inaugural meeting at the Central Hall, in Westminster, the following February had overflowed. And at the head of the column as it left Trafalgar Square on Good Friday 1958 was that doughty octogenarian, the philosopher, Bertrand Russell, even older than Aunt Rachel, who was also joining them for the final day outside the Atomic Weapons Research Establishment itself.

It was nearly five o'clock on Easter Saturday and the rain had been unrelenting. Dick had taken Ruth and Joan off early to find refuge and Flora struggled on alone, or rather with those members of the Party who had deserted with her and some fellow students from the LSE.

There had been many acts of kindness on the way. A country club had offered them overnight accommodation, and a woman from the crowd had thrown some umbrellas into the crowd for shelter from the incessant rain. The TV cameras had been busy interviewing people and among them had been Flora, who had already written her views for *The Sentinel*. Em and Luis had been with them from the start, and Paul was somewhere down the column with his friends from Manchester. Paul had recently left the factory where he'd been working because it manufactured parts for nuclear arms. Flora was very proud of Paul; proud of her family, and she chatted cheerily to those with her as the night fell, trying to inspire them to just one or two miles more.

Early the next morning, Easter Sunday, she and Paul rendezvoused with Rachel, Dick, Ruth and Joan at a prearranged spot a few miles from Aldermaston. Flora had scarcely had any sleep, she'd been so busy arguing with a group of people about the pros and cons of communism. She said she was committed to the principles of communism in her heart, but not to the Party. In fact, she felt that belonging to the Party did not square with a true commitment to communistic ideals. Paul said that she was a kind of anarchist and that he felt rather as she did.

Paul had with him a very pleasant girl called Laura. Like Paul's mother, she was Jewish, the daughter of a wealthy Manchester businessman, though Flora at that time knew nothing of her background. Laura had dark curly hair and vivacious good looks and was studying English Literature with a view to being a teacher. Flora couldn't quite decide whether she was here because of Paul or a commitment to the anti-nuclear cause. It was quite clear that Laura had no idea Paul was the Earl of Askham and he told Flora late that night that he didn't want her to know; but they had forgotten about the popularity of Rachel who, as soon as she joined the column the next morning, was met by a barrage of TV and newspaper reporters.

'Of course I support nuclear disarmament,' Rachel said, her hands deep in the pockets of a tweed coat, her face blue with cold. 'Any sensible person would.' She wore sturdy shoes and a scarf tied round her head and was willing to expound her views for as long as anyone would listen.

At three o'clock the procession, whose numbers had swollen to over a thousand, assembled outside the gates of the establishment to be addressed by prominent speakers; and then a form of interdenominational service was held before everyone dispersed into the late afternoon.

Rachel felt very invigorated by the experience and, her arms through Flora's and Paul's, joined lustily in the singing. Then she had a word with Russell, Canon Collins and some of the other luminaries before meeting Em, who had arranged to pick her and Paul up and take them on to Robertswood for the night.

Paul had explained to his grandmother that Laura had come down not as one of the party but specifically to be with him.

'Then you must bring her,' Rachel said immediately. 'Irina loves parties and there is plenty of room.' Rachel paused and looked awkwardly at Dick, who stood with Ruth and the baby, a little as though he too were part of that family.

'And Dick, dear, are you . . .'

'I'm taking Ruth and Joan back to London, thanks, Lady Askham. We're fine.'

'I'm sure Irina would love to have you, too.'

'We couldn't possibly do that,' Dick said. 'Thanks all the same. Besides, we have other plans.'

Flora looked away, guessing quite well what those plans were. Some little hotel, doubtless, between here and London . . .

'I'll take Joan, if you like,' she said suddenly.

'But Flora . . .' Rachel didn't quite know what was going on. Dick smiled.

'That would be very nice of you, Flora. Ruth needs a rest.'

'But not me,' Flora thought. It was pretty typical that he should think of Ruth and not Flora, who had spent the last two nights in her clothes. She was seriously short of sleep.

'Do you think Princess Irina would mind if we brought the baby?' Flora looked anxiously at Rachel. 'She's awfully good.'

'I'm sure she won't mind. Anyway, it's only for the night. We can all go back to Askham tomorrow.'

Em was looking at Ruth and Dick, both clearly excited at the opportunity to be alone and looking rather longingly at Dick's car, which another friend had driven along to the base. She raised an eyebrow imperceptibly at her mother and shrugged, pointing the way towards the 'Askham', which stood by the roadside. Flora was fussing about Joan, getting things from Dick's car and last-minute instructions from Ruth. Rachel and Em sat in the car with Paul and Laura, watching Flora happily pushing Joan's chair towards them while Dick followed, his arms full of clothes. Luis had gone off to take pictures.

'Looks as though Joan is going to stay for a week,' Paul said good-humouredly. 'How old is she?'

'I must say I know very little about her,' Em blew her nose vigorously because she had a cold. 'I know very little about Ruth, either, except that she shares Flora's flat with her and works for Dick. Did you know they were so thick, Mother?' Em said but, from the back, Paul scoffed.

'Don't be so narrow-minded, Aunt Em. This isn't the thirties.'

'Don't worry, people had affairs in the thirties, too,' Em remarked wryly, '*and* in the twenties, and before that.'

'Who said anything about an affair?'

Rachel was watching Ruth get into the front seat of Dick's car and sit there waiting for him. There was no doubt that she had the anticipatory expression of a lover, yet Rachel felt rather shocked and also disturbed. Angelica was her granddaughter and Dick was her husband. Where, for that matter, on this Easter holiday, was Angelica?

Dick arrived at the car with Flora and Joan and when he saw Rachel looking at him his attitude became apologetic.

'Ruth has been working very hard on the proofs of my book,' he said awkwardly. 'She could do with a day or two's break.'

Flora was too busy getting Joan into the car with the help of Paul to take much notice of what Dick was saying. Around them were the dispersing crowds, a few of whom stopped to stare at the large limousine waiting to take Rachel's party away. Flora felt self-conscious and wished they hadn't brought the 'Askham' but a smaller, less obtrusive car. Em was so sensitive in some things and rather short-sighted in others, the inevitable result of a conflict between her background and her radical views.

Dick kissed Rachel awkwardly on the cheek and shook hands with Em, Paul and Laura. Then, with a wave, he walked back to his car. Em didn't wait to see them drive off but slowly edged her way through the throng towards the A4.

* * *

Angelica lay on the sofa of the drawing-room of the Castle of Eck, watching the straggling procession join forces with the crowd already gathered outside the gates of Aldermaston. The rain was pouring down and most of them were soaked. She had seen her grandmother interviewed and caught a brief glimpse of Em and Flora with her; but too much was going on and there were the views of others to hear in a short news broadcast. Angelica had earlier watched the masses struggle past snowdrifts in the road and seen what a motley, curious, raffish crowd they looked. The CND badge in the brief time it had been around had become a symbol for nonconformity, for a change in the way of life, that was too subtle for those living through it at the moment to perceive. The word 'teenager' had given rise to a whole new generation between childhood and adulthood and this mood, a new nonconformity in dress and behaviour, was reflected in the music of rock and roll which had spread like wildfire round the world since its introduction in 1956.

It was, indeed, a very different outlook, not only since Angelica's girlhood but since 1945. Suddenly conformity and austerity had given way to a certain abandon that was very reminiscent of the twenties.

The nuclear age threatened everybody and the voice of dissent, of protest, was growing everywhere.

Angelica gave a huge yawn and took another sip of her gin and tonic.

'This is a frightful bore,' she said, as Perry Eckburgh came into the room. 'Trust my old grandmother to get mixed up in it. She used to be called The Red Countess. She'll end up as the dotty old Lady Askham if she's not careful.'

Perry sat down gingerly at the end of the sofa, just a touch away from Angelica's delicious bare feet. He wore a check shirt under his yellow pullover and a pair of Saks' grey flannel trousers. Since he had got to know Angelica so well he had taken more care than ever over his personal appearance, over his grooming and the clothes he wore. He didn't want to make himself idiotic by pretending to be much younger than he was, but he wanted to look good, a youthful and vigorous-looking fifty-five, getting on for fifty-six. He was twenty-eight years older than the young woman he wished to marry, nearly six years older than her mother.

Perry stirred the pink gin that had become a habit in the Navy, where he'd served bravely during the War in convoys, and glanced at his beloved.

'Whatever happened to Ralph's wife? I suppose she's still called Lady Askham?'

'She went to Kenya at the end of the War, taking two little evacuees with her. We haven't heard from them since, as far as I know. She spent all the family money so had none to clear off with, though I believe when Bobby sold the Kenyan estate she had most of it. I think she sends a Christmas card to Granny, but more I don't know.'

'Tragedy, that,' Perry pulled at his lower lip. 'I must say Paul Askham hardly looks the part of the young Earl.'

'Paul's all right,' Angelica never said the thing conventionally expected of her. Her besotted swain knew that after approximately nine months of courtship. When one expected her to agree she didn't and vice versa. 'I'm very fond of him. He's very independent and straight. Bobby tried to lure him into the business when Sasha and Pascal quit but he would have none of it. He's recently left a job because it conflicted with his principles. I believe he's considering starting some business of his own in Manchester.'

'Terrible place, Manchester,' Perry wrinkled his nose.

'You're a fuddy duddy, darling,' Angelica said, reaching for his hand. 'You'll have to move with the times.'

This familiarity gave Perry the chance he'd wanted to touch her feet, edge his hand up towards her knee and under her skirt.

Angelica clasped Perry's hand when it reached her knee and gave him a smile, shaking her head at the same time.

'Naughty,' she said.

'When are we going to get married?'

Perry asked the question every week and she always gave the same reply.

'Don't push things, darling. I've told you there is plenty of time.'

'Not for me,' Perry groaned, conscious of the difference in their ages. He couldn't envisage too much time with this beautiful young woman by his side.

'Darling, we *sleep* together,' Angelica sighed. 'What else does an old goat like you want?'

This offended Perry and he gazed morosely at the television set. Reception was very bad in this area and the picture was invariably a bit fuzzy. Angelica knew he was hurt and offered him her hand, her mouth in her familiar model's pout.

'Sorry, darling. Didn't mean to say that.'

'It is true, though.' Perry sat down by her side again. 'I *am* an old goat, madly in love with a woman young enough to be my daughter.'

'People would never think it, though.' She playfully tapped his nose. 'Everyone says you're terribly good-looking.'

'Dick is good-looking, too, *and* a man of your own age.'

Angelica sighed. 'Please don't mention Dick, Perry, not again as long as I'm here. If I were not so utterly fed-up with Dick I wouldn't be so interested in you. Would I?'

She opened her eyes wide and once again he thought what an amazing woman she was: talented, good-looking, well-connected. The incredible thing was that she wanted him. He still couldn't believe his luck.

Perry said: 'At the risk of sounding a bore, Angelica, may I ask you again what's preventing you telling Dick?'

'There are things to be decided; the children . . .'

'I said I'd willingly have them . . .'

'I know. But Dick might want them, too. Then there is the family.'

'They like me.'

'I know they do. There's my job.'

'I don't mind you going on working.'

'I know you don't, but . . .'

'*But?*' Perry seized her hand.

'I don't *really* like the idea of a divorce, to be honest,' Angelica soulfully shook her head. 'The scandal, the mess. I'm sure Dick isn't the gent that Uncle Adam was, who nobly compromised himself for Aunt Melanie and the sake of the family and, of course, you and I couldn't possibly compromise ourselves, could we, Perry?'

The twelfth Baron Eckburgh thoughtfully rubbed his nose. 'It certainly would be *much* better that we didn't,' he said. 'I don't want to sound snobbish, darling, but we have so much more to lose than your husband. As it is there would be no more Royal Enclosures.'

'Quite,' Angelica agreed. This was a considerable sacrifice in itself. Her dresses for Ascot usually rated several of the daily papers and society magazines. 'Dick has absolutely nothing to lose at all. But I don't think he wants to divorce. He's comfortable.' Angelica studied the tips of her highly polished nails. 'He even loves me, I think.'

But love for Angelica was not enough – love and the satisfactory physical side of marriage. Dick was a good lover and they suited each other; but there had been not too much of that recently. She and Dick had grown apart in every way.

All her life Angelica Crosby had been dogged with the feeling that there was not enough money about. She had been brought up with the idea that her family had money; but there was never much of it in evidence. There were huge houses and estates and everyone was titled. There was an *air* of affluence, but all the same a lot of scrimping went on, especially after her father died, saving ends, cutting corners.

Her mother had been left so poorly off that she had to take a job. The children had been sent to boarding-school and it was the charity of Bobby that virtually kept them going, everyone said. By the time the war came the Askhams had no money at all and Grandma Rachel and Uncle Adam, looking after a large family at Darley Manor, didn't have much, either. There was a lot of passing on of clothes between the cousins. Naturally they all made a joke of it, in a rather upper-class way.

Then the war had come and Mother had gone completely; not even holiday visits. It had been rather hard to understand for a little girl of ten years old. There was less money about than ever, scrimping and saving, rations at school. When Mother had come back Angelica hardly knew her, and scarcely recognized that pale, skeletal figure; but by then she was old enough to understand more. Her mother was a heroine: she had nearly died. Then Mother had married Arthur, who was by no means rich; they lived well, but one always felt it was because they thought they should rather than that they could afford to. There were often anxious moments when the bills came. One had the idea that Arthur lived up to the hilt.

Why, feeling as she did this need for the security that

money could bring, Angelica should have married a man with no money either, she couldn't quite fathom. It was passion, she knew, and sex. Now that had all gone completely.

Perry, on the other hand, though really terribly old, had everything: an ancient title, several homes and pots of money. He was fun to be with. He was terribly protective and considerate. He had an old-fashioned courtesy and charm. Dick, with his egalitarian views, tended to treat women as chaps, comrades. He expected them to be resilient, to stand on their own feet. For a woman like Angelica it was nice, once in a while, to feel a little frail; to need to be protected and, in his old-fashioned way, Perry admirably fulfilled this role.

Besides, Perry was distinguished-looking. She never minded being seen with someone who was a married man with children when she was born. She would never love Perry in the way she'd loved Dick; but she would be happy with him. She would be with someone who came from the same kind of family as her own, and they would mix with the sort of people she was used to – not Marxist academics and left-wing writers and politicians. She would have several homes and they would travel. She didn't want more children and nor did Perry, who was a grandfather.

To this, Angelica thought, she had been born: to be a woman of title, of wealth, as her ancestry had prepared her for. Just at that moment, glancing again at the flickering TV, she saw Dick in close conversation with Ruth Earnshaw standing just behind her grandmother, who was being interviewed, yet again, for another station.

'Of course the idea of nuclear weapons is immoral,' Rachel was saying in her forthright way, yet smiling at the interviewer at the same time, as she always did when she wanted to get a point across. She always said that one had more chance of influencing people if one did it pleasantly.

'Don't you find the thought of annihilating the human race daunting, young man?'

'Yes, Lady Askham,' the interviewer mumbled.

But Angelica was not listening to her grandmother; her eyes were on the two figures just behind her. Between them, in a pushchair, was Ruth's baby; but the baby didn't interest Angelica, either. It was the expression on the faces of the two adults that interested her most.

Two people, she would have said, in love with each other.

Perry, glass in hand, had been watching the television, too, but his eyes were fixed firmly on Rachel. He wouldn't have known Ruth even if he recognized Dick. Angelica stretched luxuriously and stirred him with her foot.

'Time to change for dinner, darling,' she said. 'The Catchpoles will soon be back.'

There were six of them altogether in the Easter house-party at Eckburgh Castle: Hugh and Larian Catchpole, who had gone fishing, Douglas and Esmée Newton-Forrester, who were upstairs in their rooms, and Angelica and Perry. Perry's married daughter, her husband and their two children were due the following day, just to make the whole thing look thoroughly respectable. Perry was a widower; but everyone knew Angelica had a husband. If one wanted an uncontested divorce one had to be very careful about appearances.

Perry fondled her foot again. 'Right ho, old thing,' he said. 'She's quite a bird, your grandmother.'

'She's quite a bird,' Angelica agreed, taking his hand as he levered her up. 'And, incidentally, I do think that quite soon we might be able to get married.'

* * *

Bobby sat rather stiffly in front of the fire in the old study at Robertswood, which had been a favourite den of his grandfather. By curious coincidence, when the house had been turned into a convalescent home for officers during the war, it had also been Ralph Askham's bedroom. Now it was back into being a study again, with all Sir Robert's furniture, paintings and knick-knacks, which had gone into storage for the duration of the war. Most of Robertswood had been restored with its original paintings and furniture; whereas everything at Askham had gone.

Bobby enjoyed spending holiday weekends with his family at the home he had spent so much on restoring. It was a luxurious home, one of the still great homes of England and far and away superior, now, to Askham Hall, which had never recovered its former grandeur, partly thanks to Cheryl Askham and partly because Hugo had nothing like the means that Bobby had to do up the Hall. Indeed, the fate of the Hall had been the subject of much speculation over the Easter break. It was partly because it was so uncomfortable, so spartan and bare that people preferred now to come and stay at Robertswood. This was a matter of quiet satisfaction to Bobby, who had wanted to buy it and turn it into a hotel, but had been stopped by the ambition of Hugo to restore it as a family home, and the connivance of Rachel and her fellow trustees.

'And a fine mess he's made of it,' had been Bobby's opinion at dinner the night before. Hugo was vigorously defended by Rachel, but she was about to move out, anyway, to the comfort of the Grange, which was being refurbished and redecorated for her. Although the Grange was small by the standards of the Hall it was quite a large house with five bedrooms and servants' quarters, no longer in use.

These reflections and others were going through Bobby's mind as he looked into the fire, impatiently flicking ash on to the hearth. Bobby was nearly sixty and life had not mellowed him. He was a clever, choleric, impatient man whose temper had not improved with the years. He was not a happy or contented man and he frequently found fault with people. He didn't get on with his wife; his daughters were indifferent to him and he had lost his only son, David. He was loveless and unloving and it showed in the grim unsmiling set of his mouth; the hard glint in his eyes; the sharp, suspicious nose he had, which could smell money or the opportunity to make money a mile away.

Bobby had been a beautiful boy and a handsome man but he had always lacked stature and this seemed to him the equivalent of status in Askham eyes. He had always tried to make up for his lack of height by the cultivation of power; to him money and possessions were power. Consequently jealousy and greed had really dominated Bobby's life and one other emotion: reluctance to forgive. He was mean-minded and he nursed grievances.

Bobby straightened himself up as there was a gentle knock on the door and called out 'Come in.' He got up and his cousin Joe appeared from around the door and quietly shut it behind him. Joe had come out of prison the week before Easter, having achieved full remission for good behaviour. In the past few months he had been in an open prison not far from Askham.

Bobby had not been one of those who found time to visit Joe; but he was aware that the times were changing. The previous September Sir John Wolfenden, in a far-ranging and well-argued report, had advocated reforms in the laws against homosexuality. It was unlikely that Parliament would approve them; but it was a sign of the turn of the tide that he dared advocate them at all.

Joe was leaving for the West Indies, where friends of

the Crewes had invited him to holiday in a private house on a private island. From there he would embark on a world tour until the public had forgotten about his case and he was free to resume his career. He would send reports of his travels to Em and *The Sentinel*.

Now he had come to say goodbye to his grandmother. Bobby and Joe hadn't met since before the trial and Bobby felt a bit awkward in shaking his hand, knowing that he was the only member of the family who had turned his back on Joe.

'Welcome,' Bobby said jovially. 'How are you, Joe? I'm very glad to see you.'

'I'm very well thank you, Bobby,' Joe said, aware of the hypocrisy behind the welcome. But he had learned a lot of things in prison, tolerance above all.

'I'm glad everything turned out all right, Joe . . . the remission, that kind of thing.' Bobby gestured awkwardly and sat down abruptly, indicating that Joe should do the same.

'Thank you, Bobby,' Joe said. 'I'm putting it all behind me.'

'That's good,' Bobby replied, with an air of relief. 'Not planning to write any books about your experiences or anything like that, I hope?'

Joe grinned. 'Not yet, anyway, Bobby.'

'Please don't,' Bobby said. 'Your mother has been very good and supportive, all the family have; but we have suffered enough.'

'I didn't think you had suffered much at all, Bobby,' Joe spoke rather harshly, 'but I know what you mean. For Mother's sake and Gran's, if not yours, I shan't be publicizing my case. Wolfenden has done that for me.'

'I don't want us to row, Joe.' Bobby was trying hard to appear reasonable. 'That's the last thing on my mind. I don't like homosexuality and I don't approve of it; but mine not to reason why. Some people, cleverer than I am, appear to think people can't help themselves with this sort of thing. I don't know and I don't judge. But that's not why I've asked to see you alone, Joe.' Bobby leaned forward, earnestly clasping his hands together.

Joe thought what a cruel man Bobby had been all his life. He had thrust his daughters out, driven his son into exile and alienated his present wife to the extent where it was rumoured she had asked for a divorce. Certainly Aileen and Bobby were hardly ever seen together these days. Joe leaned forward to hear what Bobby had to say.

'I want you to find David,' Bobby said, with a catch in his voice. 'I'm not a happy man, Joe, I needn't pretend that I am. My children don't love me, my wife always has things to do on her own and, in a way, I am a lonely man.' Bobby held up a hand. 'I don't want you to feel sorry for me, please don't think that. Some people, I know, think I deserve what has happened to me. Like the rich man in the Bible, I have everything in the world but happiness. But I want to find David. I want to know where he is and how he is. The last thing I heard was that he was in the Bahamas or maybe South America. He has stopped collecting his allowance, which makes me feel he is dead. I will pay all your expenses, wherever you travel, if you will find him for me.'

'And what do I do if I find him, Bobby?' Joe was puzzled.

'Just tell him I'd like to see him; that I love him; that I'd like him to come home. Tell him I feel I'm getting old. I'm sixty next year. Tell him I'd like to see him at my sixtieth birthday party. That it would make me the happiest man in the world.'

Joe saw, to his amazement, that Bobby had tears in his eyes. He could never remember seeing any expression of softness or compassion on his cousin's face. He didn't know him very well and it was true that Bobby was a lot older than he was. But Bobby was known as a hard man without any weaknesses.

Yet because Bobby was family, Melanie's son, and Melanie had been loved by everyone despite her selfishness, the family continued to gather round Bobby, to treat him as one of them. In many ways Bobby was the head of the family – the oldest, richest male, also a grandson of the tenth Earl.

But Joe was intrigued by Bobby's request. He could also do with the money to help pay his fare and expenses but, unlike Bobby, money didn't come first with Joe. He had had a lot of misery of his own in recent months; he had known shame, humiliation and despair, and here he saw in Bobby, his cousin, a fellow, suffering human being. Joe reached out his hand and Bobby shook it.

'I will do all I can, Bobby. Let me have all the details you can.'

'You're a good man,' Bobby said, his voice tremulous. 'Good luck.' And then he turned sharply away to hide from Joe the tears in his eyes. Joe quietly got up and left the room.

Princess Irina clapped her hands with pleasure. Her face was alight with joy.

'See how happy they are?' she said to Rachel, 'how well Stefanie is.'

'She looks very well,' Rachel nodded her head. They were in the large drawing-room, out of the cold and rain which beat upon the windows. In a far corner all the children were playing together and at their centre were Stefanie, Flora, and Paul's girlfriend Laura. Sasha, smiling with pleasure, watched from the periphery.

Flora seemed absolutely obsessed with Ruth's daughter Joan, as though she were her own. Joan, in her babyish way, seemed very fond of Flora, who had brought her up almost as much as her mother. It was odd to see bookish, serious Flora so dotty over a small child; but it did seem to bring out the best in her and ever since they'd come she'd been relaxed and happy. The family, naturally, commented on the phenomenon but there didn't seem a lot they could say, or do. Flora was Flora, after all; always had been a law unto herself.

Sasha, Stefanie and the children had travelled down for Easter mainly to see Irina, who missed them. Irina kept on making threats that she wouldn't live long – rather as Queen Victoria had done during her long life – and, gradually, the family was beginning to realize that this was a way of gettng them to come and see her more often than they might otherwise have. She was lonely in that big house with only servants for company.

All the family wanted to present a front of solidarity to welcome Joe and also to say goodbye to him. Pascal hadn't wanted him to leave the country, but Joe genuinely wanted to get away and his brother understood him. In many ways it had been a tense, emotional weekend, with all sorts of undercurrents, and Charlotte close to breaking down because Joe was leaving.

'How do you like Laura?' Rachel nodded her head in the direction of the young woman surrounded by children, although Jeremy and Jonathan were getting a little old to be lumped together with the others in the category of 'childish'. They preferred their own secret games.

'Is it serious with Paul?' Irina's eyes shone with mischief.

'Oh, no! He's *much* too young.'

'He's twenty-three,' Irina said. 'I was very well married at the age of twenty-three.' She sighed and her plump white hands fluttered in her lap. 'Of course, those were the old days.'

Rachel knew that yet another account of St Petersburg, or maybe Yalta, in the days of the Tsar was in the offing, so she hurried on.

'Laura's only a student. She's not yet twenty-one. I don't think her parents would be very pleased.'

'I don't see why not. They should be very *happy*. Paul is not only the Earl of Askham but a young man with prospects. He tells me he might go in with Sasha and Pascal.'

'*Might*,' Rachel made a face. 'None of us is very happy about it.'

Irina looked at her sharply. 'By "none of us" I suppose you mean the family, Rachel?'

'Of course.' Rachel looked at her in surprise. 'Who else? You sound rather disapproving, Irina.'

'I'm not disapproving in the least, Rachel dear.' Irina put a podgy hand on her arm. 'But I do think the family disapproves too much, interferes too much in the lives of its members. If you'd let the young alone . . .'

Rachel turned her gaze to Pascal who, happy in his wheelchair, was showing Nicky Ferov how to make a complicated model with his Meccano. Nicky loved Pascal, who seemed to understand the needs of his rather introverted nature. He had endless patience with him and detected in his young cousin the kind of inventive genius that he himself had had, although not perhaps at such a young age. Nicky showed great aptitude for science and mathematics, and had quickly risen to the top of his form at the new school, where he flourished.

'*If* we let them alone look what happens,' Rachel said softly. 'Pascal's accident is what happens.'

'But you can't control people, Rachel. I'm surprised that you, of all people, don't realize that! Sasha and Pascal will do what they will do. And Paul, too.'

'But they have no money and he has no money. They

live in a rented house near the noisy main line to London. It sounds horrible to me.'

'They seem very happy with it,' Irina said contentedly. 'I have never seen my two grandchildren so happy with each other. Think of what Stefanie was a few years ago. The change is incredible. She is loved and in love; she is fulfilled. What does it matter where they live or what they do? You should know that, Rachel, having suffered what you have.'

Rachel returned the pressure of Irina's hand. 'How very wise you are, dearest Irina. I think even at the age of eighty I have a lot to learn.'

'One always learns,' Irina said, with that air of contentment she habitually wore these days as though life had finally rewarded her for what she had endured down the years. 'I shall soon be dead, you know, and then you will have no one to advise you.'

'Nonsense,' Rachel said, 'you'll live forever.'

Laura was amazed and enchanted by Paul's family, rather daunted by the revelation that he was a lord.

'You *could* have told me,' she said. 'It's nothing to be ashamed of.'

'I think it is in this day and age.' The sun had come out and they were walking round the grounds before dinner. 'I wish there were some way of giving up a title. Anyway, I never use it.'

Laura looked at him curiously, not yet sure whether or not she was in love. They had met the previous September when Paul was dating a girl who was a friend of hers. One look at Laura and his former girlfriend had cause to regret she'd ever introduced them.

'Why not?'

'We have no money, no land, a great house that is falling to the ground. Why be an earl?'

'You have a great tradition. Your grandmother is very proud of it. She was telling me all about your grandfather and Omdurman. Doesn't it seem an eternity ago?'

'It does.' Paul sighed. 'It is.'

They were strolling through the tall forest that ran along the banks of the Thames and he had an arm round her because it was chilly.

It had not taken Paul very long to realize that Laura Cohen was the girl for him. Not the girl he had always been looking for because, in his mind, he had thought it would be years before he settled down. Yet here she was, a glorious girl, not only pretty but strong, sturdy and independent. She was clever yet thoughtful; compassionate yet full of fun. They even shared their thoughts. They had not yet shared a bed.

Paul was intimidated by Laura's family, rather than the other way around. They had a large white house in Prestbury, a fashionable village in Cheshire, and Leo Cohen had business interests of all kinds. He was a cultured and very wealthy man. Her parents were courteous towards Paul, but had not hidden their concern that their daughter should be going out, apparently seriously, with a goy. The fact that his mother was Jewish should have made him Jewish and gave him a claim to Jewishness, except that he had never been circumcised and had been baptized into the English Established Church.

When Paul and Laura came to the river they stood for a long time gazing at the muddy waters rushing by. Paul's arm tightened on Laura.

'Shall we live together?' he said.

For a long time Laura didn't reply, the she looked at him speculatively.

'Do you mean literally, or in the Biblical sense?'

'Both,' Paul replied. 'I know I should propose but I can't. I can't face marriage yet. I can't offer you anything;

your father would give me the boot. But I do love you and I want to commit myself to you. If you'll take me like this.'

Laura slipped her hand into his. That wet Easter day would remain a long time in their memories.

Paul had never been casual about girls or sex and was almost as inexperienced as Laura. She had a slim white body, small breasts and rather large russet nipples; he'd known all along what she would look like, but not what she would feel like. It had been impossible to imagine the rapture of this.

Because they'd been unprepared for lovemaking that night they had to take precautions that prevented, in his mind, the fullness of his expression of love. Its completeness. He finished outside her, emptying himself on her soft, round belly. For a long time afterwards they lay together replete and satisfied, each aware of the importance of the moment.

'You will have to get yourself fitted with something,' Paul said after a while. 'I think this is going to go on for a long time.'

'Incurable romantic.' Laura sighed. 'Is this the new language of love? If so, can I change my mind?'

'It's because I love you that I want you to be safe,' Paul protested, angry until he saw her face, 'and that when we have a baby it is because we want it. I don't want to do anything that would hurt you, because now I'm your man.'

And he put his arms protectively round her, laid his head on her breast and listened to the steady sound of her heart.

'They're a very attractive couple,' Charlotte said the following morning and Joe leaned out of the window to see what his mother saw in the garden below. Quickly she pulled him back.

'Don't let them see you!'

'Why not, Mother?'

'I think they're going to kiss,' Charlotte looked embarrassed. 'I didn't realize it was *that* serious.'

'I think you can kiss without making a firm intention to marry.' Joe began to laugh then abruptly he stopped. 'Sorry, Mother.'

'Sorry what?' Charlotte put a hand on his shoulder. She'd been helping him pack and they'd spent the morning in his room sorting through the things he'd brought up with him. Some he'd take and some he'd leave.

'Sorry that I can never give you a daughter-in-law . . .'

'Oh, Joe,' Charlotte took her hand away. 'In time, who knows?'

Joe looked grave. 'It won't change, Mother. I know it won't. It's a thing that you feel and you know.'

'I wish you'd told me before. Maybe . . .'

'Maybe . . .' Joe raised his eyebrows in enquiry but Charlotte shook her head. 'Maybe you'd have been able to do something about it. Is that what you were going to say, Mother?'

'Maybe,' Charlotte turned away. 'It's just that I'm unhappy for you, Joe.'

'But there's no need to be, Mother. I am what I am. I'm not a perverter of young boys.'

'But have you ever had . . . relationships, that kind of thing?'

'Of course, and I will. But I shan't go to court again, don't worry. I'm just sorry that I have hurt you, because I love you. You've been absolutely marvellous and I wish I *had* told you and spared you the shock. Now with Pascal . . .'

'I have grandchildren.' Charlotte began once again to

588

feel emotional. 'It isn't *that*! It's to do with happiness and fulfilment and I can't see how you can have that with another man.'

'That's because you've been conditioned to think like that, Mother. You can't imagine it. But people, men and women, can and do have happy relationships with people of the same sex and have for centuries. I think in future years fewer and fewer people will be ashamed of it and want to hide it. I think a change is on the way.' Joe put a hand on her arm again. 'I'm sorry, Mother, because you have had so much to make you sad. Pascal's accident and then me.'

'Angelica's going to divorce Dick.' Charlotte's voice sounded very hollow.

'Has she said so?' Joe looked shocked.

'No, but I know she will. She's spending this holiday with Perry Eckburgh. He is much more her type.'

'But he's terribly old, Mother.'

'There, you're being prejudiced, too,' Charlotte gave a wan smile. 'Perry is six years older than I am.'

Charlotte turned away and examined her face in the mirror of his dressing table. In times of stress she always had to look at herself as if to seek reassurance, no matter who was around or even if no one was. She wanted to look good even to herself.

'You see, darling, we *all* have our little hangups.' She went on addressing him through the mirror. 'People should be the right age, the right sex and you and Angelica are showing me it isn't necessarily so. Pascal is showing me that he can cope with disability and make a new life. I wish I could help him with the money question. Arthur can't get a bean from anyone in the City. At least that's what he says.'

'But why should he lie?'

'I never know about Arthur.' Charlotte ran a finger

589

along the dressing-table as if examining it for dust. 'We no longer have a lot to say to each other. If he *says* that people don't want to invest I must assume he's right.'

Joe sat on the edge of the bed and lit a cigarette. His cases were all packed and lying on top. Now he felt he wanted to be off; but he also felt guilty. Here he was, making a new life, while that of his mother sometimes seemed to be in ruins. She made a brave pretence but he knew she wasn't happy. With Pascal away in the north, himself about to leave and Angelica probably in Scotland if she married Perry, she would be on her own except for Jeremy and he was still too young to give her the support she needed.

'I could have left Arthur, you know.' Charlotte leaned over and took a cigarette from Joe, which he lit. Then she sat in a chair by the window facing him. 'It was the year after I married him and Jeremy had just been born. Do you remember Gran and I went to the South of France?'

'Yes, I do.' Joe looked at her keenly.

'Well, I met a man I'd known in the war, before I married Arthur but, of course, I was engaged to him. I'd loved this man very much. He was my boss in the war and his name was Marc.'

'I remember Marc. He used to come to Darley.'

'Of course you do!' Charlotte flushed slightly. 'I keep on forgetting you were old enough to know these things. Well, Marc and I were lovers and when we met again we resumed our affair. He wanted us to get married but I felt I couldn't leave Arthur. He was so good.' Charlotte paused and her eyes looked troubled. 'There was another reason, too. Marc had been responsible for shooting poor old Prince Alexei. He thought he had betrayed Hélène and me to the Boche. Of course he hadn't; but that was at the end of the war and there was a state of near anarchy in Paris. I felt I couldn't marry Marc after that, but also I knew I couldn't hurt Arthur.'

'And yet look what Arthur did to *you*.'

'Quite.' Charlotte reached for his hand. 'Joe, you are the only one who knows that and, apart from Gran, the only one who knows about Marc and me after the war. But I do sometimes wonder what would have happened if I hadn't been so noble and stuck to Arthur.'

'We shall never know that, shall we?'

Joe put his arm round his mother and kissed her. He knew that she spoke from despair and love and regret, and all those emotions that go to make up the human condition and render it so complex.

'If ever you need me I'll come back at once,' he said.

'Please don't say that,' Charlotte begged. 'You make it sound as though you're going to leave forever.'

It was still raining as Pascal looked out of the window to the swift-flowing waters of the river. It seemed to have been raining for weeks. It was a tearful, dismal sort of day. Trust Anna to choose a day like that on which to tell him.

'I always said you could go,' he said, after a while. 'I said I'd never keep you against your will. I haven't the right to expect it.'

'But it still wasn't easy,' Anna said from behind his chair. She stubbed out her cigarette, pressing it hard into the ashtray.

'Not easy for you, not easy for me.' Pascal turned his chair round so that he had his back on the melancholy scene outside, the lowering clouds and the swollen river. 'If only you weren't going back to *him*, were just fed up, it wouldn't seem so bad.'

'Because I'll be happy, you mean?'

'I suppose so,' Pascal nodded his head. 'It's easy to say

that, but I suppose I don't really want you to be happy. Yet I can't keep you, Anna. I wouldn't want to.'

'I'm very ashamed,' Anna hung her head, 'believe me, I am ashamed. I don't think I'll ever stop feeling guilty about leaving you.'

'There's no need for that,' Pascal said stiffly, 'and you were right to tell me.'

'Stefanie and Sasha would love to have you . . .'

'I see you've got it all planned.'

'Don't be horrible. I had to give it a lot of thought.'

Anna looked round the room which she had not shared with Pascal. They had slept separately for a long time. There wasn't much point. There was always so much to be done wherever he went, so many appendages and bits of equipment. That was one thing she would not be sorry to say goodbye to, one other thing. She was tired of pretence, of a marriage that was over, and now she had an enormous feeling of relief. But she felt guilty, too; guilty because a life was beginning for her, yet ending for Pascal.

She got up and straightened her skirt, already excited because by tomorrow she would be with Gunther. Already she had said goodbye to her life in England with Pascal and now she was saying goodbye to him, but no one else. Tonight a new beginning would be made.

'I wanted to tell you while the family was here to give you support.'

'It's a wonder you didn't announce it at dinner, as Bobby does when he has something awful to say like making a thousand people redundant or chopping off the allowance to his family.' For the first time Pascal let the bitterness show.

'You're making it very hard for me, Pascal.' Anna knew she couldn't keep this detachment and *sang-froid* up for very much longer. She would break. 'I wanted to tell you while Sasha and Stefanie were here, too, because they love you. Your mother and grandmother are here. You are surrounded by love, Pascal, and, in a way, I will always love you, too.'

'And I will always love you,' Pascal said, his voice soft. 'I will love you and hate you at the same time, Anna; but I will never reproach you for what you've done because I'm only half a man. I have no right . . .'

Anna quickly went over to him as he was speaking and kissed him on the forehead. Then, taking up her bag, she ran out of the room before he had time to turn his chair round and see what she was doing. She was taking advantage of a helpless man; but it would be for the last time.

Five minutes later she was in her car speeding along the road towards London, having left Pascal, and the family, and all that old, hateful life of hers behind.

CHAPTER 23

The Neri 'Sprite', high above the heads of the people standing on the ground, looped the loop, somersaulted and then, dipping its wings in a final salute, flew off across the flat Cheshire plain, its silver body gleaming like a meteor in the sunshine. It was slim, light and elegant. It was powered by twin jet engines, had a retractable undercarriage and was economical on fuel. It was quite revolutionary for its time and could fly at 200 mph. The group that had been watching it broke into spontaneous applause and Pascal reached out for Stefanie, who fell into his arms, kissing him on both cheeks.

'It's a terrific success,' Pascal said. 'It will outdo the "Dove".'

'It will easily outdo the "Dove" on my calculations.' Henry Neri, John's mechanic brother, still had his overalls on, despite the distinguished company present, and indeed the general atmosphere, now that the tension of the test was over, was of relaxed good humour.

The walked towards the hangar where the 'Sprite' had been housed until its crucial test in front of prospective backers and buyers, and where now a long table had been laid for a buffet lunch.

'I thought it was very exciting,' Laura ran to catch up with Pascal. 'I can't imagine that you designed it all by yourself.'

'With a little help from my friends,' Pascal gave her a cheeky grin, 'and a great quantity of alcohol.' What he didn't add was how difficult it had been to carry on with a crucial stage in the development of the first prototype of the 'Sprite' while in the process of being unwillingly divorced and having to rearrange his life. But now, a year after Anna had left him, life was taking off again, like his plane, the 'Sprite', conceived and designed by himself.

Pascal had never been one to allow himself to linger in the doldrums for long. All his life he had been the cheerier of the twins, the most well-balanced of the three children of Charlotte and Paolo Verdi. It didn't surprise those who knew him that he had emerged so quickly, not only from the trauma of his terrible injury, but also from the inevitable pain of his divorce. He had loved Anna and he had lost her to a man, he suspected, she had remained in love with for years. Willingly she had sped into the arms of Gunther von Spee. Pascal had gone to live with Sasha and Stefanie and, from that moment, had thrown himself into developing the prototype which was essential if they were to arrange adequate finances to go into full-scale production.

Outside the hangar the specially invited group stood to watch Sasha bring the 'Sprite' into a perfect landing and then taxiing to stop a few feet away. Stefanie waited with Galina and Nicky for the door of the plane to open and, as Sasha opened the side door and stepped on to the small platform that had been wheeled into position, the two children rushed up to him to be greeted with hugs.

Stefanie hugged him, too. 'It's a great success. Every-one was most impressed.'

'We can easily average two hundred miles an hour,' he said over his shoulder to John Neri, who had flown with him to check the readings.

Sasha and John were fêted all the way into the hangar and together they popped the first cork of champagne in celebration as Pascal, who had loved speed all his life, looked on with satisfaction tinged, perhaps, with a little envy. But this, if it were there, he kept to himself.

'I won't fizz it all around like a racing driver,' Sasha said, pointing the bottle humorously towards the crowd. 'But thanks, everyone, for being here. We had a marvellous ride and it is a terrific plane.' There was more enthusiastic applause but he held up his hand. 'I pay tribute to Pascal Verdi, whose idea it was not only to incorporate jet engines in such a small plane but who did the basic design. I know how hard Pascal had to work because he had to make quite a fresh approach to the problems of aircraft design and from a very simple premise – the need for light, fast, executive transport – I think he has designed a winner.'

There was more applause and everyone turned to a smiling Pascal, but then Sasha called for attention again.

'I also want to thank John and Henry Neri for letting us work for them, join their firm and pinch all their ideas. John and Henry are the real aircraft engineers in all this. They worked with de Havillands, the first in the field of jet propulsion, and John was one of the first to fly in the Comet. Without their knowledge and experience we would have got nowhere.' Sasha pointed to the many white-overalled men standing around the hangar, all of whom had known occasional weeks without a pay packet. 'I also want to thank our splendid team; everyone here is an expert of one sort or another and they have put in countless hours, free, to make this plane the success I hope it will become.'

There was more applause and, as champagne corks began to pop all round, Sasha and John Neri were approached by a number of men in business suits who began to engage them in conversation.

Leo Cohen was not one of these men. He stayed with his daughter and Paul, hands in the pockets of his well-cut suit, looking around him with a detached interest.

'Do you know anything about aeroplanes?' he asked

Paul who was also, for a change, in a suit with white shirt and tie.

'Not a thing,' Paul said. 'But I know nothing about parts for television, either. I believe, however, I can make a good job on a balance sheet if I see one.'

'And do you like what you see on the balance sheet of Neri Aerospace?'

Paul appeared to consider the question. He was an honest man and he knew that Leo's interest was crucial to the success of the operation, which was why he'd been invited. Through Leo, Sasha and Pascal hoped to raise enough money to carry on.

'I like what I see very much.' Paul looked Laura's father squarely in the eye. 'Otherwise I wouldn't be here. Its problems are cash flow, not talent.'

'Oh, I can see there's plenty of that,' Leo's eyes alighted on Pascal, talking to a tall elegant woman in a picture hat.

'Who's that talking to Pascal?'

'His mother,' Paul said, glancing round. 'Have you not met my aunt, Lady Charlotte?'

'I would like that pleasure,' Leo said, and Paul took him over to introduce them. First he excused himself to Pascal and then he said:

'Aunt Charlotte, may I introduce Leo Cohen, Laura's father?'

'How do you do?' Charlotte said as they shook hands, inclining her head and smiling her famous smile. She knew who Leo was, and how important. She had on a blue polka-dotted dress with a large white bow at the throat, white court shoes and a wide-brimmed navy blue straw hat with a slim white band.

'I find it very difficult to believe you're the mother of this large chap,' Leo bowed to her as they shook hands.

'How flattering of you, Mr Cohen.' Charlotte graciously

acknowledged the compliment. 'I assume you mean – I hope you mean – that I look too young.'

'Much too young,' Leo said. He was a man of medium height with iron-grey hair and was not without charm himself; the kind of cultured, clever, cosmopolitan man that appealed to Charlotte.

'I'm a grandmother, too,' Charlotte said, as if with pride.

'I find that even more difficult to believe.' Leo leaned towards the table by which they were standing and gave Charlotte a plate. 'May I give you some smoked salmon, Lady Charlotte?'

'You may,' Charlotte said, continuing to smile.

'It's very good. I own the company that imports it . . . from Scotland, of course.'

'And what else do you do . . .'

A few feet away Stefanie smiled with approval and nodded at Pascal.

'They're getting on very well.'

'You can trust my mother to make a conquest,' Pascal grunted. 'I hope she doesn't feel she has to go to bed with him to get our money.'

'Pascal!' Stefanie looked shocked, but Pascal was unrepentant.

'It's true. That's how they do things in business but, believe me, I wouldn't expect it of my mother, not even for money to develop the "Sprite".'

Money, indeed, was very hard to find. Despite the success of the public trials – rehearsed for weeks beforehand in private – and the lavish party that followed, there were no backers. There was a lot of praise, all of it genuine, and many compliments, but no one reinforced these with offers of hard cash.

Leo Cohen was quite adamant about not investing in

aeroplanes. He would like to have helped the Askhams because he was not disinterested in the family to whom his daughter might possibly one day be allied. He approved of her interest in Paul but because he thought he was a nice young man, with sound business sense, not because he was a lord. To Leo money and business acumen were of far more importance than a hereditary peerage, and also of more substance when it came to a possible lifetime support for his daughter.

He had fingers in a great number of pies, but so that there should be no misunderstanding he said immediately that he wasn't attracted by the risk of putting up a large sum of money to support the commercial aircraft industry. He believed that that was a matter for the government. Despite their popularity it was rumoured that de Havilland had no successor planned for the 'Dove' and 'Heron' or the Gipsy Six engine which had made these small aircraft so successful.

Charlotte had worked hard to woo not only Leo Cohen but other influential businessmen who were there that first day with her charm, because she so badly wanted to help Pascal to establish himself in something he loved as much as he had loved Anna. In future it was unlikely that Pascal's love would be projected towards another woman, but would remain with his talent for invention: creativity in itself. But despite her efforts, the sultry smile, the famous walk, she was unsuccessful. They were impressed; they were interested; they might even buy one for their companies, but they had no money for a venture of this kind.

Even before she was due to return to London Charlotte said they would have to approach Bobby again for funds. She had been staying at the Midland in Manchester because there was very little room at Bridge House, but Sasha had brought her over for a Russian dinner, cooked by Stefanie in her honour. Paul and Laura were also there, as well as Leo and Adèle Cohen, who was a woman almost as elegant as Charlotte and about the same age, with a tall, willowy figure and blond hair. What was more, she had been a mannequin for Captain Molyneux in London just before the War and they discovered a lot in common.

'I wouldn't ask Bobby again if you bound me hand and foot and threw me into the sea,' Sasha said firmly. 'He is out.'

'Who is Bobby?' Leo asked politely.

'Bobby is Stefanie's father,' Sasha said, after a brief pause, as though Bobby's connection with the family were somehow taboo. 'Lord Lighterman.'

'Really?' Casually Leo reached for his wine, looking interested. 'Lord Lighterman is your father? No one told me that.'

'There is no reason why anyone should tell you, Daddy.' The Askham connections were something of an embarrassment to Laura and Paul.

'You might have mentioned it,' Leo said to his daughter. 'I would like to meet Lord Lighterman.'

'Maybe some day you will,' Pascal's reply was short. He was a bit irritated by the way Leo had played cat and mouse with them; or had he genuinely wanted to try and help because Laura was anxious, on Paul's behalf, to come to the aid of the family?

'My father and I don't get on,' Stefanie said abruptly. 'To be quite frank, you are unlikely to meet him through me.'

Leo looked with bewilderment from Sasha to Stefanie. 'But I thought Lord Lighterman was a millionaire many times over? Wouldn't investing in the "Sprite" be chicken feed to him?'

'Like you, he doesn't want to throw his money away,' Paul said. 'He says he knows nothing about planes.'

'He burnt his hands with cars. We offended him over the question of the racing car,' Pascal indicated his wheelchair. 'He had asked me not to develop one and I did. My father was a racing driver.'

'Oh, I see, there *are* complications.' Leo looked anxiously at his wife. 'I'm sorry I mentioned it.'

The dinner-party had made Leo Cohen uncomfortable. He realized he was expected to offer to invest but he didn't want to. He was a good businessman and he knew where his strengths and weaknesses lay. The companies he had taken an interest in had always been connected with products he not only knew something about, but which made a good and sure return on investment: food and the catering industry, the wholesale fashion business, which was how he had met his wife. Recently he had started to diversify into toolmaking and small engineering concerns. Leo would have been quite willing to help Paul buy the small factory for manufacturing television parts he had just acquired, which only required a tiny amount of capital; but Paul hadn't wanted his money. He had done his sums very carefully, projected capital requirements and cash flow and borrowed what he needed from the banks. He didn't want to be beholden to a possible father-in-law.

The subject was quickly changed and food proved a popular choice because of Leo Cohen's connections with the catering industry, and the Askhams' gourmet tendencies. They spoke, too, of Russia: the Cohens had come from Lithuania in the nineteenth century, driven out by the pogroms, and had first of all made their money in the rag trade. Leo Cohen's father had known the father of Simon Marks, of chain store fame, who had started the penny bazaar with Spencer. They had all been young men together in Manchester. The meal contained Russian specialities, some of which were hard to come by, but most of which were made by Stefanie from old recipe books of her mother.

The *zakuski* were easy as hors d'oeuvres because they could be made from many little delicacies – salted herring, smoked salmon, pickled beetroot, cucumber, Danish caviar – all washed down in Russian fashion with vodka. *Rassolnyk* was a soup made of kidneys, which had been a favourite in Parisian days at the Ferov household because even in the war offal was usually available, and where there was no beef or lamb or pork or chicken to be had there were, for those who knew where to go, the entrails of animals not favoured by the Germans, so to be bought at a price. The greatest speciality was *pelmeni*, flat pastry filled with mixed minced meats – pork, beef and lamb – made into tiny fancy shapes and boiled in water. This was particularly unusual and delicious. It took a long time to prepare and was usually eaten alone, but today Stefanie served it with boiled rice and salad.

To finish there was *halva*, too sickly sweet for a northern English couple like the Cohens, but more acceptable were the *vareniye*, varieties of jams which were taken from their little pots with a spoon and put directly into the mouth to sweeten the black Russian tea.

It was quite late when they finished and Leo offered to give Charlotte a lift back to Manchester. 'When are you leaving, Lady Charlotte?'

'Quite early in the morning,' Charlotte said.

'My wife and I hoped you would come and have dinner with us.'

'I'd love to on another occasion. But I have to be back for a committee meeting tomorrow afternoon. Since Pascal had his accident I have become interested in the problems of people with such injuries. This country is very behind America in recognizing that such problems exist. I also have urgently to see my husband, who is in the City. Stefanie wants to try and sell some Lighterman shares. I think we feel now that this is a family matter and we have talked about it a great deal this week. I do see the reason why you, and people like you, can't help. Unfortunately the Askham family long ago lost its money, but Lord Lighterman . . .'

'Stefanie has some Lighterman shares?' Leo's hooded eyes immediately lit up with interest. 'How many?'

'I own about five per cent of the company,' Stefanie replied. 'My sisters and I were each given five per cent of the company when we became twenty-five.'

'How many sisters have you got?' Leo sounded excited.

'Two.'

'Then, between you, you own fifteen per cent of Lighterman Limited?'

'About that.' Stefanie began to look mystified. 'Perhaps a little more.'

'But you must be a millionairess several times over. The shares are worth about four or five pounds each on the Stock Market, if you can get them.'

'We've always regarded them as a nest egg against a possible rainy day, Mr Cohen,' Stefanie said slowly. 'I have had quite a lot of hardship in my life and so has Sasha. We would never have considered cashing the shares but for this emergency. But the company is Sasha's career and our livelihood. We feel now is the rainy day we were preparing for.'

'Only a small portion of the company was for sale when Bobby went public,' Paul intervened. 'He was very careful to keep control in the family.'

'Do *you* have shares, too?'

'A few,' Paul said. 'A lot were given to my family when Bobby bought out our own family interests at the end of

603

the twenties. We've had to sell some since to pay off debts – mostly back to Bobby. I assure you I'm not a millionaire and they are security with my bank for my own business.'

'I see. I see.' Leo sat back, apparently abandoning all plans to leave, despite the lateness of the hour. He sat for a while tapping his hand on the arm of the chair, while everyone looked at him expectantly. They were not disappointed.

Finally he said, 'This changes the whole complexion of the evening. I realize that you have wanted me to invest in Neri Aerospace Ltd and I have told you quite frankly that it was outside my scope of interests. I have been honest with you. As a businessman I am interested in diversification, but I have to be very careful to keep my interests in fields that I am familiar with. I not only know nothing about planes but I consider the funds needed for development on the scale you are thinking about, with jet turbine engines, are colossal. However, I think you might have a solution at hand. It is this . . .' Leo tapped his fingers again on the table and Charlotte, watching him carefully, was reminded of an actor hamming it up for an audience. Nevertheless, she liked him.

'I am not interested in aeroplanes but I am interested in obtaining a slice of Lighterman Limited. Lighterman shares are very hard to come by, just because there are so few on the market; but if you sold me your five per cent and persuaded your sisters to sell me theirs I could make you very wealthy young women. You could then do what you liked with the money.' Leo sat back with a broad smile: 'Invest in aeroplanes, for all I care.'

In so far as Bobby was fond of any of the family, he was fond of Rachel. He had known her all his life and, on the whole, they had always got on. Rachel seemed to have more time for Bobby's foibles and weaknesses than

604

others; she understood him better. She was the only person alive, since his mother died, who had known his father. This fact seemed to give him a bond with Rachel. He was about as close to her as it was possible for Bobby to be.

Bobby regarded Stefanie's behaviour as a personal tragedy that far eclipsed any considerations of mere business. She had sold out, in defiance of his express instructions, to someone who was not a member of the family. She had thrown away her inheritance to support a project he knew was doomed to failure and betrayed him in the process.

'Betrayed,' Bobby said again. 'There is no other word.'

'She only wanted to do it to help Sasha.'

'She had no right to do it.' Bobby's voice was shaking. 'She was supposed to offer them to members of the family first. It was expected.'

'It was not a condition.' Hugo was trying to be helpful. He found it hard to sympathize with Bobby, because he knew what Bobby could be like.

'Why should *I* make it a condition for my own daughter? Did you suppose that, ever in my life, I imagined she would betray her own father?'

'Bobby, it is *not* betrayal,' Rachel said, as gently as she could. 'I do agree with Hugo. Maybe you should have put up the money in the first place.'

'*That* was blackmail.' Bobby began trembling again as he had been at the beginning of the evening, like a man in a delirium. Jenny, glancing anxiously at Rachel, started to clear the plates of the main course. Rachel had been dining at the Hall, as she frequently did, when Bobby had precipitously arrived on the doorstep, having failed to find her at the Grange. He had outlined the whole business before dinner: how Stefanie had sold her shares to Laura's father, how Natasha had been persuaded to as well and how he was only just in time to prevent Olga doing the same thing by offering to buy them himself at a much inflated price.

'My daughters,' he had cried, rather like King Lear, wringing his hands. 'What have I done to my daughters that they could do this to me?'

Rachel had believed then, and she did now, that Bobby really had no idea what he had done to deserve his daughters giving a stranger the chance to buy almost twenty per cent of his cherished company. Knowing what it meant to Bobby, they must have known what it would do to him. Even Arthur had connived at the sale, having no real idea of the consequences of such a transaction. Rachel supposed that when, many years ago, he drew up the details of their inheritance Bobby had imagined that they would all remain close; though this seemed short-sighted, an act of blindness that was peculiar even for Bobby.

Nimet had listened to the story with interest. She had seemed to sympathize with Bobby and he found himself frequently addressing her. Nimet had that quality of making men feel important; she didn't have quite the same effect on women. Men were flattered by the way Nimet appeared to give them her wholehearted attention, and many a damaged or bruised male ego was reinflated on account of Nimet's apparent sympathy and concern.

Nimet considered that Stefanie was not only very ungrateful but foolish. She had nothing left on which she could fall back. This, to someone like Nimet, who had lost most of her own substantial fortune, was an act of folly that eclipsed mere betrayal of a father or his love.

'This is the end of my daughters,' Bobby continued, after Jenny had served the sweet. 'It is the end of Stefanie and Natasha. They have got their revenge on me . . .'

Rachel leaned forward to plead with him, but she could

tell by the set of his jaw that his mind was made up. She remembered when Bobby had cast out Hélène – and she had been literally cast out from his home like the woman in the Bible taken in adultery – no one would believe he could be so hard. Even his mother had pleaded with him to change his mind for the sake of his daughters, and Susan hadn't spoken to him again until after the War.

But nothing that family or friends could say made any difference; once Bobby had made up his mind he was implacable.

'Bobby, it's not revenge . . .' Rachel insisted. 'Stefanie needed that money. It has now all gone into the company, every penny. It was either that or annihilation.'

'It's annihilation, anyway,' Bobby said, regaining his composure. 'I have no interest now in what happens to Stefanie. She can be a pauper and, believe me, she will. Sasha and Pascal have no idea of business. Neither has that fool Mr Neri, with whom they have cast their lot. One day, sooner if not later, the business will fail as the last one did. If I know about anything I know about business and I can forecast that. Sasha and Stefanie will one day be paupers. Believe me, when that day comes, I shan't lift a finger to help them. As for Natasha,' Bobby shrugged, 'she is unmarried, she has money of her own. I believe she is making a very good living in Hollywood. Let her fend for herself, too. Olga can count herself lucky I got to her in time, otherwise she and her children would have been out in the cold as well.'

'What I have against that man most of all is that he's a Jew,' Nimet said coldly. 'They always have their greedy fingers in every pie.'

As Hugo froze Rachel looked anxiously at Bobby; but Bobby didn't seem quite as shocked as everyone else.

'I have nothing against Jews,' he said. 'They are very good businessmen. I have no objection to Cohen being a

607

Jew. And this time, indeed, he has made a very shrewd move.' Bobby smiled for the first time that evening and leaned across the table. 'Why, I have even done business with Turks, Nimet. Your husband was a *very* good businessman.'

Nimet gave a modest smile as though the compliment had been intended for herself and was about to say something when Hugo interrupted her.

'Excuse me, Mother, but I do take objection to your first remark.'

'But why should it offend you?' Nimet's large kohl-ringed eyes gazed at him in surprise. 'There is *no* Jewish blood in you, thank heaven.'

Hugo rose and flung his napkin on the table.

'There you go again, Mother, deliberately offensive! Have you forgotten Hitler? Can't you remember the holocaust?'

'People say that was greatly exaggerated.' Nimet put her elbow on the table and cupped her chin in her hand. 'Some wonder if it happened at all. I must say I am inclined to agree with them.'

'Mother, Em and Charlotte *saw* the evidence with their own eyes!' Hugo shouted. 'What has got into you?'

'Don't misunderstand me, Hugo, *I* am not the least bit anti-Semitic,' Nimet said, raising her voice. 'We Middle Easterners are all spiritually Semites, you know. But, please, don't expect me to support the Jews after what they have done to Palestine, robbed a people of its nation. Please, please don't expect me to *like* them.'

'I'm quite horrified with you, Mother . . .' Hugo began, but Nimet stopped him with a sharp display of temper of her own.

'*Are* you, my dear? Are you *really* horrified with me? And on what grounds? Did I not give you half of my entire fortune? What Jew would have done that? Even

Bobby, who is a generous man, only gave his daughters twenty per cent of his company and there were three of them. You were one and I gave you half. Half! And what have you done with it?' Nimet broke off and threw her expressive hands in the air. Pointedly she looked round the room – at the ceiling, the large damp patch in the corner which had warped the wooden panels. 'You go through all my money, yet what have you to show for it? This?'

There was a rasping noise as Jenny drew back her chair and, standing up, she pointed a finger at her mother-in-law. Rapidly, in Rachel's eyes, the general situation was reaching the level of farce.

'And what have *you* got to show for it, Madame Igolopuscu? You have got through several fortunes and yet and yet . . .'

'Please, Jenny.' Hugo crossed over to his wife in a few swift strides. 'Enough is enough. This isn't the place.'

'Then where *is* the place?' Jenny put a hand on Hugo's. 'When *is* the time? Your mother thinks she can insult you in your own home . . .'

'I never said . . .' Nimet crossed two hands on her bosom in an attitude of supplication and looked round appealingly. 'Why, Jenny . . .'

'Oh, I've had enough of this!' Jenny burst into tears and ran out of the room. Hugo quickly followed her.

During the silence they heard light footsteps rapidly crossing the hall, followed by heavier ones. Then came the sound of raised voices in the distance. Jonathan, who was eating with them, looked as though he didn't know whether he should get up and follow his mother or stay where he was. Rachel, next to him, put an arm round his shoulder.

'Happens in the best families, Johnny darling.'

'Especially this one,' Bobby said, grunting.

'I never heard Mother behave like that before.' Johnny's face was strained. 'Maybe I'd better go . . .'

'The meal's over, anyway.' Rachel consulted her watch. 'Why don't you go and watch TV?'

Bobby leaned back to light his cigar, as if bemused by events. Nimet remained where she was, one elbow on the table, gazing reflectively at the silver. Rachel stared at her for a few minutes then, gently pushing Johnny towards the door and whispering in his ear, went and sat next to her old rival.

Nimet smiled at her vaguely. 'What did I do so wrong, tonight? Do you know, Rachel?'

'Well, you criticized Hugo,' Rachel said gently.

'May not a mother criticize her own son?'

'It wasn't only that.' Rachel felt angry, too, but she had to try and be patient. 'It was the thing about the Jews. We're rather pro-Jewish in this family, you know, Nimet. Paul's mother was Jewish and we all loved her. Paul may marry Laura and his children will be half-Jewish, too. Besides our family were heavily involved in the War, and now that we know what we know about the concentration camps it's tactless, if nothing else, to say what you said.'

'I didn't mean what I said *exactly*.' Nimet glanced nervously at Bobby. 'I'm not fond of the Jews, but only because of what they've done *since* the War. However, I'll be careful what I say in future.' Nimet pursed her lips. 'Jenny is too impulsive. She hates me being here, you know. I see it in her eyes all the time. She's jealous. Also, what have they done about this place? They can't keep it up. It's falling to pieces.'

'I think they're both disappointed.' Rachel's tone was gentle. 'They fought to get this house and now they haven't made as much of it as they hoped.'

Bobby rose and looked at the tip of his cigar.

'Fought to get it from *me*,' he said, with a note of

610

satisfaction in his voice. 'I knew they wouldn't make it and they haven't. You've thrown your money away, Nimet.' Bobby made a gesture as though scattering something to the winds. 'The Askhams can't make money. They've no idea how. Give them a fortune and they'll lose it – just you wait and see what happens in Manchester.' Bobby glanced about him with an air of satisfaction. 'I'll wait for you in the study, Rachel. Then I'll drive you back to the Grange.'

After Bobby had gone Rachel resumed her place opposite Nimet.

'Bobby's quite right,' Nimet said indignantly. 'This could have been a beautiful hotel. Instead, the place has gone to seed. I am quite ashamed when people see it for the first time. Maybe that's why my annoyance showed. Hugo spends all his time in those wretched greenhouses.'

'Where the money is. Competition has got fiercer. Hugo is having a hard time making ends meet. Didn't you realize that, Nimet?'

Rachel's voice hardened as she looked at the still beautiful woman sitting opposite her. Her perfectly made-up face was like a mask, the russet red of her lips like a line drawn in blood. In all the years she had known her, Rachel had never seen a hair out of place on the perfectly coiffured head – black, sleek, artificial, like everything else about her. Rachel felt such a wave of dislike for her erstwhile rival that the violence of her emotion disturbed her. It was ridiculous for two old women still to be locked in enmity because of what had happened over forty years before.

Nimet, meanwhile, had folded her hands on her lap and sat contemplating her perfectly-manicured nails. She sighed heavily. 'I see, now, that Hugo is a failure. I never realized it, you know. Like his father, like his half-brother Ralph, he has gone through a fortune. I can see now that

611

Bobby is right. The Askhams have no sense of the value of money and how wise Bobby was not to invest in the latest venture. Anyone can see *that* is doomed for disaster. As for my daughter-in-law.' Nimet's expressive lips curled. 'She is obviously quite desperate about what is going on here. The place is falling apart. My rooms are damp! Yet the fortune I gave Hugo should have been sufficient . . .'

'Even *he* had no idea what needed to be done to the Hall, what structural repairs.'

'They should pull it all down.' Nimet rose to her feet. 'Or let it fall into ruins – like a tomb to the Askham family. The once great Askham family. I can see, now, that the whole structure, not only of the Hall but the family, is falling apart. Maybe it is symbolical, who knows?' A malicious smile played on her lips. 'Who knows if the fall of the Askhams was ordained in the stars?'

'That sort of talk is nonsense,' Rachel said heatedly. She rose, too, and gazed at Nimet, resolving to avoid such encounters in the future. 'Things certainly change but, you'll see, the Askhams will survive.' She stopped and looked round her as though listening to echoes of long-lost voices. 'And this house will survive, too.'

CHAPTER 24

Bad Soden was a pretty spa town in the Taunus mountains, about ten miles from the heart of Frankfurt. This was an area of luxurious hotels, clinics and the houses of well-off businessmen who had contributed to the recovery of Germany after the war and were now gathering in its fruits. Their houses were elegant, some even opulent, with high walls or leafy hedges protecting them from the gazes of the curious.

Few of the people who came to Bad Soden for a rest, a holiday or one of the cures of its spa waters and baths, would be of the kind who pry into other people's houses and lives. But still, just in case, there were electronic gates and automatic garages and all the paraphernalia of wealthy people with secrets to hide.

Anna often wondered what it was that made Gunther so worried about security. They had started to build the house soon after they were married and almost everything inside it was electronically controlled. The house was just outside the town, half-way along an unmade-up road leading into the gently undulating hills that made the area such a healthy place to holiday in or recuperate from illness. Already when they'd bought their plot of land and started to build they were surrounded by others like them, similarly security-conscious, who built white-walled houses with balconies and beautiful gardens but where everything had a lock, a fence or a roving electronic eye.

In the excitement of marriage to Gunther, the decision to sell the Black Forest house which had belonged to his first wife and was full of memories of her, and to build a new one in the Taunus mountains within easy reach of Frankfurt, Anna had not taken the security aspects of the house too seriously. But, once they had moved in, she began to realize that almost everywhere she went she was followed around by a sightless, roving eye. When she asked Gunther about it he told her it was because he was the head of a vast business, there was the possibility of industrial espionage, kidnappings were always a risk; everyone in post-war Germany was concerned about safety.

Anna thought little of it at the time. It was, in a way, an added protection when Gunther was abroad, which was frequently.

As she knew she would, Anna loved being the Baroness von Spee. She was fêted and courted everywhere she went, and admired, too, because she was one of the new breed of women – someone who worked. She continued to be in charge of the Askham agency on the Continent and remained on reasonably friendly, though distant, terms with her ex-husband. When they were in England, however, she and Gunther were not made to feel welcome by the family so they stayed at Claridges. There were no parties for them, as there had been when Anna came on what was intended to be that brief visit, ten years before.

Anna von Spee was now a poised and mature woman of twenty-nine, married to a leader of the German miracle: its post-war reconstruction. When in London they met Angelica and Perry, who were planning marriage, and they saw Sasha and Stefanie, but the rest of the family were luke-warm and Bobby blamed Anna for what Sasha and Pascal had done in setting up a business for themselves. But, in the first happy months of complete fulfilment, emotional and physical, nothing upset Anna very much.

A confident Chancellor Adenauer presided over

Germany's new rise to greatness. In England the driest, hottest summer of two hundred years seemed a harbinger of prosperity and later that same year, 1959, the Tories obtained a majority of sixty-two in the October elections.

In 1960 the good fortunes of both countries continued. In January Premier Macmillan had gone to Africa and proclaimed that a wind of change was sweeping through the continent, and in March the massacre at Sharpeville in the Cape seemed a confirmation of this prophecy: one day, but not yet, the African masses would rise against their oppressors. In February the Queen had a second son, Prince Andrew, ten years after the birth of her daughter Anne, and a few weeks later her sister, Margaret, became engaged to a photographer. That, too, seemed a sign of the times.

The fifties had been conservative years of growing prosperity and consolidation; yet it had also been the era that had seen the beginning of a new kind of music, rock and roll; and a new kind of people, the Beatnik generation, personified by the poet Jack Kerouac, who said: 'We love everything: Billy Graham, rock and roll, them, apple pie, Eisenhower. We did it all.' The contraceptive pill was radically changing attitudes towards sexuality, particularly that of women.

Anna felt very much a child of her times, a product of the new generation, and one day in the spring of 1960, as she waited in her Mercedes coupé outside the electronic gate for it to open in response to a signal from her car, she felt that she could hardly be happier.

Slowly the gate began to open and the white, modern, two-storeyed house revealed itself in all its shining new splendour, as if waiting to greet her. Anna sat in the driver's seat, her arm on the door of the open car, listening to the radio blaring out the latest pop tunes, when, in her car mirror, she noticed a surreptitious movement in the undergrowth to one side of her and the figure of a man began to crawl stealthily along by the hedge on the far side of the road, unaware that he could be seen.

Anna's immediate thought was that there had, after all, been a reason for all this security and she felt as someone momentarily paralyzed. She was aware of the slowly-opening door, the gleaming house bathed in the sunlight of late afternoon, the short drive stretching before her to the twin garage, her arm on the side of the shiny Mercedes and the latest pop tunes on the car radio. She didn't know whether she should drive in or get out and, as she continued to gaze, mesmerized, at the man creeping along, she saw a metallic gleam and knew he had a gun.

As soon as the gates opened Anna's paralysis vanished and she drove straight through the gates which immediately clicked together behind her. She had to do something similar to open the door of the garage and, once she'd closed that and parked the car, she entered the house through the garage and went straight into the kitchen at the rear where her housekeeper, Eva, was preparing the evening meal.

Eva was a jewel. She was a motherly body of about sixty and had been widowed in the war. Her son was a dockworker in Hamburg, one of the prosperous rising German working-class who backed Adenauer, conservatism and Christian Democracy. Eva was immediately all smiles but her expression changed to one of concern when Anna told her what she had seen.

'There has been no one here, Madame,' Eva answered her. 'Should I call the police?'

'By the time the police come he will have gone. Eva, I am going to go out of the back door and take a look round. Please call my husband and tell him to be careful how he comes home. It may be that someone wants to ambush him.'

'But why should that be, Madame?' Eva was bewildered, also frightened.

'Industrial espionage,' Anna said, briefly. 'The Baron is the head of a company which makes many secret components for various kinds of electronic equipment.'

Anna went straight to her room and swiftly changed into a dark jersey and slacks. She went out of the back door of the house to a gate at the side, which approached the road from an oblique angle. On this side of the house the land had been bought by Gunther to prevent development that would intrude upon their privacy. On the other side they had neighbours who were completely screened from them by a high white wall and overhanging trees which had been planted fully grown. Anna knew nothing about these neighbours and it was possible that the snooper with the gun was after them.

Anna unlocked the gate, which was also secured electronically, and peered out of it. To her right, out of sight of the main road, was a black Mercedes, some years older than hers, with Bonn number plates. A man sitting at the wheel, who had been gazing at something towards his right, suddenly looked straight in front of him but she didn't think he saw her. At that precise moment another man came up the narrow track, stopped to talk to the driver and then got into the car, which immediately roared into life as carefully, slowly, the driver negotiated the narrow path towards the main road. It passed within a few feet of Anna and gave her the chance to see that both the driver and his companion were dark and swarthy, of Middle Eastern appearance.

Gunther said: 'Your message was so mysterious I had to come at once.' He listened carefully as Anna told him what had happened, not omitting any details.

'Why should he be looking for *us*?' Gunther appeared amazed at the idea. 'Half a dozen other millionaires live up this road. The Krauses, next door, are related to the Krupp family. It is far more likely to be them than me.'

'He was opposite our house.' Anna, feeling a little foolish, accepted the drink Gunther had mixed for her. 'I had the impression that I disturbed him by coming home early.'

'My dear girl,' Gunther took her arm and kissed her cheek. 'I didn't know you had such a vivid imagination.'

'But why did you have all these electronic devices installed?'

Gunther appeared surprised. 'Because *everyone* has them. I manufacture them. No modern house is complete without a number of such gadgets. I assure you I feel in no danger from Middle Eastern gunmen, but I will report it to the police. Now, Anna,' Gunther looked at his watch and smiled at her, 'we have half an hour to change before we have to leave, and this time I will be with you.'

He kissed her again and Anna began to relax. She knew it was useless to argue with Gunther. She would change and they would go out as they did almost every night; once a week they entertained and at least one other night a week she or Gunther was away from home. It was a cheerful, frenetic kind of life, the sort she had always wanted. The beautiful house, with its mellow wooden floors of Swedish pine covered with German or Scandinavian rugs especially designed for her, the modern cubed and angular furniture by Kaare Klint, Hans Wegner and Finn Juhl was all and everything she had ever wanted. It was large and it was comfortable; it was spacious.

She would go to the airy room they shared overlooking the road where she'd seen the man. It was surrounded by a balcony approached through doors made of thick plate

618

glass. The balcony was almost purely ornamental and was full of geraniums, lobelia and hanging ivy. They scarcely ever went out on to it because, although there was very little passing traffic and few pedestrians, they could be seen from the road. But the door was always locked and the heavy net curtains always drawn.

As she slowly went upstairs to change Gunther remained behind to telephone the police.

The following day Gunther tried to dispel Anna's feelings of apprehension by telling her that a Middle Eastern potentate, a member of one of the ruling families of one of the Gulf states, was planning to move into a villa down the road. Presumably his advance guard had been doing some reconnaissance. This reassured Anna but it didn't altogether rid her of the feeling that her husband had created out of their marital home a virtual prison and, from that day on, she seldom felt secure.

Stefanie looked out of the kitchen window into that part of the garden which was sheltered from the railway line by a large yew hedge. In fine weather it became a suntrap, and when it was sunny but cold it provided shelter against the elements. Pascal had a little working room at the end of the garden, nothing more than a sort of shed that had been converted for his use. In it he had a large drawing-board, an Anglepoise light and all the paraphernalia of his craft. He also had an easy chair, and a radiogram to give him a constant background of music.

Since his injury Pascal had discovered that there were some consolations to be had from his condition. He had previously been an extrovert, keen on sports and sportsmen's activities. He had only been a thinker in the sense of being an inventor. He had never thought much about the wider, philosophical or theological implications of life and its possible aftermath, or about matters that were to do with the spirit. He had never been religious and he did not become religious now, but his perceptions altered and, as he had more time on his hands, he became deeply interested in the arts, particularly in music. He came to see that there was so much more in Mozart, Schubert, Brahms or Beethoven than one at first perceived from the charm and beauty of their music. In Mozart's piano concertos or the quartets of Beethoven or Schubert he recognized a sublimity that touched the very essence of the spirit.

So Pascal sat in his little hut, pipe in mouth, working away, listening to music, and the scene he presented was one of great peace and harmony. He was especially close to the children and sometimes, as today, they were near him. He became a kind of surrogate father to them, as Sasha was so often away. Nicky usually worked at his stool, drawing, and Galina busied herself with private games that included a world to which only she had an entrance. She would move around, whispering to herself as she played first one character then another, peopling this mysterious, silent world with inhabitants that only she could see. Galina, who had grown up surrounded by a fairly large family, seemed to have many of the attributes of the only child who creates a fantasy world through his or her isolation or loneliness. Stefanie sometimes thought that this was because she had been away from Galina at a crucial stage in her development and thus reduced her to falling back on her own inner resources.

Stefanie's two children had inherited her looks, but Galina was especially like her grandmother. She had thick fair hair like Hélène and those same blue eyes surmounted by almost black brows. Her sultry Slavonic looks, too, were from her grandmother. Galina was a thin, tall, imaginative child of nine. She had known sadness in her short life, as her mother had, though not perhaps on such a scale. She may have suspected when she was small something of the ambivalence of her mother's feelings towards her but, maybe, this was compensated for by the change in Stefanie when she recovered from her illness.

So, on this April day, with Sasha and John Neri abroad, Pascal working in his shed and the children playing in the sunshine sheltered from the wind by the high yew hedge, Stefanie felt that life had, indeed, made up to her in full measure all she had lost while she had been ill. And, having been so ill, she could appreciate it so much more. It was rather like someone who, having lost their sight, discovers it again and the world as a much more beautiful place.

She looked at her watch and, seeing that it was time for lunch, went to the door and called them to come in. Nicky jumped off the high stool on which he always sat near to Pascal and, taking hold of his chair, turned it round and pushed it out of the hut and up the slight incline of the garden towards the house. He was joined with enthusiasm by Galina and, together, the two broke into a run while Pascal began to grimace, pretending to cower with fear and, thus, a slightly hysterical group of people arrived in a heap at the back door.

Watching them, Stefanie felt her heart almost overflowing with happiness and she put out a hand to steady Pascal's chair, taking it gently from the children.

'That's enough tomfoolery,' she said. 'Calm down, now.'

'I only hope that one day they don't run too hard with me in the other direction and push me over the railway line,' Pascal said.

'Or leave you *on* it,' Galina said, with a wicked smile.

'Galina! That's a horrible remark.'

'Sorry, Mummy.' Galina ducked her head and smiled at Nicky, who put his hand over his mouth to stifle his giggles, and they took their seats at the table.

'Irrepressible.' Pascal pretended to be cross and shook his head. 'Think what a peaceful life we'd have without them.'

'Peaceful but dull.' Stefanie passed Galina her plate with meat and vegetables and told her to help herself to water.

Earlier in the morning Galina had helped her to prepare lunch. Knowing how useful her own early training had been, Stefanie was anxious for both her children to be able to help in the house and fend for themselves should it ever prove necessary, which it might be, if the business failed. Nicky was expected to make his own bed and help with the washing-up, peel potatoes and scrape vegetables. He was also in charge of shoe cleaning and had his own vegetable patch in the garden. The children took their tasks seriously and, because they'd been brought up like this, never questioned them. There were also periods devoted to the study of Russian literature and the language, which they both spoke fluently. Sasha and Stefanie often spoke in Russian when they were together so as to encourage Nicky and Galina to speak the mother tongue of the Ferovs.

They were also taught about Russian history and the history of the Ferov family right up to Hélène's bravery in the war and her disappearance.

When they came to this part Stefanie always became very sad and lingered on the life of her mother as though she were a saint. The icon that was revered in the house, always with a lamp shining in front of it, was her patron saint Helena, mother of Constantine, finder of the true cross. As Stefanie talked, she would stroke Galina's hair and hold her very close as though, at last, she had her mother in her arms and could kiss her, make up to her for the way she had behaved towards her in the past.

After lunch, the children went back to their tasks in the

garden and Pascal sat at the kitchen door with Stefanie, smoking his pipe. A train thundered past them, suspending conversation for a second or two, and Pascal looked at his watch and, when it had gone, said:

'That will be the 2.10 to London.'

'Do you wish you were on it?'

'No.' He looked at her curiously. 'Why?'

'I wondered if you missed London.'

'Not a bit! I never liked it. It was Anna who liked the high life.' He paused and Stefanie dug into the pocket of the apron which she still wore and produced a letter.

'Anna and Gunther want to come and visit us. I think Gunther is thinking of buying a "Sprite".'

Pascal's eyes lit up. 'That's good news. That will be our tenth order this month.'

'Anna thought you might mind.'

'Mind? Why?'

'Because you wouldn't let Gunther invest.'

'That was ages ago,' Pascal said stiffly. 'Anyway, there was a reason.' He puffed at his pipe, gazing at the sky. 'I didn't really want German money in our company. I didn't want the Germans cashing in on our success.'

'Don't you think that's narrow-minded, Pascal?'

'It is; but I can't totally forget the War, nor should you. Our family suffered a great deal because of the Germans. I nearly lost my mother, you lost your mother, a grandfather, and an uncle. I think we can forgive the Germans, but don't let's be too nice to them. Anyway, there was something about Gunther I never liked and, certainly, not after what he did to Anna. She must be an absolute glutton for punishment to go back to him.'

'She seems very happy.' Stefanie held out the letter but Pascal waved it away.

'I don't really want to read it. I've made my own life

without Anna and I don't especially want to be reminded of her.'

'So it did hurt,' Stefanie said softly.

'Of course it hurt.' Pascal screwed up his eyes. 'It hurt and it still hurts.'

'Do you still love her?'

'In a way.' Pascal's pipe had gone out and he began to fiddle with the bowl. 'Only remotely, as an ideal.' He looked at Stefanie and smiled. 'I know I've lost her. I don't want to keep rubbing it in by seeing her.'

Stefanie leaned back in her chair and closed her eyes to the sun. From high overhead there was the sound of a plane, a large craft, maybe from the Avro works not far away, going south. The smoke from Pascal's pipe wafted in her nostrils and the sound of the children's voices at the bottom of the garden assailed her ears: peaceful; familiar smells and sounds.

Pascal said after a while, 'I'm very happy here with you and Sasha, Stefanie, but I think I should move on . . .'

Stefanie opened her eyes and her face at once registered dismay. 'But why, if you're happy?'

'Because this is your life with your kids. I'm an interloper.'

'You're not at all! You're family and even if you weren't we should want you.'

Pascal reached for her hand. 'You're very good to me; but I think I should get my own place. I would like to be independent.'

Stefanie fell silent, aware of a feeling of panic if Pascal should leave them. Sasha was away a great deal and Pascal was a wonderful companion for her. He was so well able to fend for himself that the only thing she did for him was wash his clothes. He even insisted on making his own bed, bustling around his ground floor bedroom in his wheelchair. He fitted in.

'I'd hate to think of you on your own,' Stefanie said, at last. 'I think you'd be lonely and your mother would be very upset. But, if it's what you want . . .'

'It's what I want,' Pascal replied, 'because I must lead my own life.'

'But you do here. You're not in the way at all.'

'I know that and, believe me, I could hardly be more grateful. But as a matter of fact I've already looked at a little house near the works. It's perfect for me, a bungalow, and I can easily adapt it to my needs.'

'But what of your shed . . . the children?' The strength of her reaction surprised even Stefanie. 'We'd miss you terribly. Please think again.'

Abruptly Stefanie got up and went inside to collect the lunch plates and start washing up, trying to examine within herself the reasons for feeling such a sudden, extraordinary sense of loss.

That Easter the Aldermaston March was the biggest since it had begun, with 100,000 people taking part. Flora watched part of it on television, regretting with every step that was taken that she was not there. But Joan was ill; and Joan was in her charge while Dick and Ruth were in America.

Dick and Ruth were now a couple and they lived together. Angelica was preparing to marry Perry and become Lady Eckburgh. They were still arguing about whether, as a baroness, she could persevere with her career. Perry seemed doubtful but Angelica knew she could, and would; she had a habit of getting her own way. Her second wedding was going to be a very small affair, with only the family present.

Flora stayed where she was in the Mile End Road but Dick and Ruth moved to a rented flat in Swiss Cottage.

Flora was frequently allowed to have Joan to stay and willingly agreed to have her when they went to America.

Flora had her MSc and taught evening classes at several London colleges. She was a regional organizer for CND; but she knew that a core was lacking in her life and that she had been in love with Dick. She only realized it when she lost him irretrievably to Ruth. She wondered if it would have made any difference if she'd let him know before. But at the same time she despised herself for her weakness, for her dependence on a man, especially one like Dick, who traded on his good looks, who was superficial and, in retrospect, seemed rather spineless. She no longer even thought him a Marxist analyst of genius, but just a run-of-the-mill academic permanently on the lookout for advancement.

Flora's only weakness now was Joan. She loved her; she had known the little mite since she was a tiny baby and she was growing up into a bonny little girl. Flora moved into Dick and Ruth's flat while they were in America and she watched the TV from there, one ear cocked to be sure Joan didn't call out. The march now started at Aldermaston and ended in Trafalgar Square. Its success was a great achievement for its originators, including her. While Flora and Luis went to the meeting, Em would take care of Joan.

When Em and Luis arrived, Joan, who had flu, was a little better but still Flora gave Em minute instructions, handing her carefully-labelled bottles and a chart. Em laughed.

'I *have* brought up a child, you know.' And she looked at Luis who was very like Felipe, but had Em's colouring. Luis was now twenty-two and had left Oxford the year before with his degree in Spanish. Since then he had been a student of photography and he had his camera with him to photograph the final scenes of the Aldermaston March.

When Em was settled with Joan, Luis and Flora drove down Finchley and Avenue Road towards Regent Street.

Flora didn't know Luis very well. No one had really got to know him while he lived with his father and then he'd gone to Oxford, which was a world in itself. She had hardly ever had a private conversation with him and she was surprised when he said to her, half-way down Avenue Road:

'I suggested this because I wanted to talk to you.'

'Oh?' Flora looked at him.

'Well, you know Mum very well and I need your help.'

'*My* help?' Flora felt even more surprised.

'I want to travel abroad and I know this will upset Mum a good deal. She depends on me now. I thought you might help me break it to her when we get back.'

'But why should it upset her? You're old enough.'

'Yes, but she likes having me around. She's very lonely, you know. She missed me all those years I spent with Dad. I realize now how much my mother did for me and how much she sacrificed. I don't want to hurt her any more.'

Flora thought this showed a very nice side of Luis, which pleased and surprised her. He always gave the impression of being rather a self-sufficient, detached young man, maybe a little selfish. It was nice to know that one might be mistaken.

'I'll do what I can, willingly,' Flora said. It was nice, too, for her to be wanted.

Em said, 'Thank you for telling me, Flora, but he could have told me himself. I can take it.'

Flora took the cup Em passed her and poured a refill. She had come home by herself, using the tube, saying that Luis had remained behind to take more photographs and would pick up his mother later on. The first thing she did was rush in and see that all was well with Joan, play with her for a few minutes, then she came back and told Em what Luis had told her to say.

'I thought you could,' Flora said. 'We're very alike, you know, Em, you and I. I can take anything, too.'

'Can you?' Em smiled at her, brushing back her greying hair from her rather sad, lined face.

'Oh, yes. I can take anything. I don't honestly think I could bear to lose Joan for good, but anything else; that's why I felt you might not be too upset about Luis.'

'Luis isn't going for good,' Em said. 'Not like Joe. I think he's gone for good.'

'Don't you think he'll ever come back?'

Em shook her head. 'He's actually doing very well where he is. He likes South America and it's an under-reported continent. The despatches he sends me are splendid and he writes for Reuters and AP too. He gets to some amazing places. He likes the life and the people and I think he'll settle there, unless the Wolfenden recommendations are ever implemented, and then he might return.' Em sighed. 'Poor Charlotte. She has lost both her sons, her daughter and her husband. But she has got Jeremy and I think he may be to her what Luis is to me.' She took out a cigarette.

'She didn't lose Pascal,' Flora said.

'No, she didn't actually *lose* Pascal,' Em corrected herself. 'But Pascal has withdrawn so much into himself since the injury and his divorce. His mother feels she can no longer reach him. If he depends on anyone it's Stefanie and Sasha, not Charlotte.

'As for you, my dear Flora,' Em went on, 'I wish you wouldn't get so tied up with Joan.'

'I love her.'

'I know you do; but she's not your child. She belongs to Ruth and if she and Dick get married, and I think they

628

will, they might go to the US and take her away. Then what will you do?'

It was a possibility that Flora hadn't thought of.

'Oh, they won't take her away. They couldn't.'

'But they can and they would, my dear. Dick would like to work in America, he told me. The only thing that's stopping him getting a job is that he was a Communist. I know there's no longer any McCarthy but they're still very careful.'

'He didn't tell me that,' Flora's voice was subdued. 'He hasn't confided in me for ages. He used to all the time.' Flora sighed. 'Well, that's it, then.'

She was aware that Em had got up and, carefully putting her coffee cup back on the tray, she came and sat beside Flora, putting a hand on her shoulder.

'It was the same for me, you know, with Felipe and also with Peter Klein, Paul's uncle. I've never really had a successful relationship with a man. They're very difficult.'

'At least you had a baby,' Flora said in a small voice. She looked up at Em and nervously brushed her hair back from her forehead. 'I don't think I ever shall. I don't really like men, but I liked Dick.' She screwed up her nose; it made her look like a small girl trying not to cry. 'I don't really like the idea of the physical thing. I know it's a silly thing to say but I don't.'

'It's not silly at all,' Em said gently. 'A lot of people don't like it, but don't dare say they don't. A lot of women I've known in my life have gone to bed with a man just because they felt they should. My Aunt Flora, after whom you're named, never went to bed with a man in her life, yet had a deep and satisfying relationship with your father. No one thought the worse of her for that.'

'Yet she killed herself,' Flora said dismissively. 'What a stupid thing to do.'

629

'*Did* you love Dick?' Em asked her at last.

'Oh no,' Flora tossed her head and shook it quite firmly. 'Not at all in *that* way. I liked him very much and I admired him. I was very shocked when I found out about him and Ruth; but I'm glad I did and that it happened. It helped me to get a grip on myself. I was getting sloppy about him, working for him, doing his research . . . just like Aunt Flora did for Daddy. I admired Aunt Flora a lot, you know, what I'd heard of her. I thought for a long time that I was like her, but now I know I'm not. I am much more independent than she was. I would never, ever, kill myself for a man.'

On the way home with Luis, Em was very thoughtful. It wasn't until they got into her large bare flat in Earls Court, a kind of anonymous, rather cheerless place in which she had lived since the war, that she said to him:

'Maybe you were right to get her to tell me. Let's have a drink.'

Luis had been talking about the day, the pictures he'd taken, the excitement of the event. He hadn't even eaten and while his mother cracked some eggs over bacon in a pan in the kitchen he opened a bottle of wine and held a glass out to her.

'Cheers, Mum. So you don't mind?'

'I'm apprehensive, needless to say,' Em said. 'But of *course* I don't mind. I was like you when I was young and was dying to go abroad. Luckily Mummy was very broad-minded and let me, but thirty years ago it wasn't nearly so acceptable as it is now.'

Em paused and frowned. Was it *really* thirty years ago? Said casually like that it seemed a mouthful but, yes, it was nearly. She'd gone to Germany in 1932 just as Hitler was consolidating his climb to power. She was one of the first journalists to warn people against him, and her mother fearlessly printed her articles in *The Sentinel*. They had been great days.

'I'd like to be a photo-journalist, Mum – you know, combining both things.'

'It's terribly dangerous.' Once again apprehension clutched at Em's heart.

'So was Germany in the thirties. Hitler put you in prison.'

'Well, one is never quite so afraid on one's own account.' Em smiled, scooped the bacon and eggs on to a plate, got the toast from under the grill and put them before Luis on the kitchen table.

'I'll be OK, Mum,' Luis said, reaching up to kiss her.

'I know you will.' Em bent her cheek to his. 'And your grandmother will be very proud of you. But please, Luis, come back safely, always.'

CHAPTER 25

In the year following its first flight the Neri 'Sprite' went into production, backed by Stefanie's money and some more which the company was finally able to raise in the City on the strength of having cash-in-hand. The growing pace of industrialization around the world by the sixties had created a new wave of hope and prosperity, and travel by jet was geared to quicken the pace. The de Havilland Comet, which had launched the world's first jet-propelled passenger service in 1952, was followed in 1954 by the Boeing 707 and the Douglas DC8 in 1958. Both of the last had learned valuable lessons by the disasters to the Comet which pinpointed the hazards of metal fatigue.

Sasha began to fly round the world in the first production model of the 'Sprite' in search of orders, sometimes with John Neri and sometimes with his brother Henry, or sometimes alone. Pascal stayed behind, busy at the drawing-board, designing newer and ever better models to capture the demanding executive jet-setter who always wanted to be the first on the scent of a deal.

By the summer of 1960 Sasha began delivering models of the 'Sprite' that had been ordered as long ago as the first trade show when Leo Cohen had been asked to invest. The works near Wilmslow were expanding all the time and in the autumn Pascal moved to the small bungalow on the edge of the town that had been specially adapted for him.

Wilmslow was a little like Cheadle Hulme: a small village that had grown into a dormitory suburb of

Manchester. It was considered, perhaps, a little smarter than Cheadle Hulme, catering for a better-off population who lived in large, detached, double-fronted houses in well-wooded roads. The wealthy wives shopped in the many little boutiques that had sprung up to cater for an up-market clientele; and speciality foods began to make their appearance, continental delicatessens and greengrocers importing exotic and unusual fruits and vegetables from all over the world.

By 1960, too, Paul and Laura had set up home together, despite the opposition of Leo and Adèle Cohen, who wished for their pretty, clever daughter what any other parents wished: a normal conventional liaison blessed by priest or Rabbi with, possibly, a nice house and a shower of gifts to set the newly-weds up in style.

Instead, Paul and Laura lived in a flat on the outskirts of Stockport which was the reverse of smart: Heaton Moor. Indeed, the area they chose was rather ramshackle and Paul drove to his little factory, ten minutes away, in an old Vauxhall car that was always having engine trouble. It was not at all the kind of thing the Cohens had expected when Laura revealed to them that her boyfriend was an earl. What kind of earl, they asked themselves, behaved like that? An earl with no money was the reply they expected, and got.

The cousins, assembled, by chance, in the environs of Manchester, saw a lot of one another. Paul was interested in the Neri venture and Sasha and Pascal were anxious to see his own business grow and expand as, inevitably, it did. Paul, with his shrewd business sense, had got into television right at the beginning and there was no telling how far he could go with different kinds of colour, different models; the prospects were apparently limitless. Laura had started to teach at a state school in Stockport and there was nothing to distinguish the young couple in any way at all from thousands like them who, married or not, lived together through the length and breadth of the land. The only thing that did worry them was the opposition of Laura's parents, who had taken against Paul for not making an honest woman of their daughter. It was hard to resist that kind of pressure, but they did.

Stefanie and Laura got on very well. Stefanie admired Laura for doing something that she hadn't dared do: live openly with her lover, though that was some years ago and conventions had changed if only a little, thanks mainly to feminism and the pill. Laura was a serious girl, who loved Paul but was also interested in her job. She believed fervently in state education and the abolition of all private schools. She thought it was the only way to eliminate class differences and bring about a more egalitarian society.

By the spring of 1961 the Neri works were turning out models of the 'Sprite' at a rate that would have not been thought possible even the year before. It was due to increasing automation and the willingness of the banks to back the smaller firm. Pascal and Sasha began to discuss with John Neri the possibility of bringing the enterprise on to the Stock Market, perhaps designing an even bigger plane; a British-made jet liner to rival the very successful Viscount. It was all very heady stuff and projected far into the future.

Sasha, Pascal and the Neri brothers were passionate advocates of the move on Britain's part to join the European Economic Community with the opportunity of more favourable trading conditions with Europe.

Sasha worked long hours; he was frequently away but he was happy. He had a good, strong marriage and a satisfying job. He had loved flying ever since he joined the RAF at the beginning of the war and had served as a gunner for most of it at the back of a Lancaster bomber.

After the war he qualified as a pilot and, but for his marriage to Stefanie and the subsequent complications, he would have liked to have been a civilian pilot. Now, at the age of thirty-nine, he felt at the peak of his career with a long, satisfying lifespan before him.

He also thought it was time to move. Much as they loved the Bridge House it was inconvenient. It was rather too small and too far from the works. It was also isolated from the main part of the town and Sasha sometimes worried about Stefanie's safety.

'But there's nothing to be afraid of,' she said one night as, once again, he broached the idea of moving.

'You never know. Funny things happen. Why, the other day a woman was murdered . . .'

'Sasha!' Stefanie exclaimed, hitting him on the shoulder. '*Don't* be so stupid. I'm not likely to get murdered.'

'But it *is* isolated.'

'You never said that before.'

Sasha gazed at her and put his arm round her waist.

'I love you,' he said. 'Maybe I love you more than ever and worry about you more than ever.'

Briefly he kissed her and for a moment he clung to her as though she had become something of a talisman for him. If not a good-luck charm, at least a rock.

It was that pleasant, quiet time at the end of the day when they sat over the fire and talked before going upstairs to bed. The children were asleep, the television was off, the dog dozed on the hearthrug. It was the sort of moment of contentment that Sasha savoured especially because, at one time, he thought it was something he would never have. There were several occasions in the war when he thought he wouldn't survive and then when Stefanie had been so ill he thought she wouldn't recover. She had been hostile not only to the children but to him.

But it was no good dwelling on those bad times. It was

635

silly even to think of them when one was sitting by one's wife after a satisfying day's work, with the children upstairs and the cat asleep on the best chair. Sometimes it didn't seem possible that such perfection could last.

'It *is* a perfect life,' Sasha said, after kissing Stefanie and feeling her warm, vibrant body respond to his. 'Sometimes it doesn't seem possible.'

'One moment you're talking about murder and the next that life's perfect.'

'It's just because it *is* so perfect that I don't want anything to happen,' Sasha said but Stefanie suddenly leaned forward and put a finger on his lips.

'*Don't* say that.'

'Why not?'

'It's like tempting fate.'

'Don't be silly, darling.' He took her finger in his hand and shook it. 'We've got it made. I even think we may soon have money in the bank. You know, if we have, apart from moving, I want to pay you back what we borrowed.'

'But it was a gift.'

'I know you *thought* it was a gift, but John and I considered it a loan. We want to repay you so that if anything happens you'll have your money.'

'If anything happens?'

'Anything . . . if the company went bust,' he replied, noticing her frown.

'But it won't.'

'It shouldn't. But it doesn't mean it can't. If we build larger planes it's always a risk.'

'Why take it, then?'

'Because it's fun.'

Sasha kissed her hand and, getting up, stretched himself in front of the fire, glancing at the clock. He stuck his hands in his pockets and stared at Stefanie.

'I'm looking at a house. I'd like you to see it. It's near Pascal, that would be nice.'

'It would be nice,' she agreed, 'but not a good enough reason to move.'

'We can't stay here forever, Stefanie.'

'It's so near the school.'

'That's not a problem for people with cars. This isn't our place. I want a place of our own, somewhere where we can expand . . .'

Stefanie looked curiously up at him.

'Wouldn't you like to have another baby?'

'But Galina's ten,' she said, nonplussed.

'Exactly. Maybe one, or two, like the Queen. An old family and a young one.'

'Are you really serious?'

'Really serious. I'd love it. Now we're settled it's a good time. I always wanted several children.'

'I know you did. We never talked about it again. I suppose there were reasons.' Stefanie leaned back against the chair and swept her hair from her forehead. Thinking about babies and all that kind of thing was rather exciting. Galina was ten and Nicky nearly thirteen. It was either now, or not at all. Besides, it would be the first baby she'd really wanted. Nicky had been a mistake and Galina a compromise. Much as she loved them now a real love child from Sasha would make them both very happy.

'Why not?' she said, and gave him that distant, still slightly sad smile that reminded him of those far-off, more painful days.

Sasha always thought that like that she looked so vulnerable. Despite her habitual cheerfulness there was still an air of suffering about Stefanie, as though she had never quite got over what she'd been through. The only thing he worried about was whether another pregnancy might bring on a recurrence of her nervous trouble, though their doctor had told him there was no reason why it should. The nervous trouble was linked to a ghost, not her reproductive powers.

After a pause Stefanie went on.

'Do you ever consider Nicky as really your own son?'

'Always.' Sasha looked at her in surprise. 'I never think of him as anything else.'

'He loves you.'

'He misses Pascal.' Sasha looked thoughtful. 'I miss Pascal, don't you, living with us? I often wonder why he really went.'

'What do you mean?' Stefanie, who had started to go round and tidy up, stopped and looked at him.

'I sometimes wondered if he was falling in love with you.'

'Oh, what an absurd thing to say!' Stefanie began to bump up the cushions, fold the papers.

'I think he does love you and it made him feel guilty, also, maybe, frustrated. Perhaps he thought it was the best thing to put some distance between you and himself.'

'I thought we were all just mates?'

'We are, we are.' Sasha came over and kissed her again. 'But who can blame him, poor fellow? Incidentally,' he stepped back and produced a letter from his pocket, 'Gunther wants to come over himself and pick up his aircraft. I didn't know he was a pilot. If we have our new house I suppose we must ask them to stay with us.'

Dick and Ruth were married that summer in a Register Office. Flora, of course, was there, standing behind the bride wearing the hat she'd worn at Myles' christening. She wore the hat again when Angelica and Perry were married, a much grander affair at Caxton Hall, with a reception at the House of Lords.

Apart from Flora none of the Askhams were present at

Dick and Ruth's wedding though Em, later, said she forgot. Needless to say the whole clan, Kittos and all, gathered to see Angelica become Lady Eckburgh.

It was typical of the Askhams that once someone had voluntarily left the fold they were promptly forgotten. Even though Dick was the father of two Askham children it was as though he had never existed once the divorce papers were signed. The same thing might have happened to Adam on his divorce from Melanie had he not happened to be Rachel's brother.

But Dick had never felt part of the family. He'd liked Rachel and he'd got on with Charlotte and Em, but he had detested Arthur, who seemed to him the quintessential English clot, the sort of person he had once joined the Party to get rid of.

In many ways those years, to Dick, were best forgotten. Now he felt completely isolated from the family and wanted to slip away. A new life, a new opportunity was waiting for him in America, the land where all people, in theory at least, were equal.

The leave taking, for Flora, was very sad. If Dick felt isolated at least he had Ruth and Joan; and it was Joan that she, her surrogate mother, would miss most.

Flora and Joan spent the day together before the newly-married Crosbys left for the States. The rented flat had been given up and they were staying in a hotel off Baker Street. Flora went to help with the packing and then she took Joan to Regent's Park while her mother and newly adopted father made some last-minute arrangements.

It was a bright sunny July day, welcome after a cold, unseasonable May and June, and that beautiful park surrounding a lake, on which people gaily rowed about in boats, was seen at its best. The famous and abundant bird life was rampant in the thick heavy fronds of English oak

639

and chestnut trees, upon the banks and among the sensuous willows dipping into the water.

In the nearby bandstand the band of the RAF was playing suitably pastoral music. Flora bought Joan an ice cream and then together they stood by the water's edge to feed the ducks with some bread they'd brought. Joan was not quite five and Flora had known her since the moment she was born, coming into her mother's ward at the maternity hospital just after she'd been wheeled back from the delivery room. Flora and Joan had a special rapport that Flora knew only they shared. It was to be presumed that Joan loved her mother, but she had never been as close to her as she was to Flora.

Now, despite the excitement of going to America, Joan was aware that she and this special person were to be parted; might never, in fact, see each other again. Like Flora, Joan was small; she had mouse-coloured hair which was cut in a fringe and a pale, rather wan little face that had always made Flora anxious about her health. Joan had hazel eyes, which she must have got from her father, whoever he was, because Ruth's eyes were blue and her hair black. Above all, Joan was possessed of a very sweet disposition; she had winning ways and an anxiety to please and most people liked her, except Flora. Flora adored her and she knew that from this day her life would never be as complete again.

Joan could hardly bear to let go of Flora's hand for a second, even to feed the ducks; but Flora was determined to be gay even if she paid for it after they'd gone.

'Look at that tiny little brown one,' she cried, pointing to a duckling scurrying on the lake. 'He's trying to catch up with the rest.'

'How do you know it's a "he"?' A drip of ice cream trickled down Joan's chin.

'It looks like a boy, don't you think?' Flora crouched beside her. 'He's got that cheeky boyish look.'

Joan gazed earnestly at the duckling and then smiled, nodding vigorously. 'It's a boy,' she said. 'Let's call him Charlie.'

'Charlie, then, and that's . . . what shall we call her? She's definitely a girl.'

Flora pointed in the direction of a duckling some distance behind Charlie and Joan laughed with pleasure and gave it a name, her own sadness forgotten.

But Joan wasn't really sad. Having a daddy, at last; leaving her nursery school; moving from the flat to a large hotel; the whole business of aeroplanes, were all far too exciting a prospect to leave a little girl of four sad for very long.

She began to skip up and down by the side of the lake, soon tiring of the naming game and then, when the bread was finished, Flora took her on the small children's boating lake. After that, finally exhausted, they sat on a bench overlooking the pool, sucking iced lollies from the kiosk in the park.

'We'd better get back soon,' Flora said. 'I promised Mummy . . .'

'I *wish* you'd come, too.' Joan looked appealingly at her. 'Daddy said he'd miss you, as well.'

It was nice to hear Joan call Dick 'daddy' at last. It was nice for Joan to have a father, and nice for Dick to feel that his step-daughter accepted him instantly. Besides, he was bound to miss his own children.

'I'll miss you all,' Flora said, kissing her hair. 'I'm going to be awfully lonely.'

'Come with me, then.' Joan's little hand slid into Flora's and, unseen by her, Flora brushed away a tear.

'I will come,' she said, 'on a visit; but not for a bit. I'll have to get some money together and then I'll come.'

'Promise?'

'I promise,' Flora smiled gaily. 'And you promise to write?'

'Promise.'

'Every week?'

'Promise.'

Flora knew that maybe after a year or so, she'd probably never hear from them again.

Dick said:

'We'll all miss you terribly.'

'And I'll miss you.' Flora still had Joan's hand inside hers, though now it was a day later and they were at London Airport. Aeroplanes were still rather new and a bit frightening to someone like Flora, who had never flown. Around them was the bustle of the ever-changing crowds and the noise from the announcements over the Tannoy. It was terribly confusing.

Ruth managed a smile but her face looked strained. It was only a few weeks since she'd been married and so much had happened.

'Thanks for everything,' she said with that bright, rather artificial smile people seem to keep for departures. 'We shall miss you.'

'I'll miss you,' Flora said for what seemed like the hundredth time, and squeezed Joan's hand hard. 'I'll miss you, but . . .'

'Flora's coming over to see us very soon,' Joan said, with the confidence of the young. 'When she's got some money.'

'I'll help with the fare,' Dick said nervously. 'If you're short . . .'

'Don't be silly.' Playfully Flora tapped him on the chest. '*You'll* need all your money to settle down.'

'We'd love to see you, and you promise you'll come?'

'Promise.'

So many promises – easy to make.

Abruptly Dick moved towards her and kissed her clumsily on the cheek, holding on to her arm.

His touch reminded Flora that, if things had been different, if she hadn't been so unnecessarily kind to so many people, she would be the one at Dick's side, beginning a new life with him. Probably, yet probably not. Ruth looked very pretty in a green dress with a white hat, the outfit she'd worn for her wedding at Marylebone Register Office.

Dick stood back and then Ruth embraced her and, finally, Joan, who put her arms round her neck and clung.

'*Please* come soon,' she said.

'I will . . .' Flora felt herself near to tears as their plane was announced again and passengers were asked to report at the passport barrier.

They all seemed to listen to the announcement with relief. There were more smiles, hugs, and then goodbye.

'Goodbye, goodbye . . .' Flora stepped back as they showed their passports, gave a final wave and disappeared.

She thought the look on Joan's little face as she passed through the barrier in Dick's arms would remain with her for the rest of her life: such sweetness, such sadness, such finality.

Pascal pushed his chair to the ramp leading from the front door into the garden, turned to close and lock the door and then gently let himself slide down once again to ground level. A few more turns of the wheel and he was by his car, ready to lever himself in.

It wasn't fun being a paraplegic; but it was surprising how one could live with it. People had offered to pick him up and drive him to the aerodrome every day, but he wanted to be completely independent.

Sometimes he regretted such independence of spirit, especially when he came home at night and let himself into the dark house, having to light the fire, prepare his evening meal and spend the night alone with only the TV set for company. More often than not he went to his study and started on the plans they were drawing up for a Mach 2 'Sprite', taking more passengers with a longer range and greater speeds.

The solitary life was not one Pascal Verdi would have chosen for himself; whereas it might have suited his brother Joe very well. Pascal, unlike Joe, had always been gregarious; he'd liked to dance and play sports and date girls. He married because he was in love, but also because his nature was uxorious and he wanted a family. But now the family stakes had gone to Sasha and Stefanie: the new house, the children, the dogs, the cat and, now, a new baby on the way. It would be very easy to envy them, but very selfish, too. Sasha and Stefanie had paid a high price for their happiness and it was richly deserved.

Pascal got into his car, which was a normal car especially adapted by himself for himself, and it even had a two-way radio, as they had in aircraft, in case he came unstuck on the way. He travelled quite a lot in his car and had done all that was humanly possible to make himself mobile.

Pascal always felt a thrill of pride as the works came in sight: that very large assembly of concrete buildings and hangars that had once been just a few wooden huts. Now there was even a security guard on the gate and one had to have a pass to enter and leave.

'Morning, sir,' the guard saluted him and opened the barrier to let him pass, and immediately Pascal was surrounded by the people and paraphernalia of what some called the daily grind but he thought of as life itself.

To him work was life.

As usual, without help, he got out of his car, into his wheelchair and, collecting his briefcase and an assortment of papers, wheeled himself up to the main building approached, naturally, by a ramp, where his offices were. This morning he was greeted on the steps by Sasha, already in overalls, waving a bit of paper.

'Good news,' he said. 'A new contract from one of the Gulf states. Do you remember that bloke . . .'

Cheerfully Sasha took over from Pascal and started to push the chair along the corridor as they greeted, or were greeted by, passing members of staff. He explained about the man from the Middle Eastern state, who had come to make enquiries on behalf of a sheik and no one had taken him very seriously. Now there was an order for five of the Mach 2 'Sprites', with an option on five more.

Pascal listened and nodded, commenting enthusiastically until they got to his office where Sasha's secretary was waiting for him with a telex in her hand.

'The Baron von Spee has broken his leg,' she said, passing it to him. 'He wonders if the plane can be delivered to him instead.'

'Oh, Stefanie will be disappointed.' Sasha took the telex, studied it and passed it to Pascal. 'Winter sports.'

'That's too bad.' Pascal gave the telex back to the secretary and wheeled his chair behind his desk. 'Can we spare anyone to ferry it over? It's taking up room in the hangar.'

'I thought I'd do it myself,' Sasha said. 'Maybe Stefanie would like to come. We could have a break.'

'What a good idea.' Pascal got out his pipe and began reflectively to fill it, one of his first actions before starting a day's work. 'You could have a few days' winter sports yourself.'

Sasha moved to the wall of the office and started studying a large chart on which was outlined the flow of work for weeks ahead. He ran along a line with his finger and then said: 'Next week looks as good as anything. If she can get away. I think the kids might be able to board at school for a week. You wouldn't like to come, by any chance, too, would you?'

'Me?' Pascal shook his head. 'Thank you, but no. Winter sports are not quite me, yet.'

Sasha went over to Pascal and put a hand on his shoulder.

'There was something I wanted to say to you but maybe it can keep until we get back.'

'What's that?' Pascal, pipe in his mouth, already had his eyes on the graphs he was studying on stress tests that had been tried out on the new plane.

'We wondered if you'd like to come and live with us again.'

'No thanks,' Pascal shook his head, not even looking up.

'We miss you,' Sasha insisted. This time Pascal did look up.

'And I miss you, but no thanks. I'm very happy where I am.'

'Are you?'

'Yes, I am.'

'There's plenty of room.'

'I know.'

'Look . . .' Sasha stood up and started pacing the room. 'We bought the house with you in mind, you know. It has a cottage in the grounds. We thought it would be ideal for you.'

646

'You bought it with *me* in mind?' Pascal removed his pipe and tapped it against the bowl on the table.

'We thought it would be just right for you; you could be near us, yet independent. Now that we've been in the house for six months and have things sorted out I thought it was time to talk to you about it.'

Pascal pushed his chair back and joined his hands reflectively under his chin. His eyes, looking at Sasha, were unfriendly.

'I don't need pity, you know, Sasha . . .'

'There's *no* pity, I assure you.'

'Then leave it alone. If I say I'm happy, and I am, then you must accept it. You have your own life, Sasha, I have mine.' Pascal reached for his pipe and, after knocking out the old, stale tobacco, began to fill it with new. 'Don't think me rude and ungrateful; but I suspect there's a trace of patronage in all this and I can do without it. I *am* grateful to you both for what you did for me after the divorce, but now I am a fully readjusted man again and, as a matter of fact, I like living on my own. Now, will you forget it?'

'Stefanie will be very disappointed.' Sasha got up and took some papers from Pascal's desk. 'It was her idea.'

'Thank her for me,' Pascal said briefly, bending his head to his work again. But for a moment his vision blurred and he couldn't see what was on the table in front of him.

If only she knew.

The winter of 1961/2 was one of the worst for years. Certainly it was the worst freeze-up since 1947, some records said since 1881. Looking out of the window of the new house on the day before she and Sasha were due to leave for Frankfurt, Stefanie knew that there was no possibility of her going. Fresh snow had fallen overnight and the landscape was like a Breughel wintry scene, with people slithering down the road and skating on the pond on the little green outside the house.

Nicky had been in bed with a cold and she had arranged for her cleaning lady to come and live in while they were away. She turned to Sasha, who was still sitting at the breakfast-table opening his mail.

'I can't possibly go.'

'Darling, everything will be all right. We've kept the runway clear and Gunther says that conditions in Frankfurt aren't as bad as here.'

'It's not the flight I'm worried about. I can't leave Mrs Topling to cope with Nicky in weather like this. I shouldn't think she'd want to.'

'Oh Stefanie, Nicky is *quite* old enough. Don't mollycoddle him.'

'I wouldn't leave *anyone* in weather like this. I wouldn't leave you. Anyway, I feel happier staying at home.' Stefanie crossed her hands over her stomach and sat at the table opposite Sasha. 'I have been feeling a bit queasy, to tell you the truth. Maybe that *is* the truth. I don't really want to go.'

Sasha sat back and held out his cup for more coffee.

'If that's how you feel, darling, then don't consider it.'

'But, please, still go away with Anna.'

They'd planned to go back to the mountains to complete the skiing holiday that Gunther's fall had interrupted.

'I'll see.'

'No, I want you to, really. You haven't had a proper holiday for years, Sasha.'

'Neither have you.'

'Tell you what, let's have a nice summer holiday. Maybe go to Germany then? We can plan it after the baby is born.'

648

Sasha got up and, coming over to her, put his arms round her, nestling her cheek against his.

'You've no idea how happy I am, how happy you've made me. I . . .'

Stefanie felt a sudden spasm of fear and clutched his arm.

'*Please* don't say it,' she said. 'Please don't tempt fate.'

Sasha looked at her with concern. 'But, darling . . .'

'I mean it,' she said. 'When life is so perfect you can't bear to think of anything spoiling it.'

'Nothing will spoil it.'

'Maybe you should suspend your flight until the weather's better.'

'If I did that we wouldn't sell any planes. Besides,' Sasha pointed to the sky, 'the weather over there doesn't affect the plane. We have so many instruments now that flying is perfectly safe. The modern aircraft flies itself. You don't think that I would have considered taking it if it weren't, do you?'

'No, of course not.'

Stefanie patted his arm and turned her face to be kissed. 'Morbid fears, I guess. Relics of the past.'

Sasha found a lot of things to do at the works that day and in the evening he had a business dinner with an engineer from another aeroplane manufacturer they were thinking of employing. They had to be very careful about secrecy these days and couldn't tell him too much. Industrial espionage was a very real problem.

Sasha had the dinner alone as Pascal and John Neri had gone to a lecture in Manchester and Stefanie wanted to stay with Nicky, who was very much better. Sasha came home rather late and as Stefanie was already asleep he decided to sleep in the guest room, where a bed was always kept made up in case it was needed.

He woke in the middle of the night and found Stefanie

standing by the side of his bed. Quickly he sat up and put on the light then drew her down with him.

'Darling, what is it?' he said, worried. 'Are you all right?'

'I woke and you weren't there,' she murmured, sounding terrified. 'I was worried. I . . .'

'But, darling, everything is perfectly OK. I didn't come in because you haven't been sleeping well and I didn't want to disturb you.'

'I know. I know. I just can't explain . . .'

'Come to me, then,' he whispered in her ear and held the bedclothes back while she crept in beside him, snuggling up to him like a kitten to its mother.

'It's just that I couldn't bear for anything to happen . . .'

'But nothing *will* happen, Stefanie.' Sasha looked at her with concern. Maybe they shouldn't have conceived the baby, after all. 'What *can* possibly happen? I'm a flyer and I've flown millions of miles . . .'

'It's not that, it's just that . . . oh, I don't know. I suppose I've been worried about Nicky and not feeling too well, that sort of thing. Then I woke up and you weren't there, I thought . . . I couldn't live without you, Sasha.'

'You won't have to,' Sasha kissed her tenderly and smoothed back her hair from her hot, sticky brow. 'I'll be with you always.'

Em sat in her room at the top of *The Sentinel* building which had been the editorial office ever since anyone could remember, certainly since Rathbone Collier had taken over the paper after her father had bought it in 1910.

As far as Em knew the room hadn't changed very much since that time, except a coat or two of paint had been applied at irregular intervals and, maybe, some of the worn furniture had been replaced. Certainly the large square leather-topped desk at which she sat had been her father's, but many of the dusty books lining the shelves on the wall dated from the time of the paper's original founder in the middle of the nineteenth century.

The carpet was relatively new. Em had had that put down when she had formally taken the editorship over from her mother. Rachel had been one of the first, certainly the greatest, of womens editors, nursing the paper not only through the First World War, but the Second as well; informed, enlightened, opinionated but always on the right side: that of truth. Rachel had been one of the first to oppose Hitler when many of the papers in Fleet Street, most noticeably *The Times*, were supporting him. She had also supported Baldwin against the King; had been for the overthrow of Chamberlain, and a vigorous campaigner for Churchill during the war. After it she had immediately turned, like the majority of the British people, to the support of Attlee and the Labour government.

Not for nothing had Rachel been known in the twenties as the 'Red Countess'; but when the evils of the communist system had become apparent in the notorious trials of the thirties she had attacked them, too.

Em often thought her mother should have been given an honour for her vigorous championship of just causes, her determination always to be on the side which supported justice, but she never had. Whichever government was in power she had always contrived to offend by her independent spirit, above all by her critical and acerbic pen.

Em looked at her watch and, getting up, went to the window to check the time against the clock on St Paul's

651

Cathedral. She remembered as a little girl being taken to the office and finding the view so fascinating, up Ludgate Hill to those majestic twin towers completed in the eighteenth century by Wren. How well she could recall the scene in the far-off days of her childhood as horses and carriages toiled up Ludgate Hill, past Paternoster Row, which had been completely destroyed during one dreadful night of German bombing during the war, yet another occasion – there were five in all – when *The Sentinel* building had lost all its windows.

And that scene of desolation had remained ever since. On either side of Ludgate Hill were large open spaces of bombed-out buildings, although there was a massive scheme under way to rebuild the north side of St Paul's, behind the Old Bailey where Paternoster Row, famous for its publishing houses, had once been.

Em turned as the door opened and Charlotte walked in, just on time, as Charlotte usually was. Em went over to greet her sister and drew her to the window, pointing to the scene.

'I was recalling the old days. Do you remember how we used to come here and see Aunt Flora and look at the view and feed the pigeons?'

'And Aunt Flora used to take us to Joe Lyons in Ludgate Circus for an ice cream. Oh, yes, I remember. What fun we thought it was!'

Charlotte laughed with sheer delight and, briefly, Em could recall what Charlotte had been like then; a laughing, beautiful girl, not really all that much different from the woman who stood with her now except that the laughter was not quite as exuberant, and a good deal rarer than it had been.

Charlotte, impeccable as ever, wore a mink coat over her cream woollen dress; she had a pretty mink toque on her hair, which was a little grey at the sides now, a distinction that enhanced her attraction. She went to the window, threw it open, despite the cold, and leaned out as if recalling her own special memories of those far-off days and, for a while, the sisters didn't speak, while Em turned to her desk and got on with her work.

It was true that Charlotte seldom found much to laugh at these days. Arthur had decided not to stand for re-election at the last General Election and had taken up golf instead. Arthur seemed to have given up after Jill was dismissed from his life (no one knew what had happened to her, it was rumoured that Arthur had paid for her to emigrate to Canada where she had a married sister). He was only fifty-seven but he had become rather like an old man, with a bald head and a paunch. He had his directorships in the City and his membership of a number of prestigious clubs, but golf had become his new mistress and kept him away from home about as often as a mistress as discreet as Jill had been able.

Arthur and Charlotte were tired of each other, but they remained together: what else was there to do? There was also Jeremy, on whom they both doted, a young man now aspiring to Cambridge and a career in the law. A handsome, ambitious combination of Askham and Crewe – a good mixture, if form was anything to go by. Jeremy was everything that Pascal and Joe had never been: conventional, clever, good at games, a clean-cut, young scion of an upper-class English house. Some people said that such stereotypes were passé, but there were still a good number of them around, and flourishing in the English public schools.

Charlotte drew her head back from the window and shut it, rubbing her arms with cold.

'It's awful weather, isn't it? They say the coldest for years. Are you nearly finished, dear? Can we go?'

'Nearly finished,' Em said, looking up from her desk

and passing Charlotte a clump of photographs. 'These came from Luis yesterday. I'm rather pleased with them. I'm afraid he thinks that the war is going to hot up in Vietnam. I wish he'd get out. With our luck we don't want another casualty.'

'Oh, don't say that!' Charlotte looked horrified.

'Do you think we have had more than our share of bad luck, or do all families?' Em sat down again as Charlotte, perched on the corner of her desk, started looking through the pictures of the civil war in Vietnam, which had been going on now for years. Charlotte gazed at her over the rim of the spectacles she'd put on to examine the photographs.

'I think we *have* had more bad luck than most.'

'But it has brought us together, on the whole.' Em got up and put an arm round Charlotte. 'We're lucky. In some families grief drives a wedge. Look, do you think that Flora would like to come and live with me? I've been brooding about it.'

'Flora?' Charlotte removed her spectacles and replaced the photos on the desk. 'What made you think of Flora?'

'Maybe the association with Aunt Flora; but have you seen that little flat she lives in in the East End?'

Charlotte shook her head. 'I've heard it's horrible.'

Em nodded. 'It *is* horrible and in this weather it has been bitterly cold. It has no adequate heating. She's had two lots of flu and the last time I thought she had pneumonia.'

'You're very good to her.'

'I'm very fond of her. I often think she has no one, you know. She's not close to Christopher or Sylvia, hardly ever sees Giles and his wife. Mum would like to see more of her but we know that Mum, though marvellous, is not as agile as she was.'

Both had been worried about Rachel during the bad

winter for part of which the Grange had been frozen up and unapproachable, even by people at the Hall.

'Flora's a sad person,' Em went on. 'She was in love with Dick but would never admit it and she was absolutely dottily devoted to Joan. Of course she hasn't heard from any of them since they went to America. What work does she do? Lectures a bit at evening classes. If you ask me, she is always looking for something and I wish I could help her.'

'How would living with you help her?' Charlotte enquired, selecting a cigarette from her silver case and tapping it on the outside.

'She'd have a home. We get on well. There's plenty of room. I thought I might encourage her, stimulate her. She might even like to work for me; as features editor. I think she imagines life has passed her by. Yet she's only thirty. She often reminds me of myself when young. Maybe that's why I feel a special responsibility for her.'

'She's not a bit like you,' Charlotte protested, exhaling a cloud of smoke over her sister's desk. 'You were terribly active at her age, rushing round the world, had to be restrained . . .'

'Yes, but maybe I was luckier. I had Freddie; we had Mum. Life was very different then when I was thirty. I'd travelled a great deal. I'd seen the rise of Hitler; a terrible war in Spain at close quarters. I'd also had a wonderful love affair. Luis was born when I was thirty. I think Flora would like a child . . .'

'Well, please don't encourage her to follow *your* example.' Charlotte started to laugh when there was a knock at the door and Em's night editor put his head round the door.

'Em . . . I'm terribly sorry . . .'

'That's OK, Roger,' Em said cheerfully. 'Charlotte and

655

I are killing time until the theatre. What's that in your hand?'

Roger Garfield had been employed by Em since the war in which he'd served with distinction. As all her employees tended to become, he was a family friend and, at one time or another, had met all its members. He nodded to Charlotte, but didn't smile.

Em held out her hand but Roger hung on to the paper.

'I'm terribly sorry to give you bad news, Em,' he said, before putting the paper in her hand. 'But this came over the wire. I can't think of any other way to tell you. I'm terribly sorry.'

Em slowly took the paper from him after an agonized look at Charlotte. Luis and Vietnam. As she put on her glasses to read it Charlotte came and stood next to her, peering over her shoulder at the agency message in her hand, her arm round Em's waist.

Mr Alexander (Sasha) Ferov, chief test pilot of Neri Aerospace Ltd and a director of the firm, is reported killed in a heavy snowstorm over Germany as he was on his way to deliver one of the new Mach 2 'Sprite' aircraft, which he had helped to pioneer, to a customer in Frankfurt.

Mr Ferov, whose body was recovered from the wreckage of the plane found in the Taunus mountains was a very experienced pilot with a distinguished war record. He was thirty-nine years of age and leaves a wife and two children.

'Sasha' Ferov, as he was known, came on his father's side from a Russian princely family who fled to Paris after the Revolution. Through his mother he was related to the Askham family, and was a nephew of the millionaire industrialist, Lord Lighterman.

The paper limp in her hand, Em laid her head on Charlotte's shoulder. Her double agony was the relief she had felt that it wasn't Luis. While the twilight outside turned to dusk the two sisters clung together, vainly trying to comfort each other.

CHAPTER 26

Rachel felt that there had never been a sadder funeral and in her long life she had attended a good many. Neither her husband nor two sons had been buried in England, but their memorial services had all been poignant, each commemorating a tragedy for the family, an irreparable loss. Yet there was something specially harrowing as the coffin containing Sasha's body was laid to rest by the side of his grandmother, Melanie, whose lifespan had outstripped his by forty years.

And what was she, an old but healthy woman of eighty-five, doing here, still alive when Sasha, father of an unborn child, was dead? Sasha, who had escaped death so often in the war; was it fair that he should die in an aeroplane in peacetime?

Rachel had always felt especially close to Sasha because, in a way, she had been responsible for his being born at all. It was her suggestion that Susan should travel with her to Russia in 1921, to get over the divorce of her parents, that led to her meeting with Kyril, Sasha's father. Melanie used to blame Rachel for that marriage, as though she had not done enough to prevent it, and Rachel used to feel that she did share part of the blame. But when a marriage resulted in good things, like Sasha, a feeling of guilt turned to joy. For all his life Sasha had been joyful, had given comfort and pleasure to many. He was a generous man whose path in life had been marked by good deeds and, surely, now he would be received in the company of the blessed?

Rachel had seldom known such grief, so many

unashamed tears on the part of the large congregation who had gathered to mourn Sasha, the first member of the Ferov family to be buried in the Askham family vault. There had first been a funeral in London at the Russian Orthodox Church to be followed by a brief burial service and committal at Askham.

Stefanie, Anna and the deeply grieving Susan, supported by Bobby, led the mourners; but people had come from all over the place, industrialists and members of the diplomatic service mingling with the English aristocracy and those remnants of the old Russian nobility who lived in London and Paris.

Afterwards there was the usual reception at the Hall admirably catered for by Jenny, who was so busy she couldn't even get to the funeral. Stefanie, five months pregnant, was magnificent. Flanked by her two children, she behaved throughout with dignity, and those who had known the hysterical, depressed woman of a decade or so ago would scarcely have believed it was the same person. She was even able to comfort Susan and had spent a long time with her alone after Sasha's death. Rachel knew how well Stefanie was coping and she loved and admired her for it. However, she was one of the first to leave the reception afterwards, and drive back to Robertswood, accompanied by Galina and Nicky, to spend some more time on the way by the side of Sasha's tomb.

In many ways Gunther seemed one of the most shocked of all. His leg was still in plaster and he kept on telling everyone how unnecessary the delivery of the aeroplane had been at that time as if he wanted, somehow, to detach himself from the responsibility of Sasha's death. The plane had come down in a sudden thick, blinding snowstorm, but no one knew why the newly-installed instruments hadn't coped. The accident, widely reported, was bound to affect sales of the plane but few bothered about

658

that now, though, undoubtedly, Bobby had done some calculations.

Bobby was one of the most supportive of the family apart from Charlotte who, so close to Stefanie, had spent many hours with her. Pascal, of course, had scarcely left her side. With hindsight he felt he should have done more to stop Sasha flying, though that day, just a week ago, no one had seriously thought the weather was all that bad. It was a freak storm and it came and went leaving the sun shining over the wreck of the stricken plane.

Anna and Gunther were to stay the night at the Hall and after Bobby had driven Susan back to Robertswood and Charlotte and Arthur had left, Jenny cooked a little supper for the ones who remained: Rachel, Em, herself and Hugo, Nimet, Paul and Laura, also staying the night, as well as Anna and Gunther.

'I'm sorry it isn't much,' Jenny said, looking harassed while Nimet, dressed in deep mourning, gazed with distaste at the plate in front of her as though it were crawling with maggots. Jenny saw the expression, one familiar to her, and grimaced. Nimet, hard to please, ungrateful, seemed to dwell permanently on that time of her life when she had suites at the Ritz and the Carlton in Cannes, and was surrounded by servants. Jenny tried to ignore Nimet but it wasn't easy. She was not a retiring person; she was demanding and determined to be noticed.

'It's absolutely splendid,' Anna said, trying hard to smile. She'd wanted to be with Stefanie and her grandmother but Pascal was there, too. The following day he would travel to Manchester and then she and Gunther would spend a few days at Robertswood before going home. 'You've done too much, Jenny.'

'This is an enormous house for you,' Gunther looked around, noting the shabby furniture, the peeling plaster on the walls. 'I'd no idea it was so big.'

Rachel felt extremely tired and wished that she and Em had gone back to the Grange for a sandwich and coffee. It was one of those days of surpassing sadness, when there was very little one could add when one had said all that needed to be said. How could one comfort a young widow for a life needlessly lost, or a mother who had buried her only son, a sister her only brother?

Rachel thought that Anna looked ill, that Gunther seemed anxious about her. It was Anna who had been asked to identify Sasha's body, brought down from the mountains and the wreckage of his plane.

'I didn't realize you hadn't been here before,' Rachel addressed Gunther. 'I thought you came to look at the "Askham"?'

'No, never,' Gunther shook his head. 'Though I met most of the family ten years ago for the Festival of Britain.'

'Was it as long as that? Dear, dear,' Nimet shook her head. 'And now I suppose you know Colonel Nasser has confiscated *all* our assets.'

Gunther looked at her as though he had misheard what she'd said, but Hugo intervened quickly:

'Mother has been very upset about this. It's on her mind. She has had the few bits of property she had left taken over by the new Egyptian regime. You must forgive her . . .'

'I don't see why *I* need to be forgiven,' Nimet said with hauteur. 'I was merely telling the Baron about the deeds of wicked Colonel Nasser.'

'Yes, Mother, quite.' It had been a tiring day and Hugo looked drawn, too.

'You try to make out sometimes that I'm senile,' Nimet added petulantly. 'Quite the reverse, I assure you.'

'I can see that, Madame Ogolopuscu,' Gunther said

660

hastily. 'I can understand, too, how irritated you are with the Colonel's regime.'

'Diabolical,' Nimet said. 'Now why don't you take *this* house over and do it up? I'm sure you're a man of good taste as well as great wealth. I can tell you, it needs a benefactor.'

'*Mother!*' Hugo drew back his chair and stood up while Rachel, next to him, put a restraining hand on his arm. She wished that Nimet had had the tact and good sense to go away; but the weather was bad and there were few places left to which she could afford to go. The St Tropez villa finally had had to be sold to realize some cash.

'Why do you pretend, my dear?' Nimet said, dark eyes flashing. 'In ten years' time, maybe less, this place will be a ruin.'

'But, Madame,' the Baron leaned forward, palms of his hands outstretched. 'I assure you I have no need of a place as large as this. I don't know what I would do with it.'

'You could transform it completely.' Anna suddenly seemed excited, jettisoning, with amazing speed, her air of grief and lassitude. 'Oh, *Gunther*, I have seen pictures of Askham Hall in its heyday and it was magnificent, wasn't it, Aunt Rachel?'

'Magnificent,' Rachel echoed in a faint voice. 'But it would cost a fortune, and I don't really see . . . the point,' her voice trailed off as she saw the expression change on Hugo's face.

'It could be an excellent commercial proposition, Rachel,' Hugo said enthusiastically. 'Mother is quite right. There *is* great scope in expanding the market garden, the stables . . . are you interested in horses, Baron von Spee?'

'Enormously,' Gunther said with a half-smile and, as

he started to talk, all memories of Sasha and the reason for their presence appeared to have been forgotten.

The quick at the expense of the dead.

Gunther and Anna didn't go to Robertswood the next day or the day after that but stayed to have exhaustive discussions with Hugo. Everyone suddenly seemed fired by the notion proposed by Anna. The Baron, at first appalled by the idea, found that it had grown on him. To have a place in England, his wife's family home, would add enormously to his prestige. He would have it as the English headquarters of his company. Of course he insisted that there would be room for Hugo, his family and his mother. He would ensure that they were housed in great comfort, if not splendour. Yes, the stables were an excellent idea and there were acres of space for more greenhouses. Every day the Baron limped for what seemed like miles round the estate, viewing it from all angles. Even Rachel, critical at first, grew enthusiastic.

A new project was born. The only one who appeared to oppose it was Paul.

'It is *our* family home,' he said, bringing Laura to visit Rachel for the first time in the Grange.

'But derelict, dear. Some rooms have had to be closed. There's dry rot.'

'In a few years I'll have a bit of money.'

'But not as much as the Baron, Paul. He has millions.' Rachel's tone was gentle.

Paul impatiently kicked the rug on which he was standing, while Em, who was there, agreed with her mother.

'It's no good, Paul. At least it still will be the family home. Not a hotel.'

'*And* the headquarters of von Spee, England, Ltd.'

'That's for tax reasons.'

662

'Still, I don't like it.'

Em gazed thoughtfully at her nephew, son of her beloved twin brother, Freddie. In many ways he was like a second son, a son that Freddie would have been proud of with his unconventional egalitarian ways, the battered old car in which he'd driven Laura down from Stockport. Even that relationship he would have approved of; defying family pressures to set up home together out of wedlock. It was difficult to imagine Freddie as an earl and now his son eschewed the title. He was always known as Mr Askham.

'Might you be a *little* prejudiced, Paul?'

'I might, Aunt Em,' Paul gave her his engaging smile.

'That isn't very nice.'

'How do you know he wasn't a Nazi?'

'He was only perfunctorily de-Nazified. The Control Commission trusted him from the start, so everything must be all right. I know how you feel about Nazis, Paul, but there were lots of good Germans; your Uncle Peter was one of them. If you like, I can ask Peter to find out about von Spee.'

'Excellent idea,' Paul said. 'Let's have a witch hunt.' He sprawled in a chair between his grandmother and aunt and gazed at Laura.

'My father and mother lived their short married lives here. That's why I wanted you to see it.'

'It's a lovely place,' she agreed.

'Can I show Laura round, Gran?'

'Of course.'

Rachel was about to rise but Paul had already begun to drag Laura out of the chair in which she was so comfortably ensconced.

'Come on, lazy. Fatty lazy.'

'What a thing to say!' Rachel said with indignation but when she looked at Laura, as if to give the lie to this statement, she saw that, indeed, she was no longer the slip of a girl she had been. She glanced at Em, who did not appear to have noticed but was gazing at them with a foolish smile on her face, as if caught up in all the mystery and magic of young love.

'Don't bother to come round, Gran,' Paul said, when Laura was on her feet. 'I want to show her myself, if that's OK.'

'Of course it's OK.' Rachel sat down again. 'You may live here one day yourself. I'm going to leave it to you in my will.'

'I'm going to live in the Hall, Gran,' Paul said, eyes narrowing. 'And *you're* going to live forever.' He stood on tiptoe so that he towered over her and waved his arms around as though making some kind of magic incantation. 'I hereby make thee immortal.'

'Silly boy!' Rachel reached out to smack him but he darted lithely out of the way then, clutching Laura by the hand, he dragged her towards the door.

After they'd gone Rachel, too, sat smiling foolishly. Then she said to Em:

'They are such a sweet couple, so engaging. Do you think she's pregnant?'

'What?' Em looked at her mother in amazement.

'I think she is. If so I hope he'll marry her.'

'Oh, *Mum*, don't be so conventional.' Em looked disgusted and lit a cigarette.

'But he *is* the Earl of Askham, Em. If he died and had a son he couldn't inherit, like Johnny. I always think of Johnny as the lawful earl, Ralph's heir; and he would have enjoyed it, too, unlike Paul, who doesn't care a bit. That makes me sad.'

'Well, let's wait and see,' Em said, but it made her sad thinking, still, of Sasha.

* * *

Paul leaned over Laura on his grandmother's large bed in the upstairs room, with its view of the Hall, where they'd been kissing.

'This is where I was conceived,' he said.

'How do you know?'

'My grandmother told me.'

'She's very broadminded, isn't she?'

'She is.' Paul kissed her again. 'I think she knows you're pregnant. I saw her looking at you in that thoughtful, shrewd way my grandmother has.'

'She's a lovely woman,' Laura returned his kiss.

'I'm glad you like her. That is very important to me. I adore her, you see, and I am serious about us living in the Hall . . . one day.'

Laura drew Paul's head down to her breast. She loved him but she was afraid of what her father would say when they told him about the baby; but here and now, with Paul in her arms, on the bed where he was conceived, in the house where his parents had enjoyed their too brief marriage, it didn't appear to matter.

The future seemed secure.

Stefanie sat upright in the chair, her hands on each arm. In her grief she looked extremely beautiful, like a dark, haunted wraith. Even Bobby was moved.

'I am *very* sorry about Sasha,' he assured her. 'I can't tell you how sorry. I want to do everything I can to ease your pain.'

'Thank you, Father.' She was quite regal in her attitude; altered, somehow.

'I really want us to forget the past, Stefanie, and to become fond of each other. I know we have had our difficulties; but they are over now. You need me and I want to help you. You have been very foolish, but I will forget that . . .'

'You can never resist a little dig, can you, Father?' Stefanie's lips curled with scorn. 'Even at a time like this.'

Bobby swallowed. He felt quite nervous under this queenly, accusatory gaze of his widowed daughter. Her bereavement seemed to have imbued her with a dignity he had never seen before. In a way she reminded him of Hélène when she had been at her most obdurate and proud. There was certainly no sign of Stefanie breaking down again, as everyone had feared.

'What do you mean by "dig", my dear?'

'That I sold my shares in your firm to help the company.'

'You've probably lost all that money. The crash will do the company no good. You can't possibly go to the City now.'

'The accident was due to the weather. There was *nothing* wrong with the plane.'

'But whatever the cause it won't do it any good. Not at the moment.'

Bobby paused and, going over to the window, stood there looking out for some time. Then he turned and gazed once more at her.

'Now Stefanie, I've been thinking. You must move down here. This is your home. Your grandmother would love to have you and I am prepared to look after you. It will give Irina a lot of pleasure and, as you know, her health isn't good. Now I . . .'

Stefanie, too, rose and, coming over, stood facing her father. She hadn't worn black because she didn't think Sasha would have wished it: she had on a grey skirt and a thick blue jumper with a turtle neck. Her hair was tied at the back with a ribbon. She wore no make-up and she looked very young; fragile and vulnerable.

'Father,' she said in a firm, strong voice that belied her appearance. 'I don't think you understand me at all. I have a home in Cheshire. I have two children at school there and my life is there. I want to be near the Neris, who are devastated by Sasha's death and Pascal, who also feels a little responsible, though he isn't. I can't possibly do what you say or accept your offer.'

'But you've no money.'

'How do you know?' She tilted her chin as she looked at him. 'Do you think I threw it *all* away? I kept a little just in case; not much, but enough to see the children through school and, if necessary, I can sell the house and buy a smaller one. I'm quite determined never to be dependent on you again, Father. I love my grandmother, but I've no intention of coming back here to rot as I did ten years ago. I'm quite strong and I'm healthy and I'm going to survive. Thank you, Father, but that's what I intend to do. I don't want your charity, your money, or even your sympathy.'

'You're your mother's daughter,' Bobby said angrily, wagging a finger at her. 'Stubborn and stupid.'

As Stefanie looked at her father she realized, with a sense of shock, that her reaction was one of immense pleasure rather than of pain. 'Thank you, Father. Nothing you could have said could have pleased me more.'

Irina Ferov was nearly ninety. She was arthritic and she moved with difficulty but, mentally, she had all her faculties and she loved being surrounded by members of her family, even in circumstances as tragic as this. She hadn't gone to Sasha's funeral because she would have broken down and she knew how important it was to be strong, because of Stefanie. Besides, she couldn't believe that Sasha was really dead. Pigheadedly she stuck to the idea that one day he'd come walking through the door. Instead she had stayed behind and lit candles by the family icons in her room, just in case they were right and he really was dead.

Now, in this same room with the candles still burning, she stroked Stefanie's head lying on her lap. As usual she was stretched out on her long sofa by the fire – a relic of St Petersburg days, purchased for her at a sale by Susan – and covered by a rug. Stefanie knelt on the floor as she had when she was a child, letting her babushka brush her long, luxurious black hair.

The strokes of the brush were soothing and Stefanie, her eyes closed, was nearly asleep. It was easy to sleep like this yet, at night, it was impossible. At night she lay awake and thought of that journey that need never have taken place, that crash that shouldn't have happened. With it she also thought of the fact that she had so nearly been in the plane herself, and her two children would have been orphaned and the child in her womb unborn. There were some things, after all, to make one think that a capricious God had his good side.

With the even strokes of the brush Irina crooned a Russian lullaby she used to sing to the three Lighterman girls when they had lived with her in those far-off days in Paris. Now Olga was the mother of four children, Natasha was a famous film star and her darling Stefanie, the difficult one, was a widow. In losing a grandchild Irina felt herself doubly bereaved and, but for the fact that she was so old and near death herself, she thought she would never have survived the shock of hearing Sasha was dead, if he really was. In her heart she doubted.

'I think he knew he was going to die, Babushka,' Stefanie murmured, after Irina had stopped crooning.

'Why is that, little one?' Irina put her hand on Stefanie's head as if in blessing; that old, parchment-like hand knotted now with arthritic bumps and screwed up like a monkey's claw.

'He wanted Pascal to move back to our house. He seemed very insistent on it, as though it was very important for us as well as Pascal. And yet Pascal kept on telling him he was quite happy where he was and didn't want to move. I think Sasha knew that Pascal would look after me,' Stefanie paused and closed her eyes. 'He said the night before he died that he would never leave me. I think he knew that he was talking about his spirit.'

Then Stefanie wept as she had never wept before and, cherishing her to her breast, her old grandmother wept with her.

And that was how Anna found them some time later, and she wept too.

Anna thought that the death of Sasha was somehow to do with her. The Askhams had regarded her as cursed and she felt that, indeed, she was. She had brought a lot of trouble on them and, somehow, it was as though she and Gunther had lured her brother to his death. They hadn't needed the plane but they wanted to have it as people do who feel acquisitive over possessions, wanting to hoard and stare and gloat like a miser over his gold in a drawer or under the floorboards. They wanted to tell everyone that they had one of the new British 'Sprites' with twin jet engines, the fastest small aircraft in the world, with the longest range.

This was to be a symbol of their wealth, and so much more. Now Gunther wanted to buy the Hall, was still talking to Hugo and lawyers about it though Paul, in his role as titular head of the family, opposed it. The Hall was not for sale, he said. It was rather like the fight with Bobby all over again, though this time Hugo was on Gunther's side and so were most of the family.

When Gunther went up to London to consult lawyers and property experts Anna stayed with her grandmother and mother at Robertswood. Susan was so shattered by Sasha's death that some feared that that strong, determined woman would have her own kind of breakdown. She could hardly speak or bear to mention his name without weeping and this was to continue for some months while she fought against her overwhelming grief.

Anna did all she could to comfort her mother and, in the end, Susan perceived that Anna needed her, too. She told her it was ridiculous to feel responsible for Sasha's death.

'The family have always regarded me as cursed,' Anna said to Susan the day they returned from seeing Stefanie on the train back to Manchester.

'That's absolute rubbish,' Susan said, blowing her nose vigorously. 'The only thing responsible for Sasha's death was fate. He could have died sooner or later; but it happened when it did. I regard that as fate. He was missing in the war for six months and they even had a memorial service for him . . .'

Susan started to cry again. She would feel calm and strong and then, without warning, she would burst into tears. Anna did her best to comfort her but the only thing to do at a time like this was let her mother cry and, sometimes, she would cry, too. They tried to plan a little for the future: what Stefanie would do and what would happen when Irina was on her own just with her memories.

'In a way it *would* be quite nice if we had the Hall,' Anna said. 'We would be near Babushka and you could come and stay. The only thing is, do the family want us there?'

'They want the money,' Susan said, with the shrewd practicality of the businesswoman. 'And if Hugo doesn't object I don't see why anyone else should, especially Paul, who has hardly two pennies to rub together.'

'One day he says he will be very rich,' Anna said. 'He assured me of that. It is due to Paul insisting on the terms of the trust that the Hall will be leased and not sold. I feel, in a way, he hates Gunther because of me.'

'It's because his mother was a Jew,' Susan whispered, as if there were people around listening at keyholes. 'Some people can never forgive. It's not as though Gunther were a Nazi, is it?'

'No,' Anna replied, but she didn't press the point. Remembering the picture of Gunther with Hitler in 1932, his reluctance to say what he did in the war, she felt it was something of which she could never be sure.

After a few more days Susan flew to Venice, Anna and Gunther caught the train back to Frankfurt, as Anna hadn't been able to bear the thought of flying after Sasha's death, and Irina was left in the large house alone with her icons, her candles and her memories of the past: of Sasha as a young boy which meant that, at least in her mind, he was still alive.

Stefanie drew up by the front of the house and saw that the lights were burning. She hadn't told anyone when she and the children would be travelling north as it was just that kind of welcome she wished to avoid. Now she knew that, away from the family, she could relax, unwind and give herself up to the kind of grief and bereavement that had only been possible, and not always then, in the company of her grandmother.

The children would go to school and life would go on again.

Stefanie knew that since the accident her behaviour had been mechanical; she existed but was aware of little else. On the taxi drive home she had realized that she would be returning to a house that was empty, but full of the sounds and smells of Sasha. His clothes were in the

671

wardrobe, his wash things still in the bathroom. She would smell him, be aware of his presence for days if not years; yet she would never see him again.

Like Irina, she was still inclined to believe that that was impossible. For Sasha had been to her not only husband, lover and father of her children, but he was a cousin, a close friend she had known all her life, part of life: doubly part of her.

Once at the house she briskly paid the taxi driver, who had taken her two small cases up to the door, and Nicky and Galina bounded ahead as if they were glad to be home. They hadn't seen their dog and their cat for nearly ten days; there were the rabbits in the hutch outside the back door and the hamsters in a straw-lined box in Galina's bedroom.

As Nicky got to the front door it opened and Pascal appeared on the threshold, both hands on the wheels of his chair, his expression that of one uncertain of his welcome.

Stefanie stopped when she saw him, but Galina rushed into his arms and Nicky gave a cry and embraced him, too.

Pascal smiled up at Stefanie over the heads of the children and suddenly she smiled at him, too, and held out her hand.

'Welcome home,' he said, as she stooped to kiss his cheek. 'I've come to look after you.'

Luis Barrio sat in a darkened room by the side of a bed on which lay a man very close to death. The room stank of alcohol, vomit and something indefinable, probably heroin or a combination of the drugs from which, combined with alcohol, the man was dying. The curtains at the window scarcely met in the middle and outside the lights of Brooklyn shone like a beckoning miasma of all that was pleasurable in the world. Well, not pleasurable, maybe, or exactly good, but bright, fun-loving, enviable to a man who had once been a prominent jazz musician.

This was what had killed David Lighterman who, at the age of only thirty-five, was near his end.

Luis was only twenty-four but since he'd left England he had observed and experienced a great deal. In the past year he had travelled completely round the world and the reports and, especially, the photographs he'd sent back to his mother had appeared not only in the paper edited by her but in a number of other papers, journals and magazines as well.

Luis was one of the breed of photo-journalists who follow a wandering, peripatetic career and he was fortunate in that he had linguistic skills, a natural ability with a camera and an inherited gift for writing. Very few people were able to say that he only got published in *The Sentinel* because he was the son of the editor. He got published in a lot of other places as well. Editors clamoured for his work.

Luis had heard about David in Georgetown where his cousin Joe Verdi had come to a full stop in his search. He knew that David had been there but not for a year or more, and he was then known to be in the United States, from which Joe was barred because of his recent imprisonment. Luis had volunteered to go to New York in place of Joe and, with his inquisitive nose and natural skills as a reporter, had finally tracked David down to this small hotel in downtown New York when it was already almost too late.

Too late even for the money which David had so desperately needed. In his lucid moments David, who at first hadn't known Luis, pleaded first for money and then for help. But if he got help he'd have to give up dope and he didn't want to do that. It was hard to get a doctor to visit a bum hotel in New York but when one did come he told Luis it was hopeless, just a matter of time. Pocketing his large fee, he left.

Luis had been with David a couple of days, able to do nothing but watch him deteriorate. His conversation was rambling, disconnected and mostly to do with the past. Sometimes he imagined he was a small boy waiting for his father and, in those rare moments, Luis learned just how much David hated the man who had already spent a fortune trying to find him. It was a dreadful irony that David detested the man who loved him more than anyone. From what David said Luis knew it was no use sending for his father or mother. Besides the distress his condition would cause them they would be able to do nothing, and would only add to their son's own misery in his dying hours.

Luis, used to bunking down anywhere, had made himself a makeshift bed in the corner of the room and looked after David. He didn't need much and Luis couldn't do much, except try to get him to the lavatory before soiling the already stinking bed, and providing a bowl every time David was sick.

It was a terrible way to go, Luis thought, glad that he had this lesson relatively early in life before he was ever tempted to experiment with drugs himself. The greatest shock was that David, with his unkempt greyish hair and stubble on his chin, looked like a very old man. Luis had scarcely been able to recognize him; but David had eventually recognized Luis and, in some of his clearer moments, he continually wept for all that he had lost.

David gurgled and Luis, thinking he was going to be sick again, leapt to reach for the clean, disinfected bowl he always kept ready. David, however, gripped his wrist with surprising strength and stayed Luis in his tracks.

'Don't go,' he whispered. 'It's getting hard to see.'

'It *is* dark,' Luis said, looking anxiously at the lights beyond the window.

'Is it? That's good.' David clenched and unclenched Luis's hand. 'When I'm over this I'm going to go and stay at home with my mother and father. I'm young enough to start again, aren't I?'

'Of course,' Luis said, pressing his hand and giving him water to sip, although usually it made him sick again. David was so weak, so enervated that he couldn't keep anything down, even water. Already his thin emaciated body looked like a cadaver. Luis wondered how it was possible for a person to imagine he could survive this. It seemed, indeed, that the will to live did remain even in the most hopeless cases.

'Luis,' David said, after a long pause. 'There's a child . . .'

'A child . . .' Luis bent forward to catch the strangulated words.

'A little boy. I think his name is Tom . . . My father would be very happy about Tom and, if anything should happen to me, you know, I'd like him to know about him. Tom is . . .' David's voice trailed off and his head lolled on one side. He had many periods like this when he lapsed into unconsciousness and Luis, puzzled, waited by the side of the bed, anxious to hear more about Tom. David's child?

He waited all day and night; but David never woke up again. In a way, for a man who had abused his mind and body so much, it was merciful.

The woman who opened the door looked very much younger than David. She was a bright, rather pretty girl who seemed about nineteen, though the child standing behind her almost made that seem impossible. Luis had been on the tracks of the woman for a long time; enquiries

675

and an address in David's notebook had, through a circuitous route, led him to her.

Luis asked if he could come in and, when he had exchanged some small talk and smiled at the boy, he asked if he and the girl could be alone. The boy, aged about seven, was of a startling beauty and Luis wondered how David could have let himself go when he had so much to live for. The flat in the Bronx was neat, clean, and very tidy. It was small, consisting of no more than one room with kitchen and bathroom. The woman told the boy to go outside and play and he went obediently, no sulking or nagging as most young children sent out at an interesting moment would go in for.

'Nice boy,' Luis said, watching him exit with a polite grin and a wave. 'Is that Tom?'

'How did you know his name?'

'I know his name,' Luis said, looking round. 'But not yours.'

'I'm Mandy,' the girl said. 'Amanda Jane. May I ask who you are and why you're here?'

Luis was carrying his camera, he never went anywhere without it and, as he looked for somewhere to put the heavy case, the girl gazed at him, at it, with interest. 'Is it something to do with that?'

'Are you a model?' Luis asked and Mandy inclined her head, though he could also sense her disappointment: if he'd been here to photograph her he wouldn't have asked if she were a model.

'Would you like some coffee?' she said and, as Luis nodded, she went into the kitchen and he sat looking round the room. The furniture was cheap but sturdy and there wasn't much of it – a divan bed, a sofa that obviously doubled up as a second bed, a table with a plastic cloth on it and some plastic tulips in a vase, a sideboard and a radiogram. The walls, a bright yellow, looked as though they had been freshly painted and the carpet on the floor, though cheap, was relatively new.

Mandy came back with two cups and saucers on a tray, a small plate of biscuits by the side. Luis had the feeling that she still thought he was connected with work and, as she put the tray down, she confirmed this:

'I dance, too. Did you see my picture in one of the show magazines?'

'Look,' Luis felt awkward. 'I'm here about David . . .'

The girl stood up and Luis saw that her bright, professional smile was replaced by an expression of unease.

'David . . .' she said, sitting down again.

'David Lighterman . . .'

'Oh, I don't know anyone called David Lighterman,' she said, as if with relief, smiling again. 'The David I knew was David Younghusband.'

'I think it's the same David,' Luis said awkwardly. 'He mentioned the boy, Tom.'

'Oh, that's how you heard about me and Tom.' Mandy looked disappointed but resigned, as if this kind of thing were quite familiar to her – hopes raised and dashed time after time. However, she quickly resumed her brave smile as though nothing daunted her for very long. Luis instinctively liked her.

'David is my cousin,' Luis said. 'I should have said he was my cousin. He died about a month ago.'

'Oh, dear.' Mandy looked momentarily sad. 'What a waste of a life. Drugs, I suppose?'

'I'm afraid so.'

'That's why I left him,' she said. 'I didn't want Tom to grow up with a father like that. David made it very easy for me to leave him, anyway. Life was no picnic, I can tell you.' Mandy wiped away a tear as though for what might have been. 'No use crying over spilt milk, is there? I didn't know he'd go so quickly, though. He can't have been much over thirty.'

'Thirty-five,' Luis said. 'He looked about seventy.'

'I hadn't seen him for a couple of years,' Mandy said. 'Not since the divorce. He paid no alimony, nothing for the child. I left him to get on with it. I'm sorry, though. He had talent and it was a waste of a life.'

'Did you say divorce?' Luis said. 'Were you *married* to David?'

'Oh, yes.' Mandy looked a touch affronted. 'Tom is his child. It's all perfectly legal. I thought you knew. I use my maiden name. There's a birth certificate . . . and a marriage one, though I'm not sure I could put my hand on it.'

'Maybe you should,' Luis said, feeling a little like Father Christmas. 'How much did you know about David's family? His father for instance?'

'Absolutely nothing,' Mandy said cheerfully. 'He said there wasn't much to tell. He hated him, though. My goodness, how he hated him. I often wondered what he did to merit such hatred, poor man.'

CHAPTER 27

Charlotte looked out of the back window towards the wood that ran along Alderley Edge, a high formation of rock which was a local beauty spot and from which there was a commanding view of the flat Cheshire plain. Sasha and Stefanie's house stood about a mile out of Alderley on the road linking Alderley Edge with Prestbury, the even more picturesque village on the way to Macclesfield where the Cohens lived. Charlotte peeled off her rubber gloves and looked at the clock. Half an hour at least before they were due and time for a cup of coffee. She finished drying the plates, stacking the clean breakfast dishes, which the cleaner would know what to do with when she arrived.

After grinding the coffee beans Charlotte filled the percolator and set it on a high gas. Strangely, she felt rather nervous and fussed about in front of the kitchen mirror making sure her hair was all right, smoothing her dress, the unceasing and largely instinctive preoccupation with appearance of an attractive woman.

Charlotte went to the kitchen window again and looked out on the smooth lawn which overlooked a field in which a couple of horses were grazing. It was a very calm, peaceful scene and Charlotte was aware of a contentment stealing over her that she couldn't recall feeling quite so profoundly for years. Her mother often talked about oases of happiness that came at the most unlikely moments and, in these last few years of her life, she had learned all too well what her mother meant. In a crowded world full of anxiety and stress there were moments when one could feel utterly and serenely at peace: such as she felt now, waiting for Pascal to bring Stefanie home from the hospital with baby Alexander, born a week before.

Charlotte had gladly gone up to Cheshire to look after the children while Stefanie went into hospital to have her baby. It was an unusual role for Charlotte, not one that she was often called upon to play. Angelica was extremely self contained and well organized in her domestic arrangements, always had been especially when she was married to Dick and had two young children and a career. There had been very few calls for help from her mother then, and there were none now that she and Perry led a sybaritic life between the South of France, Paris, New York, London and Scotland, where they relaxed for the summer after Angelica's busy round of engagements.

Emily and Myles were both at boarding-schools, despite their extreme youth, and Angelica appeared largely to have forgotten about them. With Dick in the USA it was up to Charlotte to visit them as regularly as she could, and take them goodies and what other crumbs of more spiritual comfort she could offer them in the absence of both their parents.

Stefanie, on the contrary, was, since her recovery from illness, a wonderful mother; she refused to let Nicky and Galina be sent off to school and, since, Sasha's death, they came first in everything.

And Pascal? Where did he come? Pretty near the top, too, Charlotte thought as, reflectively, she turned away from the window and poured her coffee, which had been busy percolating.

Pascal had moved into the cottage shortly after Sasha's funeral. It was an ideal arrangement because he was independent, as he liked, but near Stefanie if she wanted company, a shoulder to cry on, which she sometimes did. She was brave but she was human and after the funeral, when she came down to earth and realized what was missing in her life, she began to be prey to a melancholy that was nothing like her former depression, and was little more than what most bereaved people had to endure, but it worried those who loved her, all the same.

It seemed to be the thought of the baby she was carrying that kept Stefanie going all those months, that and the help of Pascal, which was always there when she needed him. Also, because he, too, needed help, like the children, it gave her something with which to occupy herself. She was busy looking after others and that took her mind off her own misfortunes.

Charlotte took her coffee to the lounge that overlooked the main road so that she could see the car coming. The new baby had been called after his father, though he would be known by the diminutive Alex and not Sasha. This was also a tribute to his grandfather, Alexei, who had been callously murdered at the end of the war by the Resistance.

In the week since she'd been in Cheshire Charlotte had felt very happy. Not only because all had gone well with Stefanie, but because she had been able to spend so much time with Pascal. He had taken her around the factory to show her that everything was going well, with a full order book despite the crash. An enquiry had shown without doubt that the tragedy was due to the sudden intensity of the storm as Sasha was coming in to land, and a possible misreading on his part of the instruments because of freak conditions. The Mach 2 'Sprite' was still way ahead of its competitors and Bobby's gloomy prognostications about the market had, for once, been wrong.

But these days Bobby was a happy man. Luis had arrived home that year bringing with him his grandson Tom Lighterman, who Bobby had had no idea existed. The joy of Bobby was such that it had transfigured the life of that gloomy, somewhat choleric man. Many people said that for all the misery he had caused it was something he didn't deserve.

But it was nice for Tom, too, to discover a wealthy grandfather who would give him a sumptuous home, send him to school and look after his mother as well. Mandy flew over to meet Tom's grandfather with Luis, and the extent of the Lighterman fortune didn't seem to impress her all that much, which confirmed Luis's impression that she was a nice girl. In an uncharacteristic outburst of generosity Bobby settled on Mandy a large allowance and bought her a comfortable apartment in Manhattan, which would also be a home for Tom when he visited his mother. Despite his grief at hearing of the fate of David he hadn't seen his son for nearly fifteen years, and Tom more than compensated for his loss. Besides, Bobby wouldn't have known what to do with a drug addict: the very thought of the scandal would have horrified him. That was the truth and people who knew Bobby realized it. Bobby and David would not have got on; he was better off dead, with his innocent son one day inheriting what would have been his.

Charlotte got up to look out of the window but there was no sign of John Neri's estate car, which he had used to go and get Stefanie from hospital. She went to the kitchen, checked her hair and dress yet again, powdered her nose, touched up her lips and poured herself more coffee.

It was strange the way things worked out, she thought, returning to the sitting-room. Who would have thought that five months after Sasha's death Stefanie would have found happiness again? Maybe that *was* what Sasha had meant by being with her always; he had left her a son to look after her. Charlotte had dearly loved Sasha as she loved Stefanie because, most of all, she had loved Hélène

682

who had perished in the war; who had been her companion and friend through so many horrendous, difficult days. Like the daughter she had never really known or understood, Hélène's spirit had been refined by hardship and suffering and she had contrived somehow to cheer all those around her. Even some of her German captors respected her.

Charlotte, herself, had also found a way of compromise in her life. Arthur got on with his business and his golf and she busied herself with her charities, her family and especially, now, her grandchildren.

Charlotte thought that her responsibilites towards Myles and Emily were similar to those of Rachel who had brought up Paul, Flora and Giles; and that history had a way of repeating itself all over again.

And then the reflective peace of the morning was interrupted by the sound of a car's wheels on the gravel, and there was a sudden banging of doors, barking of dogs and the cry of a new-born baby.

Charlotte quickly put down her cup and ran to the front door just as Stefanie emerged from the car, carefully holding little Alexander, while John Neri went round to the back of his car to get Pascal's wheelchair and put it up for him. Galina and Nicky were clearly excited though Nicky, conscious now that he was an elder brother, helped his mother up the steps to where Charlotte stood on the porch, arms open wide.

'Welcome home.' Charlotte threw her arms round Stefanie, careful not to touch little Alexander, who had stopped crying and was looking round with a remarkable alertness for a week-old baby. It was difficult, yet, to say who he resembled. 'May I take him?' Charlotte felt almost as excited as if Alex were her own grandchild and, carefully supporting the back of his head, she took him into her arms.

Stefanie immediately turned to see that Pascal was all right, but he was already in his chair, propelling himself up the specially-constructed ramp into the house. He was smiling as proudly as if he were the father.

'Isn't he terrific?' he asked his mother.

'Terrific.' Charlotte edged back the woolly shawl to have another glimpse at Alex. 'I think he's gone to sleep. Perfectly relaxed.'

Charlotte had been at the hospital with Pascal when Alex was born so she had seen him when he was a few minutes old and almost every day since then. She felt a close sense of family with Pascal and Stefanie as though Alex were indeed the son Pascal had always wanted.

So as not to make them feel out of things Stefanie turned to her two elder children, holding each by the hand as John Neri carried her small case into the house and excused himself.

'Can't you stay to lunch, John?'

'I must go back,' John said. 'We have a possible buyer from America arriving this afternoon.'

'I have to go back, too,' Pascal said.

'Oh.' Both Stefanie and Charlotte looked disappointed.

'I promise I'll be back soon and we'll have a celebration dinner.' With that Pascal turned towards his cottage. Charlotte wondered if there were more to his behaviour than a need to get back to the factory.

She wondered if, now, he would try and distance himself from Stefanie and her new baby or if, by any chance, Alex would bring them closer?

Charlotte stayed on for a week with Stefanie and her new baby. It gave them a chance to have many an intimate chat together, to re-establish the *rapport* they'd shared so many years before. Even when Charlotte lived in Paris before the war she and Stefanie had been close, because

Angelica was friendly with Natasha and the girls had seen a good deal of each other.

In many ways they were some of the happiest days of Charlotte's life in recent years, getting to know Alex, helping Stefanie to bath and change him, seeing how well his mother was, and how happy. Stefanie's recovery from her serious illness and remarkable strength over this recent ordeal were almost incredible to someone like Charlotte, who had visited her often in the clinic, who had known how ill she had really been.

The day before she left was a perfect July day, and the two women wheeled the baby into the garden. Alex slept, protected by the sun. Galina had gone off to play with a friend down the road and Nicky with another. Stefanie sank into a deck-chair next to Charlotte, sighed and held out her hand.

'I wish you didn't have to go,' she said.

'I'll come back often.'

'It's not the same. I wish you lived nearer and we could see each other every day. You know, Charlotte, you're like a mother to me, and I miss you.' She put her head back and closed her eyes. 'Isn't it funny how Mummy left you, and Sasha left Pascal, to look after me. People do love me, after all.'

'Of course they love you! But don't you mean that Sasha left you Alex, not Pascal?'

Stefanie opened her eyes and gazed at the sky. 'I do mean Pascal. Sasha wanted to move here solely because of the cottage.'

'But he loved Pascal, too.'

'I'm sure he had foreknowledge of his death. Don't you have foreknowledge about bad events? Didn't you know, in advance, about Paolo? Didn't you feel he was going to die?'

Charlotte sat up trying, with a sense of shock, to recall

the past. Incredibly it was thirty-one years since Paolo had been killed at Monza, yet she could clearly recall her exact feelings on that occasion, when Angelica was only a few months old.

'If you're married to someone in a dangerous occupation you're always afraid; but you can live with it and I did. Are you telling me that *you* had a sense of apprehension about Sasha?'

'Oh, I agree with you.' Stefanie sheltered her eyes against the sun encroaching on their spot in the garden. 'One always has a feeling of relief when they turn up after a flight or, in your case, after a race. I didn't have any real feeling of foreboding about Sasha but I know that every time he talked about the future, how perfect things were and so on, I told him to stop. I remember thinking he was tempting fate and that feeling was particularly strong in the months before he died, because we were so especially happy. We had never been happier and sometimes I thought it was too good to last. I'm horribly pessimistic, I know, but there it was.'

There was a catch in Stefanie's voice and she stopped speaking. Charlotte pressed her hand.

'I know how you feel. Don't give in, now or ever. I never gave in and Mother never gave in. None of our family have had a specially happy life and you *have* got Pascal.' Charlotte paused, not quite knowing how to go on. 'He does love you, you know, and he'll look after you.'

'He's my best friend,' Stefanie replied. 'But for him I really don't know what I'd do.'

The following day Charlotte returned to London, driving herself, reluctant to leave Stefanie behind coping with the new baby. It was all very well to say that Pascal would look after her, but Pascal wasn't there during the day and frequently he needed looking after himself, despite his desire for independence.

When she got home the house was in silence, such a contrast to the busy scene she'd left behind.

Charlotte went up to her bedroom to unpack and stood for a long time looking round her. Really it was such an impersonal place. Everything was so neat and tidy, nothing out of place: her silver brush set on her dressing-table with its polished glass top; a decanter full of fresh water and tumbler by the side of her bed together with her alarm clock, a photo of herself with Paolo and the children when young. So as not to make Arthur jealous she had a large triptych of herself and him with Jeremy between them, taken soon after Jeremy was born. It looked a bit like a modern day Holy Family with the doting parents gazing at the child who had very little on. It was a studio portrait, clearly posed, and they were out of fashion today. Jeremy only tolerated it because it was one of the few of him and his parents together.

There was her neat bed with the purple ruched satin cover, large matching pillow exactly placed against the mahogany bed head.

She had slept alone like this for years. There were no visits from Arthur and none would now be welcome. Whether Arthur had other women she didn't know and now she cared very little. If he asked her for a divorce she wouldn't be too upset. Once it had been very important to be seen with Arthur; to go places together, to have a man by her side; but now it seemed less so. She did most things alone, especially now that Arthur had left the House of Commons. That had marked the end of Arthur's ambition. He had always hoped to be a Cabinet Minister, a person of importance, someone who people looked up to and to whom they deferred. And to some extent they had and did; but he had never been in the Cabinet and his failure had meant that his Parliamentary career had been a disappointment to him.

Charlotte sat in the chair by her bureau and began to go through her mail. There had been a note from Arthur to say he wouldn't be in for dinner and from her cleaner announcing that the French polisher had called but she had sent him away because she had no instructions. Now they had no resident staff. A bedroom was kept ready for each of the grandchildren when they came to stay but most of the rooms, unused, were merely dusted every week.

In many ways it was like a house of the dead, Charlotte thought, feeling restless and getting up again. And for what had she lived her life? For what had she suffered and endured and gone through such terrible adventures in the war? She sometimes thought of Marc and wondered what would have happened had she divorced Arthur, as Marc had wanted so soon after the end of the war, and married him?

There was a letter from Joe, happily settled in Rio, and one from an old friend she had modelled with in Paris. There were several bills, notices of meetings, appeals for money, the usual things. Charlotte consulted her watch.

It was seven in the evening and there was nothing for her to do, nowhere to go. Nowhere she particularly wanted to go. No one needed her or wanted her. She was expendable, unimportant. In the fridge there would be salad and cold meat, maybe a bottle of Chablis. Arthur would be back about midnight, probably a little tight, and she would lie in bed listening to him stumbling into his own room. Then he would stumble out again and she would hear him spending a long and very noisy penny, the sound echoing along the corridor. Then there would be the flush of the lavatory, Arthur stumbling back again, the sound of his door closing and silence.

Two people living together, but separately, as though serving a lifetime in prison.

Charlotte realized she was on the verge of being sorry for herself, giving in to self-pity. Askhams didn't do that.

The trill of the phone interrupted Charlotte's introspective thoughts and she went over to the side of her bed and picked it up.

'Hello?' she enquired in that quiet, calm, beautifully modulated voice.

It was Em.

'I've been trying to get you all day,' Em said. 'Stefanie said you left this morning.'

Fear clutched at Charlotte's heart, as it so often did. Nothing was safe, things were always happening. When Em spoke in a certain tone of voice it always filled her with alarm.

'Is something the matter with Mother?' she said. Mother, Emily, Myles, Stefanie, Pascal, it could have been anyone. She never worried much about Arthur.

'Mother's perfectly all right,' Em sounded irritable. 'It's Flora. She's been arrested and I wondered if you could get hold of Arthur and ask him what to do.'

Arthur always knew what to do, even when he was slightly tipsy, as he was when he came home at midnight. He was surprised to find Charlotte still up and fully-clothed waiting for him and at first he, too, thought something was wrong with one of the members of the family and sobered up immediately.

'Grandchildren all right?' he blinked in the unaccustomed glare of the light.

'Perfectly,' Charlotte replied. 'It's Flora. She's been arrested.'

'Oh, God, what on earth for?' Arthur slumped in a chair and lit a cigarette.

'Assaulting a policeman. There was an awful fracas in Trafalgar Square over Mosley and the Fascists and there, needless to say, was our Flora in the thick of it.'

'But Flora's not a Fascist?' Arthur blinked uncomprehendingly.

'Of course she isn't! Just the opposite. That's why she was there, opposing them.'

'I wish she'd mind her own business,' Arthur said.

'But Flora thinks it is her business. Em is rather upset and said you'd know what to do.'

'Call Makepeace.' Arthur got up and went to the telephone, turning the pages of his diary as he did. 'You'd think after all this time we'd have a lawyer in the family.'

'We have. Christopher, but we don't talk to him.'

'Maybe Jeremy ought to stay at the Bar after all.' Arthur found his solicitor's home number, dialled it, apologized for disturbing him and told him to get over immediately to Bow Street, where Flora was being held.

Rachel sat in the part of the court reserved for the public and, except that on the last occasion she was there it had been her in the dock, it was like history repeating itself.

The Bow Street Magistrates' Court hadn't changed so very much over the years, except for a coat of paint, and it was quite easy for her to go back half a century and visualize that day in 1913 when she had been accused of causing an affray in front of her own house. It had been the time of the suffragette disturbances and Rachel, smarting from her husband's infidelity, had turned to militancy.

She had been prepared to go to gaol but Bosco had refused to allow her to be prosecuted for breaking the windows of her own home. The result was humiliation for her while the rest of her comrades were sent to prison.

This time it looked as though her niece would carry her

mantle and be the first female member of the Askham family to be a convicted criminal.

Yet criminal was hardly the word for what Flora had done; scuffles with the police during the anti-fascist demonstrations in Trafalgar Square. She had attacked a policeman while resisting arrest. Normally the penalty would be a fine, but Flora was determined to be a martyr. Like her aunt so many years before she refused to be represented by Arthur's harassed solicitor, John Makepeace, who had spent a long time arguing with Flora before her court appearance.

Now here Flora was, in the dock, head flung back, hands gripping the box, lecturing the magistrate on the evils of Fascism.

'What is more, your worship . . .' Flora said, but the magistrate leaned forward and banged the top of the magisterial bench.

'*Miss* Bolingbroke, may I remind you that this is a court of law and I am a servant of the Crown. *You* are in the dock accused of a serious charge and not on a soap box in Hyde Park.'

The crowd of onlookers stirred, but didn't dare laugh. The Askham family, particularly Arthur, didn't find it amusing at all. The magistrate, looking severely at Flora, went on:

'I understand that you do not wish to be legally represented, that you are not sorry for what you have done and that you would be prepared to do it again.'

'In defence of freedom, your worship . . .' Flora shouted, while a policewoman went menacingly over to her.

Again the spectators stirred and looked at one another. Rachel felt nervous for Flora but also rather proud of her. She gave a sidelong glance at Em, who had her chin in her hand, gazing at Flora.

'I have no alternative, Miss Bolingbroke, in view of the serious nature of your offence, your lack of sorrow and your totally uncompromising attitude towards this bench to sentence you to seven days in prison. Please stand down.'

This time a gasp swept the court as the policewoman helped Flora down from the dock and the next case was called.

Flora darted a look of triumph at her family before being hustled down to the cells below.

Arthur hoped no one would recognize him as he helped his family from the court, but there was little chance of that. Outside the court in Bow Street they were pounced upon by reporters asking for a statement. Arthur knew that the sensible and dignified thing to do was to make one and, straightening his tie and clearing his throat, he said:

'My family much regret what Miss Bolingbroke has said in the court today. We apologize on her behalf, we . . .'

'I think my niece has got very strong principles,' Rachel looked contemptuously at Arthur and rather elbowed him to one side. 'What my son-in-law says may *not* reflect the view of the whole family. I certainly don't feel we can speak for my niece.'

All the reporters, including a TV crew, gleefully converged on Rachel, sensing possibly another scandal, and held the microphones in front of her. Except that in 1913 there were no microphones or TV cameras the scene was very much the same as it had been then, in the same location. Rachel had a sense of *déjà vu*.

'Do you support what your niece has done, Lady Askham?' One of the TV reporters in the background was telling his unseen audience, for the news later that day, just who Lady Askham was and what she had done. 'Lady Askham herself was in this same dock in 1913 . . .'

'Naturally I support my niece in her views about Sir Oswald Mosley and his supporters, but I do *not* approve of contempt of court. Of course I don't want her to go to prison . . .'

Arthur's car had come round the corner from Covent Garden and was waiting for them. Assisted by Arthur, Charlotte was attempting to get in. Em had stayed behind in an effort to see Flora before she was taken to Holloway and Luis, who had been covering the scene with his camera, stood back from the car, taking pictures.

Rachel was about to go on with her discourse – one always enjoyed an audience – when Arthur beckoned impatiently to her and pushed her rather unceremoniously after Charlotte into the car. When they were all in he told his chauffeur to get away from the scene as quickly as he could.

As the car leapt towards the Strand, Arthur, sitting next to the chauffeur, mopped his brow.

'What a *frightful* ordeal,' he said. 'Trust Flora to bring scandal on the family. Makepeace will send me a hefty bill, you know.'

'That's all you really think of, isn't it?' Charlotte, red spots of anger on both her cheeks, was busily trying to banish them with her compact and puff. Rachel nervously touched her arm. It was July and it was hot. Arthur was still mopping his brow, unseasonably and unsuitably dressed in a starched collar and tie, a pin-striped business suit, strands of damp hair plastered over his otherwise bald dome.

'Don't let's have a row,' Rachel said. 'It's so awfully hot. Poor Flora. Prison will be ghastly.'

'Well, it's her own fault.' Arthur gave instructions to his chauffeur to put him off at his club in St James's. 'Do you realize she'll have a prison record for the rest of her life? She'll never be able to go to America.'

'How *awful*,' Charlotte said, with heavy sarcasm.

'Really, Charlotte, one would think you are actually pleased to have a gaolbird in the family.' Arthur looked at her with irritation. 'I suppose you're sorry you're not there yourself.'

'I'm also rather proud of Flora, if you want to know.' Charlotte gave the back of Arthur's head a withering look. 'Mother tried hard to get sent to prison just before the First World War and now Flora's following in a proud tradition. You're proud of her too, aren't you, Mother?'

'I am, indeed,' Rachel said firmly. 'But I'd rather we dropped the subject now, as Arthur is so upset.'

'Don't expect Charlotte to be concerned about that, Rachel.' Arthur turned pointedly to give her a wan smile. 'Nothing pleases Charlotte more than . . .'

'Oh, *please* do stop being provocative.' Charlotte leaned forward to tap the chauffeur on the shoulder as they came into Lower Regent Street. 'Would you put me and Lady Askham off at Fortnum's, Smith? We'll have a cup of coffee there. And don't wait.'

'Yes, Lady Charlotte.' The chauffeur looked at Arthur who shook his head.

'I'm lunching at my club. You can pick me up at about three. Charlotte?'

'No, thank you.' Charlotte looked out of the window, lips pursed. 'We can find our own way home.'

It was rather late for coffee and Charlotte and Rachel decided to have a light lunch on the ground floor at Fortnum's, which was full of memories of past childhood treats and not only that. It was just round the corner from their former home in St James's Square which, since its sale after the war, had been turned into yet another club for affluent members of the male sex only. Fortnum's had been like the local corner shop in the days when the children were young, though it was the servants, not they,

694

who had to pop round for a pound of sugar or a packet of Fortnum's special tea which Dulcie Askham had been so fond of.

'Yes, Fortnum's brought back memories and certainly, at least in retrospect, they seemed happier times. One couldn't always be sure because, invariably, the past always had a roseate glow. Rachel gazed at her daughter, whose face was still pinched with vexation, cutting into her ham omelette with a fork.

'You don't get on at all, do you, Charlotte? You and Arthur? Is it *always* like this?'

'Like what, Mother?' Charlotte rather pointedly broke her roll and gazed at her mother, long elegant fingers each holding a jagged piece of white bread. On one of her wrists was a gold bracelet which Arthur had given her when they were married. He had promised her a gold charm on each anniversary of the wedding and for many years he had kept this up. But for the last few years the bracelet had remained with the same number of charms, thirteen. Arthur had given her no more after 1958 when she had found out about Jill.

'You know what I mean.' Rachel kept her eyes on the charm bracelet. 'Arguments the whole time.'

'Well, we don't see all that much of each other to argue a lot.' Charlotte spread butter on her roll and put one of the small pieces in her mouth. She still had lovely white, even teeth. On some days, but not today, she could easily pass for forty or, maybe, even thirty-seven or eight, instead of her fifty-odd years. She was elegant, poised and she had kept her figure. If only she had kept her happiness, too.

'It's an unpleasant atmosphere, though,' Rachel said.

'We don't argue when you're about, Mother, usually.'

'But I can still sense the atmosphere.'

'Well, then, what do you think we should do about it? Divorce?'

'You might be happier,' Rachel said sadly.

'Well, I tell you I wouldn't be. I don't go to many places with Arthur, but I should hate to be on my own. All the big functions and things: Ascot, Wimbledon and so on, we do go to together. We're seen and that's all that matters really. I think Arthur hoped he'd get a peerage or, at least, a knighthood; but that's gone up the spout, too. He thinks Harold was annoyed with him for not standing again, and this business with Flora is the last straw. Harold absolutely *hates* the CND.'

'This wasn't CND,' Rachel protested.

'It's the same sort of thing. Flora will support any cause that's put in front of her, regardless. You know that, Mother. From now on she'll probably be more or less permanently in gaol.'

In a way Charlotte was right. Flora loved her week in Holloway. For her it was not a punishment, but a new and exciting experience. The women she met reminded her of the hostel – they all had problems – and thus renewed her enthusiasm for doing good. She really could have done with a lot more time in Holloway: there was so much to find out and to do. So many people with difficult, complex, troublesome lives that needed sorting out. She took down so many names of those who needed help that she thought she'd have a full-time job on her hands when she got out of prison, which came all too soon. She was no sooner in than it was time to be out again with messages of goodwill ringing in her ears.

'See you again soon.'

'I hope so,' Flora said politely. It was a bit like the end of term at school.

Em had her worst forebodings confirmed when she

came home that night and found Flora retailing her experiences to Luis over a bottle of wine in the kitchen. Luis had gone to pick her up and had brought her home to Em's flat, where she now lived.

But Flora never thought of the flat exactly as 'home'. To her it was somewhere to stay and when she wanted somewhere else she would move on. She was a vagabond, a peripatetic citizen of the world. She had few possessions; few close ties. She never thought there was anything strange or unusual in her lifestyle, and when Em had greeted her and listened to her experiences she found it hard to believe that her cousin could be as carefree and wilful as she was. Rather than being chastened by her experience in Holloway Flora was inspired.

'Come round the world with me,' Luis said. 'And we'll take pictures together.'

'I'd *love* that,' Flora said, with enthusiasm. 'But not just yet. If you think Mosley is finished, he's not. This Immigration Act is the first step to a totally Fascist state. Soon you won't be able to tell Britain and pre-war Germany apart.'

Em had opposed from the columns of the paper the Immigration Act, which barred Commonwealth citizens from automatic right of entry to England. She joined with the opposition parties in condemning it as a piece of racist legislation introducing a colour bar, as white immigrants were unaffected by it. Known as the Mother Country what mother, she had argued, refused her home to her own children? It was an appalling measure though activated, to some extent, by the numbers who had come from the West Indies in the fifties, creating their own black ghettos in many deprived areas of large cities. Discriminating immigration was not the answer, but integration and education.

Em finished preparing the salads they were having for

697

dinner and sat down at the kitchen table with Flora and Luis, who poured her a glass of wine.

'I don't think there's any chance that England will be a totally Fascist state,' she said. 'We have too many safeguards against that happening. But I do think you could get too carried away by the conviction that all your particular causes are right and become a sort of anti-democrat, too.'

'Oh, *you're* a fan of Len Williams, are you, Em?' Flora, who liked prison but not the food, took up her knife and fork and tucked into the meal Em had prepared with enthusiasm.

Recently the General Secretary of the Labour Party had declared that CND had been infiltrated by anti-democratic elements.

'I'm not a *fan* at all,' Em protested. 'But he does have a point.' She leaned forward, pointing her fork at Flora. 'Flora, you can become too fanatical and I think you're in danger of being that. I don't think you will do your many good causes a service if you do. You'll become notorious.'

Flora felt hurt. Em was a favourite and had offered her a home. But it wasn't really a home. It was just a place to stay, and if Em was going to preach to her like this she wouldn't be staying there for very long. She realized that however much she liked Em and admired what she'd done she was still family and she had the reactionary, hidebound attitudes that families had. Slowly Flora was in the process of detaching herself from all close ties so that, in her quest for world citizenship, she could be totally free.

Luis realized that his mother had been rather severe on Flora. To Luis she was a kind of heroine: unconventional, odd. She was so unconcerned about her appearance that she appeared much older than she was. She had streaks of grey in her hair, and because she never used make-up, her skin had that rather leathery quality of people who spend a great deal of time out of doors.

After they'd finished eating and had washed up Flora said she was going to bed, but Em told her she wanted to talk to her. Flora looked at her suspiciously.

'Oh, not *more* telling off,' Em said. 'I love you. I really do; but I'm anxious for you and my mother is, too. We all are.'

'Well, that's very kind of you, but there's no need to bother,' Flora said. 'In many ways I've never been happier. I'm really doing what I want to do, Em: opposing tyranny.'

They went into the sitting-room and Luis put some Mozart on the record player. He had to break the news to his mother that he was off on his travels again, maybe going back to Vietnam, where he detected an escalation of the civil war. They sat down with the window open because it was hot and rather airless despite the breeze that wafted through the trees in Redcliffe Gardens. Em leaned back and closed her eyes, lulled by the sound of the music. Then she opened them and looked at Flora.

'I wondered if you'd like to work with me on the paper,' she said.

'*The Sentinel?*'

'Yes.'

'But I've no experience on a newspaper.'

'I'd teach you. I think you must have a career.'

Flora leaned forward as if she were studying something on the floor.

'Who put you up to this?' she said at last.

'Put me up to what?'

'Trying to fob me off with a job on the paper. The family, I suppose, wanting to keep its eyes on me, I guess.'

'I think that's a very nasty thing to say,' Em said.

Luis felt it was time to intervene between these two headstrong women, both of whom he loved. 'You're both getting at cross purposes. I think you'll end up by having a first-class row.' He got up to turn the record over. Then he went back to his seat and addressed Flora.

'I think Mum and Gran think you're at a loose end, Flora. I know you think that's not true.'

'It certainly isn't,' Flora said indignantly.

'I know,' Luis continued, 'from what you told me earlier on that you feel you've found your niche in life. Holloway was an enriching experience for you. CND is a vital part of your life. I think Mum and Gran and Aunt Charlotte think you may spend your whole time in gaol and that upsets them.'

'Like Pat Arrowsmith,' Em said.

'I admire her enormously.'

'Yes, but couldn't you do something better if I give you a voice on the paper? You can sound off every day for all I care.'

'Really?' Flora looked interested at last. 'My own column?'

'I was really thinking of you as a features editor.' Em was beginning to regret her impulse, yet it wasn't really an impulse but had been on her mind for some time. 'Commissioning other people, with all sorts of points of view.'

As she said that she knew the idea was hopeless. Flora confirmed it immediately.

'Oh, I could never do that! I could never commission a Tory or a Mosleyite.'

'But their points of view are interesting.'

'Not for me,' Flora said. 'You have got to take a stand, Em, and be proud of your own convictions. I'm very proud of mine. Thank you, but I could never, ever agree to work for you on the paper. I don't want a job. I'm

700

happy as I am. I have a little money of my own which I just keep for my needs, which are few, and I get what work I can. It's the kind of life I like.'

Impulsively Flora got up and, going over to Em, embraced her – a gesture that rather surprised someone who was as controlled and undemonstrative as Flora usually was.

'You can be sure,' Flora said, her arms still round Em's shoulder, 'that this is only the start of what I hope to do.'

In the course of the next six months Flora went to prison twice more. The third time the magistrate put her away for three months and nothing that the family could do could get her out. Flora had become an active member of the Committee of a Hundred, a faction of the CND movement which believed in militant unilateralism. In January 1963 Hugh Gaitskell, the leader of the Labour Party, died unexpectedly and Flora welcomed his demise because of the way he had been turning the party to the right, particularly his opposition to Clause Four, which advocated nationalization of all the means of production and distribution. Gaitskell was also violently against unilateralism and Flora had narrowly escaped arrest the previous May when she and other unilateralists had helped to break up a May-Day meeting in Glasgow addressed by the Labour leader.

Flora saw Gaitskell's removal as an act not of God in whom, of course, she did not believe, but of some benign but unknown deity who smiled on anti-fascists and unilateralists; feminists, pro-abortionists, and all the unfranchised and unloved of the world. She wasn't pleased when Harold Wilson was elected in Gaitskell's place. She thought he was a smoothie, too, like Gaitskell, but her favourite was a fellow unilateralist and Radical, Michael

Foot, and there was small chance of him ever being elected Leader of the Labour Party.

The family rather despaired of Flora, even Rachel who loved her best. Rachel took to seeing her more than usual, inviting her to the Grange to try and knock some little sense into her; but it wasn't easy. Flora usually arrived with several friends of like persuasion, many of them ex-inmates of HM prisons whom Flora met in the course of her quasi-criminal career and one of whom went off with what little jewellery Rachel still possessed. Flora begged her aunt not to prosecute the girl whose need, she assured her, was much greater than Rachel's. She did manage, however, to get most of the jewellery back, including a ring that Bosco had given her just before the Great War to mark their reconciliation, on payment of fifty pounds and a promise not to take the matter further.

All this and more marked the life of the family in these months of the early sixties. Paul and Laura had had a son in September and they called him Martin, though the name had no family connections. The government had given the go-ahead for a second TV station, and also colour TV, and suddenly Paul's business began to expand very rapidly and he was in danger of becoming a man of substance and position, a tycoon like Bobby. He had to enlarge his factory and employ more people, and he had to look around for capital. He wouldn't go to Bobby, and Arthur was no longer so influential in the City, so the only person he could really think of for good advice was Laura's father, who had made a fortune from virtually nothing after he inherited a small dressmaking business from his father, a Lithuanian Jew.

Leo Cohen was a cultured man. He had not been to university and he had had little formal education. Yet, like many people who had to work hard from their youth, he had taught himself: he was a music lover, a supporter

702

of the Hallé Orchestra, and a keen theatre-goer, going to all the plays that had their pre-London runs in Manchester. Leo had married well, an intelligent girl whose parents had been comfortably off: a kind of prototype of their only daughter Laura.

Laura's father had found a lot to like about Paul Askham but a lot to dislike about him, too. He appreciated culture and breeding but he would rather his daughter had married a comfortably-off Jewish boy with prospects, as he had been, than have formed an association with an earl who never used his title and seemed to have few prospects. Another upsetting thing, anathema to a good Jewish man of business, was the fact that Paul's family seemed to surround themselves with notoriety, events which attracted a good deal of publicity in the press. The latest was Miss Bolingbroke, frequently and flamboyantly gaoled for attacks on policemen who were bent on preserving the law while she was trying to destroy it. The death of Sasha was a tragedy rather than a scandal but, before that, there had been his cousin Joe Verdi gaoled, at about the time Laura and Paul started going together, for homosexual offences. Each and every time, beside the story in the paper, was the legend: 'a cousin of the Earl of Askham.'

Adèle and Leo didn't see as much of their grandson as they would have liked. They didn't approve of the way Laura and Paul lived or where they lived. They couldn't adjust themselves to the fact that their nicely-brought-up, well-educated, attractive daughter, with every chance in life, was an unmarried mother living out of wedlock with a man in a rather seedy part of industrial Stockport.

Of course they loved Martin, who wouldn't? He was a charming baby, already at six months obviously bright, alert and intelligent. If his father and mother had been married he would be Viscount Gore, heir to an earldom.

As it was he was nothing. The Cohens found it hard to understand.

In fact they considered it a tragedy when one saw that here was a perfect couple who, potentially, had everything – the boy was even a good businessman – and yet hadn't bothered to legalize their union.

In the spring of 1963, when Martin was just six months old, Paul and Laura took him over to Prestbury on a routine visit to his grandparents. These visits were never pleasant occasions because of the undercurrent, the air of disapproval that Leo and Adèle had about Paul and their daughter. They happened about once a month, more out of politeness than anything else, and the Cohens made martyrs of themselves and came over to Heaton Moor to return the call.

Paul and Laura usually arrived for lunch and left after tea to put Martin to bed. In the afternoon Laura spent time alone with her mother, to whom she was devoted, and Paul had a stilted conversation, usually in the pleasant drawing-room overlooking the garden, with Leo. They would smoke a couple of cigars, discuss business and engage in general small talk until teatime.

On this day in March, however, Paul had something to say. He was a direct young man who knew how Leo felt about him and he didn't mince his words. He came straight to the point, even before Leo had offered him the customary cigar and asked him how things were.

'I'd like to borrow some more money, Leo,' Paul said, standing with his back to the fire, his hands in his pockets. He was five feet ten inches tall, quite small by Askham standards. A pale, thin youth, he had grown quite stocky, with the athletic build of a fighter, and he had considerable presence by virtue of his positive and determined personality. Paul had been born in 1935, and at the age of twenty-seven he was a young man of whom both his parents would undoubtedly have been proud.

'I'd like to put some more money in the business. I need about five million,' Paul went on.

Leo sat back with a smile on his face and began to cut the end of his cigar.

'Five million is an awful lot of money,' he said. 'How are you going to raise it?'

'I thought I'd ask your advice about that. There is no end to the potential of television – bigger screens, much smaller screens, quality of picture, colour, number of lines.'

'What about all the big people?' Leo asked. 'Philips, Murphy, HMV and so on. Aren't they too competitive?'

'Well, of course, they're there, but if we left everything to the giants there would be no progress, would there? I have some brilliant electronic engineers, people who are natural inventors, who wake up every morning with a fresh idea; but I'm running out of money.'

'Five *million*,' Leo lit his cigar carefully, taking his time. Then he leaned back in his armchair, ankles crossed. 'Five million is a *lot* of money.'

Paul began to feel angry and put his own cigar down unlit. 'I'm not *begging*, Leo. I'm speaking to you as one businessman to another.'

'I know that, Paul,' Leo said, 'and I appreciate it. It is not the first time your family have come to me for money. If you remember, I helped to get Neri Aerospace on its feet.'

'You made a good deal there. You bought Stefanie's shares and they have multiplied.'

'They're worth about five million now alone,' Leo said.

'As much as that?'

'Maybe more.' Leo tapped the ash from his cigar and narrowed his eyes. 'You see, Paul, I made a vow long ago not to get involved in things I know nothing about. I know nothing about aeroplanes or manufacturing television sets. I know about food, the rag trade, merchandising, cloth, that sort of thing. I stick to the things I can do. I know absolutely nothing about aeroplanes or TV sets.'

'I see.' Paul creased his trousers and sat down. 'So you can't help me.'

'I didn't say that.' Leo's eyes were practically closed. 'I can help you; but I want, in turn, to make you a proposition.'

'What's that?' Paul said, beginning to have some inkling of what it might be.

'I want you to marry my daughter, make an honest woman of her, legitimize my grandson. I have felt very affronted by your behaviour, Paul, and so has my wife. We can't talk about our daughter in the Jewish community. We're ashamed of her, to tell you the truth, and yet we love her so much it makes our hearts break . . .'

'I find all that very old-fashioned . . .' Paul began angrily.

'I daresay you do,' Leo continued in the same flat, unemotional voice. 'But does Laura?'

'I think so.'

'Did you ask her?'

'Of course I asked her!' Paul looked indignant. 'What do you take me for, Leo?'

'I, personally, take you for a bounder,' Leo said with an edge to his voice. 'In my young day such a thing wasn't tolerated, in the Jewish community or out of it, and quite right in my opinion. It was a disgrace to live together unmarried and have children out of wedlock. You *might* have talked about it with Laura . . . or did you, perhaps, *tell* her what you wanted? And she, loving you, agreed to it.'

'She did agree to it. She felt just as I did. There was no

706

compulsion.' Paul paused and looked thoughtfully at Laura's father. 'I've had a lot of pressures put upon me in my life, Leo, and I always feel I should have resisted them. I was sent to public school and I hated it, but I stayed there because my family wanted me to. It was expected of me. I then began to realize what a sham my family's views and standards were. We had no money, we had a huge house we couldn't keep up and all because we allowed ourselves to be swindled by a cousin.'

'That would be Lord Lighterman?'

Paul nodded. 'In 1929 half the Askham money disappeared in the Wall Street crash. My Uncle Ralph, the then Earl, wanted to be a farmer in Kenya, and to get out of his responsibilities in England. Uncle Bobby was a close relation, a first cousin. Ralph went to him for advice and Bobby swindled him. He swindled us all; he got the lot. But because my family had these antediluvian ideas of loyalty Bobby is still tolerated in the family circle. It was because of Bobby that I am largely what I am. It was because of Bobby that I wanted to succeed in business because, one day, I want to get my family money back and also the Hall. That's what motivates me, to put it simply. Nothing else.'

'Bravo,' Leo said with a polite handclap. 'I like all those sentiments – power, revenge, very good. It is surely a very minor point to ask you to marry my daughter?'

'It's important. It's a matter of principle.'

'Think about it, though.'

Leo's cigar had gone out and, slowly, he rekindled it again, looking at Paul through the smoke.

'I'm not one of those Jews with a chip on my shoulder, Paul. I was born here and I'm an Englishman, as you are – an English Jew. I don't think it's too much to expect that my only daughter should be well and happily married. You may think that Laura enjoys living a life of unwedded bliss in a flat in Heaton Moor, but I'm pretty sure she doesn't. And if you don't believe me ask her mother.

'Laura loves you very much, I've no doubt about that. She loves you for being you, not because you're a peer or anything else. But I know it would be very nice for her to be Lady Askham. I don't think I'm being snobbish when I say it would give me and her mother a great deal of pleasure and pride, too. You could imagine the joy of the old Jewish pedlar from Lithuania, the honour it would shed on his name. His great-great-grandson would be a viscount, his great-granddaughter given the title of "lady". I can't tell you what that would mean to me and her mother, though to you it might seem very trivial.

'Your father was a lord. Mine was the son of a Lithuanian Jew, a pedlar who came to England with a shilling. I believe your grandfather was a hero, a holder of the Victoria Cross, and your great-grandfather a Cabinet Minister. Askham Hall is a great family possession and one day, Paul, you might be able to get it back from that German who's virtually stolen it from you. Aren't we good enough for you, Paul, we Jews? Are you ashamed of us?'

'That is absolutely absurd,' Paul protested. 'You know that *nothing* like that has ever entered my mind – my mother was Jewish. Of course I'm not ashamed. Of course you're good enough for me.'

'Then show it, Paul,' Leo said. 'Marry Laura and I will see that you have all the money you need for your business and that, one day, you will get your home back for her and my grandchildren.'

CHAPTER 28

By the spring of 1963 the renovation of Askham Hall was well under way. After coming to an agreement with the Trustees the previous year Gunther had lost no time in sending an army of surveyors and experts of various kinds to draw up plans for the Hall, landscape artists to lay out the gardens. In the autumn scaffolding had started to go up against those ancient walls and rebuilding operations began in earnest. However, the reconstruction was largely a matter of repairs to the inside of the Hall which had suffered a great deal from being a school in the war. Walls and woodwork were stripped and many rooms completely reconstructed; all winter work went on restoring the Hall to the splendour it had enjoyed before Ralph's wife had begun her programme of modernization.

Master craftsmen began embellishing the ceilings with intricate plaster reliefs: quatrefoils, lozenges, putti, pendants set in coronals of leaves; beads, rosettes and fleurs-de-lis, decorated borders filled with flower sprays, and swirling foliage all cast in plaster of Paris from reverse moulds in a time-honoured, ageless technique.

Builders swarmed over the roof, repairing large areas where the damp had begun to penetrate the interior of the Hall, fixing tiles, renewing pipes, conduits and gutters. The Hall was to be completely rewired and a new system of central heating installed.

All year Gunther and Anna came and went, sometimes together, sometimes alone, on tours of inspection, unsure of their welcome from the rest of the family. Hugo was the only one who had wholeheartedly accepted Gunther's intervention and, as the months went by, he became less enthusiastic.

For one thing the mess was indescribable. They moved from room to room in the Hall like refugees, trying to keep their distance from the builders. But it was very primitive. The heating was inadequate and for a long time hadn't existed at all. Although Nimet had supported Gunther, she felt affronted by the lack of care that he offered them; his indifference when they protested, his refusal to find them alternative accommodation. The Hall was so large, he said, surely there was somewhere for them to live in view of all that was being done on their behalf? When everything was finished he had promised them a flat in the Hall that would be quite apart from the rest of the accommodation.

For a long time Jenny, especially, had found the conditions intolerable. Johnny was away at school but Elizabeth and Anthony went to the local schools. Elizabeth was fifteen and attended the Grammar, fifteen miles away. She had a long bus journey each day and returned late, tired and exhausted, to find continual upheaval in the home, meals eaten in cramped conditions, and, in the depths of winter, always a lack of proper heating. The children got repeated colds and Nimet was either continually ill or complaining about her health.

Hugo, too, felt that Gunther wasn't honouring his promises. Instead of expanding the facilities for the market garden he was contracting them. Plans were in hand for the planning of formal gardens to rival Versailles and Hugo was being squeezed to one part of the existing land where the soil was poor.

Hugo felt that Gunther had reneged on his promises, the high hopes they had had and for which a coolness had developed between him and the family, who disapproved of Gunther taking over the Hall, even though most of

710

them realized it was inevitable. There was a general feeling of sadness that it had had to come to this, except from Paul, who was furious that the Trustees had given away what was, to him, his inheritance.

Rachel, in the Grange, near but far enough to be detached, felt that there was an inevitability about the whole thing. She was only, rather selfishly in her opinion, thankful that she hadn't been living in the Hall when all this had come about.

One day Gunther's representative in England arrived with the surveyor and the head of the building contractors who were refurbishing the Hall and went into a long conference to which they eventually summoned Hugo. They told him that the central heating would be completely shut down, part of the roof exposed to the elements, covered merely with a tarpaulin, and that he and his family would have to find somewhere else to live for the next few months. They thought Hugo's claim for compensation from the Baron, who was doing so much to a property he didn't even own, unreasonable. Hugo should be grateful that so much was being done already.

When Hugo asked about the eventual area for his market gardening operations, and where their flat would be, the replies were vague and evasive.

It was then that Hugo realized he was being squeezed out; he didn't fit in. He would have no home and no job. The Baron had merely promised him a home to get Hugo's support and his hands on the Hall. He tried in vain to remonstrate with Gunther's representatives, but they were almost as smooth-talking as the man they worked for. In the end they got into their cars and drove off and Hugo went disconsolately to find Jenny trying, as usual, to cope as best she could in the kitchen and unprepared to give him the sympathy he thought he deserved.

In the end, after a furious row, she threw up her hands and said: 'I could have *told* you this was going to happen. The only one who couldn't see it was *you*.'

'What could I do?' Hugo slumped dejectedly into a chair. 'I had the Trust against me. I had failed to make this pay, as I said I would. I squandered all my mother's money on it. Now look what's happened. If you ask me, we're ruined.'

Nimet came down to breakfast next morning, which was unusual for her. Jenny, who was still expected to serve her mother-in-law breakfast in bed, stared at her. Nimet was unwelcome at this time. Jenny had just given the children breakfast and seen them off to school, and Hugo was mixing some hen feed into a bucket. Normally this was a cheery domestic scene which had been re-enacted ever since Hugo had come to the Hall ten years before. One or two of the hungry hens had ventured into the kitchen and were anxiously watching Hugo at work.

Jenny looked up as Nimet swept into the kitchen, her hands to her head; she looked at the bell counter over the door, wondering if her mother-in-law's bell had rung and she hadn't heard it.

'I can't stand it here a moment longer.' Dramatically flinging her hands in the air, Nimet sank on to a chair as if she were about to collapse.

Hugo put the bucket down and went over to her.

'Mother, what *is* the matter?'

'This place.' Nimet looked up at him with a tragic air. 'What have I done to deserve this in my old age? Is God punishing me?'

'Mother, what exactly are you talking about?' Hugo looked at Jenny and sat in the chair next to his mother.

'Here, this place, Askham Hall. Do you know they're removing the roof?'

712

'Yes, Mother.' Hugo sighed. 'I do.'

'But I can't sleep. You must stop them, at least until I am finished in my bedroom.'

'That is never until noon,' Jenny said sharply. 'They have done a morning's work by that time.'

'The noise and the banging.' Nimet put her hands to her throbbing head. 'I simply can't stand it.'

'You'll have to, I'm afraid.' Jenny started peremptorily to clear the things from the table. 'Beggars can't be choosers, and it's going to get worse. We are beggars, you know, Nimet. Didn't you realize that?'

'But what did he do with all my money?' Nimet pointed a quivering finger in Hugo's direction. 'What did he *do* with it? There were thousands; there was well over a million. What happened to it?'

Hugo thoughtfully rubbed his chin.

'Mother, even then you needed more than a million to do up Askham Hall, and I failed. I was too optimistic. I wanted to restore the family home my father knew.' Hugo shook his head. 'It was hopeless, a hopeless task.'

'But your market garden the produce . . .'

'It was less competitive then. Now all sorts of modern methods are coming in. You can get strawberries in December without flying them over from Florida. Because I spent so much money on the Hall I hadn't enough left over for the business. I was too ambitious, Mother. I'm sorry. Gunther's agent, however, does promise me that when this is all finished we can have our own apartments.'

'And when will that be?' Nimet had begun to shout.

'I don't know, another year, maybe. Maybe more. They're being as quick as they can. I do know that.'

'And what is to happen to *me*?'

'What is to happen to US?' Jenny started to shout, too, turning on her heels and glaring at her mother-in-law.

713

'Not just you. *Us*; me, Hugo, the children. We are all being given notice to quit and all you do is bleat about not getting your sleep. Believe me, Nimet, if you were as tired as I am during the day you would be thankful to put your head on your pillow at nine o'clock or thereabouts and then you would have a decent night's sleep, as we do.'

'I couldn't possibly go to sleep that early.' Nimet tossed her head. 'Please get me some coffee, Hugo.' Ignoring Jenny she stretched past him, observing to no one in particular: 'Don't forget I have been used to life in a style enjoyed by the international set. One just began to live at nine, not go to bed!'

'Then you'd better change your habits,' Jenny said. 'Because we're all going to end up in some semi-detached house living right on top of each other.'

Swiftly drying her hands on a teacloth Jenny ran out of the door into the garden, scattering the squawking hens waiting at the door.

Rachel said:

'I couldn't possibly have her here. I could have you and Hugo and the children; but Nimet, in this confined space . . . oh, no.' She shook her head. The impression she gave was of someone repressing a shudder. Rachel had just been finishing her own breakfast when Jenny came running up the path, breathing heavily because she was out of breath. 'Besides,' Rachel put on her spectacles and reached for her telephone book, 'it is against the agreement the Trustees have with Gunther. A place is to be provided for Hugo and his family.'

'The agent says it will be a cottage in the village until the work is completed.'

'No, if you have to leave it must be to come here,' Rachel said firmly, giving Jenny a hot cup of coffee. 'I'd

714

love the company. But no Nimet. I couldn't stand it and neither, I think, could she.' Rachel looked round, feeling suddenly helpless. 'Besides there *isn't* the room. What an awful pity she sold that house in France.'

'She was offered such a lot of money for it; but it's all gone. Did you know,' Jenny looked indignantly at Rachel, 'did you know she *gambled* a lot? She got through a fortune. It's not just Hugo's fault.'

'I didn't know, but I'm not surprised.' Rachel, having failed to find the number she was after – that of the Trustees' solicitor – took off her reading-glasses again. 'I suppose it was her life and she could do what she wanted with the money. She was certainly very generous to Hugo.' Rachel paused. 'And Hugo, like all the Askhams, was not good at handling money. Never mind.' Suddenly she leaned over to kiss Jenny before pouring her more coffee. 'We shall survive.'

Jenny, feeling more at peace, as she usually did after one of Rachel's sensible talks, went back to the Hall later in the morning, walking slowly through the park, savouring the delightful things about it that never changed – the fragrant smells, the abundance of trees, the peace of the lake with the swans and ducks sailing up and down. She was greeted by an irate husband who demanded to know where she'd been.

'I went to see Rachel. She gave me some good advice.'

'What was that?'

'That we'd survive, of course.' Jenny attempted to kiss him but he backed away.

'Does she know *how*, exactly?'

Jenny went inside the kitchen and Hugo followed her. The sudden shutting off of the light gave her a sense of foreboding, that the feeling of peace had been illusory. She began the washing-up but Hugo stood behind her, demanding again how they were to survive. Finally Jenny

715

turned off the taps, wiped her hands and sat at the kitchen table, beckoning to him to sit opposite her, waiting until he did.

'Rachel has very generously suggested that you and I and the children move in with her. She wants no rent and she proposes that the rent that Gunther is obliged to pay by the terms of his agreement with the Trustees shall be used to find somewhere suitable for your mother – somewhere where she's happy and comfortable, hopefully in the South of France.'

'Why do you say "hopefully"?'

'Because I hope she does go to the South of France.' Jenny smiled across at him. 'Your mother might be your mother but she is awfully difficult to live with, Hugo. She has made life these past few months hell . . .'

'Well, they've been hell for us all; uncertainty at what was happening, disappointment that we have failed, that a person who is not strictly a member of the family is to take over the Hall that has been the Askham home for hundreds of years. I, personally, do have now a great sense of failure. It has been a very hard time for us all.'

'But your mother hasn't helped, has she, Hugo?'

'Well, she is very uncomfortable, too.'

'Yes, but she seems to think we owe her a living.'

'In a way we do.'

'*I* don't.' Abruptly Jenny stood up and draped her apron round her waist, tying it at the back. 'I have just had a bellyful of your mother; her snarls and insults, her high-handed ways. She has doubled the work I've had to do . . . rushing up these stairs carrying trays. She has been no help or consolation to you in a very trying time. I can tell you, I'm not really sorry we have to go. In fact I think it will be a good thing.'

'My mother is an old lady,' Hugo said stubbornly. 'She has not had an easy life . . .'

716

'Or made it easy for others. She drove Rachel out of here too and, believe me, I would far rather have Rachel than your mother. Your mother has made herself intolerable, Hugo, and you have no debt to her. None at all.' Jenny leaned over the kitchen table and banged on it with her fist. 'No one can stand your mother, except you, and that's because you feel so guilty; and you have *nothing* to feel guilty about. She abandoned you. My God, she left you to go to an orphanage!'

'She had no choice.'

Jenny folded her arms and looked at her husband with an expression that was very nearly contemptuous.

'Do you really believe that? Have you believed it all these years?'

'Yes, I have.'

'Well, I don't. I think she was then what she is now: a selfish woman, a parasite . . . battening on the Earl of Askham, battening on Mr Igolopuscu who, from what I've heard, was a saint where she was concerned. She has never left the Askhams alone. She has persecuted Rachel, who has always been good to her. Now if anyone was a saint, in the circumstances, that person is Rachel. She didn't have to take you but she did. Good heavens, the son of her husband's mistress . . . Not only did she take you, she loved you. She has been a true mother to you . . .'

'But Nimet *is* my mother,' Hugo said as if what Jenny said made no difference. 'She is my natural mother. She *has* been good to me. She does love me and don't think for one minute I am going to abandon her. She has only me in the twilight of her life. All right, as a younger woman she could fend for herself; she was fortunate in being very attractive to men; but what does she do now when that is no longer the case? What do *I* do with her, Jenny, throw her out . . .'

717

'Yes, as she once did you. And serve her bloody well right.'

Hugo had never hit Jenny before. He was not a violent man and she could never recall a violent gesture towards her or any of the children, even a playful slap. But the blow he gave her sent her reeling backwards across the kitchen and when she fell in a heap by the stove there was no one there to pick her up. Hugo had gone.

For a long time Jenny sat on the floor, her cheek in her hand, warming the place where he had hit her, trying vainly to comfort herself.

Anna had never wanted a baby, had never been aware of the stirrings of a maternal instinct until she married Gunther, and even after that it took quite a long time for the instinct to materialize, to be translated into fact.

What really seemed to make her wish to be a parent was Gunther's acquisition of a hundred-year lease of the Hall, home of the Askhams, and the realization that they would actually one day live there. This had seemed a moment of great power to Anna; her mother's family home, the place where her grandmother, Lady Melanie, had been born, would one day belong to her. It was her family who would grow up there and flourish and, at last, she would feel equal to the Askhams and even with them.

Anna realized that resentment against the Askhams had motivated much of her recent behaviour: she had mocked Joe, she had helped to destroy Pascal, she had upset every one of them. She had been guilty of many acts of petty spite, for which she couldn't quite bring herself to account. She thought that in a subtle, sinister way they had got their own back when Sasha was killed. Sasha was a Ferov, not an Askham. That was a cruelty that was almost too hard to bear: a shaft of pure malice from the gods. But she had borne it and, in her grief, her baby had been conceived and when the deed was done she was happy.

When finished, the Hall would be a splendid place. Gunther was thinking of living there for most of the year, filling it with his glorious pictures and commuting to Germany. The air was full of excitement and anticipation, even though, inevitably, some more people had been hurt in the process.

Unexpectedly and to the shock of the family Hugo and Jenny had split up, at least for a time. Everyone naturally assumed it would be temporary as for so long they had been such a harmonious and loving couple. Maybe the row, coming on top of so many years of discomfort and aggravation, had been the trigger which had sent Jenny back to Cumberland, where her widowed mother still lived. Johnny remained at school but Elizabeth and Anthony had gone with her, to local schools in Penrith. It was a terrible upheaval and took the family by surprise: but did it really? Jenny had been liked, admired, but she wasn't family and, somehow, despite her attitude of perpetual subservience, everlasting time done in the kitchen caring and catering for them all, she had never completely endeared herself to them.

Nimet had gone to live in a small hotel in the South of France which she thought of as home and Hugo had gone with her to try and find work. In a way it was a very sad exit for both of them as, in her time, Nimet had been both a beauty and an exceptionally wealthy woman.

But these days Anna never felt sad too long about anything. Gunther was in South America and she was alone in the Taunus house, except for the maid. It was a beautiful day in high summer and the mountain scenery was at its best; the best of rural Germany: green, fruitful, small towns and villages thriving, new businesses and industries bursting out all over the place as the Federal

Republic struggled successfully to revive itself in the aftermath of war. That his country was so successful was thanks to people like Gunther, the real barons of the new industrial empire.

Anna didn't mind her enforced idleness. It was hot in the town and there was plenty to do even if one just sat and thought about the future.

For Anna felt that at last she had achieved everything she wanted. She had found Gunther, a person as resourceful, as inventive, in a way as single-minded as herself; someone who would let very little stand in his way yet would, she hoped, be as loyal to her as she had sworn to be to him for the rest of her life.

She was quite sure that Gunther loved her and that her own feelings were unambiguous about him. Anna was not a passionate person; she was incapable of giving selflessly; but in her way she did love Gunther as much as she was able.

Anna seldom regretted the past. She seldom thought about Pascal but, in the detached kind of way some people have towards those they have never been truly attached to, she wished him well. He had taken her away from the Baron and it was inevitable that she should one day return to the only man who matched her qualities.

Anna read a lot, she walked in the garden, she took an afternoon nap, she ate early when Gunther was away. He had had to go to Brazil but she knew he hoped to be back for the birth. Even if he wasn't everything was taken care of: an obstetrician at hand, an ambulance to be summoned at once, a room booked at the clinic where no complications were expected; but if they occurred they could be taken care of, too.

As usual after a pleasant day spent in the same way as the ones before, Anna went to bed in the huge room with the canopied four-poster where their child had been conceived. After reading for a while she put out the light and was soon asleep.

How long she slept she didn't know, nor did she know what wakened her. She put on the light, looked at the clock by her bedside and saw that it was nearly three in the morning. Outside it was still dark. She lay in bed listening, wondering whether to summon her maid by ringing the bell by her bedside. She remembered the man with the gun who had frightened her some time ago, but security was even stronger. An electronic beam could pick out anyone approaching the house at any angle from a distance of fifty yards. Yet still she was aware of an uncomfortable feeling, like fear; but it soon passed and after a while she put out the light again and was soon asleep.

It was not until she came down the next morning that she was aware of what had happened, because her maid hadn't wanted to disturb her sleep or worry her unduly.

After breakfast, as she was finishing her coffee, Eva broke the news that there had been a break-in during the night and many papers in the Baron's study had been disturbed, but nothing appeared to have been stolen or anything else in the house touched. The police had been called and were on their way. Eva hadn't wanted to alarm Madame in her condition.

'Only papers?' Anna said, frowning, experiencing once more the fear that she had felt the night before. 'I was sure I heard something during the night.'

'There is no need for Madame to distress herself,' Eva assured her. 'Nothing of any importance has been stolen.'

Anna went along the hall with the servant to the room on the ground floor which was Gunther's study. A pile of papers lay on the floor and drawers and cupboards which had been ransacked were still open. Despite the reassurances of the servant she was worried and spent some hours with the police as they investigated the matter, made measurements and speculated with her on the reasons for the break-in.

'My husband never keeps jewellery or anything of value in his study,' she said in her faultless German. 'What I can't understand is why *I* should have heard the disturbance upstairs. The study is nowhere near my bedroom.'

Nor had the thieves come in from above. The access was very quickly established by a broken catch on one of the doors leading into the garden, but not the reason why the electronic eye had failed to detect the intruder.

'Such places are comparatively easy to pilfer,' the policeman in charge said. 'That's why it is important to keep nothing of value in the home, whatever precautions you take.'

However, a thorough search of all the rooms in the house was carried out, and after lunch, when they left, Anna rang Rio de Janeiro where it was breakfast time and reported to her husband what had happened.

Gunther, at first distressed and taken aback, soon recovered from the shock when she assured him she was unharmed. He also appeared to have had no doubt about the reason for the break-in, since nothing of value had been stolen.

'Industrial espionage,' he said. 'It is on the increase. Companies are more and more trying to steal secrets from other more successful ones, especially those engaged in electronics, as we are. Anyway, there is nothing of value in my study but I will fly home straight away to make sure my office and factories are fully protected, and to see how an intruder gained access to my house.'

After a few more words of reassurance he told her he loved her, would see her soon, and rang off.

For the rest of the day Anna got on with her usual tasks but she found it hard to concentrate. She did her antenatal

722

exercises to help control her breathing and her nerves and, after a light supper, prepared to go early to bed. Eva assured her that for as long as she wished a policeman would remain all night, patrolling the house and grounds.

Anna agreed it would make her feel safer.

As usual she had her bath, removed her make-up at leisure and got into a light summer nightie. She checked the curtains, locked the door and then went into Gunther's dressing-room to ensure that his windows were shut and the door barred. This done she looked into his presses and drawers to make sure that his clothes were in order and there was plenty of clean underwear for his return.

Then, satisfied, she was about to put out the light and make her way into her own room when suddenly she looked at the wall, attracted or distracted, she didn't know which, by a small empty space by the side of the wardrobe where the row of pictures taken from the Black Forest home had been hung.

Now she knew what had disturbed her the night before. Someone had been in Gunther's dressing-room. The picture of him taken in 1932 with Adolf Hitler was missing.

Alex Ferov was a sturdy child and except for obvious resilience of character, seemed to have few of the characteristics of the Ferovs. In a strange way, even at this young age, he was a bit like Paul: stocky and dark with fierce, intelligent blue eyes. Pascal loved nothing more than to sit in the garden watching Alex play round his chair or climb on his knee and, from a very early age, Alex realized that Pascal wasn't as mobile as he was and that he could do things for him. He had grown up almost with the idea of service rather than being served, and the bond between him and the man he thought of as father was very strong.

From the kitchen window Laura stood watching Pascal with Alex and Martin. The way he played with them was, as always, remarkable. It made one forget completely that he was a man confined to a wheelchair. Behind her Stefanie was cutting sandwiches for the picnic they were taking to the woods at Alderley Edge, where they would fly the kite that Pascal had designed and Paul was practising with at the end of the garden, watched by the excited toddlers. Nicky and Galina were staying in Venice with their grandmother. It had been a poor summer but the blustery days were good for the kite which, sometimes, seemed as though it would lift Pascal out of his chair altogether. He said that one day it was his ambition to be borne aloft on a flying wheelchair, maybe even the first man in space.

Pascal's sense of humour never left him though, occasionally, Stefanie glimpsed the dark side. That was when Pascal wanted to retreat to his cottage, to be on his own and, sometimes, threatened to leave her altogether. But today was not one of those black days and she stacked the paper mugs and plates in a basket together with the sandwiches, cakes and packets of crisps, bottles of beer and pop.

'Nearly ready,' she said, banging the lid and fastening it. She tried to lift it and groaned. 'We'd better get Paul to lug this to the car.'

Laura also tried the weight, staggered and grimaced. 'What on earth have you got in it?'

'Everything one needs on a picnic,' Stefanie said cheerfully. 'Including rubber pants in case of accidents.'

The two women were great friends despite ten years' difference in their ages. Stefanie managed to seem young, Laura mature for her years. She still taught at the state school but Paul was planning to move to a large house and there was a lot to do.

She went to the door and hailed Paul, who had become entangled in the string of the kite and now Pascal, helped by the two toddlers, was trying to untangle him. It was a very happy, jolly scene and Stefanie, joining Laura at the door, started laughing at the mess Paul had got himself into.

'Pascal will sort him out.' Stefanie turned to the heavy picnic box. 'If you give me a hand with this I think we can manage it ourselves. By the time Paul becomes disentangled the picnic will nearly be over.'

Laura detected a note of irritation in Stefanie's voice which was unusual and glanced at her.

'Things getting you down?' she said.

'Not a bit.' Stefanie stopped to look at her 'Why?'

'Your tone of voice. Usually you're so ebullient.'

'One can't keep in top gear all the time,' Stefanie said. 'I try but it's not always possible. My grandmother's sinking and I think she'll die. She's ninety this year and I do love her. She's always been the steady rock in my life.'

'Princess Irina?' Laura shared the weight of the basket and staggered out of the back door with Stefanie to the waiting Land Rover. 'I'm so sorry. I know how much you love her. I know she had a stroke, but thought she was recovering.'

Stefanie shook her head. 'I feel I should be with her, but what can I do? I've got Nicky and Galina's school to think of. I can't just leave them and go. Anna would go but she has her new baby. Olga has all her family, like me she's tied up, and Natasha is too busy with her career. I can't somehow bear to think of Gran all alone in that huge house, dying.'

'I'll look after the children,' Laura said immediately. 'You know we're moving very soon? It's no trouble, I assure you. You go and take all the time you need.'

'I think if you did that Pascal would be very hurt,'

Stefanie said slowly. 'You see, he doesn't want to feel he's helpless. He's already told me to go and he'll look after Galina and Nicky if I take Alex.'

'Then why don't you?'

'Because,' Stefanie shrugged and looked towards the lawn. 'If there were an accident or an emergency . . . you know, during the night.'

'But Nicky is fourteen. He'll cope.'

'I know, but . . . I can't really explain it and Pascal feels it keenly.'

Just then there was a whoop from the children. Paul became untangled and carefully began to lower the large kite and put it in the car.

Paul drove the car up as near to the Edge as he could so that Pascal wouldn't have too bad a time with his chair over the uneven ground. The two toddlers were put into pushchairs and the group set off with the heavy picnic basket with as much sense of impending enjoyment as any young family on a day's outing.

It was a week-day and there were very few people about though children were still on holiday from school. Because it had been an indifferent summer the trees were still quite green and, except for the chill, there was little hint of autumn in the air.

By the time they reached the Edge itself, a massive formation of rock, and selected a spot to picnic which was far enough from the trees for Pascal and Paul to fly the kite, they were all very hungry and the picnic was immediately unpacked and consumed. Then the grown-ups began to set up the kite with an eye on the toddlers to make sure they didn't stray. It was cloudy but not cold and there was a good wind to keep the kite aloft once it was airborne.

Laura was helping to unknot part of the string attached to the kite when Paul gave a sharp exclamation and ran

726

over to Martin, who was rapidly disappearing on his sturdy little legs down a dark footpath that went into the forest. Paul came back with the struggling child in his arms and thrust him into those of his mother.

'Can't you keep an eye on your child?' Paul said sharply.

'Why can't *you*?' Laura riposted, a glint in her eye. 'I was busy, too. Besides, I always had Martin in the corner of my eye.'

'But you didn't run after him.'

'I knew you were going to. Don't make a fuss.' Laura triumphantly undid yet another knot and gave the string to Pascal. 'Come on. Let's get going.'

'I'll look after the children,' Stefanie said. 'Don't worry. I can see you from where I am.'

'I'll stay with you, then,' Laura said reluctantly. 'I can . . .'

'No, you go ahead with the others.' Stefanie nudged her. 'I'll follow you very slowly with them.'

'OK then.' Laura trotted off alongside Pascal, carrying the ball of string attached to the large kite which Pascal had on his lap.

Stefanie felt that the sharp exchange between Laura and Paul had somehow cast a blight on the day. Just a little blight, but one nevertheless.

Paul and Laura had married very quietly in the spring. It was one of those unusual Askham occasions when hardly any members of the family had been present. Askhams always liked a fuss, particularly at a wedding, but more often than not its members were unobliging.

However, despite their disappointment, both families breathed almost audible sighs of relief: it was better than not being married at all.

After that had come the purchase of a large house, not far away from Stefanie, bought with Leo Cohen's money.

727

Stefanie knew that Leo was also supporting Paul's business and that it was his pressure that had made the two legalize their union.

There was no doubt that Paul and Laura were in love and were well suited. Yet a tension had almost immediately entered the marriage that hadn't been there before and was discernible in numerous ways; little outbursts of irritation, like today, and a general air of grumpiness about Paul which hadn't been there before.

Paul was very busy building his business and he was preoccupied with matters that were not domestic, but Stefanie felt there was no doubt that Paul, who had refused Bobby's money, resented having to take it from his wife's father.

However, following slowly behind with Alex and Martin, Stefanie put these thoughts out of her mind and, as the large kite became airborne, she was carried away by the same childish excitement that engulfed the others and made it into a happy, relaxed afternoon.

Later they had tea, even though it was much colder and they had to put on their woollies. Afterwards Paul took Martin on his shoulders and Pascal sat Alex on his chair and the male members of the party went into a nearby field to have a game with a discus so that Pascal could join in. Stefanie and Laura began to clear up.

'I've been thinking about what you said.' Stefanie folded the tablecloth on which they'd spread the picnic and put it into the basket. 'I think it *would* be nice if you could have Nicky and Galina to stay. Much less work and worry for Pascal. He's terribly busy, so he should be glad of the break.'

'Any day you say.' Laura emptied the cups and rinsed them in cold water.

'But what about the house?'

'They'll have to muck in. Paul is busy, too. Just like a

man, he expects me to do everything because, officially, I'm on holiday. Paul . . .' Laura stopped as if she were going to confide something in Stefanie and then decided not to.

'Go on,' Stefanie said encouragingly.

'Paul has never been quite the same since our marriage, haven't you noticed it?'

Stefanie was spared the embarrassment of having to reply, as Laura hurried on. 'I think he feels he had to marry me. Daddy put too much pressure on him. The shares, everything . . .'

As part of the wedding present Leo Cohen had given his daughter and new son-in-law the millions of pounds' worth of shares which he had in Lighterman Limited, so that in fact Paul now had a large stake in his own family business. 'I think Paul feels, in a way, that he's owned by Daddy and resents it. I'd rather we'd stayed as we were.'

'But you would have married, surely?'

'Yes, but it would have been nicer if it had come spontaneously from Paul. As it is, we were pushed. It was a shot-gun wedding.'

'Paul would never have left you.'

'I know, and I don't think he will now; but things are a little different.' Laura paused. 'I'm having another baby.'

'Oh, that's thrilling news.' Stefanie leaned forward to kiss her.

'Paul doesn't know,' Laura said quickly. 'I think he's got too much on his mind.'

'But it would make him terribly happy.'

'Would it, though?' Laura looked across the field to where Paul was kneeling down to throw the discus at his son. 'I think it would make him feel even more trapped. Sometimes I think things have moved too quickly in this past year and he doesn't love me as much as he did. I wish, I really do, Daddy hadn't interfered and everything had remained as it was.'

When they got back to the house Paul, Laura and Martin left immediately because it was the little boy's bedtime. They looked happy enough as they drove away, but the afternoon's conversation with Laura had worried the older woman. Pascal noticed it as he sat in the kitchen feeding Alex as she got their supper.

'What's the matter?'

'Nothing. Tired, that's all.' Stefanie stopped to pass a hand over her brow.

'There *is* something, don't say there isn't. I noticed it at once. I saw you two talking in earnest.'

'Laura's offered to have Nicky and Galina if I go to Robertswood.'

'Yes, but you told her it wasn't necessary.'

'I said it was necessary and it would be nice.'

'But I'm quite capable of taking care of them, Stefanie.'

'I know you are, dear.' Stefanie reached up for some plates from the cupboard and Pascal felt that acute sense of frustration that he sometimes did when he looked at her, how lithe, lissom and capable she was compared to him. How adorable. He sighed and his gaze returned to Alex, who sat in his chair, leaning forward, his fist clenched, mouth wide open, eyes shining. Pascal, his heart full of love, leaned closer to him, too, and popped the spoon in his mouth.

'One for Mummy,' he said, as Alex took the spoon with its helping of boiled egg and began to munch, while some yellow yolk trailed down his chin. Swallowing, he immediately opened his mouth again.

'One for *Daddy*,' Pascal said unexpectedly and, as Stefanie turned round abruptly to look at him, he said:

'Sorry, I shouldn't have said that. One for Uncle.'

Alex, as though he hadn't heard or noticed the difference, opened his mouth wide with a chuckle that transformed his face. Just at that moment, vividly, Stefanie saw Sasha – the wide smile, the brown curls, always a bit of blond stubble on his chin as though he hadn't shaved quite as well as he should.

'One for Daddy,' Stefanie repeated. 'He must always be reminded of Sasha. One for Mummy, one for Daddy, one for Uncle . . .'

Suddenly, without knowing what had happened, Stefanie felt herself overcome by grief and rushed out of the room to hide her tears.

After a while she heard Pascal come into the sitting-room and approach the chair where she sat, putting a hand on her shoulder.

'I'm very sorry I upset you.'

'I think it was as much my fault as yours. A bit too emotional after an exciting day. I know you didn't mean it.' Stefanie looked at him and blew her nose, trying to smile.

'But I think I did.'

Stefanie said nothing but went on blowing her nose, gazing at him through her tears.

'I wanted to force the "daddy" issue,' Pascal continued.

'How do you mean?'

'I always feel I'm Alex's father. I have ever since he was born. I always wanted kids and I felt he was mine as soon as I saw him and held him in my arms. I couldn't explain how it was to you because, in many ways, it was such a traumatic time. I couldn't tell you that I regarded Sasha's son as mine; but I do. You see . . .' Pascal's dark face reddened and he looked away from her. 'I feel that this family *is* mine, Galina and Nicky, too, which is why it upsets me that you wanted Laura to have them, as

731

though I couldn't cope. If I were the natural father I'd have to cope and you couldn't stop me. You'd regard me completely differently. I know you would, and I resent it. I feel . . .' Pascal paused again and Stefanie finally dried her eyes and stuffed her handkerchief up her sleeve. 'I've done what I can to help you. Probably now, anyway, you want to be on your own. It's time I moved back to the bungalow and got on with my life, instead of living so much as part of your family. So you see,' Pascal concluded with a rueful smile, 'if you *do* leave the kids with Laura and Paul, I shan't be here when you get back.'

Irina Ferov knew she was dying. She felt a little indignant about it because, inside, she felt so young, like the young woman at the court of Nicholas's father, Alexander III, when she was lady-in-waiting to the Empress Marie. She was twenty-one when Nicky became Emperor, already married himself, and had attended his bride Alix at her marriage to the Emperor four weeks after he ascended the Russian throne in 1894.

In her pretty room overlooking the river it was a pleasure for Irina to dream about the past, which became entangled with the present. So much had happened – from the court of the Tsars to the terror of the Revolution. From poverty in Paris to the halcyon days of Askham Hall in the twenties and thirties, presided over by its gracious chatelaine, Dulcie, Countess of Askham. The Hall had certainly been as large as some of the palaces of the Tsar and the nobles who surrounded him, larger than the Small Palace at Livadia in the Crimea where Alexander III had died.

From Askham back to Paris again; back to more poverty, induced by the fact that she had three additional mouths to feed, Bobby's daughters, and only a niggardly allowance from him to cope with them. Then came the war and another of those swift changes in fortune that had been so much a part of her life: friendship with the Germans, a little luxury in Occupied Paris, gifts of brandy, sausages, Alsatian ham. Then stark, awful tragedy: Alexei shot in a cellar by the Communists – a martyr like his King and master, the Emperor Nicholas. Often, at this point, Irina emerged sharply from her reverie in tears to find Stefanie by her side with words of consolation, some lemon tea served in a glass from the samovar, as in the old, old days . . .

Yet, despite the signs, the weariness and fatigue, Irina was determined not to die until she had had her ninetieth birthday. She took Stefanie's arrival with little Alex as a sign that the whole family was planning this: Robertswood would be full of guests as it had been in the days before the Great War or, even better, the heyday of Sir Robert, when he entertained the new King, Edward VII, to whom he had lent money when he was Prince of Wales. Teddy was a good man who never forgot a favour and it was even rumoured that, when he needed privacy to enjoy a flirtation with a woman, Robertswood had been his – servants, food and wine provided and discretion, that prerequisite of certain monarchs and great men of a bygone age.

But it was all a dream. Still a dream. Irina was very weak indeed, far weaker than she would acknowledge. After her stroke she had appeared to make a good recovery, which she attributed to those formidable recuperative powers inherited from a family which was even older than the Romanovs; but there was a paralysis of her left side and complications which she didn't know about, but which prevented her from keeping her balance. It would never do to have the party, such a party, in her bedroom; not a *great* party as in the old days, but certainly one attended by the family.

But, best of all, apart from planning the party which everyone suspected would never take place, Irina enjoyed the company of her granddaughter, her dearest Stefanie, always a complex and difficult girl. But not so any more. Irina was as amazed and gratified as anyone else by the transformation in her granddaughter who, many years before, some never expected to see leave the clinic where she was a patient.

In her life many things had happened to Stefanie, good things and bad: she had had an unsatisfactory and dangerous love affair, but followed it by a hasty and, ultimately, very happy marriage. That ended in tragedy. Now what was there in life for this woman who, always for Irina, remained as she had been in the old days in Paris – a young, beautiful, vulnerable girl?

Of the three Lighterman girls, Olga and Natasha had come off best, as most people predicted they would. Stefanie was too malleable, too impressionable. She felt things too keenly, suffered too much; the other two girls were adaptable, philosophical, consequently happier. When their father threw them out; when, later, their mother went away, they merely shrugged and got on with what it was they had to do. When their parents turned up again they were happy to see them; but not Stefanie. Stefanie never forgave her mother, though there was little to forgive, until too late, and, for her father, she maintained an implacable hatred. In time this did seem to have mellowed into indifference, but there was little real affection between the two.

Irina lay all the time in her bed, propped up on pillows, waited on by two trained day-nurses and a night-nurse. It was very much like the old days when she was used to attention and, rather like Melanie, though not on quite such a scale, she was enjoying her death. People would get a phone call to say that 'the Princess' would like to

734

see them and, dutifully, they would travel down at once; members of the family and the many friends she had made over the years that she'd lived in England.

Sometimes she was well enough to talk to them for an hour or more, to take tea or coffee with them as they sat by her bedside; but more often she felt tired after a short time and was relieved to see them go. What she didn't see were the tears invariably shed in the corridor outside her room, knowing that they had seen her for the last time.

Through all the coming and going Stefanie stayed, confident that all was well at home with Pascal in charge.

From time to time Irina enquired about them, too, and one day as Stefanie sat beside her reading to her in Russian the much-loved novel in verse by the great poet Pushkin about misunderstood and unrequited love, she held up her hand and Stefanie paused in the middle of a line.

'He is a good man, too,' She spoke in Russian.

'Who, Babushka?'

'Lensky, the lover of Olga,' Irina said, referring to the book.

'Good, but foolish, Babushka . . .' Stefanie prepared to continue but Irina tapped her on the knee.

'Sasha, too, was good but foolish.'

'In what way, Babushka?' Stefanie kept her finger on the page but closed the book on her knee, sensing that her grandmother was tired.

'Flying aeroplanes. It was stupid.'

'Not stupid. It wasn't at all dangerous. He was unlucky.'

'You should have stopped him.' Irina sighed and a tear rolled down her withered old parchment-like face. 'How I loved Sasha. I think God loved him, too. God called him to Himself while he was young.'

'Oh Babushka, please.' Stefanie lowered her eyes but

735

she knew it was useless. Her grandmother had the Slav love of melodrama and emotion, a need for it.

'No, he was too beautiful, too good for the world. Your Mama, too, she was beautiful and, ultimately, too good. Like the Magdalene, she paid for her sins. God called her. I often think of them together in the bosom of the Almighty and, now, they are waiting for me.'

Stefanie, tearful herself, leaned towards her grand-mother and took her hand. As she did a beam of light that had slowly been crossing the room reached the bed, enveloping them both for a moment in an almost ethereal halo that seemed, mysteriously, to have come from another world.

'I would like to think that when I go to God you are taken care of, little Stefanie. The others, I know, can look after themselves, but not you.'

'I can look after myself very well, Babushka.' Stefanie shook her head and smiled. 'I have, up till now.'

'Yes, but you have him, that good man. You have Pascal.'

'He's certainly been a help,' Stefanie bit her lip. Without Pascal she was never quite sure what she would have done.

'I think he's more than a help. From what I hear he loves you.'

'How do you hear that?' Stefanie smiled, despite herself.

Irina tapped her ears, her eyes still ringed by kohl, very bright.

'I hear things.'

'Charlotte,' Stefanie said. Pascal's mother was a frequent visitor to Robertswood, her own country home only ten miles away.

'Charlotte loves you. She loves Pascal. I know she would like you to marry. That way he can always protect

736

you, whatever anyone says. Didn't you ever think of it?' Irina gazed at her solemnly for a moment or two. 'The main thing with you now is that you need something more than passion in your life. You need help and protection. He can give you that. I wonder it's something you never thought of before.'

Irina suddenly leaned back against her pillow, indicating that she was tired. Stefanie closed the pages of *Eugene Onegin*, knowing that she would never open them again to read to her grandmother.

It was as though Stefanie's welfare had been the last thing on her mind, the last message to impart, for, from her sleep that afternoon, she never woke up. A few days later, just before her ninetieth birthday, Princess Irina of the noble House of Ferov died and an era that had spanned nearly a century, and touched many lives, was over.

CHAPTER 29

Em sat, as usual, at the desk that had been taken from her father's study after his death for her mother to work on so that every day she could be reminded of his presence.

Em had a very dim recollection of this precious man; but his children had been reared with an awareness of him and his personality. Their strong sense of duty had been imparted to them by both father and mother – even Freddie had had it and had given his life through it. Throughout their young lives their father used often to be mentioned in conversation as though he had just gone out of the room, or been seen that morning. It wasn't at all sinister. It was quite natural and, in view of what had later happened to Freddie and Ralph, the family thought it was the right attitude because Paul and Johnny were also brought up with an awareness of their dead parents.

As for Luis, he had two parents but there the advantage ended. Em knew how torn he had been between herself and Felipe and yet, in the strange way that things turn out, he had grown up into an attractive, well-mannered, pleasant, balanced young man, of whom not only the mother and father but also the family were proud. In fact the younger generation were doing well: Paul was turning into a first class industrialist; Johnny was now at Cirencester studying horticulture; Jeremy Crewe was a steadfast, reliable young man destined for a career in the City; Flora, if she could still be called the younger generation, was carrying the flag of revolution and dissent, and Giles, her brother, was a surgeon at a London hospital.

Em looked at the latest photos from Luis, just received in the morning's mail, accompanied by an incisive report on events in Vietnam, which threatened to escalate into a major war as America threw more and more troops into the area. Luis was making a name as a photo-journalist whose talents were in demand by world agencies who took the material from *The Sentinel*. Sometimes nepotism undoubtedly paid, Em thought as, with a mother's pride, as well as an editor's satisfaction, she put the material to one side, to consider later and probably discuss with her mother. She turned then to the tapes that came all the time off the wire from sources all round the world.

And, indeed, the world seemed a troubled place in the autumn of 1964 – but when had it not?

There was no significant détente in relations between the great powers; the Western Alliance was divided about its nuclear policy. Khrushchev had been ousted in Russia, and the first Labour government returned in England for thirteen years, though with a tiny majority. There was conflict in the Congo; war between Greeks and Turks in Cyprus, and confrontation in the Far East between Malaysia and Indonesia.

Winston Churchill had finally left the House of Commons at the age of 89, and it had been the hottest summer since 1959, when teenage gangs called 'mods' and 'rockers' first appeared, and drugs known as 'purple hearts' began to circulate. Some said that permissiveness was going too far and others that it had hardly started.

Em sat back and removed her glasses, rubbed her eyes. She felt tired. She didn't sleep well, but there was no particular reason for this except, perhaps, advancing age. Her mother would laugh at that; but Em was middle-aged and she felt it – fifty-six in the summer, a birthday she should have shared with her twin, Freddie. Yet Freddie had been dead for twenty-seven years. It was easier, therefore, to remember Freddie as he was than to visualize him as a man of fifty-six, portly with a middle-aged spread, maybe, someone like Arthur.

In dying at twenty-nine Freddie had kept alive his eternal image of youth, like so many millions of other young men who had perished in the terrible wars of this century.

Those who died young . . . Em looked at Luis's pictures again. He was in a dangerous place. She felt rather as Rachel must have about her when she was in Germany and Spain in the thirties . . . wishing he'd think of something else to do, somewhere else to go. Flora was certainly doing all she could to stop future wars. Flora's world, if it ever came to be, would be perfect, if a little regimented.

'Lord Askham is here to see you, Lady Em,' the receptionist on the ground floor said. She was one of the very few people in the building who ever used Em's title. To most people she was just Em, but receptionists were juniors who came and went and there had to be some respect.

'Send him up,' she said, delighted that a nephew she seldom saw was in London. He and Laura had recently become parents again of another son, Philip.

She greeted Paul at the door, flinging her arms round him and saying:

'I was just thinking of your father.'

'Why was that?' Paul returned her embrace, put a heavy briefcase on the table and sank into a chair.

'I had some pictures from Luis and an account of the escalation of the situation in Vietnam and, I don't know, it led me to think about my father and yours, and wars in general. Anyway, what brings you to London?'

'Business,' Paul said. 'Always business. I wondered if I could stay with you for a few days? I'm trying to get a contract from one of the big companies. We assemble their televisions for them; they put their name on them.'

'That doesn't sound very fair,' Em said.

Paul smiled. 'It's business, Aunt Em. I have no risk, no distribution problems, no heavy competition in the market. I know that I will make a profit. They don't.'

'You really do have flair, you know,' Em said, sitting back. 'That would have made Freddie very proud, and surprised.'

'I often think about Dad, that may surprise you, too.' Paul took out a packet of cigarettes which he held out to Em, saying as he did, 'People say you shouldn't do this and I am trying to stop.'

'With a young family you should,' Em said, lighting up. 'I'm incorrigible, I'm afraid. In my day the hazards weren't appreciated, but you should know better.'

'It's stress.' Paul took a deep breath. 'It's trying to make one's way in business. I want to make my own way, you know, and not be dependent on Leo. He's given me a lot of advice and made money available that I needed, but it's caused problems between me and Laura . . .'

'Bad problems?' Em's tone was sympathetic.

'Not bad, now. We've ironed them out; but bad at one time before Philip was born. I guess I was pretty harsh to Laura at times because of her father. It wasn't her fault, and I hate myself for what happened.' Paul stubbed out his half-finished cigarette and smiled. 'Things are much better now.'

'I'm really glad. I love Laura and I know your father would have loved her.' Em fiddled with her pen. Never having had the day-to-day minutiae of bringing up Luis – that had been left to his father, *faute de mieux* – she had not turned into a moralizing mother. As an aunt or a friend she was not a preacher either, and this made her a welcome companion to the young. 'I was thinking of your father because I was thinking of middle age. As you know, I had a birthday in the summer and I could never imagine Freddie being old.'

'You're not *old*, Aunt Em,' Paul said gallantly, but indeed dear Aunt Em was a little frumpy. Instead of a year younger than Charlotte she looked about fifteen years older: she was grey-haired, she'd put on weight and she never wore make-up, or maybe a touch of lipstick on special occasions. It was hard to believe they were sisters.

'I'm not exactly *old*,' Em said, 'as my mother is always reminding me, but let's say I feel my age, unlike Mother, who never has.'

'I'd love to have known my father,' Paul said, thinking of the picture of the cheerful, good-looking man taken on the eve of his departure for the Spanish war. 'I don't think we're a bit alike.'

'Only in some respects,' Em said cautiously. 'Your father would never have done well in business. It is not an Askham trait, so you're lucky – unless one goes back a hundred years or so when there must have been enough shrewd Askhams around to accumulate the wealth we had then. In fact, I often wondered what Freddie would have done if he'd lived, because he wasn't particularly good at anything, except friendship. I found some writings of his after he died and Mum was thinking of publishing them privately, but the war intervened and we never got round to it. He may have been a writer, who knows? He would never have made any money, whatever he did. Talking of money, incidentally,' Em paused. 'The scaffolding is coming down from the Hall, at last, I hear. Charlotte and Mum have been round and they say it is absolutely lovely. Fully restored. You ought . . .'

'Please don't ask me to see it,' Paul said icily. 'I have no interest in Askham Hall until it belongs to an Askham again.'

'I do think that is a bit unreasonable, darling. Times change.'

'Unreasonable, but there it is.' Paul nervously lit a fresh cigarette. 'If I get this new deal and some others I'm after, I might shortly be worth a few millions myself. The joint shares in Lighterman that Laura and I own are also worth millions. Already I'm a paper millionaire and I might soon be in a position to pay off my father-in-law and reclaim the family home, if only I ever could.'

'It seemed inevitable at the time.'

'Well, it wasn't, and I thank Hugo for it. Hugo, who has lost his job, his wife and everything. Kicked out by the Baron.'

'No one particularly *likes* Gunther,' Em agreed reluctantly. 'Nor Anna. Poor Anna has never been much loved by this family. She couldn't seem to help doing harm. But both she and Gunther have good taste. Excellent style. Nothing in the Hall is lacking except the furniture and they say his pictures . . .'

'Enough, Aunt Em,' Paul said, getting up. 'I'm going to take you out to dinner. How long will you be?'

It was lovely to spend an evening with Paul; in fact lovely to go out at all. Em could have had a better social life but she chose not to. Often she didn't leave the office until the paper was put to bed, and if she wasn't there she liked reading and watching television or having an early night.

Paul took her to Luigi's, an Italian restaurant in Soho, and when they got home it was nearly eleven. Em always opened the door of her flat a bit nervously as she was never quite sure who would be there. When Flora was officially in residence she was extremely generous with Em's accommodation and offered beds freely to whoever she happened to come across in need of somewhere to stay. Usually they were perfectly harmless people, but sometimes she felt she had to count the spoons, taking care not to offend Flora. Occasionally there were some spoons missing, too.

Tonight, however, Flora was alone, slumped in front of the TV, complaining bitterly about the run on sterling that had followed the election of a Labour government.

'The government has had to impose a fifteen per cent surcharge on imports, whatever that means,' Flora said, waving airily to Em and Paul as he put down his suitcase and leaned over to give her a peck on the cheek. 'Hello, capitalist,' Flora said.

'Hello, darling Commie,' Paul replied.

'Well, *you* should know what a fifteen per cent surcharge means.'

'It means bad news,' Paul said, 'for us capitalists. It means that countries which take our goods will retaliate. We shall have to expect surcharges, too. It probably means I shan't make as much as I expected to if I get the deal I'm after.'

Flora stuck her finger in her mouth and looked gloomily at the TV set, ignoring Paul and Em as she showed him where to sleep.

Flora felt very equivocal about her cousin Paul Askham. Paul was so exceptionally nice that it was hard not to like him. He was a cheerful sort of person without airs. Yet he had not only *not* renounced his peerage as she would have liked, following the excellent example set by Anthony Wedgwood Benn, but he had started to call himself Lord Askham because, he said jokingly, it increased his chances in business. Flora despised that sort of attitude. There was a side to Paul that she didn't like at all: a nice, good democrat who had hated public school turning, in her opinion, into an opportunistic capitalist.

Paul, on the other hand, felt that Flora spent a lot of time chasing shadows. He was more inclined to think there was room in the world for all sorts than she was. Like her, he supported the Labour Party but, unlike her, he felt that as long as there were nuclear weapons Britain should have them.

Em, who had a bit of a headache, only hoped that night that they wouldn't start one of their arguments. Sometimes she wondered why Paul, who had plenty of money, didn't prefer a hotel to staying with her and the possibility of sleeping on the couch in the sitting-room because Flora's friends were commandeering all the spare beds, or arguing all night with the Radical in the family.

Paul, however, on this occasion was tired and as there was a spare bed, he made use of it, not before asking Flora if she wanted to come and see the film *Dr Strangelove* the following night.

'It's about the Bomb,' he said jokingly. 'How to aim it and who to aim it at.'

'No, it's *not*. It's about an idiot who goes MAD,' Flora shouted, throwing a cushion at him, but she agreed to go just the same.

Em went to bed, for once feeling quite happy and contented. She loved family, and having the family round her was a tonic. It also took her mind off Luis, thousands of miles away in a strange, hostile country far from home.

The next morning Paul had left by the time Em got up, round about eight. He said he had an early meeting and asked her if she would like to come to the film, too? She wrote him a note saying that she wouldn't. It was one of her late nights. And then she left a note for Flora asking her if she could possibly do a little tidying up in the flat. It was such a shambles. Flora was naturally untidy. Some people said that the mess around her reflected the mess in her life; but Em argued that Flora's life wasn't messy. It was the kind of life she wanted and it had meaning and purpose. In its way it was an ordered, dedicated life. Em loved Flora; she defended her to the family and her critics. Indeed she was beginning to mother her, fussing about her if she came in too late or didn't say where she was going, or who she was with. It was a bit much for a woman over thirty who had always been independent but, in a strange way, Flora didn't mind. She had never had a mother and it was quite new being mothered now; knowing she had a base and an anchor which was Em.

Em decided that she ought by now to be a grandmother. Charlotte was a grandmother and it had made her stop fussing about her children.

However, she went contentedly to work that day, catching a taxi because she was late. Once in the office she closed the windows because it was cold, supposedly, the weather forecasters said, the coldest October since 1939, the year the war began. Em remembered that year very well indeed. She remembered Ralph going to France in September with the BEF and saying it would all be over by Christmas. Instead he came back from Dunkirk nine months later terribly badly wounded.

Em lit a cigarette, the first of many that she would smoke during the day, and started going over the various agency messages that lay on her desk. She was just about to glance cursorily at the last one before sweeping them out of the way when a name on one of the tapes caught her eye:

PROMINENT GERMAN INDUSTRIALIST ARRESTED ON CHARGES OF WAR CRIMES

LATE LAST NIGHT ONE OF GERMANY'S LEADING INDUSTRIALISTS, BARON GUNTHER VON SPEE, WAS ARRESTED AT HIS HOME NEAR FRANKFURT ON CHARGES CONNECTED WITH WAR CRIMES. IT IS BELIEVED THAT MUCH OF THE EVIDENCE AGAINST BARON VON SPEE WAS DISCOVERED AT THE TIME OF THE EICHMANN TRIAL AND THAT THE BARON, WHO HAS ALWAYS DENIED PLAYING AN ACTIVE PART IN THE NAZI MOVEMENT, IS NOW BELIEVED TO BE ONE OF THE LEADING

Horror-struck, Em gazed at the wire, shuffled through
some more to see if there were further details and then
put in a call to her mother.

The following February Hugo stood at the door of the
Grange. He had on an overcoat and his face was pinched
with cold. Outside there were still traces of snow on the
ground. Rachel looked at him for a long time, as if taking
him in. She hadn't seen him since he abruptly left England
two summers ago to go abroad with Nimet. She'd begun
to wonder if they'd lost touch.

'Nimet's dead,' Hugo said and, pausing in the act of
embracing him, Rachel stood aside to let him in, merely
pressing his arm as he passed her. Hugo looked around
the hall as though slowly refamiliarizing himself with
something that was very precious.

Rachel put her arm through his and drew him into the
cheerful chintzy lounge with its view, in winter, of the
Hall, shining and beautiful now, scaffolding down,
grounds neatly set out, ready to be occupied. Hugo gazed
for a moment at the view and then savagely turned his
back on it.

What might have been.

'I'm terribly sorry.' Rachel sat down and clasped her
hands in her lap. 'What can I say?'

'Nothing, really.' Hugo looked tired, his eyes blood-
shot. He also seemed to have aged. It was very hard to
recall the tiny urchin playing in the garden of a run-down
house in Streatham, whom she had brought to her home,
adopted and come to love so much. But she had always
shared him with Nimet and, finally, Nimet had won.

Now she was dead.

'How did she die?' she said.

'She was run over on the Promenade des Anglais. We lived in a small hotel just off the front and she was coming home. I don't know if she fell or had a stroke or something happened; the French are hopeless, really. She was dead when she got to hospital.' Hugo shrugged. 'That's all there is to it. It was all over very quickly – death, burial. I had no reason to stay on.'

Nimet dead. It was a shock – also, dare one think it, a relief? The existence of this woman had been a torment for the greater part of her life; yet now that she was no longer alive it didn't seem to matter very much. Sad Nimet. Run over by a car, dying all alone. No family, as she had.

'I'm terribly sorry,' Rachel said again. 'Believe me, I grieve for you, Hugo. You were always very good to your mother.'

'And she to me.'

Rachel acknowledged what he said with a slight smile.

'Have you come home now? I hope so. You know there's always a place for you here.'

'I don't know if I've come home.' Hugo didn't return her smile. 'I don't know where I belong any more. All this gone,' he gestured towards the Hall, 'all my dreams.'

'Why don't you have a bath and a rest?' Rachel said. 'I'll get us some tea. I want you to stay here for as long as you feel like it. You know you always have a home with me. Besides, I've something to tell you.'

But, somehow, as she saw him up the stairs, he no longer seemed like her son. Something had happened.

Later he said to her: 'Have you heard from Jenny?'

'Occasionally she writes.'

'How are the children?'

'I think they're very well,' Rachel said carefully.

'It wasn't my fault.'

'Whose was it, then?'

Hugo looked at her and for a moment Rachel thought he was going to get up and leave. There was a wildness in Hugo's eyes that she couldn't remember seeing before and she wondered if he'd taken to drink.

An ineffable sadness remained always in her heart about Hugo because of the promise he had shown not only in his youth but in later life as well. Then everything seemed to go wrong. Hugo had given in, the fight too much for him.

'Jenny worked far too hard for too long,' Rachel said sadly. 'I don't think we ever understood her properly.'

'I don't think she ever stopped loving Ralph, that's the truth,' Hugo said. 'She married me out of pity.'

'I don't believe that at all. I just think she became a beast of burden and the Hall was a prison to her. Do you remember all those parties without much help – Jenny never out of the kitchen, cooking, waiting, washing-up? It was too much. She just broke when you broke.'

'She was certainly no help to me. I think I saw her then as a rather bitter woman. I wondered what she had wanted in life and I'm afraid I didn't understand her. How's Johnny?' Hugo's face softened. 'I think I missed him most.'

'Oh, Johnny's fine.' Rachel smiled with pleasure. 'He loves his course. He is going to farm. He often comes to stay.'

'And the rest of the family?' Hugo said and, at last, Rachel could feel the tight coil that had bound him begin to unwind.

'The family are all fine . . . well,' Rachel paused and looked at the clock. It was nearly six. 'Why don't you get us a drink? I said I've something important to tell you.'

Hugo got up and went over to the sideboard where

Rachel kept a few bottles with which she entertained people when they came to visit her.

'Sherry for me,' she said.

'As usual. I remember, Mum,' Hugo smiled across at her and then she knew that it was all right again. It was just Hugo's strangeness on returning after a silence of nearly eighteen months that had made him seem different. She noticed that he took only a small whisky. Of course Hugo wouldn't take to drink! He was much too resilient for that.

'Now, what's up?' Hugo gave her her sherry and came and sat next to her. She took his hand, pressing it in her own.

'Gunther is going to be tried as a war criminal . . .'

'*What?*' Hugo interrupted her.

'If he's guilty all his possessions will be confiscated. He'll lose all his money. Anyway, without any doubt, he will never move into the Hall.'

'How on earth did they find that out?'

'We only pieced it together gradually. Em saw it on the wire a few months ago, and the next day it was all in the papers, underlining the connection with us, needless to say.'

'Needless to say,' Hugo echoed, returning the pressure on his hand. 'Poor Mum.'

'Not me particularly. The "Red Countess" came out of it quite well. But Bobby was furious because they raked up all the old pre-war thing about Askham Armaments selling weapons to the Nazis. Susan, of course, left everything and went to Anna straight away and what we know we have heard from her, a strange tale.' Rachel took a sip of her sherry and went on.

'Apparently Anna felt all along that something was wrong with Gunther but she didn't know what. He blinded her as he had before. They built this house outside

750

Frankfurt and it was full of all sorts of electronic gadgetry to keep people out. Nevertheless it was burgled at least once. Many years before, Anna had seen a picture of Gunther taken with Hitler. He kept it on his wall as though he were proud of it, even when they moved house, and she thought this was strange.

'The Israelis, it seems, had been on the track of Gunther, and many others, trying to get evidence for a number of years. Anna had once seen a man of Middle Eastern appearance with a gun near the house. She couldn't understand it. Gunther always fobbed her off with some explanation. Of course she loved him and she wanted to believe him.

'Then one day, last October, the police appeared at the door and arrested him. They claim that he was one of the very instigators of the Final Solution, working closely with Eichmann and Hitler. He was never at the Front; he never personally killed a Jew, but he undoubtedly helped to plan the whole thing. He was a very clever, very evil backroom boy, who nearly covered his tracks. But for what they found out from Eichmann they would probably never have got him.'

'My goodness,' Hugo said. 'And he nearly came to live at Askham Hall. What an irony.'

'We think,' Rachel could hardly keep the note of excitement out of her voice, 'that we may get the Hall back very soon. Paul has just made a lot of money. If it happens he's going to restore it with all the right furniture. He's going to settle some money on Anna and little Hans by way of compensation because he says he doesn't want to live in a place paid for by Nazi gold.'

'And what is Anna going to do?'

'She's sticking by Gunther so far. She doesn't believe any of it. But Susan feels it's a watertight case. Anna doesn't *want* to believe it. But these people never act without proof and Gunther hasn't a chance.'

'Well, well.' Hugo got up and looked out of the window again at the Hall, gleaming with paint paid for by a German war criminal. 'I don't *think* I could start up there again, Mum, even if I had the chance. My heart isn't in it.'

'What will you do, darling?'

'Stay with you a few days if I may, go up and see the children, go back to France. You remember Charlotte's friend from the war?'

'Marc?' Rachel said sharply.

'Marc la Forêt. That's right. He has this boat business. I like boats, remember Dunkirk?'

'Don't I just,' Rachel said. 'The memory still makes me shudder.'

'I did a bit of work for Marc and he'd quite like to have me full time.'

'Did he talk about Charlotte?'

'He mentioned her; but he has family of his own.'

'Twenty years ago, anyway.' Rachel sighed; another might-have-been.

'I met him in a bar in Cannes. We knew each other straight away. He said to remember him to you and her; but he has a very pretty wife.'

'And what about *your* wife?' Rachel enquired. 'Might you not get together again?'

'I very much doubt it. Like you, I think she had enough of everything, me as well.'

Jenny said:

'I was never free of work in the house.'

'That would all change if we go back to France. I promise you you need never do any housework again.'

Jenny shook her head. As she looked at him her expression was almost chillingly impersonal.

'I don't love you any more, Hugo. That's really all there is to it. I haven't pined for you and I haven't missed you.'

'I don't think you ever loved me.' Hugo's tone was bitter. 'You married me because it was rather convenient, a father for Johnny.'

'That's a horrible thing to say.'

Jenny turned away from him and looked stonily towards the bar of the hotel in Keswick where they were having a drink. She had wanted to talk to him before he saw the children, explain to him how things were: that she was happy and settled in Keswick, working as a nurse in a home for elderly people. Elizabeth wanted to go to university and Anthony was happy at school.

Hugo had listened glumly, unable, in a way, to believe her. It was a Jenny he had never seen before: a calm, detached, very mature woman, older than him; the kind of competent nursing sister with whom Ralph had fallen in love during the war, yet extraordinarily unfriendly towards the man who, after all, was still her husband.

'I never liked the family,' Jenny went on after a while. 'And they hated me. "Common", I bet they thought, "after Ralph for his title". Well, I never wanted to be Lady Askham and, thank God, I never was. I never fitted in.'

'Rachel was very fond of you. It's an unkind thing to say. She sent you lots of love.'

'She was fond of me *eventually*, but she made it hard for me, always. Never quite good enough for her sons. As for Charlotte, I think she always thought of me as a servant, whose place was definitely in the kitchen . . .'

Hugo stood up. 'I can't take a lot of this,' he said. 'Can I get you another drink?'

Jenny held out her glass. 'Same again, please.'

* * *

It wasn't a very successful visit. Neither Elizabeth nor Anthony seemed particularly pleased to see him. They felt he had treated their mother badly, even though he said she had walked out on him. They liked the north country, the Lake District. They liked their mother's family and the new friends they'd made at school. Anthony had even developed a Cumbrian accent. He was a tough rugger-playing boy whom, Hugo realized, he scarcely thought of as his son. Yet it was scarcely eighteen months since it had all happened.

It was very difficult indeed to think he was Elizabeth and Anthony's father. He loved them, and they had spent so many years together. But, undoubtedly, they had been very hard years; years when he had managed to lose his mother's fortune, and perhaps his anxiety, the tension of life in the large crumbling Hall, had been too much for them.

After all those years of pretending to be an Askham – of fitting in first with Ralph's family then Hugo's – Jenny was her own woman at last; happy among her own, her kith and kin. She had loved Ralph, but she had lost him. Maybe she hadn't loved Hugo as much, but what young woman with a child could resist such a kind and gentle man? Yet Hugo's gentility had been his own undoing.

Jenny had made a new life in her own familiar niche. She had never felt an Askham and sometimes, Hugo realized, with a sense of loss as well as bitterness, he had never felt one either. Before he left she asked for a divorce.

He was quite glad to go back to London and get a plane for the South of France.

Sometimes in the winter, the mist stealing in from the Adriatic Sea, across the waters of the lagoon, seemed to envelop the city of Venice in a shroud, its ancient buildings silhouetted in the encroaching gloom like spectres. At other times, driven by the wind, those erstwhile calm waters lashed against the boats anchored along the Riva degli Schiavoni, flooding St Mark's Square.

But usually in winter Venice was a pleasant, temperate place to live, free of tourists and the crowds that clotted up its meandering ways in summer, filling the bars and restaurants to capacity and driving the residents away to the hills on the mainland.

Anna, who had seen Venice in all its moods, in all seasons for a great part of her life, now thought of it as home, as a welcoming, protective and compassionate friend. By now she felt that she knew every stone, every bridge, every statue, every waterway, every building, large or humble. She had come to Venice when she was a baby and now, like a baby in need of succour, she had returned.

The muddy waters of the sluggish little canal which wended its way slowly past the Palazzo Quinducale gleamed palely in the wintry sun. There had been a great deal of rain. It was said that Venice was sinking; that one day it would be engulfed completely by the sea unless something was done to save it. But for Anna Venice was timeless and indestructible and the Palazzo Quinducale was both her fortress and her prison.

Anna had been in Venice for over a year, ever since Gunther had been brought to trial. She didn't want to be hounded by the press, the subject of malicious and speculative articles that would be agented across the world. Neither had she wanted to sit in the court daily watching him because, even before the verdict, she had known that what he was being tried for was true. With hindsight she knew it was all true; the thefts, the electronic gadgetry, the spies at the gate. There was a meaning for them all now.

It had emerged that Gunther had never expunged his Nazi past. He had continued to support key figures in the former regime who had evaded capture, which was why he had made so many trips to South America. Millions of von Spee marks, her son's inheritance, had been transferred to Rio, Buenos Aires and tiny places in Paraguay and Peru, where the wanted men still lurked.

The fact that Gunther had deceived her so much and for so long was what finally cost him Anna's allegiance. For the second time he had lied to her and she decided not to stand by him – an object of ridicule and pity, an Englishwoman who should have known better than be deceived by an enemy of the country.

To Venice she fled, taking her small son with her.

Anna had reverted to her maiden name of Ferov and was known as 'Principessa'. She was, in fact, a princess because her father had been a prince and it suited her very well.

Anna liked to begin the day alone. She seldom saw Hans before noon, when she also saw her mother. As Anna had been, Hans was brought up by servants; as a tiny baby he had been exclusively cared for by nursemaids, Anna a mother in name only. Anna hadn't cared for small children and nor had Gunther. For lonely, neglected, unloved little Hans servants were all the company he had.

Melanie in her turn had been a bad mother – children relegated to the nursery from birth, so that Anna was only following in a family tradition. Such things did seem to go in families, like alcohol or violence, or evil.

Susan had grown reclusive; Sasha's death had changed her personality from an outgoing, forthright woman to an introverted, misanthropic hypochondriac. She saw none of the family and allowed none of them to visit. She was a very wealthy woman, her business in good hands, and she needed no one except her daughter and her pathetic little grandson Hans. She didn't ignore him quite as much as Anna did; she was fond of him – as one is fond of a pet dog or cat, and allowed him to play in her bedroom in the mornings. It was whispered around in the family who knew of her state of mind, especially by Bobby and her other brother Christopher, that her grief over Sasha and Anna had been such that she might have gone a little mad.

But Susan was not mad; she was bitter and angry, humiliated by what had happened to Anna, and until that mood evaporated she was content to stay in this old palace, giving her daughter what comfort she could. Both she and Anna had been let down in their lives by men and, like two grieving, betrayed women, they stayed together.

Denton had died the previous year. He had simply faded away like a piece of old parchment and what had been left of his remains was buried on the island of the dead, San Michele in the Lagoon. Tucked away in a corner overgrown by trees, Denton's grave would languish, forgotten until in time he was joined by his son Jordan, and the bones of the two odd isolated men, who had never acknowledged each other in their lifetime as father and son, would spend eternity together.

Jordan was fifty-seven and had lived for over twenty years in his attic in the Palazzo Quinducale. He was a white-haired, gentle man who had acquired a tranquillity he didn't perhaps deserve in view of his past. He read a lot and enjoyed visits from his great-nephew Hans, whom he admired for his blond Aryan looks and aristocratic, Teutonic breeding.

Hans spent hours playing in Jordan's room with bricks and toys, or being read to, sitting on his uncle's knee.

Jordan scarcely ever left his suite of rooms where he felt safe. Now, because of the changes, the new staff, he seldom came downstairs and never went outside. He hadn't been outside in the streets and alleys of Venice for over fifteen years.

It was an odd, melancholy household, even by Venetian standards – and Venice had a lot of secrets and concealed many old mysteries of the past. Yet it seemed to suit all its occupants existing in a circumscribed, claustrophobic atmosphere of mutual need, self-pity and self-protection.

One morning Anna came down to breakfast after a poor night. She seldom slept well and this particular morning she felt depressed as well as tired, and the sight of a letter with a German stamp addressed in Gunther's hand did nothing to cheer her up. Gunther very seldom wrote unless it was about their divorce, to which he had at last agreed. Gunther, in his odd, detached way, didn't appear to blame her for the attitude she'd taken towards him, and seldom enquired after the son whose arrival he had greeted with such joy. It was as though Gunther, incarcerated probably for life, wanted to obliterate all past contacts. He was said to be studying philosophy in prison.

Anna sipped some black coffee in an effort to revive herself and then she opened the letter.

It was a curious letter without any preliminaries, no personal news or enquiries. It was just a story as though, in some cruel way, he wanted to make the maximum impact, leaving her totally unprepared for what he had to say:

My dear Anna, [*he wrote*]
I know what happened to your father. It came about like this. I told you that for many years my family had a house on the

outskirts of Berlin on the Potsdam Road? This was occupied after the fall of our city by the Russians and I never saw it again.

It so happened that yesterday, as I was exercising in the prison yard, I was approached by a man who used to be a servant in our Berlin house and was there all during the war and immediately afterwards. He is now some minor official in the prison but he recognized me at once. He is a little older than I am. His name is Fritz Wengel.

Fritz and I were reminiscing about the past – he knew my father well – when we had servants who had worked for us for generations, rather like the Askhams, in what is termed the good old days. Then he related a very strange tale which I repeat to you exactly as he told it to me:

After the fall of Berlin, he said, our house was occupied by a Russian Colonel who spoke excellent German and also English and French. His name was Colonel Ferov and he had fought until the fall of Berlin – or so he said. Fritz had the impression that Colonel Ferov was anxious about something and also lonely, because very few other Russians visited the house, which was large enough to billet many people and relatively unscathed by war damage. There was some mystery about the Colonel; he drank a great deal and told Fritz something of his life: how he had been imprisoned in Siberia but how he remained a true Communist and had to cheat, and even kill, for his beliefs.

One day Colonel Ferov appeared more excited than usual and told Fritz to prepare a meal for a guest of his. As a matter of fact the Colonel told him he was an Englishman, a relative of his, and it was their first meeting for many years.

Fritz did what he could to provide a meal fit for such a meeting, in the circumstances; but food was not easy to get in those days immediately after the fall of Berlin. Germany, as you know, was decimated. However, Fritz set it out as best he could; those were the Colonel's instructions and also he was told to keep out of the way while the Colonel had his visitor with him.

But, naturally, Fritz was curious to see this English officer and, as they were leaving, he looked out of the window and saw them preparing to get into the Colonel's car and drive off. The Englishman was tall and, without his cap, fair. He had on the uniform of an officer in the British Army and as he got into the car with the Colonel there seemed a constraint between them, before the Russian Colonel and his guest drove off.

When Fritz went downstairs he found that the meal was only

half finished, the wine scarcely touched. He had the impression there had been an argument and that they had left in a hurry. Anyway, he cleared up and prepared the Colonel's night things for bed.

But the Colonel never came back. His things remained in his room untouched.

Some days later some Russians appeared, to clear out the Colonel's things. They were very meticulous, Fritz assured me, in making sure that no trace of him remained.

Just as they were going Fritz was emboldened to ask what had happened to his master and whether he would have the pleasure of seeing him again. The Russian replied that the Colonel had met with a road accident and was dead. Fritz was told not to tell this to anyone and given a hundred marks in compensation, a sum which was already worthless. Maybe this is why he told me.

Anna, I think, by now, you can be in no doubt, as I am not, that the Russian Colonel was your father Kyril and the Englishman your cousin, Ralph Askham.

You can make what conclusions you like but, in my opinion, and as we know that Ralph suffered from a severe gun wound, he and your father succeeded in killing each other. Your father, therefore, is dead.

I know that this news will put your mind at rest if, at the same time, it saddens you.

Gunther had formally signed it with his full signature, like a confession.

When Anna finished reading, her coffee was cold, her brioche untouched. She thought about everything the family, she knew, said about her and now she wondered how much of it was true. She walked to the mullioned window and peered through the small thick pane to the muddy canal waters meandering beneath her. She knew that they said she'd brought bad luck; she was ruthless, unprincipled, with a touch of evil.

Maybe they'd been right, the family. Maybe it was all true and that the terrible legacy of her father – traitor and murderer – had left its mark on her.

Well, if it had, if the sins of fathers did, fairly or

unfairly, visit their children, then justice had brought its own retribution by imprisoning her in this gloomy palace, hiding from vengeful Israelis or Russian hit-men, for the rest of her life. She would always be scared to go out.

Anna was not one for tears, nor did she cry now. She left the embrasure of the window, Gunther's letter clenched in her hand. She walked across the long, light, airy, paved salon that ran the whole length of the front of the Palazzo overlooking the canal, her high-heeled shoes tapping on the floor.

As a *principessa* Anna had never let herself go. She dressed smartly and well, even though she scarcely ever left the house: the maids did all the shopping and she seldom bought clothes. Sometimes at night she would slip out in a dark raincoat and walk across the Rialto bridge, along the narrow streets past the market on the other side; or along the Merceria with its smart fashionable boutiques whose brightly lit, shuttered windows attracted without holding out the temptation to spend. Anna had to be careful with her money.

Anna crossed the hall, with its ancient coats of arms emblazoned in marble on the tiled floors, and climbed the stairs to her mother's room. Susan had moved into the bedroom once occupied by Lady Melanie. Except that it was the nicest room in the house Anna didn't know why her mother had decided to use it. All the furniture was as it was and in the same position as when Melanie had been alive, and there was a gloomy, sepulchral air about the room overlooking the stagnant canal, the faint effulgence of death.

Susan was reading the morning paper, having just had her breakfast, which was brought up to her on a tray by her maid. She had the same light breakfast as Anna, rose at about eleven, had her bath, dressed with her usual care

761

and came downstairs at about noon. She looked up and smiled as she saw her daughter crossing the room towards her.

By her side little Hans played with his toys on the floor, as he normally did in the morning. He looked up rather anxiously as he saw his mother making this unscheduled visit, in case she told him to stop, but Anna smiled kindly at him and patted his head. It was about as close as she ever got to him, a little pat. She never kissed him or cuddled him or had him in her bed. Her own childhood had been similarly starved of affection. But then when she'd grown up she'd become very close to her mother and she supposed that, in time, Hans would to her.

'Good morning, dear.' Susan put down her paper, removed her reading glasses. 'How did you sleep?'

'Not well.' Anna stooped to kiss her mother and as she did Susan saw the letter in her hand.

'Not bad news, I hope?'

'When is news good?' Anna said. 'These days?'

'It *is* bad news, then.' Susan sighed and held out her hand.

Anna gave her the letter and sat by her bed as she read it. Her mother's face remained unemotional; she scarcely seemed to blink and hardly a muscle moved. Then, when she had finished, she rested the letter on her lap, her spectacles on top of it.

'I always thought it was true about Kyril killing Freddie.'

'But you said it was a *lie*!'

'I had to, didn't I?' Susan looked with compassion at her daughter. 'I daren't give the *slightest* indication I thought it might be true. I knew in the thirties that Kyril was deeply involved in some sort of political trickery, as you did with Gunther; one knows, one suspects. Kyril had these funny, secretive meetings, as Gunther had; he

762

came and he went as Gunther did. He disappeared for long periods, years. They're all the same, these people. They live by treachery; they have a passion for secrecy, for double-dealing, for lies.' She looked up at Anna, her face creased with pity. 'I'm so sorry, my dear; but I'm afraid Kyril *must* have killed Ralph. Ralph was shot. Someone shot him. What happened to Kyril afterwards we shall never know, except that he's dead. I always thought he was. It appears that, somehow, they died together.'

For a moment Susan paused and looked thoughtfully towards the window. Then she replaced her glasses and picked up her paper.

'Ah, well, I suppose it's just as well we know for sure. It happened such a long time ago – over twenty years if this letter is correct. So I'm a widow, after all, but it doesn't really seem to matter much now, does it? One thing, though,' she looked solemnly over the paper at Anna. 'The family must *never* know. This is a secret that you and I must take with us to the grave.'

EPILOGUE

Happy Returns

August 1967

CHAPTER 30

Rachel was awake early on the morning of her ninetieth birthday and lay for some moments, as she customarily did, listening to the sound of birdsong in the garden. Then she got up, drew back the curtains, saw that it was a nice day and, donning her housecoat, went downstairs to the kitchen and put on the kettle. Then, taking some secateurs and a pair of scissors, she went into the garden and began energetically cutting off the dead heads of the roses, snipping at the petunias, delphiniums, antirrhinums and geraniums so as to give them more room to grow.

That done, Rachel straightened up and looked at the scene before her, breathing in the fragrance of the day. Over the years the Hall had practically become obscured by the trees in summer so that only occasionally, when they stirred in the wind, one could catch sight of it gleaming in all its pristine glory. For so many years the scaffolding had seemed to be part of it; now it had all gone, a construction at the corner removed only as recently as the spring.

Because the day was so calm, the trees so still, she caught only a glimpse of the Hall but clearly to be seen was the marquee half way down the meadow, which had been constructed especially for the party to be held for her birthday.

Ten years ago, when she had been eighty, Rachel had never expected to see this day. Now she confidently expected to see a hundred.

The years recently had been good to her. She had settled comfortably in her old home and, since Paul had moved back to the Hall, there was once again the sense of family on call, combined with her own independence which was so precious. Almost each day, or every other day, she saw her great-grandchildren. She had only to telephone and a car came round to take her to wherever she wished to go. Once a week, at least, she dined at the Hall and frequently the children's nanny brought them over to be with her.

She had had a fall, but she had recovered. She had bronchitis but antibiotics stopped it turning to pneumonia. They were the new miracle drugs that would revolutionize medicine. She knew that she no longer moved as quickly as she used to, that neither her hearing nor her eyesight were as good. She had to watch her blood pressure and needed more rest in the afternoon. But the doctor's opinion was that, at ninety, Lady Askham had the constitution of a woman many years younger. But more important was her spirit. Rachel was a survivor; she had overcome much sorrow, many vicissitudes. She was already a young woman when Queen Victoria died, and now her great-great-granddaughter had been on the throne for fourteen years.

No, all in all she felt well and strong, young in spirit. Capable, for example, she thought as she went back to

768

the kitchen, of taking tea up to her niece in bed, who was fifty-five years her junior.

But no, it was too early and too nice a morning to interrupt Flora, and after Rachel had brewed her tea she took it out to the front lawn and put it on the table beside the pond that Paul had thoughtfully reconditioned for her only the previous year. The pond had always been there, but when her own children had been small Bosco had had it boarded over. It had remained like this for years, certainly when Freddie and Marian had Paul; but now it had been freshly excavated, concreted, filled with water and supplied with goldfish, so that his grandmother could feed them every morning.

This she now proceeded to do, sprinkling the fish food fairly thickly, as it was her birthday, and gratified to see by the reaction of the fish, the snapping of jaws, that her gesture was appreciated.

Rachel sat down, luxuriating in the glory of the morning, and sipped her tea. Ninety. It was quite an age. Like Queen Victoria she'd never expected to live so long after her husband died. Her own mother had died young. Yet the years passed – two wars that had seen a complete upheaval in the world, and six monarchs had sat on the English throne in her lifetime. There was no one left alive whom she knew who could remember her as a young woman. She had outlived them all. Occasionally she would read in *The Times* of the death of a near contemporary but few, if any, had reached ninety years of age.

Yet she didn't feel ninety, an old, old lady. It would be absurd if one did.

When Melanie had died Rachel had soon expected to follow her. Yet Melanie had been dead eleven years. One couldn't live forever but she hoped that when she did go it would be peacefully in her sleep, slipping away gradually like dearest Irina.

Rachel poured herself another cup of tea and sipped it by the pond, grateful that it was such a fine day. Then she went indoors again, had a bath and got dressed before calling Flora with a cup freshly brewed.

'Nine o'clock,' she said, bending over her sleeping niece.

Flora opened one eye and then two, gazed at her aunt, at the clock and sat upright in bed.

'Oh, Auntie Rachel! *I* meant to do it for *you* on your birthday.' She reached up and, as Rachel bent down, put both her arms round her neck. 'Your ninetieth birthday . . .'

'Ssh,' Rachel said, smiling. 'I was just telling myself, sitting in the garden, how young I felt. Don't spoil it.'

'And you are young,' Flora assured her, sitting up and taking the tea from her. 'The only thing is,' she screwed up her face as Rachel sat beside her on the bed, 'although you're so young and everything, I don't like you living here all by yourself.'

'But why not?' Rachel enquired. 'I am surrounded by people if I need them. Mary comes in every day to do the housework. Laura calls or comes over at least once a day. Sometimes I yearn for a bit of peace. Now that I have television I am quite addicted. I never thought I would be but if anything has gone it's my eyes, and needlework is not quite the pleasure it used to be. But ever since Paul has given me that lovely new colour TV,' Rachel clasped her hands together and gazed at the ceiling, 'I'm in heaven. This year, for the first time, they had the tennis at Wimbledon in colour! I'm extremely fortunate. Paul says there are only a few thousand colour TV sets in the country.'

'Auntie!' Flora shook a finger at her disapprovingly. 'It rots the mind.'

'Not at all. There are some very good programmes on.

770

Things I learn, at my advanced age, for the very first time. The nature programmes are wonderful.'

'But if anything happened, in the night . . .'

'I have a bell by my bed wired directly to the Hall. Paul has been so good.' Rachel joined her hands on her lap. 'So very good. I never, ever, thought I'd have my grandson living at the Hall again with his lovely family, and Laura is such a sweet girl. So thoughtful and sincere. I like her mother, too. She has excellent taste. It's thanks to her that the Hall's interior is as good as its exterior. She never stops looking for suitable items and pieces of furniture. How much it all costs I can't think.'

Flora got out of bed and ran to the window, flinging it open and sniffing, as Rachel had.

'And such a lovely day! Oh, Aunt Rachel, I'm so pleased for you.'

'And I'm especially pleased that you're here.' Rachel got up from the bed and, crossing over to her niece, put her arm round her. 'I wish you could stay here with me. That I *would* like.'

'Oh, Aunt Rachel . . .' Flora played with a lock of her long straggly hair. 'You know I can't settle. I'd get terribly bored down here, even with you and the coloured television set!'

'Well, you get dressed now and meet me downstairs for breakfast,' Rachel said, stooping automatically to pick up Flora's dressing-gown from the floor. 'And leave your room tidy, please.'

'Yes, Auntie,' Flora said meekly. 'You'd think I was seventeen.'

'Sometimes you behave like it.' Rachel shook her head as she left the room; but she was still smiling.

Flora wasn't seventeen; she was thirty-five. Her efforts to find peace and justice in the world grew accordingly more frantic as the world became a more violent place.

The six-day war in June between Israel and Egypt had seemed to threaten the very fabric of civilization. The Tories had gone – a blessing from Flora's radical point of view, but the Labour Party was unpopular. There was disenchantment with Harold Wilson's leadership and a lack of confidence on the part of Britain's allies. Once again de Gaulle had said a firm 'non' to Britain joining Europe. It was very disappointing for those who had hoped for a Socialist revival that would lead the world.

Rachel laid the breakfast table: cornflakes, sliced bread for toasting, pots of honey and marmalade. Flora drank orange juice while she had more tea.

Flora was a true child of the sixties, a radical, a feminist whose lack of conventional attitudes reminded Rachel of herself when young. She had travelled abroad alone before she was twenty. Her independence had been one of the things that had shocked Bosco's mother when she met her in Cairo in 1898. She had actually come out there by herself: shocking.

Rachel had been a suffragette, a reformer – not a scholar like Flora but a well-read, well-educated woman. She had been willing to go to prison for her beliefs but had failed. Flora had succeeded and Rachel wasn't so sure this was such a good thing. She was rather addicted to prison, as she was addicted to doing good and, consequently, her views seemed to make less impact on those who called her a professional agitator, a publicity seeker.

But Rachel loved Flora and admired her. She was almost the closest to her of all her female relations, except Em and Charlotte. She worried about her constantly. To have her living at the Grange would be reassuring, but it was an impossible dream. Dear Flora, Adam's daughter, was a maverick.

Unlike Flora, Rachel was a meticulous person and had been all her life. Having to run a family, a newspaper and cope with her various commitments and duties had required a degree of organization which she maintained in her old age. Even though it was her ninetieth birthday chores had to be done, beds made, dishes washed, regardless of the fact that her daily woman would have been quite glad to have done the whole thing.

With little to do after she moved to the Grange Rachel had felt that if she did absolutely nothing she would stagnate and, for an active person, stagnation was death. So she made each day into something important with tasks to be done.

At eleven Rachel and Flora had a cup of coffee with Mrs Anderson from the village, who had brought Rachel a selection of home-made jams for a present and which were duly opened, tasted and their exquisite flavours admired. After all these years Mrs Anderson didn't need to be told what to do, Rachel just liked to remind her about this little job or that although, as she was also going to the party in the afternoon, there wasn't much time. She, too, had to be off to don her finery and at noon Rachel went upstairs to prepare herself for Johnny, who was coming to collect her at one.

Like Rachel, Paul, too, was meticulous. This party had been planned for months with the precision of a military exercise involving placement of forces, i.e. the staff, and logistics, i.e. the refreshments. As he was a very busy person, a tycoon, skill had been required to make sure that the whole thing went like clockwork. Because the occasion was to honour his grandmother he felt his personal touch was necessary.

When Rachel came down Johnny was already there chatting to Flora whose party dress was an ankle length, beltless garment made of bleached calico. With her long black hair tied at the back, she looked like an early

Christian martyr, an impression helped by the strong leather sandals on her bare feet.

But one would not expect Flora to look other than herself for whatever occasion. She was uncomfortable in finery and despised and deplored the mini skirt, which she thought was a chauvinistic exploitation of women.

Rachel, on the other hand, wore a pretty georgette dress with a striking pattern of large blue flowers, secured by a white belt round the waist. It was a simple, summery dress with buttons up the front and revers, that was not new, but which she kept for best. Unlike Charlotte and Angelica, Rachel had never been the least interested in clothes and this shirt-waist style of dress in different colours and materials was almost a uniform for her. She seldom wore a hat. Her hair was now quite white, with a soft natural wave and secured in a large bun at the nape of her neck. It had scarcely changed since she was a young woman. In the twenties she had once rashly tried the bob but then couldn't wait for her hair to grow again; no other style seemed to suit her.

The fullness in her figure that Rachel had briefly developed in middle age had disappeared and she was now very thin, with a slight stoop; her skin was wrinkled and deeply tanned, due to the many hours she spent gardening; but those brilliant blue eyes which had first captivated her husband nearly seventy years ago were practically undimmed. As she came into the lounge, Johnny thought this was how he'd always remember his grandmother: relaxed, smiling, welcoming, with just that touch of extra tenderness that advancing years had given her.

'Happy birthday, Gran.' Johnny took her hands and stooped to kiss her. He had just had his twenty-second birthday and the sight of him always gave his grandmother mingled pleasure and pain because he was so like Ralph, the father who had died before he could see his son.

Johnny was tall, fair, thick-set, muscular, easy going, not particularly cerebral, a lover of animals and the land. The cousins, though very different, got on well, and Paul wanted Johnny to manage the farming side for him that Hugo's departure had left neglected. There were acres of good arable land round the Hall that Paul wanted to develop along with the stud that had never been revived since the war.

Johnny placed a carefully-wrapped parcel in Rachel's hand and watched her as she eagerly undid it. Rachel held it in her hands and looked at it for several moments, her eyes shining with pleasure, that wonderful smile on her lips. It was an exquisitely-wrought, lovingly-executed wooden carving of the Grange, complete in every detail and mounted on a bronze base.

'Johnny, *darling*.' Rachel carefully put the carving down and threw her arms round his neck. 'I know you did this yourself.'

'Every bit, Gran.'

'It's absolutely lovely. It must have taken hours,' Flora said, as her aunt passed it to her. 'I didn't know you were so clever.'

'Good with my hands, they say,' Johnny smiled shyly. 'No brains.' He consulted his watch. 'Come on, ladies. There is a terrific reception for you at the Hall. It's rather as though they were expecting royalty.'

Royalty was indeed what Rachel felt like as Johnny's car rounded the bend in the drive and she saw the whole family drawn up on the steps to greet her, as though posing for a formal portrait. In the middle were Paul and Laura, with their two boys Martin and Philip standing and the latest baby, Sandra, in her mother's arms. Next to them were Charlotte and Arthur, with Jeremy slightly to one side talking to Galina who, at sixteen, was not only a beauty but bore a marked resemblance to her grandmother. By her side, looking for somewhere to sit, was Bobby, who kept on mopping his brow against the heat and, just as the car swept round the drive his thoughtful grandson, Tom, brought out a chair, placed it on the steps and Bobby thankfully sank into it.

Lower down from Bobby was Stefanie just behind Pascal, who was bending down to admonish Alex who, by the look of it, would not keep still and kept on trying to get the attention of his best friend Martin, a step up and a few feet away from him

On the other side of Bobby Em was talking to Aileen and Adèle Cohen, whose dark good-looking son, Derek, down from Cambridge where he had just taken his law finals, was trying to engage the attention of Galina, perhaps without realizing how old she was, because she looked about twenty.

Leo Cohen was standing next to Paul and just behind him was Luis, newly returned to England with an exquisite little Vietnamese bride, Lin-Su. Lin-Su, dressed in a beautiful gold and turquoise cheongsam, looked totally overwhelmed by the whole concourse, as she spoke very little English and had not yet quite appreciated the kind of family, or the size of it, that Luis came from. Angelica Eckburgh, looking absolutely beautiful in a pink moygashel dress, and wearing the kind of wide-brimmed straw hat that she was famous for modelling, was trying to help Laura with baby Sandra, who had started to cry. Perry Eckburgh, some paces away, kept on mopping his brow and finally asked thirteen-year-old Myles to go and get him a seat like the one that had been procured for Bobby.

There was a hum from the family as they saw Johnny's car and, as he stopped it in the drive, everyone surged down the steps, upsetting Paul's carefully-drawn plans, which included a speech of welcome to greet the lady of the day, each one wanting to be there to give her the first kiss of greeting.

In the days before the First World War the summer party given annually, usually in August, by the Earl and Countess of Askham was one of the highlights of those weeks after the official ending of the London Season. It was then that those privileged young ladies who had been presented returned to the country homes of their families, and more splendid parties were given, some of which rivalled those that had been held earlier on at their parents' London houses.

These were usually the months when arrangements were made between families, rather as alliances were cemented by the nations of the earth, whereby scions of the great and noble promised to marry into one another. For a young woman to become engaged in her first season was a much sought-after cachet. Such had been the case when Dulcie Kitto met Frederick, Viscount Gore, heir to the nineth Earl of Askham.

Frederick Gore had married the then Dulcie Kitto in 1873 so, very probably, the party at which they'd met had been held in 1871 or '2, nearly a century away from the summer party of 1967 to celebrate the ninetieth birthday of the woman who had married Bosco, the eleventh Earl.

But throughout the nineteenth century nothing really disturbed the even tenor of those far-off halcyon days when the British Empire was at its zenith, the nation secure in peace and prosperity. The battlefields of Ypres, Verdun and the Somme were very far away.

And, indeed, from her marriage to Bosco in 1905 up to 1914 Rachel could recall the Askham summer parties very well. She and Bosco would ride over from the Grange, rather as she had today, though not in motorized transport, with their young children and they would mingle among the great and famous, the not-so-well-off, the menials and servants, and the downright poor who came from the locality, because on the day of the summer party the gates to the Hall were open to everyone. Only the local constable in his best uniform and white gloves directed traffic and made sure that law and order were maintained, the few inebriates despatched swiftly down the road towards the village.

After the Great War there had been no attempt by Dulcie to resume the summer party until 1923. It had not been felt that, until then, the nation or the Askham family, which had lost its Head in the war, were in a fit state or condition to entertain. The 1923 summer party had been notable for many things, as has so often been recalled and, although there were parties after that date, none was on such a scale until this party held by the current Earl, the thirteenth, in honour of his grandmother.

Rachel, perched on a straight chair on the terrace, felt rather as though she were sitting on some kind of throne surrounded by acolytes, her grandchildren and great-grandchildren, assisted by numerous young Kitto and Crewe cousins who took her presents: the bowls and baskets of fruit and bunches of flowers, the offerings of jam, honey, homemade cakes and much more expensive or elaborate gifts, some of which had taken months to make or embroider.

In the great days of the Hall the entire village of Askham depended on the inhabitants of the big house; but two wars and a long period of disuse had done away with that. Many of the villagers kept their houses in the village but worked in Salisbury or Winchester; but some had moved away altogether and the houses were let as weekend residences to wealthy city dwellers or put up for sale.

One of the things that had contributed to Hugo's failure was the fact that there was no help to be had on the land or in the house that had some thirty bedrooms and, in pre-war days, had employed a staff of fifty. Paul, howver, had begun to change all that. He had installed many labour-saving devices produced by a modern electronic age, which cut down the need for servants – dishwashers, clothes-washing machines, eletric floor polishers and gadgets of every kind. He also improved the servants' quarters, installing hot and cold water in every room and a television set in the servants' hall. There had not been a servants' hall for many years – since 1939 – but there it was again, with TV set, billiard table and comfortable chairs. Together with the high wages he offered, Paul was able to attract foreign personnel and he thus had a staff of Filipinos, Malays, Yugoslavs, Italians, Spaniards and others from that part of Europe which now lay behind an iron curtain.

Some of the staff were English. Paul's wife's personal maid was from Manchester and he had, of course, an English butler. His gardeners were mostly English because they were local men and, gradually, he was hoping to build up the village of Askham again to make it part of a unity with the Hall. But times had indeed changed and, in some ways, one could never quite, entirely and successfully, put back the clock. It was doubtful if the relationship between Hall and village would ever be as it had been in the days of his forebears.

However, this party, unlike those held when Hugo and Jenny lived at the Hall, was run on almost pre-war lines. The staff did not wear livery but a uniform of a sort: the men in black trousers, white shirts with black bow ties, the women in short black dresses with white aprons. And then the hierarchy of the party was very carefully and subtly planned and organized, with the marquee in the grounds for the lower orders and tea on the terrace for those who had received embossed invitations.

Although there was a Labour government in power and this was the age of the Common Man he was not expected to penetrate, at Askham Hall as elsewhere, into those areas reserved for the family and its friends. Hands could be shaken, but only over an invisible barrier of class.

For instance, the publican of the Askham Arms would never have dreamt of stepping on to the terrace to wish Lady Askham, whom he knew well, a happy birthday; but he waited along with the rest – the owner of the village store, the chemist, the church vergers, the policeman's family, the garage attendant and other sundry workers, mechanics at the Askham motor works – in the lower meadow outside the marquee. There Rachel at last made her way, slowly, between ranks that parted for her like the waters of the Red Sea drawing back to make way for the hordes of Israel.

Rachel was flanked by the Earl, his wife, her grandson Johnny and her granddaughter Angelica, all bowing, nodding with gracious smiles as they passed through the lines, stopping occasionally to talk to people they knew. Those familiar with post-war Royal Garden Parties held in the grounds of Buckingham Palace would have recognized the picture that the Askham family presented, smiling and waving, as they strolled towards the marquee where Rachel was prevailed upon to have a cup of tea.

There she was able to greet, with utmost sincerity, all the many friends she had in the village – real friends, women she had consoled if a son or husband had been lost in the wars, as hers had; children she had comforted for the death or illness of a parent. Rachel had always been popular in the village and there were so many acts of kindness on her part that it was impossible to recount them all. She had lived among them, in the Grange, for so many years; never the great lady, although always treated with respect but, above all, affection. Many had gone to her in need and come away much better off spiritually and, sometimes, materially. She would never let anyone down and now it showed in the countless tributes and gestures of affection she received from all and sundry on her birthday.

Finally it was time to return again, slowly, the way she had come, grasping hands, kissing cheeks, loving and being deservedly loved. Once back on the terrace she sank rather gratefully into a more comfortable chair and asked for a fresh cup of tea.

'You did that *beautifully*, Granny,' Angelica said approvingly. 'I don't know how you remember all the *names*.' She nodded at Stewart Kitto, a cousin who had just returned from abroad. He stopped and she drew him over. 'You remember Stewart, don't you, Granny? He's just come back from Kenya.'

Rachel screwed up her nose and then seized Stewart's brawny arm.

'Stewart! When I last saw you you were a tiny baby. Tell me about Kenya.' Rachel drew him down next to her. 'You know my son Ralph, Johnny's father, was there in 1928 . . .'

Johnny Down, to whom all this would have belonged had his father and mother been married, stood just behind his grandmother, absorbing everything that was going on. He knew how he had missed his inheritance, but he bore no grudge. His mother had always told him that she and his father would have married had Cheryl given him a divorce.

Now, by new divorce laws, she would not have been able to refuse him his freedom unreasonably; but they

781

had come twenty years too late. Johnny, however, did not miss something he had never expected to have. Paul, ten years his senior, had inherited the title on the death of Johnny's father. He was then only a few months old and had always looked on Paul as an elder brother. Paul, an only child, loved Johnny as much as if he had been.

However, Johnny did miss the man he had come to know as father, Hugo, who had brought him up. Hugo had taught him to love the land and become a man who worked with his hands. He had loved Hugo unreservedly and devotedly and when he and his mother split up Johnny had to call on vast, hidden reserves of character not to break down, even though he was nearly grown up. It seemed, then, that he had no home until Paul came along and restored it to him. Now he lived in his own suite in the Hall and concentrated on Paul's plans for development. People who knew them both said, privately of course, that it was a good thing Paul had succeeded and not Johnny, who was too like his father; too nice and soft and would have given in. Paul had the will as well as the mettle to succeed, and a certain ruthlessness that emulated his cousin Bobby rather than any member, past or present, of his immediate family.

As for Hugo, he was making a new life for himself in the South of France, about to marry a young French girl, who was having his baby.

Paul Askham looked, indeed, extremely comfortable in his beautiful home, refurbished with such skill and care, mostly by Laura and Adèle, who travelled the country visiting sales and antique shops. There were now pieces of Chippendale, Hepplewhite, Channon, Paine, William Kent and Matthias Lock. Old masters on the wall – Reynolds, Sargent, Stubbs – as well as the Impressionists of whom Paul was particularly fond: Monet, Manet, Pissarro, Sisley and Seurat.

There were Aubusson carpets and rugs from Persia, India and Afghanistan. There were tapestries from the Balkans and silverware from Russia, much of the latter provided by Susan. Many of the walls had been completely repanelled in oak or walnut; others had been stripped and rehung with William Morris wallpaper exactly copied by master craftsmen. The plasterwork, those intricate quatrefoils, lozenges and pendants, had been restored to the ceilings and huge, heavy chandeliers, some with many thousands of tiny, polished pieces of glass, rehung. Not only was the interior of Askham Hall the same as before: it was better than before – safer, more splendid and in good order. Other things being equal it would survive several more hundreds of years.

Paul, saturnine, thickset, stocky, full of nervous energy, didn't resemble the sort of British earl of whom people had a stereotype. But he did play the part admirably because he was only ten when he inherited his uncle's title in default of his dead father, and, accordingly, he was used to the concept of authority and handled it well: gimlet-eyed, sharp, sensitive, missing nothing.

After the progress across the meadow was over and Rachel was sitting on the terrace he felt he could relax, drink a glass of champagne and make sure that everyone was enjoying themselves.

At this point, just as Paul was approaching one of the waiters carrying glasses, Bobby came up, saying he wanted a word.

'Not *business* on the day of a party, Bobby!' Paul exclaimed.

'It won't take a minute.' Bobby felt expansive, and tucked his arm through his young cousin's. 'There's always time for business. If we just have a little wander round the grounds I can tell you in a few seconds.'

Paul took a glass of champagne from the waiter, held it

towards his grandmother, who smiled, and then he stepped back to allow Bobby to precede him. Just at that moment Tom walked past with Nicky, Johnny and Jeremy clad in whites, going across the lawn for a game of tennis. They waved their rackets at him.

'Not enough women around,' Bobby grumbled. 'In the old days it would have been mixed doubles.'

'There are *plenty* of girls,' Paul said. 'They've just got together for a knock-up because I said Nicky was very good. He's a class player, even though he's so young, and could make Wimbledon.'

Paul watched Nicky, who was very tall, trotting off beside his cousins. Young Tom, the comparatively new boy, was shy but he had quickly adapted to life as part of a large family. It was a strange experience, however, for one who had been brought up in another country and solely in the company of a single woman.

Like some stray animals, however, who are given refuge, Tom was adaptable and grateful. Moreover, Bobby was very good to him and Tom had grown to love him and his grandmother.

'Tom has settled in very well,' Paul said to Bobby as they rounded the house whose beautiful white Chilmark stone had been newly washed, repointed, and was as splendid as it had been the day it was built.

'Very well.' Bobby puffed at his cigar. 'Tom is a splendid lad, a chip off the old block – me, of course, not David. It's really about Tom that I wanted to talk to you.'

'I thought that might be it,' Paul said.

They reached the front of the Hall, away from the crowds, and sat down on one of the benches on the newly-turfed lawn. In the old days Dulcie's rose garden had been one of the outside splendours of the Hall but during the war it had been dug over and given up to cabbages, cauliflowers, carrots and peas to feed the hungry young people at school there.

Now it had been restored as a rose garden again and this was the first year of flowering of the magnificent standards which stood like sentinels on either side of the drive.

Bobby and Paul sat on one of the wrought-iron benches which Hugo had long ago discovered in a back shed, restored, and placed at points in the garden where strollers could take rest and shade. Bobby relit his cigar, offering one to Paul, who shook his head.

'I shouldn't be too long away. It looks rude.'

'Of course,' Bobby nodded. At sixty-eight he had become rather a grand old man, plump and florid, but in his expression there was a serenity that few people ever remembered seeing before and which few thought he deserved. This serenity had come from Tom; the gift of an heir, a grandson, blood of his blood, whom he hadn't even known existed.

'I'm coming to the point, Paul.' Bobby contentedly studied the end of his cigar and tipped his white straw hat over his eyes to keep out the sun. 'You know I'm very fond of you and Laura?'

'I know that, Bobby, and we're fond of you.'

'You're real family to me and I'm proud of you; proud of you and her – she'll be a wonderful companion to you. You've made a magnificent job of restoring this Hall, even if the groundwork was done by our German friend. You've established it as a family house, seat of the Askhams, as I hoped you would and above all, you've restored the dignity of the Earls of Askham, which in my day underwent a sad decline.

'Now I want to put a proposition to you, Paul, and I don't want you to speak until I've finished.' Bobby put a plump hand on his arm. 'I know you've done very well. I hear you're a millionaire now, one of the first to make television sets in colour in this country. Now, what I would like to say is this: I suggest that you have outstripped your present interests. You are capable of far, far more than running a little company making television sets.'

'A *big* company,' Paul corrected, mildly.

'Yes, but only television sets. I would like you to consider, quite seriously, merging it with Lighterman Limited. We have many similar companies in the electronics business. I'm without a really good man and I'm getting old. I would like you to run it in trust for my grandson who, hopefully, one day will join it. Already he shows an aptitude . . .'

As Paul held up his hand Bobby stopped.

'What is it?'

'Not in *trust*, Bobby. I am not surprised at your suggestion, which I'd already anticipated. I thought one day you'd ask me again and vertical integration suits my business perfectly. But I will not run it in trust, for Tom to sweep me to one side whenever he wishes. Oh, no. I am prepared to run it as managing director but not in trust, not to be swept aside. If, in time, Tom joins the business and is good at it he *may* succeed me. But so may any of my sons. You see what I mean, don't you, Bobby? Lighterman Limited must be Lighterman-Askham again, as it was in the old days before you bamboozled my uncle.'

Paul paused and gave the discomfited Bobby an enigmatic smile. 'The business must once again be shared equally with the Askhams. Life, you see, has a habit of coming full circle.'

Bobby didn't like the word 'bamboozle'. It had a crudity about it that he found offensive; but he knew Paul. Paul was a blunt man and a plain speaker, and that was why Bobby not only liked him so much but also trusted him.

After more discussion he and Paul continued their amicable promenade, ending up on the terrace again just as the local band, far down in the meadow by the water's edge, had finished a rendition of the works of Gilbert and Sullivan. Everyone was clapping.

Charlotte and Arthur had gone down to the marquee and, as they came up arm in arm, Rachel wondered whether it was for mutual support up the hill or whether their marriage was showing signs of improvement. It was seldom one saw them together, never mind arm in arm. In particular Arthur, who had looked very weary a year or two ago as though he were a candidate for a heart attack – that kind of grey look on the face that often presages ill health – seemed much better.

Rachel had always been fond of Arthur, but she knew he did not feel he had had a happy life. Although he had made money he hadn't made a lot of it; he hadn't become a captain of industry like Bobby because he had diffused his energies into the House of Commons. And, although he'd been a successful MP, he'd never achieved more than minor ministerial rank, never the Cabinet office he'd coveted, despite his connections. Arthur, in reality, seemed to have reached his peak of achievement as captain of the golf club, which he ruled with the authority of a dictator.

Neither had he had a very happy marriage to a woman he'd once adored. He'd soon realized that Charlotte was only happy when she was doing something; when she was really busy, not just attending committees or opening charity fêtes but doing a real job of work as she had for Chanel before the war, or for the special services during it.

787

Rachel recalled Marc, whom Charlotte had rejected for Arthur and, as she had helped be a party to that decision, she had often during the course of the next twenty years wondered if she'd done the right thing. Charlotte in her perpetual search for happiness had often seemed to her mother more a casualty of peace than a contented woman; someone made for danger and excitement, only real when it was present.

As Charlotte and Arthur reached the terrace they both observed that she was watching them and each waved. Then Arthur went to the bar, a place where he was very much at home, and Charlotte went over to help Stefanie, who was coping with Alex in a tantrum.

On the other hand Em, sitting next to her and trying to converse with her new and delightful, but totally unexpected, daughter-in-law – Luis hadn't even cabled them that he was coming home, never mind that he had a wife – had made the best of her life, given the sort of person she was. Em was one of the great post-war editors, a worthy successor to Rachel and was consulted, as Rachel had been, by the eminent of all parties. Em was a solitary; a dedicated, clever woman who had known love and action in her life and, unlike her sister, had managed to enjoy the peace.

Rachel leaned over to try and help Em with Lin-Su who was trying hard to please, to understand her mother-in-law, hand firmly clutching Luis's. Luis, very tanned but much thinner, looked supremely happy to be home, to be with Lin-Su, whom he had rescued after a Vietcong retaliatory raid on her little village near Haiphong. She had been in a camp and he had been covering the aftermath of the attack with his camera. First pictures of Lin-Su showed her emaciated and terribly frightened. But love, as much as good food, had made her blossom.

Flora was very taken with Lin-Su, very excited about

meeting her and hearing Luis's account of President Johnson's escalation of the war. America was in it, now, up to the neck and 'Americans out of Vietnam' was Flora's new cause. She had already been arrested for causing a disturbance outside the American Embassy in Grosvenor Square in 1965. One magistrate had threatened to put her away for good unless she stopped appearing in front of him for disturbances of the peace. Leftwing papers took up this remark and pilloried him, much to Flora's satisfaction.

Flora now was chatting away to Luis with an account of her activities, not listening as Luis tried to tell her there were two sides to the picture in Vietnam. 'Oh, no,' Flora said, shaking her head. She knew who was to blame, didn't everyone? America.

Rachel saw Luis winking at her. She smiled and surreptitiously winked back. They knew Flora. When Flora had a cause nothing would make her change her mind – especially reason.

'Alex is very fractious today,' Stefanie said to Charlotte. 'I think it's the heat.'

'Where's Pascal?' Charlotte looked around her. 'He'll know what to do.'

'He's supervising the younger children in the new swimming pool. Paul went back to the marquee to take part in a darts match, I believe. I must go back there soon, else they'll think we're snooty,' Stefanie said, then, at an anxious look from her mother-in-law, reassured her. 'Don't worry. There are plenty of people at the pool, though Pascal would be very hurt if he even suspected that we thought he couldn't save them if anything went wrong.'

Charlotte smiled and linked her arm through Stefanie's as they left the terrace of the pool which Paul, a keen swimmer himself, had had constructed at the side of the house, extending the library so that it could be approached from indoors.

The marriage of Stefanie and Pascal had been one of the most happy events in Charlotte's recent life. Her beloved son had married a woman she herself had loved all her life and thought of as a daughter. The marriage, though brought about by necessity and mutual need, perhaps, had been ideal. Pascal loved Stefanie and he loved her children. At last they were his own and called him 'Daddy'. They all lived in the house in Cheshire in the greatest domestic harmony. Pascal went less and less to the aerodrome, concentrating on inventions at home. His enthusiasm for flying had waned since Sasha's death, and even more since he'd married his widow. One day he wanted to move away altogether, perhaps to Scotland where no one knew them or their history; where people might think the children really were his, and they could start life from the beginning – the simple life they both liked.

By the side of the pool Galina was preparing to dive in, watched with admiration by a number of young men including Derek Cohen. She knew how she affected men and she not only enjoyed it but played on it. Arms outstretched, but thrust forward, she prepared to dive off the side.

Charlotte looked on with amusement but, once again, felt unable to overcome the feeling of astonishment she always had when she saw Galina at certain angles, in certain moods. She reminded her so vividly of her grandmother – tall, fair, beautiful, with those fascinating dark eyebrows. This was Hélène as she might have looked in 1923, the year that, at the summer party, Bobby first had eyes for her. Hélène, flirtatious too, was aware of her power over men – a power that was to be her undoing.

Charlotte sighed and Stefanie, glancing swiftly at her, squeezed her arm.

'I know what you're thinking,' she said. 'And I'm glad, aren't you?'

'That she's so like your mother? Yes. I'm glad for her and I'm especially glad for you, my dear.' She returned the pressure of Stefanie's hand, not wanting to add that if her beloved daughter became too like her mother, there could be trouble in store. There would not automatically be wars to make heroines of adventurous women.

Adèle Cohen, too, was by the side of the pool with Laura, who was helping to dry the younger ones. Aileen Lighterman sat in an easy chair next to them, her eyes concealed by dark glasses. Two years before she had had a successful operation for cataracts. Since then, as she was able to wander less, she and Bobby had settled down to an attempt at mutual tolerance and the admiration and enjoyment of their newly-discovered grandson.

Leo Cohen had buttonholed Bobby after he left Paul, always anxious, if possible, to discuss the stock market. Bobby drew Leo into the shade by the pool and, over two large Pimms, gladly outlined his ideas for Paul taking over Lighterman Limited. Leo thought it an excellent idea.

'He already has shares, you know.'

'I know,' Bobby said. 'I was irritated at the time the way it all came about, but now I'm pleased.' He looked shrewdly at Leo. 'You've done a lot for this family, Leo, and I like you. I like you and your wife and I'm very fond indeed of your daughter. Not only is she pretty and accomplished, but she's sensible. She's an excellent foil for Paul. You know, in the twenties we had an injection of new blood with our alliance with the Ferov family. You may not know that my first late-lamented wife, Stefanie's mother, was a Ferov, a Russian princess. My sister Susan married her brother, Kyril. The Ferovs enriched this family, though they were a bloody nuisance, too. I must admit they were at times a really bloody nuisance.' Bobby clapped his hands to his brow. 'Temperament! Awful. My daughters have all inherited some of it, though all have made good.'

Bobby paused and looked at Pascal swimming in the pool, like any other healthy person, surrounded by toddlers. Pascal, dark and tanned, devastatingly good-looking, was throwing a ball and laughing at Stefanie, telling her to come in. She touched the water with her toes, pretended she was cold, shivered, but leapt in, nevertheless, to be seized by Pascal who, holding her in his arms, kissed her with unashamed joy. It was a moving moment for Bobby, for all those who were watching, wishing so much that Pascal had the mobility on the land that he had in the water. At the other end of the pool the lissom Galina was making long strides towards her mother and stepfather, pursued by Derek Cohen.

Bobby's eyes narrowed, his hand remaining on Leo's arm.

'Incidentally, the way I see your son making eyes at *my* granddaughter Galina makes me think a healthy infusion of Cohen blood might not be a bad thing either.'

'I'm gratified you say that, Bobby,' Leo said emotionally. 'We Jews are not always liked or accepted, I must confess it to you, especially by the English aristocracy.'

'Nonsense,' Bobby said, slapping his back. 'Paul's mother was Jewish. He looks Jewish, doesn't he?' As Leo nodded Bobby went on. 'He's always been very proud of his Jewish heritage and *I* always say that's where he got his excellent business sense. The Askhams were hopeless, quite hopeless, about money; but with a little help from the Kleins and the Cohens . . .' Bobby winked and gazed around him with satisfaction, at the gleaming house, the well-laid-out grounds, the spacious new swimming pool, 'I say we got a good deal.'

By six o'clock the crowds in the grounds were beginning to thin. Up at the house most of the young people who had clustered round the swimming pool had gone indoors to change, and nannies had come out to reclaim their small charges. There had been ball games, and cricket games and races. Croquet for the older members and donkey rides for the young. It had been a truly happy day, leaving many contented hearts.

On the terrace Rachel looked round, noting the depleted numbers. Below her the band was packing up, preparing to leave to a polite splattering of applause from those stragglers who were reluctant to depart, and the white-shirted waiters, helped by garden staff, were collecting litter from the lawn and stowing it in large boxes. On the lake swans, freed from the deafening irritation of loud music, swam up and down, interrupted by a few rowers and punters who remained. Everyone had had such a good day they were naturally loath to go home.

'In the old days the lake was the attraction, remember?' Rachel put a hand on her daughter's arm and as Charlotte, who had returned to be with her mother, nodded, she said: 'Now it's the swimming pool.'

Rachel sighed. 'It's been a lovely day. But I do miss Hugo. I've felt his absence. All my sons have left me now, you know. I think he might have written or telephoned.'

'I'm sure he will, Mother,' Charlotte said comfortingly, 'later on.'

But Charlotte wasn't really sure. Freddie and Ralph had left the fold by death, but Hugo voluntarily. Charlotte felt there was a deep wound in Hugo that would take a long time to heal. She hoped his new life and baby would do that because, like Rachel, she loved him, too.

'I miss *all* the family who are absent today,' Rachel went on in a nostalgic mood. 'Poor Anna, Susan, of course, and dearest Joe.' She gazed at Charlotte. 'I wish that Joe had come back, now that everything is all right.'

In July after ten years of fiercely fought debate and controversy since Wolfenden, the Royal Assent had been given to a bill legalizing homosexual acts between consenting adults.

'I don't think Joe will ever come back.' Charlotte sadly shook her head. 'Not to live. Arthur and I may go out in the winter to see him. We thought we could have a nice cruise down the coast of South America, calling at Rio.'

'What a splendid idea.' Rachel suddenly shivered as the sun began to sink behind the trees. 'I think I'll go in, dear, and have a little rest before dinner.'

'Are you OK, Mother?' Em looked at her anxiously but as Rachel got to her feet she stood quite straight, feet firmly on the ground, adjusting her belt.

'I feel a bit fat with all the cream I've had, but I'm perfectly all right, dear. Something tells me, however, that, with a family dinner party and a dance for the young people afterwards, the day's jollifications have just begun.'

Inside the hall Flora was talking to one of the Crewe cousins, Julia, who was engaged to a young Rhodes scholar from America. The place was full of people coming and going, young girls in trousers or very short mini skirts, which Rachel had never quite got used to. She thought they were ugly, showing a bare and rather ungainly expanse of leg, unless one were very fortunate. There were many unusual hair-dos and peculiar kinds of make-up.

Many of the younger people had gone indoors to listen

to their favourite pop musicians – Bob Dylan, Joan Baez, the Righteous Brothers and, of course, the Beatles. The thump of noise echoed across the house as, once upon a time, it had been the restrained sound of string music that went with the long dresses and large picture hats of a more leisured, elegant age.

Rachel didn't really mind. She loved young people, especially this new independent, concerned generation, typified for her by Flora and Johnny, Galina, Jeremy and Nicky. They lived in the shadow of weapons that could destroy the earth; and their values were not the ones she'd had as a girl, even though she herself had been considered a rebel. Bosco and Adam in 1898 had fought against men armed only with spears, and Flora Down, her sister-in-law, had not been allowed to travel by herself abroad even though she was over 21. Rachel seemed to have lived more than a lifetime in her ninety years and it was almost impossible to imagine what the next ninety years could bring.

Few people even seemed to know who she was as she walked across the hall towards the staircase. Indeed, it *was* a bit like the hotel that Bobby had tried to make of it twenty years before.

'Are you all right, Mother?' Arthur called, coming out of the study with Perry Eckburgh just as Rachel was about to mount the stairs.

'Please don't think of me as an old lady, Arthur,' Rachel replied, rather sharply. 'I intend to have my hundredth birthday here in ten years' time. *Then* you may help me up the stairs.'

Arthur stepped back, laughing, joined by Bobby, Perry, Paul, who had just returned from the meadow, Johnny and Jeremy, who were still in tennis whites.

They all stood and watched her go up the stairs to the room Paul had made available to her to rest and change in and, on the landing, she turned and waved. For a moment it was like a tableau in which the various generations of her family stood before her: near contemporaries of hers, like Bobby, and Perry; those who were middle-aged, then the young and the very young. At the last moment Laura appeared with Sandra in her arms, lying bathed and contented with only a nappy on because of the heat. Rachel blew them both kisses before proceeding along the corridor to her room.

Alone at last.

Suddenly it seemed very quiet in the vast house, although the rooms would be full of people changing and, in the reception rooms, staff would be busy setting out the cutlery, plates and the glasses for the evening's buffet, while in the kitchen all day preparation would have been going on for the party.

Rachel realized she had never even popped her head into the kitchen. It was remiss of her and she would do it on the way down. When Jenny was here she spent her time in the kitchen and expected everyone to help. Everyone did; but it was Jenny's undoing. There was too much to do and too few to help. It was odd how completely Jenny had disappeared from their lives.

One had to have money and vision and also flair to maintain a house of this size. Rachel sighed. She was sure Paul would, but in many ways she thought he had found it too easy to make money, to become a millionaire. The Askhams had always been good at spending and losing it, but not at making it. It always seemed a vaguely ungentlemanly thing to do, a whiff of trade and the market-place. She herself thought that money made on such a scale, so easily, must have been dishonestly made. She thought of how Bobby had made his, what suffering his greed had brought on the family. But Paul was very different. He was straight. She knew he was because she had brought him up. She admired his spirit and integrity, his drive and his forcefulness, but she was still rather astonished at his financial acumen, his flair for getting rich.

She opened the door of her bright, pretty room with its view of the back of the Hall, the meadow with the marquee, and the lake. She'd stayed in this room before, but in less happy circumstances. The place had been falling apart, the furniture needed repair and the roof had been leaking. Things had not been well with Hugo and Jenny, and then there was Nimet. Better not to think of her.

Now, a few years and many millions of pounds later, the situation had changed completely.

She took off her dress, sluiced her face in the bathroom next to her room and ran the bath. Then she slipped on a robe and went to the window and leaned out, unseen by those beneath her on the terrace. Arthur, Perry, Bobby and Leo Cohen were enjoying a drink in the cool evening air. Charlotte and Em were perched on the parapet, also with drinks in their hands, chatting. Em was never far away from Luis and her new daughter-in-law, but just occasionally she had moments for someone else, particularly her sister. But Em kept on glancing at Luis as though to be sure he was still there.

Laura, still with Sandra in her arms, was talking to Angelica. She was a happy, self-contained, calm kind of person who seemed able to cope with everything: a busy husband, children, a huge house. In a way she was rather similar in temperament to Rachel's granddaughter, who was a world-famous model. Happily, Laura did not have the single-minded egotism of Angelica who, it was said, commanded fabulous sums of money and, as far as one could see, she and Perry were happy. No one ever mentioned Dick, perhaps they never thought of him. All day Emily and Myles had hovered round their mother, as if glad to see her again; to have her company for more than a few hours.

Angelica had removed her hat. Her pink dress was like a beacon because she, too, attracted the men, as Galina did, that new temptress in the family. The men were standing around wanting to get a word in, a glance from Angelica, who was pretending not to notice.

Luis and Lin-Su were once again with Flora, and two other guests. For a moment Rachel's eyes rested tenderly on Flora, her child of the sixties, brave, rebellious little thing. What a contrast with Angelica, her exact contemporary and once close friend, a few feet away. As they got older the two women had increasingly little in common though, being family, they would each have dropped everything to come to the aid of the other, if needed.

The family was the really good, positive thing, Rachel thought, as Paul came on to the terrace looking cool and elegant in his grey flannels and blazer, shirt open at the neck. Around him people were moving, some into the house, others for a saunter in the park in the cool of the evening. The sun had sunk well below the trees, casting a pink glow on the lake on which the ducks and swans were now thinking of bed, gracefully heading for their homes on the bank. Lights had started to go on on the terrace and one or two white-coated waiters were circulating with trays. Some people had begun to appear, dressed already in evening clothes. Charlotte and Em finished their drinks and decided to go and change, and Emily tugged at her mother's arm. Angelica beckoned to Perry, who glanced at his watch.

Paul looked about him with satisfaction, acknowledging people, and then chatted for a few moments to Luis and Lin-Su. After a while they decided to go and change, too, though Lin-Su looked lovely in her dainty oriental dress.

Paul lit a cigarette before following them and, briefly, Rachel caught a glimpse of his handsome face, bent thoughtfully to the task, a face so reminiscent, in that flickering half-light, of another that she hadn't seen for thirty years. But she would never forget it.

Was it fair that a son was so long dead and the mother still alive?

That day, on her birthday, Paul had shown her Freddie, as Johnny had earlier shown her Ralph. The best present had come from her grandsons.

Rachel felt close to tears and was glad she was alone. But she also felt surrounded by love, by the presence of loved ones of the past and by the family. Around her were the grounds and gardens she loved so much, had known for so long, and above them the Grange; a home from which no one, now, would ever dislodge her.

The present was certain; the future, even if it ended for her tomorrow, secure for those she loved.

Once again, for the first time for nearly a century, a youthful, energetic Lord and Lady Askham lived in the Hall with small children who could carry on the dynasty begun hundreds of years before. Once more there were servants, horses, stables, beautiful furniture and priceless possessions, as in the days before the First World War; an ambience of elegance and ease.

It was certain that these things didn't matter so much in the modern world, and to Rachel, personally, they never had. But when the family had been in decline, the Hall, scene of so much pleasure and beauty, decaying and sad, a certain sense of happiness and satisfaction had vanished, too.

The past could never be fully recaptured; things never be as they were, and nor would one want them to be. But this family was part of a very old and great tradition.

Now it was as though the clock had indeed turned back

and the rooms of this great house, for so long empty and derelict, echoed no more to the voices of the dead, but to the vital, vibrant sounds of the living; to future generations yet unborn.